STEEL DEMONS MC

BOOKS 7-10

USA TODAY BESTSELLING AUTHOR

CRYSTAL ASH

Copyright © 2021 by Crystal Ash

Cover Art by MoorBooks Design

Published by Voluspa Press

This is a work of fiction. Names, characters, places, and incidents either are the products of the author's imagination or are used fictitiously. Any resemblance to actual persons, living or dead, businesses, companies, events, or locales is entirely coincidental.

All rights reserved. No part of this publication may be reproduced, distributed, or transmitted in any form or by any means, including photocopying, recording, or other electronic or mechanical methods, without the prior written permission of the publisher, except in the case of brief quotations embodied in critical reviews and certain other noncommercial uses permitted by copyright law.

SDMC SERIES PLAYLIST

All American Nightmare - Hinder
Notorious - Adelitas Way
Hail to the King - Avenged Sevenfold
O Death - Ashley H
Joan of Arc - In This Moment
Radioactive - Imagine Dragons
Bad Company - Five Finger Death Punch
Love Me to Death - No Resolve
(Don't Fear) The Reaper - HIM
David - Noah Gunderson
Apocalyptic - Halestorm
Blue on Black - Five Finger Death Punch
Machine Gun Blues - Social Distortion
Wanted Dead or Alive - Chris Daughtry
I Get Off - Halestorm
You Shook Me All Night Long - AC/DC
Nobody Praying for Me - Seether
Loyal to No One - Dropkick Murpheys
Crazy in Love - Daniel De Bourg
Be Free - King Dude & Chelsea Wolfe
Raise Hell - Dorothy
Coming Home - Skylar Grey

Listen on Spotify at:
crystalashbooks.com/sdmc-playlist

Content Warnings

This series is set in a dystopian world and contains graphically violent scenes throughout.

Please note the following content warnings for each book in this set:

Senseless:
Past child abuse,

Ruthless:
War and battle scenes, hostage situation, combat injuries

Merciless:
Physical and psychological torture

Endless:

SENSELESS

STEEL DEMONS MC BOOK SEVEN

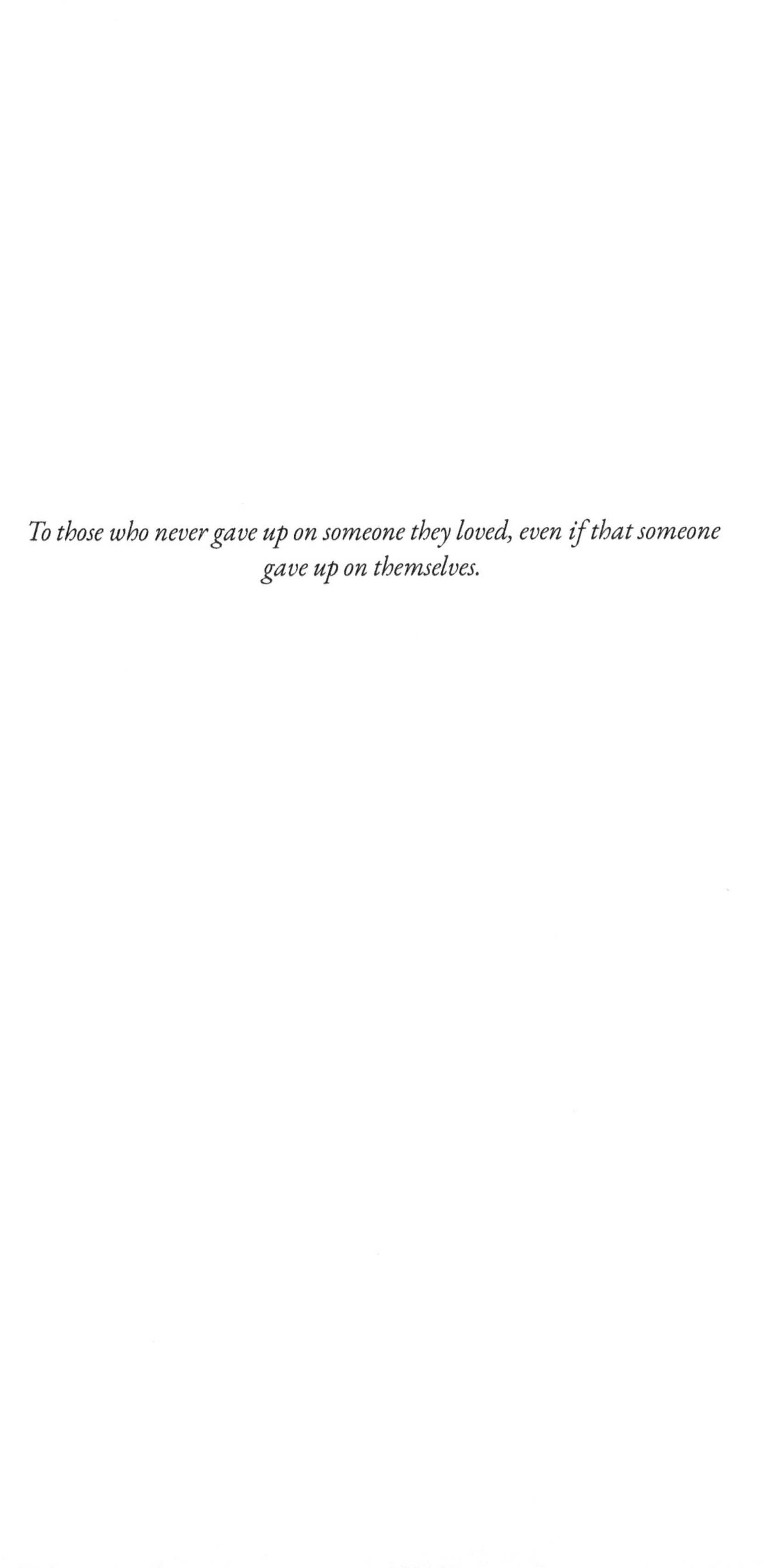

To those who never gave up on someone they loved, even if that someone gave up on themselves.

PROLOGUE

THE BLOOD BAG

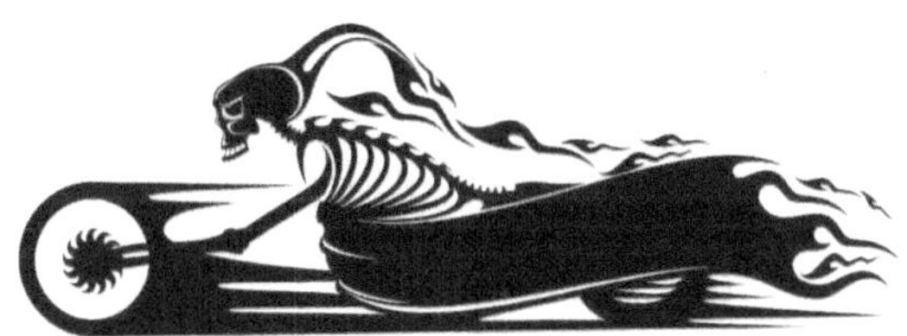

NINE YEARS EARLIER

They cut deeply today, so much so that it made me almost grateful that I stopped feeling anything years ago.

Using the corner of my ragged shirt, I wiped at the blood still seeping out of the red line running from my shoulder to halfway down my arm. The cut throbbed, the skin red and angry around it. It would probably get infected, if it wasn't already.

I looked to the far corner of my cage, where my water container sat with a dangerously low amount of liquid. The cut would feel better if I washed it, but that was also my drinking water. It could be another day, maybe more, before they refilled it. This was a predicament I ran into often—drink or wash my blood away.

Cleaning my cuts always seemed like a waste. The concrete floor of my cage was painted with years upon years of my spilled blood. And the cutting would never stop.

The last man who shared the cage with me said I was already dehydrated. Malnourished. Words he had to explain to me because I hadn't encountered them in my reading yet.

He was surprised that I grew so tall after spending my whole life in here. I had no perception of how tall, short, or malnourished I was compared to other people, and didn't know what to tell him.

The man was a doctor, or so he claimed. They were always different, but their occupations and life stories started to blur together after a few years. It was nice to have company in my cage that didn't want to cut me, but it was always brief. The men would spend a couple nights in here with me, a week at the most, before being taken away, never to be seen again.

I used to cry. I had begged, pleaded, and clung to their legs as they dragged the men out. After the first dozen or so, I learned to stop being attached to my temporary companions. The result would always be the same.

"Those women are brainwashed," the doctor had told me, pacing back and forth in our shared cell. "Not mentally ill, most likely, but manipulated. The old woman, the one up in the chair, she's the master manipulator. The cult leader! Now that one's got a whole slew of mental issues, narcissistic personality disorder for damn sure. Oh, and she's a total sociopath, I'd bet my whole practice on it!"

"It doesn't matter," I'd said, watching his pacing feet scrape a trail through my dried blood on the concrete floor.

"And you." He stabbed a finger in my direction. "You must have a serious case of Stockholm Syndrome, kid. How long have you been in here?"

I'd peered at him from where I sat against the wall. "I've never been anywhere else."

"Oh, Jesus..." He turned back toward the bars, peering around the room beyond the cell as if looking for some way out. "Am I gonna die in here?"

"No." *Not in here, exactly.* I went back to picking the scabs at one of my cuts. "Your stay won't be much longer."

He had been given a hearty meal later that night, a whole roasted chicken with piles of vegetables, rice, and an entire bottle of wine. More food than I ate in a week, usually. I'd learned to stop looking on enviously as they ate their last meal too. It only earned me more bleeding.

"You honor us," the women had told the doctor with their pretty smiles. "Please eat and drink everything. You are our honored guest and will be released tomorrow."

He fell for it. They always did. None of the men placed with me had known hunger and hopelessness for as long as I had. Their lives had given them reasons to hope. They all had something they wanted to return to. Usually a family, children, or some other purpose.

For me, hope was a foreign word. A concept I didn't understand.

The women took him before sunrise the next morning. Hungover, he stumbled out willingly, hesitating only for a moment. "What about him?" he asked with a glance over his shoulder at me.

Sometimes my cellmates asked about me on their way out. Most didn't care.

"He is a prisoner," the woman holding his arm told him. "He hurt one of us, and is being punished for his crimes against us."

I would have laughed if I had known how to.

The doctor was guided out of the dungeon, a woman on each of his arms. All the usual shuffles and thumps as they guided him to the top floor played out like clockwork. The first ray of sunlight poured through the crack in my wall as I passively listened to the monthly ceremony above my cell. Just one more out of so many hundreds of times I heard it before.

"Let me go! What—what's that for?" I heard the doctor ask over the scuffling as he tried to struggle. "Why do you have a knife?"

"You honor us," came the rough, warbling voice of the elder woman, "with your sacrifice."

"*Sacrifice?!* I thought I was being released! Ahhh, fuck!"

"You honor us," she continued, "with your fear."

"What the fuck is wrong with you?! Stay away from me!"

"You honor us with your blood."

Next came the wet, sucking, squelching sounds as she stabbed him. I never saw the ceremony, only heard it. To me, it sounded like she always took deep, long stabbing motions through them. I wondered if she did it to maximize the pain and fear of the victims. Wouldn't surprise me.

"Agh—God! Stop, please!"

The man's blood began dripping through the floor at that point, raining through the roof of my cell like a dark waterfall. I scooted to the corner to stay out from under it. Being covered in my own blood was enough when I had limited water.

"You honor us with your death."

Then a final, wet slicing sound, which could only be across his throat. The doctor only made choked gurgling sounds now as his blood streamed through the cracks in the boards above me.

The doctor's body made a heavy thump as he collapsed on the ground. He flailed a bit, slapping the ground a few times. The flailing gave way to twitching and then, dead stillness. They would leave him there until his blood stopped draining before taking his body to discard it. I never knew what they did with them.

"Because the only good man is a dead one."

Like all the times before, I wondered why they insisted on keeping me alive if that was true. I'd come to my own conclusion years ago, with the help of another man who had shared my cell temporarily.

"You're a training dummy," that man had said. "They get to practice on you before doing the real thing."

It made sense, especially as to why none of my cuts were lethal. Why the ones who cut me were usually the youngest. Some of my earliest memories were staring through the bars of a much smaller cage, my eyes locked onto a girl's roughly the same age as me.

We were both just children, staring wide-eyed at each other, while an older woman pulled my skinny arm through the bars, placed a knife in the girls' hand, and ordered her to cut me until she drew blood.

Sometimes the girls would cry and say no, but they always did eventually. They grew swift and efficient with it, the horror in their eyes morphing into cold hatred as the years passed.

The doctor had been sacrificed last week, so I was surprised to hear more male voices shouting above me as I contemplated my water rationing. The words weren't clear and there seemed to be multiple men, which was odd. Sacrifices were only conducted once a month, the morning of the full moon. My cage was cramped with two people, so the women rarely imprisoned more than one man at a time.

A series of loud pops rang out, and then many voices screaming and shouting. High-pitched feminine ones, and deeper voices rumbling as they shouted things too fast for me to decipher. Dozens of rapid, running footsteps *thump-thump-thumped* over the ceiling of my cage, running back and forth over the popping noises. My ears started to ring, the pops were *that* loud.

Nothing had ever occurred like this in my lifetime and I didn't know what to make of it. I'd never heard the women scream before, and the sound was jarring. Nor had I ever heard running around like everyone was in a mad rush.

Eventually, the footsteps ceased running. The screaming and the popping faded away to nothing. It became eerily quiet—I'd never heard anything like this either. Not even at night when most were asleep. Someone was always talking, cooking, or doing some other chore that I could hear through the walls. Was this what death sounded like?

At some point I heard voices and footsteps again, and that was a small comfort. But these steps were louder, heavier than I'd ever heard before.

The door to the basement slammed open with a loud crash, the wood bouncing against the wall as the heavy footfalls made their way down the stairs to my dungeon.

"Whoo-wee! Smells worse than the whorehouse your mom came from, Jensen." It was definitely a man, dressed in some kind of tactical uniform with all kinds of items hanging off of the thick vest he wore. He held a long, dark object in both hands as he examined the corner of the basement by the door.

"Shut up, Lopez." The reply came with a crackling sound from a small, black box on the man's shoulder. "Just clear the area so we can get the hell out. This place is fucking creepy."

The man chuckled to himself as he finished rummaging through whatever supplies he'd found and started making his way toward me. I kept still, barely breathing, and at a complete loss as to what I should do.

"Holy...shit!" The man stumbled back at the sight of me, eyes wide as he pointed his long, black stick in my direction. "Who are you?"

"I'm..." I stared back at him, noticing how his hands shook and how large his eyes became. "I'm the blood bag."

"What?" He brought a slow, shaky hand to the black box on his shoulder. "Jensen, get your ass down to the basement. Someone's in here, a guy. Looks like a prisoner." He repositioned his grip on his weapon. "I'll ask again. Who are you?"

I didn't know how else to answer. I was a man, and therefore unworthy of an identity, or even a name.

"I'm just the blood bag," I repeated.

"You got a name?"

"No."

"How long have you been here?"

"I've always been here." Why did every man assume I had spent time somewhere else?

"Oh...shit. Okay." He started lowering his stick to point away from me. "Fuck me. They really did a number on you, huh?"

I didn't know what that meant, so I said nothing.

"How old are you?" he asked next.

I coughed, my throat hoarse from how infrequently I spoke. "I don't know."

He blinked several times, his blue eyes narrowing. "So you're tellin' me you've always been in this," he waved his stick around, "in this cage?"

"Yes." Every man that came down here always asked a variation of the same question, and it was tiring.

"Well, huh. Guess we're breaking you out of jail then." His lips pulled to the sides, revealing white teeth as he spread his arms wide. "Every one of those cunts up there is dead. You're free."

"Dead?"

That couldn't be true. The women had always said the blood sacrifices would make them live forever, immune to all earthly suffering. The sacrifices of men were a gift to the goddess and she rewarded them with immortality. So how could they all be dead?

And free? I knew the dictionary definition of the word, but like *hope*, it was a completely foreign concept to me.

"Yeah!" His mouth pulled open wider at the sides. Was that what a smile was supposed to be? "We thought these broads were crazy, but damn." He gestured at me. "Guess they really got what was coming to 'em."

"They're really dead? All of them?"

Dead meant they would never come back. She would never see me again. Never yell, spit on me, or try to hurt me as badly as she could without killing me.

I will never see her again. The thought was never one I'd considered before. It made me feel strange. Heavy. Like I was unraveling from the inside.

"Yeah, man! You should be doing a jig right now. Ah, step aside. Allow me."

I moved to the corner as he raised his long stick, pointing it at the padlock holding my cage doors together. The lock broke apart with a loud clang as something was ejected out of his stick. I covered my ears and shut my eyes at the ringing echoing through my skull.

"There you go, man." I peeked one eye at the man spreading his arms wide as my door swung open. "You're free."

I lowered my hands slowly, the uneasy, unraveling sensation in my body only growing heavier at the sight of the open door. She used to leave it open to test me when I was younger. Even years later, those scars were still the most prominent ones on my back.

"Where do I go?" I looked at the man. "Is there another Sisterhood that needs a blood bag?"

"Jesus Christ..." His lips came together again, face making an expression I didn't understand. "They really fucked you up, man."

Again, I didn't know the meaning of what he was saying. "I'm sorry. I just don't know where to go."

The man scrubbed a hand down his face with a sigh. "It's alright. We'll, uh, we'll figure out some place to take you. I'll be right back."

With that, he headed for the stairs, taking two at a time. I still didn't leave my cell, the only home I'd ever known. I leaned against the wall, listening to the hushed voices outside as they decided what to do with me.

CHAPTER 1

MARIPOSA

PRESENT DAY

"Okay, are you ready?"

The boy nodded, his face serious and determined. I stole a look at his father sitting across the room, and we shared a smile.

"Okay, here goes." I stuck the syringe in his arm where I'd just cleaned with an alcohol wipe and pressed down on the plunger.

The boy hissed at the needle's poke and bit the inside of his cheek against a whimper, shutting his eyes tight.

"All done!" I dropped the syringe in the wastebasket, grabbed the sky-blue band-aid, and laid it carefully over the injection spot. "That's your last vaccine, Jason. You're so brave!"

"It didn't even hurt," he scoffed as he slid off the exam table and returned to his father's side.

The man chuckled as he ruffled his son's hair. "Thank you for squeezing us in at the end of the day, Mari."

"It's no problem at all." I peeled my gloves and white coat off before heading to the sink to wash my hands.

They hesitated by the exam room door. "Do you want us to wait with you?"

"It's okay." I smiled as I dried my hands. "My husband should be outside. Thank you, though."

"Have a good evening, Mari."

"You guys too!"

The door closed softly after them as I pulled on the large, black hoodie. I didn't have to put my nose to the fabric to know that Shadow's scent was fading from it. Trying to catch a whiff of him would only make me feel worse, so I did my best to find comfort in the heavy weight of the fabric. Over the sweatshirt, I pulled on my leather jacket, adjusting the hoodie so it didn't bunch up underneath.

I said goodnight to Rhonda, Dr. Brooks, and the other medics with a smile, like I did every night. A smile that I hoped didn't betray how numb I felt inside.

The rumble of Jandro's bike filled the chilly air as I stepped outside, and my man was leaning against the machine while he waited for me.

"Hey, *bonita*." He wrapped around me, warm and strong. "Everything okay?"

"Yeah, I just had a last-minute vaccination." I tilted my face up, accepting his kiss.

His lips lingered on mine tonight, one warm hand reaching up to caress my cheek. "You want to drive?"

"Sure."

I threw a leg over the bike and gripped the handlebars, Jandro easing into the seat behind me. Riding felt like second nature to me now that I'd had weeks of practice. These days, being in the driver's seat and with Jandro were the only times I felt remotely alive.

The road led us to the house far too soon—that cheery, cozy facade mocking me as we approached. What was supposed to be my home with my four husbands was actually an empty shell. A place to crash in the evenings after I spent most of my day working at the hospital.

Such a waste of a beautiful house.

So many times I wished to make a different turn at the bridge leading into this development. I fantasized constantly about leaving town, riding off into the sunset to find the man I missed so badly that my chest physically ached.

But Jandro would never let me go. And Horus kept telling me it wasn't time yet.

So every night I kept returning here, to this house that filled me with resentment, and continued to wait for when the time was right.

"What's for dinner?" I asked, removing my helmet. Not that I was *feeling* hungry, I hadn't truly felt hungry in weeks. I just knew that my body needed food.

Jandro scraped the mud off his boots on the mat outside the front door. "Chicken *pozole*."

I narrowed my eyes.

He laughed, cupping my face to kiss me. "Not *our* chickens, don't worry. Joe is thinning out his flock, so he gave me a couple."

I relaxed, making my way inside the house that I knew would be empty. Jandro started up a warm blaze in the fireplace while I quickly showered and changed out of my scrubs. He had two bowls of *pozole* doled out when I made it to the kitchen.

"Thank you, *guapito*." I kissed his cheek before taking a seat in front of my bowl.

"Of course."

I felt his eyes on me as I started to eat. I ate fast, spoonfuls of broth, hominy, and chunks of chicken breast came robotically to my mouth. Food barely tasted like anything to me lately, it was just a resource. A means to an end. So I ate quickly.

"Mari."

I readied myself with a quick swallow of broth. Jandro was going to try this again today.

"Yes?"

"Slow down, *mi amor*," he urged, his voice gentle. "If you wait, if we can all eat together—"

I shut him down quickly. "No, thank you. I'm tired, and I'm just going to go to bed."

Jandro sighed, clearly disappointed, but didn't push the issue.

We ate together in silence, him mostly poking at his food while I consumed my sustenance like a robot. When my bowl was empty, I thanked him again with another kiss on the cheek, and cleaned up after myself.

The distant rumbling of motorcycles had just begun as I set my bowl in the dish drying rack. I dried my hands and immediately headed toward Jandro's room, feeling his eyes on me the whole way.

The growling engines were just outside the window as I got undressed for bed, pulling sheets and blankets over me as I curled up on the mattress.

When the engines cut, and I heard Reaper and Gunner's murmured voices from the garage, a pain slashed hard through my chest.

I missed them. I missed them both so fucking much.

But right on the heels of my longing came a different pain, one heated by anger and betrayal.

How could they?

It was that second pain that kept me from springing up and running to them, no matter how badly I craved Reaper's rough touch and Gunner's bright sweetness.

Jandro's voice mingled with theirs through the closed bedroom door as they came inside. All of their voices were low, murmuring and serious. I could only pick up a few *fucks* from Reaper. He sounded angry, his tone harsh and biting.

It hurts to go without your wife, doesn't it? I thought cruelly. *Now you know how I feel, losing a husband.*

Shame flooded my senses, making tears well up in my eyes. When did I become so mean and spiteful? I still loved Reaper, so fucking much. I missed him with every cell in my body. But I also had these moments of hating him so intensely, I felt like a completely different person.

A soft weight dipped the bed near my feet, and then a rumbling purr filled the air.

I reached a hand out for Freyja, her furry head bumping into my palm and rubbing against my whole arm affectionately. She kneaded the mattress directly in front of my chest before flopping down and snuggling against me.

I pet her as she soothed me with that purr. I didn't ask her any questions, nor did she speak to me. Maybe she knew exactly where I was in my grief, anger, and heartache, and simply allowed me to be there. Maybe she knew how touch-starved I was for the three husbands I felt like I no longer had. Whatever the case, Freyja seemed to sense that I didn't want advice, just some comfort to dull the now-permanent ache in my chest.

Jandro came in roughly an hour later, his weight dipping the bed behind me as he shucked off his clothes for the night. The heat of his chest kissed my back as he got settled in, broad body wrapping around me protectively.

"I know you're awake." He brushed a kiss along the back of my shoulder.

"Mm-hm."

Jandro sighed deeply, his breath fanning over my hair. "Mari, how long are you going to keep this up?"

"Keep what up?"

"Come on, babe. I'm serious." His head flopped down on the pillow. "I know you're angry, but it's been almost a month. You have to talk to them at some point."

I curled into a tighter ball, pulling my knees up toward my chest. "I'm not ready."

"Mari." His arm came around my waist, lips light on the back of my neck. "I can tell how much this is hurting you. It's hurting them too. Fuck, it's hurting *me* seeing you all like this."

"And Shadow?" I said. "How much do you think he's hurting?"

"Read his letter again," Jandro said after a few moments of silence. "He wanted you to heal, to be loved by your men. He wouldn't—"

"Stop talking about him like he's dead," I snapped. *He's still out there and he's still mine.*

"I'm not even saying you need to forgive Reap now, or anytime soon. But this whole avoidance thing isn't doing anybody good. Just talk to each other, that's all I'm saying."

"And say what?" I scoffed. "That I'm still angry? That I still want Shadow back? He'll just dig his heels in and stand by his actions like he always does."

"You don't know that. Reap would do anything for you." Jandro brushed a small kiss along the back of my shoulder. "It's killing both of them to not talk to you. They want their wife back."

"Oh, great. Now we've reached the guilt-trip stage," I huffed bitterly. "Well, guess fucking what? I want my husband back. The one *he* sent away when he knew I couldn't do anything to stop him."

"I understand, *mi amor*. You're not the only one who wants him back." Jandro squeezed his arm around my waist. "I miss him too. I don't agree with what Reaper did. I don't think it was right."

"But you still support him." The bitterness coiled deep in my gut, turning all the food in my stomach to acid. "Because you're a good, loyal vice president."

"I understand wanting to protect the woman I love from anything that would harm her, even our own club brothers. Especially if I nearly lost her, and I could remove the cause of her harm for good." Jandro's arm slid from my body as he rolled onto his back. "So no, I don't support it. But I get *why* he did it."

"It was an accident." I felt like I was stuck in an endless cycle of repeating myself. We'd had this conversation so many times already. "It wouldn't have happened again. Shadow would never allow it to happen again. He *never* wanted to hurt me."

"I know," Jandro said gently. "I believe that just as much as you do. On some level, I'm sure Reaper knows it too. He reacted emotionally, as he tends to do. His woman, his whole world, was threatened. So he followed his instincts to eliminate that threat as soon as possible."

"And he did so proudly. He thought it all out. He made a plan, which he carried out in several steps. He could have stopped at any point, but he didn't. He could have waited until I was cleared from the hospital to see how I felt about it, *but he didn't*. He was deliberate about the whole thing, and he will stand by his actions until the day he dies. That's just the kind of person he is."

"*Mariposita*, you won't know that unless you talk to him. He's made mistakes. He does have regrets about actions he's taken. He would never want to hurt you, or jeopardize his marriage."

"Maybe he should have thought of that before, you know, doing exactly that."

Jandro sighed heavily behind me, and I knew he was rubbing his forehead or his eyes. These arguments going in circles were exhausting, and I was sick of them too. At some point, the cycle would have to be broken. I just couldn't bring myself to take that first step. It was easier to be angry, to shut down and wallow in the hurt and bitterness.

His defense of Reaper's actions made sense, and I could see the reasoning behind them too. Really, it was just as I expected from my passionate, protective first husband. But to admit that felt like defeat. It felt like I was excusing his behavior and letting Shadow down. Shadow needed more people on his side, not less. His letter all but told me he would never defend himself in this matter. He accepted Reaper's exile because he believed he deserved it.

If he wouldn't advocate for himself, then I would. I didn't care if I was his victim. I loved him and I knew his heart.

"What do you want to happen, Mari?" Jandro sounded defeated. "How do we fix this?"

"I want Reaper to apologize and admit he was wrong. I want Shadow to come back, and us all to move forward."

"And if that doesn't happen?" he pressed. "We have no way of finding Shadow. For all we know, he could be out of the country now."

"I don't know."

Jandro rolled toward me, resting a hand on my arm. "You have to make a decision, Mari. It's not fair to keep dragging this on."

"What do you mean?" I knew what he was getting at, but I wanted to hear him say it. I needed to know he was serious.

"You have to decide if…if you want to stay married to them or not." His hand fell away. "And to me too, I guess."

It wasn't a complete surprise to hear. The gods knew I had fleeting thoughts of leaving them over the past few weeks. But it still hurt, hearing it spoken into reality. Panic clamped down in my chest as I flipped over to face Jandro in the dark room.

"I love you." My fingers found his face and those plush lips I adored. His arms came around me and pulled me into a deep, emotionally-charged kiss. "I'm sorry this has been so difficult, and you're caught in the middle. But thank you for being here while I need you."

"I love you too," he whispered, stroking over my back in a soothing pattern. "With my whole heart, Mari."

I believed every word as our mouths found each other again. Our kisses were warm, passionate, and loving, but not escalating into lust. I wanted comfort and love, but I couldn't bring myself to do anything sexual since Shadow. Jandro was more than understanding, content to hold me and kiss me while I spent many nights crying.

"But," he murmured at the end of our last kiss. "You know I'm not the only one who loves you."

There it was, the reminder. The reality I couldn't escape from. I did *not* want Reaper or Gunner like I had Jandro right then. I didn't trust myself to even look at my two other men without screaming out all my rage at them.

But I wasn't anywhere near ready to end things either. The mere thought of losing them, setting them free to love other women, ground my heart into dust.

"I'll make a decision," I promised Jandro as I turned onto my opposite side. "Soon. Just not yet."

He kissed between my neck and shoulder as he settled in for sleep. "Okay. Goodnight, my love."

"Goodnight."

Morning came quickly. I got out of bed before Jandro, our usual early riser. His bedroom was on the first story, just a short walk to the kitchen where I started making coffee and a quick breakfast for us both. If Reaper or Gunner's bedroom doors opened on the second floor, I'd be able to hear them and zip back to Jandro's room before they could corner me.

The two of them tried getting up early to talk to me at first. When I kept retreating to my safe space with Jandro, they eventually stopped. I couldn't decide if I was relieved or disappointed at that.

Avoiding them wasn't the only reason I got up early, though. Horus's perch was in the kitchen, mounted high near the vaulted ceiling to resemble a cliff ledge, where falcons usually made their nests.

The bird preened his feathers, pointedly ignoring my staring up at him while the coffee maker gurgled. My patience wore out when the pot was full. "Well?"

Horus fluffed up his feathers before smoothing them down, peering at me with those razor-sharp eyes.

Today is not the day, daughter. The time is not right.

I grabbed the coffee pot's handle and jerked it toward me, frustration and disappointment bleeding into my movements as I slammed a cup down on the counter. Another fucking day of waiting.

And so the cycle of numbness and heartache started again.

CHAPTER 2

REAPER

My eyes wouldn't stop aching no matter how much I rubbed them. Exhaustion was setting in hard. I probably only got a single night's worth of sleep in three fucking weeks. Next to me, Gunner didn't look much better. The whites of his eyes were red, dark circles underneath them making him look like a raccoon.

The two of us looked, and most likely felt, like ghosts. Haunted and empty.

"What are we gonna do, Reap?" It wasn't the first time he'd asked that question, his voice coming out like a sad whimper.

I gave him the same answer I always did. "I don't know."

"Is this it?" he went on. "We're coming up on a month of this. Is she done with us?"

Two weeks ago, maybe even days ago, I would have told him no fucking way. Mari was angry and just needed time to cool off. She had Jandro firmly in her corner. He'd make her see reason and come around.

Then the days of silence stretched on. Night after night, I went to bed alone. The closest I got to touching my wife was running my finger over the stone on her ring, which rested on my nightstand. Every single attempt to talk to her was met with a door slammed in my face.

I wasn't ready to give up. Not until Mari looked me in the eye and told me to my face that I wasn't her husband anymore. If she wanted to avoid me and slam doors in my face for another year, so be it. I would wait until she gave me an answer.

But fuck if this weird limbo wasn't taking its toll on me. I fucking missed my wife, everything from her hair drifting over my skin as we slept, to her snappy little comebacks when I teased her. All my waking energy was spent being pissed at Jandro because he was the only one she talked to. Just the fact that he had her in his bed every night made me see red. I fucking hated feeling like an outsider in my own marriage.

It wasn't even about sex. My drive had shriveled down to nothing the moment she called me a heartless piece of shit and took her ring off. I wanted only her, and only if she still loved me. Jealousy burned in me knowing she still loved Jandro, and probably even Shadow, for all the fuck I knew.

That was the worst part—that I no longer *knew* if she still loved me or not.

"Reaper," Gunner whined again after I didn't answer him. "I'm near the end of my rope, man. I can't handle this shit, I *need* to know where I stand with her."

"I. Know." The words came out with a biting growl. "You don't think I feel the exact same way you do?"

"You're the pro at this shit, not me." He lifted his hands, elbows resting on the conference room table. "What would your parents do in this situation?"

"No fucking clue." I rolled my head around on my tired, aching neck. "Nothing like this has ever happened between my parents, or anyone in my community."

"I wouldn't wish this on anyone," Gunner groaned, pinching his forehead. "I feel like I'd fall on my knees with relief if she would just look at me."

"Yeah," I agreed. That was how desperate we were. She could throw us scraps, any small acknowledgment of our existence, and we'd eat it up like starving dogs.

The conference room door opened, and I peered through my bleary eyes to see my dad walking in. He came through with something held high above his head, like a victory trophy, then subsequently dropped his arm when he saw our faces.

"You boys look shittier by the day," he remarked, approaching the table with one of his lieutenants behind him.

"You got somethin'?" I nodded at the folder he placed on the table, not caring to hash out my marital problems at work.

Dad nodded, his grin returning. "Andrea has made contact. So she's alive and carrying out her part of the mission." He turned to his lieutenant, a slender south-Asian man who radiated a calm, understated strength. "This is Anurak. He developed the code and will be translating Andrea's messages. I figured you boys would want to be the first to know what it says."

"Yes, please." Gunner reached over and shook Anurak's hand. "Thank you for working with us on this."

"It's my pleasure." Anurak took a seat and opened the folder, examining the full page of foreign characters while my dad got him a pen and plain sheet of paper.

I leaned over to look at the glyphs Andrea had written, my weary eyes quickly blurring all the symbols together. "Is that a made-up code or a real language?"

"It's based on my native language, which is Thai," Anurak explained. "But it's altered slightly, so that even if a Thai speaker were to find the message, they would not be able to decode it."

"I didn't know Andrea spoke Thai," Gunner mused.

"She doesn't," Anurak said with a polite chuckle. "She's using the phonetic sounds of the characters to compose a message in English. Because Thai and English consonants don't match up exactly, we did have to invent a few."

"She learned it pretty fucking fast," I remarked.

"We gave her a copy of the codex to carry with her," my dad said. "But encouraged her to memorize it and destroy it at the first opportunity, so her messages wouldn't be compromised."

"Here." Anurak dragged his finger across a row of characters. "She says she burned the codex, and this message is composed entirely from memory."

Dad clapped his hands once. "That's our girl."

The three of us waited as the lieutenant transcribed the message onto the piece of paper, capping his pen with a definitive click. "Would you like to do the honor, General?" Anurak slid the translation across the table to my dad.

General Bray accepted the paper, his eyes scanning it before relaying the information. "Everyone here worships General Tash like a god," he read aloud, his brow pinching. "From food and clothing, to weapons and victories in battle, everything is attributed to his greatness. However, no one seems to have direct contact with him. Everyone is a messenger, or a foot-soldier. The only ones who speak to him directly are a small group called the General's Council. They have immense power and influence, and are the ones who relay the general's orders to the rest of the army. I have met several men in saloons who claimed to be General Tash undercover, keeping a watchful eye over his citizens. It's clear, however, that no one knows who the general truly *is*. He stays out of sight and gives commands from on high like a deity."

Dad paused in his reading, noticing as Gunner and I exchanged a look. "You two said you traded goods with this guy?"

"Yeah." Gunner stroked his jaw, his eyes more focused than they had been in weeks. "It was always the same guy, his uniform decorated in medallions and with general's stars. He claimed to be Tash, and his soldiers referred to him as such. But apparently that's not the case, huh?"

"It was probably one of these council members acting in his stead." I drummed my fingers on the table. "What else does Andrea say?"

"She says, 'I'm getting close to some of the unit leaders, but must tread delicately. I can't dig for intel too aggressively, or else I risk my position. Below are current estimates based on what I've already found out.'" Dad proceeded to list numbers of Jeeps, ground units, sniper units...and other shit my exhausted brain was too tired to catch, before setting the message back down on the table. "Her message ends there."

"Nothing about Big G's fuckery, huh?" Gunner shoved his hair back. "I still can't wrap my mind around that."

"If she's getting close enough to unit leaders to bring us these numbers already," Anurak tapped his fingers on the original coded message, "she's likely not being regarded as a suspicious person. Is it possible Big G may have done what he did to throw suspicion off of her?"

"Maybe," I sighed. "I hope she gets closer to these council people. I need to know how to topple Tash himself."

"It's just the first message, son," Dad reminded me. "This is a long game. Every message will give us a clearer picture of what's going on in there."

"I know, you're right," I sighed. "Anything else?"

Dad's smile wavered. "Yeah, that was the good news. We're also getting reports that Blakeworth units are mobilizing. They're moving toward us, but staying just out of our reach in the neutral territory north of here. It's looking like they want to draw us out for a skirmish."

"Great." I went back to rubbing my eyes. "Just fan-fucking-tastic."

"Gunner, I'm gonna want your input on the best way to engage them," Dad said. "How many units we should send, what kind of artillery to bring. We want to shove them back, but be mindful that we're dealing with conscripts and don't want overkill. Regardless, they won't go away unless we respond. Can you meet with us this afternoon?"

"Yeah," Gunner said blankly. "Sure."

Eying us carefully, Dad turned to Anurak. "Thank you, lieutenant. I'll leave you to bring these numbers to our tactics teams. Can I have a word with my sons?"

"Of course, General." The man swiftly excused himself from the table and Dad turned on us the moment the door closed. "What the hell is going on with you two?"

"Just the same old shit," I grumbled. "Mari's still not talking to us after the whole exiling-Shadow thing."

"And you still haven't done anything to fix it?" He glared at us. "What kind of husbands are you?"

"I'm sorry, what the fuck are we supposed to do?" I spread my hands out, my voice rising. "No one knows where Shadow went, so we can't exactly drag him back here so everyone can kiss and make up."

"You can be a man and quit with the fucking excuses." Finn Daley was the only man in the world who could make me feel small, and I felt like I was under the stare of a giant right then. "You do whatever is in your power to make this right. Camp outside her door. Spend an entire week on your knees begging for forgiveness, I don't care. Your woman is the center of your family and you have wronged her. You caused her this pain, so it's on you to fix."

"But—"

"Ah!" Dad cut Gunner off swiftly with a raised finger and a look that dared him to keep arguing. Smartly, Gunner shrank into his seat and kept his mouth shut. I knew he'd been happy to bond with my dad, but good father figures weren't always warm and loving. Finn was giving us a much-deserved tongue lashing, and I hoped Gun understood that.

"I know you boys know you fucked up," Dad said in a gentler tone. "You've given her space to be angry, and that's good. But enough time has passed now that you need to assert yourselves as men, *her* men. The longer you let her shut you out, the less respect for you she'll have." He leaned back, crossing his arms over his chest. "And no woman wants to fuck, much less be tied down to, a guy she doesn't respect."

"What if..." Gunner hesitated, chewing his lip. "What if she doesn't want us back?"

"She would've kicked your sorry asses out already if that was the case," Dad replied. "I know how much this hurts, boys, I do. But you gotta fight for your marriage and not let all this bitterness drag out and fester. And when you overcome this, your relationships with her *will* be stronger."

"You've been through stuff like this?" Gunner asked, wide-eyed.

"I've never forced out one of my wife's men behind her back," Dad laughed. "But have I gotten the silent treatment after being an idiot? Oh hell yeah."

"And doing this...worked for you?"

"Every time," Dad nodded. "For smaller things, Lis would come talk to me on her own when she was ready. But when I *really* fucked up, it was on me to *make* her see how much I wanted to set things right. Otherwise, I knew I'd lose her."

"I'm scared of pushing Mari away," Gunner admitted, raking his hands back through his hair. "Like we're already too far gone and there's no coming back." He looked to me for confirmation and I nodded, letting him know I had the exact same fear.

"You want to make that a self-fulfilling prophecy, just keep doing what you're doing." Dad brought his palms to the table as he stood up. "Your marriage is withering away. You can either keep neglecting it and allow it to die, or put some fucking effort in and bring it back to life."

With that sage advice, he left us to make our decision.

Chapter 3

IVAN

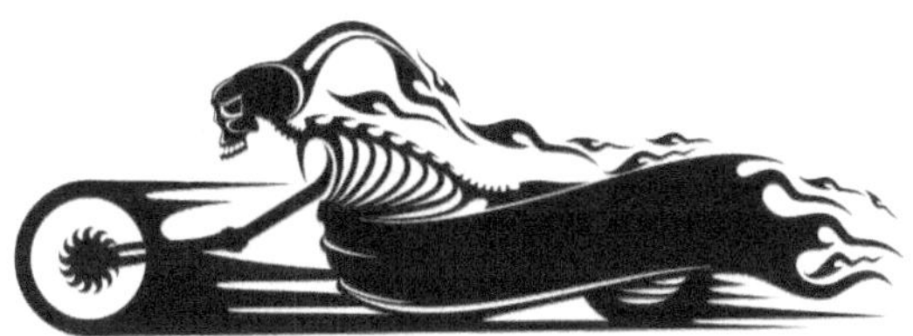

"Remove the bandage in a few hours. Wash it thoroughly with soap and water, and moisturize it at least twice a day until it heals." I gave my client's skin another wipe before pressing the bandage to her fresh tattoo, holding it in place with one hand while I peeled strips of tape with the other. "It's going to start itching after a few days and that's normal, but avoid scratching it. The itch means it's healing." I finished taping the bandage in place and sat back to pull my gloves off. "If it becomes red or painful, beyond the usual soreness, see a medic, or an artist with a good reputation, if you can."

"Got it! Thanks, Ivan." My client hopped off the table, stretching her arms over her head when her feet hit the floor. "I left your payment with the bartender, like you said."

"Great. Thank you." I made a half-hearted attempt to smile, but the expression didn't feel natural anymore. "Enjoy the rest of your stay."

The woman went off to find her fiancé, who was most likely appraising some of the vehicles in the junkyard. Like most of my clients, they were just traveling through. Apparently this couple had heard my name from another tattoo client a few towns over. Good tattooists seemed to be a rare find out here, so they came to this service center specifically to seek me out.

That had been happening more often lately. And my one-week stay soon turned into three weeks. But it wasn't just the tattoo work keeping me here.

I glanced at the clock above the bar as I cleaned up my supplies, anxiety gripping my chest at what was to come in the next half-hour.

Once my area was tidied, I parked at my usual spot at the bar and waited for Jen to finish with her current customers.

"Hey big guy, you want your payment?" she asked me.

"Yes, please." I tried not to outwardly bristle at the nicknames she gave me.

"Always so polite," Jen mused as she reached under the bar and set my whiskey in front of me. "Your mother must have taught you well. You want a glass?"

My mother never taught me anything remotely useful, but she didn't need to know that. "Yes, thank you."

"Want me to pour?"

"Thanks, I got it."

"Such a gentleman." Jen smiled, stretching her forearms out on the bartop next to me.

The bar was slow, which meant she'd likely want to hang out and talk. Her arms were covered in black outlines that I'd started a few days ago, along with small bits of color filled in for her sleeves. In another two weeks, she'd be covered in bright floral designs from shoulder to wrist.

I liked Jen, which was not something I thought I'd ever feel about another woman. She was friendly and talkative, protective of the service girls when men came to stay, and a hardass when it came to cutting off liquor for sloshed bar patrons. I could have done without the nicknames like *big guy, big boy,* and *handsome,* but other than that, she was a good client and bartender.

"You seein' Doc soon?" she asked, her voice lowering.

"Yeah." I swallowed my first mouthful of whiskey and poured another.

"How's that been going?"

I paused to throw back my next drink before answering. "It feels like hell when it's happening but...I think it's actually working." I started pouring my third shot. "So I keep going back."

"That's good!" Jen's arm slid across the bar to nudge against mine. I fought back the urge to pull away from the touch. It would've been rude, or at least that was what some niggling voice in my head told me.

"I give him shit for being a dirty old man, but I swear Doc saved my life," she continued in a near-whisper. "I was having nightmares, panic attacks set off by the littlest shit. Got hooked on booze, pills, anything I could get my hands on to make it go away. Fuck, I wanted to end it all." Jen nudged her elbow into my arm. "What's your flavor of misery?"

"Um." I felt fine to talk to her about mundane things, but absolutely not this. "Nightmares, mostly. Sorry if you've heard me at night."

She raised one shoulder in a shrug. "Hey, I get it. And I haven't heard a peep out of your room in a week, so that's somethin', huh?"

"Yeah." I stared at my bottle and empty glass, debating on one more drink before going to see Doc. It was still early on in my treatment, so I couldn't be sure if it was Doc's bizarre therapy letting me sleep through the night or simply my old habit of drinking myself into oblivion. "Maybe it is."

Jen lifted her chin, her eyes focused on my other arm. "Your nightmares got anything to do with her?"

I followed her gaze to the fresh tattoo inside my left forearm, where a beautiful, dark-haired woman stretched from my elbow to my wrist. I did it in a pin-up style, the woman's large eyes were sultry and inviting with her lips curved into a coy smile. She wore a cropped T-shirt with a horned skull on the front, black jeans with rips in the knees, and motorcycle boots with her feet crossed at the ankles.

"No," I told Jen absently, my gaze fixed on the image embedded in my skin. "She has nothing to do with the nightmares."

I loved her, and then became her *nightmare.*

While I had no regrets about it, the tattoo was done in a moment of weakness. I had been here a full week, drunk in my room at night, my brain unwilling to let me sleep. I was missing her so badly, the ache in my chest made it difficult to breathe. I stared at the drawing I made of her for hours, tracing the pencil lines with my finger over and over, remembering how I'd mapped her body during our last night together.

The more I drank, the more I sank into the memories. Her voice, her laughs, the sounds she made in her climax. The taste of her, the warmth of her lips on my scars. The way she looked at me—without fear.

The paper wore so thin that it ripped.

I flew into a panic, immediately grabbing a pen to copy the drawing onto my forearm. Another empty bottle later, my tattoo machine buzzed late into the night, making the woman I loved in a past life a permanent fixture on my body. I could barely bring myself to think of her name because of how much it hurt, but not even Ivan could fully let go of the woman Shadow had loved.

Looking at the tattoo brought me no joy, no nostalgia of a better time. It only brought me sorrow. All it reminded me of was how much I lost, how badly I fucked up the one good thing I had. How much I deserved to be here, far away from the woman I missed so much.

With a resigned sigh, I stood from the bar. "I better get going. Thanks, Jen."

"Hey." She reached for me, her hand landing softly on top of mine. Again, I fought the urge to snatch my hand away. "If you ever want to talk after the bar's closed, or you know, get something out of your system..." her fingers stroked over mine, "I'm here for you, Ivan."

It took me a moment, but from the way she kept trying to touch me, I could figure out what she was implying. I tried to see her from the perspective of a normal man—the attractive, edgy bartender with her piercings and tattoos, damaged in her own way but not completely unlike me. She was a good friend, and if I was anyone else, maybe I would take her invitation as a way to distract myself.

But there was only one woman whose touch I craved. Maybe that would change in the future, but right then I was content to wallow in my self-flagellation. Torturing myself with the ink on my arm as a constant reminder, and holding on to memories I wasn't ready to let go of.

"Thanks, Jen," I repeated before sliding my hand out from under hers, unsure of what else to say.

Turning away from the bar, I headed for a side door that could have passed for an office or supply closet. In truth, it was a basement.

Ducking my head and squeezing down the narrow staircase, I reached the basement floor to find Doc waiting for me.

"You keep coming back," he stated, leaning against the chair in the center of the room. "That's promising." The frizzy gray hair on the top of his head was illuminated by the long, tungsten light tubes hanging from the ceiling.

"Let's get this over with." I went to the chair and sat down. The metal frame didn't budge under my weight, due to being bolted down to the concrete floor.

"Had a couple drinks?" Doc asked casually as he wrapped the attached metal cuffs around my arms and legs.

"Yes." I watched him shackle me in, always making sure to slide two fingers between my skin and the cuffs to check my circulation. "Why do you suggest drinking before this, anyway?"

"Alcohol depresses the central nervous system." His matter-of-fact tone reminded me of *her*.

I swallowed the lump in my throat and shoved thoughts of her away. There was no room for her here.

"With the physical senses dulled and inhibitions lowered, it's easier for the patient to go *inward*." Once I was fully restrained, he tapped my forehead with one finger and gave me an unnerving smile. "That's where we go during these treatments, Ivan. Are you ready?"

I was never ready, not really. I hated, dreaded, *loathed* every second of this. But I could feel it changing me. The monster created within me lashed out in full force during these sessions, but I could feel it weakening, like its energy was being spent. The nightmares still came, but they didn't send me on a destructive rampage like they used to.

She had told Shadow something once, that he—I—had to address the root of my fear, the cause of what morphed me into this creature, before I could get better. Taking sleeping pills hadn't protected her from me, so she was probably right. But I couldn't imagine this being what she had in mind.

"Yeah." I lifted my eyes to Doc. "Go ahead."

The man took his glasses off and stuffed them in his shirt pocket. From the same pocket, he pulled a length of string with one end tied through a hole in a coin.

"Take a few deep breaths, Ivan." The coin spun on the string before Doc held it still with his opposite hand.

I pulled deep lungfuls of air through my nose, releasing them through my mouth as he'd instructed me on our first day. After a cycle of ten breaths, Doc released the coin and held it from the top of the string, roughly a foot in front of my face.

"Continue your breaths," he said as the coin began to swing in slow arc from left to right. "Let your eyes follow the coin as you listen to my voice."

Doc stood just outside of my field of vision, letting my eyes focus only on the coin swinging in front of me, and the empty room beyond. Eventually the two began to blur, my focus pulling inward at the lack of stimulation from my surroundings. I wasn't sure how Doc knew, but this was always the spot where he guided me further.

"Good, Ivan. I'm going to count backwards from ten now. With each count, I want you to descend into yourself. Like stepping into an elevator going down. Ten...nine...eight..."

My eyelids grew heavier as he counted, shutting to the point of not fully closed, but where I could barely see through my eyelashes. I didn't strain for sight, knowing now that my eyes wouldn't show me my physical surroundings, but what I shoved away deep in my mind. That was where my internal elevator was descending.

"...Five...four...three..."

All physical sensations fell away until it felt like I was floating. I didn't feel the chair underneath me or the cuffs locking my limbs down. New sensations took over that felt like they were in my body, but I knew they weren't. It was unnerving how *real* things could feel, deep in the recesses of my mind.

"...One."

Doc's voice fell away and the best way I could describe the feeling was coldness. A chill on my skin and also within me, along with a deep, gaping emptiness. I now knew that feeling to be profound loneliness.

"Where are you, Ivan?"

I didn't need to force my eyes open to know exactly where I was.

"I'm here, in my cage." My body felt small in this place, this time, the voice coming out of it sounded too big.

"Is anyone with you?"

"No, I'm alone."

"Can you tell me how old you are at this point in your life?"

I moved my head slowly, taking in the surroundings of the prison embedded deep in my memories. Iron bars covered in dark specks of my blood. Dark stains on the concrete floor—more of my blood. A small pile of bones in the corner of the cage, some animal I'd eaten and picked clean two days before. I was starving again.

"I...don't know."

"Can you read and write?"

I observed my cell some more, noticing a short stack of books in another corner. Loose papers were tucked between the pages. Oh yes, I remembered now. If I went over there, I'd find a small groove in the floor where I kept a pen. I used it to practice writing, copying sentences from the books. I'd had it for years and it ran out of ink a long time ago, but it was the only one I had, so I kept it. I just pressed hard to make indentations in the paper.

"Yes," I answered Doc. "I'm...teaching myself how. So I must be around thirteen."

"And how do you feel right now?"

"I feel...sad. Hungry. Lonely. I..." I resumed my breathing as he taught me, using it to navigate this other overwhelming need I didn't have words for at the time. "...I *want* something. No, someone."

"Can you tell me more about that? Are you wanting a particular person? Or more of a general wanting someone to keep you company?"

"No...I mean, I wish someone, anyone, was with me. But there is a person I want too."

"Who is that?"

"I don't know...I can't..."

It was just *there*, the person I wanted to see. Like someone was standing on the other side of a thick fog. I knew they were there, but I had to reach. My mind couldn't seem to—

"Fuck!" I jolted away when her face broke through into sharp clarity.

"Ivan, what is it?"

She appeared out of thin air, like a ghost, standing just outside of my cage. I could feel myself shrinking back against the wall, fear riding my system as she casually spun a knife in her hand. But it wasn't just fear, it was immense relief. A feeling so sweet, I wanted to cry. *Finally, she came to see me!*

The past feelings of relief rolled through me alongside the current ones, like oil floating on top of water, existing together but never able to mix. I *hated* her, hated that I had been waiting like a desperate puppy for her attention again, when she always just came to hurt me.

A violent anger simmered, held back on a tight leash by my breathing and this metal chair restraining me. *How could you?* I wanted to say to her. *I never did anything to you. I* needed *you, and you left me to rot down here!*

"Ivan, tell me what you see." Doc's voice grounded me, reminding me of my true location. "You're safe here, son. No one's gonna hurt you. Just tell me what you see."

"I see *her*," I whispered. "She's standing right outside my cage, trying to decide where she'll cut me today."

"Which one is it today?"

"*Her.*" I emphasized the word. "The one who cut my face and tried to take my eye. The one who always cuts me the deepest because she hates me so much."

"And how do you feel seeing her? What's going through your head?"

"I'm scared," I admitted. "I can't feel pain anymore, but I'm going to bleed a lot and that won't be good. But also I...I'm so happy." A shaky laugh escaped. "She hasn't come to see me in weeks. I'm so relieved she came back."

"Why?" Doc couldn't keep the disdain from his voice. "Why would you be happy to see her?"

"Sometimes I think she cuts me so deeply because she loves me. Why else would she keep coming back? She yells and screams that she hates me when no one else does. She's the only woman who talks to me at all. Maybe it's because I'm so alone and going crazy, but I *want* her to love me. I want her to keep coming back. I get so sad when she's gone for weeks."

Another laugh floated up from my chest, this one weak and embarrassed. "I feel stupid and weak for being happy to see her. I hate her. I hate that I want love or anything from her, but she's the only person in the world I have."

Doc was silent for a few moments. "Why do you want her to love you?"

"Because." I stared back at the woman with hollow, hateful eyes. "She's my mother."

Chapter 4

MARIPOSA

"Alright, you brave little lady." I scooped up a crying, fussing Vivian and turned to place her in Tessa's arms. "Here's your mama."

Tessa shushed and bounced Vivian against her chest while rubbing her back. "It's okay, sweetie, no more poking. Auntie Mari promises to be nice from now on."

I smiled at the familial term while I cleaned up debris from Vivian's shots. "Normally she'd have boosters in a few years, but there's no telling when new vaccines will be made. So you're off the hook for a while, little miss."

Tessa smiled as Vivian started to calm down. "How's everything going?"

"Eh." I shrugged and flung my hand in a noncommittal gesture, not eager to get into the fact that I hadn't spoken to two of my husbands in a month. "How are you holding up?"

"I won't say it's been easy," the young mother sighed. "But now that Andrea's made contact, it's a little easier."

My eyebrows lifted into my hairline. "Oh, she has? That's great!"

"You didn't know?" Tessa frowned. "They translated her first message yesterday. T-Bone didn't tell me what it said, but she seems to be okay, which is all that matters to me really." She gave me a strange look. "I figured Reaper would have told you."

"Oh yeah, you know." I shoved my hands into the pockets of my white coat, trying to lean casually against the counter. "We've both been really busy."

Tessa wasn't fooled, her stare was as hard as a sledgehammer while I tried desperately to not shatter into pieces on the floor. I could fall apart again tonight in bed, with Jandro holding me. Not here at work.

"Mari, you'd tell me if something was going on, right?"

I pulled in a heavy breath. "Yeah! Yeah, of course. I mean, it's—" My chest shook, my resolve threatening to unravel. "It's just things are still kinda tense since..."

"Shadow?" Tessa guessed.

"Yeah." My chest deflated and I preferred not to elaborate. Word spread quickly after Shadow left. My guys didn't put out to the club the details of what happened, but people speculated and put pieces together on their own. Shadow was gone without a trace, but my injuries didn't fully heal until a week later. They saw the cuts on my nose, the bruising on my forehead and neck, and drew their own conclusions.

I would have loved nothing more than to set the record straight, but the Steel Demons were Reaper's men, not mine. They would stand with his decision, no matter how I felt about it.

And it didn't feel right to hash it out with Tessa, who I had encouraged to leave her own husband. As shitty a partner as Big G was, he never hurt her in the way Shadow hurt me.

Thankfully, Tessa didn't press me to talk about it. She stood with Vivian in one arm, diaper bag in the other, as she gave me a quick hug. "You've been with me through so much. Remember I'm here for you too, Mrs. President."

"Thanks." I gave her a half-hearted smile. "I'll walk you out. Is T-Bone picking you up?"

"I dunno. One of those crazy bastards is," she laughed with a roll of her eyes.

It was actually Dyno, the sides of his head freshly shaved and topknot of dark hair pulled tight at his crown. He was all decked out in black leather, sitting atop a rumbling, stretched out Fat Boy in front of the hospital.

"There's my baby!" He grinned, reaching gloved hands out toward us as we came outside. It took me a moment to realize he was talking about Vivian, not Tessa.

"You'll hold her when we get home." Tessa smacked his hands away, but allowed him to take her diaper bag and secure it in one of the compartments.

"But Vivi told me she wants to drive." Dyno unwound a black scarf from his neck and proceeded to wrap it around the baby's head.

"I should've known you spoke Babbling Infant," Tessa cracked, helping him secure the scarf around Vivi's ears to muffle the noise of the bike.

It was cute and wholesome watching them, looking established in this routine like they did it all the time. I couldn't tell right off the bat if there was anything romantic between those two or not. It was pretty clear that the three Sons of Odin were all in a relationship with each other. But there was apparently some degree of openness to it, as I found out on the ride back from Blakeworth. Grudge had helped watch over Shadow when I caught Dyno and T-Bone in bed with a service girl.

"I'll see you guys later," I said with a wave.

Tessa and Dyno waved back as they pulled out of the lot, Vivi strapped to her mother's chest and looking stylish with her black head wrap.

"There you are, Mari." Dr. Brooks came up to me just as I returned to the hospital lobby.

"What do you need, Doctor?" I was itching to get back into work mode and stop thinking about relationships, especially mine.

"Just updating you. General Bray is sending a few units north to engage with some activity from Blakeworth. We want to have some field medics within reach just in case—"

"I'll go."

"Uh." The doctor blinked, taken aback. "You don't have to, we have a team ready. The mission is expected to take a few days, maybe a week. So I figured you'd want to stay here with your family."

"Is Rhonda staying?" I asked.

"Yes, she's retired from combat medic duties."

"Then the hospital is in good hands. If anyone on the field team would prefer to stay, I'll swap places with them."

Dr. Brooks' warm gaze turned piercing as he looked at me. "Are you sure, Mari? You've already been pulling a lot of long hours in the past few weeks. I was actually going to suggest you take some time off."

"I don't want time off. I want to work," I insisted. "Put me out in the field, Doctor. It's what I know and what I do best. My family understands."

His narrow-eyed stare continued to probe but he eventually nodded. "The team heads out tomorrow at five a.m. They're setting up ahead of the army, which is due to leave at six."

"I'll be here."

"Thank you, Mari." He gave a friendly squeeze of my shoulder. "Four Corners is in good hands with you. Go on and head home early if you don't have any appointments."

"Thanks, Doctor. See you in the morning."

Going home early was the last thing I wanted to do, so I killed time in the cafeteria with the other hospital staff on breaks until Jandro came to get me.

The evening wrapped up like every other one. I drove us home, washed up, we ate dinner together, and went to bed. I told Jandro where I'd be going tomorrow and while he didn't seem happy, he didn't fight me too much on it. Right before falling asleep, he agreed to let me take the dirt bike and ride to the hospital on my own. He didn't have to be at the garage until three hours later, and I insisted he get some much-needed sleep.

The world was still dark and cold when I crawled out of bed. After getting dressed, I wrote a quick love note for Jandro to find on the nightstand. It was little more than, *Love you. See you in a few days.* I was still half-asleep when I opened the bedroom door and crashed directly into a wall.

A solid wall that was warm, and smelled like cloves and whiskey.

"What..." My brain was slow to make the connection until a hand with strong, callused fingers clasped around my wrist.

"Mari, please." Reaper's voice was hushed. "We need to talk."

Even with how quietly he spoke, his voice was still a shock to my system. My heart jumped into my throat the moment he breathed my name, breath frozen for a moment until I composed myself.

"I don't have time for this." I pulled my arm out of his grip and tried to move around him, but he blocked my path, bracing a hand on each side of the door frame.

"I'm not leaving until you talk to me," Reaper growled. "This has gone on long enough."

"How did you even know I was getting up this early?"

"I didn't. I slept on the couch so I could catch you." He angled his head back, and I could see the pillow and messed up blanket on the long sectional in the living room behind him.

I also saw Hades and Freyja, their animal eyes bright as they watched us like a couple at a sports match.

Great, so our marriage is just as entertaining for gods as it is for humans, I thought bitterly as I went to duck under Reaper's arm. He stopped me, catching me around the waist. My temper spiked as I struggled to get away, but so did something else.

If my skin could talk, it would be crying out in sweet relief. I didn't even realize how much I missed Reaper's touch. The smell of him and the solidness of his body. It all came rushing back to me like a drug high as he pinned me against his chest with one arm, softly closing Jandro's bedroom door with the other.

"Let me go." I hardly dared to make my voice louder than a whisper, not wanting to involve anyone else in this. "You fucking let me go right now, Reaper!"

"No." His breath was hot, voice harsh against my ear. "You are my wife and I'm *never* letting you go." The fight started to drain from my body as I heard the deeper meaning in his words, loud and clear. The more I sagged against him limply, the tighter he held me. "I love you, and I'm never letting you go."

My legs wanted to give out, to let my strong, capable husband support me and make everything better. But just as my longing for him ripped open like a scab on a fresh wound, so did the resentment and the burning anger. He was stubborn enough to make good on his word, but I'd fight him every step of the way if he insisted on holding me captive.

Sometimes he could be reasoned with, and now that he was desperate, I hoped this was one of those times.

"I can talk for a minute, just get off me."

Reaper's arms released me slowly, like he was afraid I would bolt at the first chance. And I wanted to. We stood outside of Jandro's room, tension wrought between both of us in the dark, early morning.

"Do you, uh," Reaper's voice was harsh and raspy like he'd been smoking too much, "want to sit down?"

I sidestepped toward the couch he'd been sleeping on, pulling the blanket over my legs like it would shield me from him. Hades and Freyja, in their front-row seats to our mess, watched him move to sit on the far side of the couch. Looking at Reaper expectantly, I folded my hands on top of the blanket and waited.

"I..."

So eager to talk just a few moments ago, Reaper now seemed at a loss for words. His forearms rested on his knees, eyes flicking up from me and back down to his hands.

"I really have to get going soon," I told him. "And not just because I'm avoiding you."

"I understand. I just, I..." his head tilted back with an exhausted sigh. "I miss you so much, Mari."

I miss you too. So fucking much. My teeth came down hard on the inside of my cheek to prevent the words from coming out.

"I want my wife back." Reaper's hand moved to the couch cushion next to him, a small motion toward closing the distance between us. "I want *us* back." His hand slid a whole inch toward me, stopping as I scooted away. The hurt on his face cut like glass.

"You...*hurt* me." The words came out through gritted teeth, my nails biting into my palms to remind me of just how much it hurt. "And you might not have killed Shadow, but you *destroyed* him. I loved him, Reaper. I knew it wouldn't be easy, that he would be a work in progress, and that he'd need help, possibly for the rest of his life. And you undid *all* of it."

"I know." His hand returned to his knee, fingers clasped loosely as his head hung low, his throat worked in heavy swallows. "I'm so, so sorry, Mari."

I didn't want to acknowledge that apology. It sounded half-hearted and cheap, so I said nothing. Silence passed between us, no sounds except for our breaths sawing in and out of our chests.

"I thought I was protecting you. I thought sending him away was my duty, as a president and a husband, to do things right." His voice, now heavy with sorrow, cut through the silent air. "That was wrong of me. I should have trusted your word, instead of writing you off to protect my ego." Reaper's head lowered until his hands touched his forehead. "I'm sorry. I never would have done it if I knew it would hurt you so much." His head lifted slightly, eyes turning toward me. "If I knew it would damage us like this, I'd have never let it cross my mind."

I could hear the aching hurt in every one of his words. He sounded sincere and truly pained by his actions. It dulled the edge of my anger a little, but not fully.

"Shadow is the real victim in this," I said. "You, me, Gunner, and Jandro? We all have the same things we started out with—the club, our jobs, this house, the favor of the governor. But *he* has nothing anymore. Do you realize that?"

Reaper nodded tiredly. "Yes, I know."

"I want to believe that you're sorry. I want to believe that you regret what you did and want to make things right. And I..." My breath shook as my chest tightened. "I want our family back together too."

"But?" he prompted me gently.

"But I can't just let this go while Shadow is still out there, suffering for the consequences of *your* actions." I stabbed a finger toward his chest. "At the end of the day, we still have beds to sleep in and food on our table. We still have a community that supports and cares for us. But *he* doesn't. And that," I shook my head, "means I can't go back to being happily married to you and Gunner. Not until I have *all* the men I love back where they need to be."

"I understand, sug—Mari." Reaper sighed deeply, rubbing his eyes. "If I allow him to come back into the club with no questions asked, would that be a step in the right direction?"

"Do you really mean that or are you saying it because it's what I want to hear?"

"I mean it. He can return to his original position, no questions asked. It's just..."

"What?"

"After knowing what he did to you, seeing it with my own eyes..." Reaper swallowed. "It...might be difficult for me to work with him, to trust him like I did before." His fingers clasped tighter together. "But I'll do it anyway. I'll welcome him back and I promise not to make any issues for him. It's just...something personal I have to get past."

"That's a nice sentiment," I said, skepticism coloring my voice. As long as he followed through on his actions, it didn't really matter to me how he felt. "Now, how are you going to let Shadow know he's welcome back in Four Corners with open arms?"

Reaper spread his hands. "I'll put the word out as far as I can. Governor Vance probably has more reach than me. But even *if* the message reaches him, it's gonna be up to Shadow to come home."

"Right." He wasn't wrong about that, but it hurt too much to think that Shadow might not *want* to come back. I pushed the blanket off my lap before I stood up. "Good talk, Reaper."

"Wait!" He jumped to his feet, panic crossing his face. "Is it...can we..." He swallowed again, the pulse in his neck firing rapidly. "Can we just...start talking again? Please?"

I grabbed my backpack by the front door and pulled it on, purposely stalling while trying not to look like I was. My chest ached with the need to scream *yes*, to run at him with the knowledge that he would catch me, take me to bed, and make everything better.

Instead, I fiddled with my straps while he stood there waiting, like I was about to sentence him to death or set him free.

"I'm going to be gone for a few days," I said. "Maybe a week. I'm going with the field medics to support your dad's units engaging with Blakeworth." My weight shifted on my feet. "We can talk more after I get back."

Reaper pulled his lips between his teeth. I saw his fists close at his sides and brow pinch in the start of his signature, disapproving scowl. I already knew what was going through his head—that he wanted to prevent me from going, or at the very least, send one of the guys with me.

But he dragged a hand down his face with a resigned nod. "Okay. When you get back, then." He seemed unsure of what to do with his hands, settling for resting them on his hips. Normally he'd be holding me tightly against him, hands on my ass and his tongue down my throat, making sure I got a goodbye worth remembering. "Be safe out there."

"Thanks. You be safe back here."

"I will. You, uh," Reaper cleared his throat. "You might see Gunner out there," he called after me as I headed for the garage. "Not in the first wave, but he'll head out there if the troops need backup." He ran a hand through his dark hair, rubbing the back of his neck. "I know he'd really love to talk to you too. Just for a moment, if you're up for it."

I didn't answer as I went through the garage door and headed for my dirt bike.

CHAPTER 5

MARIPOSA

I rode to the hospital, helped pack supplies for the field medic team into a couple of Jeeps and vans, then rode my little dirt bike north alongside the other vehicles. Being alone on my little bike, with the open road in front of me and the sun slowly rising, only deepened the yearning in my chest.

It wasn't just my men I wanted back, but our old life. I missed seeing them on their roaring bikes riding next to me and whoever I was clinging to. The grins on their faces and their wild yells as we tore across the landscape. Hands holding mine as I wrapped around them, or stroking my leg as we rode. We'd always had enemies, that was no different now. But Reaper was right about how our family had been fractured. A tear ran through us, separating us. We'd never be the same, but maybe we could move forward into something new.

Once *all* of us were back together.

I'd heard nothing new from Horus that morning, just like every morning before it. The more time passed, the more my emotions seemed to shift. I was growing tired of waiting for the right time, impatient and eager to have Shadow back. Something Reaper said this morning unnerved me though.

What if Shadow didn't want to come back?

What if he found a place to stay? A place where he could be safe, maybe even work as a tattoo artist? What if…

My dirt bike jolted forward, a result of my hand closing into a fist around the throttle. I eased my grip and the breath that had been stuck in my chest with where my mind went.

What if Shadow met someone?

I definitely wasn't the only woman in the world who was attracted to him. And he was confident now, expressing himself with ease. And that said nothing of how generous he was in the bedroom.

My pulse sped up, stomach flip-flopping at the memories of how he kissed me, how much sweetness and care he treated me with. A fresh knot formed in my chest at the realization that he might kiss someone else like that, touch another woman and please her using what he learned from me.

It only dawned on me then that he might be happier wherever he was. He might have found a whole new life to give him fulfillment and meaning. And if that were the case, what right did I have to demand that he return to me?

I leaned over my handlebars, refocusing on the road ahead. My plans wouldn't change. I would wait for Horus to tell me when it was time, then head out and find him. If Shadow was truly happier where he was, I'd leave him be and return home. I would find a way to forgive Reaper and move forward with my three husbands, not four.

No matter how wrong it felt to not have Shadow as mine.

I moved on autopilot when we reached the site in neutral territory to set up the field hospital. Having a team and being fully stocked with equipment was a luxury I never encountered while working alone. Four people got the canvas tents set up quickly, while the rest of us unloaded supplies and stored them where they'd be easiest to access in case of an emergency. We set up beds, gurneys, and curtains to divide sections of the tents for privacy. We had just finished when the sun was rising high, and were finally settling into having breakfast and coffee when one of the Four Corners Army Jeeps pulled up.

"Good morning, medics!" The lieutenant in the passenger seat hopped out to greet us. His name tag read GONZALEZ.

"Morning, sir. Coffee?" asked one of the younger medics, a woman named Cynthia.

"No, thank you. General Bray just recommended I stop by and let you all know essentially what to expect." He pulled in a breath and squared his shoulders back. "Blakeworth's scouts have been meeting with ours in the past couple of days and engaging with hostility."

"Meaning what, exactly?" Cynthia asked.

"Their scouts have started shooting at ours," I said. "Initiating all the firing, even when they're both in neutral territory, from what Jandro has told me."

"Correct." Lieutenant Gonzalez nodded. "Their numbers and hostility have been increasing in the past week. No serious injuries to our men yet, but they're sending a clear message that they want a fight."

"So this war has actually started?" Another medic paled. "Like, this is the first actual battle?"

"We're hoping it's nothing more than a small skirmish," Gonzalez said. "They're showing off their firepower, trying to provoke a reaction from us. Our goal here is to show them we're just as strong, just as organized. We're still open to peaceful negotiations, if Governor Blake is willing."

"I wouldn't hold my breath on that," I muttered. Then, "Lieutenant, may I add something?"

"Of course, ma'am." He brought his hands together behind his back and stepped aside as I turned to face the wide-eyed group of medics.

"My brief time in Blakeworth showed me that their most vulnerable, their most disenfranchised citizens, will likely be the ones our soldiers meet in battle." I looked at Gonzalez, who confirmed my words with a nod. "It's our duty to tend to *all* the wounded, not just our own. If you are treating a Blakeworth soldier, give him the same care you would anyone coming into the hospital. Most of them are not thrown into this conflict because of love or loyalty, but because they have no other option. If you have someone who is conscious, let them know there is possible refuge in Four Corners." I cast one final glance to Gonzalez. "They'll be interviewed and evaluated by the army for citizenship once they're well enough."

I stepped aside and allowed the lieutenant to hold the team's attention once again. "We will engage the enemy just over that ridge." Gonzalez turned and pointed at a hill in the distance. If you see us coming down this side toward you, be ready. It means we've got injured."

"What if they completely overwhelm you guys?" asked another young medic. "And it's them coming over the hill on their way to capture or kill us?"

"Welcome to being a combat medic," I said sharply, turning toward the young man who spoke. "Being captured or killed is a risk that comes with this job. We're basically soldiers, only we try to keep people alive instead of killing them. As for defending yourself against a hostile enemy, you have scalpels, syringes, and lethal amounts of drugs. I've had to use all of them at one point or another, you probably will too. If any of this is too much for you, you're better off being a medic somewhere else."

Everyone was as still as a statue, except for Gonzalez, who was trying hard not to laugh.

"Understood, ma'am." The medic who asked the question lifted his chin and squared his shoulders.

He was *so* young, barely into his twenties, most likely. I saw a flash of myself in him for a moment, the bright-eyed nursing school graduate who left Texas for better opportunities, who wanted to bring some goodness back into the world. Nothing could have prepared me for the horrors I found along the way. My life on the road molded me, hardened me into someone who shut away all emotional responses when faced with battle injuries. It wasn't who I expected to become—the smiling, joyful labor and delivery nurse who would proudly place a newborn baby into its mother's arms.

Still, I preferred embracing the role of the hardened combat medic to the alternative—falling apart at the horrors of war and being unable to help anyone.

Lieutenant Gonzalez leaned toward me, a smile still playing on his lips. "You'd make a good drill sergeant, ma'am. No wonder General Bray likes you so much."

I snorted out a laugh. "He has to, because I'm his daughter-in-law."

The words stung my throat as they left. I hadn't thought about it until now, but I missed my kind, smiling father-in-law too. Shutting Reaper out also meant cutting off other members of my family. My in-laws and I were still only just getting to know each other, so it wasn't exactly the same. Even so, I had to remember my relationships with Reaper and Gunner weren't the only ones affected by our issues anymore.

The lieutenant only smiled as he headed back to his Jeep. "Thank you for supporting us, medics. And hang tight. The action could start in a matter of hours or days."

He drove off, leaving us to stand outside our tent.

"You heard him," I said to the others. "Be ready. Let's double-check the solar chargers and make sure everything's sterilized."

The rest of the day was uneventful. Gonzalez's men rotated patrol shifts every few hours, with the 'off' soldiers still required to stay nearby. Some of them came over the hill to hang out with us, drink coffee, take naps, and just shoot the shit.

It was early the next morning, roughly twenty-four hours later, when the first shot was fired.

We heard the *pop-pop-pops* of rifles over the radio of a soldier having breakfast with us. Then Gonzalez's voice ordering all units to the front line, and everyone sprung into action. The soldiers on break dropped everything and scrambled into their Jeep, tires kicking up mud and slushy ice on their way up the hill.

I yelled at all the medics once again to be ready. We were about to get very busy, very quickly. Returning to an operating table, I sprayed everything down again with an alcohol solution. I had just set the bottle down when a loud *BOOM* crashed through my eardrums and sent the ground shaking under my feet. It had some medics, myself included, falling on their butts.

"What was that?" someone cried.

"Was that the enemy or us?" another medic asked.

"Not us," I said, scrambling to my feet. "General Bray wouldn't be that aggressive right off the bat. It's Blakeworth."

"Bombs?" The young medic sounded panicked. "They're *bombing* us?!"

"Shh! Hey, hey!" I grabbed her shoulders and made her face me. "The soldiers *need* us. Stay with me, medic."

Another blast went off, this one slightly further away, but an ominous plume of black smoke rose up from the other side of the hill.

"They have backup units," I said, more to myself than the others. "If they're in trouble, help will come."

The first truck loaded up with injured soldiers came about fifteen minutes after the first explosion. I winced at the sight of the vehicle coming down the hill at lightning speed, fishtailing precariously through the mud and ice. The driver seemed to hit every boulder and uneven bit of terrain, which was no help to our patients that he carried. He swung around when he reached the flat plain of our camp, backing toward the main tent where we waited.

My worst fears were already confirmed as medics touched fingers to the necks and wrists of unmoving soldiers.

"Take the deceased to the black tent," I ordered quietly, my voice suddenly feeling like it lost all power. "There's nothing we can do for them right now."

Living soldiers were quickly rushed to different areas to assess and treat their most serious injuries. I helped two other medics lift a larger man onto a bed. He seemed dazed, but otherwise uninjured.

"Watch his head," I instructed, my nursing autopilot taking over. "Check for internal bleeding."

Blasts and gunfire raged on for hours. It was a special kind of torture listening to the variety of weapons and shouting voices, but being completely unable to see it. We only saw the effects of it as the injured and casualties swarmed our tents. The first wave of fighting stopped, but our work only carried on.

The medics took catnaps in rotating shifts, catching a few hours of sleep under a blanket or thick coat wherever we could. I couldn't tell how many days had passed, only that it was sometimes night and daytime at other points. My team was reaching their limit, as evident by the dark circles under their eyes and hollowness in their cheeks. They needed time off and rest, and soon, before the fatigue would start affecting their care.

You do too, my brain seemed to remind me in a small whisper. *You need the love of your men to bring life back to the zombie you've become.*

I shook it off, returning my focus to the tasks of my surroundings. If I put too much thought into how much I missed being surrounded by warm bodies when I woke up, having my feet rubbed and a glass of wine placed in my hand after a long day, I just might give in. I might relent to the fantasy that my body and soul craved, rather than remember the cruel reality.

There was a brief lull in the day during one afternoon. All current patients were stabilized and at the moment, there wasn't a truck hauling a bed full of bodies to us. I took a seat on top of a cooler that had stored some of our food, willing my torso not to slump over and crash in the dirt. Some field medics had developed the talent of sleeping while sitting or standing up. I never seemed to acquire the skill.

My eyelids slipped closed and I just as quickly snapped them open. Shit, I thought my two-hour power nap earlier would be enough to sustain me, but that was apparently not the case.

A few more minutes, I pleaded with my exhausted body. *If another truck comes, I need to be able to help.*

Biology wasn't having it. My head dipped low as I slumped over, forehead nearly coming in contact with my thighs. I couldn't seem to muster the strength to sit up, I was so damn tired. *Just another day in the field.*

Something happened the moment my eyelids slipped fully closed.

I was instantly dreaming that I could fly, soaring high over a vast landscape of rocky terrain. My eyesight was incredible! From up here, I could see rabbits diving into the dense brush, prairie dogs hiding in their burrows. My body felt light but immensely powerful. I was fast enough to catch one of those animals if I was hungry, kill them swiftly with my talons—

And then, bodies.

Lifeless forms were strewn across black, scorched earth. The few that were still alive would be gone soon, bleeding out or broken beyond repair.

"What is this?" I heard myself ask. Was I actually asleep and dreaming, or was this something else?

Look, daughter.

Below me, someone was digging frantically at a mound of dirt and rock where it looked like one of the blasts had made a crater that had caved in. He started using a shovel, then tossed it away to move handfuls of earth away in a panic.

I circled down lower, taking in every detail with my sharp vision, from the scratches on the man's motorcycle helmet to the dirt under his fingernails. His breaths were ragged, labored, and he was alone. When the exhausted, panicked man looked up and met my eyes, I nearly fell out of the sky.

"Gunner!" I tried to cry out, but only a screech left my mouth. "What happened?"

"Horus!" my blue-eyed man rasped. "Get Mari and other medics! The blast caved it in and they're trapped!"

Like a slingshot, I propelled back into my own body. The momentum was so strong, I fell right off the cooler to the ground. But seeing him and hearing those words sprung me to action.

"Get the van and load it up with oxygen tanks, masks, and shovels!" I yelled, starting for my dirt bike. "Every available medic, follow me!"

I got some confused looks in return, but they sprung into action as I kicked the little bike into gear. Rest would have to wait.

Such was the nature of war.

CHAPTER 6

GUNNER

Everything had been fine until the Blakeworth lieutenant ordered the use of explosives for no good goddamn reason. Horus felt the effects of the blast through his wing feathers, and I swore the sensation echoed through my human body as I came to in the Four Corners conference room.

"You okay, Gun?" General Bray asked me.

Reaper and I had decided to come out with my abilities to his father, considering that we planned to use Horus' sight to our advantage during the war. I was more than okay with this, as Finn was not only my family now, but one of the best tacticians I'd ever seen, and that included the many decorated generals I'd learned from at McAlister.

"Ugh, yeah." I pressed a hand down on the table, closing my eyes for a moment to get my bearings. "It's not good. They're blowing shit up."

"What?" The general paled, his face betraying the fact that I'd said his worst fear.

"We need to send the second wave out now," I said. "Our guys need backup or they're going to get demolished. I can ride out and be there in two hours."

"Go." With that, he turned to Reaper. "Ride out to the hospital. Tell Dr. Brooks they need to send more medics."

"Fuck, Mari's out there." Reaper brought two fists down on the table as he stood, stilling only when his father reached out to touch his forearm.

"Keep your head on straight. If they send more medics out, she'll be able to come home. Dismissed, both of you."

"If Blakeworth wants to be taken seriously as a territory, they won't attack the medics," I said to Reaper as I followed him out of the room. "Targeting medical staff has been a war crime for centuries. No one will want to ally with them if they pull that shit."

"I don't know if they care," he answered with a shake of his head. "None of the rules apply anymore, Gun. If they didn't make that clear when they kidnapped a governor's daughter, they sure as hell did when they brought bombs to a gunfight." Reaper paused next to his bike, releasing a sigh as he pulled riding gloves on. "I'm just worried about her, and even if she is okay, I know things are still gonna be shitty when she gets home."

"You talked to her, though." I sat astride my ride, pulling on my thickest jacket for the long journey to come. "That's getting somewhere."

Reaper shrugged, turning his engine over with a roar that leveled out to a rumbling purr. "Maybe. It didn't feel like much changed. Her being away just makes it feel worse. Like..." His hand slapped his chest pocket in search of a cigarette. "Like she's already left us."

"I know, man."

He wasn't wrong. The house had felt even more empty the last couple of days, knowing she wasn't at the hospital or hiding in Jandro's room. Even the smallest traces of her presence were gone, like her coffee cup in the sink or the damp towel hanging in the bathroom after her shower. Of course I missed actually talking to her, seeing her, hearing my wife's laugh and squeezing her in a hug, more than anything. But it was the absence of those little things that really made all the other stuff hurt.

That was what made it feel like we really lost her. That she was gone, and not ours anymore.

"We'll get her back." I raised my voice over the sound of our engines as we pulled out toward the street. *We have to. Or I'm gonna go ballistic if we don't fix this and she actually walks away.*

"Be safe out there, Gun." Reaper slipped into the flow of traffic and peeled out with a roar toward the hospital.

"Yeah you too, pres." I made a wide left turn and headed in the opposite direction, picking up speed as I raced toward the second wave units' camp. They would be ready to mobilize as soon as they saw me.

Hang on, guys. Hang on, Mari. I accelerated faster. *We'll be there soon. Just hang on for us.*

A SENSE OF DREAD SETTLED LIKE CONCRETE IN MY STOMACH as we approached the battlefield. I'd seen the black smoke from twenty miles away, now the air was thick with it and tasted like gunpowder.

"Fan out to the north and south!" I yelled to the unit leaders. "Stay on the perimeter and close in from the outside! Alpha unit, with me!"

Jeeps and motorbikes split off to either side at my instructions, while I led my team straight through the middle.

"Don't let me fall off, man," I mumbled, aiming my bike straight ahead while I slipped into Horus's point of view.

Oh...fuck.

So many dead and dying. Blakeworth's ground units moved over the scorched landscape with rifles and daggers. They shot and stabbed anyone clinging to life, but it wasn't mercy killing. One soldier tried to limp away on one good leg while the Blakeworth soldiers threw daggers at him. Another man crawling on the ground screamed as the enemy shot through his hands.

I returned to my own body, and the rage waiting for me there. My teeth ground like stones in my jaw, my grip painful as I accelerated my bike to its limit.

"Orders, sir!" the lieutenant yelled next to me, struggling to keep up with my speed.

I looked over my shoulder at him. "Protect the injured, respect the dead. And kill them all."

An embankment with a steep upward incline loomed up ahead of me. I kept my speed the same, heading straight for it.

"Sir!"

I ignored those around me, riding up the densely packed dirt like a ramp until I reached the crest and launched into the air. The carnage I saw through my falcon was laid out beneath me, the details dulled through my human eyes, but no less horrific.

In midair, I pulled the rifle from the holster across my chest and started spraying bullets at the Blakeworth ground units. Some shots I missed and the foot soldiers took off running. Thankfully, the perimeter units were already in position and started picking them off.

I landed hard on the ground, my bike's shocks protesting, but I managed to stay upright, shoot one Blakeworth coward in the back, and run him over. *Thank you Jandro, for the all-weather tires, even if they are ugly.*

My rear tire spraying up gravel and mud, I circled around and picked off more Blakeworth guys. They clustered together as they retreated, which was great for us. I did a quick check of all units through Horus before I grabbed the small radio clipped to my cut.

"Beta unit, this is Gunner. They're coming toward you," I said into the receiver. "You'll have a visual in about thirty seconds."

"Roger that, Gunner," Lieutenant Fields replied. "Shall we drop them a present?"

I smiled before responding. "Please do."

After the lieutenant confirmed my order, I returned my attention to the state of my surroundings. This area had been blown to bits, and from the looks of it, at least twenty people along with it. Several of my team were already tending to the injured, tying off limbs that were bleeding out or plugging up large wounds with whatever they had on them.

"Where's the field hospital from here?" I asked my lieutenant, a guy named Davis.

"Just over that hill," he pointed behind me. "There's been a truck going back and forth, transporting people."

"Good, so it's on its way back?"

"I think so, it—"

A deafening *BOOM* made my eardrums cry out in pain, Davis and I covered our heads as we fell to the ground. Dirt and gravel rained down on us, the little stones landing hard like mini-projectiles.

"Fuck, I hope that was ours!" I lifted my head carefully to take a peek when the shower ended.

Lieutenant Fields' voice crackled through my radio a moment later. "They were blown away by our gift, sir."

I couldn't help but laugh. "Good man. Keep your eyes peeled and I'll let you know about more clusters when I see 'em."

"Roger that."

"Sir, the truck!" Davis pointed, and I turned to see the white pickup truck coming down hard over the hill.

The driver turned, backing the vehicle up toward us with a bed covered in blood and viscera.

"Damn, wish we could spray that down," I muttered. I wondered how Mari felt about piling people with open wounds on such an unsanitary surface. Or did she even have time to think about stuff while working in a war zone?

"No time, sir. These people are clinging to life."

Davis and I worked quickly, lifting people in all states of consciousness as carefully as we could into the truck bed. The driver, a sergeant by his insignia, got out to help too.

"Hey, have you seen a woman with the medics?" I asked him. "Long dark hair, really pretty face? She might be the one in charge down there."

"I dunno," he grunted, lifting an unconscious—or dead—soldier and placing him gingerly in the truck bed. "Half of the medics down there are women. I just drop off and pick up."

"Has the field hospital been targeted at all?"

"Nah. The action's all up here."

I nodded. That was a relief, at least.

The sergeant took off once the truck bed was full, and I damn near had to stop myself from jumping in his passenger seat. Even if it was through a bloody, mud-caked windshield, I wanted to see her. Just for a moment.

Two more trips later and no one remained in our area except for the ones who were unmistakably dead.

"We shouldn't leave them here," I said to Davis as I leaned down to close the eyelids of a soldier who looked barely eighteen. "Once this is over, we should have all the bodies recovered and ID'd."

"They deserve a hero's homecoming," he agreed, his voice rough.

I patted his shoulder as I went back to lean against my bike. "Give me a moment, lieutenant."

He stepped away, probably thinking I needed to compose myself, while I slipped into Horus again for a larger aerial view.

Our perimeter teams were doing a good job of ambushing the Blakeworth soldiers from behind. They expected us all to rush into the center, assuming they predicted we'd have backup at all. Without a doubt, the formations and weapons they used showed that they planned to massacre us. So much for this being a small skirmish. Like Reaper said, they had no qualms about fighting ugly. Unfortunately for them, neither did biker gangs.

If they wanted to fight dirty and underhanded, fuck yeah we'd give it to them.

"Keep pressing in on them, perimeter teams," I said into my radio when I came back to my own body. "We'll take no prisoners today."

"Some of Blakeworth's injured got tossed onto the medic truck," Davis said.

"That's fine. We'll give them a chance to recover and see how much better they'd have it if they were loyal to us."

"And if they try anything?"

I smiled. "I'll leave that up to the governor and my president."

Sudden movement caught my eye behind the dirt mound I'd just jumped off of. A head poked out from behind the hill and I pointed my rifle in that direction, but they ducked down and threw something from where they hid.

"Run!" I screamed, realizing immediately what it was. "Everybody move!"

Davis and his soldiers took off, but it was too late. The grenade bounced once, rolled a few feet, and detonated with an ear splitting boom.

The force sent me flying, and I knew other bodies had been launched in the air too. Ringing filled my head and I landed hard, pain shooting up my shoulder. Grinding my teeth against the pain of the beating I took, I rolled and climbed shakily to my feet. My legs wobbled unsteadily beneath me as I made my way back to my unit.

"Guys," I rasped, nearly falling to my knees. "I got you guys, don't worry."

A shallow crater had formed at the base of the hill I had jumped from. A few members of my unit lay motionless, but Lieutenant Davis and half a dozen others still moved. Some rolling in pain, others screaming. "Don't worry." My hands shook as I reached for the nearest man. "I got you guys."

I was in shock, most likely. Speaking nonsense to myself, as well as the men. It wasn't until a hand clasped my arm that I realized a fine rain of dirt and gravel had continued to fall down on us.

"It's gonna collapse," Davis told me with a strangled cough as he shoved me away weakly. "Run, captain."

"No, no. Come on." I tried to tug him toward me. "I gotta get you guys to the truck. Can you walk?"

"Go, captain! Anyone who can move, go!" He shoved me more forcefully, and I was already so unsteady that I fell back, landing on my ass. "The hillside won't hold any more weight! You have to get away now!"

It dawned on me only then what he was saying, as pebbles and dirt began falling in earnest, rolling down the hillside in bigger chunks.

"No," I whispered. "No, come on! You'll be trapped!"

"So will you if you come any closer!"

I grabbed my radio receiver with a shaking hand. "Any available units, we need assistance at the southeastern side—"

"Negate that!" Davis yelled. "More bodies will mean a bigger landslide..."

His voice was drowned out by a low rumbling sound. It reminded me of the avalanches I'd seen at my father's ski resorts when I was young.

But this time it was made by an avalanche of mud, loose earth, and rocks.

"No, fuck!" I scrambled forward, trying to get my useless legs underneath me, but it was already too late. They were getting buried faster than I could run, the soft bottom of the crater giving way so they sunk even deeper.

"I need men!" I shouted into my radio. "All available men and shovels! They got buried."

A crackling, heartbreaking reply came over the speaker. "We have our hands tied here, Gunner! Will assist when we can, but we can't spare anyone at the moment."

"Fuck!"

I crawled forward and started shoveling loose dirt away with my hands, my movements feeling heavy and too damn slow. My shoulders and arms cried out with fatigue and probably a few injuries from the blast as I dug like a dog in search of a prized bone. None of it seemed effective, I only found more dirt as I dug. Panic spurred me on. They probably couldn't breathe, couldn't move with the weight of a small hillside on top of them. Fuck, what if I was compacting the dirt and making it worse? But what else could I do, stop?

It was awful and probably hopeless. But no way in hell was I about to just sit on my ass and wait for help to come.

A screech from the air somehow reached through the ringing in my ears and I looked up, spotting my falcon circling overhead.

"Horus!" I cried out. "Get Mari and other medics! The blast caved it in and they're trapped!"

I didn't know if he heard me or if he even could do as I asked, but I was out of options. Help wasn't coming from the other units. I couldn't reach Reaper or General Bray from here. These people were dying, if not already dead. If that turned out to be because I couldn't reach them in time, I'd work that out with myself later. I just had to try, I had to put everything into getting them out.

My ears were so fucked, I didn't notice the arriving vehicles until I saw movement at the corner of my eye. Even then, I didn't stop. My arms were numb, movements clumsy and inefficient, but I could not fucking stop.

People came into the corners of my vision, wearing camo uniforms with red crosses—the medics! They came in from the sides with shovels, tossing huge clods of dirt over their shoulders. Still, I didn't stop.

Not until a small, gloved hand touched my arm, the other hand on my cheek to turn my face gently. My wife's face filled my vision, so beautiful even with the dark circles under her eyes and her brows knitted together.

"We're getting them out." I could barely hear Mari's voice, but watched her lips move slowly so I understood her. "Rest, my love. Let me help them, then I'll check on you."

I nodded, the fatigue settling deep into my joints with painful aches. Leaning away from the cave-in, I fell unceremoniously on my ass again and stayed there.

Cloudy sky filled my vision now, soft, gray, and endless. Before my exhausted eyelids closed, I saw Horus's dark shape as he circled over us.

CHAPTER 7

IVAN

"Keep your knees slightly bent. Elbows too." I didn't stand too close to Jen, but touched my fingers to her elbows as a small reminder. "Don't hold your breath. You want to stand firm, but keep some flexibility. Try not to lock anything."

Jen nodded tightly, her shoulders relaxing a few centimeters away from her ears as she remembered to take a breath. She was still tense, but wasn't shaking anymore at least. Guns made her nervous. Almost as nervous as women used to make me.

Now she could hold one, and I could stand by and observe, teaching her a few things. Even touch her to help fix her stance, without worrying I was doing something wrong.

"Line up the sights like I showed you," I said, taking a few steps away. "And squeeze when you're ready."

She took a few more breaths before pulling the trigger, her eyes squeezing shut and her whole body startling at the noise. But she shot again and again at the rusted metal target we set up in the junkyard, until her magazine clicked empty.

Jen laughed as she set the gun down and removed her ear and eye protection. "I totally suck."

"You're getting better. You just need practice," I said, bringing over the case to put the gun away. "No one becomes a perfect shot overnight."

"How long did it take you?" She watched me remove the mag and return it to the foam placeholder.

"Two nights." She laughed and my chest relaxed, relieved that she understood I was joking. "I did take to weapons and bikes pretty quickly, to be honest. But I suck at plenty of other things."

"Like what?" Jen tilted her head as she peered up at me, chewing at the metal jewelry through her lip.

"Like people."

"I don't think that's true." She placed a hand on my arm, the second time she did that within a week. "Everyone here likes you."

"Because I keep to myself and don't bother anyone." I closed the case and slowly turned to move out of her reach. I liked Jen, but not to the point of touching each other regularly. Still, I didn't want to be abrupt and hurt her feelings.

"Well yeah, but not in the way you think." Her hand fell to her side. "All the girls are comfortable around you, and that's saying a lot for most of them who've escaped abusive men."

"I'm...glad for that. But it doesn't mean I'm great at socializing."

"Oh, stop being so hard on yourself."

Jen reached out to touch me again, and I let her fingers rest on my forearm. Not because I was open to anything from her, but when she said that, it reminded me of someone else.

The one person I *wanted* to touch me.

Jen stepped in closer to me, closer than we'd been even during tattoo sessions, and I followed my gut reaction to step away.

Shit, I thought at the flash of hurt crossing her face.

"Jen," I started, eager to soften the blow. "You've been a good friend to me—"

"It's alright, Ivan," she laughed sheepishly. "I can take a hint. I'll leave you be."

"I...just..." Fuck, this was difficult. I wish I could disappear into a hole in the ground.

"You're not over her." Jen nodded matter-of-factly, gesturing toward my arm. The arm that had the tattoo of *her* on the inside.

"I...guess not." Nor would I ever be. Not entirely. "How'd you know?"

"All the signs are there," she remarked with a shrug. "A man shows up alone, doesn't respond to any attention, though it's clear he's missing something or someone. But he keeps it all wrapped up, only finding comfort in drinking and staying busy."

"I'm that obvious, huh?" I rubbed at my forearm absently.

"I've been a bar wench a long time," she chuckled. "I've seen all kinds. Yours seems like a hell of a story, though." Her smile dropped and she asked quietly, "Are you gonna go back to her?"

If that was an option, I would in a heartbeat. If I had even the faintest sign, a whisper in the breeze or a vague note in one of those folded up cookies that I could be with *her* again, I'd be gone in a cloud of dust.

But it wouldn't happen. Happiness didn't come for people like me.

"No." I shook my head. "I'll move on from this place eventually, but there's no going back for me."

Jen's eyes widened. "Is she...?"

"No, she's alive. She's fine, actually." I forced my hand away from my forearm, to stop petting my tattoo like it could will Mari into real life. "She's much better off without me around."

Jen tilted her head again, giving me a skeptical look this time. "Not sure if I believe that."

"She is," I insisted. "That's not just me being hard on myself."

"If you say so, big guy." She nudged her shoulder into mine as we started walking back toward the service center. I recognized it as a friendly gesture I didn't need to step away from. "You seeing Doc today?"

"Yeah, as soon as I drop this off in my room." I held up the gun case.

"You want a drink before seeing him?"

"No thanks. He said he wanted me sober for this one."

"Ooh, interesting," Jen mused. "Trying something new?"

"I think so." I swallowed, my thoughts turning anxious. I had just started to feel like I was gaining control on these trips through my subconscious. Every time I made progress, Doc pushed me a little more. I'd come to sweating and panting, but my mind felt a little quieter after every session. A little bit less of the poisonous, evil place that I tried to shove down at every opportunity.

"Well, good luck." Jen made her way behind the bar once we got inside. "If you need me, you know where to find me afterward," she added with a wink.

"Thanks. I'll see you later, Jen."

I didn't want to encourage the idea that anything might happen between her and me, but if the tight clamp in my chest was any indication, drinking it away would be a necessity after tonight.

"Where are you, Ivan?" Doc's voice permeated my subconscious, true and clear, solid, like an anchor for me to hold onto.

"My cage." The answer was usually the same, but the feeling was different today.

"How old are you at this time?"

I looked down at myself, at my skinny arms and legs covered in dirt and the infected cuts across my thin body. Cuts that *hurt*.

"I'm young," I said, my voice sounding foreign in comparison to the small body it was coming from. "Eight, maybe ten years old?"

"What do you notice about your surroundings?"

"There's...there's not much." My cage was nearly empty, no books or reading material like the ones I taught myself from in later years. A dirty container of water was nearly empty. My threadbare blanket was laid out neatly in the corner. In front of me was a stick, the end sharpened to a point. A crude drawing was made in the patch of dirt just outside my cage—a simple face with eyes, a mouth, a nose, and long hair. A self-portrait of sorts.

"How are you feeling at this moment in time?"

"The cuts hurt," I said. "They're red and swollen. My whole body aches and I feel so tired."

"So you've been cut recently?"

"Yes, I think yesterday. And she..." My throat closed up at the memory, teeth grinding down and tears springing up at the painful memory.

"Who, your mother?"

"Yes."

"Can you tell me what she did?"

"She..." I lifted my hand to my face, feeling the puffy flesh, the tender soreness around my eye and cheekbone. "She started off being so nice. She said she wanted to give me a hug."

"And what did she do?"

"She...hit me." Doc didn't respond, so I continued on. "She said if I was a girl, that she would love me and hug me. She would protect me and never hurt me. But I'm a boy who will turn into a man. If I was free, I would just hurt girls, so I don't get hugs. That's why I have to stay down here."

"Ivan." Doc's voice sounded strained. "Have you ever been hugged by anyone?"

"No...Wait, yes." Another memory came forward, one from a different, more recent time. I could feel the gentle pressure of a face resting on my chest, and small hands on my back.

"Do you remember how it felt?"

"Yes, it was...nice. It felt good." It was better than good. It felt like the warmth of sunlight on my skin.

"Good. I'd like you to try to visualize this person who hugged you. Imagine they're there with you, in your cage now."

"No." I shook my head. "She doesn't belong here. She shouldn't be in a cage with me. She's too good."

"It's just an exercise I'd like you to try, Ivan."

"No, I don't want her to see me like this."

"Ivan, take a deep breath. You're okay. You're safe."

My breaths were heavy, panicked and ragged as they sawed in and out of my chest. But after several rounds, my racing heart began to slow down. The bite of the metal cuffs on my chair reminded me of where I was.

"Are you with me, son?" Doc's voice pulled me further out of the panic, the fear, and the shame.

"Yes, I'm here."

"Good. If it's alright with you, I'd like to keep trying."

"Okay."

"You're still in your cage, yes?"

"Uh-huh." I could feel the swelling in my face now—my eye was swollen shut from the force of the blow. My face ached with every dull throb.

"Would you like a hug now? No tricks, no hitting. Just a bit of comfort from someone who showed you kindness."

The thought of such a thing made a sob rattle though my child-sized chest. It was *all* I wanted, just for someone to show me they cared.

"Yes," I choked out. "I wish I had that."

"Picture it, Ivan. While you're here, imagine that person wrapping around you. Soothing you. Telling you it'll be okay. Start with one small detail you remember, and then add another."

I thought of Mari, standing in front of me after I completed her back tattoo. She told me she was proud of me, then shyly asked if she could hug me. I said yes and she approached me, turning her head to place her cheek on my chest, and then her hands on my back.

I could feel it again—the light pressure of her body against me, her fingers moving over my back. It was easy to think of, I'd only thought of that moment hundreds of times.

"Is that helping you, Ivan?" Doc's low voice floated in. "Do you feel a bit better? A bit safer?"

In my memory, now morphing into some kind of fantasy, Mari not only hugged me, but treated my wounds. She put ice on my face and cleaned my cuts. Her touch was warm and gentle, and she always asked permission before doing something. Her brows knitted with concern, eyes just as sharp and focused as when she always treated someone.

She healed me—the eight-year-old me, alone, scared, and confused —just as she healed me as a man, with patience, warmth, and kindness. For the first time since beginning these sessions with Doc, I didn't want to leave.

"Ivan, are you still with me?"

"Yes," I answered. "She's making me feel better. So much better."

"Good. How are you feeling now?"

"I feel...safe. Cared for. I..." My breath hitched, like hitting a road-block in my chest.

"What is it, son? Go ahead."

"I...miss her." Everything started fading away. Mari, the cage, my pain, all of it. And fuck me, I didn't want it to. "I miss her *so* much."

"Okay, Ivan? You're coming out of it on your own. Take it easy, slow. Remember your breaths."

My leg kicked out, a reflex that jolted me out of my hypnosis with a start. Doc, the room, my chair, everything came sharply back into focus. And my sweet fantasy was already fading, like a dream I'd just woken up from and started to forget.

Doc knelt in front of me, unshackling the chair restraints as he peered up at me. "You alright?"

My skin had broken out in a cold sweat and my heart pounded furiously in my chest like I'd just ran for miles. I was back and had mixed feelings about it.

"Yeah, I think so." I stretched out my leg once he released it. "What was that?"

"Just a little visualization practice." Doc stood from the floor with a groan and went to unbind my arms. "If you like that technique, we can try it again next time."

"I...didn't want to leave," I admitted, rubbing my forearm once freed. "I'd never felt anything like that before, at that age, and it was all I really wanted."

"That's the power of your mind, son." Doc leaned back with a small smile. "We absorb things that other people tell us, then we tell ourselves those things, not realizing that not everything we think is true. By replacing the internalized message with something else, we can unlearn what we thought we knew."

I blinked at him, sort of following, but not really. "What was I unlearning just then?"

Doc's face softened even more. "That you were at fault for the abuse you received. You internalized that belief at a young age, Ivan. But have you ever stopped to think it wasn't true?" The older man gave my shoulder a soft pat. "You were just a kid who needed a childhood, needed hugs. And visualizations like this can help shift your thoughts into something less destructive."

I nodded slowly. His words weren't fully sinking in but they made logical sense. Mostly, I was just trying to recapture the feeling of Mari's embrace, grasping for it as it slipped further out of my reach.

"Would you like to try it again next time?" Doc asked.

"Maybe, but…"

"Yes?"

"What if…the person I thought of, visualized…" The words felt stuck in my throat, but I forced them out. "What if thinking about her is also painful? The memory of her hug was comforting to me, but…"

"Has she also harmed you in some way?"

"No, but…" I sucked in a breath. Doc knew about my violent sleep-walking episodes, but not the extent to which I injured Mari. It felt wrong somehow, to use her in my therapy, even if it was our good memories from before I hurt her. I felt like I was taking more from her, keeping her shackled to me when I should have been setting her free.

"She is someone I…had feelings for," I finally said, watching Doc's slow nod. "It's my fault that it didn't work out, but I want the best for her and I'm…trying to move on. I just worry that thinking of her like this isn't actually good for me. Or her."

"Well, thankfully, no one can police your thoughts," Doc said with a warm smile. "You can rely on another visualization if you think it would be better. The power is really in your hands here." He stroked his goatee. "As for moving on from that relationship, I don't believe a positive memory will hinder your progress in that regard." Doc gave me a curious look. "Time and distance seem to do the job best."

I lowered my gaze. The weeks spent away from Mari only seemed to deepen the ache of losing her. Every passing day that she didn't greet me with a 'good morning' felt emptier than the last. My spontaneous tattoo of her certainly didn't help.

"I'm sure you know," Doc continued, "that people from our past never really leave us, even long after they're no longer in our lives."

A derisive snort left me before I could contain it. If I could escape the people from my past, I wouldn't be in this situation right now.

"Every person we meet shapes us into the people we are. Even brief relationships can have a lasting impact on our lives. If this woman made you happy, well, what's so bad about holding on to the good memories? Especially if they can improve your wellbeing."

"I don't know." I stood from the chair, stretching from my cramped sitting position. "It feels like I don't have the right to them."

"But you do, Ivan." Doc approached me and touched his index finger to my forehead, something Mari had also done before. "You have *every* right to good memories because you were there. You experienced them, they're yours." He tapped his finger twice on my forehead before dropping his hand away. "And no one can take them away from you."

CHAPTER 8

MARIPOSA

With quick work and oxygen at the ready, we were able to save everyone in the cave-in who had survived the initial blast, about half of Gunner's unit.

Those with the worst injuries were quickly transported back to the field hospital. Everyone else, we told to sit tight until the van came back. Even with oxygen and rest, they were no longer in fighting shape after what they'd been through.

Gunner too had been rattled. He was covered in dirt from trying to dig them out, had clearly been in shock, and seemed to experience some hearing loss from the blast.

"We shouldn't stay here," Gunner said, his voice a rough rasp. "The perimeter units are holding off Blakeworth, but we're still in the middle of a battlefield."

"We'll get them moving soon," I said, not wanting to argue. "Let me check you over."

He thankfully kept still while I moved my hands and stethoscope over him. I had to feel under his clothes and tried to remain as clinical as possible, but something passed between us as my gloved hands pressed on his abdomen.

This was my husband, not just any patient in my care. This was a man I hadn't touched in weeks, despite how intensely I craved him. He let out a soft grunt at the pressure from my fingertips and I fought hard to not recall the last time I heard him make such a noise.

"Any pain when I touch you here?"

He snorted, and I knew he was holding back some wisecrack reply. "No, no pain."

"Any ringing in your head?" I moved to his side and shined my penlight into his ear canal.

"Oh yeah. It's pretty much all I hear."

"Yeah, that'll probably last for a few days."

He snorted again. "Great."

I slid my stethoscope dial up his back, under his shirt, resting it over where he wore the tattoo that matched mine. "Breathe deeply for me."

Stepping away after he took a few breaths, I pulled the eartips out while making sure I put some physical space between us. Being close to him, touching him, it was intense, bordering on too much. Like with Reaper, it was annoying how much his close proximity affected me. I resented all the attraction and chemistry with these two men, hating the possibility that it might influence my judgment of their actions.

"You might have inhaled some particulate tossed up in the air from the blast," I explained clinically. "Take it easy for a week or so. You might have a cough for a few days. Let me know if you cough up any blood."

He lowered his blue gaze to his lap, an ironic smile on his face. "Does this mean I'm allowed to talk to you again?"

I released a sigh and crossed my arms over my chest, knowing this conversation would have to happen sooner or later. "You talked to Reaper, I take it?"

"Yeah." He lifted his shoulder as if to shrug, then winced as he lowered it back into place.

"I'll get you an ice pack for that," I said. "So did he tell you what would set this right for me?"

Gunner nodded. "Yeah, he did." He went quiet after that, looking at me as if waiting for me to explain myself. When I didn't and just continued to meet his stare, he lowered his gaze again with a sigh. "Mari, I love you—"

"Stop right there." I raised a hand. "This isn't a negotiation,

Gunner. I know you're good at that, but you won't convince me that I'm better off forgetting Shadow. Frankly, it feels manipulative."

"I'm not—"

"I said, *stop*. Let me finish."

A muscle feathered in his jaw as his mouth clamped shut. He looked determined to speak, but thankfully held back.

I lowered my hand, my throat tightening with emotion. "And it… hurts that you took Reaper's side over listening to me." I sniffed, batting my eyes as I willed the tears not to fall. "That hurt a lot, Gun. So can you understand why I don't want to hear you say you love me? Or are you going to ignore that too?"

His mouth dropped open, brow knitting with tension as his hands wrung in his lap like he was fighting the urge to touch me. With a sharp breath, his jaw closed, teeth clicking with how hard his mouth shut.

"I'm sorry, Mari." Gunner blinked and I saw the beginnings of tears welling in his sky-blue eyes. "I'm sorry I didn't listen to you. I should have. I should have spoken up and told Reap it wasn't what you wanted. I hurt you and we," he paused to swallow thickly, "we probably fucked up his life when there was another way."

The air seemed to whoosh out of us both. It was like a small crack had formed in the tension between us over the last several weeks. We weren't out of the woods yet, but it was something.

"I'm not trying to make excuses, just explain," Gunner said with another shaky breath. "We were just…convinced it was the right thing to do. The *only* thing to do. We wanted to protect you, baby gi—Mari. But I understand," he nodded to himself, "the damage was already done and it wouldn't have happened again. Shadow is the type of guy who will go to extreme lengths to protect you from himself." Gunner met my eyes again, the blue depths filled with sadness. "What Reaper did—what we did—was wrong. It was badly thought out, and we should have listened to you."

"Thank you for referring to Shadow in the present tense," I said softly. "But you know this can't stop here. *Anything* that comes up between us, you will have to listen to me. You can't just steamroll over me when you've already decided what to do. When something concerns me, you have to actually listen to what I want."

"I know." Gunner nodded again. "You're absolutely right, Mari. I'm sorry it took such a painful event for me to realize this. I promise I'll do better." He extended a hand, and I held back as long as I could before placing my fingers in his. His hand wrapped around mine, long fingers stroking over my palm. "It's good to talk to you again."

I nodded, but felt like I'd be unable to voice the same sentiment without bursting into tears, and thus letting myself fall against his chest. "I should check on your unit," I said instead, pulling my hand out of his.

He reluctantly let me go, sad eyes watching me as I turned my back. Even without looking at him, I could feel his stare as tangibly as the kisses he used to leave on the back of my neck.

Further away from him, I could focus better as I checked oxygen levels and injuries. When the truck returned, we helped people into the bed carefully and moved out to return to the field hospital.

"You coming with us, or staying?" I called to Gunner as I straddled my dirt bike.

He stood next to his bike, talking into the radio clipped on his cut. "I'll meet you back there in a bit. Maybe, um—" He shoved a dirt-covered hand back through his hair. "The hospital is sending another team of medics so you guys can take your leave soon. If it's okay with you," he pulled his lip between his teeth, "maybe we can ride home together?"

Oh, how I wanted to. I yearned to ride off to some beautiful, secluded place and catch up on all the time I lost with my golden gunman. But the hurt wasn't completely gone, only slightly healed from his apology. I wasn't ready to go back to being a happy family again. Not until our whole family was back together.

"We'll see," I answered noncommittally. "I'll have to give reports to the new head medic when they arrive."

He nodded, reluctantly accepting that answer as he turned to continue listening to his units through the radio.

"Be safe," I told him, turning my bike around. "Don't make me come out here to pull you out next." I saw the hint of his gorgeous smile before I drove off, kicking my bike into gear to catch up with the supply van.

I heard a high-pitched screech rolling through the air, even over my engine, as I spotted Horus dive bombing like a missile for some food. The memory of soaring, of seeing the whole battlefield through a bird's-eye view came to the forefront of my mind.

It wasn't a dream, was it?

No, daughter. You needed to see, so I lent you my eyes.

The answer came clearly through my head as though Horus had been flying right next to my handlebars.

"What's the point?" I demanded, my voice low and barely audible over my bike. "I don't understand any of it. Shadow being exiled, my marriage falling apart. Just why?"

The point is growth, daughter. Just as there is no flying without falling, there is no growth without pain.

He said nothing after that, and I didn't inquire further. The next few hours were a busy hustle-and-bustle of treating new patients. The new medic team showed up just before nightfall, and not a moment too soon. My exhaustion had returned with a vengeance, and I was nearly falling asleep on my feet.

"At ease, Mariposa." The head medic of the second team, a tough woman named Tori, patted my shoulder. "Get some sleep before you head home."

"Has, uh," I forced my eyes to stay open, despite how heavily my lids drooped. "Has my husband come back?"

"He's been radioing updates. The battle is pretty much over. I think he and the remaining units will be heading straight back to deliver intel to General Bray, last I heard."

I nodded as I meandered to a corner of the tent to lay down on a cot with a blanket. A big part of me was disappointed that Gunner didn't come here to ask me again about riding home. Seeing and touching him had reawakened so much *feeling* that had been numbed over the past few weeks. I wanted both of my husbands that I'd pushed away in all of my senses, to consume them like drugs.

The only thing I wanted more were the wrongs committed against Shadow to be reversed, for my beautiful, scarred man to return home to me.

I pulled the blanket over me and curled my legs up to my chest, fluffing the lumpy, cheap pillow under my head into something marginally more supportive. Lying there, settling into my exhaustion, I wondered where Shadow was right then, what he was doing.

Did he still think of me as much as I thought of him? His letter said he would never forget me. I couldn't forget him if I tried, despite him telling me that I should. Did he even have a tent over his head and a blanket like me? Was he hungry or lonely? Or maybe he was just fine, living a life that never would have been possible if he hadn't been freed from the SDMC.

I drifted off to sleep with memories of kissing scars over warm skin and corded muscles, and swore I jolted awake only seconds later to Horus' voice.

Wake up, daughter.

Blinking at the early dawn light coming through the tent, I pulled the blanket tighter around me against the chill. Medics were already up and about, making coffee and breakfast over camping stoves, chatting quietly, and tending to patients.

"Coffee, Mari?"

Someone pushed a steaming cup into my hand before I could answer, and I wrapped my hands around it gratefully. A few careful sips warmed me up enough to get moving, and I was unsurprised to see Horus perched on my bike just outside the tent. He faced east, the same direction as the rising sun.

Make your preparations, daughter, his ancient voice echoed in my head.

"Preparations?" I repeated. "For what?"

For a long journey. The falcon stretched his wings out to the sides, sunlight illuminating the long, graceful feathers. *Tomorrow is the day.*

"Tomorrow?" I gasped. "You mean...?"

We leave to pull a man from the shadows, he said. *And begin a new stage of growth.*

CHAPTER 9

JANDRO

I hated empty houses. They always felt fucking weird, like ghosts were lurking, because homes were meant to be filled up with people. With a family.

My house growing up was wild. If me or one of my sisters wasn't causing a ruckus, my aunt and uncle would be yelling at each other across the house from different rooms. It was just how they had a normal conversation.

In Sheol, I didn't spend a ton of time at home until Mari came into our lives. But that place was different. The clubhouse and my bike shop were just as much my home as the place I shared with Shadow. Our club thrived because of the sense of community there.

But here? I didn't know how the fuck we ended up here.

Mari had been gone for going on six days straight to run the field hospital for the Blakeworth skirmish. Four days in, Gunner headed out with the backup units. Back at our so-called home, Reaper and I were just in and out, barely interacting.

I spent most of my days at Dave's garage, tuning up the club's vehicles and helping Dave out with his workload when I had spare time. Coming home to a dark, empty house was the worst. I ate enough to get by, showered and got into bed to start the whole day over. Reaper usually got in later than me, and I didn't care enough to keep tabs on his whereabouts.

Even before Mari left to work out in the field, it was like I could feel the life in our home slowly suffocating. She spent all her free time at the hospital, avoiding the other guys and barely talking to me beyond surface level stuff.

Our new house had been lively and bright the night of our homecoming party, filled with happy people and good cheer. It felt like a turning point for us, a chance to put roots down and become a real family unit. I never expected our sense of home and togetherness to start dying that very same night.

For weeks, I went back and forth between feeling pissed at and sorry for Shadow. We all hated that Mari got hurt, but the big dude never had a say in what happened to him. He didn't have control over how the abuse from his previous life would affect him. Shadow was a victim too, and what happened to Mari was a long-festering symptom of the damage that had been done to him.

But Reaper was president. My bullheaded best friend would have thrown *me* in a damn jail cell if I tried to stop him. I knew him even better than I knew Shadow. The one thing I knew that Reaper would never admit, was how fucking scared he was.

Losing his parents had almost broken him. Losing his brother *did* break him. Finding Mari had helped glue some of those broken pieces back together. If he were to lose her? Nothing would bring him back from that.

He was terrified of losing those who mattered most to him. That kind of fear turned a rational man into a creature who reacted on instinct, relying on past events as a means to protect his future.

Like the parts of a motorcycle, I knew Reaper well enough to fit together all the pieces of his history. The sum of which spurred actions and a mindset that didn't surprise me in the least.

It didn't mean I had to like it. We'd exchanged few words over the past weeks, mostly him asking how Mari was, and me always giving the same answer, "Fine."

I felt like a robot, like those automated machines I heard stories about that used to build cars and computers. My mind was blank, empty and numb as my body went through the motions it was supposed to. Eat, sleep, feed chickens, shower, work.

The emptiness of the house didn't even register when I came inside that evening through the garage door. It would send me on a downward spiral if I let it, and I couldn't. It felt like I was the only one keeping this family together, albeit by fraying threads. Distantly, I knew Mari was due to come home after a week. With six days that had passed now, I'd have to find out if anyone knew if she was on her way back.

I ate a cold dinner, checked the heat lamps in the chicken coop, showered, and got ready for bed. No sooner than my head hit the pillow did I hear the high-pitched rattle of a dirt bike pulling into the garage.

I sprang out of bed and yanked on a pair of shorts, feeling something close to alive for the first time in days. I didn't even notice the cold as I whipped the garage door open.

"*Mariposita!*" I declared with a genuine grin of happiness that felt strange on my face.

"Hey." She turned off her bike and pulled her helmet off, making her long hair stream out like the tail of a comet. "Sorry, did I wake you?"

"Nah, I just went to lie down." I approached her, the concrete floor icy on my bare feet, but I didn't give a shit. "Welcome home. What do you need, *mi amor?*" I rubbed the arms of her jacket, planting a kiss on her forehead. "You hungry?"

"No, I'm okay." She glanced up at me with a weary smile. "I think I'll just shower and go to bed."

"Sounds good to me." I slid my arms around her in a loose hug, dropping another kiss in her hair. I didn't even care that she smelled like dirt and sweat, my girl was home. "I'll keep your side of the bed warm."

"Thanks, love." Mari brushed a soft kiss under my jaw before pulling away. It was nothing like the passion we shared before all of this shit went down, but I would take it.

We got inside and I set out a clean towel for her before slipping back into bed. Her shower was long, probably the first one she had in nearly a week. I nearly fell asleep before hearing the water shut off, but scooted to my side of the bed to make room for her. Mari padded softly across the dark bedroom to her side, lifting the sheets before sliding between them.

"Thank you for warming my side." She scooted to the middle, nestling between my arms for our nightly cuddle.

"*Siempre*," I murmured sleepily before blinking my eyes open, pulling her tighter against my chest. "Do you want to talk about your week?"

"Not really." Mari's lips brushed my chest, her fingertips trailing lightly across my ribs.

"Want to talk about anything else?" I played with the ends of her hair trailing down her back.

"Not tonight. Just…" she trailed off, burrowing into me closer than she had in weeks. "I love you, Jandro."

"*Mariposita*, I love you so much." I reached under her hair to cup the back of her neck. "And I missed you like hell while you were gone."

"I missed you too." She drew in a shaky breath. "I miss…*everyone*."

"They miss the hell out of you right back." I rubbed into her neck, rolling my fingers over the knots there. "And I'm including Shadow in that."

Mari pulled back to look at me, her gaze finding mine in the darkness. "If he comes back, would you accept him? Into the club, our home, our life again?"

"Yes," I said without hesitation. "I would, if only to see you happy again."

She stiffened slightly. "What about for him?"

"I'd love to have Shadow back in general, but you are my priority." My palms spanned across her back. "Having him around and in…a better mental state would be great, *bonita*, don't get me wrong." I tapped a finger to the tip of her nose. "Just as far as reasons go, you are at the top of that list. Always."

"Jandro…" Mari sighed, her lips landing on my neck when she leaned in again. "When you say that, I actually believe you."

"Good, 'cause it's the truth."

She didn't say anything else, so I shifted into the mattress, pulling the blankets higher over us to settle in for sleep. It was expected to be a cold night, and I silently hoped she'd sleep in late with me after her long, hard week out in the field.

Mari kissed my neck again, lips lingering sensually. Her tongue flicked out against my skin and I let out a soft groan, my body already heating up a few degrees.

"Babe?" I muttered, the hope clear in my voice.

"Mm-hm?" She kept kissing me, her short nails now making trails of heat over my chest.

"Are you seducing me?"

"What do you think?" There was a tone of playfulness in her voice I hadn't heard in so long.

I slid a palm over her hip, taking a handful of her flesh there before pausing. "Has something changed?"

We hadn't done anything sexual in weeks. With how messed up things were, it wasn't like I had an insatiable drive anyway. A couple of half-hearted tugs in the shower was the most action I'd had since the awful night of our housewarming party. Of course I wanted my woman more than anything, but seeing her so heartbroken killed any selfish desire I had.

"I'm just tired of feeling miserable." Mari slid her leg over mine, resting her thigh on my hip. "I love you and I want you. I want to feel good again."

"Say no more, *mami*."

With a deep kiss, I rolled us to her back. She slid her other leg out and wrapped them both around my hips, already drawing me to her core.

"No, no, not yet." I was already fully hard and aching, my body just as desperate to be with my wife as I was. "I won't last if we go straight to it."

"I don't care, I need you." She pressed up, lining her body flush to mine with another one of those damn neck kisses that never let me think straight. "I just need to feel you, Jandro."

"Mari..." I grunted out a weak protest.

She was so soft and warm. Her need for me sent the primitive part of my brain wild. I wanted to give her what she asked for, to drive deep into her silky heat and just rut until my release.

But I also hadn't touched my wife like this in weeks and I wanted to celebrate it. To spend the whole night savoring and pleasing her. I wanted this to be a new corner we turned, the start of healing our family again and putting the painful weeks behind us.

"Please, Jandro." Her hand grazed down my body to stroke me—fuck—no, to direct me toward her entrance.

"Wait." I grabbed her hand, unwrapping it from my cock. "Let me give you a few orgasms first."

"A few?" Even in the dark, I saw her eyes narrow at me. "How many is 'a few'?"

"Hm." I brought her hand to my lips and kissed her wrist. "Three?"

"No. I want you so bad, I know I'll come when you fuck me."

"Two, then?" I bit lightly on the tip of her finger.

"Jandrooo..." Then she giggled. "I can't believe we're arguing about this."

"Beats fighting over other stuff, right?" I kissed the center of her palm. "So, two it is?"

She smiled wickedly. "One."

"Hmm." I released her hand, running a long caress down the gorgeous curves of her body. "One and a half?"

"A half? What are you—uh, fuck..."

I rolled her clit under my thumb, watching how her hips rose off the bed to meet my hand.

"Fuck yes," I said in a harsh whisper, utterly mesmerized at how she moved. "I want to watch you come like this."

"It's not enough," she whined, fisting the sheets at her sides while her hips chased the pleasure my hand was giving her. "I need more, Jandro."

"I got you, babe. Don't worry." I turned my hand, my fingertips quickly finding her slick entrance.

Her satisfied moan sent my cock twitching as my hand pressed through to the center of her heat. My woman quickly grew needy again as my fingers curled and stroked inside her, my thumb resting next to her clit.

"Jandro..." Oh, how I wanted to hear her say my name like that all fucking night.

"Uh huh, I'm right here." My left hand pressed her thigh to the mattress as I fucked her with my right. My cock twitched again, as if jealous of the other body part that got to touch her.

"Come on, I need you." Mari shifted her hips, an attempt to direct my thumb to move on top of her clit, but my grip on her thigh kept her in place.

"You never said there was a time limit on our orgasm agreement," I informed her with my most charming smile. "What if I don't want you to come until dawn?"

"Ugh." Her head flopped down heavily on the pillow. "I never even agreed to a stupid orgasm deal. I just wanted sex before sleep!"

"And I want to make up for over a month of not pleasing you." I leaned down and drew a pert nipple into my mouth, sucking on the tight bud until she gasped, then releasing it with a pop. "As a husband should."

"I should have known you would," she laughed, scratching lightly over my neck and upper back.

"Trust me, babe." I mouthed my way to her other nipple, bringing that delicious peak under the same treatment of my tongue. "I'm dying to be buried inside you. But it's like I just told you." I scooted up to kiss her lips, our mouths locking for a moment with sweet pulls and tongue caresses. "My priority is you." I kissed her again quickly before making my way back down her body. "Always you."

My fingers dragged along the walls of her channel and her hips shot up from the bed, crashing against my mouth. I took the opportunity to suck a kiss low on her pelvis, a few inches away from her clit that was begging for my attention.

Mari's whines grew guttural, desperate. Her fingers raked over my scalp as my mouth hovered closer to her clit, her thighs already shaking. The reaction was instant when I finally kissed her there, her scream undoubtedly reaching the second story of the house. I secretly hoped Reaper was home, listening to what she wanted with me and no one else.

I heard Mari's panting above me, her pussy starting to close around my two fingers, despite me spreading them wide. Her clit was a small pebble under my tongue, the one hard spot on her supple body that tried to squirm and thrash under my hold.

She came with another beautiful scream, her body going rigid as she convulsed around my fingers. Thighs clasped to my ears, that succulent pussy bucked against my mouth. I sucked at her tender flesh until she pushed my head away and whimpered at me to stop.

Drawing up her body, I lined myself up with her and pressed inside with slow ease. I kissed her mid-gasp as I settled between her thighs, her body so warm and receptive to me.

My first few strokes were long and slow, drawing out all the way before filling her back up. When her thighs squeezed tighter around me, hips tilting up for more friction, I slid my hands under her back and rolled us so she was on top.

"Show me how you were gonna seduce me." I grinned breathlessly, relaxing one arm behind my head while keeping the other glued to her hip.

Mari's breath was still coming in short pants, the movement of her ribcage and breasts utterly erotic in the dim light. She ripped my hand from her hip, reaching over to pin it next to my other hand behind my head. My woman stared at me with a fiery intensity as she rolled over the length of my cock in a seductive rhythm, while keeping my hands pinned next to my head.

"Is this what you wanted to see?" she asked, lips hovering over mine. "Riding you for myself?"

"Yes," I groaned, lifting my hips to meet her as she crashed down. "Take what you want from me."

The tight buds of her nipples skimmed up and down my chest as she moved. My fingers curled with the need to touch them, to draw them into my mouth and hear her resulting yelps. I could have broken her hold on my wrists easily, but didn't dare. It was so hot being used by her, watching her take her pleasure while I laid back and enjoyed the view.

Mari eventually released my wrists after a few more minutes of vigorous riding, dragging her nails down my chest as she sat upright. Her movements slowed to a more languid, back and forth motion, fluid and hypnotizing.

"You're close again," I rasped, my hands running up her thighs to her waist. I could feel it in how tightly she wrapped around me, the quickness of her breaths and heat in her skin.

"Uh huh." Her hands covered mine. She didn't seem to be chasing the release, but riding the feeling out slowly as she rolled over me. "I just want to keep feeling you."

"Ride me all night if you want to." My touch extended over her ribs, her breasts, and the long curve of her spine. "All I want is to feel you too."

I reveled in every lowering of her hips, her slick heat enveloping me so sweetly. My breath stuttered for control with each long drag out of her pussy, fingers digging into her flesh as I fought to keep the control in her hands. This was for her, after all. This was all about giving her something good, something to start us on the path of healing.

Eventually, Mari's patience wore out and she began rocking back and forth on a vigorous ride again. Her hands braced on my chest as her brow pinched with tension, grinding her body into me with harder crashes and more friction.

"Oh yes, yes," I encouraged her, driving up with hard thrusts to meet her need. "Let me see you come all over my cock."

Her pussy wrung me out with its release and Mari nearly took me with her, crying out and writhing over me. I held back long enough to roll us over once again, pressing her back into the mattress as I pounded into her with everything I had left.

"Fuck! Yes Jandro, more!" She was limp and breathless from her orgasm, soft and pliant for me to pound into, but her hands dug into the backs of my arms, thighs still squeezing my hips.

I crashed into her until my rhythm naturally stuttered, the need too great to ignore as I chased it higher and higher. Lightning zipped up my spine and my heartbeat thundered in my ears. My release pulsed through me into her, rendering me lightheaded and unable to breath for a few moments of pure bliss.

I took in big gulps of air as I rolled off of Mari, weeks worth of pent-up tension now drained from my body. Mari curled into my side, her head on my chest with her cheek over my still-rapid heart beat.

"I love you, Jandro." Her hand slid over my torso and I threaded my fingers with hers, my other arm draping down her side.

"Love you more than anything." I kissed the top of her head and squeezed her hand. "Tomorrow's another day, alright?"

"Yeah," she murmured. "It is."

CHAPTER 10

MARIPOSA

I knew it would be hard to pull away from Jandro's warm body, his embrace loving even while in sleep. I just didn't think it would be *this* hard. But I had to. Horus said it was time.

Slowly, painstakingly, I peeled away from my lover in the dead of night and dressed silently in the dark. I had already written the note I would leave, carefully pulling it from my jeans pocket and leaving the folded piece of paper on the pillow next to him. It was short and to the point. *I've gone to find him. Don't worry, Horus is my guide. We'll all come home together. I love you. —M.*

I could only say so much to convince him that I *had* to do this, and do so alone. He'd never let me leave if I said anything first, and no one else seemed to get the message from Horus that it was time. This mission was only meant for me.

I had to dig deep to find the old Mari, the woman who'd never met the Steel Demons before and traveled on her own for three years. I had to introduce her to the woman I was now, who knew how to ride and could protect herself with a gun and a dagger. I needed to draw strength from both sides, to combine what I learned to scrape by with what taught me to thrive.

My weapons had come from the remnants of the Steel Demons

armory we carried with us. They were the same weapons Gunner had me practice with multiple times, so I'd be better at handling them than anything else. The knife slid easily into my boot while the small .40 caliber handgun fit in a holster under my jacket.

I packed enough food, water, and fuel to last me around three days, plus enough pills to earn my keep somewhere for a month if I had to. It would have felt nostalgic if I didn't keep looking back at Jandro's bedroom door as I packed. How many times had I left one service center with these same items—minus the weapons—without any idea how far away my next stop would be?

Even after everything that happened between Shadow, Reaper, and me, I wouldn't have gone back to my old life for a second. The Steel Demons were my home and my heart. I just had to draw on that old resilience, the tenacity to keep moving, in order to bring our family back together.

Assuming Shadow still wanted to come back.

Horus wouldn't lead me on a wild falcon chase if Shadow didn't want to come home, right?

Who was I kidding? Nothing about this was certain at all. My gut still screamed at me to not be foolish, to tear off all my clothes and weapons and dive back in bed with Jandro. But I couldn't keep living like the past few weeks either. Something had to change, and it would begin by finding Shadow.

Dawn was just starting to lighten up the sky as I walked my dirt bike out of the garage, closing the door by hand as silently as I could. I walked down to the end of our long driveway before throwing my leg over the bike and starting up the engine. The high-pitched growling cut through the early morning silence as I kicked my heels up and sped away, praying the noise hadn't woken up my men and spurred them to come after me.

Because if they did, I might not have the courage to leave again.

BY THE SECOND DAY, I REALIZED WHAT A CRUEL MASTER Horus was.

He pushed me *hard* on the road. Unlike when I was traveling before, I didn't go at my own pace, but at his. I had no compass or map, just the falcon flying ahead of me as my only guide. We were heading east-ish, as far as I could tell.

Every time I wanted to stop to pee or stretch my legs, he just kept flying. I'd hurry back to my bike in fear of losing sight of him and we'd carry on until dark.

At night was the only time I could rest and refuel. Conveniently, Horus always flew down near the end of the day when we were coming up on a service center or some other kind of lodging. To let me know it was time to stop, he'd swoop down at dusk to perch between my handle-bars, making soft chirps rather than the loud screeches he threw at me if I got too far behind him.

It got tiring quickly, this journey was feeling aimless.

"Was this the same way and pace that Shadow took?" I wondered aloud early on the third morning, stifling a yawn as the falcon tore apart a squirrel for his breakfast.

He peered at me, beak smothered in blood and squirrel guts, but didn't give me an answer.

We carried on for another grueling four days. The desert landscape turned into flat plains, the air cold and dry as the grasslands stretched on for endless miles. Gradually the plains gave way to humid marshlands full of greenery and thick, heavy air. The sky was covered by clouds and when rain started to fall, I was still warm enough to ride for a full day without my jacket on.

I thought I'd seen abject poverty in the Southwest, but all of the Texas and Arizona territories were lush with riches compared to this area. People lived in tents and broken down trailers next to the road, watching me ride through with empty stares. I saw children with distended bellies and living conditions that were hazardous at best. These people had no one to advocate for them now, which was the worst part of it. Not even a mayor or a congressman to fight on their behalf. These people were the real victims of the Collapse, the ones that everyone forgot about.

My heart squeezed in my chest, the instinct to stop and provide help riding me hard. But Horus was a dark speck in the sky and every rotation of my tires brought me closer to Shadow. I couldn't save everyone, nor could I let myself get distracted. A spark of determination fired me up, making me bear down hard on the accelerator. The sooner I saw Shadow and convinced him to come home, the faster I could provide help for these people on the way back.

By the sixth day on the road, Horus veered north, the oppressive cold returning to settle deep in my bones. Looking to the east, warm, sandy beaches gave way to a rocky, jagged coastline. The road grew rockier too, and I started to fear all the weathering on my tires from this long journey.

The seventh day was by far the hardest. I was sore and stiff from riding all day for a full week. My bike started to make a grinding noise, the suspension rattling underneath me.

"Come on," I patted the bike's fuel tank as if trying to encourage a living thing. "We made it so far, don't give up on me now."

A few miles later was when my front tire decided to give out. I heard a loud pop, then smelled burning and saw sparks flying near my feet.

"Fuck!" My balance started to wobble, the tire shredding as the rim met the road with an awful grinding sound.

Fortunately I stayed upright long enough to slow down and pull over to a grassy field. I was nowhere near as knowledgeable as Jandro about bike maintenance, but even I could tell it wasn't drivable in this state. I didn't have a spare tire and the metal wheel was already scratched from running along the road at high speed.

The best part of this situation? Horus kept on flying like nothing had happened.

"What the fuck am I supposed to do now?" I called out to the sky, all my frustration and exhaustion leaving my throat in a strangled scream.

Have you forgotten your feet, daughter? The sky god's voice almost seemed to be mocking me.

"What? Walk the rest of the way?" I demanded. "How much farther is there to go?"

Does it matter? Is there any distance you would not go?

No, there wasn't. I knew that answer instantly.

I'd walk the entire journey from Four Corners if it meant I would see Shadow again. I'd cross that freezing-looking ocean on a life raft if that's what I had to do. I shouldered my backpack and started walking, leaving the dirt bike on the side of the road without a second glance. It likely wouldn't be there on the way back, but Shadow and I would find a way home together.

We had to.

It was only another few miles before I started to feel the ache in the soles of my feet, the feeling soon traveling up to my calves and hips. I wished I'd brought my hospital sneakers instead of my riding boots. Even then, running around on flat floors had nothing on this barely maintained road and constant changes in elevation.

I ended up putting on all of my warmest layers, the coldness growing sharper as the sun started to set. I even pulled my shirt over my nose and mouth, the frigid air starting to hurt as I took deep breaths.

Walking was not only slower, but used up all my physical energy. I was more exhausted, hungry, and thirsty than I ever would have been on the bike, and covering far less ground. Moving so much slower also caused me to think more. It made me realize how much I missed my men. My last night with Jandro felt like a distant dream now. I couldn't recall his warm touch anymore, not out here while I shivered in some foreign territory all by myself.

Reaper and Gunner, my heart ached heavily with missing them too, if even more than Jandro. I hated that it felt like so long ago that they were truly my husbands, when we were actually happy. This divide between us seemed to gape even wider with each step I took, every mile of distance I put between us. Even if I did make it back with Shadow, was there any going back with me and my men?

I pulled my arms inside my sleeves, hugging them against my body as I kept walking, although I was so cold, tired, and weak that it was more like shuffling. I tried to draw on memories of warmth, of waking up between multiple bodies pressing into me on all sides. If I shivered at all while in bed with them, someone would always wrap around me, even while dead asleep. Sometimes it got stifling, but I would kill for the heat and company of another person right then.

The sun finally dipped below the horizon, the temperature plunging even lower. I didn't hear wings flapping, but the clicking of talons sinking into wood near me. Horus had settled on a fence post, sharp eyes and beak pointing to a structure up ahead.

Rest here, daughter.

A service center, out in the middle of nowhere, but with blue and red neon lights in the windows advertising cold beer and spirits. I shuffled forward, any signs of life more inviting than the frigid wasteland out here, even if they were from an old motel attached to a dive bar.

The heat inside was almost suffocating compared to how cold it was outside, even though it probably wasn't any higher than seventy degrees. Laughter and conversations abruptly stopped as I shivered just inside the front door. I looked around, but my eyes seemed unable to focus.

"Holy shit, hun! You okay?" A female voice called out to me. "Doc, go check on her."

"Jen, get a blanket and heat up some water," a male voice answered. Then the weight of a hand rested on my arm with the same voice saying, "There's a chair to your left. Take a seat and we'll take care of you, alright?"

Too weak to argue, I followed his lead and sat down in a large armchair, my feet screaming with relief as I took my weight off them. The man who spoke knelt in front me, his hair and goatee mostly grey. Crows feet lined blue eyes behind thick glasses as he clinically checked me over for injuries, and then my pulse and temperature.

A medic, I realized. *Maybe even a doctor.* The woman had called him Doc after all.

"How long were you wandering out there?" he asked, pulling up on one of my eyelids to check my pupils.

"A w-w-week," I stammered, my teeth still chattering hard.

"Damn," he breathed, rocking back to look at me. "Where'd you come from, the girl's camp?"

"N-no. F-f-four..."

"It's alright, hun. You don't have to explain now. You'll be safe here." His tone was gentle, soothing, something I wanted to trust even though I probably shouldn't yet. I didn't know this man, and plenty of people were good at pretending to be trustworthy.

"I c-c-can p-pay…"

"We'll worry about that later," the man said with a kind smile just as a woman walked up, unfolding a blanket to wrap around me.

"There you are," she said, bundling me tight. "Don't worry about a thing. Believe it or not, we're used to all sorts walking through our doors."

I found myself fixated on her sleeve tattoos. They were beautiful, intricate flower designs decorating her from shoulder to wrist. Parts of them were fresh, still scabbed and healing. The ink fit her overall punk-rock look with her dark burgundy lipstick, ripped stockings under her shorts, and piercings through her lip, nose, and eyebrow.

"Th-thank you," I said, finally allowing myself to relax a little. Horus's screeching be damned, I would need at least two days to recuperate. My body had met its limit on this fucking trek. I hated that it would be even longer until I saw Shadow, but I couldn't keep pushing myself like this.

"Jen." The man with glasses turned to the tattooed woman. "Is Ivan out there?"

"No, he crashed early tonight," she answered. "Otherwise I'm sure he would have swooped this lady up and carried her inside."

"I was wondering why he didn't," the man chuckled. "You got a name, miss?"

"M-Mari," I said, my shivers finally slowing. "M-Mariposa, but call me Mari."

"Alright, miss Mari. I'm Jen and this is Doc." The tattooed woman pressed a glass of room-temperature water into my hands. "We'll get you set up with a room. You should sit tight with us for a couple days. If you see a big, scary-lookin' guy walking around, that's Ivan. He's a gentle giant and will likely be more scared of you than the other way around."

"Huh," I mused, trying to gulp down the water without drinking it too fast. "I'm kind of looking for someone who fits that description."

Jen and Doc seemed to exchange a look, but I was already slipping too far into exhaustion to notice.

CHAPTER 11

———————

REAPER

The morning was so bitterly cold, I forced myself to get up early to light multiple fires in the house—one in the potbelly stove in the dining room, and the other in the regular fireplace in the living room.

Electricity was still unpredictable when it came to heat, especially in the winter when we didn't have as much solar power. A good, old-fashioned fire was the best heat source, at least until we had reliable utilities like before the Collapse.

The house was cozy before too long, or as much as it could be with Mari still giving me the cold shoulder. My heartbeat accelerated when I heard Jandro's bedroom door open. It was still early enough for her to be sleeping, and she was supposed to be back from the field mission now. Gunner said she left earlier than him when he got in last night. Her dirt bike had been in the garage and Jandro's door was shut. The same scene we'd become accustomed to.

But that morning it was only my VP padding over to where I was making coffee in the kitchen, naked except for his boxer shorts, his expression blank like a zombie.

"What?" I grunted at him.

He said nothing, but held a slip of paper out to me. I took it, recognizing Mari's neat handwriting instantly. The momentary excitement of having her back home quickly died as I read the brief note. I looked back up at Jandro, bewildered.

"What the fuck is this?" I demanded. "What does this mean?"

"She's gone." His voice was flat, his disbelief manifesting as numbed shock. "She went to find him."

"How?"

Before I could properly fly off the handle, Gunner came racing down the stairs, dressed only in a pair of flannel pajama pants.

"Hey, have you guys seen Horus?" he asked in a worried tone. "I just tried to see through him, but I can't. It's like he's shutting me out or—."

"Apparently, he's with Mari." I held the note out to him, letting him take it so he could read and join us in our stupor.

"The...fuck?" Gunner kept staring at the slip of paper as if the words might change. "She went to find *him?* Shadow? And my bird is her guide?" His hand fell to his side as he stared at us helplessly. "What the hell do we do?"

"Send the club out to get her back." I stroked my jaw as a plan began to form in my mind. "Let's get the Sons of Odin on it too. We've got to branch out—"

"No."

I whirled on Jandro, his eyes now dark and burning into me. "What did you say?"

"I said no, Reaper." His arms crossed over his chest. "She chose to do this on her own. We're not sending people out to find her because she clearly doesn't want to be found. Not until *she* finds Shadow."

"I don't care—"

"Yeah, that's your fucking problem!" Jandro stepped closer to me, his cool, collected temper now surging. "You don't care. You don't *think.* Someone does something you don't like, and you do everything possible to put them back under your thumb. Fuck the consequences, fuck how other people feel. Am I wrong?"

"Fuck off, I don't want her under my thumb! I want her safe. I want our wife home with us."

"Some fucking home this is," Jandro scoffed, scrubbing a hand down his face. "This isn't a home, it's a mess. It feels like I'm in a fucking nuthouse."

"What are you saying, Jandro?"

"Just fucking think for a minute!" he bellowed. "Think of someone other than yourself, other than what *you* want! Put yourself in *her* place. *Dios mio*, I don't blame her at all for leaving."

I backed up against the kitchen counter, thinking back to my last conversation with Mari, nearly a week ago. Fuck, it felt like an eternity ago, and even longer since I touched her.

She was adamant that nothing would satisfy her except bringing Shadow back, that he was the one who suffered the most in this situation, despite her being the one who was nearly strangled to death.

Even then, she still had us, I remembered. *While Shadow has no one.* A man she loved and wanted to build a life with, was cast out into exile without warning. *I* did that. By hurting him, I hurt her.

And that mattered.

I should have known how much it would matter. I saw how intensely she loved her men, how much work she put into drawing Shadow out of his comfort zone so he could live a full life without fear. Had it been me, Jandro, or Gunner in Shadow's circumstances, she would have done the same for any of us. That was how deep her love went. That was how badly I hurt not only her, but all of us.

My actions told her that her love meant nothing, that it was something meaningless and easily discarded. It hit me right then like a brick to the stomach, just how utterly wrong I had been.

"I...drove her away." The words came out a weak whisper.

"And exiled one of your own men, someone we can never replace." Jandro's gaze bore into me, daring me to argue. "One of your best and most loyal fighters, tossed out on his ass for something he couldn't control."

I could only lift my head up and down in shamed agreement. "Yes, you're right. Shadow was nothing but good to us. Good to *her*, and I threw it all away." I scrubbed a hand down my face, barely able to look at the two of them. "I get it now. *I* did this. I ruined everything, I know."

"We should have listened to her," Gunner added mournfully. "She *told* us she wanted help for Shadow, not punishment. We completely disregarded her wishes, and that's the real reason why everything's fucked."

"I know. I know." A massive sigh left me, my entire body feeling like it was deflating. "So what do we do now, just wait?"

"Don't look at us," Jandro scoffed. "You're still the pres."

"This is pretty fucking bad, actually." Gunner looked at both of us. "We were depending on Horus' sight to plan our battle tactics. Now we're basically blind."

"You can't see through him at all?" I asked.

Gunner shook his head. "It's like he closed a door. He's not letting me in, no matter what."

"That's gonna fuck us," I groaned, pinching my forehead. "We have to tell my dad."

"Keep trying," Jandro told him. "Or I dunno, see if you can look through Foghorn as a backup?"

"This doesn't make any sense." Gunner ignored Jandro's attempt at a joke and frowned at Hades and Freyja, sitting next to each other as they watched. "Why didn't Freyja go with her?"

She does not need love, she has that already. She needs sight, not love.

The answer threw all of us off-balance, grabbing for something like an earthquake had hit.

"Holy shit." Gunner stared wide-eyed at the cat.

"Nice of you to say hello again," I grumbled.

We belong to none of you. Hades' voice cut through our heads next. *We assist at our own discretion, nothing more.*

"I already figured that," I said. "But Gunner has a point. How are we supposed to win now? We're outnumbered, surrounded, and now blind."

You will find a way. Hades' tone was dismissive. *Humanity is good at that.*

"Fuck me." I turned away, stabbing my fingers through my hair. "Get dressed, Gun. We better tell the general sooner rather than later."

"Need anything from me?" Jandro folded his arms, Mari's note between his fingers like a precious relic. "From the club?"

I thought for a moment, rubbing my jaw. "Get all of our bikes fitted with off-road tires and the biggest fucking mufflers you can find. I want our bikes as silent as you can make 'em. Maybe even camouflage paint, if you have time. With an army this big, we're better off with a divide-and-conquer approach, and we gotta be stealthy."

"You got it." He nodded sharply before a half-smirk pulled at his lips. "That's the fucking president I know."

"Yeah, well." I headed toward my bedroom to get dressed for riding. "Let's hope he's still around when his old lady comes back."

"Wait, wait." My dad's eyes pinched shut as he raised a palm. "Say that again."

Gunner swallowed. "I can no longer see through Horus. He's left with Mari to find Shadow."

"And you don't know where they've gone or when they'll come back? *If* they'll come back?"

"There's no *if*," I snapped. "They *will* come back." *They have to, or else there's no fucking reason for me to fight for this place at all.*

General Bray slumped back in his chair, a posture I rarely saw him in, while he rubbed his temple. "I thought I ran through all possible worst-case scenarios, but *this* fucking tops all of them."

"We'll make do." My eyes slid over to Hades, who returned my gaze impassively. "We'll figure something out."

"Son..." my dad sighed, tipping his head back. "We've lost not only our trump card, but our best medic. My daughter-in-law and your wife! How can you be so calm?"

"I'm not calm, I'm...I'm numb." The realization from this morning settled even heavier on me, like boulders pressing in on all sides. "She's gone because of me. This is my fault." My fingers itched for a cigarette but I closed my fist at my side. "So I'm gonna fix it. We'll figure out a way to win, and make this a place Mari wants to come back to."

My father nodded slowly. "I hope to all the gods you hold on to that, son. Because I'll be honest—things look pretty bleak here."

"Jandro's working on stealthing up our vehicles," Gunner chimed in. "I suggest your army mechanics do the same. We're going to need off-road strike teams."

"That *might* help." Dad pushed a manila folder across the conference table to us. "Considering we got this news this morning."

I flipped the cover open and Gunner leaned in to read with me. The typed words in the memo made logical sense as I read them, forming coherent sentences in my mind, but I couldn't muster up any emotional reaction. I was already too numb.

"They're demanding our surrender?" Gunner voiced angrily, looking up at my dad.

General Bray nodded, his face blank. "Blakeworth, Jerriton, and New Ireland have formed an official alliance. All three of them have pledged to march on Four Corners if we don't surrender by sundown tomorrow."

Gunner shoved the folder away, leaning across the table. "You're not actually considering this?"

"Son." My dad folded his hands on the table and looked at Gunner with a grave expression. "That is a combined army of roughly six thousand troops, to our *one* thousand. A good chunk of which are still recovering from injuries in the skirmish last week."

Gunner sat back, his face despondent.

"If we had eyes in the sky, knew when they were coming and in what formations," Dad continued, "I might say we still had a fighting chance. But like this," he gestured to the message, "even if they don't invade and slaughter us, they could just surround the whole territory and starve us out."

"The alliance doesn't matter," I bit out.

Both of them looked at me. "Reap?" Gunner's voice was tinged with hope.

"General Tash's army is the biggest, best trained, and well-financed," I said. "The other two barely matter."

"Blakeworth is well-financed too—"

"No, they just appear that way because everything goes to their city and elite class."

"You weren't there, Reap." Gunner shook his head. "They came well-stocked with explosives to that skirmish. People got buried, caved in, blown apart. They pulled *no* fucking punches. Whatever we thought of them before doesn't apply. They're serious about taking us out."

"What about Jerriton?" I knew I was grasping at straws, but I had to grasp at fucking something. "Tash has taken over your uncle's army, right? Were those troops loyal to him, your family?"

"I dunno," Gun sighed. "My uncle treated regular citizens like shit, but he kept the army well-supplied I think. Now that it's Tash's, I imagine he's doing the same."

"So what, we just let the three of them come in and divvy this place up to their liking?"

"Rory, just think ahead for a moment," Dad said. "We don't want to risk a bunch of lives for no reason. If we start making a plan now, to strike back at a later date when we've gathered more support—"

"And our wife comes back home to what, exactly?" I demanded. "Tash's soldiers informing her that Four Corners is theirs now? That we just gave it all up while they do fuck-knows-what with her?"

"Son, I love Mari. You know I do," Dad pleaded with one hand raised. "And I know you're heartsick about her, but I'm talking about the whole territory. We have to think 'big picture' here. We're responsible for not just the army, but everyone here."

"I'm with Reap on this one, general." Gunner tilted his head toward me. "You've been telling the governor we need to be ready to fight. Well, we're fuckin' ready. We've always had smaller numbers. The odds have always been stacked against us. We've had losses that hurt really fucking bad, and we still keep going. Sometimes we've gotten out by the skin of our fucking teeth, but we are still here."

"We can't meet them out in the field like a regular army," I added, clarity finally beginning to dawn on me. "We have to fight like an MC."

CHAPTER 12

IVAN

I got up early, following the smell of coffee from my room down to the bar. Jen always made a strong pot first thing in the morning, and Heidi, the cook, made a mean plate of bacon and French toast.

The eggs were okay, but not all that impressive compared to the fresh ones from Jandro's flock. They didn't keep chickens here, but had eggs delivered from some market down south. It wasn't until I tasted the difference that I realized how spoiled I'd been before.

A plate of eggs might do me good today, though. I had a full day ahead of tattoo appointments, and a potential buyer was coming by to look at the Indian motorcycle I had restored in the junkyard.

The pang of missing Jandro flashed through me. I owed a lot to my old friend about what he taught me about eggs, bike repair, and more.

"Morning, Jen," I grunted out, approaching the bar when I hit the bottom of the stairs.

"Morning, Ivan!" she returned with her usual perky chirp. "You want your usual?"

"Yes, with a side of eggs, please."

"Coming right up, big guy."

I glanced down the length of the bar as she set the coffee pot in front of me, then did a double-take when my heart stopped at the recognition of the woman a few seats down.

No...No, it can't be.

I had to be dreaming, but I'd never had a dream this sweet before.

There she was, hunched over a steaming mug with a blanket over her shoulders, hair a tangled mess, and hazel eyes that rooted me to my spot.

The last time I remembered her looking at me, she was falling asleep on my chest and telling me I deserved happiness and healing.

"Good morning, Shadow." Mariposa lifted the steaming cup to her lips and paused. "Or is it Ivan now?"

"Mari..." Stunned didn't begin to cover the state I was in. A feather could have knocked me over. "What...are you doing here?"

"I came to find you."

An answer that was succinct, simple. Too simple for the racing questions in my head.

My mouth was much slower to catch up, to process that she was *here.* "How?"

"Horus led me here."

Jen came out right then, her stance cautious as she set my breakfast on the bar, watching the exchange between me and Mari.

"You two know each other?" the curious bartender asked.

"Yes," Mari answered quickly. Then to me, "Can we have a word in private?"

Private, what a loaded word. I decided on my first day here that I'd never be alone with a woman again, not after what happened with her.

But she was here, right in front of me. After what I did, she wanted to talk to me. Led by a god that guarded me and renewed my sight, but for what purpose?

I didn't dare hope. I didn't dare dream. I deserved nothing from her, not even the tattoo under my sleeve that started to itch at that very moment.

The hows and whys didn't matter—I had to make her leave.

Jen quickly made herself scarce, but we weren't the only ones in the dining area. I didn't want to embarrass Mari with what I had to tell her, so I grunted out a, "Yes," and made for the side door heading to the junkyard.

Mari's steps sounded odd, a bit of a shuffle, as she followed me, like her feet were hurting her. *Fucking hell, Horus. Don't tell me you made her walk here all the way from Four Corners?* It took all my resolve not to sweep her up and carry her to my room, a much better private place, where I could tell her in a hundred different ways how sorry I was. How much I missed her.

Instead I pushed open the door with a jerk of my shoulder, letting it swing wide so she could walk through. I walked until we would be out of earshot of anyone at the service center, then turned to face her with my arms crossed.

She pulled the blanket tighter around her shoulders, the drape of the fabric reminding me of how my hoodie had engulfed her when she wore it.

I squeezed my fingers into my own biceps, fighting the overwhelming need to touch her.

"Why did you come here?"

"To bring you back." Mari never was one for beating around the bush, lifting her chin as she looked me squarely in the eye. "To bring you home, where you belong."

I shook my head, looking down at my boots. It was just as I had feared. "I don't belong in Four Corners. I'm not a Steel Demon anymore, Reaper made sure of that."

"Reaper was wrong to do what he did—"

"No, he wasn't." My gaze returned to her. "He was absolutely in the right. I deserved—" I swallowed. "I deserved much worse than this, actually."

My life at the service center wasn't happy by any means, but it was fine for living in exile. I was kept busy, fed, and sheltered. Plus I hadn't sleepwalked in over two weeks, which I most likely owed to Doc's therapy sessions.

"That's not true." Mari started to blink rapidly, her eyes filling with tears. "Shadow, I know it was an accident. I forgive you—"

"Stop." I held out a hand, dropping my gaze. Seeing the hurt on her face was too fucking much. "Don't say that, please."

"I do, Shadow." She started coming closer, my body was bristling both with panic and yearning. "I...miss you. So much."

"Did you get my letter?" I took a few steps backward to widen the distance between us.

Mari's feet stopped moving, her face crestfallen. "Yes, Jandro gave it to me. I've only read it hundreds of times. And you know what I've realized?" A tear spilled down her cheek. "I can't heal. Not until you're back with the club. With me." She quickly wiped her face. "That is, unless you've truly moved on, and you're happier here. I want you to be happy, to thrive. That's all I really want."

Lie to her. Tell her yes, I've never been happier than in these last six weeks. Let her go home with that peace of mind, so she can be free of you.

But I couldn't lie, not to her. Not when she stood right there, looking so sad, and I was dying to be the one to put a smile on her face again.

"Even if I could...be with you again..." The words came out tight and strangled. "Reaper would never allow me to rejoin the club. He made it abundantly clear I was to stay away from Four Corners and you."

"No, he'll let you come back." Mari spoke with an eager hopefulness as she took another tentative step toward me. "He told me he would, no questions asked."

Puzzled, I stepped away from her again. "Why would he do that?"

Mari's face hardened, a coldness settling over her that didn't suit her warm personality. "Because I didn't speak to him or Gunner for over three weeks." She looked down at her feet. "I thought so many times about leaving them."

"You...did? Because of exiling me?"

She nodded and I couldn't believe what I was hearing. I injured her to the point of putting her in the hospital, and here she was, tearfully asking me to come back. They locked me away, then exiled me to protect her, and she nearly left them over it. None of it made any sense to me.

"I think they're finally understanding, especially now that I've come here," she went on. "You don't need punishment, Shadow, you need support. All the hard work you've done doesn't need to be thrown away over an accident—"

"Stop." I closed my eyes, the sight of her too much to bear. Another second of looking at her and I'd fall to my knees, begging her to stay. To be mine and no one else's. It would be completely unfair to ask, but that didn't diminish how badly I wanted it.

"I'm sorry, Mariposa." I turned away, intentionally using her full name. "We can't ever go back to how things were before." I started to walk away, pausing only to add, "I'll see about getting you a ride home."

"You said you would never leave."

I stopped in my tracks, her words hitting me like the Blakeworth arrows that once embedded poison into my back.

"You promised to come back if you ever had to leave," Mari called after me.

Turn around, some voice told me. *Turn around and keep your fucking promise to the woman you love.*

I didn't turn around. I clenched my fists and kept walking.

I FOUND DOC A FEW HOURS LATER, TINKERING WITH ONE OF the laundry machines that had started leaking.

"Hey, Doc." I approached him, carefully stepping over his tools laid out on the floor.

"Ivan, what can I do for ya?" He barely looked up, elbow-deep in the guts of the machine. "We don't have a session for a couple of days."

"It's not that. I, uh, could use a favor."

He paused in his work, shoving his glasses up the bridge of his nose as he looked at me. "I'm listening."

"Mariposa, the woman who got in last night," I said.

"Uh huh?"

"She could use a lift back home, to Four Corners."

"Clear across the country?" Doc scoffed. "Why don't you take her? Your joints are much younger than mine."

Damn it. I knew he would ask that.

"It...wouldn't be a good idea," I said. "She and I have some...history."

"Uh huh." Doc leaned back, saying nothing else, as if waiting for me to elaborate. When I didn't, he remarked, "She calls you Shadow, I heard."

"Yeah," I sighed. "It doesn't really matter, but maybe you can arrange someone from town to give her a lift?"

"She's who you're running from." Doc clasped his hands together, a smile pulling at his face from the small epiphany. "Your past has caught up to you, son."

"No," I shook my head. "She has nothing to do with...what I've been seeing you about."

"I never said she did." He continued to observe me in that quiet, curious way that he had since the first night I walked into the service center. "Does she know about it?"

Since talking to her that morning, I felt like I'd been keeping everything bound up tightly with string, and Doc's questions were slowly beginning to unravel it all.

"Not everything," I admitted. "She's a medic and gave me sleeping pills for my nightmares."

Doc nodded sagely as he continued to unravel the thread. "But that's not all, is it?"

I shook my head. "No. We...we got close. Really close." I swallowed. "I hurt her, Doc. Badly."

"I see." A small acknowledgment to the biggest regret of my life.

"She's safest when she's far away from me," I explained. "That's why I left. So please, help me find a way to send her back home."

"You must mean a lot to her," Doc remarked, wiping his hands on a rag. "For her to come all this way."

"Doc," I pleaded, sucking in a breath. "You know my mind better than anyone. You're the only one who knows how fucked up I am to the core. You *must* see that she's not safe here."

"If she's not, then neither are any of the other women." He stroked his goatee. "Are you telling me you're really no better than the camps that Jen and the others escaped from?"

I blinked, taken aback by the comparison he was making. "No, that's different—"

"Listen, son." Doc took his glasses off and wiped the lenses on his shirt. "I've been providing hypnotherapy to trauma victims for over thirty years, and I'll be honest—your case is one of the longest and most extreme I've seen in my whole career."

"Huh, I figured."

"But also." He pointed at me with his glasses. "Your progress has been remarkably fast compared to other patients with such extensive trauma."

"It has?"

"Yes, and that's all due to the work you've done before ever stepping foot into this place. Somewhere along the line, you had a support system. You felt safe and had people you could trust." He placed his glasses back on his face, peering at me over the rims. "Is it fair to say that Mariposa had something to do with that?"

My fists closed at my sides, as did my throat. "Yes," I choked out. "She had everything to do with it."

"Something I try to tell all of my patients," Doc said softly. "You are not your trauma, Ivan. You are not your nightmares, you are not your regressions or your flashbacks."

"But—"

"Are you a man who wants to hurt others? Who enjoys doing such a thing?" Doc's arms crossed over his chest. "Tell me, is that who you are, deep in your soul?"

"No." It was almost shocking how easy that answer was. "I don't want to hurt anyone. I never have."

"Then that is who you are," Doc said. "Everything else is a symptom of what has been done to you." He gave a small smile. "And we're working on that."

"I...think I understand, but," I scrubbed a hand down my face with a groan. "Mari still can't stay here, and I'm still worried about..." The guilt was still as present as ever, choking away any glimmering hope of happiness. "I can't risk hurting her again. I won't, Doc."

"Good. We'll continue with our sessions then." He picked up a wrench and resumed digging into the washing machine. "Mariposa will need a few days to recover from her journey, anyway. Once she does, I'm sure she's perfectly capable of coming to a decision on her own."

I left him to his work, feeling something between reassured and only more confused.

MARIPOSA

"You might want to cut back on acidic foods, like tomatoes," I said, handing a glass of water and two antacid tablets to the pregnant mother. "It'll help with the heartburn."

"Oh no, really?" The woman rubbed her belly with a crestfallen face. "But Heidi's tomato soup and grilled cheese is the best! It's all I've been craving during this pregnancy."

I offered a smile. "Cut back doesn't mean giving up for good. I'm just a medic, not the food police."

The woman looked relieved and thanked me as she waddled away with her heartburn tablets. She was the last of the ones who sought my advice this morning, after I had a full day to recuperate and let Shadow's rejection from yesterday sink in.

I didn't know what to make of our conversation, other than the fact that it *hurt*. So fucking much. I would have much rather dealt with another nightmare than hear him crush every hope I had.

What did you expect? I asked myself, wandering the dining room slowly, meandering toward the bar. *He sees himself like Reaper did— an abuser and a monster, even when that couldn't be farther from the truth.*

I slid onto an empty barstool, blankly meeting the eyes of the bartender with piercings and dark lipstick. It took me a moment to remember her name—Jen.

"Want some lunch?" she asked.

I nodded. "Sure, thank you. Anything's fine."

"I'll see what Heidi's got stashed." She disappeared through the swinging doors behind the bar, leaving me to look around the room.

There were a lot of women here. More than I ever imagined Shadow would be comfortable with. Come to think of it, he and Doc were the only men I'd seen since getting in two nights ago.

Small groups of women were spread out through the lobby, mending or knitting clothes as they talked. Some read worn-out paperbacks, painted their nails, put on makeup, or just chatted with each other. I could pick out the service girls pretty easily—they were more primed in their appearance and sat by the windows to look out for potential customers.

Was Shadow ever a customer?

Jen returned right then, pushing open the swinging door with her hip as her arms were full of plates.

My eyes widened at the multiple plates of food she set in front of me, and me alone. "Oh no, this is too much."

"Hey now, don't insult the cook," she cracked with a grin. "Heidi's orders are for you to eat everything you can, and I'm inclined to agree. You keep walkin' up the eastern seaboard, you're gonna need some meat on you." Her tone had a friendly tease to it and I decided that I liked this bartender.

"I think my days of walking around in the middle of winter are over," I said in return.

Jen laughed as she began washing glasses. "Well eat up, anyway. You need the energy."

I helped myself to the first plate she set in front of me, a rich broccoli-cheddar soup. "What territory is this, anyway?"

"They're calling it New Greenland these days. But it was once the great state of *Nawth Carolynah.*" She exaggerated the southern accent.

"Wow, is nobody original with coming up with new names?" I remarked between spoonfuls of soup.

"Seriously! If you're gonna run a militia through a town of innocent people and claim it as your own, at least put some thought into what you're naming it."

I laughed, tearing off a chunk of bread to dip in my soup. "So are you from here, Jen?"

"Nah, I'm a Midwestern girl from the mitten." At my blank stare, she clarified, "Michigan."

"Oh, gotcha. Yeah, Texas here."

"Well, giddy-up," she cracked. "Is that where you and Ivan met? I heard they make 'em big down there."

My next laugh was forced, the recent interaction with Shadow still a fresh wound. I couldn't even bear to think of him with another name. This Ivan person was a stranger to me.

"No, we met in Arizona." I tried to keep my tone light, despite the tightening in my throat. "After nursing school, I traveled west for a while."

"Never been to the southwest," Jen commented, the tattoos on her arms dancing and jumping as she wiped bar glasses. "Dunno about that desert heat."

"Summers can be rough, but it's not so bad," I said distractedly. "Sorry for my staring, I just love your tattoos."

Jen beamed as she propped her arm on the bar to show me. "Aren't those pretty? Ivan did 'em all."

"He...did?" I had suspected, but having it confirmed seemed to suck all the air out of my lungs.

"Yeah, he's the best." Jen turned her arm over to show me the full extent of the design. "Amazing artist and such a sweetheart." Her eyes found mine. "But I'm sure you knew that already."

I did. And I hated this feeling crawling through my body, this twisting anger and jealousy that another woman knew him like I did.

Both of Jen's sleeves matched, so Shadow had clearly worked on both arms. That must have taken hours, over multiple sessions. Which meant many hours of him touching her. Sitting with her. Drawing on her skin and talking to her about the design, among plenty of other things most likely.

I felt ridiculous for being jealous, but compounded with how he rejected me yesterday, and how our relationship had blossomed over his tattoo sessions with me, it was another twist of the knife already deeply embedded in my gut.

Was there more to this? Did their tattoo sessions lead to anything more intimate? Did he worry about causing her pain like with me? Did they hug afterwards, or do anything else?

I didn't dare ask, afraid of what Jen's answer might be. My once-delicious soup now sat like a brick in my stomach and I lost my appetite for the rest of the food.

"Does Sha-uh, Ivan do a lot of tattoo work here?" I took small sips of tea, hoping it would settle my stomach.

"Oh yeah!" Jen returned to her glass-washing. "He's inked up almost all of the girls."

I nearly choked on my drink. "All of...the...girls?" I thought hearing he had other clients might make me feel better, but it certainly did not.

"Yeah, they made it a little tradition after he got here," Jen went on with a smile, oblivious to my discomfort. "A bunch of them got little matching tattoos to celebrate being freed from the girls' camps. Others were like me," she gestured to her arms with a smile, "and went all-out."

"Oh." I forced a smile. "That's...nice."

"It was a big step for a lot of them," Jen agreed. "Especially trusting a big scary-lookin' man to get it done, but they saw pretty quickly that Ivan's a teddy bear underneath it all." Her voice quieted, hands slowing over the bar glasses. "And it doesn't take a genius to figure out he's been through some shit himself."

"Yeah..."

Jen snorted out a laugh. "I'm sorry! Here I am talking your ear off about him when y'all already have a history. Hey!" Her eyes narrowed. "You look a lot like the girl in *his* tattoo."

I met her gaze, frowning. "What tattoo?" I had seen both of his, and neither of them had resembled a woman.

Jen paled, her brows lifting for a moment before returning to her glasses. "Never mind, I probably should have kept my mouth shut."

I picked at my food, desperate to know more, but also unwilling to ask her those questions. It disturbed me how much she knew about Shadow already.

He's still mine, a feral, possessive part of me whispered. But that voice was becoming diminished, crushed into silence due to his rejection yesterday, and by his apparent ease with making female friends now.

I felt like I wasn't special to him anymore, as juvenile as that sounded. Just him saying good morning to Jen yesterday sparked both pride and a stab of jealousy. He used to say it to me, *only* me. He never would have been able to say it at all if it wasn't for me.

I sat up from my food and began sliding off the stool. Jen and the other girls didn't deserve this vitriol from me. Shadow never believed he would see me again. I had no say over who he talked to, or whatever else he did with other women.

"Want me to box that up and keep it cold for you?" Jen offered, breaking the silence.

"Sure, thanks." I put on a smile, hoping to convey that I wasn't mad at her. "I'm just gonna lie down in my room, I think."

"I gotcha, Mari. Go on and rest."

I left the dining room to the sound of Jen scraping my leftovers into storage containers, and quickly decided I didn't want to stare at the four walls of my room. It was the middle of the day, so it shouldn't be too cold outside for a brisk walk. This was my second full day here and I had yet to properly explore my new surroundings.

I bundled up in all my layers and headed out the side door to the junkyard where Shadow and I talked yesterday. I wasn't exactly *hoping* to run into him again, despite still missing and craving him like mad. Even if I did, I wasn't sure what I would say.

What I really wanted was a reset button. A quick rewind back to the night of the housewarming party. Before drifting off to sleep, I'd remind him to take a pill, and all of this would be avoided.

Or just kicked down the road to deal with later, the more cynical part of me said.

Regardless, Shadow was not in the junkyard, but Doc was. The older man was bent under the propped hood of some ancient sports car in pristine condition, the cherry red paint still glossy, and the whole body of the car lowered close to the ground.

"Afternoon, Doc," I greeted, walking up.

"Ah, hello Mari," he returned. "You're looking much better today."

He scratched his forehead as he studied me curiously. "Looking for someone?"

"No, not really," I said, avoiding his gaze to look at the piles of scrap metal surrounding us. "Just out for some fresh air. Exploring a bit."

Doc nodded and gave a polite smile. "You look like a smart cookie. Do you like books?"

"Oh, definitely! I love to read."

He turned and pointed down the main road the service center was on. A weathered brick building, clearly pre-Collapse, stood on the next block.

"We take pride in our library here," he said softly. "About five years ago, me and a bunch of the townspeople prevented an invading army from burning it down. When others invaded to take over, we protected it with guns. It's sacred to us, and one of the few intact libraries left for hundreds of miles."

"That's amazing," I breathed. "You must be so proud to still have something so important."

"Immensely," he nodded. "And there's no use in hoarding knowledge to ourselves, so," he spread his hands, "it's open to you, if your exploration takes you there."

"Don't mind if I do." My feet were already heading in that direction, fingers itching to trail over spines and flip through pages. "Thanks, Doc."

"Enjoy yourself, just put everything back where you found it." With that cheerful quip, he returned to working on his car.

I felt near tears the moment I walked into the library, just from the nostalgia alone.

The smell of books hit me first—there were thousands of them here in one place. Paper, glue, and the hushed atmosphere brought me back to long nights studying in nursing school. When my friends and I needed breaks from pouring over anatomy textbooks, we'd head over to the fiction section and devour young adult novels.

I walked through the main aisle now, hardly daring to breathe, as if it would blow away the magic of this place. Other people perused the shelves, though I didn't see a librarian on duty.

In the children's section, I spotted one of the service girls I saw that morning, gently helping a young boy sound out words in a picture book. Down another aisle, two young women giggled and whispered to each other behind books with shirtless men on the covers.

I didn't know where to start looking. When was the last time I read for pleasure? Probably in nursing school, devouring the adventures of a young heroine while I pulled an all-nighter.

I soon reached the back wall of the building and decided to turn down the left aisle. This was a small library, but no less worth treasuring when so many had been burned down in the chaos following the Collapse. Scanning the spines as I walked slowly, this section seemed to be about travel and foreign countries. I paused to flip through a book on the Maya culture through Mexico and Guatemala—something close to my and Jandro's heritage.

Jandro.

My chest squeezed uncomfortably tight at the thought of him. I'd been too exhausted or too focused on my destination to give him much thought since I got here. Now I sank into it, our last night together and how good he felt that I almost didn't leave. Guilt filled me up at how hurt he must have been to find my note in an otherwise empty bed. He was so happy to have been intimate again after weeks of nothing.

Reaper and Gunner were one thing, but Jandro...I hated hurting him most of all. He'd been there for me and Shadow, and didn't deserve to get caught in the crossfire.

Setting the book back on the shelf, I ran a finger down the spine. "I'm coming back to you, *guapito*. Probably sooner rather than later."

I kept making my way down the aisles, passing a row of glass-walled study rooms that people could rent out for meetings or private study groups. Most of the rooms were empty, but two people in one had me looking with absent curiosity, which turned into dread.

Shadow was impossible to miss, organized chaos surrounding him in the form of his open sketchbook, small pots of ink, markers, and his tattoo machine.

But it was the woman with him that made my stomach drop. A pretty—no, beautiful—brunette sitting on the study table, her shirt pulled up past her waist, and her butt perched on the table's edge.

Directly in Shadow's face.

He touched her waist as he leaned over to tattoo her lower back. Their position to each other was close, if even intimate.

The entire wall facing the inside of the library was made of glass, so I quickly slid behind a bookshelf so they couldn't see me. The glass was thick, so I couldn't hear much of their conversation. Those rooms were meant for some privacy after all. Still, I heard the buzz of Shadow's machine and their murmured voices talking to each other.

He said something that made her laugh, looking over her shoulder at him.

My heart drummed a powerful, aching beat in my chest, growing more painful the longer I watched.

I saw Shadow smile at her before his hand returned to her body, resting on the center of her back as he tattooed just above her ass.

It's nothing. It's just tattooing.

But my heart didn't seem to get the memo. It raced painfully, like I was watching something much more nefarious. My eyes only saw one of *my* men touching another woman in a private room.

And I couldn't bring myself to believe anything else as I walked hurriedly out of the library, blinded by tears.

CHAPTER 14

JANDRO

Gravel and small stones crunched under my tires, my body shifting on the bike with the uneven terrain. Sitting behind me, Slick held onto my waist, doing his best to move with me and not throw us off-balance. But it was clear he hadn't done much off-road riding before, and especially not with an arsenal of weapons weighing us down.

We were in neutral territory, roughly two hours northeast of Four Corners, looking like a pair of redneck hunters. The spare bike we rode on was covered in desert camouflage tape, and our borrowed uniforms from General Bray's army had a similar pattern. Even our weapons and gear had been taped and painted to blend in with the landscape. The whole idea was for the opposing army to never see us coming. They had bigger numbers than us, so we had to be smarter.

I wasn't sure about this attempted stealth thing, but me, Slick, and a few other Steel Demons volunteered to scout as close to Blakeworth and Jerriton as we could. Without Horus' eyes, it was the best chance to gather intel on our enemy. And with us going, we wouldn't put more of General Bray's soldiers at risk needlessly, not until we knew more about what we were dealing with.

We had no orders, except to get as close as we could, find out what we could, and defend ourselves as necessary. That, I could do.

I was a defensive fighter. I didn't have a raging temper like Reaper, the strategic mind of Gunner, or Shadow's innate ability to kill swiftly and efficiently. But I knew how to defend and protect.

As soon as the long city wall came into view on the horizon, I veered sharply to the left, signaling the four other riders spread out behind us to follow my lead.

"Where you going?" Slick asked through the cloth mask covering his face.

"Nothing stealthy about walking up to the front door and ringing the doorbell," I answered. "We're gonna peek through the back door."

This city was once called Grand Junction, Colorado and was technically Jerriton territory, but it straddled the current border between Jerriton and Blakeworth. From our previous intel, we figured that Grand Junction was a hub used to direct troops and goods between Blakeworth, Jerriton, and New Ireland. If Tash was supplying Governor Blake with weapons and soldiers, it was likely through this city. And likewise if Blake was sending payment, it mostly likely came through here too.

The best case scenario would be disrupting a supply chain, maybe blowing up a freight of ammunition or other supplies. Anything to send the army scrambling and buy us some time. The worst case scenario would be getting discovered, probably by their own scouts, and getting captured or killed.

Our odds weren't great, as Gunner emphasized to me while we poured over maps before leaving. It was a risk we felt forced to take at this point, but I was confident in the guys backing me up. Steel Demons were crafty. We fought dirty when necessary. General Bray's men were skilled soldiers, but I didn't have their loyalty and trust as I did with the men behind me right now.

It was another hour of riding to circle around toward the back-end of the city. I took us to a ridge overlooking a sprawling housing development, which might have been a nice suburb at one point, but now looked slummy and for the most part, abandoned. The buildings got taller and more condensed up ahead, with activity bustling through the streets. Mostly people walking or on bicycles, but I noted a few civilian cars among the armored trucks rolling through the streets.

I held up a fist, signaling our team to stop at this lookout point. We'd observe here for now, and get closer if it was safe. Everyone cut their engines and quickly hopped off their camouflaged bikes, eager to stretch their legs.

"Fan out and make sure no one's peeking on us," I ordered. "Slick, stay with me." I crouched at the edge of the ridge, pulled out a small set of binoculars, and spent a whole minute adjusting the damn things to focus. What I would give to have vision like a bird of prey right now.

"See anything interesting?" Slick hovered over my shoulder.

"Maybe." I handed him the binoculars. "That caravan moving through the city center look important to you?"

He watched through the binoculars for several moments before answering. "I dunno, maybe? If it was so important, you think they'd be moving it through the busiest part of the city?"

"It's the fastest route." I shrugged. "Most direct way if it's heading to the Blakeworth capitol. You think they'd be worried about disgruntled civilians?"

"Hm, maybe not." Slick lowered the binoculars and handed them back to me. "Gunner made it sound like his uncle really had the citizens under his boot. I imagine Tash wouldn't be much better once he took over."

"I bet you're right."

A single gunshot popped off just as I lifted the lenses to my eyes. Slick and I dove and flattened ourselves to the ground, both of us reaching for our guns as a few more shots fired.

"You think that's us?" Slick rolled up to his knees and went to crouch behind our bike, weapon close to his chest.

I rolled the opposite way, ducking behind a boulder. "Fuck, I hope so. We could use a win."

Several long seconds passed with no more gunfire, only oppressive silence. Approaching footsteps made me hold my breath, index finger curling around my trigger.

"All clear, it's just us," I heard Brick call out. "Took out a couple of Blakeworth lookie-loos."

"Jesus Christ." I let my hands and gun flop down to my lap, releasing my breath. Slick did the same, relief smoothing out his features. "You scared the shit out of us."

"Sorry, we didn't want to make any noise and signal to others that you were here."

I nodded, coming out from my hiding spot to clap Brick on the shoulder. *This* was why I felt best with Demons at my back. "Good work. Thanks, man."

"How far away could people hear those shots, you think?" Slick looked between the two of us, worry furrowing his brow again.

"Ain't nobody around for miles," Brick said dismissively. "Those Blakeworth fucks must have caught sight of us and started following about an hour ago. Found 'em hiding in the tall grass like a bunch of pussies. None of us heard shit, so we figure they must have left vehicles behind and tracked us to this spot on foot. I got Wells out lookin' for their wheels now. If there's anyone else out there, we'll know."

Two more shots rang out, much further away than the previous ones.

"Ah, guess we found some more," Brick added cheerfully.

"So they are stalking us when we get close," I mused, rubbing the stubble on my chin. "And being stealthy about it."

"It's not *that* stealthy," Brick huffed. "Kinda amateur, really. If Reaper sends his dog out, he could probably sniff out all of 'em hidden in a field before any of us get close."

"Maybe," I offered skeptically. I'd bring it up to Reap, but didn't have high hopes for that plan. Hades was not a dog that he could just send out on a hunt.

"Hey VP," Slick called. "You might wanna see this."

I went to his side, looking out over Grand Junction again. The caravan of armored trucks had left the city center and was moving through the residential area just below us. I didn't need binoculars to see the heavily armed soldiers in the Jeep leading the procession. Another matching Jeep drove slowly behind the pack, the soldier in the passenger seat hanging his arm out the window, casually waving his weapon at frightened families in threadbare clothes.

"That's our target," I declared. "It's headed straight for Blakeworth and we're gonna blow it up."

"It's turning off the main road," Slick observed. "Headed for the single-lane highway winding through the mountains. They're definitely not looking to be out in the open."

"All the better," I said, grabbing the handlebars of my bike and straddling the seat. "We're gonna head 'em off. Brick, you guys hang behind and cover us. Do *not* get close enough for them to hear you. Not unless you can shoot them before they call for backup."

"You got it, VP." The man turned to relay the orders to the other Demons.

Slick climbed on behind me, slow and apprehensive. He took his time settling in while Brick and the others hustled and drove off in seconds.

"Something wrong?" We had to ride fast to get ahead and couldn't afford to dally, but Slick had good instincts and it was clear he had something on his mind.

"I dunno, something just doesn't feel right." He chewed his lip, watching the caravan down below. It was almost out of our line of sight and we'd have to hurry. "You don't think it's weird that this opportunity has just presented itself to us so perfectly?"

"I've learned not to look a gift horse in the mouth." I started up the bike and turned it around, speaking louder over the muffled engine. "But what are you thinking, a set-up?"

"I dunno, maybe. It's probably nothing." He didn't look convinced by his own words. "Just be careful, VP."

"Always, kid." I tapped his thigh once. "You're my best apprentice. I won't let anything happen to you."

He snorted in response. "Worry about yourself, man."

We drove down the ridge back the way we came, Brick and the others were already out of sight, as they should've been. I headed north, straight for the mountain pass the caravan was heading for. To make decent headway without being seen, we'd have to ride for another hour, maybe two. Then we'd have to set up the explosives and lie in wait to trigger them.

As long as we got there fast enough and no scouts caught us off-guard, it should have been easy.

Maybe too easy.

I accelerated hard, making the landscape whip past us. Grinding my jaw, I pulled my neck gaiter over my face so as to not catch any bugs with my teeth. Slick's words had set me on edge. I didn't have any doubts about this until he said something. Now my stomach clenched with unease.

Damn you, kid. Why'd you have to make me paranoid?

It wasn't uncalled for though, after everything that had been happening. Before Mari took off, I had just regained full mobility of my shoulder and leg after being shot. Reaper was paranoid about me taking her out on the bike then, after just getting stabbed, and he turned out to be right.

We need a break, I thought stubbornly. *Just one small win.* This had to work. It felt easy simply because our people were good at their jobs. We were diligent, and we thought outside the box.

Not a soul could be seen when we reached the mountain pass, a long-abandoned road with train tracks running alongside it. I followed it, heading northbound toward Blakeworth for another ten or so miles. Even though the caravan was moving relatively slowly, putting more distance between them and us just gave us more time to prepare. Plus, if those rich fuckers over in Blakeworth heard the explosion, even better. Maybe they'd heed it as a warning.

I stopped the bike and let it idle, the quietness and lack of any other people around feeling ominous. *Brick and the others are out there,* I reminded myself. *They're watching out for us, lying in wait.*

"Here's as good a place as any." I dismounted the bike and headed for the cargo.

"How long d'you think 'til they'll be here?" Slick already had his gun drawn, head swiveling in all directions for any threats.

"Half-hour, maybe a little more." I carefully unloaded our explosives, sweat already gathering at my temples. I had to be precise with this shit, just like with an engine.

We couldn't just throw grenades or timed bombs out on the road either. A well-trained military like Tash's would expect that, and mitigate accordingly. No, I had to make sure this puppy was hidden, and detonate it with a remote at the right time. The patrol Jeep in front would be watching for anything suspicious in the road and move it out of the way.

"Start grabbing handfuls of dirt and sand," I instructed Slick. "And little things, like rocks and brush you would just drive over."

He got to work quickly while I set up the device. "What if we put something big in the road that they have to move?" he suggested halfway through pouring sand and swishing it around to make it look natural.

"That way they stop exactly where we want them to," I said, following his train of thought with a grin. "You don't think it'll be obvious?"

"We can make it look like there was a rock slide," he suggested, looking up at one of the embankments. "Shit, I can cause an actual rock slide. It'll look totally normal that way."

"Do it," I said. "Careful, though," I added, watching him scramble up the rocky hill face.

"I wanna yell timber so bad," he laughed, pushing loose rocks of various sizes down the hill.

"That's for trees, dumbass, not rocks. Hey, watch it!" I jumped out of the way just as a head-sized rock came tumbling down the wall to the road below.

"Careful, VP. I can't control where they go."

"Just hurry up with your damn rock slide and be quiet." I looked anxiously to the south. No sign of anyone coming yet.

After making a convincing display of a natural rock slide, Slick and I rolled a larger boulder into place on the road. It was off to the side, not directly in the center, but just enough of an inconvenience that it would need to be pushed out of the way. Roughly three car lengths behind of it, I carefully laid the explosive hidden under one of many smaller rocks littering the road. We dumped more sand and brush to cover the long wire to the remote trigger—which I would hold and press when the time was right.

And then *kaboom.*

Slick kept on covering the wire with sand as it moved off the road while I hid the bike and any other evidence of us being there. We found cover, wedged between two boulders and a tree, and hunkered down. We masked up, trying to blend into the landscape until only our eyes were visible, then sat and waited.

And waited.

It wasn't a half hour like I initially thought, but at least two hours before we saw anything.

"Here they come," Slick said in a tense whisper.

I raised the binoculars, looking south down the length of the road. A speck of black appeared, growing slowly larger.

"They're driving *really* fuckin' slow," I remarked after a few moments. "Like twenty miles-per-hour, max."

"About the same speed they were rolling through the city." Slick squinted at the oncoming vehicles. "You think they're just watching out for obstacles and enemies on the road?"

"Maybe." If that was true, it didn't bode well for us. If they stopped before our supposed rock slide to clear the road of any threats, our bomb would be discovered. I wasn't a fan of any of these people, but I'd rather blow up supplies than a person just trying to clear the road.

If my gut was uneasy about Slick's earlier suspicion, it was screaming at me as I watched the leading Jeep creeping closer up the road, the procession following along behind it. It was like watching toy cars moving along a track—a slow, constant ambling that seemed almost...automated.

I looked through the binoculars again, peering as hard as I could through the windshield of the lead car. It was still too far away to see the driver clearly, plus a black mask covered most of his face. Even so, I could tell there was an eerily un-human stillness to him. No shifting of hands or arms on the steering wheel, nor gentle movement of the head or shoulders that all living people had.

"Fuck!" I threw the binoculars down in frustration, forgetting all about being quiet. "Man, I think we got fucking duped."

"What do you mean?" Slick picked up the lenses and peered through them.

"They got crash-test dummies in the seats. The cars must be locked on some kind of cruise control."

"What? How?"

"I dunno." I rubbed my temples, already dreading having to bring this news to Gun and Reap. "The caravan through the city looked legit, but I bet they switched on us when we lost sight."

Slick lowered the binoculars, looking at me with a harrowed expression. "So they knew we were watching."

I nodded gravely. "Brick must not have gotten all of them."

"Well, shit."

"Yeah."

"What now?"

"Stay put for a sec." Slick looked like he wanted to jump out from our hiding place, so I placed a hand on his shoulder to keep him still. "Let's see how this plays out."

The decoy vehicles looked so obvious as they got closer, and I wanted to kick the shit out of myself for not realizing our mistake. Maybe using decoys was standard procedure on transports to Blakeworth. This road was not easily accessible, but I still should have known they wouldn't have put precious cargo on a direct route. Shit, Blakeworth might have cut a whole network of hidden roads just to transport goods for this alliance. Fucking stupid.

Gravel and dried brush crunched under tires as they approached our fake rock slide area. I wasn't even holding the trigger button anymore, there was no point. Crash-test dummies were indeed outfitted with black uniforms and masks, and placed in the driver seats of the escorting Jeeps. The three armored trucks in the middle had black-tinted windows that were impossible to see through. They might still be worth checking out, but I wasn't about to hold my breath on anything valuable.

"You think it has a sensor for anything blocking the road?" Slick asked as the leading car slowly approached our biggest boulder obstacle.

"We're about to find out."

It did not, as a matter of fact. The Jeep continued on, delayed briefly as the left side of the bumper hit the rock, metal crunching and bending in as the wheels insisted on continuing forward. Whoever set these cars to autopilot did not account for the need to swerve around obstacles. The Jeep continued straight forward, the boulder only nudged to the side slightly. A high-pitched screech echoed throughout the canyon as the boulder drew a deep scratch along the side of the car.

It was like a train wreck happening in slow motion— fascinating and horrifying. The short halt caused by the front car's collision allowed the armored truck behind to catch up, giving a love-tap on the Jeep's rear bumper, and then the second car got scratched to hell by the rock.

Slick and I exchanged a short laugh together. Despite the utter disappointment at the failure of this mission, it was still kind of funny to watch.

"Alright, now can I go check out these cars?" he asked.

"Yeah, go ahead. I gotta make sure I disarm this thing now." I shifted to the side so Slick could jump out. He approached the road at a jog while I pulled the detonation wires from the trigger. I was preoccupied with insulating the wires so nothing else would set them off when I heard the series of shots.

"Ah, fuck!" Slick shielded his head with his arms, turning abruptly to run back toward me, then he fell.

"SLICK!" I roared, scrambling to get out of my crevice, but more rapid fire popped off and I was forced to duck back between the rocks for cover.

"Jandro—ughh—they're up top!" Slick started pulling himself on his elbows, his legs bloodied and dragging behind him.

"I know, buddy. I'm coming to get you." I barely had the arm space to pull my gun out, but fuck if I was about to leave him out there.

"No, stay covered!"

"Shut *up*, Slick!"

I jumped out, not giving a damn that I was making myself a target. Gunfire rained down around me as I grabbed the back of Slick's cut and dragged him to the bottom of the rocky wall we'd hidden in. Miraculously, nothing seemed to hit me.

"VP, you need to get *out* of there!" I recognized the frantic voice as Brick's, shouting from the top of the ridge.

More gunfire filled the air—some pointed down at us, while other shots exchanged above us. I had to stabilize Slick first but fuck, I prayed Brick and the others weren't overwhelmed.

"You're gonna be fine," I told Slick, taking off my cut and then my long-sleeved shirt. "Your first time getting shot, huh?" I watched his face, trying to make sure he was still lucid while I wrapped my shirt around his thigh and used the sleeves to tie a knot above his bullet wound.

The kid was squirming and nearly gnawing his lips off in pain, but nodded tightly.

"No one tells you this but *now* you're a real Demon," I said, pulling and tightening the knot. "You know how many times I've been shot? I've lost count at this point. One little slug to the leg ain't gonna do shit to you, man."

I started wracking my brain, trying to remember the major arteries in the leg Mari told me about, when Slick placed a bloody, scraped hand on my shoulder and shoved me hard to the side.

"Dude, what—"

He raised his opposite hand—his shooting hand—and fired three times in rapid succession. The next thing I heard was something heavy tumbling down from the rocks across the road, a body, with his weapon clattering down alongside him.

When another shooter popped his head and weapon out from his cover, I was ready. I fired first at the rock he braced his arms on, then at his chest when he jumped away. He fell dead, stuck in the crevice where he hid.

I looked back at Slick with a shaky smile. "See? You're watching my back like it's just another Tuesday."

He laughed dryly, then immediately winced in pain. "I gotta keep you sharp, VP."

"You're doing a good job." I tapped my palm to his chest, trying not to show my worry at his face growing paler. "You always have, and will continue to do so when we get back. 'Cause this little scrape ain't no big thing and I need you, okay?"

He nodded, more weakly than before.

"Stay put for a sec. I'm gonna check on Brick." The gunshots above us had ceased and I didn't know whether to dread or feel good about whatever that meant.

No sooner had I started climbing up the ledge than shots sent tiny explosions of dirt and gravel into my eyes. I curled up on instinct, spinning and forcing my eyes open to the coward hiding on the opposite ledge. My shots were wild and panicked, but the shooter slumped limply over a boulder, leaving a red smear.

I looked back down at Slick, making a small noise of disbelief as he shakily lowered his gun and gave me a weak thumbs-up with the other hand.

"Kid needs a promotion," I muttered, finishing my climb to the lookout area.

Staying behind a rock, I quickly reloaded and peeked around cautiously, but soon figured out it was all for naught. I stood, coming out slowly to find several bodies laid out across the ground. Too many. Too still.

"Ugh, Jesus..." I rubbed my mouth, stuck somewhere between wanting to vomit, cry, and scream.

Soldiers clad in black camouflage were lying dead. But Brick was also lying face down. His nephew Wells was a few feet away. I spun around, looking to the ridge across the road, and saw more bodies there too.

Ours and theirs.

Anger and hopelessness hit me like a fist to the chest. Fuck it all. Just...fuck everything.

My knees buckled and I let myself fall, a choked sound escaping my throat. I wasn't crying, I was too stunned, too angry.

Why?

I couldn't stop looking at them, that infernal question on repeat in my head. *Just, why?*

They would need proper burials, but I couldn't carry them all back with me. I needed to get Slick medical attention right away or I'd lose him too, but my knees felt cemented to the ground.

It felt like we had no chance of winning.

I wanted to lie down and give up.

Mari... I wasn't sure why my thoughts turned to her in that moment. *We need you back so bad. We can't do this without you.*

Something answered me.

A warm breeze passed over me like a soft caress on my cheek, and I felt the distinct pressure of something wrapping around me. Supporting me.

Your love will return to you. Freyja's voice seemed to whisper in my mind, while also echoing across the mountains. She spoke gently into my ear and vibrated over my skin. *Your men are at rest. Their sacrifice was not in vain, but you must get the young one home now.*

"I don't know if I can do this," I confessed to the bodies lying in front of me, to the air and mountains surrounding me. "They're just killing us all."

I cannot make you, but you can, Jandro. You must. Dig deep, my son. I promise you, the strength of your love is there and it will not fail you.

I wanted to lean forward and hit the dirt like all the bodies lying facedown. I wanted to scream about the unfairness of it all. I wanted to hold Mari against my chest and hear *her* voice instead of Freyja's.

But I braced one hand against the rock and brought one foot underneath me, then the other. Then I headed back down to the road to get Slick and my bike.

CHAPTER 15

MARIPOSA

I paced back and forth in my room, all but certain that I was wearing new grooves into the floorboards.

My bed was made, and on top of it sat my packed bag. I should have been *in* bed, getting a good night's sleep so I could catch an early ride back to Four Corners in the morning. Because I clearly was not needed, let alone wanted, here.

But I couldn't sleep. Nor could I leave now in the frozen dead of night. And I sure as hell could not ignore the pull to the room down the hall and to the left of mine.

I had come back to my room and packed things up in a hurry after seeing Shadow in the library. I heard his footsteps, more heavy and solid than anyone else's here, make their way to his own room a few hours ago.

I wanted to say goodbye. I wanted to cry and scream and punch at his chest. I wanted to leave without saying anything. So I settled for pacing, back and forth.

Horus had been noticeably absent and silent ever since I got here. For all his insistence that *now* was the time, and all this growth that was supposed to be happening, the whole trip seemed pretty pointless.

The only point I could see was about hurting myself deeper. To keep my hopes alive, come all this way, only to be completely dashed by Shadow himself. Why would he ever want to leave? He did work he loved and was surrounded by women. He didn't need me anymore. He didn't *want* me anymore.

That last thought slowed my pacing to a halt, the ache in my chest spreading like ice through the rest of my body. Oh, it hurt, and I sucked in a shaky breath.

"Fuck it," I muttered, grabbing my doorknob and turning it with a hard pull.

I forced every step, marching toward Shadow's room, the pain of his earlier rejection thumping with every beat of my racing heart. I had no plan of what to say or do as I raised my fist and knocked at his door. Maybe I'd just put a smile on and say goodbye, that I wished him well. Maybe I'd cry and make an utter fool of myself. With the luck I'd been having, maybe I'd be interrupting him balls-deep inside Jen or that pretty brunette from the library.

Whatever the outcome, I knew it was unlikely to change this all-encompassing ache throughout my whole body. I wasn't really hoping for a different outcome. Mostly, I was just so sad that I'd failed and wanted to see him one last time.

The door pulled open and Shadow stared at me, for a moment looking just as frozen as I felt. His hair was damp like he recently had a shower, the snug, heather grey T-shirt still had a few wet spots on his shoulders. He wore black sweatpants and was barefoot.

"Mari-posa." He forced out my full name with an air of surprise. "Are you okay?"

"I'm..." *No, not okay at all.* "...leaving. In the morning."

The door groaned as Shadow seemed to grip it tighter, swinging it open a few more inches. At least there was no else in his room. "You are?"

I gave a shaky nod, my body hovering in a weird limbo between wanting to flee and feeling nailed to my spot. "There's no point in me staying. I can't force you to go anywhere you don't want to, so." I jerked my shoulders up in a shrug. "I just want the best for you, really. I'm glad you've found some...some contentment here." Now felt like a good time for a smile and an escape, so I plastered one on. "So goodbye, Shadow. Best of luck to you."

"Wait," he bit out as I turned to leave. He was gripping the doorknob so hard I saw veins popping in his forearm.

His *tattooed* forearm.

The sight of the familiar pin-up art clicked into my mind just as he started talking.

"It's not that I don't *want* to go back with you," he began softly. "That I don't want...*us* again. Because I...I do, Mari."

Sudden commotion in the hallway had me jumping, barely able to process what he said. Giggles, whispers, and heavy footsteps traipsed carelessly through the hall of rooms. A service girl, most likely bringing a customer to bed.

"Want to come in?" Shadow asked.

I nodded gratefully and stepped over the threshold, close enough to catch a whiff of his soap, as he closed the door softly.

"You get used to those noises living here," he muttered a bit sheepishly.

Shadow's room was tidy and neat, like all the living spaces I'd seen him in previously. His bed was large, the sheets only turned down on one side. *So he hasn't been sleeping with anyone.*

I brushed the hopeful thought away just as quickly as it came. Cleaning staff made the beds every day. It didn't mean he'd been the only one in his.

I could only awkwardly look around his room for so long before addressing what he'd said.

"You still...want to be with me?"

The only light on in his room was a desk lamp aimed down at his open sketchbook. Deep shadows carved out his imposing form standing across the room from me, and accented the scar cutting through his face.

"Of course I do," he said in a low voice. "You are...simply the best thing that has ever walked into my life."

"Then why—" A hand flew to my chest, a futile effort to stop the sob that wracked through my lungs.

"You know why," he said mournfully.

"Tell me!" I demanded, my teeth clenched and aching.

"Because I *hurt* you. Because you mean too much to me to ever risk that happening again." Shadow's breaths now sawed in and out of his chest, every muscle accentuated in the dim light.

"Is that really why?" I fired back. "You have no problem touching every woman here, but *I'm* the one you want, and you just blow me off?"

"What?" His brow furrowed with confusion. "I'm not—"

"Jen's sleeves are nice work. Those must have taken *hours* to complete." Every pent-up, racing thought came pouring out of my mouth now and I was helpless to stop it. "And matching tattoos for *all* the girls, huh? That must have kept you busy."

"It's just tattoos. What do you think I'm..." Shadow's eyes narrowed at me before widening with clarity. "You think I'm sleeping with all of them?"

"Are you seriously gonna tell me you're not?"

"No! I mean yes, I'm telling you I'm not. Mari—"

"Not even the girl from the library?" I crossed my arms, feeling no triumph in the surprise on his face, only sickening dread. "Yeah, I saw you two looking cozy together in the study room today."

Shadow looked to the ceiling with a sigh. "Telisha is the librarian. She lets me take books in exchange for tattoos. We're friendly, that's all."

"Telisha, huh? That's a pretty name."

"Mari." Shadow returned his gaze to me with a growl of my name. "I'm not fucking her, or anyone else here. I haven't been with anyone since —" He cut himself off abruptly, pausing to swallow deeply. "Since you."

I believed him. I only needed to take one look at him to know he was telling the truth. For some reason, that knowledge wasn't a relief. It only made it harder to leave.

"I miss you," I blurted out with a pained breath, my stomach and all my emotions feeling like they were hurtling off the edge of a cliff. "I've missed you so fucking much."

"Mari." He was close enough for me to smell again, to feel the heat of his body, to see the scar cutting through his face, so near and kissable. "I have missed you during every moment of being away from you."

Fuck, was this really happening? It couldn't be. But I lifted my hand

and found it pressed to a warm chest and a thundering heartbeat underneath my palm.

Shadow's knuckles grazed my cheek to wipe a fallen tear, and I gasped at the contact. His lips hovered inches away, my eyes fixated on them as he spoke again.

"I have never wanted anyone but you."

Our kiss connected with softness, and then with all the power of a storm.

Shadow crushed me against his chest with a powerful arm against my back. His mouth devoured me, tongue surging deep in a passionate war against mine. I clung to his wide shoulders, fists curling and pulling at the thin T-shirt covering his body. My own shirt twisted and lifted from the friction of him holding me closer and closer, despite us being pressed flush together already.

Bare skin slid hot and firm against my navel and I was done for, fumbling down the length of his torso in search of his shirt's hem to pull over his head.

Our kiss broke momentarily as I yanked the fabric up, then reconnected with the same fervent need, even as Shadow was still peeling his shirt down one arm. His skin was scorching hot, almost feverish as my hands ran down the familiar planes I was only just starting to know before he was ripped away from me. I broke away from his mouth to kiss under his jaw, lingering long, drawn-out kisses on his neck as my touch ran up his back.

"Fuck..." he ground out, working the hem of my shirt up past my waist.

Knowing how much he loved it, I kissed his neck for as long as he would allow me, before my own shirt came off. Once it did, I pressed my lips to his chest, kissing scars that I knew I had missed the last time we were together.

Shadow only allowed that for a few seconds before drawing my mouth back up to his, one hand holding my cheek with the other anchoring my hip against his. While no less passionate, his kisses began to slow. His mismatched eyes were partially open, watching me every time our lips locked together and then peeled away. When he didn't lean in to kiss me again, I closed my eyes, unable to take another rejection from him.

"Please don't stop," I begged with a whisper.

I felt the weight of his forehead lean against mine, then his hand on my hip sliding between us to the button on my jeans.

"Not a chance, Mari."

His kiss devoured me again, stealing my breath as he flicked open my jeans and started easing the fabric over my hips and ass. I took off my bra while he did that, enjoying his temporary distraction as his kisses made a path to my breasts, his hands going still below my waist.

"You're still mine," I groaned, voice tinged with a whimper at his careful bites and rough tongue flicks on my nipples.

"I've always been yours." Shadow took a seat at the edge of the bed, his bearded mouth tickling the undersides of my breasts before his kisses moved on to my ribs and waist. "Never anyone else's."

And you'll always be mine. I didn't dare voice the thought, not wanting to bring attention to any point in the future, anything that wasn't happening right now. This could still be a goodbye for all I knew, and I might still be heading home alone tomorrow. But we both needed this—just for once to have what we wanted more than anything else.

I ran my fingers over Shadow's scalp, enjoying the feel of his long, jet-black strands as he resumed peeling my jeans and underwear down my legs. His kisses swept over my waist and belly, trailing lower with every brush of his lips.

"I missed you too, beautiful little scar," he murmured softly, pressing a lingering kiss on my hip while rough fingertips trailed their way up my legs.

Something shifted inside me then, like a dam bursting. And I knew right then I could *never* let this man go.

I pushed hard on his shoulders, sending him flat on his back as I yanked his sweatpants down to his knees. His cock bobbed out, already hard and hitting his stomach with a soft slap. I crawled over him, my knees outside his thighs as I took his thick length in my hand.

"Mari, wait." Shadow pressed up onto his forearms, pupils wide and fixated on where I hovered over him. "You're not—I haven't—"

"Please don't make me wait anymore," I begged in a whimper,

stroking him as I touched my sex just over his silky head. "I thought I lost you. I need you, Shadow."

"I need you too, I just...ohh, fuck..." His head dipped back as I lowered onto him, fists clenching the sheets.

The thickness of him stretched me wider than I remembered, a pinching pain making me stop with a gasp. Shadow's gaze immediately returned to me, his hands reaching for my thighs.

"Come here."

"It's okay." I shook my head. "I just need a second to—"

Shadow curled up, wrapping his large hands around the backs of my thighs and dragged me off his cock, pulling me up his torso toward his face as he laid back down.

"Shadow, what—ohh..."

He pulled me up until my knees splayed on either side of his head, his intention clear when he pressed a long, open-mouthed kiss to my sex. I bucked against his mouth with a sharp cry, the pressure so instant and heady I could only move on impulse.

Shadow let out a satisfied groan, his eyelids sliding closed as he devoured me from below. He licked me from bottom to top, tongue teasing my opening before it lashed at my clit. Lips pulled and sucked at my flesh, working with his tongue in a dizzying rhythm to kiss and lick me to bliss.

I quickly got over the shock and rocked against his mouth, my fingers clasping through his hair again. Shadow didn't seem at all worried about suffocating, one hand wandering up to knead my breasts while his mouth devoured me greedily.

His tongue focused on my clit just as he plucked a nipple with his fingers, the combined sensations building almost too fast for me to catch up.

"Fuck, that!" I gasped, grinding hard against his face. "Don't stop, Shadow! Oh God, don't..."

I came apart so hard that I fell forward, my shaking legs unable to keep me upright. Shadow's hands caressing up my spine sent more delightful shivers of pleasure zipping through me. His touch ran over my ass and down my legs as I panted for breath, hanging over him limply, my pussy now seated on his chest. He kissed my belly and waist again, fingers pressing gently on my knees. I took the cue and wearily crawled backwards, down over his torso.

"Now you can ride me if you want." His lips quirked playfully, caressing my cheek when we were face-to-face again.

I huffed out a laugh, still catching my breath. "Is that what you were trying to tell me earlier?"

"Maybe."

Our lips connected in a slow kiss, this one reminiscent of the last time we were in bed together. We spent that night exploring, talking, kissing like we had all the time in the world. Like we'd wake up the next morning and everything would be fine.

I wanted to hold on to this feeling, this sweetness and warmth of just being with a man I loved. Shadow seemed to be right there with me, his eyes closed and hands moving indulgently, lovingly, over my body.

Never breaking a kiss, I slid a hand down his firm abdomen and swallowed his moan as I took his cock in my fist. Our kiss broke away at the last moment as I settled over him, gripping his waist with my knees as I lowered onto his length.

My body, well foreplayed now, took him easier, but I still had to go slowly and ease into how well he stretched me. Shadow was still as I braced my hands on his chest, letting me set the pace as I raised and lowered my hips, taking more of him every time I sank down. Only when I took him completely did his hips roll underneath me, letting out a choked groan to the ceiling while his fingers dug into my thighs.

"Fuck, you feel so..."

Whatever he was going to say died on another moan as I dragged up his length and slowly sat back down.

"Move with me," I whispered, leaning down to kiss him. "Do what feels good."

His hands slid around my back, holding me to him as his hips surged up, hitting new depths that made me cry out into his mouth.

Shadow broke the kiss abruptly, his brows drawn tight with concern as he pulled nearly all the way out. "I don't want to hurt you."

"You're not," I rasped, earning another moan from him as I sank all the way down again. "Please don't stop. I want you so bad."

Still, he hesitated. "You'll tell me if I'm hurting you?"

"Yes, yes of course! But you're not, you feel so good." I kissed the scar cutting through his eyebrow, then his cheek, then his mouth. "I want you to feel good too."

"Just seeing you feels so good." His mouth skimmed to the edge of my jaw, pausing to kiss me there before moving on to my neck. "Holding you, having you, it feels too good to be true."

Through our kisses, our movements below the waist resumed. Shadow's light, roaming touch found its way to my ass, guiding me on his cock while he rose up to meet me from below. Our breaths and kisses were accented by soft slaps of flesh, his hands on my skin and the steady drag of his cock through me lighting my nerves on fire. I ended a kiss and sat upright, face toward the ceiling as I drove down harder, wanting to take him deeper.

My observant Shadow noticed the instant my pleasure started to build. His hand came between us, giving some extra friction to my clit as I rode him. I rocked hard against his hand, taking my fill of him as his other hand skimmed up my body, running over a breast and teasing my nipple as we crashed together.

"Oh fuck, I can feel you..."

I barely heard Shadow over my pleasure cresting, my pulse thundering in my ears and my scream reaching the rafters. He was so solid and hot inside me, pressing so thickly against my walls, they could barely squeeze around him in my orgasm.

I slumped against his chest, my skin now slick with sweat as my head rested over his heart.

He rubbed my back, brushing a kiss along my forehead. "Again?"

I huffed out a breathless laugh, weakly swatting his chest. "Shut up."

His breath ruffled my hair as he laughed, and he waited all of ten seconds before lazily rolling us over, turning, and scooting us up the mattress to let my head rest on one of the pillows.

"Don't go down on me again," I whined. "My poor clit can't take it."

Shadow laughed lightly, lips tickling my skin as he brushed kisses along my collarbones. "Then where would you like me?"

He was still inside me, so I squeezed my legs around him in reply, bringing his mouth to mine because I couldn't get enough of his kisses. "Right here."

His tongue thrust into my mouth just as his hips rolled forward, filling me with a delicious, sweet ache.

"Yes," I moaned, wrapping my hands around his back. "More."

He answered with a hungry growl, drawing his hips back and snapping them forward, making me see stars with the rough crash of his body into mine.

"Oh fuck, yes!" I clung to the wide muscles of his back, my ragged panting returning. "Like that, Shadow."

"Fuck," he grunted out in return, lips catching mine in a rough kiss as his steady, measured thrusts became frenzied rutting. When he wasn't kissing me, he moaned into the pillow next to my head, finally lost in the pleasure he took from my body.

"Oh fuck, don't stop," I pleaded over the slaps of our skin, the headboard thumping against the wall. "Fuck, that's so good, Shadow..."

I was being extra vocal because I didn't want to leave any room for doubts. He was so careful, so worried about hurting me, I didn't want a single whimper or cry to pull him out of this moment, to make him stop and think instead of just feeling good with me.

"Yes...oh, yes..." I dragged my teeth along his neck and shoulder, digging into his back with my nails, knowing he liked some pain with his pleasure.

"Oh fuck, Mari..."

He drove into me harder, the rougher friction and his cock swelling sending me hurtling toward another orgasm.

"Shadow!" I cried weakly, my whole body taut as a wire as he fucked me wildly.

Then sweet, explosive release, Shadow's chasing right after mine with stuttering thrusts and ragged, gasping breaths.

CHAPTER 16

SHADOW

When Mari's eyelids started to droop, I rubbed a thumb across her cheek and kissed her forehead to rouse her. "Want me to take you to your room?"

She made a soft grunting noise as she rubbed her eyes. "Why would I go to my room?"

I lowered my forehead until it rested on hers. "Don't make me remind you why."

She blinked at me, eyes more alert than a moment ago. "When was the last time you had a nightmare?"

"Um." I pulled away from her, rolling onto my back as I thought. "Three nights ago. But one where I also sleepwalked?" I scratched my head. "Two and a half, almost three weeks, I think."

"Really?" Mari actually sounded unsurprised as she scooted closer, propping her chin on my chest as she smoothed a hand over me. "What's changed?"

"Doc," I admitted, clasping my hand with hers where it rested on my side. "He's been...working with me."

"I knew it." She grinned triumphantly, letting her cheek fall to my chest.

"How?"

She shrugged. "I know doctors. I can spot 'em in a crowd."

Mari nestled against me with a contented sigh, making no move to leave. My arm wrapped around her back, hand resting on the side of her hip. It felt so good to have her lying here with me, I never wanted this to end.

Just a little longer, I thought, my lips brushing her hairline. *It could be the last moment I have with her.*

That last thought was sobering. She had initially come to my room to tell me she was leaving. Was she still planning to, after what we just did?

Mari's eyelids were drooping closed again, her breaths deepening and blowing warm puffs of air on my chest. Fuck, the last thing I wanted to do was disturb her, but I couldn't let her fall asleep on me. This night would *not* be a repeat of our last one together. If that meant I had to unwrap her body from mine, severing the warmth and peace of this moment, then I would.

"Mari," I murmured against her hair, running a light touch up her arm.

"Hm." She barely opened her eyes at all and just snuggled against me closer, sliding her leg over mine.

"I can't let you sleep here," I said with a frustrated groan.

Her eyes finally batted open, peering up at me. "After two-and-a-half weeks of nothing, you're still worried?"

"It could be two-and-a-half years and I still wouldn't risk it."

She stiffened at that, then the warmth of her body peeled slowly away from me. I watched her long spine straighten up as she turned to sit on the edge of the bed, wordlessly pulling her clothing back on.

I needed a distraction, otherwise I'd tell her to forget it and tug her back into bed with me. So I rolled up and proceeded to get dressed myself. "I'll walk you back to your room."

"No, it's okay." She looked over her shoulder, her smile appearing strained. "It's just down the hall. Get some rest."

My hands gripped the edge of the mattress as I sat frozen, unsure of what to do. Was this it? Was she just...leaving?

"Are you, um..." I pulled in a deep breath like Doc had taught me.

Sometimes they helped with the tightening in my chest like I was feeling now. "Are you still leaving in the morning?"

Mari didn't answer for a few long moments as she pulled her shirt back on, then stood and buttoned her jeans closed. She walked around to the side of the bed I was sitting on, regarding me with an expression I couldn't read.

"What do you think I should do, Shadow?" she asked quietly.

Stay with me, my thoughts said in answer. *We'll never be able to sleep in the same bed, but I* am *getting better. I miss you. I crave you. It's been hell not seeing your face, and I'll strive to be worthy of you every day.*

She'd never agree to it. She had nothing here and a whole life waiting for her back in Four Corners. But the temporary illusion felt nice. Feeling her curled up in bed against me made it seem more real.

"Maybe...stay one more day?" I reached for one of her hands, enveloping her slender fingers in my palm. "So we can sleep on this and maybe...talk it out tomorrow after we've had some time to think."

Even that felt like a long shot. So what if she enjoyed sex with me? She had that and more back home.

But Mari's lips quirked into a small smile, her other hand reaching for my face. "I suppose another day won't hurt."

Temporary as it was, relief finally loosened the tight ache in my chest. I wouldn't have to say goodbye to her yet.

I grabbed her hand that came to rest on my cheek and pressed a kiss to her palm. "Let me walk you to your door."

She sighed and laughed lightly, but otherwise didn't protest as I stood and finished getting dressed. Her room was a mere fifty feet away down the hall, but I couldn't fully relax until I knew she was safe on the other side of that door.

The hall was dark and quiet, all the service girls had finished exhausting their clients hours ago. Mari held onto my arm, trusting my night vision to guide us just like when I showed her the night-blooming Cereus. Fuck, that felt like years ago.

We reached her door too soon, and she spun in front of it to face me. "Thanks for walking me."

Her hands slid up my chest at the same moment my fingers skimmed over her waist. The ease of touching her sent a deep ache rippling through me. Why the fuck did everything have to feel so natural if I was never meant to keep her?

"Sleep well." I bent low, touching my forehead to hers before finding her lips with my own.

I *loved* kissing her. Maybe because it was something I'd only ever done with her, or the simple fact that a kiss was the fastest, easiest way to get my fix of her. I was an addict of many things—alcohol, violence, and misery. But nothing gave me a high like her.

Mari's tongue shoved into my mouth, lips scraping over mine with a need punctuated by her grip around my neck. She was on her tiptoes to reach me and I banded my arms around her back, holding along that sweeping curve of her spine as her body pressed to mine.

I was moments away from pulling her legs around my waist and carrying her back to my room for another round, when her mouth broke away and her palms flattened against my chest to create distance. My hold around her loosened and her shoes found purchase on the floor once again.

Mari pulled away from me slowly, her hand reaching for the door-knob. "Goodnight, Shadow."

"Goodnight, Mari," I returned. "See you tomorrow," I added, almost like a reminder to not leave too soon.

She nodded and started to unlock the door. I had just turned in the hall when she called out, "Shadow?"

I whipped around. "Yes?"

Mari was standing in the middle of her open doorway now, her hand still on the knob. "Will you tell me tomorrow if you sleepwalk tonight or not?"

My teeth ground against each other before I bit out, "Sure."

She disappeared inside and I returned to my room, my elated mood suddenly sour. I would tell her, but didn't see how the information would be useful. It wouldn't change anything.

None of this changed anything.

The realization hit me hard as I fell back into bed, the side where she laid still warm and smelling lightly of her. Now alone, without her voice and her touch allowing me to fantasize about a different life, cold, harsh clarity settled over me. The sex distracted both of us, and only delayed the inevitable.

She would still have to leave.

And I could never be with her.

HAVING BARELY SLEPT, I WAS ALREADY AT THE BAR WHEN Mari came down the next morning. My breakfast was cold and untouched in front of me, my mood clearly sour, although Jen was kind enough not to pry this morning.

I could barely bring myself to look up at the sound of Mari's light footsteps. My hand clenched around the coffee cup in front of me, which had also gone cold. If I turned to her, if I allowed myself to relax in her presence, I might end up kissing her again. Getting distracted, and selfishly taking more of what I could never have long-term.

"Good morning, Shadow." She slipped into the barstool next to me, helping herself to the coffee pot Jen left in front of us.

"Morning," I grunted out.

Silence passed over us, with Jen and the others thankfully giving us plenty of space. Did they know how things had changed? Or could they just sense the regret and despair rolling off of me?

"Well?" Mari prompted after a few sips of coffee.

My heart beat painfully in my chest and my throat wanted to close up until I could say nothing. But it had to be done.

I had to let her go.

"Mari, I—"

"Did you sleepwalk?"

We started speaking at the same time and both abruptly stopped. I stole a look at her for the first time, noticing the tiredness under her eyes. It seemed I wasn't the only one who slept poorly.

She returned my gaze but said nothing, waiting for my answer.

"No, I didn't," I admitted, scrubbing a hand down my face. "But that might have more to do with barely sleeping at all."

"What kept you up?" She set her coffee cup down, folding her hands in her lap.

"This." I gestured between her and me. "Us, and...what we did."

"You don't sound all that happy." Fuck, she was starting to sound like Doc.

"I'm always happiest when I'm with you, it's just..." I paused, subtly scanning the room to make sure we had no eavesdroppers. "We both know I can't come back to Four Corners. And you can't stay here, so..."

Her eyes hardened, lips pressing into a thin line that I wanted to kiss away.

"I told you you *could* come back. Reaper told me himself he'd let you back in. He won't go back on his word."

"That's not as simple as it sounds. He would have to rewrite club law and get a vote to have it approved. And even if he did that, Mari..." I ached to touch her, to take one of her hands or just wrap around her in a hug. "I can't be yours."

"You *are* still mine." She dropped a hand to rest on my thigh and I couldn't bring myself to remove it. "You told me yourself last night that you've always been mine."

It was so fucking hard to talk. My heart felt jammed up my throat, but she deserved to know the truth—that I was a lost cause who would never deserve her.

"I loved last night Mari, but," I curled my hand around hers and removed it from my leg, "it shouldn't have happened. It's just making things harder."

The look crossing her face hurt worse than the most painful cut I'd ever received.

"Shadow, why does it have to be like this?" Emotion choked her voice and that sound killed me. "I want to be with you. You want to be with me. Why should anything else matter?"

"Because I've already hurt you," I bit out. "I can't ever forgive myself for that, and now I can't ever trust myself to sleep next to you. I want you more than anything else in my life, but I don't deserve you."

I turned away, closing myself off from her as I faced the bar. Focusing on a random speck of paint on the wall, I took my deep breaths and willed my chest to stop collapsing in on itself. I silently hoped she would slide off the stool and leave, putting both of us out of our misery.

I should have known better when she placed a hand on my arm and leaned in closer, when every nerve in my body screamed at the light touch from her. This was the woman who forced me to say good morning to her after all.

"That's not true, Shadow. You deserve *so* much. You deserve to be loved."

"Mari, please..." I didn't know what I was begging for.

"You've gone nearly three weeks without sleepwalking when it used to happen, what, three, four times a week? Shadow that's *amazing* progress."

"It doesn't mean anything," I argued. "If it happens once a month, or once a year even, it's still putting someone in danger if they're near me."

"We can take precautions. Maybe a combination of Doc's therapy and sleeping pills. We can figure something out, Shadow. It doesn't have to condemn you to a life without any happiness."

"It already has." I stole another look at her. "That happened the moment I hurt you. I can't *ever* take that risk again, do you understand? You mean too much to me."

"Shadow." Mari shook her head with a huff of breath, clearly frustrated, but nothing she said would change my mind. My thoughts had already run in circles about this hundreds of times before. "It was an accident. I *know* you would never hurt me."

I shook my head in response. "Consciously, no, I would never. But my subconscious is a deep, ugly place. I see it with every therapy session and it's...I never want to expose you to that. It'll never go away, Mari." I swallowed deeply. "That violence you experienced at *my* hands is part of me. It's who I am."

"I don't believe that," she said quickly, just as stubborn as me. "It might be part of you, forced on you by what you endured, but that person who hurt me was *not* you." Her voice lowered as she spoke closer to my ear. "Would you let me sit in on a therapy session?"

"No." I forced the word out through gritted teeth. "Absolutely not."

"Shadow, I'm willing to do this." Both of her hands wrapped around my arm now, her cheek nudging my shoulder. "I want and accept all parts of you. Let me prove it. Let me be there for you."

"No, Mari." I forcibly removed her hands from me, sliding off my stool to put distance between us. "It was fucking hard enough letting Doc see what happened. You? No, I could never show you that."

She remained unfazed, crossing her arms in front of her. "So is it that you don't trust yourself, or you don't trust me?"

"What?" I blinked at her. "What do you mean?"

"Of course, I see it now." Mari tilted her head slightly as she regarded me with some new understanding. Whatever that was eluded me completely.

"What are you talking about?"

"You've set yourself up in a perfect, self-destructive cycle," she said. "You've convinced yourself that you're so undeserving of love, that I'll run away screaming if I get a small glimpse of your trauma, right?"

I bristled, unsure of the point she was trying to make. "Maybe not that exact reaction, but yes. I think it'll change what you think of me and...I don't want to burden you with that knowledge."

Mari held up two fingers. "One of two things needs to be true if that's what you expect to happen. One, you think I'm a fool, that I don't see you for the walking textbook of childhood trauma symptoms that you are, and that I don't understand the weight of what you've been through."

"I don't believe that at all." I stepped toward her, the impulse against my earlier reaction to step away. "You're not a fool, you're brilliant. You and Doc understand me better than anyone else."

Mari put a finger down, her chin wobbling slightly. "Then it's the other thing—that you don't trust me."

"That's not true either!"

"You don't believe that I care about you enough to stick around if I see what's in your past." She blinked away the tears accumulating in her eyes. "You're so convinced that I could never love you, it doesn't matter how many times I tell you. It doesn't matter that I followed a bird across the country *for you*. You'll stand here and tell me I deserve better, because that's what *you* already decided. But your thought patterns affect other people too, Shadow."

She spun on the toe of her boot and headed for the stairs, the reaction I was hoping for just moments ago. But I felt no sense of relief or victory now. I felt gutted, flayed open and exposed. It was like she reached into my mind and laid bare what I had failed to see this whole time.

She'd been trying to tell me I was worth something, worth *wanting*. And to keep rebuffing her like I was, only added insult to injury.

I started after her, my heart pounding in a wild panic. Because I knew after this time, she wouldn't try to convince me again.

"Mari." She was almost to the first landing, ignoring me as she quickened her pace. "Mari, wait!"

The floorboards creaked under our weight. As she neared the top of the stairs, I swore I heard something else among the creaks. Something more like a *click*.

My instincts kicked into overdrive and I lunged up the stairs, grabbing Mari's ankle and pulling her back toward me.

"Get down!" I bellowed.

She fell hard with a scream, knees and forearms hitting the stairs just as bullets sprayed holes in the walls over our heads.

CHAPTER 17

MARIPOSA

I n one moment, I was walking away from Shadow for what I was certain was the last time. In the next, I nearly face planted on the stairs to the rapid *pop-pop-pop* of gunshots.

"What's happening?" I cried, arms around my head.

"Traffickers," Shadow grunted out, his voice near my ear. I hadn't even realized he had splayed over me, shielding me with his body. "They come to retrieve runaways from the girls' camps."

"What?" I hissed. "You mean this is a regular occurrence?"

"They didn't get close last time, about three weeks ago. I saw them coming and fired off warning shots from the roof." Shadow's arms tensed on either side of me. "Sounds like they brought bigger guns this time."

Another round of gunfire popped off, forcing us to slide lower down the stairs while making our bodies as flat as possible. This time I heard the panicked screams of the service girls on the main floor and in their rooms.

"Well, fuck! What do we do?" I demanded.

"*You* do nothing," he growled. "Get to your room and wait until it's safe. I have weapons stashed by the bar."

"Do you know how many there are?"

"No, but I bet it's several."

"And who's gonna back you up?"

Shadow's teeth ground in his jaw. "Doc's an okay shot, he's probably loading up now. I know he's scared, though."

I twisted underneath his massive body to the sounds of men shouting outside. "I brought a gun. Let me help."

"No, Mari," he barked. "Just wait for me in your room."

Someone had barricaded the front door and now it buckled under the heavy slams of boots from the outside.

"You know I can shoot," I continued to argue. "Gunner taught me."

"Fine!" he yelled. "Just shoot from your window. I won't let them get past the stairs."

"Okay, be careful."

I didn't know who moved first, but our mouths crashed together in a rushed, clumsy kiss, and then I was crawling up the stairs while Shadow slid down. He was barking at the terrified women to hide and diving behind the bar for his weapons before I fully realized what happened.

The pressure and taste of his mouth still lingered as I finished scrambling up the stairs, crouching low under the hallway windows on the way to my room. I went inside crawling on the floor, trying to stay hidden as I reached for my gun and the holster zipped into my bag on the bed. Wearing it was bulky and cumbersome for me, and I hadn't percieved any danger when I first got here. I was far from making my gun a daily part of my outfit like my men.

I checked to make sure my little .40 caliber was loaded and clicked off the safety, listening hard as I crawled my way around the bed to the window.

I heard shouting and commotion, and what sounded like footsteps running down the hall as more girls surely went to hide. It was impossible to tell if the majority of the male voices were coming from inside or outside the building.

Once I crawled directly under the windowsill, I squeezed my grip on my gun as I dared to take a peek outside.

"Shit," I muttered under my breath. I couldn't see the front door at all from this angle.

It took less than thirty seconds, and more gunshots and screams, for me to make a decision. I slid the window open and popped my head out to see better.

A section of the dining room's roof was directly below my window. It wasn't terribly steep, and the corner of the building would give me enough cover to shoot at the assholes trying to storm through the front door.

I rose to stand, stepping one leg over the windowsill and testing how it held my weight before I brought my other leg to join it. A single loud shot startled me, and I grabbed the windowsill for support.

"You're a fucking Steel Demon," I muttered to myself, pressing my back to the building as I walked carefully along the roof shingles. "Keep your shit together."

Shots volleyed back and forth, likely Shadow and Doc battling the traffickers from inside. With my heart feeling like it was going to beat itself out of my body, I reached the corner and dared to peek around it.

Six men were positioned at the front, the windows already smashed and the door still partially barricaded. They used this to their advantage, using the walls and partially obstructed door for cover as they shot inside. Two of the traffickers lay dead already, bleeding out on the front porch. Shadow's work, mostly likely.

Their vehicle was a pickup truck with a wire cage fitted like a camper shell over the truck bed. A single, dirty blanket was spread out on the bed, with chains attached to the sides of the cage, complete with collars at the end of the chains resting on the blanket. Like they were farmers coming to pick up their livestock.

I thought such a sight would churn my stomach, but an eerie calm settled over me instead.

Mindful to keep out of sight, I raised my gun and braced my arm along the side of the building for stability. The traffickers' backs were turned so they wouldn't see me. Shadow was a great shot even with all the obstacles, but these assholes were clear, open targets for me.

I waited until three of them ducked to reload, the other three taking aim while I did the same. Lining up my sights, I aimed between the shoulder blades of the closest man to me, who was aiming a rifle through the window, and fired.

"Gahhh!"

"What the fuck?!"

I pulled my arm close and turned out of sight, flattening myself against the wall as I tried to listen over my pulse roaring in my ears.

"Petey, d'you get shot in the fuckin' back—Ahh!"

The man's distraction with his friend's mysterious wound cost him his life as two more shots rang out, and I heard the slump of a body falling on the porch.

"Spread out and head for side doors and windows! Cover your fuckin' heads, someone's tryin' to snipe us."

Fuck, fuck, fuck.

I tried to run back to the window while keeping against the wall and not slipping on shingles. But no amount of roof balancing would make me faster than men running on solid ground, two of which were headed straight toward me.

My body froze while my mind raced. The window was a good fifteen steps away--I'd never reach it before they saw me. They'd see me regardless within seconds, and then I'd be dead, or worse, thrown in that truck and having a collar forced around my neck.

The only advantage I had was if I caught them off-guard. My element of surprise was quickly slipping away, but in these few precious seconds, I still had it.

Forcing a deep breath of air into my lungs, I raised my gun and aimed it at the men running toward my wing of the building. The two of them stuck close to the side of the building for cover, but never bothered to look up at the roof.

When they paused next to a support column almost directly under me, I opened fire.

"Fuck!"

One managed to duck under a small section of overhang. The other guy slapped a hand over the bleeding wounds on his chest and fired back at me with an insurmountable rage in his eyes.

I turned and ran, no longer caring about balance and stealth. His shots were going wide but I was still open and exposed.

"Bitch on the roof!" I heard someone bellow. "Found our sniper!"

I ran for my window, ready to sail through it like an Olympic tumbler. It was only ten steps away, then five, then—

My leg swung out behind me, all my momentum crashing down. I landed hard on my chest and hands, the wind knocked out of me as I realized too late that I'd slipped on a loose shingle.

I couldn't afford to stay still, I had to fucking move even though I could barely breathe.

Pop-pop-pop-pop!

Shots kept whizzing over and all around me. My chest ached so badly when I tried to push up, so my fear and adrenaline-stricken body settled on rolling down the roof.

That was a bad fucking idea.

Holding on to my gun, I started scrambling for a hold with my left hand. My body rolled to the very edge and no amount of kicking and scraping stopped my momentum. I was temporarily in freefall, heading toward the ground, when I somehow managed to grab hold of a gutter.

Now the breaths came, ragged and painful as I dangled by one arm, my boots less than six feet away from solid ground. My relief was short-lived as I heard a gun cock. I swung my free arm wildly in front me, firing off shots at the first sign of motion I saw.

Thankfully it was a trafficker, now dead on the ground.

I released the gutter, collapsing onto the ground, where I fell with an aching left arm. Pulling my arm against my body with a hiss, I rubbed my shoulder that was screaming in pain. It wasn't dislocated, but those connective tissues sure weren't happy.

I only noticed then how quiet it was, and strained to listen. Seconds stretched on without any gunshots. Did that mean it was over?

A nearby door slammed open and I scrambled to my feet, ducking behind a patio chair for cover. I heard the sounds of a struggle, of feet kicking desperately for purchase along the ground. And the most haunting, harrowing cries and screams of protest I'd ever heard in my life.

One of the traffickers had emerged from the front door and headed toward his truck. Behind him, he dragged a wailing, pleading, terrified Jen along the ground.

Her wrists were bound with rope, blood already running down her tattooed arms from how hard she pulled and tried to get away.

I ran out into the open without a thought, only her tortured screams filling my head as I raised my gun and emptied the rest of my magazine into the man's chest. He fell with barely a sound, only a choked gurgle of blood as life left him swiftly and his hold on Jen's rope went slack.

I went toward her next, unsure if I was running or walking. My body felt too slow, like I was in some kind of daze. It didn't matter.

I never made it to her.

A shot rang out and pain exploded up my leg. Suddenly I was on the ground, my eyes level with Jen's terrified, wide-eyed stare a few feet away. She wasn't looking at me, but past me.

I looked over my shoulder just in time to see the man walking up with his gun pointed at my head.

CHAPTER 18

SHADOW

A shower of splinters rained down on me as I ducked behind the bar to reload. I brushed broken glass out of my hair, barely giving a thought to how the tiny shards cut up my hands.

"Jen!" I barked at the scared-witless bartender, who was curled up in a ball and trembling as she clung to Doc sitting next to me on the floor. He was trying to soothe her as best he could, rubbing her back and making shushing sounds in her ear.

"Jen, get into the kitchen with Heidi." Another round of shots sent splinters and glass falling over us, and Jen let out a pained whimper.

"Sweetheart, do as Ivan says." Doc tried to loosen his hold, but she just clung to him tighter. "Heidi's back there, you two stay together."

"I don't want to go." Jen's lips quivered as she stared at Doc with wide, unseeing eyes, a look I recognized in myself. "I don't want to go, please don't let them take me."

When the firing ceased, I rose up and fired a series of shots just over the bartop. The fuckers were staying outside, using the walls and front door for cover. The window panes had been shot out, and one of them had smashed a head-sized hole in the front door with an axe. I was able to get two head shots through it, but the smarter guys were staying out of my line of sight. If they kept this up, the winner of this fight would be whoever had more ammo stocked.

And my supply was running dangerously low.

My magazine emptied and I'd only managed to graze a guy's shoulder. I ducked behind the bar again, a bullet whizzing past my head and only narrowly missing me as it tore through more glass liquor bottles.

"Jen!" I yelled more insistently. "You could get shot out here. Get back in the kitchen with Heidi *now*."

Her wide, unblinking eyes stared back at me, tears staining her face. I grabbed her arm in a motion I hoped was gentle, but she still recoiled at the touch.

"Doc, go back there with her," I said, releasing her.

The older man nodded, his own hands shaking slightly as he started to crawl across the floor with his arm around Jen. "Come on, sweetheart. My old knees can't do this without you."

Together they shuffled through the swinging kitchen door and I breathed a sigh of relief knowing they were slightly less in harm's way. Maybe it'd let me focus and aim better.

Another shot rang out and I quickened my reloading, but a male curse of pain from the other side of the bar was not what I expected to hear.

"What the fuck?!"

I looked over the bar, seeing two of them in plain sight in front of the window and didn't miss my chance.

"Petey, d'you get shot in the fuckin' back—ahh!"

The guy fell dead over the windowsill with one well-placed shot to his chest. His last observation before death set my teeth on edge. If his friend had been shot in the back, that had to be from Mari's gun.

"Spread out and head for side doors and windows! Cover your fuckin' heads, someone's tryin' to snipe us."

"Shit." I ran along the length of the bar, keeping low as I tried to track the guys, but we still had four of them to deal with and one of me.

Two of us, I reminded myself. *Mari can handle herself.* I needed to believe that she could, at least until I could reach her.

A rattling sound alerted me to one of them running through the junkyard, making a shit-ton of noise. I waited for him by that side door and picked him off easily.

"Bitch on the roof! Found our sniper!" I heard someone yell.

God fucking damn everything, why the fuck was she on the *roof*?

I started to run in that direction, the sound of gunfire just as rapid as my fucking heartbeat.

"Ivan! Oh god, Ivan, *help*!"

The terrified cry had my feet skidding to a stop, quickly pivoting to head back toward the bar. I jumped it and slammed my shoulder into the swinging kitchen door.

It didn't budge.

I heard Jen's screaming on the other side, and Doc pleading with someone to let her go.

"You shut the fuck up," the trafficker answered and a single shot was fired.

Fuck! I pushed harder on the door, using all of my body weight, but the fucker must have shoved the refrigerator in front of it. I ran again, my mind set on the back door they used to receive food deliveries. It was the only other way inside.

Going that way wasted precious time, but I could only hope he didn't intend to kill Jen or Doc. Jen was precious cargo to them, at least. Doc was more expendable. By that same logic, Mari should be able to buy herself some time until I made it back out front.

I reached the backdoor to find it open and swinging. Doc was inside, on the ground with a bleeding cut on his forehead. He seemed otherwise unharmed, but he was alone.

"Where's Jen?" I demanded, my eyes darting around the kitchen that was now in ruins.

A scream across the kitchen answered me, sounding like it was coming from the back of the bar.

"He took her through the swinging door as soon as he saw you leave," Doc said with a pained groan.

I ran through without another word, jumping and climbing over counters and machinery that had clearly been pulled out to slow me down. Fuck, I hated that I fell for such a simple trick, and now Jen would be the one to pay for my mistake.

When I burst through the door, he was already across the dining room, dragging Jen across the floor with a length of rope that bound her wrists together.

"Ivan!" she cried with body-wracking sobs as she struggled and kicked for her life.

"Stop!" I fired a single shot that would have hit if he hadn't suddenly crouched low, wrapping one arm around Jen's middle as he hauled her up to use her as a shield.

"Shoot again and she dies, Tonto."

I raised both hands, holding my finger away from the trigger. The fucker kept his eyes on me, walking backwards as he dragged Jen out the front door, but my gaze was rooted on her. I recognized the stricken fear in them and hoped she understood that I wasn't surrendering, just buying another opportunity.

He shut the mangled front door and I didn't wait a second longer, crossing the room as fast my legs could carry me. I heard a thump and another cry of pain as he dropped Jen and proceeded to drag her again. When I touched the doorknob, four shots fired in rapid succession, each of them filling me with cold dread.

Fuck, Jen!

I pulled the front door open, weapon raised, to find Jen's abductor dead on the ground.

And Mari standing a few feet away, her gun pointing at the bleeding man on the ground. She didn't see the guy running up behind her.

"Mari!" I bellowed.

He fired, the shot low and clumsy, but it hit.

Shock and then pain spread across Mari's face as she went down, blood quickly spreading up her pant leg.

He shot her.

She got hit.

She was hurt.

Someone hurt *her.*

I didn't know when I lost control. The whole event seemed to play out in slow motion, and then fast-forward in a senseless blur, to the point where I was looking down at a misshapen mass of flesh and blood. I blinked several times, realizing I was sitting on top of an unmoving body. The bloody, fleshy blob in front of me had once been a man's face. My fist was bleeding and clenched tight, a few teeth embedded in my knuckles.

I scraped them away with my other hand and took a careful look at my surroundings.

"Mari!"

"Shadow," she whimpered, still on the ground a few feet away, pale and clutching at her bloodsoaked leg.

It was impossible to tell, but my disassociation must have only lasted seconds. I scrambled over in a panic and went to hold her, but immediately froze. I didn't know what to do here.

"I...I need to wrap something tight around my leg," she explained through pained, wheezing breaths. "I'm...I'm bleeding a lot."

"Okay, just tell me where." I tried to keep my voice calm as I shrugged off my holsters and pulled off my shirt. But my hands shook as I tore down the middle of the garment to make it a longer piece of fabric.

"Around my thigh," she told me. "It's—ah! It's...just above my knee."

She ground her teeth and did her best to sit still as I wrapped my shirt around her leg, but every whimper and wince cut through me worse than any blade.

"I'm so sorry. Am I hurting you?"

"No, tighter," she hissed. "Make it tighter, you have to cut off circulation."

Doc finally stumbled out the front door, followed by a few of the service girls who quickly rushed to Jen's aid. She was still tied up on the ground, but otherwise uninjured.

"Doc, please tell me you have actual medical knowledge," I growled at him, pulling tighter on the knot around Mari's leg.

He took one look at the state of Mari's leg and gulped, running a bloodied hand over his goatee. "It's been about five years since I pulled a bullet out of someone, but I *have* done it before."

"My kit's in a duffel bag in my room," Mari gasped. "I'll walk you through it."

Doc nodded sharply and went to retrieve what she needed. The others were helping Jen inside, leaving us momentarily alone.

"Should I move you?" My hands went to Mari's waist, ready to lift her up if needed.

"Ugh, maybe," she grunted out. "A sanitized surface would be much safer."

"Okay, I got you." I'd only lifted her a few inches off the ground when her howls of pain nearly pierced my eardrums, and I set her right back down. "We're not going anywhere," I decided right then.

"Fuck! Oh fuck!" She shook like a leaf in my arms, forehead rolling across my chest as she writhed from the pain.

"It's okay." I wrapped around her, squeezing tight. Before I knew it, I was rocking her in my arms and kissing her forehead. "I'm right here. Doc's going to fix you."

"Ugh, it *hurts*..." Mari was hunched over and small, her brows drawn tight over her delicate features. "And he's gonna dig in there and I know it's gonna be worse."

"I'm sorry, love." The word slipped out, the same term of endearment she used for me. "I'm so sorry. I wish I could feel it instead of you." I stroked her hair back, holding her face against my chest. "But Doc's going to make it better. Just hold on with me."

He returned moments later and set to work efficiently with Mari's instructions. First, he cut away her pant leg without issue. When he started to clean around her wound with alcohol, that's when things got difficult.

She screamed and thrashed hard, nails digging into my arm as I tried to restrain her against my chest.

"Mari." I touched my lips to her ear. "You didn't bring any local anesthesia with you?"

Her head shook back and forth, her face in a grimace of pain that I couldn't even fathom, and it broke my heart.

"I can't get it out if she keeps kicking," Doc said with a worried frown. "I hate to even suggest it but...should we knock her out?"

"No," I bit out, holding her with one arm while the other worked to pull apart my belt buckle. "The pain could wake her up, anyway."

Doc watched with a puzzled expression as I pulled my belt through my belt loops and folded it in half with my free hand. "What the hell are you..."

He got his answer when I held the folded strip of leather in front of Mari's mouth. "Bite down on this for me."

She understood, taking the belt eagerly between her teeth.

I returned to holding her with both arms, petting her hair and stroking down her back. "Listen to my voice and breathe deeply for me."

Her breaths came out harsh and ragged, but I felt her body calm slightly. I continued the same pattern of stroking her hair, rocking her upper body gently as I continued to talk to her.

"You're safe with us. You'll get through this, Mari." I pressed my lips to her forehead again. "You're so brave. You know what to do. Let Doc get the bullet out, okay?"

I felt her head nod against my chest, the rest of her body still except for her tremors. Taking a deep breath for myself, I nodded at Doc for him to proceed.

Mari whimpered and bit down on my belt as he finished cleaning her wound, but otherwise remained still enough for him to work.

"Might not wanna look, sweetheart," he said, quickly sanitizing her forceps with more alcohol.

Mari pressed her forehead into my chest, aided by my hand on the back of her head. "You're doing great," I told her, dropping another kiss to her hair. Doc finished cleaning the instrument and started poking around the entry wound, prompting more whimpers and sobs from Mari. "Shh, you're okay, love." I lowered one hand to her ankle, trying to be comforting as well as helping keep her leg still. "You're okay, I'm here. I'm not leaving you."

It felt like hours dragged by. I hated every minute of Mari's sounds of pain, the sweat and shivers erupting on her skin. She burrowed in my chest, blunt nails clawing at my skin and teeth grinding down on my belt. But I'd hold on and keep her steady for as long as she needed me.

After what seemed like an eternity, Doc victoriously held up a metal slug in his forceps. "Got it!"

I stroked Mari's cheek, but didn't loosen my hold on her. "Bullet's out. We're so close to done. Just let Doc close you up, okay?"

She nodded slowly, cheek dragging on my chest. The pulse on her neck beat steadily under my hand, though I was worried it might have been weaker than normal.

Doc finished quickly, placing a thick wad of gauze over her wound and winding tape around her leg tightly to hold it in place. He wiped his brow and looked at us tiredly. "Not as nice of a job as you, sweetheart. But we're not losing you yet."

Mari slackened her jaw, releasing my belt, which now had deep grooves in the leather from her teeth. "Thank you," she said in a barely audible whisper, her eyelids fluttering closed.

"What now?" I looked between her and Doc. She still looked pale and was clearly exhausted.

"She needs rest and that wound needs to stay dry for a few days." He closed her kit and kept the tools he used in his other hand. "I'll sterilize your stuff, Mari. Don't worry."

I still had plenty of worry. She was slumped against me and looked close to death. "What about food? Water?" I asked Doc. "Should she eat?"

"If she's up for it, yes." He climbed to his feet. "But rest is most important. Her heart's gonna work overtime to replenish the blood she lost."

"Mari." I leaned down, touching my forehead to hers. "We're getting up, and I'm carrying you to my room, okay? Tell me if I hurt you."

"Shadow..." Her lips brushed my collarbone as she mumbled my name. "Don't...don't leave me..."

"Never." I slid my arm under her thighs and lifted her carefully from the ground. "Never again. I promise."

Mari made no pained sounds as I carried her through the battered front door and trashed dining room. The others had already started cleaning up, but I barely took notice. I watched every step as I took the stairs, not wanting to jostle her body.

When we reached my room, I was about to lay her down on my bed when her fingertips curled into my chest. "Wait."

"What?" I froze, hovering her a foot above the mattress. "Are you okay?"

"I'm…I'm all bloody." Her tongue flicked out to wet her dry, peeling lips. "Do you…think I can…clean up?"

"I don't care about the sheets getting dirty," I told her. "Doc said you need to rest, and your wound can't get wet."

"I know, but if…if you have a tub…and can…help me." Her eyelashes batted slowly. "I just want to wash it off."

"Okay," I relented, returning her to my chest and walking around the bed to the attached bathroom. I did have a tub, and a detachable shower head at that.

I paused, still holding her just over the empty bathtub. "How, uh." I cleared my throat. "How do you want to, uh…"

"I'll need your help undressing." Mari's arms went around my neck. "Let…let my good leg down. I'm gonna lean on you."

Slowly, painstakingly, I allowed her uninjured leg to touch the floor. She kept one hand on me for support as she started unbuttoning her pants. Right away, I could see how weak and uncoordinated she was, and went to help her.

Once her clothes were off, I made sure she was stable as I bent to turn the water on. I lifted her around her waist and placed her in the tub as it started to fill. She kept her injured leg bent and hanging over the lip of the tub as she carefully sat down.

"Comfortable?" I took the shower head and ran the warm water over her skin, carefully rinsing away the dirt and blood that coated her.

"As much as I'm gonna be." She gave a weak smile as she leaned against the edge. Relaxation—or just pure exhaustion—began to settle into her limbs.

I drained the tub once to clear the dirty water when she finished rinsing off, then refilled it so she could soak for a while.

"Do you want something to eat?" The thought of leaving her side punched up my anxiety, but I wanted her in the best shape to heal, to have the best possible chances of recovery.

I needed her healthy and well again. Fuck, I just needed her, period.

"I probably should." Mari nodded tiredly. "Something light…I dunno. Just bread or…something."

"I'll be right back." I squeezed her arm resting on the tub's edge, then kissed her shoulder before reluctantly climbing to my feet.

In the cleaning and repairing madness downstairs, I was able to find part of a sourdough baguette, clean water, and some grapes. I was barely gone five minutes, but still breathed a sigh of relief to find Mari in the exact same position I left her. It almost would have been funny if I hadn't nearly lost her—seeing her slouched low in the tub with her leg dangling over the edge. Jandro would have thought of some funny comment to make.

"Here." I handed her the bottle of water first, then sat on the floor next to the bathtub.

"Are you going to feed me?" There was some brightness in her expression after all, humor in her exhausted smile that made my chest ache.

"Yes," I decided, tearing off a chunk of the baguette and holding it in front of her lips. She ate it all, as well as the grapes I fed her.

When she started sliding down lower in the tub, I cupped the back of her head, making sure her face stayed above the surface. "Ready to get out?" At her tired nod, I got a large towel ready and helped her stand.

Mari leaned on me again, her good leg shaking with effort as I dried her off. "Here we go," I said, scooping her up into my arms again.

It was a short trip to the edge of my bed, where I sat her down and dug out a clean shirt and pair of my shorts for her to wear. When she finally laid down to rest, scooting gingerly toward my pillow, I was at a loss for what to do next.

"Come here, Shadow," she murmured, more asleep than awake.

"Just for a little bit," I relented, moving to lay on my side behind her. At first I made sure not to touch her, then she rolled back toward me slightly, her shoulder colliding softly with my chest. Her hand found mine, then our fingers intertwined, and my arm found its way around her waist.

I let out a breath and closed my eyes, her hair tickling my lips. If only I could stay here, continue to be someone she needed even during sleep. But here was where my usefulness ended. The last place she needed me was asleep in a bed next to her.

When her breathing became deep and steady, I lifted away from the mattress and carefully worked to unlace my fingers from hers. I'd take a nap in her room, or find any empty spot to crash for a few hours before checking on her again.

The moment our hands separated though, she snapped awake.

"Shadow." She looked over her shoulder at me, eyes wide and fearful as her hand scrambled for mine again. "Where are you going? Don't leave me."

"I'm not, love. I'm just—" My other palm found her cheek, mouth trailing over hers in a ghost of a kiss. "I'll be close. You need to rest."

Mari's grip wound tightly around my forearm, all the fear from the day's events seeming to hit her hard now that the adrenaline wore off. "Please don't leave me. I don't want to be alone."

"I can get someone—"

"No, I want you." She turned over, a pained groan escaping her with the movement of her injured leg. But she was kissing me before I could tell her to be careful.

"Mari," I sighed, sinking into the soft presses of her lips more than I should have. "I can't stay. It's not safe for you."

"You've kept me safe all day," she whispered, hands trailing over my neck and face. "Please, Shadow. I only want you here."

"Mari, please understand—"

"Please don't leave me."

Even if I moved to leave, her grip around my hand threatened to hold on anyway. With a heavy swallow, I lowered back to the mattress and let her nestle into me. Her eyelids fell closed and her body relaxed again, but I kept my eyes open, focusing on the falcon staring at us from the tree outside the window.

I would not close my eyes. I wouldn't fall asleep.

I'd never sleep another day if it meant keeping her out of danger.

CHAPTER 19

REAPER

I stuck a cigarette in my mouth only to have it immediately yanked away by my mother. She just glared at my disapproving grunt. "Not in the house. You want to be a chimney, do it outside."

"Fine."

I started to roll up from my parents' couch when my dad's palm smacked my shoulder, shoving me back down to the cushions. "What are you, eighteen? You don't speak to your mother that way." His glare was murderous.

My impulse was to shove him right back, make him get the fuck out of my face so I could go smoke in peace. But if the last miserable several weeks had taught me anything, it was that I shouldn't give in to my impulses. All it ever did was hurt the people around me. So I clenched my hands against the desire to lash out, and looked at my mother.

"I'm sorry, ma. I'll be outside."

My parents' stares felt like the tips of knives on my back, another weight to balance precariously on top of everything else. First the alliance, then the losses at the skirmish, then Mari leaving without a word, and now, more of my own men dead.

I feared the worst when I saw Jandro riding back into town alone, with only a bloodied, limp Slick on the back of his bike. Gunner and I zipped through town, clearing the way for Slick to get rushed to the hospital. The medics told us he might not have lasted another hour, but they were able to stabilize him. That was the only silver lining to that dark cloud.

When Jandro told me about the decoy caravan and the ambush, I couldn't even muster up the strength to react. Those guys were among our best, and they got slaughtered. It was just one blow after another, and I couldn't help but wonder if this was some kind of divine punishment for what I did to Shadow.

Hades, of course, provided zero insight.

After Jandro got back, my dad, his lieutenants, Gunner, and I tried to re-think our tactics *again*. For days we'd been going around in circles nonstop. Without Horus' eyes, we just had no efficient ways to track the enemy. The skirmish had hurt our army's numbers, which were already small by comparison. If I kept sending my men out, the Steel Demons MC would dwindle down to nothing.

And I still had no fucking idea where Mari was, or if she'd ever come back.

My throat was raw from all the stress-smoking. My sleep was fucked, only catching moments of rest here or there. I was a snapping, irritable prick to everyone I ran into, even my own mother. Gunner and I went at each other's throats a few times, and needed to be physically separated by my dad and Jandro. None of us were doing well in the slightest.

There *had* to be something. Had to be a way our little territory could stand a chance against the giant threatening to crush us. But I didn't know what else we could do. Gunner had put forth several formations, but we still only had guesses as to the enemy's numbers and locations. Andrea hadn't yet made contact with more information and I was starting to lose hope in her too.

I thought the despair was bad when Mari wouldn't talk to me. Now, it was crushing. This weight had slowly grown heavier over the weeks and I had finally reached my breaking point.

A door swung open, and I heard both paws and booted feet approaching. My dad stood a few feet away from me in the small patio garden, Hades at his side. *Even my dog has abandoned me.* The melodramatic thought bubbled up from some nonsensical place in my exhausted brain.

"Sucks, doesn't it?" Dad remarked casually, like he was commenting on the weather.

"What?" I grunted.

"Everything. You're lost and not finding a way out. You're exhausted. You're fighting with your loved ones at every turn. You're heartbroken and feeling alone."

"So what, you came to rub it in?" I shot back.

"Nah, son." He shook his head, eyes never leaving me. "Just empathizing."

"Yeah, I know you've been through shit too. Being taken away to that labor camp, losing Carter, escaping with Mom. I get it. You've had it bad, if not worse than this. Doesn't change dick about where we are now."

"No, it doesn't," he agreed. "But the lesson is the same." He came close enough to touch a finger to my chest. "You have *got* to keep fighting, son." I snorted and he growled. "No, listen to me. It's easy to fight when you're winning. It's easy to have hope when you feel good. But right now?" He tapped his finger to my chest a few times. "Now is when you need to fight the most. I can see that dark cloud in your eyes, Rory. I know you're sick of it all, and it feels like it'll never end. But it will. You've gotta dig deep and find it in you. For Mari, for your family. Fuck, for *yourself!*" He backed away, turning quickly as he wiped his eyes. "I'm not losing another son. Don't give a fuck if it's on a battlefield or by his own depression. I need you around, Rory."

"Dad..." My cigarette had long since turned to ash and I dropped the butt in a tray on the patio table. "I just don't see how we can win."

"We can," he insisted. "You have gods with you."

At first, we only told him about Gunner's ability. After Jandro came back and we had nothing left to lose, I ended up spilling *everything*. From the moment I found Hades and started hearing his voice, to the accelerated healing that seemed to be powered by Mari and Freyja's bond. I even told him about when Shadow and I looked up the gods in books to try to make sense of it all. All this time later, I didn't feel any closer to understanding why they were here, or what they were really doing for us.

"We have gods who only step in when it suits them," I argued. "Maybe this shit is fun for them, I dunno." I gestured a hand to Hades. "He tells me who to kill, big fucking whoop. I don't need him to tell me we have to kill three-thousand troops, to our sub-one-thousand."

"There must be more to it," Dad said, sounding a lot like me back when I actually had hope. "Why can't you see through him like Gunner does with Horus?"

"I don't fucking know, Dad!"

You've never tried, my reaper.

My head jerked to stare at the dog, sitting calmly on his haunches. He stared back with that unsettling human gaze, and then I was somewhere else.

WHAT THE FUCK? WHERE AM I?

I tried to yell but my jaw was rigid, like it was wired shut. No part of my body could move, as if I was paralyzed. In the next few moments, I realized I wasn't breathing. I went to suck in a breath, but my lungs didn't expand. My heart wasn't pumping. There was no activity going on in my body at all. It was utterly strange to feel panicked with zero physical responses.

What the fuck, am I dead? Hades, what did you do?!

Look.

It was the only answer I got.

I was lying on the ground, not in my parents' yard, but some place I didn't recognize. Someone's boots were inches from my face. I heard gunshots and felt the *instinct* to duck for cover and reach for my holster, but it felt like I was encased in cement.

The boots in front of my face stepped away, the soles tacky with the blood that I realized had pooled around me. *What the fuck is going on?*

More gunshots fired off somewhere further away, like a shootout was going down behind me. In front of me, I saw a pickup truck with a wire cage fixed over the bed. It still had a pre-Collapse license plate that I didn't recognize. I couldn't squint, but tried my best to read it. Did it say West Virginia?

A woman's scream gradually became louder, and I couldn't even grit my teeth at how harshly the sound hit me. A door slammed and booted feet stomped down the porch I was facedown on. Some guy was dragging a woman along the ground by a rope tied around her wrists.

I couldn't see well from my angle, but she was clearly terrified and fought like hell. Her wrists were already chafed and bleeding, red lines dripping down her tattooed arms. The guy was dragging her straight to the truck with a cage on it, and apparently no one was stopping him.

Hades, what the fuck is happening? Do something!

His life is hers to take.

What?!

Someone ran up, arms outstretched toward the man, with a well-trained shooting stance. If I didn't already feel cold and dead, my heart would have stopped at the sight of the woman with long brown hair billowing around her.

Mari?!

The man dragging the other woman paused, but Mari didn't give him an opportunity to draw a weapon. She pulled her trigger and emptied the gun into him—six shots with no hesitation, her expression calm, if even cold.

That's my girl.

My pride was short-lived as I saw movement behind her, and then a shot rang out that wasn't hers. Mari fell, shock and pain on her face as she reached her palms out to break her fall. A dark stain began coloring her pant leg.

Hades! I cried out mentally as loud as I could. *Let me move! She's fucking hurt!*

No movement came, no matter how much I begged and pleaded. It dawned on me too late that I was watching this scene through someone else's dead body, likely one of these fuckwads who had gotten shot.

The man who shot Mari walked up to where she lay on the ground, trying to drag herself to the tattooed woman, his gun pointed toward her head. I'd never felt worse or lower in my life than at that exact moment. What kind of cruel joke was this, being forced to watch the woman I loved die?

HADES, PLEASE! PLEASE DO SOMETHING!

Her life is not yours to take. The ancient god's voice reverberated through my mind, angry and protective.

Footsteps crashed near my head, nearly kicking me. A shot fired and Mari's attacker went down, clutching his stomach. Then a giant of a man crossed the distance with nearly inhuman speed until he crashed into the shooter. From there, the huge man sat on him, punching and crashing the man's skull against the ground.

It went on and on. I saw blood and brain matter flying from the force of the blows. I quickly put together that it was Shadow, turning Mari's attacker into ground meat with a barbaric violence that I had never seen before. Shadow had always been a clean killer, nothing like this.

He finally stopped, pausing to stare at his hands as if coming out of a trance. When he finally went over to cradle Mari in his arms, putting pressure on her wound while his blood-speckled face frowned with worry, it was all I needed to see.

So she found him. And he really does love her.

The dead are your vessels, my reaper, Hades said to me. *Use them to see what you must.*

In a sudden jolting sensation, I was back.

"Rory?"

Both of my parents were staring down at me, concern on Mom's face and curiosity on Dad's. I blinked. I could fucking move again! I sat up with a groan, my head aching slightly.

"You alright, son?" Dad asked. "You went down like a sack of potatoes."

I nodded, smiling genuinely for the first time at the sight of Hades, looking regal with his belly on the ground and front paws stretched out.

"I think...I know how we can win," I said in an excited whisper.

Chapter 20

MARIPOSA

The excruciating, burning pain in my leg had dulled to a pulsing ache when I awoke. My whole body was stiff as I attempted to stretch and move. A quick glance out the window told me little—it was cloudy and gray.

I turned over in bed to see Shadow reclined on the opposite end. He was on his side facing away from me, at first looking like he was wearing some kind of jumpsuit. It took a few moments for the realization to dawn on me.

He was wearing a straitjacket?

"Shadow," I croaked out hoarsely. My voice quickly became a whispered cough, and I searched the nightstand for my water bottle.

Shadow stirred and turned toward me as I took a few greedy gulps. He was indeed strapped into a full-body suit, arms bound in front of him, and even his legs were encased.

"Good morning," he said.

I burst out laughing, spitting water all over the sheets, but cracking up too hard to care.

"What's so funny?" Shadow stared at me. "Careful, your leg."

"You...look...like," I took desperate gasps of air between peals of laughter, "a *mummy*!"

He frowned, looking down at himself and then at me. "It's funny to you that I look like an ancient Egyptian corpse?"

"Yes!" I shrieked, falling back down to the mattress. "Why on earth are you wearing that?"

"You wouldn't let me leave." A smile finally curved his lips. "And I didn't want...you know, anything to happen if I fell asleep. So Doc found this thing and strapped me in."

I laughed into the pillow. "What an ingenious idea."

"I figured I'd fall on the floor, squirming around like a caterpillar, and by then you'd be awake."

Grinning at him from across the bed, I propped my head up in my hand. "So how long have I been out?"

"Almost two full days. You were kind of in and out the first day, but you never had a fever or anything, so Doc said to just ride it out." Shadow swallowed deeply as his eyes trailed from my leg back up to my face. "You look much better today."

"I feel better." I stretched long again, mindful of the dull throbbing above my right knee. "How are the others? Is Jen okay?"

"Shaken up, but she'll be fine."

Shadow's arms pulled against the restraints holding his arms to his chest. He wiggled from side to side in an effort to sit up higher, which prompted another laughing fit from me.

"Would you like to be freed from that?"

His lips quirked again. "As much as I love hearing you laugh, yes please."

I crawled across the bed toward him, keeping most of my weight on my left leg. Even then, after everything that had happened and how ridiculous the straitjacket solution was, it was oddly erotic pulling apart the straps of the garment. He even let out a pleasured groan when his arms came loose from the sleeves. When I helped pull the top part of the jacket down to his waist, I saw that he was shirtless underneath, still wearing the red marks on his chest from where I gripped him so hard during the bullet extraction.

"Shadow, I'm sor—"

He grabbed my hand on its way to his chest. "Don't be."

"I was so..." He flattened my palm to his skin as the disjointed memories returned to me in a rush. Most of them sensations rather than images. "It feels like I wasn't even really there. I just get flashes of pain and feeling so scared."

"It's okay." His fingers stroked over the back of my palm. "Whatever you're feeling is okay." He looked a bit sheepish at my evident surprise at hearing such a thing coming from him. "It's something that Doc tells me a lot. To just...*be* with whatever you're feeling rather than try to fight it." Shadow's warm caress over my hand continued. "Fighting just makes it worse."

"Shadow..."

My lips fell to his in a desperate, needy kiss, one he returned with equal fervor and a moan that almost sounded pained. His large hands came to my arms, pulling me closer while my fingers dove through his hair. I remembered how he held me, soothed me as Doc dug the bullet out of my leg. How he helped to undress, bathe, and feed me, thinking only of my comfort and care.

"Shadow." His name escaped my lips again when we parted for a breath. "Shadow, I love you."

"Mari, no."

Rather than meeting me for another kiss, he tore away, holding me back by my shoulders. He looked so sad, sorrowful, and pain sliced through me like another onslaught of bullets.

"Shadow, why? What's wrong?" I held his face, making him look at me. "I've loved you even since before—"

"No." He shook his head, his jaw clenched hard. "Don't tell me that. Don't...feel that way for me, please."

"Too late," I whispered. "I already do." He just kept shaking his head, the hurt and rejection making me blurt out, "You don't feel the same for me."

That caused him to stop and look at me. "No, that's not it at all." He looked at my hands like he wanted to grab them again. "I do...I do feel the same way."

"Then what is it?"

He looked to be struggling so much, like he was fighting against something that was clawing to come out of him.

"You don't...know me." Shadow's voice was small, hesitant. "You don't know what led to the me you see now, all of this." He rubbed a hand over his arm, scars running over scars. "And I'm scared to death of you knowing that part of me."

I scooted closer in small movements, his eyes watching me like a wary animal backed into a corner. "If I told you nothing will change how I feel, would you believe me?"

"I want to." He pulled in a deep breath. "More than anything, I want to believe that."

"Then trust me." I placed a hand on top of his, threading through his scarred fingers. "If you feel the same way about me, please take this chance. Trust that I would never hold your past against you."

He stared straight ahead, his hand passive in mine as he spent a few long moments thinking. Finally, his fingers curled around mine in a light squeeze. "I'll tell Doc to meet us in the basement."

I STOOD OFF TO THE SIDE AS DOC METHODICALLY SHACKLED Shadow into the metal chair, like they'd done this dozens of times before.

"Are the restraints really necessary?" I asked.

"I don't think so, at this point," Doc answered cheerily. "But Ivan insists on it. The therapy works best when the patient is at ease, so I do as he asks."

"The first couple times, I would have been violent if I wasn't restrained," Shadow muttered. "It's not a risk I'm willing to take."

Doc tossed a smile my way at that. "I take it you've heard this before?"

"A few times," I said with a returned smile.

"Okay, Ivan." Doc reached into his shirt pocket and produced a string tied through a coin with a hole in the center. "Are you ready?"

"Yes."

I folded my arms, leaning against a side table as I watched with fascination. Doc stood off to the side, holding the string in front of

Shadow's eyes as he began to swing the coin back and forth like a pendulum.

"Begin to take deep breaths." Doc's voice took on a soothing, even tone. "Match your inhales and exhales with each swing of the pendulum."

Shadow's broad chest rose and fell with each breath, his gaze fixated on the coin.

"Very good. I'm going to start counting backwards from ten. With each number, your eyes are going to get heavier, and your gaze is going to turn inward. Ten...nine..."

Shadow's eyelids drooped, his breaths remaining steady and even while the older man counted. Doc hadn't even reached the number one when he put away the pendulum. Shadow had already reached a hypnotic state. By the time he finished counting, Shadow appeared to be asleep sitting up in the chair, his eyes closed and breaths deep and even.

"Can you tell us where you are, Ivan?" Doc asked after a few silent moments.

"My name is Shadow."

The declaration made me jump. It was still his voice, yet completely different. He sounded younger, more timid.

Doc however, didn't seem fazed. He just smiled. "Alright, Shadow. Can you tell us where you are?"

"I'm in my prison cell." Shadow tipped his head back as if to lean it against the wall behind him.

"The one you grew up in?"

"No, I'm in the mental health unit at the men's prison." A small smile came to Shadow's face. "Jandro just snuck me a flask and I drank it all. I'm numb and it feels good."

I released a tight breath at that. Vaguely, I knew this prison was one of Shadow's better memories. It was where he first met Jandro, where his life improved because he wasn't tortured on a daily basis.

"Mariposa is here," Doc said, keeping that even, calm quality to his voice. "You know who she is, yes?"

"*Yesss...*" Shadow drew the word out like he was experiencing something that felt utterly heavenly. Like a massage or a hot bath. Or...

I bit the inside of my cheek to hide my smile.

"Good. Would you be open to answering some questions from her?"

Shadow's mouth twitched, the smile fading as his face hardened. I thought he might refuse until another, "Yes," slipped past his lips.

Doc turned to me. "He's aware of everything and knows who you are. Just think of it as his subconscious being in the driver's seat while his conscious mind is taking a step back."

"So he'll remember this?" I asked.

"Yes," Doc nodded. "He remembers everything. Ask him whatever you'd like."

I moved away from the table I was leaning against to stand in front of Shadow. From here I could see that his eyelids weren't fully closed. Even so, his eyes shifted back and forth under his lids as if he were dreaming.

"Hi Shadow," I began.

"Hello Mariposa."

It didn't sound like him, the Shadow I knew, and that was jarring. I just had to remember that I was speaking to an earlier version of him. Hearing him address me in that strange voice seemed to make all the questions in my head vanish.

"You can ask him open-ended questions, but it helps if they are a bit specific," Doc prompted me gently. "Going too broad might pull the thinking mind forward and take him out of the hypnotic state."

I nodded, trying to maintain my focus and come up with something simple first. "Can I ask, when did you first start getting cut?"

"I don't remember." Shadow's voice became flat, monotone. "In my earliest memories, I already had scars and cuts that were freshly bleeding."

I pulled in a breath, fighting the wave of anger, the hurt on his behalf, to have been abused so young, as a toddler mostly likely. This was what I needed to know, and it was just the beginning.

"Who cut you?" I asked next.

"Everyone," he answered. "Every woman drew blood from me during the days she bled on her monthly cycle. I deserved it. Men had been cruel to women for ages and it was only fair to make me bleed when they did."

A hand came to my shoulder and it took me a moment to realize it was Doc, steadying me as I started to shake. He gave me a knowing, sympathetic look. He'd heard all this before, and from the tightness in his brow, it wasn't any easier to hear the second time around.

"Where were your parents?" It was an impulsive question, a demand through gritted teeth. "How could they let you be treated like this?"

Shadow began to laugh.

Again, the sound was foreign to my ears, like someone else had possessed his body and was laughing through his mouth.

"Loving parents are a myth," he scoffed. "I read about them in books, but they're not real. Do you really want to know where my parents were?"

Doc's hand squeezed my shoulder, a small warning. Even subconsciously, Shadow was trying to deflect. But I had to know. This information was probably the core of everything.

"Yes," I said firmly. "Tell me about your parents."

The strange grin faded from Shadow's face, hardening into a scowl that I knew well.

"My mother became pregnant with me at fourteen years old," he said. "You want to know who my father was? Her grandfather, who raped her."

Air rushed out of my lungs like I had been kicked in the chest. My hand flew to my heart, pounding with a crazy mix of sympathy and fear as Shadow continued on, unprompted.

"He tried to kill her when he found out about the pregnancy, but she escaped and ran away from home." Shadow sounded detached, almost robotic as he spoke. "The Sisters of Bathory found her and took her in. They were a refuge for girls like her, a community that sheltered and protected women from men.

"She was too far into the pregnancy to terminate me, and when I was born, she wanted to kill me the moment she saw that I was male." Shadow's lip curled. Not with a smile, but with disdain. "But the leader of the Sisterhood convinced her not to. She gave my mother a better idea, to let me live so I could suffer." Shadow's eyelids lifted slightly, peering through the thin gaps with an unfocused gaze. "To take the punishment that all men deserved for abusing women."

"Shadow..." My voice escaped in a cracked whisper, all my fiery anger gone and replaced by blank shock. If it wasn't for Doc still gripping my shoulder, I probably wouldn't have been able to stay upright.

"How..." It took a few tries to find my voice again. "How do you know all this?"

"Oh, my mother told me," he answered in that same eerie, flat voice. "Several times. She loved talking about how much she hated me. She hated that I invaded her body and grew inside her, the living result of a man who preyed on a child." Shadow's head tilted to the side. "She both hated me for existing and loved to make me suffer. She cut me the deepest, you know. She blinded me by puncturing my eye and gave me this handsome face."

Shadow's pale eye swiveled under his half-closed lid, the one with the scar cutting through it. A scar that *his mother* gave him. The person who was supposed to love and protect instead delighted in his pain.

"You want to know what her favorite game was?" It was like a dam had burst, and he could no longer hold back everything he'd bottled up.

"What?" I asked with dread.

"She'd leave the door to my cage open. If I tried to escape, she'd come out from a hiding place and whip me with a cat o' nine tails until I collapsed. My back was all scar tissue before I turned twelve years old, by my estimate."

I had to turn away and cover my mouth then, fighting back the bile that rose in my throat.

It wasn't like I didn't know horrible parents existed. In nursing school, I even had a lecture on identifying signs of abuse in children. But this senseless violence went so far beyond child abuse. He was subjected to a lifetime of torture, just for existing.

"The...the other men you've told me about." I turned back to him when I composed myself. "The botanist. The ones who taught you how to read and write. What about them?" Maybe it was a morbid fascination, but I still had to know.

"They were kept with me temporarily and then killed at every full moon," he answered. "A ritualistic sacrifice." Shadow talked over my shocked, gasping breaths this time, the words spilling out of him as if rehearsed. "Only the spilling of a man's blood could slake the thirst of the angry goddess. She demanded vengeance for the harm that had been done to her daughters since the dawn of history."

Shadow's head rolled slowly on his neck, eyeballs still moving actively under his lids. "The sacrificial altar was positioned above my cell. Not that I was ever let out, but I could see a little through the grate in the floor. And I heard *everything*. The chants, the struggles, and the screams. I heard the knife sink into their skin and their last pleas for life. Then I felt their blood."

His head stopped moving, staying upright with his unseeing eyes looking straight at me, and leaned forward as far as his restraints would allow him. "Blood ran over the floor, dripping down through the grate into my cell like rain. Every single month I felt it."

Shadow leaned back. "I used to try stopping them. I used to grow attached to the men who taught me things and told me about the outside world." He pulled in a labored breath. "When that didn't work, I begged the women to sacrifice me. I offered myself freely to their goddess if it would end my miserable existence. But they *refused*."

His voice cracked with clear agony at that final word. "I wasn't even good enough to be sacrificed because I was a product of evil, born of an attack on someone innocent. I was destined to live and suffer."

Shadow's head slumped forward, chin nearly resting on his chest. I couldn't tell if he had fallen asleep or come out of the hypnotic state. All I knew was that I'd heard enough.

"Take him out of it," I said to Doc. "And let's put him in bed to rest."

CHAPTER 21

MARIPOSA

"More?" Doc held the bottle of whiskey over my empty glass, pausing before pouring.

"Yes." I nodded. "Please."

I didn't usually have a taste for whiskey, but nothing was appetizing at the moment. I just wanted to chase away this ache, this awful hole ripped open from what Shadow told me. I wondered if this was how he felt when he tried to drink the nightmares away—chasing sweet, empty numbness.

Doc kept him in the hypnotic state so we wouldn't have to haul him to bed with brute strength. Shadow followed his gentle instructions up to his room, and once settled into bed, Doc talked him out of the trance. I felt awful that Shadow wouldn't let himself fall asleep while I'd been recovering from the gunshot. So I followed Doc back down to the bar, so Shadow could rest up without being put in another straitjacket.

"They called themselves the Sisters of Bathory." At my confused stare, Doc elaborated. "The cult that kept Iv—Shadow, and sacrificed men."

"You knew about them before meeting him?" I took a sip of whiskey, savoring the fire burning a path down to my belly.

"Rumors, yes, but nothing substantial." Doc stroked his goatee.

"You never want to believe stuff like that, you know? You hope, you *pray*, that it's just tall tales." He gave a slight shake of his head and sighed before taking a long drink.

"Is the cult still around?" Panic flashed through me at the thought. What if there were others like Shadow? And more men being kidnapped and sacrificed?

"I don't think so," Doc said. "The rumors stopped roughly ten years ago, about the time Shadow was rescued."

"Rescued?" I repeated. "By who?"

"From what he describes, it sounded like a mercenary army hired by a governor looking to claim the area at the time. They just rolled in, gunning down everyone they saw above ground. Which is damned horrific if you think about it from the army's view—they shot up a remote village full of women and girls."

My stomach dropped at that. "Could they have known it was a cult?"

"I doubt it." Doc gave me a sympathetic look. "Cult leaders kept a tight lid and brainwashed their followers into total obedience. They operated for years under total secrecy. It's not likely anyone spilled."

"So, this Sisterhood built a following out of abused girls? Like the girls' camp runaways?"

Doc nodded gravely. "A girl in Shadow's mother's situation was a typical follower for them, if I were to guess."

I made a sound of disgust as I drained the rest of my whiskey. "I want to hate her but...she was just the victim of one predator and then fell into the hands of another."

"Mm-hm." Doc polished off his whiskey, then quickly refilled it and mine, without asking this time. "It's a shitty situation all around."

I rolled my palms across the glass, thoughts tumbling as I stared blankly at the wall behind the bar. "It's a good thing he came to you," I mused, my eyes flicking to Jen as she swept up shards of glass with a broom and dustpan. We were still finding bits of glass here and there from the shootout with the traffickers. "You seem like you know how to treat people who have been through similar situations."

Doc smiled, looking down into his drink like he was being shy. "All the girls here have faced their own traumas, some brainwashing too.

When my license was revoked, I felt lost. Adrift. But this place..." He looked around the dining room with an affectionate gleam in his eye. "It's nice to have a little refuge. And to be able to help people again."

"Okay, now *this* is a story I need to hear." I leaned back in my barstool, turning to face him. "You're a man. How did *you* get your license revoked?"

He shrugged modestly. "Hypnotherapy has always been controversial. The mind, and the subconscious specifically, are so intricate and difficult to study. I used to be a psychiatrist, but..." Doc cleared his throat as though sobering. "Drug manufacturers started offering me and my colleagues *a lot* of money to prescribe their products. The FDA had been completely dismantled by then, so there was no telling what was in these drugs and the effects they would have on our patients. Lots of us suspected politicians were the ones pulling the strings."

"Makes sense," I agreed. "With how the world was going."

"It never sat right with me," Doc said. "Even before, I always had mixed feelings about treating mental illness with drugs. Once those bribes started rolling in I said, 'to hell with it! I'm opening a private hypnotherapy practice.'"

I smiled at him. "Good for you, Doc."

"It was good." He nodded. "For about twenty years, I helped people in a way that didn't conflict with my conscience. I gave them their own tools to face their traumas."

"And then...the Collapse?" I ventured.

"And then the Collapse," he confirmed with a dry laugh. "The first governor that claimed this area sent a notice to my office that said I could go back to prescribing pills at his discretion, or I'd be declared a quack and my hypnotherapy practice deemed illegal."

"Sounds like a typical governor," I remarked, before quickly remembering Vance. For all his imperfections, he was at least fair and wanted to do right by his people. A pang of longing thumped in my chest. I missed Four Corners, my home. And my men.

"Yeah, we've gone through about three governors since then," Doc said. "The latest one doesn't seem to care about anything except gaining more land. It's not like he protects us, but at least he leaves us alone."

"You might like Four Corners," I offered. "And not just you, but everyone here. It's fair, and relatively safe. I'm sure Dr. Brooks would love to have you practicing."

Doc's smile faltered. "I've heard about this fabled Four Corners, but unfortunately, so have half a dozen governors hungry for territory. I'll be honest, Mari, I'm a little worried for y'all out there." He glanced toward the stairs leading up to Shadow's room. "Everyone's heard about the prosperity out west, the good infrastructure, the citizens with flourishing businesses. It's like a beacon for governors and their generals who want war. A *real* war for a prize worth conquering, not these little border skirmishes."

"I know," I sighed. "We've already been dealing with it. My father-in-law is the general, and my husbands have been supporting his defense effort."

Doc didn't comment on my implication that I have other lovers. "You and Shadow are welcome to stay here until it blows over. I don't expect more traffickers to bother us again." He chuckled. "Or anyone really. They must've heard that gunfight up in Boston."

I gave a regretful shake of my head. "Honestly I'd love to, but they need me out there. They need *us*. Although," I frowned with my next thought, "I wish we could clone you so Shadow can keep receiving his therapy."

"I may have a colleague out that way who can help." Doc winked with a smirk. "But really, I'm confident Shadow only needs supplemental therapy at this point. He knows how to stay lucid in his memories. He knows how to ground himself and pull himself out if it becomes too much."

"The violent sleepwalking is his biggest concern."

"Ah, right." Doc stroked his goatee. "It's *possible* those episodes may return, the chance of it is greater than zero. But I don't expect it to happen unless he backslides significantly."

"What are the chances of that?" I asked.

"It would have to be quite the traumatic event to trigger such a regression. The sudden death of someone he loves, or being abused again in a similar manner as the cult did." He gave me a warm smile. "Something tells me he feels safest with you, and will go to great lengths to prevent any sudden-death situations."

"I hope he feels that way with me." I spun my glass idly on the bar. "It's the least he deserves after everything he's been through."

Doc reached for one of my hands and clasped it with friendly affection. "His mind is stronger than he believes. And with each passing day in a healthy, supportive environment, he heals a little bit more. All he really needs is that constant, gentle reminder that he matters. That he is a person worthy of love and care."

I nodded, returning the squeeze of his hand. "I'll do my best to remind him of that every day."

CHAPTER 22

SHADOW

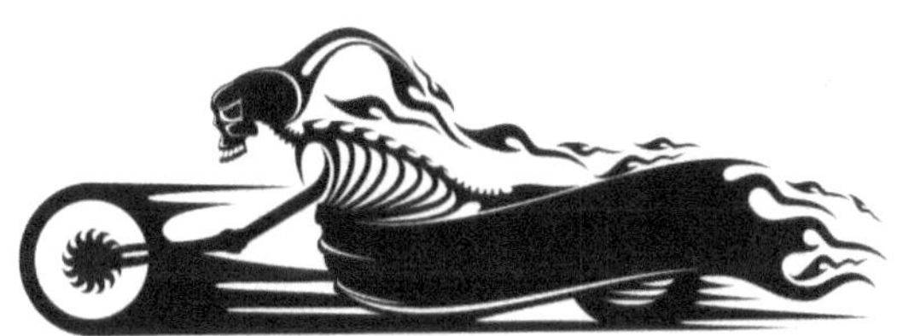

I woke with a start, my legs kicking out with a falling sensation before I jolted upright. My heart pounded as the room snapped into focus. Chairs and furniture remained in their places, nothing broken or scattered on the floor.

Another day of no damage. That was good.

Before I could sag with relief, my eyes landed on Mari sitting at my desk with one of my borrowed library books in her hands.

"Good morning," she greeted me.

"Why are you in here?" I snapped instead of returning her greeting. "I told you it's not safe—"

"Your therapist disagrees," she returned snippily, shutting the book.

"My therapist," I repeated. "You mean Doc?"

"Is there anyone else giving you hypnotherapy sessions?" she teased.

I rubbed my hands down my face with a groan, both to finish waking up and also to block myself from seeing her. "No, I guess not."

Doc *had* told me the chance of me acting out my dreams again was unlikely. The lingering fear that it still *could* happen never abated, however. Even a one-percent chance felt like too much.

Now that my surroundings and Mari had survived the night without harm, a different fear was riding me hard. For the first time since meeting Mari, I wanted to shrink away, to put as much distance between us as possible. To become small and invisible until she would forget me.

She had been there. She asked me questions, and I answered her. I told her everything and now she knew. She was one of two people alive who knew how I turned out this way, and why.

I was dying to know, and yet terrified to find out what she was thinking, looking at me from across the room like that. Would my worst fear be confirmed, and she was here to tell me we couldn't be together after all? Or was everything she said true—that she loved me before and still did?

I wasn't ready to feel the hurt that would cut through me if it was the former, nor did I dare hope for the latter. So I sat in the middle, caught between the two outcomes that awaited me, until I couldn't stand not knowing anymore.

"Well?" I said, filling the oppressive silence that expanded between us. "You know my past now. Has...has anything changed?"

Mari took a deep, shaky breath, like she was composing herself. I expected that.

I did not expect the tears that followed.

"Shadow..." She hiccuped and sobbed with great gasping breaths and I forgot about everything else.

"Mari." I shoved back the sheets and got out of bed, thankfully still dressed, and went to her. My knees hit the floor in front of her as I took her face in my hands, brushing away her tears with my thumbs. "What's wrong?"

"They..." she breathed shakily, "...*hurt* you."

Her fingers went to my face, shoving back my hair and stroking over my skin like she'd done so many times before. But she was seeing me differently now and it made dread pool in my gut like a well of poison.

"They did this to you," she sniffed, hands moving over me, tracing my scars. "Fuck, you were just a kid. A baby! You should have been loved and all they did was hurt you. Your own mother hurt you..."

I stopped her, taking her hands from me and gently pressing them between my palms. "I'm sorry that I upset you."

"Upset me? No, Shadow." She shook her head and leaned forward until her forehead touched mine. "I just hate that someone I love had to suffer so much."

My breath froze in my chest, rendering me as still as a statue. Did she really just say that? She couldn't have. Not after everything I had told her, everything she now knew about me.

Mari let out a small, sad laugh. "Yes, of course I still love you. I told you I would."

"How?"

The word came out choked, my breath still stuck in my body. My eyes had closed at some point, like I was afraid to see a different reality than what I was hearing. Meanwhile, my hands closed tighter around hers, clinging to the feel of her really being here.

The weight of her forehead lifted away from mine, replaced by the soft touch of her lips. "Because you're still you."

Only then did a rush of breath enter my lungs, filling me up with a hope and relief that I never dared allow myself to feel before.

"I love you, Mariposa." The sentence felt both strange and thrilling to say, a flipping sensation happening in my chest as the words left me. "I love you, and I want this. I want a life with you."

Mari inhaled sharply, still a bit of a sniffle in her nose. I saw a quick flash of her smile before our lips found each other. My hands released hers and fell to her thighs before running up to her waist. She scooted forward in the chair, leaning into my embrace as her arms wrapped around my shoulders.

She was still crying, salty tears coloring the taste of our kisses. I broke away and wiped my thumbs over her cheekbones, desperate to fix whatever was wrong. But she was still smiling, which confused me a little.

"Are you...unhappy?"

"No." She shook her head, then tilted her face to rest her cheek in my palm. "A little overwhelmed, but not unhappy." At my frown, she kissed my palm. "I'm glad you showed me. What happened to you was awful and I hate it that it happened, but I'm glad I know now. I understand better."

She looked at me so sweetly, with the same warmth she always did, and I started to wonder why I never wanted her to know my past in the first place. This was Mari, who never treated me differently, no matter how abnormal I perceived myself to be. My impulse was to open my mouth to warn her, to let her know that I'd still mess things up and not get everything perfect. I would do my best, but she was still the first woman I was ever truly *with*, the first one I loved. I'd fuck something up again. I always did.

Then I realized none of it needed to be said. She knew I wasn't perfect and loved me anyway. This woman never saw me as lesser than her other men, even before we became friends. She forgave me for hurting her even before she knew the whole story. Now she knew all there was to know about me and, like the sun setting every day, she always stayed with me.

Suffering and bleeding were the constants in my life that I never expected to change. I fully expected to be a caged animal until I died. The only other constant I'd experienced was Mari's care and kindness, which grew into a love that strengthened me like nothing else. Because of her, I broke down barriers that I caged myself in. I became more than a broken-down shell that was only useful for its blood.

I became a person, someone with their own wants, dreams, and desires. Someone who wanted to experience what else life had to offer, like loving another person.

"I feel...better, now that you know," I said, still stroking her cheek even though her eyes had dried. "I don't want to keep anything from you anymore."

She nodded her agreement, cupping her hand over mine. "That's the only way this works. Being honest and open about everything." Her eyes darkened as she lowered our clasped hands to her lap. "That's what hurt most about Reaper exiling you. The dishonesty of it."

"Will you forgive him?"

Her gaze flicked from our hands up to my face. "Do you think I should?"

I thought for a moment, curling my fingers around hers and stroking over the small digits with my thumbs. I just loved to touch her and was entranced with the feel of her skin, now that the huge weight of guilt had been lifted away.

"He acted with your best interest in mind," I said. "Not only that, but your physical safety. I can't fault him for that." Mari's eyes narrowed and her lip curled with a cute snarl. It brought a smile to my face, probably my first real one in months. "So yes, I think he's deserving of forgiveness when you feel ready."

She made an even cuter grunting sound, fingers stroking over mine and the simple returned affection brought an elated, weightless feeling to my chest. "I think how he treats *you* when he sees you again will be a determining factor in that."

"Fair enough. When do you want to ride back?" My smile faltered, a quick stab of anxiety hitting me in the chest. "Doc and I meet twice a week. Maybe if we do more sessions—"

"Shadow, he told me he has a colleague near Four Corners who can help." Mari's grin grew wide. "And even then, he said you only need supplemental therapy now. You have all the tools and your mind is strong." She untangled her fingers from mine, wrapping her warm touch around the back of my neck. "And you have me, always."

The anxiety morphed in my chest, becoming a heavy ache, but not one made of fear. It was like a dense brick of emotions wanting to burst from my body, even making my eyes water. Now I understood why she cried even when she wasn't unhappy.

"I would be nothing without you," I said through the tightness in my throat.

"That's not true." Her eyes began to water again too. "You're amazing just as you are."

Our bodies collided with a force that we couldn't have fought even if we wanted to. She crashed against my chest and my hands pressed to her back like we were made to be joined as one. And right then, it was the only thing I needed in the world. More than air, I needed to be inside my woman. I *needed* her lips on my scars and to feel the heat of her skin on mine.

Securing her with my hands on her ass, I rose from the floor and turned us toward the bed. I didn't need to think about kissing her correctly anymore. Even our clumsy, frenzied rush of lips and tongues felt natural and right.

I lowered her back to the mattress, our mouths locked in a tight seal until she clawed at my shirt to pull it over my head. Some part of me wanted to go slowly with undressing her, make it a slow, drawn-out exploration like our first night together, but mostly I just wanted her so fucking badly.

"Tomorrow," Mari said, her touch grazing down my stomach to the button on my jeans.

"What?" I grunted distractedly, revelling in her smooth, unblemished skin as I lifted her shirt away and peeled it off of her arms.

"Let's ride back to Four Corners tomorrow." She had me unbuttoned and unzipped in seconds, shoving my jeans and boxers down my thighs a moment later.

"Okay." I helped her get my pants off and then pressed her shoulders back down on the bed before she got any ideas. My fingers hooked into her waistband and I paused. "How is your leg?"

"Fine, just get those off, please."

Her eagerness was sexy and I felt myself grinning as I leaned over, planting a kiss on her sternum as I worked her pants down her legs, still taking care around the bullet wound wrapped in gauze. Once we were both free of clothing, she hummed and sighed, clamping her thighs around my ribs while her fingers raked over my scalp.

It felt *so* good to be wanted by her. I ran my hands up her sides, palms finding her supple breasts as I dragged my mouth over her belly. I was lost in tasting her skin, kissing her, and feeling her wonderful touch on me. A touch that felt so right, especially after weeks of starving and craving her.

"Come back up here." Her voice was low and husky, fingers running down my arms to squeeze around my hands that were on her breasts.

"Not yet." I kissed the beautiful little scar above her hip, tightening my hands as she prompted until her pert nipples were pinched between my fingers. At her gasping breath I released them, smoothing my touch over her flesh as I brought my mouth lower.

"Shadow..."

"Mari," I answered, utterly in love with the way she said my name, the sight of her back arching off the bed, everything.

Her legs hooked over my shoulders as I kneeled at the edge of the bed. I skimmed one hand down her body, never missing any chance to touch her, bringing it between her legs. She drew in a sharp breath with a moan at the pressure of my hand just stroking her, caressing down the center of her pleasure.

"Shadow, please." She tried to wiggle against my hand to increase the friction. "Seriously, don't tease me too much. I just want you."

My cock was heavy and aching, she was slick and wanting me, but more than anything else, I didn't want to hurt her. I sucked a harder kiss at her hip crease, letting my beard drag over her skin until she shivered. "You know I never tease."

"Liar!" she laughed.

My smile remained until I kissed her pussy, releasing an indulgent moan at her heat—oh fuck, and her *taste*. Was it only three days ago when she rode my face? I felt like an addict needing his fix, my tongue taking long greedy licks through her folds.

Mari started bucking then, and I clamped a hand around her thigh to hold her in place. I heard her ragged breaths, felt her small fingers curl in my hair, smelled her everywhere, and tasted her sweetness on my tongue. I was torn between eating her until my jaw went numb or pulling away to sink my cock into her.

We have the rest of our lives, a voice reminded me. And it was true. This wasn't like our last time in bed together, when I thought it might've been the last time for good. We weren't saying a desperate, confusing goodbye. This was the beginning of something new for us.

I released her pink lips from a long, sucking kiss and nudged my mouth higher, at the same time moving my fingers in to stroke and test her entrance. Her clit was begging to be kissed itself, so I sealed my lips around that spot as I pressed my first finger through her folds.

"Shadowwww!" she cried out, hands tugging in my hair and sending thrilling tingles down my spine.

I moaned against her sex, pressing another finger inside and curling both of them against her slick walls. She pulled harder on my hair and my cock was already dripping. A bit of pain with pleasure, the sensation I couldn't get enough of from only her.

Mari's thighs squeezed around my head, though they barely muffled the beautiful sounds she made as I pleased her. Her breaths came in increasingly short pants, and then seemed to stop altogether as her whole body went rigid, then shook and shuddered in her release.

She squeezed rhythmically around my fingers, hips tilted up to chase more sensation. I kept my mouth glued around her clit until she shoved my head away. Even then I couldn't back away far, removing my fingers from her channel only to replace them with my tongue so I could taste her again.

"Stop that," she panted, squirming further up the bed. "Come up here."

"Do you need a minute to recover?" I couldn't fight the smug smile as I sat up, wiping my jaw with my hand as I looked at her stretched out on the bed.

"Very funny," she snorted, rolling onto her stomach. "No, what I need is you."

She propped up on her hands and knees, a deep arch in her back and glossy, wet sex on display. I was *almost* put off by the position. It was the same way I'd fucked women other than her, the ones that meant nothing and didn't matter. I didn't want her like that. I loved seeing her face and feeling her skin on mine when we were together.

Mari must have sensed my hesitation because she pressed up to kneeling and leaned back, the tattoo on her back kissing the matching one on my chest as she looked at me over her shoulder.

"You good, love?" She reached an arm up, her small hand coming to my jaw to angle my mouth for a kiss.

"Yes." I pressed into her kiss, answering her sweet tongue flicks with my own. "I was just enjoying the view."

My hands ran up the front of her body, pulling her lightly to me until the full length of her back pressed against my torso. Always, at any given time, I wanted to feel as much of her on me as possible.

"You'd enjoy it a lot more if you were fucking me," she teased, darting her tongue out to the tip of my nose.

I snapped my teeth like I was going to bite her tongue and she laughed, kissing me again. Her legs nudged closer together, hugging my cock in the slickness and heat coating her inner thighs. The groan leaving my chest was a direct result of her smooth flesh gliding over my length, teasing me. I released her from my embrace, my hands finding a hold on her hips as she fell forward to her hands and knees again.

I realized then that this was completely different, even if the position was the same one I'd done with others. My woman lowered her face to the mattress, looking back at me with a plea in her eyes while her ass lifted higher in the air. I'd never had anything like this before. Mari *wanted* me. She *loved* me.

And fuck if I was going to deny her what she wanted.

I splayed one hand on her lower back, using the other to guide my cock to her sex. Her sensitive flesh parted for my blunt head, hugging around it like her mouth had done before. Mari whimpered and tried to rock her hips back toward me, but my hand on her spine kept her place.

"I love that you want me," I said, just staring at where her flesh met mine and fighting the urge to plunge through. "But let me go slow so I don't hurt you."

She let out a cute, frustrated groan. "I know how much I can take."

"I thought I was the dominant one in this position." I gave a playful swat to her ass.

Mari laughed, grinning up at me. "I knew I should have just climbed on top of you."

"You can next time." I pressed forward with a short thrust, watching in fascination at the change on her face. Her mouth fell open, eyelids falling shut as my head nudged inside. I pulled back and it felt like her pussy was trying to suck me back in. When I pressed in a little deeper, my head tipped back with the feeling of her. She was all slippery and hot, delicious pressure on all sides of my cock, with little resistance.

"Oh yes, Shadow..." Mari rocked her hips back and this time I didn't stop her, meeting her in the middle as I pressed forward. She was a sight to behold, arched and stretched out in front of me, the curving lines of her waist and hips more hypnotizing than Doc's pendulum.

And she's mine. She enjoys this. She wants me. The thoughts kept repeating in my head as if to remind me that this was real. I'd never have awkward, transactional sex with a stranger again, but join with the woman I loved because we wanted each other. This was my life now.

Mari reached back, her hands finding my thighs as my short thrusts gradually filled her deeper. I leaned over, my forehead touching the back of her shoulder. The sensation of her wrapped around me and everything she made me feel was dizzying, consuming. Overwhelming in the best way.

"I love you." My arms wrapped around her middle, mouth brushing her shoulder blade. "Fuck, I love you, Mari."

"I love you, Shadow." She twisted in my arms, angling back to kiss me, I assumed. With my arms around her and not supporting us, the momentum took us sideways and we landed softly on the bed. "Shit! Are you okay?" she laughed breathlessly.

"So much more than that," I promised with a kiss to her neck. I could touch more of her now that we were lying on our sides.

Still inside her, I rolled my hips against her plump ass, making her gasp and arch against me. She moaned when I resumed my thrusts, and my mouth found hers to swallow the beautiful sound.

I like this position much better, I realized. I could play with her clit easily here, tease her nipples, and kiss her. Mari's entire beautiful body was in reach of my touch and I made every effort not to leave any part of her ignored.

My hand ran leisurely down her thigh, and I lifted her leg to see if that would allow me to sink into her any deeper. It did, and judging by her resulting moan and the frantic gripping of whatever she could hold onto, it was very well-received.

"Good?" I checked in with her anyway, my mouth against her ear. Despite her clear body language of wanting me, the lingering fear of hurting her remained.

"More," she begged. "Fuck, please. More."

I rested my head on the mattress, letting her hair tickle my face while I dragged my lips along her neck and upper back. Mari kept her leg lifted while I gripped her waist, holding tight for leverage as I started to fuck her wildly.

Her first scream almost made me stop, but she immediately began crying out *yes* and *more,* and I gave in to the need to rut and fuck *hard.* My hips crashed against the soft flesh of her ass, the slapping sounds and Mari's screams filling the small room. I found a nipple with my free hand, plucking the tight peak to see if I could get any different noises out of her. Mari gasped in response, a strangled moan escaping her like her scream was stuck in her throat.

She was already so snug and tight around my cock, the feel of her squeezing me even tighter just about made me lose my mind with pleasure. I wrapped around her in a tight embrace, my hips driving into her wildly and uncontrollably and my face buried in her neck. Mari grabbed my forearm across her chest and I swore she used the leverage to push back on me as I pressed into her.

"Fuck…" I growled into her neck, squeezing around her tighter with one arm while the other slid down her belly. The reaction when I touched her clit was instant—breathless whimpers and the stuttered rocking of her hips, her pussy closing around me, making me swell and throb.

Her orgasm spurred my own, the grip and slide of her just too fucking good. Sensitivity and aching pleasure raced down my spine, releasing through my cock in a violent rush as I crushed her tight to my chest.

Then I released her, my arms limp and heavy as my pulse thundered and echoed throughout my whole body. I rolled to my back, sucking in great lungfuls of air as the heady wave of pleasure ebbed away.

Mari curled into my side after we started catching our breath, nudging her head onto my chest. I stroked down her back, nestling my hand into the small dip of her waist. Once the haze of pleasure started to clear, I brushed my lips along her forehead, a question weighing heavily on my mind.

"Would it bother you if I slept in another room tonight?"

She lifted her head, looking up at me with a puzzled frown. "Doc said you don't need to."

"I know." My hand ran along her jaw and I took a fast kiss, her lips still swollen and flushed. "But it still makes me nervous to sleep next to you. And I'm honestly not fond of the straitjacket."

Mari let out a soft laugh, returning her cheek to my chest. "Can't say I blame you." Her hand slid over my body until her fingers clasped with mine. "Would you be willing to get a second opinion from Doc's colleague when we go back to Four Corners?"

"Yes." I brought our conjoined hands up to my lips and kissed her fingers. "It's just hard to break the habit. I don't plan on sleeping away from you forever."

"Better not," she huffed, sliding a leg over mine. "You're such a wonderful cuddler."

"I don't know how that happened," I mused, bringing both hands to her back. "You didn't exactly teach me that."

"You can't really teach cuddling," she laughed, nuzzling into my neck before kissing me there. "It's just kind of innate, natural."

"Does it always feel this nice?" I murmured, my eyelids already weighing down. Fuck, how amazing would it feel to stay wrapped up in each other all night?

"Hmm, I think it's kind of like sex." Mari placed more kisses along my face and neck. "It's better when there's something more between the people involved."

I hugged tighter around her, catching that sweet, beautiful, luscious mouth in a deep kiss that I never wanted to end. "Then this is the best," I whispered against her mouth.

"It is," Mari agreed, her lips pulled back in a smile.

We kissed and held each other for a time that seemed entirely too short. It felt like a crime to leave her alone in bed for the night, but I would not risk her safety with me again. Not until I was absolutely sure I wouldn't become a danger to her in my sleep.

"I'll be just down the hall in your room," I said, sitting at the edge of the bed as I reluctantly got dressed.

"Okay." Mari had pulled the sheet up to her chest, her hand on my back as sleep pulled down on her eyelids.

I leaned over to kiss her before leaving, fighting every urge to dive back in bed and pull her warm body to me.

"I'll get up early and be here when you wake up," I decided right then, brushing a strand of hair out of her face. "How does that sound?"

A slow, drowsy smile formed on her lips. "That sounds wonderful."

"Good." I cupped her cheek and kissed her again. *This isn't goodbye. Not anymore,* I reminded myself.

"Goodnight, Shadow." Her eyelids finally fell closed, dark lashes sweeping over her cheeks.

"Goodnight." I slowly drew my hand away from her face. "My love."

CHAPTER 23

MARIPOSA

Shadow made good on his promise.

I roused slowly, stretching and intending to roll over in bed —if it weren't for the long wall of muscle blocking my path.

"Good morning." He sounded amused and at ease. Even happy.

"Morning, handsome," I groaned through my stretch.

Shadow set aside the book he was reading and scooted down in the bed to lie next to me, sliding a large hand over my waist to turn me toward him. He pulled me into a breath-stealing kiss, holding nothing back. It caught me off-guard for a moment, just the unexpected boldness of it. But in the next moment I melted, sinking into his affection and soaking up every morsel until we both came up for air. A woozy smile came to my face when we parted, and I swore right then I'd never take his confidence for granted.

"I don't want to get out of bed now that you're here," I admitted, curling into him and nuzzling into his neck.

"Don't you miss the others?" It felt like a loaded question, even though I knew he didn't mean it as such.

"I do." I played with the collar of his shirt, dipping my fingers in to touch his bare skin. "But I'd be lying if I said I wasn't worried about how things are now. With all of them." I frowned, stilling my hand.

"Things will be different when we get back. I'm just not sure how. I worry that...Reap and Gun might have moved on."

"They would never," Shadow said with a low growl. "They'll be overjoyed to have you back, and eager to make things right."

"Even so," I said hesitantly, running my hand down his chest. "I'm still not sure how eager *I* am to make things right."

"If you can forgive me, you can forgive them." Shadow pressed a soft kiss to the bridge of my nose.

"Apples and oranges," I retorted.

"Are you saying you want breakfast now?"

I laughed, leaning my temple against his shoulder. "It's an expression. It means the two situations are completely different."

"I know. I'm just teasing you." His chest shook with his laugh as he pressed a kiss to my hair.

"From the man that never teases?" I said with fake shock. He just pulled me closer, and I happily snuggled into him for a few blissful moments I wished didn't have to end. "I guess we better start saying goodbyes soon, huh?"

"Yeah." He sounded wistful in his agreement.

I leaned up, kissing under his jaw. "It's okay for you to miss this place. They've taken good care of you here."

"They have," he said, resting his chin on my head. "I'm glad I was able to find this place."

"I am too." So much of my worry before coming out to find Shadow had to do with him having basic necessities like shelter and food, let alone a caring community and a doctor to look after him. It put me at ease that he had all of those things the entire time we'd been apart.

"But it's not home," Shadow added, brushing a strand of hair out of my face with his left hand. The motion drew my eye to the new tattoo inside his forearm, the pin-up that looked remarkably like his drawing of me.

"What made you do this?" I asked, tracing the lines of ink with my fingers.

He sighed, lowering his arm. "Missing you."

"Aww." I took his chin in my hands, kissing him deeply.

Shadow returned my kisses with tooth-aching sweetness before elaborating. "When Reaper told me to pack and leave, the drawing of you was the first thing I grabbed. I looked at it all the time when I first got here." He stroked my cheek, eyes warm and loving. "Then I accidentally ripped the paper and I...couldn't stand the thought of not having something to remember you, so I tattooed myself that same night."

I slid my palms around to the back of his neck, pulling him closer to kiss him more deeply. He followed my momentum, rolling us down until I was on my back and he was on top of me. His hands slid between my back and the bed, holding me against his chest as our tongues surged, trying to taste and feel even more of each other. My legs parted to make room for him between them, but he pulled away on the next breath, slow and reluctant.

"We better get going," he said regretfully. "We have a long week of travel ahead of us."

I nodded and allowed him to lift away from me. Most of my things were still packed from the first time I had planned to leave, so I was pretty much ready after a quick shower and change of clothes. Shadow needed some extra time to pack clothes and tattoo supplies, so I told him I'd wait for him downstairs.

I'd barely hit the bottom step when Jen called out from the bar, "So you're leaving us and taking our hero with you, huh?"

I approached her with a smile, grateful for the spread of breakfast and coffee at the bar. "Word travels fast, I see."

"Doc didn't reveal *too* much, but we were able to read between the lines." She smirked.

"Jen..." I started, but she held a hand up to stop me.

"No, no, none of that. This isn't goodbye, just a 'till next time'. Any time y'all come back this way, make sure to stop here. We'd love to have you."

"I owe you big time." I was trying not to get emotional, but my eyes welled up and my throat was tight anyway. "My history with Shadow is...a lot to explain, but I'm glad you were here for him. All of you. You've all done wonders for him."

"Well he literally saved our lives. You did too." Jen held up her arms, wrists still bandaged from her rope burns. "I'm a sucker for a good romance, so I'm glad you came out this way and got your man back."

Shadow came quietly down the stairs a few minutes later, dressed in all black like the silent assassin I knew, but also different. There was clear confidence in his steps, his face lighter and less tense than it usually was. He beamed at me, one hand brushing along my back while the other set his duffel bag on the floor.

"Jen, I have a parting gift for you." He unzipped his bag, pulling out a square case slightly bigger than a lunch box.

"Shadow! Whatever it is, you shouldn't have."

It secretly pleased me that she called him by his real name so easily.

"I insist." He set the case on the bar and opened it, revealing a black handgun inside. "It's the one we've practiced with. I left ammo in the safe too, but you'll need to restock eventually." Shadow gave her a hard look. "You're the best shot here. You shouldn't have anyone bothering you anytime soon, but in case someone does, you should be ready."

Jen's smile wobbled a little. "You have too much faith in me. I cowered like a baby and nearly got dragged away last time."

"No, Jen," he told her kindly. "You're brave. I've seen how you protect everyone here. Those assholes won't be coming for you again. Keep working with Doc, you'll be just fine."

She nodded, blinking away tears as they leaned across the bar to hug each other.

"Oh, uh." Shadow dug into his bag when they released each other and pulled out a stack of books. "Can you make sure Telisha gets these back?"

"You can hand them back yourself!" The pretty librarian herself walked through the dining room, a toddler with a curious stare on her hip. "Thanks, Iv—er, Shadow. I'm kinda mad to lose my tattoo artist, but I guess I'll live," she joked.

"Go see Phil, he's just as good as me," Shadow told her. When she pouted and held an arm out for a hug, his eyes slid to me first.

I snorted and helped myself to coffee and breakfast to allow them their parting hugs and words. Doc came down when we were finishing up, taking a hug from me and a handshake from Shadow.

"Just remember what I told you," the older man said, clapping him on the shoulder.

"I know." Shadow nodded. "Thank you Doc, for everything."

Doc just beamed like a doting father. "You did the hard work yourself, son. I'm proud of you." He handed Shadow a small slip of paper. "That's my colleague's information. She's actually a bit northwest of Four Corners in currently neutral territory, but well worth the visit, should you need it."

We ate our fill, packed up Shadow's bike, and said our final goodbyes. Horus screeched from a fence post in the junkyard, where Shadow's growling engine filled the air as we prepared to leave. I watched the bird sail off, becoming smaller as he flew higher. Aside from when I first came upon this service center, I'd barely seen him. Apparently the sky god was content to be our guide and nothing more.

It was *the right time*, I realized as we began a slow, gentle drive out of the yard. *Just as he said it was.*

I hugged my arms and legs around Shadow, my heart swelling when he released one of the handlebars to rest a gloved hand on my leg. The smile I wore against his back was uncontrollable. For the first time in so long, I felt overcome with happiness. I had Shadow back. Nothing was perfect or completely fixed by any means, but we were on the right track again.

The world flew by us on his motorcycle, the wind whipping as we took winding roads home. We rode hard, but the way back seemed easier than the journey to find him. Maybe I just found comfort in having someone with me, but the long hours in the saddle with Shadow weren't nearly as lonely or painful as being on my little dirt bike. The first couple of days even felt like a vacation. We took scenic roads winding through the southern territories, stopping to sleep at service centers for the night.

Shadow made sure to book us separate rooms to sleep in, but every morning when I started to ask, he told me no. He had the occasional nightmare, but still did not sleepwalk. My hope grew with each passing day, but he wanted a second opinion from Doc's colleague and I'd give him that before broaching the subject again.

The air whipping past us on the bike started to feel different on the fourth day. Humidity turned to dryness. The winter cold hurt more, but didn't seem to cling to me like it did when we were further east. When I saw the faded, discarded Welcome to Texas sign next to the road, the pang of longing and homesickness shocked me. I hadn't considered this place my home in years, or so I thought.

Observant as always, Shadow held me close and squeezed my hand during one of our pit stops. "Do you want to take a detour? Maybe see your old home?" he asked.

I thought about it for a bit, then shook my head. "No. I already know my parents aren't there. There's nothing for me to see here."

"You're sure?" He nudged me and placed a kiss on my temple.

"Yeah, let's keep going."

My parents were out there somewhere, just not here. Absently, I looked to Horus in the sky when we hit the road again, and he spoke to me for the first time in nearly two weeks.

They are not far, daughter. But your instincts are correct.

I swallowed down a hard lump with that knowledge, more questions filling my head. *Does that mean they're together? What instincts, that they're alive?*

Horus didn't provide any more insight, and we rode on like normal. I got nothing from him again until near the end of the day, when we had to be nearly out of Texas and near the Jerriton and New Ireland borders.

I was leaning against the back of Shadow's shoulder, fatigue taking over, when I was suddenly flying over a darkening landscape.

Look, daughter. You must see. Horus' voice in my mind was as clear as my own, as certain as if I had wings outstretched to the sides and eyesight that could spot mice in tall grass.

What am I looking for? It was freaky that Horus just seemed to pull me in whenever he wanted me to see something. Unlike Gunner, who was able to see through him at will.

Look below.

I first saw us—me and Shadow on his bike. Somehow I stayed upright, arms still wrapped around his waist despite no longer being in my own body. Speaking of freaky, watching myself from an outside view had to top the list.

Shadow and I continued to follow the winding road, he seemed none the wiser about my out-of-body experience. My aerial gaze lifted to the horizon ahead of us, where the sun was nearly disappearing behind the mountains.

There.

The shock of it sent me jolting back to my own body, my arms jerking around Shadow as I took a great, gasping breath.

"You okay?" I heard him over the wind whipping past us and felt the squeeze of his hand.

"Stop the bike." I lifted from my seat to yell in his ear, clutching tightly to his leather jacket.

He slowed immediately, pulling us over to the shoulder, then turned around to face me when we stopped. "What's wrong?"

"We have to go a different way," I said, still catching my breath. The ground and sky tilted dangerously in my vision, like the sudden return to land from air had given me vertigo.

Shadow's brow furrowed. "I don't know if there is. We have to go through either New Ireland or Jerriton to reach Four Corners. This road is mostly abandoned—"

"It's not," I insisted. "There's an army a few miles up ahead. I saw them through Horus."

"An army?" Shadow turned more to face me head-on, his face hardening with concern. "How many, could you tell?" It was strangely comforting that he didn't find anything weird about me seeing through the falcon.

"I dunno, thousands." I shook my head. "They stretched all across the landscape as far as Horus could see, forming a long, unbroken line."

"Fuck." Shadow's fist clenched as he realized the severity of this news. "Were they moving? Or camped out?"

"They were moving," I said, my gut churning. "Heading west, toward Four Corners."

CHAPTER 24

SHADOW

We'd be fucked if we got within sight of that army. I cut the engine after pulling over, oppressive silence filling in the space in my head as I tried to think of our next options.

"So we have to head north or south to try to get around them," I mused.

"South wouldn't be good," Mari said. "We'd have to cross into Mexico and could end up captured there too. You never know who border patrol is working for."

"North, then." I stroked my beard, turning my body in that direction. "Into Jerriton."

Mari looked concerned. "How bad do you think it is up there?"

"I'm not sure," I admitted. "The territory only fell under General Tash's control recently, so his hold may not be as well established as New Ireland."

"Sounds like it's our best chance." Mari was looking past me to the horizon, the warm glow of the sunset on her skin slowly fading as dusk approached. "You don't think we're too late, do you?"

"No." I touched her cheek, bringing her attention back to me. "If you saw them only a few miles away, they're not in Four Corners yet. But we have to move fast."

Mari nodded, accepting a quick kiss from me before I turned back around and started the bike up again. *Thank you, Jandro,* I thought to myself as I turned off the interstate, accelerating over the untamed desert wilderness. *You kept my off-road tires on. I owe you, friend.*

The world fell into darkness quickly, with my headlight bouncing over the landscape as the only light source. I had to find a north-bound road at some point to not totally kill my tires, but staying off the road would help us get into Jerriton undetected.

We rode north for a few hours, the cold biting hard at my nose and ears. Mari slid her arms under my shirt for extra warmth, but I could still feel her fingers trembling. As the night wore on, I felt her grip on me loosen from fatigue and knew we had to stop.

She was already nodding off, jerking up when the bike came to a complete stop with nothing but dark desert in all directions.

"Why are we stopping?" Mari mumbled against the back of my shoulder.

"Because you need to rest. I don't need you falling off and becoming roadkill." I swung a leg over to dismount then lifted her out of my seat by her waist. She smiled groggily and I thought back to the moment she told me she liked when I picked her up. "Can you handle unrolling the sleeping bag while I start a fire?"

"Uh-huh," she said with a yawn.

There wasn't much room to lay out anywhere with all the shrubs and rocks surrounding us, but Mari didn't take up much space. Still, she kept shoving rocks and debris out of the way next to the bike to make a bigger sleeping area.

"Are you sure you need that much space?" I teased her, feeding our fire a healthy amount of kindling.

"No, but you do." Finally satisfied, she unfolded my sleeping mat and laid the sleeping bag on top of it.

"Mari." I watched her cautiously. "I'm not sleeping."

"Don't be silly, of course you are." She sat down on top of the sleeping bag and unrolled a blanket, wrapping it around her shoulders. "Come over here and keep me warm."

"Mari, there's no service center around for miles. I can sleep far away, but—"

"And freeze to death? Absolutely not." She stuck a hand out from under the blanket. "Come here."

"You know that's not what I'm worried about." Still, I rose from the fire, now roaring with a healthy blaze as I walked around it to sit next to her.

Mari lifted my arm to snuggle into my side. "How long's it been now?"

"Almost a month, I think?" I let my arm drape over her shoulders as I glanced up, like the glittering night sky would give me answers. "Yeah, about four weeks since I sleepwalked."

The flames danced in Mari's eyes as she looked at me. "And you'd rather risk freezing to death than try *one* night snuggled up with me."

"Yes," I answered quickly. "Because you have much better odds of surviving the night if you sleep alone."

She let out a weary sigh, leaning heavily against my shoulder. "How long, really, until you'll let it happen?"

"I don't know," I admitted, rubbing her arm. Before Doc's therapy, spending a night with her, or any woman, was something I'd never risk again. Now it felt like the final barrier between us, one I was desperate to break through, but not at the risk of her safety. "I think I'll feel better if Doc's colleague tells me the sleepwalking isn't likely to come back."

Mari leaned up, planting a small kiss on my neck. "What's one of your favorite memories from staying at the service center?"

The question wasn't completely out of left-field, but I still gave her a bemused look. She was trying to drum up positive associations to the forefront of my mind, right before sleeping no less. I wondered if this was our new game, instead of saying good morning to each other.

"About a week before you got there, Doc was going to scrap this old Indian motorcycle for parts," I said. "I convinced him not to and was able to get it running."

"You did?"

I nodded. "It was a beautiful little bike by the time I was done restoring it. We were able to trade it for a new chest freezer for the kitchen."

"Look at you." Mari beamed at me with genuine pride. "Jandro will be so happy to hear that."

"Nah. If I tell him details, he'll work himself up over everything I did wrong."

"Oh, whatever." She stretched her legs across my lap and draped the blanket over both of us. "How did it feel to turn that engine and hear it come to life?"

"Amazing." A smile burst onto my face at the memory. I recalled the pulse of elation in my chest when I turned the key and heard the sputter and then the roar, rather than the lifeless clicking sound. "It felt like I brought something back from the dead."

Mari stroked a gentle finger along my jaw, turning my head to bring my mouth to hers. Her lips were cold from the night air and I kissed her deeply, bringing my hand to her cheek to stave off more of the cold.

"How long until we're on the road again?" she asked when one long kiss ended and right before another began.

"Not long." I took another lingering pull from her lips. "It's just a few hours 'til dawn."

Her arms slid under my jacket, pulling her chest flush to mine. "I don't want to sleep alone," she whispered, forehead nudging mine. "We'll be warmer this way too. Do you think you can try tonight? Please?"

"Mari..." I started to shake my head and pull away, but my woman held onto me tightly.

"You trust me?" Her lips skimmed over mine as she spoke.

"You know I do."

"I trust you too, you know." She placed a soft kiss on the bridge of my nose. "I'd love to see you start trusting yourself."

"It's not about that."

"Yes it is, love." Her mouth skimmed up my face to kiss the scar cutting through my eyelid. "You're more in control than you realize."

It was going to happen sooner or later. This leap of faith, this trust I was putting into myself to not harm the woman I loved. I already had a sneaking suspicion that Doc's colleague would just confirm what he'd already told me. The idea of talking to another doctor was a safety precaution more than anything. I trusted Doc and Mari more than any other medical professional anyway.

Mari believed in me, and she was usually right.

Still, it took a long while and an enormous effort to nod my head and breathe out, "Okay."

Her grin was brighter than the fire and she kissed me again. "Don't worry. Just think about that motorcycle you brought back to life."

"I'm going to think of that and a million other things," I admitted. "Because I won't be able to let myself sleep."

Mari's lips drifted up to my forehead. "Try to get a little rest for me. I need you sharp tomorrow."

"I'll try." My eyelids did feel heavy. Her uncanny ability to calm me, plus the heat from the fire, started lulling me into relaxation.

Without another word, Mari unzipped the sleeping bag and we both slid inside.

I WOKE WITH A START, LIKE I ALWAYS DID. THE FAMILIAR jolt of panic flashed through me as I looked around to assess the damage I'd surely caused in my sleep.

But there was none.

I was still zipped snugly into the sleeping bag, Mari bundled up against me with her face in my chest.

"Good morning," she mumbled, jostled awake by all my moving around.

"Morning, sorry to wake you." I smoothed a hand over her hair, overwhelmed by the sheer relief that she was still here, safe and unharmed. With *me*.

"S'okay. We gotta get moving, right?" Mari yawned and groaned as she stretched within the confines of the sleeping bag. "Do you have coffee?"

She was speaking so casually, but this was huge for me. I tilted her mouth to mine, enamored with the taste of her despite the slight dryness to her lips in that moment.

"I did it," I whispered. "I just...slept. With you right here. Without...*using* anything."

Mari smiled, sleepiness pulling her mouth in an adorable, crooked way. "I knew you would."

My mouth pressed to hers, tongue licking out to seek more of her taste. "You have no idea what this means," I choked out with a laugh. "Fuck, I love you so much."

"I love you so much." Her fingers rubbed over my beard, which was growing coarse and longer than I preferred, but she seemed to enjoy touching it. "And this means you've suffered enough. You've worked your ass off to heal, and now it's paying off."

"And it'll be even better once we're home." I still had some lingering doubts that all would be well once we stepped into Four Corners, but as long as I had Mari with me, I didn't care what the outcome with the Steel Demons would be.

"Not much longer." Mari started unzipping the sleeping bag as she sat up, the furrow of concern returning to her eyebrows. "Although I guess that depends on what we find in Jerriton today."

"We'll make it through." I rolled up behind her, hooking an arm around her waist and dropping a kiss to her shoulder. "We snuck into Blakeworth, after all."

"Ugh. If one of us has to play slave again, I will scream."

After coffee and a quick breakfast we hit the road again, or the terrain, rather. We didn't find a road until the sun was high, and I think we were both grateful for a smoother ride again.

Horus offered no confirming or dissenting advice about our change in direction, but we could see him soaring high above us as we rode. I could only hope the gods were invested in our wellbeing enough to not lead us straight to our deaths. Freyja certainly seemed to be, but Mari only had the sky god with her on this trip to find me. Last night was the first I'd seen Horus offer his sight to anyone but Gunner. I didn't know it could be done with anyone else, but there was probably plenty I didn't know about our companion gods.

A few miles outside of the last known border, which had been the Colorado state line, I pulled over to the side of the road and turned to Mari in my seat.

"We're a couple miles out of Jerriton. Can you see anything through the bird?"

"Oh, I don't know." Mari frowned. "I've never tried to see through him. He just kind of pulls me in."

"Can you try?" I gave a light squeeze to her knee. "We'll be going in blind otherwise."

"I don't know how, Shadow."

"Try what Doc did with me," I suggested. "Close off your senses and take some deep breaths. Let your consciousness take a backseat and remember what it felt like to be a bird."

She didn't seem convinced, but gave me a tight nod. "Count me down?"

"Sure." I waited until Mari's eyes closed and she grew eerily still, only her chest moving with steady breaths. "Instead of descending into yourself, you're going to float. Lifting up from your body, higher and higher until you're flying. Ten...nine...eight..."

I counted all the way down to zero and didn't even blink as I watched her. Gunner lost control of his body, twitching and going limp when he went into Horus. Mari's eyeballs moved under closed lids as though she were dreaming, but she held herself upright in the seat, calm and still.

She stayed like that for several minutes and I had no idea if it worked, or if she had just been put in a hypnotic state. How long should I wait until trying to bring her back?

More minutes ticked by and I started growing anxious. I knew Doc's sessions with me lasted roughly a half-hour, but he knew what he was doing. What if this was harmful to Mari's brain?

Just as I was about to touch her, start talking to give her external stimuli to bring her back, her eyes flew open and she drew in a big gasp of air.

"Mari!" My hands shot out to grab her arms and keep her from falling. "Are you okay?"

"Yeah, I'm fine." She brought a hand to her chest, panting like she was out of breath. "I saw, and border security is tight. Their army is well-stocked, just like the one I saw last night."

My chest deflated at that. "So we're dealing with the same thing up here?"

Mari shook her head. "No, not exactly. They're not in a long line."

Her breaths slowing, she focused her gaze on me. "I think...I know how we can get in. There's a...can I get something to draw with?"

"Yeah, left saddle bag." I watched her dig to the bottom where my sketchbook was stashed, a strange kind of excitement building in my chest as she flipped to a blank page and started sketching out long lines. "Got a plan in mind?"

"I do, just give me a second." She paused in her diagram, looking up at me with a smile that was both coy and endearing. "Would you be upset if I said it involved helping people?"

"Not at all." I leaned in and pressed a kiss to her forehead. "Are we going to need a lot of guns?"

Mari's grin grew wider. "We probably will."

"Even better."

I hopped out of my seat and went to load my weapons while waiting to hear her plan.

CHAPTER 25

MARIPOSA

"They have these six towers here, and fenced-off, open areas in between." I pointed them out to Shadow using a pencil on my crude drawing. "The fences converge up here, to these buildings."

"Those are prison yards," Shadow mused, his mismatched eyes carefully inspecting my diagram. "So they have a prison complex right at the border."

"That's what I thought it was," I said. "And what are the chances you think the people in those yards are actually criminals?"

"None. Last time we were here, providing protection to Gunner's uncle, we found out that he kept a lot of his citizens in prison. Women, mostly."

Shadow checked the magazine of yet another gun and inserted the weapon into his holster. He may not have had a Steel Demons cut, but was just as intimidating with a tactical vest loaded with weapons and ammo.

And just as hot.

"So you're planning on a prison break?" Shadow asked as he slapped a reloaded magazine into my little .40 caliber pistol and handed it to me.

"Uh, yeah." He must have caught me staring, and grinned while I blushed. "At the very least, we can create a diversion to move through the territory undetected. And then free some people as a bonus."

"Works for me." Shadow seemed calm overall, if even pleased about going to battle again, but right then his face looked grim. "Will we have to separate?"

I looked down at the drawing, chewing my lip as I tried to think like a strategist. Like Gunner, who I missed with a fierce ache at that moment. We were roughly a day's ride away from Four Corners, but crossing through Jerriton was a huge obstacle we could not afford to fuck up.

The last time Gunner and I talked, which felt like centuries ago, he finally seemed to understand where I was coming from, how I wanted everything to be fixed. Maybe it was odd to have hit me right then, bent over a crude diagram and chewing on the end of a pencil, but the realization was crystal clear—I did forgive him.

Now Reaper, I was less sure about.

"At the beginning, I think we have to," I said in answer to Shadow's question. "Once you start shooting the guards in the towers, I'll run in and cut through the fences. I'll deal with anyone on the ground while they scramble to get more people up in the towers. It's the only way they'll be able to see us in the chaos." My forehead met his as I started to look up at him. "What do you think?"

"It's a good plan, probably the best we can do with just the two of us." Shadow grazed the backs of his fingers over my cheek. "I just don't like the thought of my woman in danger."

"Better get used to it," I snickered. "You're fucking with a biker chick, in case you forgot."

"How could I ever?" Shadow's voice was a low rumble as his fingers wrapped around the back of my neck. His grip was strong, but not overly possessive as he pulled me in for a long, deep kiss. Just as swiftly as he planted it on me, he broke away with a growl. "As soon as you see me come back around, you run like hell and get back on, okay?"

"Yes." The word came out more breathless than I intended, my lips tilting up for more.

Shadow chuckled, indulging me with one more kiss before untangling from me and closing up his compartments. "Let's do this so we can go home."

MY FISTS TIGHTENED AROUND SHADOW'S SHIRT WHEN THE first prison tower came into view. He squeezed one of my hands, a small reassurance before holding his palm out. I handed him the rifle like a Bonnie to her Clyde, and felt grateful for my earplugs when he opened fire.

Shadow was inhumanly accurate with a gun, and it seemed to be thanks to that pale, scarred eye of his. He didn't shoot recklessly, spraying bullets like an action movie hero. He was methodical and precise, firing a single round through the open window of the first tower. The guard on duty fell out of sight, though I couldn't tell if the shot was lethal or not.

We picked up speed, accelerating toward the towers and barbed-wire topped fencing with a roar. I held on to Shadow with one arm while brandishing my gun with the other. Shadow fired at the next two towers along the fence line before a blaring alarm sounded.

He pulled over at the base of the first tower, coming to an abrupt stop. "Go."

I jumped off and ran toward the fence line, the roar of his bike already growing quiet and distant as Shadow peeled off to take out the other towers. Over the constant blaring of the alarm, a broadcasted message rang out through multiple speakers.

"Inmates, get off the yard and back in the building! Get fucking inside now or get shot!"

"Hey, hey!" I yelled and waved my arms at one group of people getting in line to file into a building. They were all dressed in the same matching gray sweats and seemed to be young adults and teenagers.

A few heads turned in my direction, and I pulled out the bolt cutters that I'd stuck in the back of my pants. My gun returned to my holster for the time being while I started cutting through the links in the fence.

Please, please. I wished I could project my thoughts to them, speak directly into their minds like the gods could. *This is your chance. Fight back and escape.*

A bullet hit the dirt next to me, and I rolled, scrambling for cover behind the guard tower. The memory of getting hit in the leg was still fresh, and even though I healed quickly, that kind of pain was something I never wanted to encounter again.

More shots zipped around me, coming from the yard as they blasted off small chunks of concrete from the edges of the tower. Fear started to overwhelm me as the shots intensified, the shouts of the guards growing louder. *I can't do this.*

I must have overestimated my ability to fight like this. Maybe with more backup I could've handled it, but not with just Shadow and me. I was supposed to be covering him, keeping the guards distracted while he took out the towers, but couldn't bring my shaking hands to raise my gun and turn to face what came for me.

See, daughter.

It was a quick flash, under five seconds, but I was in the sky again. I saw the two guards heading for the tower, for me. They left the prisoners in the yard unguarded and I could count how many steps they'd need to reach me. I saw the angles they were coming at me from, and which parts of their bodies were exposed even with bulletproof vests on.

In the next moment I returned to my own body, and knew exactly what to do. There was no time to think, to hesitate. Only to move.

I spun away from the wall, arms outstretched with my weapon raised and fired before my human eyes even settled on my targets. My shot landed in the neck of the first guard and he went down silently. The other guard ducked and changed direction, running for cover. Now I had time, seconds to set up my next shot, and I took it.

He fell dead a few feet away from his partner, the crowd of prisoners across the yard all staring at what just happened. I ran back to the spot in the fence where I began cutting, holstering my weapon and picking up my bolt cutters again. I had the advantage now, but more guards would come, and I never knew when Horus would give me his eyes again.

"Come on!" I yelled, snapping the tool through the thick wire links. "We're breaking you guys out!"

Finally the prisoners quit staring and started running toward me. I cut a hole roughly my own height, and held it aside for people to come through. A young woman at the front of the group hesitated, eying me suspiciously as she held her arms out to the sides to halt the others. "Who the hell are you?"

"We're just trying to get through the territory to go home," I said. "You guys are kept here on orders from the new governor, right?"

"No, some fucking general who invaded us," the woman snarled.

"Oh, even better." I pulled back harder on the cut-away fence, trying to bend the wires back so the opening would stay. "I can't stick around, but freeing you guys keeps the guards distracted while we ride through."

The woman's expression softened but she still didn't usher everyone through. "What territory you from?"

"Four Corners." I bent the chain links back as far as I could, then picked up my bolt cutters and started jogging toward the next yard. "You're all welcome there if you'd like. Good luck," I called back behind me.

The next yard had already gotten all of its prisoners inside, but the two guards were racing across the field to man the tower. I shot them both, I was moving quickly so my hits weren't as accurate. They went down clutching their legs and radioing for backup as I cut through the links on that fence too. Hopefully the people inside could break a window or unlock a door to escape.

Our plan was working. The guards scrambled to refill the tower positions to search for us after Shadow had taken care of them, while also keeping inmates contained. I heard over the radio calls that even contained prisoners were fighting back against their guards. The people could hear what was going on before I ever reached them.

By the time I got to the last yard, there were no guards in sight, only people in gray sweats jumping for joy near the fence line. They cheered when I ran up with my bolt cutters and stood back to give me space.

"I dunno who you are, ma'am, but thank you," said an elderly man with tears in his eyes as he leaned heavily on a cane.

"She's an angel, that's who!" called another man in the crowd.

"Just someone trying to help and get back home." I gave him a weary smile. Cutting this fence was going much slower. My hands were cramping and fatigued from the heavy tool and thick chain links.

"Here, allow me." Another man, about Reaper's dad's age, with silver hair, held a rough hand out through the small hole in the fence.

I handed him the bolt cutters without a second thought, grateful for the rest as he easily sliced through the wires that kept them all caged. When the hole was big enough, everyone stood aside while the most frail and elderly men were helped out first.

"Here, I got you." I grabbed the free arm of the first man who spoke to me.

"Thank you, darlin'," he beamed at me. "Never thought I'd live to see freedom and a beautiful woman in the same day."

"I have to go," I said with a returned smile. "Good luck to all of you."

My bolt cutters were returned to me and I took off running along the perimeter, listening intently for the roar of Shadow's bike. The alarms continued to blare in their repetitive, monotonous screeching. Excited voices of freed prisoners shouted over the panicked orders and frantic radio calls of the guards. A motorcycle the size of Shadow's should have drowned them all out, but I heard nothing.

"Fuck, where are you?" I looked around everywhere, even skyward to see if Horus would lend me his view again. My adrenaline was running too high to get into a hypnotic state, plus there was no time. We had to get the hell out.

"Shadow!" It wasn't smart to call out his name, to draw attention to myself, but panic started riding me hard. If he had been captured or shot, this whole plan was for naught. I could not, *would* not, go on to Four Corners without him, even if I managed to slip through the territory undetected. I had come too far, watched him make too much progress to abandon him now.

"Shadow!"

Something slapped over my mouth, a large hand that was also

pulling me backward behind a small shack just beyond the fence line. My flight response kicked in, trying to jerk free for a moment before I heard a familiar, "It's me, Mari."

Shadow's hand slid away from my mouth and I took ragged, grateful gulps of air. "Where's your bike?" I demanded in a harsh whisper.

"I stashed it and took the towers out on foot," he whispered back. "It was too loud and they would've heard me coming."

"Guess I should have thought of that," I muttered.

"It was still a good plan." Shadow's gloved fingers ran over my arms and sides. "Are you hurt at all? I heard shots early on."

"I'm good." I smiled back at him. "Some of those were mine."

He squeezed my shoulder affectionately. "That's my girl. Ready to go?"

"Yeah."

Our hands clasped together and I followed as he took off in a run slow enough for me to stay on his heels. His bike was stashed inside another shack just outside of the prison's perimeter—an abandoned pump house by the looks of it. We both jumped into the seat, and Shadow handed me his rifle. I squeezed my thighs around him as we peeled away from the prison, keeping an eye out with the rifle, ready for any guards who spotted us.

No one came after us, the alarms and shouts soon fading into nothing as we made our escape. But we weren't out of the woods yet and I kept my grip tight on Shadow's gun, ever vigilant. We didn't know what else waited for us in this hostile territory.

Only an hour after leaving the prison complex behind did I allow myself to relax a little. This stretch of highway seemed long abandoned —covered in gravel, potholes, and discarded belongings that seemed to have fallen off trucks. Rocky hillsides rose up on either side of the road and I kept my gaze lifted for anyone who might try to snipe us from above.

Shadow must have been thinking similarly because out of nowhere, he braked so hard and suddenly that I crashed against his back. "Fuck!"

I looked ahead of us on the road and cursed out my own agreement. "Fuck."

The wind had blown away some debris lying across the road about twenty feet ahead of us, revealing a spike strip underneath. And roughly fifty feet beyond that, a metal barricade cut across our path. Braced on top of the barricade were long black rifle barrels pointed at us, the shooters crouching on the other side of the wall. Armored trucks took up the road behind the shooters at the barricades, more soldiers in camo uniforms covered behind their vehicles with weapons drawn on us.

Fuck it all, we weren't fast enough. The prison staff must have contacted the nearest army base and told them to be ready for us.

"Shadow..."

"Stay behind me," he instructed under his voice. "Just follow my lead. We'll be okay."

But I heard the apprehension in his voice and it only worried me more.

"Drop all your weapons and get off the motorcycle," one of the soldiers commanded through a megaphone. "We'll let you live as long as you follow orders."

Shadow didn't move right away, and I only tightened my grip on his rifle. A sound behind us had me turning to look—three more armored Jeeps drove up behind us, spreading out across the road to block us in. Soldiers opened the car doors and swarmed out systematically, bracing weapons over doors and across the hoods of their vehicles.

"Shadow?"

"Do as they say, Mari." Shadow slowly removed his two handguns from the holsters at his sides, dropped them on the ground, and raised his hands in the air.

"Shadow, we can't."

"We can't die here either," he replied. "We'll figure something out, but we're not in a good position here."

"They'll throw us in that prison!"

"Then we'll throw riots and rebel until we get out." My big, stoic man even tossed a smile at me over his shoulder. "I know my way around a prison, we'll be okay. We already have supporters on the inside."

"Last warning," the megaphone wielder called. "Drop the weapons and step away from the motorcycle, or we *will* open fire."

I knew that if I dropped that gun, it would be the end. Something twisting and turning in my gut told me there would be no getting out for us. No seeing Four Corners or any of my other men again. I just had to decide if it would be better to die within concrete walls and iron bars, or out here on the road, filled with bullet holes.

At least this way, I had Shadow with me.

"I love you," I whispered. "And I'm so fucking proud of everything you've done."

"Mari," he hissed. "Drop the guns, *now*."

"Duck behind the bike and make a grab for yours," I said in reply.

My decision made, I did step away and into the road as ordered, but I did *not* drop my fucking guns.

"Mari!" Shadow yelled, reaching to pull me back behind him, but stopped when I stretched my arms out to either side of me. One hand wielded his rifle, the other my small handgun, pointing at the soldiers blocking our path both in front and behind us. The rifle was heavy and definitely not meant to be shot one-handed. Good thing I didn't plan on holding it for long.

Time seemed to go still for a single beat, neither Shadow nor our enemies believing what I was doing. Then I squeezed the triggers on both guns, opening fire and letting chaos erupt.

Shadow must have finally ducked for cover behind his bike—I wasn't sure, I couldn't see him. I had tunnel vision, hyper-focused on taking down a few soldiers with me, maybe even clearing a path for Shadow to keep going. They must have returned fire, I didn't know. I stood in the middle of the road shooting forward and backwards, all sound in my ears muted and my mind feeling oddly calm.

I did my part, I thought, watching soldiers duck behind their barriers in slow motion. *I saved lives. I healed wounds of the heart and body. I loved more deeply than I ever thought possible. I'm ready.*

I saw men aim their guns and shoot back at me, but none seemed to hit. I was still standing in the road, firing so rapidly that my guns burned hot and my hands ached. I felt nothing but my final desire to do my last bit of good in the world—take out some fuckers who would torture and kill me.

Then the ground swung out from under my feet and slapped me in the face. Heat burned my cheek, and the smell of asphalt and gunpowder filled my nose. I could hear everything now, a cacophony of gunshots and shouting voices. A heavy weight pressed down on top of me, smashing my face and chest down into the road.

"Even for an avenging angel, you're pretty damn ballsy," said a voice near my ear.

I twisted my neck to look up, recognizing the silver hair of the man who helped me cut through the fence.

"What...what?" It was all I could stammer out in my disbelief.

"Let's get off this road, darlin'. Your work ain't done."

He lifted up, allowing me to scoot out from underneath him, but kept an arm around my back as we hurried in a low crouch together to the side of the road. The man practically dragged me behind Shadow's bike, where my man gave me a very disapproving look as he reloaded a gun.

"What happened? How...?" I stared at the silver-haired man, who'd escaped the prison complex with a bunch of older men barely an hour ago. "How did you get out here?"

"Stole some wheels and boomsticks of our own." The man grinned, tilting his head upward.

I followed his gaze to the top of the hills running alongside the road. Nothing was there at first, then a few faces—and guns—popped into view. They fired at the soldiers, most of whom were either dead or retreating. More and more freed prisoners looked over the ledge at us, pumping fists and cheering. All I could do was stare with my mouth open—these people lined the hills as far as the eye could see.

I spotted the young woman from the first yard I freed and she waved at us with a smile.

"My daughter up there," the man nodded at her, "told me y'all were heading for Four Corners, so we figured you'd come this way." He looked at me, a bit amused and patronizing. "Didn't know our angel was on a suicide mission, though."

"I wasn't, I..." My gaze fell to my lap, where my sore, bruised hands shook. Shadow grabbed one of them, squeezing gently and rubbing my palm. "I just knew we wouldn't survive if we let them take us."

"Well, maybe y'all got angels watching over you too." The man held a hand out to Shadow, who clasped and shook it gratefully. "I'm Samson."

"Shadow," my man answered, then tilted his head toward me. "This is Mariposa."

"Mari," I told Samson, holding my own hand out to him. "You saved us. All of you."

"Just returning the gesture in kind." Samson helped us both to our feet with a smile, earning more cheers from the people lining the hills.

Relief swept through me as Shadow and I exchanged a glance, then raised our fists in victory with the crowd.

"There's gonna be more army coming," Samson warned, his expression turning serious. "We'll be happy to escort you out of Jerriton. They won't touch you in neutral territory without orders."

"Come to Four Corners with us," I urged him. "You'll be safe there, everyone will."

"Thank you, but no." The older man shook his head. "Now that we're out, there's more friends and family that need us here."

"Four Corners is yours then," Shadow said. "We're on the brink of war, but will support the people of Jerriton however we can."

"Oh, I'm well aware of the governors playing war games with our lives." Samson crossed his arms. "And let me assure you right now, the people of Jerriton stand with Four Corners."

CHAPTER 26

GUNNER

"This shit is so ugly," Jandro sighed mournfully at the camouflage painted bikes. "And it's gonna double my workload painting them back to normal after this is all done."

"Oh, we're still planning on being here after *all this* is done?" It was like we didn't want to say what was actually happening—war. Fighting for the simple right to live and exist on our own terms.

I sat on the hood of some rusted out car in Dave's garage, where Jandro had been working out of.

"Yeah, I know." Jandro grinned sheepishly as he wiped his hands on a rag. "Can you imagine it? Getting some time off after saving everyone's lives?"

"Yeah..." I let the word trail off, paying attention to the unease in my gut. Saving Four Corners and everyone within it was a big deal, to be sure. But I couldn't shake the feeling there was something more.

What could be *more* than saving thousands of lives? I didn't know. But plenty of other wars had been fought without gods involved. Without uncanny abilities like fast healing and seeing through eyes other than your own. I'd venture a guess that no gods had appeared during any of the major wars throughout history, so why were they getting involved with a bunch of unimportant bikers?

"I know that look," Jandro called from across the shop. "What are your two brain cells telling you, blondie?"

I ignored his ribbing. "What do you think it means?"

"What what means?"

"Reaper can see through the dead now? I used to see through Horus, but now I can't anymore? Hearing voices and obeying commands?" My hands flailed at my sides. "I mean, we've all been kind of *whatever* about gods coming into our lives over the past few months, but now we're on the brink of war and it's just like, hey we got super-human abilities, that oughta help!"

"You picked a hell of a time to have an existential crisis," Jandro scoffed.

"Why now?" I continued. "Why us, of all the fucking people who can actually make a difference in the world? Like, I'm starting to wonder if we're being used for something bigger than us."

"Maybe." Jandro shrugged. "But that kind of stuff might be beyond our scope of things, right?"

"They don't want us to lose, but why does that even fucking matter?" I stabbed my fingers through my hair, releasing a frustrated groan. "If they're gods, why the fuck do they care if Tash lays waste to Four Corners? If they're above this petty human shit, why are they even here?"

"Dude." Jandro shook his head. "You need to chill the fuck out. The last thing we need is your head exploding, double-brain-celled as it may be."

"Actually I think it's a perfect time to freak out, I've been fucking chill all this time." I pressed the heels of my palms into my eyes. "To be honest, I don't know how Reaper's seeing through the dead even helps us. It's been over three weeks and there's still no sign of Mari—"

"She'll come back." Jandro's voice dropped to a growl, all humor gone. "She will. She has to."

"After how me and Reap treated her, I don't blame her if she's just gone." I sighed, closing my eyes with my palm against my forehead.

I felt so heavy with regret and guilt over not listening to her. Especially with this foreboding sense that gods were using us for something beyond saving people and ending senseless violence. The outcome of this war was important to them, and fuck me if I could figure out why.

"I'm going for a ride," I muttered, sliding off the car hood and heading for the open bay door.

"Careful out there," Jandro called.

"I know, *Dad*."

We'd already seen glimpses of scouts creeping in closer from Blakeworth and Jerriton. After Slick and Jandro got ambushed, these fuckers just seemed to get bolder. They stayed in neutral territory for now, but tiptoed closer to our borders with each passing day.

One of General Bray's men even shot down more drones coming from Tash's direction. They didn't carry weapons or explosives, but the cameras on them had already been wiped by the time we inspected them. They must have programmed to send back any images they captured and then delete the storage.

Shit like that made me feel like we were cavemen, fighting with sticks and spears against guns and bombs. Reaper was optimistic about his newfound ability, but it was still limiting in my view. T-Bone's raven could provide us with an aerial view to a point, but his bird didn't have nearly the eyesight Horus has. We were still limited, disadvantaged.

And war was coming for us within a matter of weeks, if not days.

This leisurely ride around the territory could very well be my last, so I needed to make it count.

My bike was already painted to blend with the landscape, and I physically cringed as I got on. Jandro was right about them being ugly.

I took off with no destination in mind, just following where the road led me. The landscape was beautiful, turning a golden-orange with the late afternoon sun. I wished to be able to enjoy it, but everything just felt fucking wrong.

Mari wasn't here. The absence of her grew vast and overwhelming with every passing day that she wasn't here. How was I supposed to figure out how to win a war without my reason for everything by my side? I hadn't been able to think straight since she came home from the hospital that night, all the hurt and anger on her face upon seeing Shadow's empty room. How I was supposed to strategize and inspire our army to victory when I'd let my own world crumble before my eyes?

The beauty of my surroundings might as well have been an ash-covered wasteland. It was going to become exactly that in a matter of weeks, anyway.

I reached a bend in the road and turned around, heading back to the city. Less than a mile on my way back, the sky began to darken, like night was falling or a storm had started to roll in. But the sky remained clear of clouds and dusk was still hours away. It simply got *dark*.

A chill ran over my skin, all my hair follicles raised at the cold, heavy presence in the air.

"What's happening?" The words were lost, whispered under the roar of my engine, but *something* answered.

AHAHAHAHAHAAAA! HAAAA-HAAAHAHAHAHA!

I nearly lost control of the bike with how hard my head rang. It felt like something was loose inside my skull and rattling around. Pain exploded behind my eyes, my temples throbbing like they were being crushed in a vice. The laughter was unhinged, maniacal and wild like the Joker from the old Batman cartoons. And it would not stop.

HAHAHAHAHAHAHAAAAAA!

"Stop, stop!" I slapped a hand to the side of my head, the sensation of wetness immediately coating my palm. I pulled my hand away to see the smear of blood that came from my ears.

Gotta get back...warn them. My own thoughts were drowned out by the nonstop, crazed laughing in my head. It felt like someone else had taken up residence in my mind and was shooting up everything with a machine gun, an invader laughing with victory over newly claimed territory.

I pushed the bike hard, accelerating to the machine's limit as I hunched over it and prayed I wouldn't lose control at such high speed.

I'm going to die, I realized as black dots multiplied in my vision. My head hurt so fucking bad, I wanted to smash my forehead between the handlebars for some relief. I couldn't feel my hands or feet, only pins and needles, like they'd fallen asleep. *No, no. They have to know...have to...reach them.*

AWW. ARE YOU DONE ALREADY?! HAAAAAAHA-HAHAHAHA!

"Get out." I gritted my teeth with what little of my strength remained. The outskirts of the city were just a few hundred feet away. I could barely see the buildings but I had to keep going, had to get in sight of someone, anyone to call for help.

And do what?

Was it my own voice or the thing inside my head that asked the question so cynically? Did it even matter? I was moments away from death, and if this thing destroying my mind was what was coming for us, then we were all fucked.

Between the numbness and pain shooting off from my skull throughout my whole body, I felt the motorcycle lean dangerously to one side. And I knew I didn't have the strength to pull it back up.

I'm so sorry, Mari. Sorry Shadow, about everything. I wish I got to make it right.

The road hit me with a force that could have turned my skeleton to Jello. And then I felt nothing. No ground, no pain. The laughter was gone, and I both hated and loved how peaceful it felt. I didn't want to open my eyes and face the reality that I was dead.

Look, son.

The voice was masculine, warm and calming like my grandfather's had been. I'd never heard it before, but recognition flooded through me as I dared to open my eyes.

Horus?

I did not abandon you. She just needed to see.

I looked, and the landscape below me was vast. A surge of wind carried me upward, floating northeast over the stretch of road that looked like a thin black stripe from this high up. Gone was the darkness that had fallen when I first heard the laughing—everything looked beautifully normal.

Is Mari okay? Is she coming back? My thoughts raced frantically once I realized that Horus had lent me his eyes again. I felt the tether to my human body like a lifeline—going back would be as easy as a simple pull.

Look and see, Horus instructed, sounding oddly amused.

I flew closer, my gaze following the length of the road cutting through the landscape. At first I only saw movement, dark specks like ants from far away, inching closer. They had to be at least five miles out, and Horus beat his wings to fly us closer, as if sensing my urgency.

Is it her? Is it them?

If I hadn't already left my body, I would have once the details came into focus. A single motorcycle with two riders. A big hulk of a man driving, and a woman with long brown hair sitting behind him.

The laughter ringing through my head was my own now, elation and relief filling me up so completely, I didn't care if I was dead. Mari was back, she was safe.

As intense as the euphoria was, the duration was brief. That thing laughing and taunting me in my head was gone for now, but would it come back?

I hovered over Shadow and Mari in Horus's body, not wanting to take my eyes off of them for a single moment. As they got closer, I saw Mari wipe at her ear, blood trailing down her neck. She leaned forward in her seat, inspecting the side of Shadow's head where he too was bleeding.

That was both comforting and completely unnerving.

I waited until they were less than a mile out from Four Corners before making the return back to my own body.

"Owww…"

My head pounded like a drum, but nothing was rattling inside anymore. I blinked several times, focusing my dulled human vision on the clear blue sky above me, where I'd just been a moment ago. After a quick extremities check and finding that my fingers and toes were still attached, I rolled painstakingly up to a seat.

"Fuck, nope. Too fast." The world spun a circle around me and I promptly laid back down. Staying on my back, I gingerly tested bigger movements of my limbs. Ankles, wrists, knees, and elbows were all intact, albeit sore as hell.

A rumbling purr grew louder, that comforting sound spurring movement into my body again. But it was nothing compared to what I heard next.

"Gunner? Fuck, it's Gunner! Stay there, I'm coming!"

The sound of her voice was so fucking sweet, I wanted to cry. It felt like I hadn't spoken to her in years.

"Hey, baby girl," I said to the quickly approaching footsteps, and drew in a sharp breath when Mari's beautiful face hovered over me.

"What happened, did you crash?" She touched a hand to my forehead, the other moving swiftly over my abdomen, then arms and legs.

"Did you hear it too?" I reached up with one hand to touch the drying blood on her ear.

"The laughter? Yeah, that was nuts. But we'll worry about that later, let me make sure you're okay."

"I'm fine," I insisted, hardly daring to blink in the off-chance she was a mirage, or my head trauma making me hallucinate.

Mari looked the same, but something had changed. Maybe her cheekbones were a little more prominent like she'd lost weight. Her mouth seemed to be pressed a little tighter as she examined me for injuries. Her eyes were definitely sharper, harder. More ruthless. I'd find out eventually what happened, but for now, all that mattered was that my girl was back.

"I'm fine, baby girl, really." My fingers rested on her cheek, thumb trailing over her lips to her chin, turning her face so she'd look at me.

Mari's gaze stole my breath, lower lip wobbling and sharp, ruthless eyes filled with unspilled tears. "Gun..." She reached for my face with a shaking hand, pushing my hair back and touching her fingertips to the trail of blood under my ear.

"Fuck, it's so good to see you." I pressed up, leaning into her without thinking. The moment I remembered and halted, she closed the distance herself, slamming her lips to mine with a ferocity that released just as much pent-up longing as I'd been holding onto for weeks.

More elation and relief filled me as my mouth clumsily, desperately sought out her taste. I'd been starved, wasting away to a husk, and she breathed precious life back into me. I almost thought I was flying again but I was here, right here with her.

"I love you," I said between desperate sips of air. "Fuck, I'm so sorry. About everything."

Mari pulled away slowly, her head turning toward the man behind her. Shadow looked just as I remembered, massive and imposing as he stood guard on the side of the road. With Mari's help, I climbed gingerly to my feet and walked over to him without another word spoken.

Shadow stopped looking down the length of the road and regarded me with a blank expression, like he always did.

"Hey Shadow. I'm sorry." He didn't look eager to shake hands, so I stuck my hands in my cut pockets. "Reaper made the wrong call, and I was wrong to follow his lead. Emotions were running high and we were all panicking, but that's no excuse. You're one of us. You belong with the Steel Demons and we should have treated you fairly, brother."

A sigh deflated my chest. I had imagined what I would say to Shadow if I ever saw him again, but it all went out the window. I could only speak to what I honestly felt.

"We made a bunch of bad decisions that hurt both you and Mari. This whole thing was one-hundred percent our fault. I can't speak for Reaper, but I am so incredibly sorry. If it comes to a vote, you have my word that I will advocate for your return." I swallowed. "If that's what you want."

Shadow's expression didn't change as I spoke, but his eyes flicked to Mari when I was done. I didn't dare peek behind me at what she was doing, but Shadow's hand stretched out in front of us a moment later.

"It's forgiven," he said quietly. "I accept your apology, Gunner."

A breath whooshed out of me as I clapped my hand firmly to his. "Thank you. Welcome back, brother."

CHAPTER 27

MARIPOSA

I almost didn't let Gunner drive himself into town. That crazy laughing, combined with the ear bleeding, meant some serious damage had been done to the inner ear. Shadow and I felt fine, but it could have affected everyone differently. Only when Gunner demonstrated to me that he didn't have vertigo or other symptoms did I allow him to get back on his bike.

"Ride straight to the hospital," I told him, climbing on behind Shadow. "We'll meet you there."

"Damn, I love hearing you boss me around again." Gunner grinned before his lips twitched and went serious again. "Should I let Jandro and Reap know you're back?"

I hesitated before answering, locking my hands together on Shadow's stomach as I rested my head on his back.

"Just head straight to the hospital so we can all get checked out," I repeated. "I'll see them at home."

Gunner jerked his head down in a nod and took off, his engine roaring.

Shadow squeezed my hands once before starting up his bike. "Are you nervous about seeing them?"

I didn't want to be. It didn't seem like there was a reason to be nervous. *Reaper should be nervous to see* me, *for fuck's sake.*

"A little," I admitted, my lips against the back of Shadow's shoulder. "I just...don't know how they're gonna react."

"They'll be happy," he assured me before returning both hands to his grips.

I had hoped seeing familiar faces like Rhonda and Dr. Brooks would ease me into being ready to see Reaper again later. But I had no such luck.

The moment we walked through the hospital front doors, the front desk clerk jerked her head up. "Mari! You're back!"

"Hey Natalie," I greeted as she grabbed her handheld radio—the best way to communicate over distances these days—and reported into it. "Dr. B, we've got Mari and Shadow back, if you can believe it! Same symptoms, blood from the ears."

Dr. Brooks' voice crackled over the speaker a moment later. "Thanks, Nat. Send 'em in."

"Exam room five, Mari," Natalie relayed to me.

I thanked her and led Shadow down the hall that way, noting that it was one of the biggest exam rooms in the hospital. Knocking at the door to announce us, I walked in, unsurprised to see Reaper, Jandro, and Gunner, all having their ears examined by Dr. Brooks and two medics.

Hades and Freyja were in the room too, sitting calmly against the far wall.

"Mari, welcome back!" Dr. Brooks beamed at me as he pulled the otoscope from Reaper's ear and threw the disposable tip away. "Your sabbatical was enjoyable, I hope?"

"Uh..."

I couldn't pull my gaze away from Reaper, who stared at me wide-eyed, like I was a ghost. The Steel Demons president was still strikingly handsome but looked...awful. His eyes were bloodshot and rimmed with dark circles. His cheeks looked more sunken in, like he'd lost weight. And the smell of his clove cigarettes filled the room.

Jandro unfroze from his stupor first, pulling away from the medic to approach me and wrap me in a crushing hug.

I slid my arms around his broad back, letting myself lean into his strength. "I'm sorry," I whispered, only for him to squeeze me tighter.

"I'm so glad you're back, so glad you're okay," he rapidly muttered, his breaths tight. "Thank the gods, all of them. Jesus, him too."

Jandro's grip finally loosened on me with my tired laugh, and he immediately attacked Shadow with a violent, leaping bear hug that sent Shadow stumbling back a few steps.

"And holy shit it's good to see you again, big guy."

Shadow not only humored him with a returned hug, but actually lifted Jandro off the floor with a throaty chuckle. "Missed you too, Jandro."

"Okay, now you're just embarrassing me. Put me down, asshole."

Dr. Brooks turned to me with a sheepish grin as Shadow placed Jandro back on the floor. "Should I leave you all alone for a bit?"

"Yeah, if you could, thanks." I pointed to my ear. "I think we're okay, but just to be sure—"

"Haven't found anything alarming yet, but we'll come back when you're ready." The doctor patted my arm and left the room, the medics following after him.

The door clicked softly closed and I was left alone with my men.

All of my men.

Shadow's presence at my back was like a shield, impenetrable and safe, while it was Reaper in front of me who I still felt unsure of. Fortunately for me, he looked just as unsure, and seemed content to hang back and say nothing.

I approached him first, slowly, as I would a cornered wild animal. He remained frozen stiff as I opened my arms to the sides and placed them around him in a loose hug. The contact seemed to shock life into him, a gasping breath leaving his lungs as his hands tentatively rested on my back.

I hugged him a little closer and he returned my gentle squeeze, thankfully not escalating to anything more. I wasn't sure if I could handle a kiss or an ass-grab from him yet. Before Shadow and I walked into this room, I wasn't sure if I still wanted to see him at all.

But the hug felt good, and the ache in my chest loosened. It was a first step I was willing to take, as long as he was respectful of my pace.

Reaper's cheek brushed against mine, seeking permission for a kiss. I took that as a cue to end the hug, stepping off to the side until he and Shadow faced each other head-on.

Reaper didn't look wounded at my rejection and released me without issue. A few tense seconds passed while the two men stared each other down, the Steel Demons president and the man he exiled. This time it was Shadow waiting to see how Reaper would react, the tension palpable on both of them.

Finally Reaper stepped forward, extending his hand. "I owe you one hell of an apology."

Shadow didn't answer, nor did he accept Reaper's hand. His mismatched eyes only flicked to Reaper's hand and then back up to his face as he continued to wait. The room was dead silent, but inside I was cheering. *Don't give him an inch. You deserve more,* I thought.

Reaper blew out a long breath. "I was wrong to exile you without properly considering the situation. We could have come to a different solution, like Mari had suggested at the time." He cocked his head toward me. "I was selfish and short-sighted to ignore you. I made you both suffer, and neither of you have any obligation to forgive me. But I see now how wrong I was and I'm deeply, deeply sorry."

While Shadow considered his words, my fingernails bit into my palms. Part of me wanted to hug him again—properly this time, as my husband. As I watched Shadow accept his outstretched hand with a curt nod, I almost did. My hands even swung forward a tiny distance, but I drew them back.

The wound he caused was still there, a raw and vulnerable sensation in my body. It was healing, slowly. But these apologies had only slowed the bleeding. The hurt would need diligent, consistent care before it healed. And I still didn't know if he'd be patient enough to stick around long enough for that to happen.

"Thank you," I said softly and then, ready to move on for the moment, opened a cabinet to pull out a pair of gloves. "Now that that's out of the way, did we *all* hear crazy laughter and get bloody ears?"

"Felt like my head was getting bludgeoned from the inside," Jandro offered up.

The others nodded their agreement. "Thought I was a goner for sure," Gunner added softly.

So it was the same for all of us. I too felt that rattling, slamming pain inside my head and wondered if it would be our end right before we reached home. Shadow and I had been riding when it hit us, and he didn't want to stop and risk injuring us further. Somehow we both managed to stay on the bike until it stopped, and soon after that was when we found Gunner.

"And everyone feels okay now?" I took a spare otoscope from its hook on the wall and added a fresh tip to it, receiving nods from everyone in the room. "Did anyone aside from us experience this?"

My gut knew the answer even as the guys looked at each other before answering.

"I was just down the hall from here, visiting Slick," Jandro said. "He and his nurses weren't affected at all."

"Slick?" I repeated, staring at him. "Stephan? What happened to him?"

"Gunshot. He's fine." Jandro rubbed his eyes then pinched the bridge of his nose with a sigh. "It's a long story, *Mariposita*, but he's okay."

"I'll have to visit him later."

Jandro smiled tiredly. "He'd love that."

Reaper cleared his throat. "I was in the conference room with my dad and some lieutenants. I was the only one hearing it and freaking the fuck out."

"So we can safely assume it is just us." I turned around to find the ancient, penetrating stares of Hades and Freyja across the room. "Those of us who've heard the gods."

"Hades." Reaper regarded the dog cautiously, more so than I'd ever noticed before. He seemed almost afraid to touch Hades now. "Is there anything you can tell us about this?"

The time is nearly here.

Everyone in the room heard, as evident from their wide-eyed reactions. The chance of Hades answering a question always seemed slim, but he did not hold back now.

"The time for what?" Reaper asked.

The confrontation that will determine the fall or survival of all. Gods included.

My men and I all looked at each other, disbelief and worry settling over us with a heavy weight.

"That laughing sound, that pain, we all felt like we were about to die," I lowered to a crouch on the floor, coming to eye level with Hades, "was it another god?"

Freyja stretched, her back arching as her curved claws extended.

It is like us, but different, she answered. *We do not know what name or face it takes, but it is a human concept that has personified and taken form.*

"What is that concept?" Shadow asked the question on everyone's mind.

Chaos. The reply came from Hades. *Senseless violence. And the destruction of everything in existence.*

I DID A PRELIMINARY CHECK ON ALL THE GUYS' EAR CANALS, then let Dr. Brooks check over them and me more thoroughly. By the time he cleared us, I was more than ready to go home.

Who was I kidding? I'd been ready to go home that first day I followed Horus into the great unknown. But every minute of that journey was worth it to have us all back under one roof. Even Reaper, as shaky as my trust in him still was. His presence too, felt comforting and *right* in our home.

"You probably know we're all dying to hear everything." Jandro cupped my hands as we walked inside, joy and relief washing over me at the sight of the familiar walls and fixtures. "But what do *you* need right now?"

"Hmm, excellent question." I pondered for a moment while letting my gaze bounce all over the familiar touches of our home—things I didn't even know I'd miss, like the bronze sculpture next to the stairs, and the throw pillows on the couch.

"A bath," I decided at last. "And then food, and then cuddles and a long night of sleep."

"You got it." Jandro kissed my forehead. "But tomorrow you and Shadow are telling us everything, deal?"

"Deal," I agreed, tilting my face up for a real kiss. "Fuck, I've missed you *guapito*.."

"*Bonita*, missing doesn't even come close." He wrapped me in a tight hug, kissing me deeply. "Even before you took off, shit wasn't right. It was just...wrong not having all of us here."

Gunner squeezed past us right then, sending back a lighthearted smile. "I'll get the tub filled for you, baby girl."

"Thank you, Gun." A pang cut through my chest. Reaper was usually the one I took baths with. Things still weren't all better, but I hoped they would be soon.

I *did* want Reaper back. I wanted to believe he truly saw how wrong he'd been and felt remorseful. I just...couldn't yet.

He and Shadow did seem to be getting along fine, though. The door leading out to the garage was slightly ajar, and I heard them both tending to the bikes and unpacking supplies.

"You want a different bedroom?" Reaper asked gruffly. "We can trade, if you want."

"I'm okay with keeping it, but maybe ask Mari," Shadow answered. "If she's comfortable being in there, I can just rearrange the furniture to make it feel different."

"Sure."

Reaper sounded anything but sure about talking to me again, and guilt sliced through me at the uncertainty in his voice. Once so confident and self-assured, the Steel Demons president had nearly lost everything and couldn't seem to find his footing again. With the chaos and senseless violence to come, he *needed* to be able to lead.

I got my towel and headed for the bathroom with the now-filled tub of deliciously hot water, undressing once the door closed.

"He needs *me*," I said aloud as I stepped into the water. "But what about what *I* need?" My chuckle echoed off the bathroom walls at this conversation with myself. Maybe that laughing, chaos god had shaken some things loose up there.

"If he's still the man I fell in love with," I muttered, sliding my legs through the water, "he knows I'll need time to let this go. And he's strong enough to carry us all through whatever comes next."

The longer I soaked in the tub, the smell of spices and marinated meat wafting in from the kitchen became stronger and more decadent. I scrubbed and rinsed off when I couldn't stand it anymore, then quickly toweled off and pulled on a robe to join my men in the kitchen.

"There she is." Jandro beamed from across the counter, steadfastly chopping a head of lettuce. "Hope you're in the mood for tostadas."

"I'm in the mood for anything you serve on a plate." I ran a hand across the back of Shadow's shoulders, who was already seated and scooping up the remains of his tostada with his tortilla shell. His hair was damp and he smelled freshly showered. I pressed a kiss to the corner of his mouth before moving on to Gunner.

"How was your bath?" My golden, beautiful man leaned back and tilted his lips up, a different question in his sky-blue eyes.

"Wonderful." I planted a chaste kiss on his lips, not wanting to rub our affection in Reaper's face, who appeared hyper-focused on his own food and whiskey in front of him.

"Shadow was just saying he was restoring bikes out at the service center he was at." Jandro waved his chopping knife at him in a mock threat. "Trying to put me out of business, homie?"

"Like you even have a business," Shadow taunted back.

Gunner and I nearly choked on our food laughing, and even Reaper chuckled at Jandro's open-mouthed, exaggerated horror.

"Out!" Jandro pointed the knife out the window to the backyard. "Get out of my house. You're sleeping with the chickens tonight."

"Mari will come out with me. Would you do that to her?"

"Don't drag *me* into this!" I shrieked, swatting Shadow's arm.

The jokes, the food, the stories—all of it was cozy, blissful normalcy for the next hours. Even Reaper was not completely sullen and silent, making playful jabs at Jandro and laughing occasionally. I couldn't tell if it was intentional on the others' part or it just happened, but as dinner wound down and the guys dispersed, Reaper and I ended up in the kitchen alone together.

"I'll wash those. You should rest." Reaper placed a light touch on my waist, but otherwise gave me space in front of the sink.

"It's okay." I gave him a tight smile over my shoulder, but found myself feeling bashful at how intensely he looked at me. "Gives me something to take my mind off looming chaos and destruction, you know?"

"Right," he said with a forced scoff, but stayed hovering behind me.

I returned my attention to washing the dishes, unsure of what else to do under his heavy gaze. A few agonizingly long seconds passed, and it seemed like neither of us could handle the tension any longer.

"Reaper—" I started to turn to him.

"Mari—" He said my name at the same time, reaching for my hand. "Go ahead," he urged with a small nod of his head.

"No, you." I brushed my hand alongside his, my heartbeat accelerating at the contact. "I'm...not even sure what I want to say."

Reaper pulled in a deep breath, his fingers curling around mine for a loose, gentle hold. "Whatever Shadow needs, I'm willing to help. I'll listen to you, and to him. I know it's not worth much right now, but you have my word." His grip tightened on my hand just slightly. "And I have been taking the consequences to my actions into account since realizing how wrong I was. Not just in personal matters, but everything."

I listened with rapt attention, watching his full lips move and seeing the sincerity in his eyes as he spoke. I swallowed, nodding as my pulse stabilized just slightly.

"Thank you for saying that."

My fingers stretched for release, the heat from him too intense, and he removed his grip quickly. I wrung my hands in front of me instead, dropping my gaze from his.

Who am I? I used to have no problem standing up to him, telling him exactly what I thought with no filter. I didn't recognize this meek, insecure person I turned into, only in front of him.

He hurt me and I'm still licking my wounds.

"Wait," I said just as Reaper was about to turn away.

He spun back around, hope bright in his green eyes. "Yes?"

"I..." My throat clammed up and I forced out breath before trying again. "I...haven't given up...on us. I just—I just need time. I don't want to be angry at you anymore, it's just..."

"It's okay, Mari." He returned to stand directly in front of me, feet nearly touching mine. "This is on me to fix." Reaper reached for one of my hands tentatively again, allowing plenty of slack for me to pull away if I wanted to. "It's on me to earn your trust again. To—" His voice cracked and he swallowed. "To win back your love again."

My next breath released a little more of the painful ache in my chest, and I lightly squeezed his fingers. "One day at a time, right?"

"Absolutely." Reaper smiled and sent my heart fluttering again. He was always so broody and serious, I forgot how beautiful his genuine smiles were. "For now, I'm just happy you're home safe. And that you're talking to me again."

"Me too."

I kept still as he leaned down slowly, giving me every opportunity to move or stop him. But I had no desire to. I even lifted my chin slightly, so his kiss could land on my forehead.

It wasn't much, and he didn't try for more. But that small, sweet gesture took me one step closer to healing.

To forgiving.

CHAPTER 28

SHADOW

"Come in," I said to the knock at my door, setting down the pieces of my tattoo machine.

The door swung open to show Reaper standing hesitantly in my doorway. "Hey. Mari said she's fine with this room, given that, you know, it changes up a little." His eyes swept over my furniture. "Which I can see you've already done."

"It wasn't difficult," I said, leaning away from my desk. "Jandro and I did it in an afternoon."

The desk had now been pushed against the opposite wall as before, just below the window. It worked out better this way. I liked using natural light when I sketched tattoos. My bed, dresser, and side tables had all been shifted to different walls and configurations too. It felt like a completely different room from before, one that I hoped Mari would feel safe spending time with me in.

"Good. Great." Reaper leaned a forearm against the door jam. "And we can still trade rooms later, if Mari ever changes her mind."

"Sure." I watched him, his body language curious to me. "I'm sure she knows that."

"Yeah." Reaper hovered in my doorway, not entirely comfortable, but in no rush to leave.

"Was there anything else, president?"

"Oh! Yeah." He snapped his fingers. "I swung by the seamstress today. We got you a cut and she's going to embroider all your patches, matching the original designs. You'll be properly covered by the end of the week."

"Uh, thank you, president." I couldn't hide that I was taken aback. "So, you're not putting it to a church vote?"

"Nah." Reaper shook his head. "It's not club business. It was—" He ran a hand over his jaw, pulling in a deep breath. "It was my foolish and short-sighted actions that led to your exile. The club's got nothing to do with it, this was my error." His hand dropped to his side as he leveled a heavy gaze on me. "I'm just trying to make things right."

"Reaper, you don't have to..." I stood abruptly from my desk, feeling like this conversation needed a better setting than my bedroom. "Is anyone else home?"

He looked over his shoulder, arm still propped up in my doorway. "Don't think so. Why?"

I angled my head toward the kitchen. "Want to have a drink?"

A smirk crossed his face and he thumped the wood of my door frame. "Hell yes I do."

Moments later, we were seated next to each other at the breakfast bar, each with our own glass of whiskey and the bottle between us. The house was quiet, with only the clucking and occasional squawk from Jandro's chickens in the backyard.

"I never blamed you for exiling me," I said to pick up where we left off. "I was never angry at *you*, Reaper."

"Doesn't change that it was wrong." He shifted his glass in a sunbeam on the counter, watching it throw light reflections everywhere. "Mari was pissed at me, and rightfully so."

"I had no idea." I turned my own glass, the amber liquid sliding around. "That everything was so bad here. I thought you would all just...move on like I was never here."

Reaper shook his head, throwing back his whiskey in one gulp before slamming it down and pouring another. "Even before I made you leave, I knew Mari would be pissed for a while. She fought me on it every step of the way. But I just..." His palms flopped to the countertop, staring at his whiskey like it had suddenly become unappetizing. "The truth of it is, I wasn't thinking of anyone but myself. I told myself and anyone who would listen, that it was for her. Her safety and wellbeing, but really, it was just me grasping for control. And you, her, the other guys," he sighed, "you all got caught in the crossfire of my selfishness."

I sipped on my whiskey to let his words sink in. "I appreciate you saying that. It still wasn't wrong for you to be concerned about her safety. If you still are—"

"I'm not." Reaper shook his head, tight-lipped. "Not when it comes to you being with her."

"I still am," I admitted. "I've got a better handle on my sleepwalking now, but the nightmares will probably never fully go away. I want measures in place so she can get away from me if something happens."

"We'll think of something." Reaper rubbed his chin. "Jandro can probably rig a panic button or whatever. You've got us supporting you, man."

"Thank you." I polished off my whiskey, my anxiety releasing its grip on my chest as the liquid heat made its way to my belly. "I mean it, Reaper. Thank you."

The president inclined his head, peering at me with an odd smile. "You know why I trust her with you? The real reason?"

I just stared back at him, unsure of what he was getting at.

Reaper's smile grew, eyes on his whiskey as he swirled it around. "I saw what you did to that guy who shot her."

My eyes narrowed, confused. "You mean...at the service center?"

Reaper nodded, biting his lip like he knew some tantalizing secret. "I saw when he had the gun pointed at her head. And then you ran out there so fucking fast and silent, like a black blur. Well, a shadow." He laughed, bringing the glass of whiskey to his lips. "I saw you turn the guy's head into raw hamburger meat. Skull and brains flying everywhere, it was beautiful."

"How?" I demanded, equally perturbed and fascinated. "Through Horus?"

"No." Reaper downed his glass. "Through the eyes of a dead man on the porch."

"A dead man?" I repeated. Then it hit me. "Hades?"

"Yeah." He scoffed like he couldn't believe it himself. "Seems he was waiting for the perfect moment to show me that little trick."

"You can see through the dead," I said, mostly to cement the reality for myself.

"And what I saw was you," Reaper pointed at me, "unleashing hell to protect the woman you love. Your wife."

My wife. A warmth spread through my belly that had nothing to do with the alcohol.

"I barely remember doing it," I admitted. "I saw he was about to shoot her and it was like instinct took over."

"Even better." Reaper leaned back in his seat. "I'm no scientist, but in my opinion, that means even at the subconscious, cellular level, despite all this other shit you've got going on, you'll do anything to protect Mari." He reached over and slapped my shoulder. "That is why I'm not worried about her safety with you."

"Thanks, Reaper." I understood and appreciated what he meant, but I was still stuck on the whole *seeing through the dead* thing. "Do the others know? About your...sight?"

"Yeah, we were gonna tell you and Mari once you all got settled in." Reaper tilted back on the rear legs of his barstool.

"Have you...used it again?"

He nodded, looking at nothing straight ahead of him. "Jandro and Slick got ambushed last week and I looked through some of the dead at that scene. Blakeworth guys, not ours." He let out a weary sigh. "It doesn't feel right to look through our own men after they've passed. Like it's invasive and they deserve to rest."

"Who did we lose?"

"Brick, his nephew, couple others." Reaper scrubbed a hand down his face. "Jandro had to leave them to bring Slick back to the hospital. It'll be suicide to get the others' bodies, as much as it sickens me to leave them out there."

"We'll still hold memorials for them. We can do it here at the house."

Reaper nodded. "Governor Vance wants to put a memorial plaque in the City Hall building. Their names and the date and everything."

"That's nice of him to do."

"Yeah, he's a good guy."

Silence hung over us for a few moments, in this rare display of... could this be called friendship?

I didn't know if I'd ever considered Reaper a friend before. In the years I spent in the club, he and I never shared a drink just between us like this. I was his assassin, and he was my president. I knew my role, my usefulness. He had my complete respect and trust as a leader, but it was Jandro who I turned to when ordinary things confused me. Likewise, Reaper treated me with the same cordiality as everyone else in the club, but I wasn't constantly rubbing shoulders with him like Jandro and Gunner.

Now we shared nearly everything. A home, a wife. And now a bottle of whiskey.

"This ability of yours," I said, breaking the silence. "Do you think it'll be useful in...what's coming next?"

Reaper refilled our whiskeys as he answered. "You mean all the fucking enemies surrounding us, or this manifestation of chaos and destruction coming for everyone?"

I shrugged. "Do we know they're completely separate issues?"

"You know." Reaper straightened, his gaze down in his whiskey as he pondered. "They're probably not." He took a quick sip and added, "You know, fuck it. I'll bet you they're not."

"I agree with you." I swirled my own whiskey. "If we have gods working with us, it only makes sense there could be gods working against us."

"Fuck, man," Reaper huffed. "With you, Mari, and Horus back, and now this crazy sight thing, I just...hope we can turn the tide on this war. Because let me tell you, it has been *rough* being without all of you here. These last few weeks have been like we're fighting blind, then our arms are tied up, then our toes get broken, then we catch a cold, and it's just non-fucking-stop."

"We are stronger together," I agreed. "Not just the Steel Demons, but *us*."

"Yeah." He gave a wry smile. "Our little family." His smile faded and his gaze flicked away, as if temporarily in pain.

"She will forgive you," I said. "She's trying."

"I know. It's not even about that, really." Reaper rubbed his mouth. "Not to make this into a woe-is-me bitch-fest, but with all the gods and the crazy shit we've seen? I wish I could undo it all. Hurting her. Exiling you." He leaned his forehead into his hand. "This is the probably the most valuable lesson I'll ever learn, but fuck, I just wish you two didn't have to suffer for me to learn it."

"It wasn't just you that learned an important lesson," I said. "I wouldn't be sitting here if I was still stuck in my old thinking pattern."

"Oh yeah?" Reaper leaned his temple on his fist to look at me. "What did you learn?"

I sipped my whiskey as I thought of how to sum up all the ways that Doc and Mari had changed me.

"That I'm not everything my past told me I was," I decided. "I'm not inherently evil just because I'm a man. I don't *have* to believe in all of the abuse I internalized. My thoughts about myself aren't always true." My gaze dropped to my whiskey glass, swirling around the last sip. "And I don't have to sabotage happiness for myself. I...have a right to be happy."

"Damn right you do." Reaper slapped my shoulder again. "Shit, I know a few people who could afford to learn that." His face was flushed from alcohol, his voice growing louder and more boisterous as it often did when he drank. But then he lowered his voice again, his face serious. "I never did say thank you, Shadow."

"For what?"

"Just," he flung his hands up, "for being you. For being there for Mari, being someone she needed. For loving her when she couldn't rely on me."

"Reap—"

"Don't fight me on this. Just, thank you, Shadow."

The front door lock turned right then and opened, Mari and Jandro's voices floating across the house a moment later.

"Where have you two been?" Reaper nearly stumbled sliding off his stool but quickly saved himself.

"Shopping." Jandro dumped four large bags of groceries on the counter. "Now that we're feeding two-and-half more people again," he added with a wink at me.

"You talking about that spare tire you're growing?" I jabbed a hand out to slap his stomach, earning a glare in return.

"No, I'm talking about you, Hulk-Smash! And it's still winter, okay? My fluff adds a protective layer of warmth."

"Shadow!" Mari came in with the rest of the bags, digging into the bottom of one with a determined grin on her face. "Have you ever had goat cheese?"

"No." I leaned across the counter to kiss her. "Is it much different from regular cheese?"

She groaned into my kiss, taking a small bite of my lip. "It is a whole other *level* of cheese! Hey, why do you taste like whiskey?"

"We've been catching up," Reaper said, hovering nearby. He relaxed when Mari turned to squeeze him in a brief hug.

"Is Gunner still at City Hall?" Mari asked. Her arms loosened around Reaper, but didn't entirely let go.

"Think so." Reaper draped an arm around her shoulders, his gaze at her full of longing. "Why?"

She looked back at me. "Did you tell him while you were catching up?"

"Not yet," I said. "I wanted to wait until we were all together."

"Tell me what?" Reaper's eyes flicked up to me.

"Go ahead, Mari." I started digging through one grocery bag to help with the unloading, curious about this goat cheese she was so wild about.

Mari pulled away from Reaper and made sure Jandro was listening too. "I know the oncoming war is going to be rough, but we *do* have allies out there. They helped Shadow and I break through Tash's army on our ride back."

"Well shit, don't leave us in suspense now." Jandro made a valiant attempt at juggling bell peppers and promptly dropped all of them.

"Jerriton," Mari said.

Reaper looked confused. "I thought the territory was under Tash's control."

"It is, but the *people* of Jerriton don't support him. Why would they? Gunner's uncle mistreated them, and a bunch of them were in prison under Tash's rule."

"We broke them out," I added. "At first only to create a distraction, but they overwhelmed the border patrol and allowed us to escape the territory."

"They escorted us all the way to neutral territory," Mari said. "They're wanted fugitives in Jerriton now, but they're crafty, and there are a *lot* of them."

"Damn," Jandro muttered.

"Fuck," Reaper agreed. "This…could be huge. We gotta tell Dad and Gunner."

Mari squeezed another hug around him. "We can win this, guys. Whatever happens, we're strongest together."

Reaper rested his chin on her head, soaking up and returning the embrace. "I do believe that now, more than ever."

Epilogue

HADES

Horus's presence was frazzled, energy coming off of him in harsh waves of tension as we watched over the humans. The falcon body he inhabited couldn't sleep, its feathers puffed out and eyes still alert, despite the darkness of night. Freyja noticed it too.

"What's troubling you?" she asked him.

"We've reached that point," he answered. "It's a black wall from here. Not even we can see what happens next. Without our foresight, I'm concerned about the humans."

Gods existed outside of the bounds of time. Since our inception, we had seen all that occurred up to this point. But from now in the present, we could look back, but see no further ahead.

Whatever happened next would depend on them, these humans we had formed bonds with.

"They will prevail," Freyja said. "They have each other. They have love."

She reached out toward the sleeping humans. We didn't have bodies, or forms in the physical sense, but her presence drifted over the three people in the bed. As if prompted by Freyja, the two men, Jandro and

Gunner, scooted closer to Mariposa, wrapping tighter around her with their limbs. Freyja's cat form purred contently at the foot of the bed.

"It doesn't matter what happens next," I said. "All that is meant to happen will happen. They will prevail, or this will be the beginning of human extinction. And ours."

Gods didn't die. We either existed, sustained by human belief, or we faded into obscurity. Sometimes gods were renewed, rediscovered long after their followers' devotion faded into nothing. But if there were no humans left at all, we were done for.

No god had a chance of re-emerging from nothing. We arose from thoughts and ideas. Our inception began when humans took a sharp evolutionary path away from the other animals. When they began learning, conceptualizing, and scheming.

"Come now, Hades," Freyja chided me. "It's alright for you to admit you've grown attached to them. Even your reaper, as bullheaded as he is."

I did not answer, merely observed the humans in their sleep state. Many thousands of generations ago, Reaper's ancestors invoked me into existence. They entrusted me with their dead, and gave me the purpose of shepherding souls into a final resting place. To ensure the balance, I entrusted human reapers to take lives as needed. This one, supposedly the last one I would need to carry out my hand, was one of the worst I encountered.

Historically, humans had been honored to carry out my commands. The balance of survival was so delicate—billions of threads intertwining into a rich, complex fabric. Plucking the wrong one could send the whole thing crashing down, plunging all beings into nonexistence. Reaper's stubbornness almost did that, more than once. For all their innovation and brilliance, human beings were just as remarkably good at destroying themselves.

And in spite of it, I did grow attached to him and the humans he surrounded himself with. I wanted these people to survive, to leave their mark on history and carry their species into a new age. Not only because their survival preserved the existence of gods, but because these five infernal, short-sighted, ridiculous creatures were willing to fight for it.

I recognized devotion when I saw it. The devotion of these humans to each other and to their cause was awe-inspiring, even to us gods. It was no fault of theirs that the whole of human existence rested on them. The balance had been sliding toward chaos for generations, and the tipping point just happened to be in their lifetime.

"We have done all we can for them," I ultimately said in response to Freyja's remark. "We have put them through trials, and all have emerged victorious. They have our eyes, our wings, and our hearts. Now the choice is theirs—to fight for humanity, or submit to the chaos."

Just at the fringes of my perception, I felt the ghostly echo of wild, uncontrollable laughter creeping in.

RUTHLESS

STEEL DEMONS MC BOOK EIGHT

PROLOGUE

JANDRO

FIVE YEARS EARLIER

"Where are you going?" I stood in the doorway, watching my sister Angelica throw clothes into a suitcase on her bed. She ignored me and grabbed a small wooden box next, one that I knew was stuffed with letters. "Angie, come on, answer me."

"Oregon." She flashed me a glare but otherwise remained steadfast in her packing, tucking clothes around her letter box as if it were a precious relic. "Not that it matters to you."

"Why wouldn't it matter?" I crossed my arms, watching her from the door.

"Because it's clear you're happy here." Angie jerked her chin at me. "In this wasteland with that vest, those patches, all your guns. Not all of us can play gangster, Jandro, so I'm out. Alma and Josie decided to come with me too."

I leaned my head back until it thunked on the doorframe, closing my eyes with a resigned sigh. I'd seen this coming for months, but still wasn't prepared for it to be real. All the women in my family were scared, frustrated at being cooped up in the house, and always needing a man to look out for them. Me and my club brothers stepped up to protect them without complaint, though we still hated that it was needed at all.

Years had passed, a decade almost, since it was considered safe and normal for a woman to go somewhere alone. The Collapse had only made it worse.

"You'll be safer if you stay," I argued. "The club will protect you. We've already secured this whole block so everyone who lives here can come and go without issue."

"Yeah? And what happens if someone bigger than you rolls up, huh?" My sister paused in her packing to stand squarely in front of me, hands on her hips. "What if the fucking Steel Demons finally meet their match one day?"

"It won't happen," I insisted. "It's been almost a year since anyone's tried to fuck with us, and we're just getting stronger. Our protection is secure."

"Right," Angie scoffed, turning back to the suitcase on the bed. "Denial won't get you anywhere these days."

"If a militia threatens this area, we'll get you all out," I said. "You can stay with us, where you'll be safest. Look at Reaper's sister, Noelle. She's adjusted fine to MC life."

"I don't *want* to adjust to MC life, otherwise known as squatting in hotels when you're not riding around on your loud-ass motorcycles!" Angie's fists balled up at her sides. "You think our fifty-year-old aunt and uncle would be up for that too? Praying with their rosaries in a filthy room while you bang your whores next door?"

"It's not like that," I protested. "Well, not *all* the time," I amended. "One of the guys is married with a kid and has another on the way. It's pretty family friendly actually." I decided against telling her about Big G's wandering eye but the point was, his kids *were* safe and taken care of.

Angie unclenched her hands and took a deep breath, her voice softening. "I just want to live a normal life, and not worry about getting kidnapped or raped every time I walk outside."

"You think there's none of that up in Oregon, sis?" I gave her a hard look. "You think it's some kind of utopia up there? *Nowhere* is safe anymore. The safest place you'll be is with us. We're armed to the teeth and we'll protect our own. That's the whole reason Reaper started up the club in the first place."

"Oregon was establishing independence before the Collapse ever happened," Angie shot back. "They saw this coming and they prepared. And even if it sucks," she shrugged, "oh well. It's close enough to Canada."

"How are you gonna get there?" I demanded. "'Cause I ain't giving you a ride through Nevada. You think here's bad? *That* desert is a fucking wasteland."

Angie wrung her hands in front of her, looking nervous for the first time. "Drew's picking us up. Tonight."

My jaw fell open at the same time my hands fell limply to my sides. "So *that's* what this is about."

"Don't, Jandro." Angie's jaw clenched with the warning.

"You give me this whole spiel about safety when you're about to run off with some guy you've never met? Taking our sisters with you? Unbelievable, Ang." I rubbed my forehead with a groan.

"He's not some stranger, Jandro. He's my boyfriend. You've talked to him!"

"On the phone," I reminded her. "He could be anybody! Most likely, he's a trafficker getting a three-for-one deal."

"I said, *don't*!" Angie moved with lightning speed to square up in front of me, dark eyes murderous and jaw set tight. She only came up to my chin, but was older than me by two years and wouldn't hesitate to pop me if she got pissed enough. When we roughhoused as kids, she was always the scrappiest fighter.

"Damn it, sis." I shook my head at the expression on her face. "You're really gonna do this, huh?"

She and this kid Drew started talking on the phone last year when he accidentally dialed a wrong number. When all the phone companies went bankrupt and the cell towers stopped working, they kept in touch by writing letters. I should have known he put this in her head the moment she stashed that box in her suitcase.

Angie's face softened just a fraction but she didn't back up. "I know you're worried, but you're suspicious of the wrong person." She stepped away, returning to her suitcase. "You should worry about those bikers you're rolling with now."

"Don't try to deflect, Ang," I warned, my temper flaring. "I've known most of the guys for years. Plus, Reaper's a hardass about club law. We do what we have to, and that does *not* include luring women to the so-called safety wonderland called Oregon."

"He is *not* luring me, it was my idea!" Angie slammed the suitcase closed and whirled around, dark curls whipping her shoulders. "Anyway, what are you gonna do? Keep me prisoner here?"

"No." I slumped against the door, defeated. "If you're gonna go, I won't stop you."

"Then why are you being so up my ass?"

"Because if you go," I let all the sadness bleed out into my voice. "I know I'm never gonna see you again."

There was a long pause as my sister and I just stared at each other. "Jandro," she finally said, as if chastising me. "I'll write to you."

"Not if you're dead," I answered curtly. "Not if you're chained up in some sicko's basement, or drugged up constantly 'til you're a zombie."

She sighed, the sound heavy and tired. "Is there anything I can do to make you feel okay with this?"

"Stay," I pleaded one final time. "Just...don't run off with him. Hell, he can even stay here for a few days so I can meet him properly before you go."

Angie shook her head and my heart sunk. "I can't stay here another fucking day, Jandro. I'm so, so sick of it here."

"I'm sorry, sis. That's just how the world is now," I told her sadly. "You've heard the radio reports. The whole country's fucked."

She shook her head adamantly. "I don't believe that. There has to be a better place, Jandro. And for me," she pulled in a shaky breath, "that's in Oregon, with the man I love."

I'd never felt anything like that moment before—that awful paradoxical feeling of knowing my sister was already gone, despite standing right in front of me. Nothing I said would make her budge. Trying to talk her out of it would only drive her further away.

So I did the only thing I could do at that moment—pulled Angie into a hug for the last time.

"God, please, *please* be careful," I begged her. "You get even one weird feeling, you hit the dirt and run back here, okay?"

To my relief she hugged me back, the anger melting out of her as she patted my back. "I've thought about this for months. Trust that I know what I'm doing."

I bit down hard on the inside of my cheek, not wanting my last moment with her to be an argument. After one more tight squeeze and a kiss on her forehead, I released her.

"Write me as soon as you can," I said on my way out of the room. I didn't bother with goodbye. I couldn't just stay and see her off all hopeful and positive and shit. I all but knew she was walking out to her death, and taking my other two sisters with her. As the youngest and the only male sibling, I was woefully outnumbered in this fight.

There was one more thing I had to do for her, but she couldn't know about it. I left my aunt and uncle's house without another word, hopped on my bike, and headed straight for the Steel Demons compound, which was just an abandoned hotel we took over.

Angie was right about that, at least.

I crashed through the front doors, heading to the bar where Reaper was parked. "Yo, Reap." I smacked his shoulder to pull his attention away from the girl dancing on the stripper pole off to the side of the bar. "I need to run an errand, it'll take a few days. I'll take Shadow with me, that should be enough."

Reaper's green eyes narrowed at me through the haze of cigarette smoke surrounding him. "What's going on?"

"Angie," I admitted with a sigh, scrubbing a hand down my face. "She's finally had it and she's taking off."

He straightened in his seat, looking more alert as he turned to me. "You sure you don't want more of us?" Reaper had a brief fling with my sister a few years ago that went nowhere, but it wasn't even about that. She was my family, and by extension, his too. The whole club would rally to protect her if he said the word.

"Nah." I shook my head. "We're gonna hang back so she won't know we're tailing."

"Why?"

"She's taking off with that guy she's been penpalling," I grumbled. "Can't get in the way of her fucking prince rescuing her. I'm just gonna make sure she gets to Oregon like she believes she is and not straight to a trafficker's compound."

"So you're not stopping her?" Reaper looked curious.

"She's a grown-ass adult, what am I gonna do?" I leaned on the barstool next to him. "Would you get in Noelle's way if she pulled this shit?"

"Huh, no." He took a drag on his smoke and said loudly, "Those psychopaths can have her."

"I can hear you, asshat!" Noelle called from somewhere behind the bar.

"Whatever. D'you find that bottle of Beam yet?"

I tapped Reaper's shoulder again to get his attention. "Back in a few days. Me and Shadow."

He waved an arm to dismiss me, his attention returning to the girl on the stripper pole. "I hope Angie's guy is alright. But if he's not, put an extra bullet in him for me."

"Oh, I was planning on it," I said, heading to Shadow's room. A dim light spilled out through the crack under his door, where I rapped my knuckles twice. "Hey man, it's Jandro."

I barely heard his footsteps as he approached the door and it still baffled me how such a big dude could be so silent. He didn't open the door for me, but the deadbolt sliding out from its locked position was my cue to come in. When I entered, Shadow had already returned to his desk, hunched over his sketchpad with his hand sweeping over the page.

"Hey." I closed the door softly behind me. "You've been cooped up in here a while. Let's go for a ride, get you some fresh air."

"Where?" he grunted out, not even looking up from his page.

"To Oregon and back. I gotta watch over someone heading out that way."

Shadow paused in his drawing, turning his head to look at me suspiciously. "Who?"

"My sister," I said, then swallowed. "Three of my sisters, actually."

"No—"

I raised a hand to calm him before he started freaking out. "You won't have to talk to them or be near them. They'll be in a car. We'll be on our bikes, just following to make sure they get there safe."

Shadow's hand clenched around his pen. I could hear the agitated breaths rushing in and out of his lungs.

"You won't interact with anyone but me," I continued to placate him. "Come on, man. You need to get out of these four walls, and I need some backup."

He took a long time to respond, and I could see the internal battle as he spun the pen in his hand. The big dude loved having freedom—the open road and flying sensation of riding, even just the ability to come and go as he pleased. But that kind of freedom was still unnatural to him, even spiking his anxiety sometimes. Shadow always picked the smallest rooms when we moved around, and I figured the cramped space was comforting to him, if only because it was familiar. Once he retreated to his hiding place, it was always a battle to coax him out again.

On the upside, winning that battle got a little bit easier every time.

"Promise?" he asked finally. "Just you and me?"

"I promise," I said with a sigh. We had come a long way as far as him trusting me, but sometimes Shadow fell back into thinking I was trying to trick or deceive him.

"We're going through Nevada, right?"

"Yeah, so?"

"No women," he said, teeth clenched. "I mean it, Jandro."

"You sure?" I couldn't help but tease him, grinning as I leaned against his door. "I could've sworn I heard you say you wanted to swing by the bunny ranch."

"No," Shadow repeated. "Maybe another time, but I'm not in the mood for...*that*."

"Fine, be a cock block," I sighed in mock disappointment. In all honesty, I wasn't in the best of moods for fucking some random woman either, definitely not with my sisters on my mind. "We'll just go there and back, crash when we need to. Cool?"

"Okay," Shadow relented. "I'll get dressed."

"Meet you in the garage." I turned to leave, closing his door again behind me as I stalked down the long, dark hallway.

My mind was elsewhere as I checked the tire pressure and fluids on Shadow's bike, my movements on autopilot. All I could think about was Angie, how I was just going to watch and hover until she was gone for good.

Sure, this Drew guy *might* be okay. She could end up safe and happy with him for all I knew. I had to hope for a good outcome.

The Collapse last year was still fresh on everyone's minds, the lingering effects of it continuing to ripple out across the country. We no longer had a national currency, no more government agencies to help people in need. Everyone was wondering about the economy, infrastructure, and if we would unify and rebuild.

No one talked about this—families splitting apart because they had no other options. This world made people cling to fantasies, like Angie did with this guy. It drove people to seek out anything better than their current situation, even in people and places completely unknown.

"At least she's going for something," I muttered to myself. "At least she still believes in something better."

I opened the garage door and went to sit on my bike to wait for Shadow.

MARIPOSA

PRESENT DAY

I held onto Jandro's arm, squeezing around his bicep as we watched the men drill the commemorative plaques into the wall. He placed his fingers over mine, a deep breath filling his lungs. On the other side of him, Slick leaned on his crutch and bowed his head when the final bolt secured the plaque into the concrete.

A small crowd had gathered while the plaques were being installed, curious onlookers between me, my men, and the Sons of Odin, who got their own plaque for the loss of their own people.

Silence filled the City Hall foyer once the drilling was done, only the soft echoes of footsteps filling the open building.

"Thank you for doing this," Jandro said softly, turning to Governor Vance. "Honoring our fallen is so important to us."

"It's both my pleasure to do this for you, and a regret for your men and their families," Vance said, his face full of sympathy. His daughter Kyrie stood next to him, hands clasped demurely in front of her.

"We apologize for the delay in commemorating your fallen people," she added, inclining her head toward the Sons of Odin, standing across from her in our small semicircle. "The Sons too deserve remembrance in Four Corners' history."

T-Bone nodded politely, a thick swallow working in his throat. "Thank you, Miss Vance."

His reply was stiff, formal. Kyrie looked briefly taken aback but smoothed out her features quickly.

Not wanting to dwell on the tension between them, I released Jandro's arm and stepped forward to lay my bouquet of flowers at the wall under the plaques. My guys and other club members who came to pay their respects stepped up after me. Cigars, patches, silver rings and pendants, lighters, more flowers, and even small glasses of whiskey were laid down for Brick, his nephew Wells, the other Steel Demons we lost, and for the fallen Sons of Odin.

Jandro and Slick's faces were the most somber I'd ever seen them. The bodies of the men they'd lost on that mission were never recovered, hence the plaques. A recovery mission had been shot down because it was deemed too dangerous. Secretly, I was glad that it hadn't been approved. It could have been Jandro and Slick commemorated on a plaque too, a poor replacement for the men at my side. I slid an arm around Jandro's waist, his arm coming to rest on my shoulders as he pressed a kiss to my temple.

"I would never rush any of you through your grief," Governor Vance said slowly as the crowd began to disperse. "But this war is not waiting for us to be ready." His eyes scanned over my men and the Sons. "If you're able, please meet us in the conference room. We have much to discuss."

Gunner walked up to my opposite side, fingers twining gently with mine. "Coming, baby girl?"

I glanced at him in surprise. "You think I should?"

He nodded insistently. "They need to hear about what you and Shadow ran into on your way back. And honestly," he blew out a long breath, "we need all the fresh ideas we can get."

"Then I'll be there."

He smiled roguishly at me, then leaned down to brush a quick kiss on my lips. Under the guiding weight of Jandro's arm, I turned to follow the others down the hall to the conference room. Reaper and

Shadow were already ahead of us, walking side-by-side as they spoke to each other in low voices. Those two had grown closer since we got back, more like friends than a president and his foot soldier.

Reaper reached up and swatted Shadow on the back at one point, his palm slapping the freshly printed Steel Demons patch on Shadow's cut. The grinning skull stretched wide and menacingly across the expanse of his back. Shadow's already-imposing figure was amplified now that he was decked out in a cut and patches again. People walking past us steered clear, taking one look at him before jerking their gaze away and hurrying their steps.

I almost wanted to laugh. It was such a contrast to how he was with me privately—arguably the most loving, gentle man in existence. I couldn't lie to myself, it was hot as hell that he came off as so intimidating, but was truly anything but. Like he could hear my thoughts, Shadow glanced at me over his shoulder, a smile pulling at his lips.

"You guys talking about me?" I demanded.

"Never." The sarcastic reply came from Reaper, who tossed me a charming smile over his shoulder.

My stomach did flips at the sight of those green eyes. I felt like I did when I first met Reaper, so inexplicably attracted to him but also completely unsure of where we stood. Only this time, the power was in my hands and it was him waiting for me to make things clear.

For every urge to run up and kiss him, to erase all the uncertainty of him being mine, there was an equally strong force pulling me back. It was like reaching out to touch a stove after I'd already been burned, trusting that it wouldn't hurt me again. I *wanted* to move on— Shadow clearly had. I wanted to forgive and have my first husband back.

But the hurt wasn't gone. It still cut through me when I thought about what Shadow had endured, how he must have felt when he was made to leave Four Corners and travel across the country alone.

It was getting a little easier every day. Shadow was back home and happy. Reaper and I were talking now, even flirting from time to time. He never pushed for anything physical, though he looked at me with such longing and I wanted so badly to give in. The wall between us was slowly crumbling, but it was still there, an invisible barrier.

"Slick." I turned my attention to Jandro's apprentice, the young Demon who had saved Jandro's life. "How's the leg?"

He shot me a good-natured smile as he walked tirelessly alongside us on his crutches. "Better, thank you, Mari. Rhonda's whipping my ass in physical therapy. She said I should be off these in another week."

"That's great news!" I looked down just in time to see a small black blur walking along Slick's other side.

Freyja's tail was in the air, large eyes fixed on him. Slick made soft clicking sounds at her and she meowed in reply. Jandro and I laughed softly, exchanging a knowing glance. Slick's recovery from his gunshot had taken longer than any of ours since the gods came into our lives, but I was hopeful that Freyja's presence would speed things up for him.

"I told him he's not a real Demon 'til he takes a gunshot," Jandro told me smugly.

"Don't say that," I grumbled with a smack on his arm. "Just because you've been shot a dozen times."

"It builds character," Jandro insisted with a straight face. "Puts hair on your chest."

"Huh." I looked down while tugging the collar of my shirt. "Where are my chest hairs then?"

Jandro chuckled and wrapped both arms around me in a protective embrace. "You're the exception, *Mariposita*. You're a Demon because you save all our dumb asses. I'd never in a million years wish for you to get shot."

"I know." I lifted on tiptoes to kiss his cheek. "You're not entirely wrong, though. Getting shot...changed things."

I had never come so close to death, nor had been in so much pain in my entire life. The aftermath still came to me in flashes—blinding pain, Doc digging into my leg, the worn leather of Shadow's belt between my teeth.

And Shadow, holding and soothing me. The solidness of his chest like an anchor, the sound of his voice keeping me from losing my mind to the terror running through me.

As painful and horrifying as that experience was, it was also moving. A shift had occurred that day, one that brought us back together. It gave Shadow the chance to see for himself that he was capable of so much more than killing. That he was a deserving partner of me, from the moment he beat my shooter to death, to holding me during the bullet extraction, and then the aftermath and my recovery.

I had a feeling he'd never believed himself worthy of caring for someone until circumstances forced him into doing so. And for that alone, I'd do it all over again.

Governor Vance's assistant, Josh, held a heavy door open as we filed into the conference room. Reaper's father, General Finn Bray, was already seated at the head of the long table, surrounded by a few of his lieutenants. Reaper and Gunner took their seats to the general's left, knowing instantly where to go, like they'd done this hundreds of times before. Jandro led me to the general's right, pulling a chair back for me before he sat down next to my father-in-law.

Finn leaned over the table, smiling at me and mouthing a *hi, sweetheart*. I smiled and mouthed hello back as Shadow sat on my opposite side, the table quickly filling up with people. I hadn't seen much of my in-laws since Shadow and I returned, and while I missed them, I was grateful for the space. The fewer people digging into my and Reaper's relationship, the better.

"Thank you all for coming," Finn addressed the room once everyone had been seated. His fingers drummed on top of a manila folder in front of him. "I'll start with the good news. Andrea has made contact once again, which means she is still alive and her position has not been compromised."

The whole room seemed to let out a sigh of relief. I couldn't wait to tell Tessa when I had the chance.

"I'm afraid the good news ends there," Finn continued in a grave voice, flipping open the folder. "The information she gives does not bode well for us." His eyes scanned the document as if making sure it hadn't magically changed to better news. "Two-thousand of General Tash's troops have mobilized as of a week ago, heading directly west." *Straight toward us*, were the unspoken words hanging in the air. "Most of them are foot soldiers, but she estimates sizable motorized and aerial units as well."

"Aerial?" Reaper barked, his face drawn in a scowl. "Does that mean drones or...?"

"Yes," his father confirmed. "Andrea has also made note of at least five attack helicopters as well."

No one made a sound in response to that, but Reaper dropping his head into his hands must have summed up everyone's thoughts.

"And that's just their first wave," Finn added, leaning back and folding his hands. "Who knows what Tash is still holding back?"

"Meanwhile, we've got Blakeworth creating decoys and hiding in the grass like ninjas to the north," Jandro chimed in. "After that first skirmish, they're keeping their soldiers *very* close."

"I wonder if they're hoping Tash flushes us to the north, then they can pick us off, like shooting fish in a barrel." Gunner rubbed his jaw. "It makes sense. We can't exactly flee in any other direction."

"We're not fleeing," Reaper growled. "We're fighting."

"I don't disagree, son. But we're at a huge disadvantage," Finn said.

"There is still Jerriton," I piped up.

All eyes in the room turned to me, and I felt Shadow give an encouraging touch of my thigh under the table.

"Jerriton is Tash's territory now," one of Bray's lieutenants informed me.

"It's under his control, yes," I said. "But the people of Jerriton are not loyal to him. They're organizing a resistance."

"I'm sorry, but how does that affect anything? The citizens don't have any—"

"Let her speak," Shadow snarled to the lieutenant across the table.

The man in question shut right up, and the entire row of soldiers seemed to shrink in their seats. I allowed myself a small, smug moment to squeeze Shadow's hand on my leg before continuing.

"Tash had citizens imprisoned. We," I tilted my head toward Shadow, "freed them, at first to create a distraction so we could get back to Four Corners undetected. Tash's border patrol caught up to us, but the citizens saved our asses."

"How?" another soldier blurted out before withering under Shadow's glare again.

"We killed a few prison guards," I said. "It was chaos, so the prisoners were able to arm themselves and steal vehicles. Knowing their territory, they knew exactly where we'd be blockaded and came to our aid. Their leader, Samson, told us himself that they stood with Four Corners."

"Did they inform you of any specific plan?" The question came from Finn, who was looking at me intently. "Or any way to keep in contact, at least?"

That was where my confidence faltered, and I wanted to shrink down in my seat. "No, General. I invited them here but they wanted to continue helping others in their own territory. I wanted you to know we have someone else supporting us, but as far as specifics to help us in battle? I'm afraid I don't have anything."

Finn smiled kindly at me, but I noticed the downturn in his lips. He was disappointed I didn't have anything substantial to offer, and I was kicking myself for not thinking of it when I had the chance. At the time, all I wanted was for me and Shadow to get home.

"Maybe we could send a bird out," T-Bone suggested. "See if there's a secure way we can exchange messages."

"If we can get a direct line to their leader, that would be the best," Finn agreed. "But in the meantime," he sighed, "we need to decide how to split up defenses to the north and the east." His fingers dragged across the map in the center of the table. "I will not let us be corralled and herded like livestock for General Tash. So what do we do?"

Gunner leaned over the map, his eyes sharp and calculating. "Send heavy artillery toward Tash. It'll do the most amount of damage."

"But will it be enough?" the general challenged.

Gunner steepled his fingers, holding them to his lips as he stared at the table. I knew dozens of scenarios were playing out in his mind and like a true tactician, he was filtering down to the most effective ones.

"If we act fast enough," my golden man said, "I think so." His eyes shifted toward Reaper, and I knew he was considering the president's newfound ability to see through the eyes of the dead. Something we didn't want made known to this packed room.

"Heavy artillery with the fewest possible amount of people," Gunner decided. "I'm talking going all-out, like planting IEDs in their direct path and picking the rest off in the chaos. But we have to act fast, before they get too close to us."

"What about Blakeworth?" someone else asked.

Gunner snapped his fingers, turning toward the speaker. "The exact opposite. Large numbers but sleek weapons. Just rifles and handguns. We'll comb the landscape and flush those sneaky fuckers out of their hiding places. Now that my boy's back," he paused to pet Horus' chest feathers while shooting a grin at me, "I can survey the area better. We'll be able to spot more of them before they spot us."

"Sounds viable," General Bray mused, rubbing his palms together.

"We can set up field hospitals outside of the northern and eastern borders," I chimed in, eager to be useful. "Just let me know where."

"Excellent." The general beamed at me. "Steel Demons officers," his eyes swept over my four men, "Sons," he nodded at T-Bone across the table. "Stick around to discuss the logistics of this and receive your unit assignments. The rest of you are dismissed."

I started to get up when Finn clicked his tongue. "Sit down, Mrs. President."

All of my guys were grinning when I plopped back down into my chair. "Never thought I'd get a seat at the big boys' table."

"Honestly." Jandro leaned in to kiss my cheek. "You should have been here since the beginning."

CHAPTER 2

MARIPOSA

The meeting went on for most of the day, long into the afternoon. Finn sent for several meals and beverages to be brought up to us. No alcohol, much to my men's disappointment. They were planning to strike Blakeworth and General Tash that very night.

"I can have emergency medics on-site with you guys right away," I said. "But it will take a few hours for a full-on field hospital to get set up at both locations."

"We'll take whatever you can support us with," Finn said. "As long as we have some medics there once things get ugly."

"I can definitely do that." I nodded. "You want people who can ride bikes?"

"Reaper's team should have the experienced riders." Gunner jerked his chin across the table to the president. "Your guys will need to move fast, since you don't have the big numbers covering you."

"Makes sense," Reaper agreed.

"I'll be with Gunner's team then," I decided. "To even things out, since he'll have less medics on his side."

"Good idea." Finn smiled warmly at me. "You've got a good mind for this, Mari."

I lowered my eyes to the table bashfully, still feeling slightly out of place despite being among friends and family. "Thank you, I'm trying."

"Alright." The general's eyes scanned over everyone in the room. "Does everyone know where they're going?" When no one said otherwise, he rose from the table. "Good. Inform your units, then spend the last few hours of daylight with your loved ones. Eat a good dinner, but don't get shitfaced." He looked pointedly at Reaper. "We start moving at nightfall."

The Sons of Odin stood abruptly after the general finished speaking. "We'll inform the soldiers and the medics," T-Bone announced. "Don't worry about it, Demons. Steal a bit of extra time together."

"You guys don't have to do that," Jandro protested. "You're fighting with us, you're not our messengers."

T-Bone shrugged, sending quick looks to Dyno and Grudge with a smirk. "Y'all have been separated long enough, and while we're optimistic about the battles, none of us know how it's gonna go. Spend the time together now," his voice softened, "while you know you still have it."

"If it's gonna be that way then," I huffed, making my way around the table with my arms out. "Gimme hugs now. I won't see you guys until after it's over."

T-Bone chuckled, his gaze watching the men behind me before wrapping his broad, tattooed arms around my back and crushing me in a tight squeeze.

"Be safe," I whispered in his ear, hugging tightly around his neck. "Come back to us, all of you."

"You too, little lady." He kissed my cheek. "Bring yourself and all your bastards back home in one piece."

We released each other and I moved on to hug Grudge and Dyno. After my men said their goodbye-for-now's, the Sons left to inform the troops of their assignments, and it was only my men and my father-in-law in the room with me.

"I'll leave you all to it," Finn said, taking his cue to leave next. "See you in a few hours."

And then there were five.

Jandro came up to me first, locking his hands around my waist as he pulled me closer. "Anything you want to do in our free time, *Mariposita*?" He lowered a kiss to my neck and heat filled my skin, like a match had been lit.

Over his shoulder, I saw Reaper pull his gaze away to shuffle papers on the table. Shadow watched us with a kind of cool curiosity. He didn't look *not* interested, but it wasn't the clear desire I saw when we were alone. I realized we'd never really discussed group bedroom situations. Of course he knew he wasn't my only husband, but he might feel differently about sex. So far our time together had only been with each other, and always so intensely intimate.

Reaper and I still hadn't done anything sexual since I came back. I wanted more one-on-one time with him too, when I came to that point in healing those stubborn past wounds. With everyone here now, I wasn't about to leave Reaper out. Nor was I about to potentially make Shadow feel uncomfortable.

The only one who looked at Jandro and I with clear interest was Gunner, teeth sinking into his lower lip as he grinned at us. For all his initial hesitancy about this relationship, lately he seemed to love sharing me the most. Gunner's main priority in the bedroom was having fun. He and Jandro together ensured that I would be laughing just as much as I'd be having orgasms.

"Honestly." I pressed lightly on Jandro's chest. "I just want to relax at home with all of you. *Actually* relax, like cuddling," I clarified.

Reaper's eyes lifted to me, relief in his gaze. Shadow's face relaxed too, and I knew quality non-sex time was the right decision. We'd all been so busy since Shadow and I returned, it was rare for us all to be together at once. With just a few hours, I sure as hell didn't want to waste it.

"Home, it is." Gunner pet Horus on his shoulder as he whirled toward the door. "Jandro, can we have tacos?"

"Make 'em yourself." Jandro released me to grumble after him.

I walked up to Shadow first, hugging around his waist as I propped my chin on his chest. "See you at home."

He smiled knowingly, swiping his thumb over my cheek in a quick caress as he bent to kiss me. "See you there, my love."

Reaper was already following Gunner and Jandro out to the parking spaces when I untangled from Shadow. I jogged to catch up to his long strides, slipping my hand into his. "Can I get a ride with you?"

Reaper smoothed over his surprise quickly with a cocky grin. "You sure can, sugar."

This was another baby step forward for us. I didn't know when riding behind one of my men became something intimate. Maybe it always had been.

On the ride home, the memory of Reaper fucking me on his bike drove my thighs to squeeze tighter against his. That felt like an eternity ago, when my feelings for him were at an all-time high. When I thought nothing could shatter the bond between us.

He'd always be groping me, grabbing me, and whispering sweet, filthy things in my ear. Now, he kept his hands to himself. And my hands, resting on his stomach, couldn't seem to stroke his chest, nor dip under his shirt to tease and touch him like I used to. I *wanted* to. More than anything, I wanted to break this wall between us and go back to being happy together. But the thought of doing so made my heart race with anxiety.

To let myself love him wholly again opened up the possibility of being heartbroken again. The one thing I wanted most also terrified me beyond words. So my hands never moved, and neither did his. Every day that he was patient and accepting of my coldness only made me feel worse about it.

Reaper braked slowly as we pulled up our driveway, the others falling in behind us. "You good?" he asked, pausing while I climbed out of the seat.

"Yeah, thanks." I dusted myself off, mentally kicking myself. He probably wanted to help me off the bike, and have another excuse to touch me. Another baby step forward.

I hated that this all felt so awkward. He was my *husband*, not some guy I started dating yesterday. Still, Reaper didn't seem bothered as he shut off the bike and headed for the front door. Everyone left their steeds in the driveway, since they'd be back on them soon anyway.

Once I kicked off my shoes by the front door, a large arm wrapped around my waist from behind and lifted me off the ground.

"Shadow!" I shrieked with laughter as he swung an arm under my knees to carry me. "Where are you taking me?"

"The couch," he answered flatly. "To cuddle."

I let my head flop against his chest with a smile, just curling up smaller as he sat down with me across his lap. My legs stretched out to find another lap, Jandro's. The VP placed my feet on top of his thighs and immediately set to work rubbing them. The other two were rummaging in the kitchen, by the sounds of it. I shifted and scooted between my two men, making myself comfortable to the sounds of cabinet doors closing and murmured voices.

"Whatever you guys get, bring some for us," Jandro called, running his thumbs up my arches.

"There's not much, besides eggs and liquor. And we have orders *not* to drink," Reaper scoffed.

"We can drink, your old man just said don't get shitfaced," Jandro reminded him.

"There should be ice cream," I yelled. "Unless one of you dicks ate it all."

"I could go for some ice cream," Shadow mused, his fingers making delicious circles of pressure on my back.

I heard the refrigerator doors open, and then Gunner's voice over the machine's hum. "I kinda want scrambled eggs. Easy comfort food."

"Make me some!" Jandro called, his hands still doing wonders to my feet. "And don't forget to season that shit with salt and pepper. We should have cheese too."

"Yeah, whatever. Baby girl, you want eggs?"

"No thank you, just ice cream."

Not twenty minutes later, we were all piled around the couch with our very grown-up dinners of scrambled eggs, ice cream, and whiskey. I held the tub of cookie dough ice cream in my lap and fed hearty spoonfuls to Shadow, which he chased with small sips of whiskey.

"I'm tellin' you, bro." Jandro scraped his plate of eggs clean. "You gotta cook it on really low heat, folding it the entire time. You want perfect scrambled eggs, you gotta cook 'em for like forty-five minutes."

"Fuck that," Gunner scoffed from the armchair across from us. "I like my eggs crispy anyway."

"See, I don't understand that." Reaper, in another armchair, set his whiskey on his knee as he looked at Gunner. "You grew up with butlers and chefs and shit, and you eat like a garbage disposal. If it was anyone who demanded perfect eggs, I figured it'd be you."

"Nah, food is food. If it doesn't poison me or taste like Satan's asshole, I'll eat it."

"Food is not *just* food, it's culture," Jandro protested. "It's love. It's bringing a family together. It's an experience brought on by a chain of events, leading to what's on your plate." He pointed at Gunner. "You ate those eggs because I rescued—"

"You mean stole?" Shadow interjected with a chuckle.

"Fine, whatever. I *stole* my girls from the Sandia outpost and trekked across the desert with them. They miraculously survived the attack from Razor Wire, then got transported again to this place, where they'll finally live happily ever after. Those aren't *just* eggs, man. My girls went through hell to reach paradise, so you could have deliciousness on a plate."

"I get it man, I'm just saying," Gunner laughed, raising his palms in the air in mock surrender. "That I've never discriminated against what's been on my plate, whether it came from a personal chef or a dumpster."

"It is really sweet that you love those chickens so much," I said, digging my toes into Jandro's thigh.

"Sometimes I do, and then there's days like yesterday," he sighed. "Where those little dumbasses chase and peck the shit out of me for no good reason." Jandro lifted his chin. "Cream me, babe."

"Excuse me?"

"Ice cream, let me get some."

"What's the strangest thing you've ever eaten, sugar?" Reaper was relaxed and leaned back in his chair, eyes following me as I fed Jandro a spoonful of ice cream.

"Hmm." I spooned some of my healthy dinner into my mouth while I thought. "You heard of calf fries?"

Reaper took a pensive sip of whiskey, looking all too sexy while doing so. "Don't think so."

"That's what we called them in Texas. You might know them as Rocky Mountain oysters."

He nearly spat out that sip he just took, as did Gunner who was already red-faced and laughing. Jandro cackled at Reaper's reaction while Shadow just looked at me curiously. "What is that?"

"*We-ell...*" I purposely drew out the word while scratching the rough beard on his jaw. "You take a bull's testicles, deep-fry them—"

And then Shadow was choking on his drink, trying not to spit it all over me, which only made the other guys laugh harder. Gunner and Reaper were sliding down to the floor, clutching their stomachs. Jandro would have done the same if it weren't for my feet in his lap.

Those few hours passed by too quickly—talking, laughing, and just relaxing with my loves like we had all the time in the world. My ice cream ended up getting passed around until it was finished. The sun was less than an hour away from setting by the time Gunner was scraping the last of it out of the tub.

"We should head out," Reaper voiced what everyone else was reluctant to acknowledge.

I had shifted directions on the couch and slowly lifted my head from Jandro's lap, pulling my feet out of Shadow's hands as I came to a sitting position.

"Be careful," I managed to whisper to the VP before he pulled me in for a deep kiss with a hand on my neck.

"Don't worry," he murmured against my lips. "I promise I won't get shot more than once."

"*Jandro,*" I growled as low and threateningly as I could manage.

"I mean I'll *try* not to get hit at all, but you never know." His mouth pulled into a wider grin, still teasing me.

"No getting shot," I insisted. "Not even once."

He kissed me again, slow and lingering, while holding the sides of my face. "I'll be careful, *Mariposita.*"

Knowing I wouldn't get more of a promise than that, I slid across the couch to Shadow. Those massive, solid arms wrapped around my back while my arms braced against his chest.

"Come back to me." I ghosted a kiss over his lips.

"I'll never leave you." The promise rumbled from deep in his chest before his mouth pressed solidly to mine.

It was hell to stop kissing him and pull away, both because of how physically addicting he was, and the simple fact that I was seeing my men off to battle. A *real* battle.

I rose from the couch and went to Gunner, who was already up and strapping on a bunch of weapons.

"Be careful," I repeated, the sentiment sounding lame and empty at this point.

"Always, baby girl." He placed his hands on my waist and pulled me closer, the easygoing smile never leaving his face. "I'll have you and Horus watching over me. How can we lose?"

"Don't tempt fate like that," I warned. "But I know you'll be smart."

"You know me well, then." We shared sweet and playful parting kisses, then I turned to Reaper.

Except he was already gone.

"What?" I spun around the living room, a quick flash of panic rising.

Jandro cleared his throat. "He, uh, went outside while you and Shadow were making out."

I headed out the front door without wasting another moment, finding the Steel Demons president checking the tires on his bike.

"You were *not* about to leave without saying good-bye," I accused, folding my arms as I approached him.

Reaper stood up and shrugged sheepishly. "Didn't want to, uh, ruin any of your goodbyes with them." Meaning he didn't want to stand around awkwardly and watch me kiss and whisper promises to everyone but him.

"Come on." I opened my arms and approached him for a hug like I had with the Sons earlier.

But when his arms came around me, there was nothing platonic about that hug. Chemistry fired between us from his hands on my back, to my breasts against his chest, to the breath of air tickling my neck from his mouth.

I found myself clutching hard to his back, fingers digging in, while I buried my face in his shoulder, inhaling his signature scent of clove cigarettes and leather. I wanted to linger there, to pull the shirt away and taste the heat of his skin again.

It took all my resolve to pull back, and I immediately hated losing the solidness of his body against mine.

"You need to come back too," I said, stepping further out of the embrace. "You're just as important. Just as needed."

Reaper's hands fell away, dropping to his sides with a small smile. "To Four Corners or to you?"

"Both." I rubbed my arms and hugged myself against the cold, fighting the urge to burrow into his chest again. "You're still my husband."

His smile brightened at that. "As long as you keep telling me that, sugar, I'll keep coming back home to you."

CHAPTER 3

REAPER

It didn't seem feasible at first glance, taking on a couple thousand troops with just a few hundred of us, some howitzers, and some strategically placed IEDs. But Gunner obviously put a lot of thought into it, covering all angles to maximize an effective attack while putting a minimal amount of bodies at risk. That same night as the meeting, when we started putting the plan into action, I wasn't exactly feeling *optimistic,* but certainly better about this war than I had in previous weeks.

Gunner and Dad split up units between the northern and eastern fronts to best utilize the skills of those involved. Those dealing with Tash specialized in stealth and scouting, with a select few heavy artillery experts manning the howitzers. The Blakeworth front consisted of nearly everyone else, specialized or not. They needed numbers to keep their advantage, while we needed tight coordination and precision.

I was heading east no matter what Gun or Dad told me. I knew it wasn't likely to happen in *this* battle, but I wanted the chance to hurt Tash myself regardless.

Shadow and I were leading the eastern units together, with his sight giving us an advantage in the dead of night.

"Where did Mari see the line of soldiers when you all were out there?" I double-checked all the straps and tie-downs on my bike, ensuring nothing explosive would fall off on the ride.

"Hm." Shadow tilted his head, looking skyward as he thought. "Two, maybe three hundred miles from our border."

"And it was all on foot? One long, unbroken line, she said?"

"Yes," he confirmed gravely. "And that was days ago, so I don't suspect we have to go far. They might be right on our doorstep, with vehicles and attack helicopters not far behind."

"Let's go greet our neighbors, then."

Shadow started up his bike with a roar, with mine and a chorus of hundreds of others filling the air after him. With his night vision as our guide, he'd lead us to the first site to plant a bomb. Gunner was using Horus on the northern side, so we didn't have an exact location on Tash's movement until there were some dead folks for me to see through.

We just had to pray that we didn't run into Tash before we were ready.

I mentally scoffed at the idea of prayer, then shifted the thought immediately. I knew gods existed. Maybe praying wasn't so far-fetched after all.

Yeah, right. It's not like the gods have answered half of the things you've prayed for.

Hades offered no comment as I kicked my feet up and followed Shadow out of the army base's lot and onto the road. We kept our headlights on low power, and the dog nearly turned invisible in the dark landscape. In the corner of my eye I only saw flashes of white teeth as he ran alongside me.

Despite my cynical thoughts about prayer, I couldn't completely write off the gods as cruel puppet masters. I had my parents back. I had Mari back. Who knew how much the gods played a part in those events, but they had certainly been out of *my* control. And having Shadow back too...

I hit the throttle, speeding to catch up to his tail light on the road ahead of me. So many times I replayed that confrontation with Hades in my head, before I attempted to kill Shadow. The big guy was still needed for something, either in this war or something else. It had to be bigger than just him and Mari getting back together. No god would step in to prevent his death for only that, would they?

After roughly an hour's ride, Shadow pulled over to the side of the road, with the procession of bikes filing in after him.

"We start planting them here," he called out. "Moving further up and covering until someone has a visual. If you do, you know the signal."

"Look at you giving orders," I chuckled, sliding out of my seat to begin unloading.

"Heh," Shadow said dismissively. "It's getting easier, I guess."

"You're good at it," I told him.

He paused, seemingly taken aback by the compliment. "Thank you, president."

We and our units fanned out in a wide zig-zag pattern to plant the bombs a quarter-mile apart from each other. The landscape was mostly flat with only gently sloping hills, which wasn't great for our ground cover. Canyons or rock formations would be ideal, but Tash wouldn't be stupid enough to lead his troops where they could be easily sniped from above.

Planting the explosives took most of the night. We set them up at very specific coordinates so everyone knew not to accidentally drive over them. Dawn was peeking over the horizon when the radio call came.

"This is Stealth Unit 2, we've got a visual at 3-o'clock. Roughly two miles out."

I couldn't grab my receiver fast enough. "Y'all heard him, get into your positions. Unit 2, can you confirm it's Tash's army?" I released the button and waited for a reply while my heart jammed against my ribs.

The radio hissed for a few seconds that felt like an eternity before the answer came. "It's definitely an army marching on foot. I see no insignia or flags to indicate any allegiance. Do you want me to wait until I can see better, president?"

"No, proceed," I answered. "That's exactly who we're supposed to be fighting. Get into positions and stand ready, everyone."

"Coming from three-o'clock means they'll hit these first." Shadow pointed at the map marking all of our bomb placements.

"Should've concentrated 'em all there," I mused.

"We had no way of knowing," he reminded me. "And anyway, they'll scatter in a panic and set the others off."

"I hope you're right." I went to lean against my bike and idly scratched Hades' head before setting up a long-range automatic rifle against my seat. Shadow got to working on setting up his own gun, and all there was left to do was wait for the boom.

About twenty minutes later, the first boom came.

The earth shook beneath our feet at the explosion, and I gave a quick tug at the straps holding my gun to my bike seat. "Shadow, you got that for me if it starts to slip?"

"Yes, president. I have no visuals yet, so go ahead."

The act of leaving my own body never stopped feeling strange. I couldn't even explain how I did it, aside from closing my eyes and simply stepping out of my own skin. It was nothing like what Gunner had with Horus, from when we tried to compare experiences. I wasn't sharing consciousness with another living thing, but temporarily filling a space where consciousness once existed.

The time between being in my own body and into the dead person I'd be seeing through felt like zipping through a dark tunnel. And when I emerged on the other side, I could see, hear, and feel the movement of my surroundings, but all other senses were simply not there. I had no heartbeat, no breath in my lungs, and of course, I couldn't move. It was eerie, especially now when I still felt the warmth of a body that had just been killed.

The first dead man I slipped into was face down on the ground. Panicked shouts and running footsteps surrounded me, but I couldn't see for shit, so I went through the dark tunnel again before finding another host. This next one was facing straight up at the sky. I saw quick flashes of people running, but because I couldn't move my eyes, I missed the directions in which they were going.

This ability sucks. I'd much rather see through a bird.

The third time was the charm, the deceased bastard was lying on his side and giving me a front row view of our work. It was just the panic and chaos we were hoping to create, people running around wildly and unaware of the dangers right under their feet.

Another boom went off to my right, sending a small cluster of people flying.

"It's a minefield, stop moving!" Someone was smart enough to figure it out, but no one paid him any attention. The more explosives set off, the more heightened their panic became.

I surveyed what I could before returning to my own body, jolting up from sitting against my bike.

"You back?" Shadow asked.

"Yeah." I blinked several times and came slowly to my feet—the vertigo always lingered for a bit. "Let me see the map."

Shadow handed it to me and I was quickly able to triangulate where my dead body host had been. Grabbing the radio, I barked out firing and movement orders to the units nearest where the body had been.

"Like shooting fish in a barrel, boys, but stay covered," I said into the radio. "Remember, this only works if they don't get the upper hand and figure out our positions."

"We've got incoming," Shadow warned, swinging his assault rifle to aim between his handlebars.

I looked in that direction, at first only seeing a dust cloud, but the shape of several Jeeps became clearer as they got closer.

"Their backup is hauling ass," I noted. "Easy, man. Don't shoot yet."

"I know, just waiting for the..."

BOOM!

The explosion went off louder than any of the previous ones, the affected Jeep rolling to its side and quickly becoming engulfed in flames.

"Oh shit," I remarked. "That's gonna—"

BOOOOM!

Shadow and I both ducked on instinct, the force of the blast rocking the ground beneath our feet. Despite being over half a mile away, I still felt the heat of the blaze scorch my skin. The other Jeeps were blown off their wheels, two of them still rolling across the landscape like children's toys.

"Damn, that might have done most of the work for us." There was too much dust and smoke in the air to see bodies, but no one close to that blast could have survived it.

"You going back out there to see the damage?" Shadow leaned down to peer through the scope on his rifle.

"Fuck no. I'm not about to find out what it's like to be cooked alive."

A corner of his mouth quirked up. "It's not like you're *technically* alive."

"Yeah, yeah, man. You don't need to tell me how smart you are."

My radio stopped hissing as calls started coming in.

"Holy shit, did you *see* that explosion?!"

"Ugh, bro, I was taking a piss and it made me fall in it!"

"All units come in," I said into the receiver. "Give me numbers, any casualties or major injuries from that blast?"

"Nothing major here, President. Medics are standing by."

"Scared the piss and shit out of us, but we're good."

One by one, everyone reported that they were fine and damn if my heart didn't soar a little. *We're okay*, I realized. It was too soon to feel like we might actually win, but not being utterly fucked from the start was damn better than the luck we'd been having.

"Keep to the plan and stay calm," I ordered. "All the dust and smoke puts us at an advantage. The less they see us, the better."

"I hear helicopters, can't see 'em yet," someone reported. "Sounds directly overhead, but hard to tell. This is Unit 5."

"Howitzers, that's you," I answered. "Take your shot when you see 'em."

Another boom sent the earth shaking not five minutes later. Tash's soldiers scattered madly as a dark form hurtled down from the sky. The falling helicopter only sent more smoke into the air, obscuring everyone's vision too much to get away. It hit the ground and started rolling, then must have hit another one of our bombs, setting off another explosion that knocked us off our feet.

"Feels like goddamn Fourth of July!" I yelled, my ears ringing. "All units, how we doing?"

They all reported in positively again, with only minor burns and shrapnel injuries to treat. But we were still alive and kicking ass. I clipped the radio to my belt and returned to watching the horizon with Shadow.

"I got a few clear shots," he reported, one eye squinting shut while the other looked through the scope.

"Take 'em." I knew he wouldn't miss.

Tash's units on foot were still advancing, the majority of them still unaffected by our bombs due to their sheer numbers. They were definitely nervous though, their marching all out of step and their tight formations breaking. And the closer they got, the thinner their numbers would become.

The unit heading straight for us had to be one of Tash's best. They never broke formation once, their marching steady and robotic. They were clad in black and wore masks and hoods—not unusual for trekking through a dusty desert, but the sight of them coming remained unsettling. They had missed all the previous detonations without breaking a sweat, but if they continued marching in a straight line they'd walk right over one.

My finger hovered over the trigger on my rifle. They knew what was going on by now, their defenses had to be up. But they were laser-focused, and I didn't want them alerted to my position yet. By the time they got close enough to see us, they'd hopefully be blasted sky-high.

I stalked them from my position, checking my scope and pulling away to gauge their distance. They were heading directly for the IED and would be stepping on it within the next twenty feet.

Closer, closer, and closer they came. I no longer needed a scope to see them for a clear shot.

"Come on, come on..." My trigger finger was cramping from how badly I wanted to squeeze. Shadow was next to me, taking people out from a distance like a true assassin, and I just wanted to mow down some Tash followers.

The masked soldiers kept marching closer and then my heart started to race with panic. Why wasn't it detonating? They were walking right over it! I couldn't take on the whole unit myself and everyone else was spread out too far to help.

"Fuck, Shadow, I'm gonna need—"

BOOM!

Shock and relief hit me in equal measure, the blast raining down pebbles and dirt as I ducked under my arm. Something must have been fucked with the detonating mechanism for such a delay, but fucking finally! I went to re-aim my gun, and what I saw made me freeze.

They were *still* marching.

The soldiers toward the center and back of the formation had been hit, their bodies scattered around with either mortal injuries or dead. But the unit leader and the ones in the front carried on like nothing had happened.

No panic. Not a single sign of being shaken or afraid. It wasn't even like they acted *determined* to keep going, but more like they were machines with a single purpose. Human beings didn't act like this. Something was very, very wrong with these men.

"Reaper, shoot them!"

Shadow's command brought me out of my stupor, and I squeezed that trigger with all the fucking strength in my hand.

My initial shots went wild—I was unfocused and thrown off my axis. But thankfully with an automatic rifle, I didn't need to be all that accurate. Some of my shots hit the soldiers in the lower legs. When they fell, the men behind walked on top of them to continue marching.

"Reaper, the leader—"

"I see him," I assured Shadow.

The soldier front and center, the only one with some kind of gold insignia pinned on his all-black uniform, drew his gun and aimed the short barrel at me. Thank all the gods I was faster.

My rapid fire never stopped, all I had to do was aim the rifle at the man's chest to see him go down. His guys kept marching, stepping on him like all the others, and drawing their weapons as soon as they caught sight of us. My ears rang painfully from all the blasts and gunfire. My hands were burning up and cramped with my constant, rapid-fire shooting. But fuck no, I wasn't about to stop until they were all dead.

With Shadow's help, the whole unit fell, until no more men marched like creepy zombies toward us.

"I want that unit searched when it's safe, especially the leader." My hands were surprisingly steady as I checked my gun and reloaded, especially considering how fast my heart was hammering.

"Yes, president. How are the others doing?"

"I think all of our bombs have detonated." I picked up the radio. "All units come in, give me a status update."

The replies came a few agonizingly long seconds later.

"We've got minor injuries, just some debris from the blasts but medics are on it."

"All good here, president."

"Minor injuries here, couple bullet grazes and a twisted ankle but no casualties."

"Same shit here, Pres. It's like target practice."

I looked at Shadow with disbelief as the calls came in. "Are you hearing what I'm hearing?"

"No casualties." He sounded just as awed as I felt. "Despite being massively outnumbered."

"Holy shit, Shadow." I lowered the radio to my bike seat and turned around in a slow circle. "I think...I think we actually won this one."

"It looks that way."

The world surrounding us was hazy, thanks to all the dirt, smoke, and gunpowder being thrown in the air. I heard shouts and pops of gunfire but no longer felt the dread of wondering how many men we'd lose. At the end of the day we might still lose a handful and it would be tragic, but that was war.

Our losses could have been so much worse. Just one soldier panicking and forgetting the plan, allowing his unit to get overwhelmed —that was all it would take. But everything was perfect, seamless.

"President." My radio crackled from one of our unit leaders. "They're surrendering. Your orders?"

"Call in the vans and have them brought back to Four Corners," I answered. "They'll be questioned and tried." If there was anything these people knew about Tash, I wanted it at any cost. After giving my orders, I looked to Shadow. "Shall we search them?"

"Yes, president." He sounded pleased.

We kept our guns on us—in case of any surprises—as we walked out to the battlefield. The landscape was riddled with craters now, thanks to our explosions. Surviving members of Tash's units were on their knees as our guys searched them and bound their wrists while waiting for the army transport vans.

Shadow was already searching through the bodies of the unit that came straight toward us, while I took a moment to just look around and marvel.

We did it.

It may have been just one battle of many, but this victory was *ours*.

"Anything interesting?" I asked Shadow, kneeling next to the unit leader. Hades had been searching with him, sniffing out the bodies.

"No." He almost sounded disappointed. "No photos, letters, jewelry, or anything personal on them at all. Not even tattoos, although..."

He shoved back the sleeve of one man to expose an extensively scarred forearm. Nothing like Shadow's scars, but the man's entire arm had been severely burned at one point.

"This guy *had* tattoos," Shadow remarked. "I can still see ink spots where his skin wasn't burned as badly." He placed the man's arm down at his side. "A couple others have burn scars too."

"So they've had all unique identifying markers taken away." I scanned the dead men's faces, all of them individuals that had acted as mindless drones.

They are now free and at rest.

One glance at Hades told me the answer to the question I didn't know I had. These men may have died just minutes ago, but they certainly hadn't been alive before.

"What do you make of them marching over each other like that?" I asked Shadow. "Not responding to any of their surroundings."

Shadow's hands paused in his quick, efficient search of the soldiers' clothing. "It reminded me of when I'd been hypnotized but...different."

"Different how?"

"It's like..." He cocked his head as he searched for the words. "Hypnosis is not control. It's like being guided through a dream. I was aware the whole time and could stop or wake up at any point. But on the surface, it looked like Doc could control me." He glanced down at the man he'd been searching. "I don't think any of these guys could have stopped if they wanted to."

"So something *was* controlling them."

"I think so, yes." Shadow's mouth hardened as he gazed at each of the dead men. "And erased their individuality in the process."

I reached for the pin on the unit leader's jacket, ripping the fabric as I yanked the gold thing off—it wasn't like he needed it anymore. The more I stared at the golden brooch thing, the more confused and unsettled I got. Whatever the thing was, it wasn't *right*.

"You ever seen this?" I held it up for Shadow to see.

"No. Actually, well," he squinted, "it looks kind of familiar, but I can't recall ever seeing it anywhere."

"Same here." I laid the pin flat in my palm, as though looking at it from a different perspective would jog my memory.

It was little more than a stick figure of an animal, but nothing I could place for sure. The animal looked roughly like a dog, it had four legs, a head, and a tail. But the tail was forked—splitting in two halfway down the length. The ears were triangular like a wolf's, but in reverse, so the thinner ends attached to the head and widened at the tops. The head itself had a long snout like a canine, but the nose and overall head shape was wrong.

I closed my hand around the pin and slid it into my pocket. Looking at it was disorienting in a way, like I was staring at some paradoxical thing that should not have existed, but did. I'd make sure to give it to my dad and his lieutenants later.

"You ready to get out of here?" I rose to my feet and started back toward our bikes.

"Yes." Shadow followed after me. "Can we check in on how the northern battle is going?"

"Excellent idea." I picked up my radio. "Let's hope they've had as good a day as we have."

CHAPTER 4

GUNNER

"Listen up, fuckers!"

"Jesus, Gunner, do you *have* to call them that?"

I couldn't see Mari behind me, but had the image with crystal clarity in my mind—hand rubbing her forehead, groaning but trying not to laugh at how I addressed the soldiers.

"Yes, it's protocol," I whispered under my breath. Then to all the unit leaders in front of me, "You should all know the plan by now. I want no stone unturned, no blade of grass uninspected, between here and Blakeworth. Is that understood?"

"Yes, Captain!" came the chorus of replies.

"Killing blows are only to be made in self-defense. If your unit finds a Blakeworth scout, I want them detained and brought back to me alive. Anyone with injuries should be brought immediately to the field hospital, whether Blakeworth or our own. Any questions?"

T-Bone cupped his hands around his mouth and hollered, "When you gonna come sit in Daddy's lap, pretty boy?"

"You can fuck right off." I grinned as I waved my middle finger at him. The other soldiers allowed themselves a tittering of nervous laughter when they realized we were just fucking around.

"Mari said we could borrow you," T-Bone egged on, draping his arms over Grudge and Dyno's shoulders. The two of them just shook their heads at his antics. T-Bone was clearly the flirt of the trio, although who knew how successful he was with lines like that.

"Shut up, you have your own," Mari fired back.

"Man, I *hope* Blakeworth captures your ass," I laughed before waving my hand to everyone at attention. "Dismissed. All of you to your posts. We head out in thirty."

T-Bone's hounding certainly lightened the mood, if nothing else. Everyone had been serious, if downright somber, about the two battles going on today. Now everyone seemed a little more relaxed, a little more confident as they filed out of the meeting tent.

We were just outside the Four Corners northern border already, gearing up in massive numbers to take out Blakeworth spies and scouts in neutral territory. Mari's field hospital was the tent next door, and she'd use this one for overflow if the medics needed it, although we were hoping it wouldn't be necessary. Our large numbers were meant to flush Blakeworth's spies out from hiding, cut off communication to their territory, and question them for more information. Just on sheer numbers alone, the odds were stacked heavily in our favor.

My thoughts turned to Reaper and Shadow, heading east to confront Tash. They were in the much riskier battle, relying on more complex tactics to balance out their smaller units. But if anyone could pull it off, I knew it was them. I just hoped that whenever these battles were over and I got to go home, that my family would still be intact.

The sky was still dark, but the sun would be rising soon. No one knew exactly where Tash's line was, so they could have been engaging with the enemy already.

Slender hands ran around my waist while my thoughts were on the others. I returned Mari's hug with a squeeze around her shoulders, soaking up the last little bits of warmth and love before a day full of carnage.

"You ready, captain?" She propped her chin on my chest to look up at me.

"Keep calling me *that*," I sighed. "And I never will be. I'll ditch the whole thing to stay here with you."

She laughed lightly and turned her head to place her cheek on my chest. "Be careful out there."

"I will". Horus clicked his beak from his perch on my shoulder. "*We* will," I amended. "You be careful back here too. We shouldn't have much to worry about, but we keep underestimating how sneaky these fuckers are."

"We'll be fine. Jandro's hanging back and I've told all the medics to stay sharp."

"Good." I cupped her face, allowing myself a long gaze at her beautiful features before I lowered a kiss to that mouth. She returned it, holding on to the edges of my cut to keep me in place. I closed my eyes to savor her, to really feel the accelerated pounding in my chest when she kissed me.

Weeks ago she probably would have watched me ride into battle and hoped I never came back. Never again would I take this woman and the family we created for granted.

"Captain."

Some lieutenant calling me from outside the tent jolted me out of the moment. "What?" I growled.

"They're ready for you."

"I'll be right there." My touch slid down Mari's arms, our bodies separating with slow reluctance. "I'll see you when it's done, baby girl," I sighed out, my forehead heavy on hers.

"You better." Her face was tense but a smirk pulled at her lips. "Or Horus is gonna get an earful from me."

The falcon chirped from my shoulder, fluffing up his feathers once before smoothing them down again.

"Let's get this over with then." I headed for the tent flaps, my hand still connected to hers. "So we can move on and finally start our lives."

Mari followed me, her hands squeezing mine as we exited the tent together. Before we could separate, she drew up next to me and kissed me again for all the units to see.

"I love you," she said as she pulled away, untangling our fingers at the last possible moment. "Come back to me."

"I love you more," I called back, not giving a damn about our audience. "And you're the only thing worth coming back to."

Oh yeah. I see you, Blakeworth fuckwads.

Horus soared over miles of rolling hills and endless plains. Our units were still a couple miles south, moving in while T-Bone and I scouted through our birds up ahead.

From up here, it was easy to see how the spies snuck up on us so quickly. They used flashlights with colored film taped over the lenses to communicate messages without making a sound. Most of them were positioned at various points in elevation so they had eyes from every possible vantage point. These fuckers must have seen Jandro and Slick from miles out, and tracked their movement by relaying the coordinates to each other through their lights.

It was genius in its simplicity, really. I was a little annoyed that I never thought of something similar.

Sending my focus back to my own body, I felt heavier and a little disoriented. Next to me on his bike, T-Bone blinked rapidly and gripped his handlebars as he also got his bearings.

"D'you see 'em?" I asked when he came to.

"Oh yeah," he chuckled, flexing his wrists. "We got this in the bag, pretty boy."

Now that we knew where the Blakeworth spies were, it should be a slam-dunk to round them up. I wasn't about to go tempting fate by speaking it out loud, though.

"Take your units around to the east and west to surround them," I said, marking the locations on a map. "We'll come up the middle."

"Yes, sir." He turned his bike around, grinning as he went to relay the orders to Dyno and Grudge.

I hit the receiver on my radio and told my unit leaders all the points we'd be hitting. "If a target isn't at one of those points, let me know and my falcon will find them. We don't want any of them getting back to Blakeworth."

"Roger that, captain. We're on the move."

I stuck the radio in my cut and revved up with a loud roar before tearing across the landscape. My units' Jeeps picked up speed too, racing to give our hiding enemies a rude awakening.

The first ones heard us coming as we got closer, but running on foot and their little dirt bikes had nothing on us. We hunted them down like it was a sport. One of my lieutenants swung his Jeep around, cutting off a couple of runners so close that they bounced off his doors. They weren't badly injured but were quickly surrounded, dropping to their knees with their hands in the air.

I drove on, heading right for another small group trying to zig-zag through some tall weeds. One of the ballsier ones turned around and fired shots at me, all of them going wide in his panic. I rode right up to his ankles, laughing directly in his ear.

"Do you know who the fuck you're shooting at?"

I eased off the throttle, letting him get ahead of me while I pulled out one of my smaller handguns. He looked over his shoulder as he ran, relief in his eyes as he thought he was losing me. But I just wanted some target practice.

I aimed low, where the weeds were the most dense and his legs were barely visible as he ran. I popped off three shots before the grass stilled and a scream rose up.

One of my lieutenants, Gonzalez, walked up as I leisurely drove forward to check my target.

"Four scouting units captured so far," he reported. "We've lost track of a few."

"Gotcha, I'll find your hidden ones in a sec." I was in a good mood, and in no hurry. None of them would be able to escape Horus' sight.

My target was lying on his back, gripping his leg and wincing when we approached. I grabbed his arm and turned him over roughly, patting him down for weapons while inspecting his leg wound.

"Only one shot out of three?" Gonzalez clicked his tongue at me. "You're losing your touch, captain."

"I know, just haven't been practicing." I started searching through my pockets, finally settling on a spare rifle strap. The injured Blakeworth man started crawling away as I approached him with it.

"No, no! Don't kill me."

"Quit squirming and calm down." I pushed him to the ground with a boot on his back, then turned to face his legs as I sat on top of him. "I'm tying this around your leg so you don't bleed out. But feel free to untie it any time if you do prefer to die."

"Wha...what? You're not gonna kill me?"

"Nope. We're not gonna torture you either," I said cheerfully with a pat on his butt. "We will detain you and ask questions, though. Cooperate and you'll be fine."

The man stilled, dumbfounded as Gonzalez and I hauled him up to stand on his good leg.

"I'll track down your escape artists if you're good here."

"Go ahead." Gonzalez bound up the man's wrists and started guiding him toward the other soldiers. "Holler if you need back up."

He had just disappeared through the tall weeds when I planted my feet wide and turned my face toward the sky. "Show me, Horus."

My eyes closed and I was weightless, with the sun on my back and air lifting through my feathers. When my eyes opened, I could count every blade of grass from three hundred feet in the air. Our army swarmed the landscape, just as we intended, but a few had broken past the line we tried to corral them in.

Three Blakeworth scouts ran on foot, their camouflage no match for my falcon's binocular vision. I could count their eyelashes from here. They were fast, I'd give them that. And with the distance they were clearing, they had great endurance. But no human could outrun a motorcycle.

I dove through the air, not to get a closer look, but to touch base with another being who had eyes on them.

Munin waited for me on the branch of a tree in the runners' direct path. I landed next to the glossy black raven just as the humans ran underneath. T-Bone's bird stared at me with its dark eyes and cawed once. Horus screeched back.

In the next moment, my awareness was hurtling through space back into my human body. I caught my footing after a quick stumble and ran back toward my bike. I had that machine between my legs and drove her hard straight north, flattening the tall weeds in my path until they gave way to the rockier terrain.

Not a minute later, I saw T-Bone cutting across the landscape until he fell in next to me. He shot me a maniacal grin, accelerating hard to pull up ahead. His bike was fucking loud, the roar reverberating off of every rock and tree for miles. The runners definitely heard him, and I hoped they were pissing themselves knowing they were being hunted.

The two of us stayed in tandem as we gave chase, following on the heels of the sneaky fuckers we saw through our birds. We could see them with our human eyes now, their forms growing bigger as we kept closer.

"Feel like playing with fire, pretty boy?" T-Bone yelled over our engines.

"What do you mean?" I glanced over to see him flicking a lighter on and off with one hand.

"It's all dry brush up there." He nodded ahead toward the runners, the distance between us and them shrinking with every second. "It'd be a mighty shame if a little brushfire was their last obstacle before making it home."

"You crazy fuck," I laughed, patting at my cut in search of my own lighter. "Let's do it!"

The runners would have to go up another hill before they were technically back in the Blakeworth territory. The city was still miles further up ahead, but we had agreed to fight in neutral territory only.

"Let's split up," T-Bone yelled. "Make a wall of fire they'll need brass balls to jump through."

"Fuck yeah." I was already veering to the right, going around the runners to head them off. T-Bone did the same on the left side of them.

The runners skidded to a stop, grabbing hold of each other's arms and panting with exertion as they watched us pass in front.

"Keep running, little cowards! You're so fucking close," T-Bone taunted. He held his lighter out to the side as he drove, the flame instantly catching the dry bushes like kindling.

The scouts started backing away, darting to the right in an attempt to go around the flames, but we headed them off that way too.

"Ah-ah-ah." T-Bone shook his index finger at them. "That way's not gonna work either."

My brushfire was already bonfire-sized, the flames licking six feet up in the air. The scouts tried darting for an opening between T-Bone's fire and mine, but he quickly blocked them with his bike.

"You want to run home so bad?" he continued taunting them. "Where your governor sits high on the corpses of those who built his city for him?"

"Come on, T. Let's just grab them." I pulled out zip-ties to bind their wrists, but he apparently wasn't done.

"You want to run to a territory that kidnaps women and forces them into marriage?" he went on. "Go ahead!" He gestured toward the fire. "Run through it, jump over it. Let's see how important your home is to you."

Holy shit, he was making this fucking personal for some reason.

"T-Bone," I yelled louder. "These fires could get out of control. Let's just grab them and go."

"Let them get out of control!" he roared at the top of his lungs. "Let these people see what it's like to have everything they love go up in smoke!"

"T-Bone, dude!" I rode up next to him and clapped my hand around the back of his neck, forcing his head to turn until he faced me. His gaze was wild and unfocused, with pupils like pin pricks. "You're not with me right now, man." I slapped his cheek. "Get it together! I need you to focus."

He blinked rapidly, eyes dilating as he focused on me. "Gunner?"

"Help me tie them up and let's get the fuck out before we choke to death." The smoke was already stinging my eyes and throat, our visibility getting hazy. Maybe I shouldn't have been so quick to jump on the fire idea.

"Go!" T-Bone pointed at the Blakeworth runners making a break for it up the last hill. I didn't blame the guy for still grieving those he lost, but he had cost us valuable time.

We spun our bikes around in a cloud of dust and exhaust as we took off after them. The incline grew steeper and I grit my teeth hard as I fought gravity, the rocky terrain, and now the smoke in my throat and eyes. We could still catch them, but were right on Blakeworth's doorstep. We could not afford to dally anymore.

My bike was more lightweight than T-Bone's and I pulled ahead of him, closing the distance on our runners just as they began cresting the hill. If they made it to the bottom, they'd be firmly across the Blakeworth border, and we could not capture them without nullifying our original agreement and causing a much bigger problem.

Steering the bike with one hand, I pulled out my handgun and took aim. A couple of non-lethal shots would end this chase quickly, and we could go home before sundown. I curled my index finger around the trigger as the runners reached the top and started running down the other side. Only by the grace of Horus or some other god watching did I have the sense to look beyond my targets at what awaited us just a few hundred yards away.

"Oh fuck, fuck!" I swerved and braked hard, struggling against my momentum and all the force now carrying me downhill. "T-Bone, turn around! Fucking go back!"

But he couldn't hear me over both of our vehicles running on such a high gear. We nearly crashed into each other as I started my way back up, and he began his way down.

"What are you doing?" he roared before looking past me, his determined expression falling to stunned disbelief. "Oh no..."

"Go! Gooo!"

We started back down the way we came up, and with a confirming glance over my shoulder, I saw my worst fear coming true.

Blakeworth's army was hot on our heels.

Chapter 5

GUNNER

A fucking trap.

We should have known.

T-Bone yelled something like, "They're catching up!" but I couldn't make it out over the *hundreds* of vehicles hot on our tails now. Mostly motorcycles, but I saw some Jeeps and Hummers too. And knowing Blakeworth, these vehicles were souped up, powerful and fast.

In essence, T-Bone was right. We couldn't outrun them.

Fuck it all, this was *not* how this battle was supposed to go.

We pushed our bikes to their limit, but riders on some kind of crotch rocket-dirt bike hybrids zipped around us like it was nothing. Two long lines of riders converged ahead of us to surround us and cut us off.

T-Bone glanced at me and I gave the tiniest shake of my head. We could plow right through them, probably killing a couple people and hurting ourselves in the process. But that would also lead them straight to Four Corners. We were miles ahead of our army, and most of them were probably heading back to base at this point.

No, I'd rather let myself be captured before bringing an army right to our doorstep when our people were unprepared. I began to slow down and T-Bone did the same, his face hard-set and determined. At least we were of one mind about this.

The riders ahead of us already had guns drawn, pointing them directly at us when we came to a stop.

"Off the bikes," someone yelled through an opaque black helmet.

T-Bone and I dismounted with our hands in the air, the two of us getting immediately shoved to our knees and patted down aggressively for weapons.

"At least buy me a drink first," the Son muttered. He got a punch to the stomach for that, doubling over with a groan.

I tensed under my own rough patting and groping, fighting the instinct to rush to his aid. My heart drummed wildly as Blakeworth soldiers closed in tighter around us, and I tried to force calming breaths through my chest.

Captured doesn't mean dead, I thought. *And it doesn't mean you'll never get back home again.*

Oh fuck. I promised Mari I would come back.

Sorry, baby girl. Looks like it won't be happening today.

"Why do you look so familiar?" A looming figure stood over me, the uniform decorated with war medals and an opaque black helmet blocking out the sun.

"I dunno. If you used to be a woman, we probably had a good time at some point—ugh!" Apparently it was my turn for a punch in the gut. I didn't see the hit coming and it knocked the wind out of me. "You hit hard for a Blakeworth pussy," I wheezed.

"Ah, I've always wanted to punch a Youngblood." After shaking out his fist, the figure removed his helmet. The face underneath belonged to a middle-aged man with blue eyes and grey hair at his temples. I stared at him for a few moments but the recognition never came.

"Haven't had the pleasure of meeting you before but," I coughed, "I would love to punch you as well." Sadly, my hands were now zip-tied behind my back.

"Your father and I have some...history," the man sneered down at me.

"Yeah, well, join the club, dude. Oof!"

I earned a fist to my cheek for that one, his ring cutting across my face with a stinging pain.

"I knew you were his the instant I saw your pretty fucking face," he went on. "I gotta say, it's such a joy to see how far Youngblood's golden boy has fallen."

"I haven't fallen," I hissed, spitting blood on his shoe. Like I cared if he kicked me in the face with it. "I've risen."

"Huh." The man looked around at his army, now completely closed in on T-Bone and me. "Doesn't look that way to me, kid."

"You'll never get it." I shook my head at him. "Dogs like you will never understand."

"Understand what?" he humored me.

"Let me guess. You hate my old man because he burned you on a deal. Either that or you're jealous of him. You wanted his life—the contracts, the money, a different mistress for every day of the week." I shook my head, ready to welcome whatever hit came next. "Just another sad little man who wanted everything Jon Youngblood had."

"And look at his sorry shithead for a son." The man, who I figured was a general, regarded me with disgust. "Born into the best possible life and he threw it all away."

"And I'd do it again." I leaned forward, a thrill running through me at his retreating steps and the flash of fear in his eyes. Hands clapped down on my shoulders to hold me in place, but I paid them no attention. "I traded my life and my name for freedom, general. For the open road and the sky. For integrity. Things you can't even imagine."

"What an ungrateful child," the general scoffed.

I grinned at him, knowing my teeth were stained red with blood. "No argument there."

"And to think I almost promised my daughter to you."

"I hope she finds her freedom too." I didn't know where this conversation was going anymore, if I was stalling or just pushing his buttons for the hell of it. This guy wanted to gloat, so I wanted to knock him down. Adrenaline was still riding me hard and I was just spouting jabs at him without thinking. "I hope she finds a man you'll never approve of. One who loves her deeply and worships her pussy with his tongue every —oof!"

There came the second punch across my other cheek, pain ringing through my teeth and up to my skull.

"She's thirteen, you fucking brute!"

I spat out more blood before peering up at him. "Are you fucking joking?"

"Do I look like I am?"

"Think about this for a minute." I paused to spit out more blood. "You'd marry her off as a child bride to someone she doesn't even know. Who do you think is the bigger piece of shit between the two of us?"

"I would have secured her future with the Youngblood name! Set up my legacy for life, if only your father had kept *you* under control!"

"Yeah, that's the thing." My grin grew wider. "No one controls me."

This general was getting hot under the collar, but managed to calm himself after taking a few steps back from me. "Some control will do you good," he promised with the creepiest fucking smile.

All his posturing was getting boring, so I slid my gaze over to T-Bone, who was not having riveting conversations like me. His head was tipped back, eyelids heavy and twitching. I hissed in a breath of shock. Was he really seeing through Munin *now?* That was some risky shit. I knew I was vulnerable out of my own body, so I'd never look through Horus while in a compromising position, much less in the hands of the enemy.

But the soldiers posted on T-Bone paid him no mind, apparently waiting on orders from their general who was obsessed with riding my dad's coattails. He had his back turned to me at the moment, talking in low voices with his unit leaders when T-Bone finally came to. The other biker slid a glance and an amused smirk in my direction.

"No worries, pretty boy," he muttered under his breath.

That phrase could have meant anything, but he didn't elaborate. He did seem calmer though, taking a deep breath that puffed his chest out. His zip-tied hands stretched out behind him like he was waking from a nap.

"You okay, dude?" I asked him.

"Peachy," he grunted back. After a few beats of silence he added, "Sorry about that."

"It's alright," I said. "That stuff sneaks up on you."

"When you least expect it," he murmured.

One of the men speaking with the general whipped around right then. "Do I have to cut your fucking tongue out?"

T-Bone's expression morphed into a rage I'd never seen on his face before. "You think that's funny? Come and try, Blakeworth pussy."

The memory hit me right then—Grudge couldn't speak because his tongue had been removed. And T-Bone took that threat *very* personally.

Everyone had stopped talking and turned to look at us now. The man who threatened T-Bone laughed lightly as he pulled a knife from his belt, the small, silver blade flicking open and closed. "I'll find you much funnier when you can't talk anymore."

"Come get it, then." T-Bone stuck his tongue out and wagged it, taunting him. "Take it from me. You take everything else from people tied up and on their knees!"

"T-Bone, shut up!" I hated how he flipped on and off like a light switch. Grudge and Dyno must have kept him even-keeled, because he was a fucking maniac without them.

"I recognize him too," the general mused, narrowing his eyes. "He's one of the thugs who stole the governor's daughter-in-law."

"She was never his!" T-Bone roared, face red and veins popping in his neck. "She never belonged to your fucked-up territory."

The general was the epitome of calm compared to my friend foaming at the mouth like a rabid dog. "Captain, go ahead and remove his tongue." His eyes drifted to me. "Make sure Youngblood Junior is watching."

"No, no, no, no." They turned my body toward T-Bone as the captain approached him, brandishing the knife. "Stop this. He won't talk anymore."

"He sure won't," the general said with a quiet sort of glee.

"Take it from me!" T-Bone goaded, not helping his own case at all while pulling against his restraints. "Show me what a big man you are to silence me, tied up and on my knees with all these fuckers holding me back."

"Stop it, T! He's not fucking around."

"Oh I know, pretty boy." T-Bone's gaze slid toward me, and I was stunned to see his eyes were sharp and fully aware. He wasn't somewhere else like with the runners and the fire. He was all there, and he actually *wanted* this. "I told you, it's alright."

He refocused on the captain in front of him, the man flipping the knife in the air like a taunt. With a lurch of his body, T-Bone somehow got a leg underneath him and started pushing himself to stand.

"Hold him! Fucking hold him!" the captain ordered.

More soldiers rushed in to push T-Bone back down to his knees. One person wrapped an arm around his neck in a triangle choke hold. Someone else started binding his ankles together. Altogether, there were five people restraining him. He just grinned at the captain, not at all disturbed by the knife now hovering inches in front of his face.

"Can't make it too easy for you now," T-Bone goaded. "Otherwise you'll still look like a pussy to all of your men."

The captain only scowled. Everyone was watching to see what he would do. I couldn't help but wonder how the soldiers would feel if he actually went through with it. Some men could be intimidated into falling in line, while in others, the same act could spark a rebellion.

"Hold him still." The captain stepped closer. "Hold his head and open his mouth."

"That's it. Gimme a kiss, captain," T-Bone said before a soldier grabbed his jaw and forced it open.

"Don't!" I struggled against my own bonds, the zip-ties just digging tighter into my wrists while more soldiers came to hold me in place. "Don't, please. Take my tongue instead."

"No, we can use Youngblood," the general said in response to his captain's questioning glance. "This scum," he jerked his chin at T-Bone, "we don't need for shit."

"I'm useless too!" I insisted, desperate enough to say anything at this point. "My father wants nothing to do with me. You'll never get access to his fortune through me. I'm just a fucking biker like T-Bone."

"We'll see," the general said dismissively. "Get on with it, captain."

"No!" I fought and wiggled a shoulder loose, only to have a foot crash into my back. I landed facedown in the dirt and then felt the punishing weight of a boot on my head.

I could only see the captain's shoes a few feet in front of me, and T-Bone's knees. Any second now I expected to hear his screams and watch the blood drip down his body. God, why the fuck would he ask for that? So Grudge wouldn't be the only one?

Someone yelled from a distance, but I couldn't make out the words with a rubber sole crushing my ear. The shoe on my head was gone in the next second, and all the boots in front of my face started running around, people shouting in a panic.

T-Bone had been shoved down and was now lying in the same position as me. He coughed out a mouthful of dirt and grinned at me, his tongue still very much intact.

"What's happening?" I grunted out, trying to push myself up, but I was too hogtied.

"These fuckers were so focused on cutting off my tongue, they didn't see the cavalry come to our rescue," he chuckled, then winked at me. "Told ya, it would all be alright."

CHAPTER 6

MARIPOSA

"Is that smoke?" I shielded my eyes, squinting far across the landscape. There was definitely a plume of gray smoke rising up in the distance. "Was making a fire part of the plan?"

Lieutenant Gonzalez shrugged, his eyes never leaving the Blakeworth prisoner I was treating. "It's dry as hell out there. Even just hot ammunition could spark something."

"It looks big," I noted. "Could it be a signal of some kind?"

"Maybe. I'll check-in with Gunner when the POWs are secure."

I waved a hand over the man on the hospital bed, who was now firmly under general anesthesia. "He's not going anywhere, lieutenant. Can you check-in with him now, please?"

Gonzalez ducked his head with a sheepish grin. "I'll be right over there." He pointed outside the hospital tent flap.

"I'll scream if I need you," I promised. I also had my little handgun in a holster and one of Shadow's daggers strapped to my calf under my scrub pants. Chances were I could take this drugged up gunshot victim by myself, but I didn't want Gonzalez to feel inadequate.

He stepped outside and spoke with a low voice into his radio as I cleaned up my station. Like Gunner had expected, we only had a few injured come through the field hospital. Most of them were the Blakeworth scouts they'd been sent to capture, primarily minor injuries but some gunshot wounds. So far nothing had been fatal, which was a huge relief to me.

I looked toward the battlefield again with crossed arms, frowning at the smoke reaching higher. The day was nearing its end and some of the soldiers were coming back already, their assignments complete. But there was no sign of my husband and his falcon.

"Captain Gunner I repeat, do you copy?" Gonzalez said into his radio. His voice sounded tense and my heartbeat began to accelerate.

I hurried out of the tent. "What's going on?" The lieutenant turned to face me but said nothing, his lips pressed into a tight frown. "Gonzalez, please don't even *think* about keeping information about my husband from me."

"He's not answering," he admitted. "My unit met up with him about an hour ago. He was going to fetch a couple of runners. They were on foot and he was riding. It should have been easy, but we haven't heard from or seen him since."

"We have to find him." My feet started moving, instinct taking over, but Gonzalez grabbed my arm, halting my movement.

"We will, Mari, but *you* can't go out there."

"I have been in battles before. Let go of me!" I yanked my arm from his grip.

"I'm sorry, but your husbands would never approve of me letting you out into that field."

"Well, they never approve of a lot of the shit I do. They're used to it."

"Mari." Gonzalez's jaw ticked. "General Bray will come down on *me* if you do this."

"No he won't, I'll explain it to him. But we're wasting time here arguing. Which units are heading back out? I'll join them."

"You will *not*!"

"What's going on?"

I whipped around to see Shadow and Reaper walking up, my hope soaring. "You guys are back!"

"We nailed it, sugar," Reaper grinned, opening his arms in a subtle motion for a hug.

I went to squeeze around him briefly, then pulled back. "I'm so glad! But no one has heard from Gunner and I'm worried."

"Is that smoke?" Shadow squinted at the horizon much like I had.

"Give us the rundown, lieutenant," Reaper said to Gonzalez, who repeated the same information he gave me.

"You're right, Mari should stay here." Shadow glanced at his president with a cool, neutral gaze. His assassin's gaze, I realized.

"Why?" I demanded. "I can help. What if he's injured out there?"

"If it's anywhere near that smoke, it's not that far. It's better if you're here, with all the tools you might need." Reaper reached out and brushed his fingers against my hand. "If he's in bad shape, we know how to keep him stable until we bring him back here."

"What if you don't, though? What if Blakeworth ambushed him and you guys are walking into a trap?"

"All the better that you stay here." Shadow approached me, all imposing and predatory to the point that Gonzalez took a step back. But I stayed put and allowed him to tower over me, his hand coming out to rest on my hip with a comforting weight. "Let us ride into danger while you stay safe, for once."

"I don't like it," I said with a shake of my head.

"Yeah, well, we don't like you running off either," Reaper chuckled. "Stay, sugar. We'll keep you updated over the radio."

"Hey, guys?"

We all spun to find Jandro walking up with a grim-faced Dyno and Grudge. My heart sank as I silently wondered, *Oh no, what now?*

"T-Bone's units are back, but no sign of the man himself," Dyno reported. "He didn't rendezvous with us at the agreed-upon spot."

"Gunner is missing too," I said.

"Well, shit. What are we waiting for then?" Jandro spread his hands. "We're taking prisoners, Blakeworth probably is too."

"Not if we can help it," Reaper growled. "Let's go."

Everyone followed his lead and my frustrated groan mostly fell on deaf ears. But Jandro hung back, wrapping me in a warm embrace and tilting my face up to press insistent kisses to my mouth.

"We still outnumber them," he whispered, forehead against mine. "We'll be fine, and back before you know it."

"I know I'm more useful back here," I admitted. "I just hate that all of you are going. I can't lose you all in one swoop!"

"Not gonna happen, *Mariposita*." He cupped my face sweetly, but his smile was devilish. "You softened us up, but the Demons are still crafty bastards when we fight. With two of the Sons with us, we can't lose."

"Stop tempting fate and just get them back." I shoved him away roughly. "The sooner the better."

"We will." His promise was solemn, sealed with a final kiss before he hurried away to join the others.

DUSK CAME. AND THEN NIGHTFALL, WITH NO SIGNS OF my men.

I was exhausted but knew I couldn't sleep a wink. Most of my time was spent pacing around the hospital tent, listening to the static of the radio in my hands.

As promised, Reaper had given regular updates until roughly three miles out. Last I heard, they still hadn't spotted Gunner or T-Bone. One lieutenant speculated that Blakeworth had put some interference out that messed with radio waves. Whatever the case, the silence made the hours pass by torturously slow.

Nightfall eventually turned to early morning, with no news and no sight of them. At four AM, I said, "Fuck it," and marched out to where my dirt bike was parked. Unfortunately, it was near the officer's meeting tent, and I hoped I could take off quickly enough before any lieutenants spotted me.

No sooner had I grabbed my handlebars and started walking it out toward the battlefield when I heard a distinct rumbling fill the once-quiet air. Headlights turned on in the distance, which would have looked remarkably like fireflies if I wasn't so desperately hoping.

It wasn't just a few lights, or even a dozen. More and more switched on, creating a festive line that shined upon our camp. There were at least a hundred of them, motorcycles and Jeeps from the looks of it. People started coming out of their tents to look, and I stiffened for a moment. Were these our people returning to us? Or was it Blakeworth invading? It was too dark to tell, the headlights too bright to make out anything on the vehicles they shone from.

Somehow, over the rumbling growing louder, I heard, "We got him, *Mariposita*!"

My knees buckled, threatening to give out from under me as I sagged from relief. They found him, and they were coming back!

I returned my bike to its parking spot and went back to the hospital tent, setting up sutures, forceps, scalpels, local anesthesia—whatever Gunner might need for the shape he was in. I had just scrubbed my hands and pulled on gloves when my men burst through the tent flaps.

"Gunner!" I choked out a sob at the sight of him.

He was filthy, covered in dirt with dried blood on his cheeks, lips, and chin. But he was standing there, on his own, smiling easily like it was just another day.

"Sorry to keep you waiting, baby girl," he rasped. "But I told you I'd come back, didn't I?"

"Y-you asshole," I hiccuped through my sobs, rushing over to him. "What happened?"

"Runners lured us to the waiting Blakeworth army just outside their border." His arms came around my back, rubbing up and down soothingly. "They had me and T-Bone captured for a hot minute but—"

"Captured?!" I cried.

"We were okay, honestly." He cupped my face, bright blue eyes staring down at me before glancing at the others over his shoulder. "They were chatty fuckers, so we kept stalling. T-Bone distracted their attention enough so they didn't even see anyone running up on them."

"It was still a hell of a battle," Reaper huffed. "But we made it through, and captured ourselves a general and a captain."

I looked at the rest of my men for the first time since they arrived. They did look worn out and dirty, like they'd been scuffling for hours. "Are any of you hurt?"

"Nah, sugar. We're fine."

I sagged with relief against Gunner's chest. "And T-Bone?"

Gunner frowned. "We got separated in the chaos. I sure as fuck hope he's okay."

"I saw him riding back with Dyno," Shadow confirmed.

"Thank fuck."

"So what was the smoke? Some kind of signal?" I asked.

Gunner shook his head with a soft laugh. "A total fucking accident that ended up saving our bacon. If you guys hadn't seen it, T-Bone and I would be in a Blakeworth cell right now."

"But you're not." I untangled from him to grab alcohol wipes for the blood on his face. "None of you are, and that's what matters."

"So I'm not a super smart math guy or anything but," Jandro scratched the back of his head. "Did we win *two* battles today?"

There was a beat of silence before Reaper answered softly, "Yeah. We sure as fuck did."

I paused in cleaning Gunner's face so he could turn and face the others, his grin infectious and bright. "Holy shit, guys. We did it."

"We can't afford to celebrate yet," Reaper said. "Tash has a lot more in store for us, and I'm sure Blakeworth does too. But for now?" He looked at the dust covering his arms, then at his fellow men. "We deserve a fucking shower at least."

"I need some fucking sleep," Shadow grunted out.

Reaper laughed and thumped Shadow's chest. "Go on and get a solid few hours. We'll need to brief my dad on everything later today."

"We'll be right after you guys," I said. "I want to make sure this one is medically cleared before we head home." I returned to dabbing at the cuts on Gunner's cheek.

"I won't say no to a beautiful medic fussing over me." Gunner smirked.

"We'll see you at home then." Reaper nodded curtly, then quickly stepped out of the tent.

The sudden departure had me staring at the tent flap for a few seconds. A familiar discomfort coiled in my gut. He was doing that moody, hot and cold thing. Again.

Don't read into it, I told myself. *We've all been up for over twenty-four hours. He's exhausted.*

But Jandro and Shadow came over to give me quick kisses goodbye before heading out after Reaper. I sighed before returning my attention to Gunner's wounds. Reaper and I were still complicated, messy. I couldn't get upset over every little thing when I hadn't fully allowed him back in yet.

"You okay, baby girl?" Gunner's eyes were watchful as I cleaned his face. He had deep scrapes on both cheeks that had bled, but they didn't appear to need stitches. His lower jaw was bruised and swelling on both sides, but nothing appeared broken.

"All things considered, yeah." I dabbed ointment on his cheek. "What happened here?"

"The Blakeworth general popped me a couple times," he grunted out. "He had rings on."

"Who wears gaudy rings out to a battlefield?" I grumbled.

"Someone who doesn't actually fight," Gunner scoffed, then went quiet for a few moments. "He knew my dad."

"Oh?" I paused, watching his expression. "Is that...bad? Good?"

He shrugged and let out an indignant huff. "Doesn't matter to me. Never has. My old man's just a sperm donor as far as I care."

"Something about it is bothering you enough to mention it," I noted, returning to treating the cuts on his cheeks.

"He was going to cut out T-Bone's tongue and then beat him to death, most likely. He only wanted to keep me alive because he thought he could use me," Gunner sighed out tiredly. "My whole life used to revolve around strengthening my dad's power. Or people using me as a stepping stone to access my dad for their own gain. It just," he raised a hand and let it flop back down to his thigh, "sucked to be reminded of that. I thought I got away from that life." Gunner used the heels of his palms to rub his eyes. "Sorry, I'm whining like a little bitch while you've been worried about me. Sorry about—"

"Hey, stop." I grabbed his wrists to pull them away from his eyes. "You were almost captured by the enemy today. That's going to bring up a lot of upsetting shit. You don't have to apologize for anything."

"Yes, I do." He freed his wrists from my hands and laced his long fingers with mine. "I'm not done apologizing for failing you as a husband."

My breath stuttered in my chest for a moment. "Tonight, you *are* done. Believe it or not, I'm not mad at you today."

Gunner let out a soft chuckle, lowering his forehead to mine. "How was I lucky enough to end up with you?"

"Because I know you're more than your name and your family's wealth," I said. "I've never met your father, but I know you're a hundred times the man he is."

His grin grew. "It wasn't until you that I really felt like I could be."

"You are." Finished with his face, I lowered my hands. "Did you get hit anywhere else?"

"No."

"Good." I peeled my gloves off with a triumphant snap. "You're cleared to go home. Might want some ice and painkillers for your jaw soon."

"Okay," he said absently, reaching for my hands again. "Hey, can I take you somewhere before we go home?"

I raised a brow at him. "Take me where?"

"A place I used to stop at on supply runs. It's not far from here. I've been meaning to take you out there, just," he lifted one shoulder, "we never got the time."

"I'd love to, Gun, but I'm exhausted. I need a shower and—"

"This is a great place to rest. And we can uh, wash up." He smirked. "It's totally secluded. There won't be anyone else but us, promise."

My eyes narrowed. "Okay, really. What is this place?"

"You'll see." His eyes lit up. "I don't want to ruin the surprise."

Chapter 7

MARIPOSA

The ride was cold, even for how early in the morning it was. The sun wasn't even up as Gunner drove us roughly a half hour through a small, winding canyon, and I shivered as I clung to his waist.

"How did you even find this place?" I asked at one point. I'd lost all sense of direction miles ago. There was no trail here, we drove over completely wild terrain. The twists and turns through the rocky formations seemed endless.

"Had to hide some contraband a couple years back," he answered. "I figured if *I* got lost the first few times up here, thieving MCs definitely wouldn't find our stuff."

"Mm-hm." I lifted off the seat and leaned forward to stick my tongue in his ear. "What kind of contraband?"

"Weapons, mostly."

"Mostly."

"And a certain green herb, occasionally." He smirked at me over his shoulder. "Never anything harder than that, though."

"Amateur," I teased him, kissing his cheek as I settled back down in the seat. The guys and Noelle loved to joke about me about trading prescription drugs, like I was the most hardcore dealer ever to join the Demons.

A few more twists and turns later, I saw what looked like fog in the distance, hanging thick and heavy, only in this section of the canyon. Gunner slowed as we approached it, warm air brushing my cheeks the closer we got. It was a shocking contrast to the cold on the entire ride here, and took me a moment to figure it out.

"Is that steam?"

"Damn right it is." Gunner stopped the bike a few feet away from where the steam cloud hung in the air. "This is a natural hot spring, baby girl."

"Oh my god!" I couldn't scramble off the bike fast enough. Gunner laughed as I ran directly toward the steam cloud, the warmth now coating my skin in dew like I was in a fancy spa. There was a gentle slope and more rocks to climb over but sure enough, the steam rose from a small pool filled with glassy, crystal-clear water.

"Told you it'd be great for relaxing." Gunner came up behind me, already shrugging off his cut and pulling apart his belt buckle. "And washing up," he added with a lascivious grin.

"Is it safe?" I asked him.

"Oh yeah. I've been up here dozens of times. It's pretty hot, but you get used to it after a few minutes." He pulled his shirt over his head and gave me an intent look. "It's shallow, and you're a fine swimmer now anyway."

I didn't have to say anything and he assuaged my worries anyway, coming up to me and wrapping me in a hug. "I won't let anything happen to you regardless," he added with a kiss on my forehead.

"Fine, you've convinced me." I smacked his abs once and started shedding my own clothes.

"Just think of it like a hot bath." He bent over to unlace his boots and remove them, then shoved his pants down his legs. "From nature."

Once both down to our birthday suits, Gunner took my hand and started leading me down to the pool.

"Watch your step. Some of these rocks are sharp," he cautioned. He let out a hiss as he stepped one foot into the water and then the other. "Been a while. Feels like it's gotten hotter."

"Probably 'cause the air is colder," I mused. My skin erupted in goosebumps the moment my clothes came off, and my hand that wasn't holding Gunner's was clenched in a fist against the cold.

"Whenever you're ready, baby girl. Try a foot. Take it slow."

I pointed my toes and reached, skimming across the surface of the water. "Yeesh, that's hot!"

"My feet feel okay now." The water was so clear, I could see Gunner's toes wiggling a few inches below the surface. "Just let your body acclimate."

I nodded and, tightening my grip on his hand, lowered my foot into the scorching water next to his, making the same hissing sound as he did.

"Just a few degrees below being cooked alive," he laughed, wrapping both arms around my waist.

"Sure feels that way." I wrapped an arm around his shoulders and waited until the water felt pleasantly warm enough before dipping my other foot in.

Together we eased in slowly. He was right about it being shallow—the water only came up to waist-height while standing. Working our way down to sitting, I finally let out a satisfied sigh once the water rose past my shoulders.

It was ten times better than a hot bath. The constant heat soaked into all my tired muscles and made me utterly relaxed, languid. Gunner splashed water over his face and shoulders, then dipped his head back to wash the rest of the battle out of his hair. I did the same and oh, that heat felt incredible on my scalp too.

"This is amazing," I told him, sitting sideways in his lap once we finished rinsing the past day away. "Thank you for bringing me."

"I didn't want to wait," he admitted, fingers dipping in and out of the water as they traced patterns on my back. "Who knows when the next battle will be? Or how long this war will drag on for? I want to make time for things like this whenever we can."

"Me too." I nuzzled his neck and kissed him there, lacing my hands on his opposite shoulder.

"I want you and Shadow to come up here," Gunner went on. "I've always thought of this place as mine, but I want it to be a refuge for you." His arms circled my waist under the water. "A place you can run away to when some of your husbands are driving you crazy."

"Gunner." I lifted my head from his shoulder and pressed my forehead to his temple. "I don't need apology gifts from you. Or sacrifices or whatever. This place *is* yours, and I'm grateful you shared it with me."

"Well there's not much else I can give." He chewed his lip. "And I owe you. Because I contributed to taking him away from you."

I wrapped tighter around his neck and kissed his cheek. "All I want is for you to be honest with me, love me, and love the other guys."

"Loving you is easy, baby girl."

"And the rest?"

"Of course, but loving you is easiest." He turned his head, nudging his nose against mine. "You ask so little of us."

"Well at the end of the day, you're all pretty great men."

"Huh." Gunner let out a small breath of laughter as his hand slid up my back to grip the back of my neck. "At the end of the day, we're a pack of outlaws who found ourselves a queen."

His mouth came down on mine with demand and heat that rivaled the water we sat in. Our tongues dove and crashed, lips sliding against each other with a friction that lit me up even hotter. I turned in his lap to straddle him, his thickening cock stroking my lower belly as our kisses stoked the fire that always burned bright within us.

In fact, I was getting a little *too* hot.

"Gunner," I gasped, breaking off a kiss, then forgetting what I was going to say as his tongue teased the spot below my earlobe.

"Mari," he groaned back, nipping me before dragging his mouth down the side of my neck.

"Gun, can we, um, get out?" My hips rolled forward despite the request, my core seeking the solidness of his cock between us.

"Yeah, if you want." His tongue laved my collarbone, hands lifting me higher out of the water so he could kiss the swells of my breasts.

"Yes, please!" The cooler air was a shocking relief from the hot spring, which had started to get overwhelming. "It's too hot now."

"Hold on." Gun's face remained firmly in my chest as he lifted us out, my arms and legs clasped around him.

It was such a sensory delight, the cool air caressing my overheated body, and still having the heat of Gunner's bare skin on mine.

"Careful," I told him as he walked us out of the pool.

"I know where I'm goin'." The skin of my chest was reddening where he kissed and teased me, his fully engorged cock now pulsing between us.

I glanced over my shoulder to see that he was heading straight for his bike, and a thrill bolted through me. Gunner went for the back end of the motorcycle, perching me on the edge of his seat, and returned to kissing my mouth with a ferocity that had me aching between my legs.

Mid-kiss, he reached behind him and forcibly unlocked my ankles from each other. Holding my thighs apart, Gunner ignored my whimpers and pleas to be fucked as he began to descend down my body. He went back and forth between each breast, sucking and running his teeth along my nipples until I begged for more. That wicked tongue dragged down my body until he finally devoured my pussy in a long, succulent kiss.

"Fuck!" My screams echoed off the canyon walls as Gunner probed me with his tongue, running it from my opening to my clit and back down again. My thigh muscles were no match for his hands splaying me apart, no matter how badly I resisted his grip in an effort to clamp my legs around his head.

"Gunner, Gunner..." I reached for him, fingers sinking into the wet, golden strands of his hair. "Gunner, please..."

His eyes met mine and he shook his head no, dragging that scorching hot tongue across my clit in a way that made my head fall back on the bike seat. I must have sounded like a wounded animal with how much I whined and begged. My core closing around nothing was pure torture.

He dragged my orgasm out for as long as he could with that tongue, finally giving my poor clit some relief with some fast, flicking magic that I never felt another man replicate. But even as the release swept over me, shooting out through my limbs, I still felt too hollow and empty.

Gunner stood upright, towering over me as he licked his glossy lips and fisted his cock. "You want this, baby girl?"

I was almost afraid to say yes, out of fear that he would deny me. My lips parted as I watched him stroke up and down that thick, beautiful length. Jesus, he could have been a porn star just with how pretty his cock was, never mind his actual bedroom skills.

Apparently impatient for an answer, Gunner released himself, letting the dense weight of his cock fall onto my clit with a soft slap. I was still incredibly sensitive from my orgasm and squirmed with a groan. He grinned, held around his base again and repeated the motion. That one was more of a direct hit and it sent sparks through me.

"Yes!" I cried out, almost in tears. "Yes, I want it. Please, please fuck me, Gunner."

"That's my sweet girl," he praised, drawing his hips back until his blunt head slid through my folds.

When he pressed forward it was the sweetest relief, almost better than an orgasm. The ache inside me was replaced by such a satisfying fullness that my head fell back with a reverent moan.

"Fuck..." It was Gunner's turn to bite out curses, his eyes locked on where our bodies connected as he dragged slowly out of me. "I can never get over how fucking incredible you feel."

"More, don't stop," I breathed, rocking my hips as he returned to sheathe himself in me.

"Not a chance, baby girl." His voice was always lower, rougher during sex. I loved how being together this way brought out a growly, possessive side to my sweet, always-smiling husband. He anchored one hand on my hip as he picked up the pace, using the other to grip one of the compartments next to the seat. "I can't believe it's taken this long to fuck my woman on a bike."

"Better late than never," I grinned up at him. Only Reaper and I had sex directly on a bike before. A passing thought of doing it with all my guys, like filling up a punch card, made me giggle.

"Something funny?" Gunner arched a brow and he slammed into me harder, that cocky smirk showing how much he enjoyed my attempt to reply—words turned into moans and curses and babbling that made no sense because *holy shit,* I was going to come again.

His skilled fingers went to my clit and he never fell out of rhythm with his thrusts, sending me hurtling over the edge with a few quick swipes that turned me into a quivering mess.

I didn't even feel the cold anymore. The heat of our fucking, our connection, our love, roared like a bonfire.

Gunner pulled completely out of me when my aftershocks dulled to hot pulses and I whined at the loss of the delicious fullness. In the next moment he grabbed me and flipped me over onto my stomach, my arms and legs now straddling the back of the bike as he re-entered me from behind with a deep thrust.

"Holy fuck, that's so fucking sexy," he grunted, hips crashing into my ass while his hands dug into my waist. "I need a picture of this, or for Shadow to draw it at least."

"Yeah? Ahh…" I held on to the edge of the seat, taking and relishing in all of Gunner's hard crashes into me.

"I love this view," he panted. "My gorgeous woman with these hips and her sexy tattoo. My bike's pretty sexy too," he added with a laugh. "And fuck me, I just love watching your sweet pussy take my cock." His thrusts slowed as he moaned loudly and I looked back to see his head thrown back, eyes shut as his grip tightened on my flesh. "You look so fucking amazing, it's gonna make me come too fast."

"Don't stop, I'm getting close again…"

Gunner's growl was primal as his hips slowed, his grip tightening on my waist as he forced himself to take long drags of his length through me. I trembled around him, my release so close but just out of reach. His breaths were labored, ragged as he fought for his own control.

"I want to make this last," he rasped, running his palm up my back. "I don't want to go back to war and meetings so soon."

"Then fuck me again after this."

He laughed breathlessly and leaned over to brush a kiss along the back of my shoulder. "I think I just might."

Gunner stilled inside me as his lips teased the back of my neck, my earlobes, wherever he could reach. I arched up to kiss him, and his hands swept underneath to my breasts, plucking my nipples to aching peaks in the cold air.

With his hands and mouth occupied, I did the moving for him—pressing back on his length so I could feel that delicious stroke inside me.

"Oh fuck," he groaned, forehead heavy on mine. "That's, fuck, that's gonna do it."

"Me too," I whined, holding the edges of the seat while my lower body rocked back and forth. The dull roar from our short breather fired up into a demanding blaze again, the need too great for me to stop or slow down.

"Oh fuck yeah, use me," Gunner growled, his arms tense and straight on either side of the bike as he held himself still for me. "Take what you need from me, baby girl."

"I need all of you," I whimpered, my backward thrusts desperate and frenzied on his stiff length. He swelled inside me, the pressure making me breathless with need.

Gunner reached around and between my legs, finding my clit and keeping his fingers pressed there so I could rock onto his cock and his hand with every movement. I didn't even have time to take a breath and shout *yes* before my pleasure reached its peak. My limbs shook with the release, Gunner's hand remaining firmly in place as he finished with a last few stuttered thrusts through my aftershocks.

His forehead came to my back with a heavy moan, panting breaths making my skin shiver. We remained locked together, our bodies pulsing gently where we connected. Gunner's hand eventually trailed up my arm, his fingers curling through mine.

"Wish we could stay here," he murmured, stirring gently as he dragged lazy kisses on my back.

I brought our joined hands to my lips and kissed his palm. "One day we can."

"One day," he agreed before carefully sliding out of my body.

CHAPTER 8

SHADOW

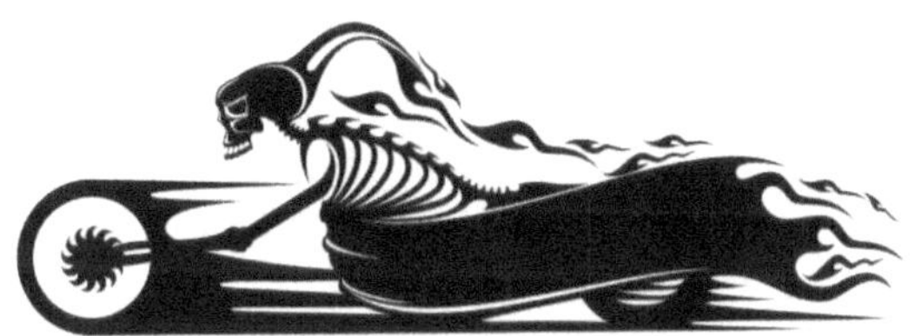

I woke up to a soft weight resting along the length of my back. Warm skin covered me like a heated blanket, and the smell of some floral lotion filled my senses. And then kisses rained down lightly on my shoulder blades.

"Mm, morning," I murmured into the pillow, unwilling to move and disrupt the sweetness I'd woken up to.

"It's afternoon," Mari informed me, her lips on my spine and hands running down my sides. Strands of her hair dragged lightly over me, cool and damp in contrast to the warmth of her skin. She must have just gotten out of the shower.

"Huh, napped longer than I thought."

"Good dreams?" She kissed the back of my neck before laying her cheek down on my shoulder blade.

"Better than that." I reached a hand back to touch her leg straddling my waist. "No dreams at all."

Mari made a soft humming noise before returning to her task of kissing my back. A smile pulled at my lips. Did she see me sleeping and decide to come in and lay on top of me? Just because she wanted to?

"Did you just get home?" I circled my fingers around her knee, tracing the scar tissue from where she'd been shot.

"Gunner and I got back a couple hours ago. We took a detour to a little hot spring in one of the canyons."

"Oh, his secret place."

"You know it?"

"Know of it, but never been there."

I waited for the jealousy that never came. It used to cut through me, sharp and biting when I saw her with the others, when they would talk within earshot about being with her. Now I realized that feeling came from wanting what I never thought I'd have—the love and attention of this woman right here.

"He wants us to go there," Mari said. "You and me." She paused in the middle of a kiss. "He still feels guilty about what happened."

"He'll get over it," I murmured, not wanting to dwell on negativity during such a sweet moment. "Let's take him up on his offer when we have a free day. I've never been to a hot spring."

"Neither had I, before today." I felt her smile against my skin. "It's a date."

Mari's mouth lingered on me sensually, indulgently, in the same places where blades had sliced me and my mother's bullwhip had ripped my flesh away. All the while, her hands ran leisurely up and down my back, pausing to rub tighter areas. In some places, her fingers curled up as she lightly scratched me, the feeling sending a pleasant buzzing up into my scalp. She was in no hurry, lips placing kisses instead of telling me urgent, worrying news like this morning on the battlefield. A rare moment that I wanted to last forever.

I still had to get used to the fact that, with what little free time she had, she *chose* to spend it with me.

"You're really enjoying this?" My words slurred as though I were drunk. Her touch had lulled me into utter relaxation.

She laughed softly, the air from her mouth blowing softly over my skin. "What do you mean by *this*?"

"This right now. Touching me like you are. Kissing all of...*that*."

Mari slid off me then, crawling up the bed to lie on her stomach next to me. She was topless, wearing nothing but a pair of panties. No wonder I felt so much of her beautiful skin on mine.

"You're mine and I love you," she said. "Of course I enjoy kissing you and touching you." She reached out again, smiling as if she couldn't help herself, and ran a hand from my shoulder down the length of my back. "I can never get enough of you."

I rolled to my side, freeing an arm from under my pillow so I could wrap it around her. "So does that mean I've been...satisfying you?"

Mari looked confused and then started laughing. "You really need to ask?"

"Yes," I admitted, glancing away from her face. "You always seem happy with me, but for my own peace of mind, tell me honestly if you are?"

"I'll answer your question with a question." She scratched lightly at my jaw, fingers trailing over my beard as she scooted closer to me. "Is water wet?"

My gaze found hers again. "Yes."

"Does a bear shit in the woods?"

Her smile was so contagious, I couldn't stop myself from mirroring it. "Yes."

"Does Freyja snore when she sleeps upside down?"

I started laughing then. "Yes."

"Does a rooster—"

I leaned in to cut her off with a kiss, which she returned eagerly before her lips pulled back with another smile.

"You're perfect for me," Mari whispered before planting another kiss on my lips. "Don't ever question that."

"I won't anymore," I promised, stroking down her back. "I just want to make sure I'm doing this right. That I'm keeping you happy."

"You are." She kissed me again, her mouth warm and succulent on mine, before moving on to my neck, the spot she knew drove me wild with wanting her. "You are, you are..." The whispered words became a chant, soothing and repetitive, punctuated by kisses. "Am I satisfying *you*?"

Her question took me by surprise, making me pull back slightly to see more of her face.

"Of course you are." I slid my hand up her back until I cupped the nape of her neck. "You make me happy beyond what I thought was ever possible. Have I made you doubt that?" A knot of anxiety tightened in my chest while I waited for her answer.

"No my love, never," she assured me with more kisses, warm hands stroking my chest and relaxing me again. "But your needs are important too. If you're checking in with me, it's only fair that I do the same with you." Her nose nudged against mine. "This is a partnership, Shadow. We take and give to each other."

"I just want to give you everything." I cupped her face with one hand and dragged the other to her hip, pulling her flush to me. "I love you."

"I love you," she answered in a quick breath before I swallowed her mouth in another kiss.

Our hands roamed each other lazily, our kisses long and indulgent. The world might have been a war zone outside this room, but everything about this moment with her was perfect. I knew she'd been with Gunner recently, so I was in no rush for sex. To know she wanted me, *loved* me, was more than enough.

My fingers traced her necklace at one point, running along the small links in the chain to the colored glass on the butterfly pendant.

"I should get you something like this," I mused, kissing the space between her collarbones.

"You don't have to get me anything." Mari scratched over my scalp in long, luxurious strokes that felt like pure heaven.

"I can't be the only one of your men that doesn't give you a gift."

"It's just stuff. It's a nice gesture, but I don't need it." Her palms swept forward, cupping my jaw for another kiss. "I have everything I need right here."

Determined now, I shook my head. "No. I'll think of something."

Mari groaned, a playful, exasperated sound. "You've already given me tattoos."

"I've given lots of people tattoos," I scoffed. "No, I want to give you something unique to us."

An idea did strike me then of what I could give her. Finding it in a jewelry piece would be nearly impossible, unless I had it custom-made. But the only decent jeweler I knew was Reaper's mother, and I didn't want to risk Mari finding out about it before I could surprise her.

If I tattooed it on her, however...

I ran a hand down Mari's side, picturing the design in my head and imagining it transferred to her skin. Oh, it would be beautiful. Perfect, even. And doing it myself would ensure it looked exactly as I wanted it to. The only catch would be the element of surprise.

"Question for you," I murmured after lying quietly for a few moments in each other's arms.

"The answer is yes." Mari kissed my forehead and returned to stroking her fingers through my hair.

I laughed, pushing up to my elbow. "Don't be so quick to answer before you know."

She just smiled, dragging a gentle touch along my ribs and abdomen. "What's your question?"

"Would you let me tattoo you without seeing the design until it's done?" I rested my hand on the side of her hip. "Or choosing where it goes?"

Mari's eyebrows lifted. "Oh, interesting." She pursed her lips for a moment, then came to a decision quickly. "Yes. I trust you."

I knew she did, in all the ways that mattered. But hearing her say it sparked all kinds of emotions in my chest. *She trusts me.* It felt like such a gift.

"I take it back about the tattoo." My hand slid up to hold the beautiful, dipping curve of her waist. "I just thought of something, but I want to surprise you with it."

"Ooh, color me intrigued." She grinned. "I like that idea. And it is still unique to us."

"Yes, it will be." My hand slid back down to rest on her thigh as I pictured it on her skin. Already, I was itching to sketch it out. Next to the drawing of her I put on my arm, it just might end up being my favorite piece of artwork.

"Can you tell me where you'll put it?" she asked, watching me drink in her skin.

"I'm thinking here." I returned my hand to the top of her hip, and slid it back down to her upper thigh. "About this big."

"That's pretty big," she mused.

"Mm-hm. Some of it might go here." I slid my touch behind her, helping myself to a squeeze of her ass.

Mari groaned as if annoyed but she was laughing. "I'd expect nothing less."

"You're really okay with not seeing it until the end?"

"I'm already dying to know what it is, but I know it'll be worth the wait." She scooted closer, nuzzling her head into my chest. "I know it'll look amazing. And knowing you, it'll be so meaningful and unique."

"I hope so." I wrapped both arms around her back, holding her tightly to me. "I hope you'll like it."

"I'll love it." Mari lifted her head and kissed under my chin. "You could get drunk and tattoo a bunch of squiggly lines on my ass and I'd like it."

"Don't let Jandro hear you say that," I scoffed. "He'll think it's a great idea and try everything to make it happen."

Mari laughed into my chest again, then went quiet for a few moments while she touched and kissed me some more.

"I have a question for you now," she said.

"The answer is yes." I leaned in to nip at her ear.

She chuckled, a bit of nervousness lacing the sound as she held the sides of my neck and kissed my mouth once. "How would you feel about Jandro coming to bed with us?" Before I had a chance to think, she quickly added, "If you don't want to, that's okay. I'm just wondering."

I paused to study her expression. "You mean sharing you with him during sex?"

Mari nodded, a dark flush running up her neck.

I shrugged, playing absently with the ends of her hair. "I figured it would happen at some point since we're all with you."

"That doesn't mean it *has* to happen," she said. "If you wouldn't like it, if you prefer our time together being just me and you, we can absolutely do that."

"Hmm." I rolled to my back to look at the ceiling, keeping her close to me with one arm. "I didn't know I had a choice in the matter."

"You always have a choice." Mari leaned over me, brushing another kiss against my chest. "Always."

This woman was so perfect, how could I not share her? This blissful, sparking feeling in my chest—she made *three* other men feel this way. She deserved more than I alone would ever be able to give her. And still, she gave me the option of being selfish enough to keep her to myself in the bedroom.

"You don't sound thrilled." Mari smiled lightly at my silence, trying to hide her disappointment. "Forget I brought it up."

She slid down, moving to place her head on my chest, but I pulled her back up, my mouth landing on hers with a rough crash.

"I told you," I growled, heat and want lighting me up like a bonfire. "I want to give you *everything*."

Mari's lips pulsed against my own, her breath coming in soft puffs from the harshness of my kiss.

"If my wife wants more pleasure in bed," I continued, dragging my thumb along her swollen bottom lip. "She can bring a hundred men into the bedroom."

Mari laughed a bit breathlessly. "We don't have to go *that* far."

"Yeah, that's probably too many." I chuckled and kissed her again, more lightheartedly. "But yes, Jandro or any of them are fine with me."

"You're sure?"

"Yes." I banded my arms tightly around her again, feeling beyond touched and loved that she would be so considerate of my feelings. "I knew what I was getting into, Mari."

"I just don't ever want you to feel neglected or...unimportant." Her brows knitted together with concern.

"You could never make me feel that way." I brushed my knuckles against her cheek, just utterly in love with this woman and marveling at the fact that she was mine.

"Still, I want you to tell me if I do." Mari opened my fingers and leaned her cheek into my palm. "If I make you unhappy in any way, I want to know so I can correct it."

"There is nothing to correct." I tipped her chin forward until her lips just barely grazed mine. "You are perfect."

She traced my mouth with a smile. "The rest of our lives is a long time, hopefully."

"Hopefully," I agreed.

"There's bound to be some moments where not everything is perfect."

"I'm sure there will be." I used my other hand to brush the hair off of her shoulder. "But that's not right now."

"No." Mari smiled wider, keeping her lips connected to mine. "Everything about this, right now, is..."

"Perfect," we said together.

CHAPTER 9

———

MARIPOSA

My stiff legs were happy to see our home at the end of the long, winding driveway, but the rest of me wished the ride could be longer. I just loved being wrapped around Shadow, flying down the road with him with the wind whipping past us —even if I must have looked like a child-sized jetpack strapped to his back.

I squeezed around his waist once when we came to a stop, then groaned as I threw my sore leg over the seat to hop off.

Shadow reached for my waist, pulling me close once I was steady on my feet. "Thanks for coming with me," he murmured, nudging his forehead against mine. "I think having you there made me feel a lot better."

I grinned, running my hands up his broad shoulders to wrap around his neck. "Of course. I'm always here when you need me."

He drew me against him, winding both arms around me like a shield of muscle at my back. "I'm actually starting to believe it when you tell me that."

"Good." I planted a quick peck on his mouth. "You should."

We had a free morning the day after the battle and decided to take a day trip to visit Doc's colleague, Dr. Ellis. She was far enough away in neutral territory that it was deemed safe by the other guys. Blakeworth was no longer spying on us, and Dr. Ellis' practice was well out of their sphere of influence.

Shadow had been nervous when we arrived, but Dr. Ellis immediately put us both at ease. She had served us tea, was barely five feet tall even with her mane of white frizzy hair, and made it feel like a social visit with a grandma rather than a therapy session.

"Sorry to waste your time, but there's nothing you need from me, dear," she'd told Shadow with a smirk. "It seems old Bill Harman worked you through the most difficult part. You're in fine shape to continue the work yourself." Dr. Ellis then beamed at me. "A loving, patient, supportive environment is so important for continued progress, and it seems you have that in spades."

We spent another hour small-talking with her before we took off for the hot springs. Gunner had written down directions for us, and we were lucky enough to run into a taco truck before winding through the canyon. Shadow and I had lunch, made love, and soaked in the spring. I couldn't imagine a more perfect day with him.

Now at home, Shadow's smile, full of genuine happiness and warmth, was so beautiful to see. He leaned in to pull a longer kiss from me—slow, delicious, and lingering. I indulged him for the first few, loving how the gentle pulls of his mouth contrasted with the roughness of his beard.

When we parted for a breath and he leaned in for more, I patted his chest to pause him. "Get off that bike and come inside."

"Inside the house or...?"

"Shadow!"

He grinned at my peals of laughter, thoroughly pleased with his joke as he dismounted his steed and grabbed my hand as we headed for the front porch.

"Jandro is a bad influence on you," I teased.

"I think I stole that one from Gunner, actually."

"Oh yeah?" I widened my eyes dramatically. "And who was Gunner offering to *come inside*?"

Shadow tried to put on a serious face, but he was still smirking. "Oh, no one important. Some random woman long before you came along."

"Oh *really*?"

"I don't think she took him up on the offer, if that's any consolation."

"Hmph. I'm not sure it is." I flipped my hair over my shoulder, maintaining my sass as we walked up the porch and through the front door. The sight in the living room made me stop in my tracks, and Shadow nearly crashed into me.

"What happened?" I demanded right away.

T-Bone and Dyno were sitting next to each other on the loveseat, their arms intertwined and clasped together. Jandro and Gunner sat across from them, and Reaper stood next to the couch. All of them wore grim, worried expressions.

"Grudge is missing," T-Bone said with a hard swallow.

"Missing?" I cried.

"Grudge?" Shadow gasped at the same time, moving out from behind me. "Since when, the battle?"

Dyno nodded, his thumb stroking over T-Bone's hand. "When he didn't report back afterward, we thought he might have been laying low. We all technically went behind enemy lines, so we figured he'd take his time getting back to us, to not alert anyone from Blakeworth. But it's been almost two days."

"I couldn't find him with Munin," T-Bone choked out. "I even went out to the battlefield and called for him with our distress signal. He didn't answer."

"I just searched the area over the past few hours with Horus too," Gunner added softly. "And nothing."

"Well that's...that means he's still alive right?" I babbled out, my heart already hurting for Grudge. "If he's not out there..."

"Then he's been captured," T-Bone spat out, confirming my fear. "By fucking *Blakeworth*."

A heavy silence filled the room. So much implied meaning was held in the name of that territory, the place that built an elite class on slave labor and whose scumbag governor approved the kidnapping of Kyrie Vance. Blakeworth's working-class had few rights, and harsh punishments were inflicted for the most menial of crimes. I didn't dare imagine how such a territory would treat a prisoner of war.

But that wasn't the worst of it. If anyone in the military recognized Grudge from when we took Kyrie back months ago, stealing a piece of Blakeworth property as they saw it, Grudge would be more than just a war prisoner.

He would be a political prisoner, someone who directly undermined the authority of Governor Blake. I had no doubt in my mind he would be made an example of, tortured beyond any lines that would be considered ethical.

From the expressions on everyone's faces, it was clear they had already been thinking of all this.

"What can we do?" I asked the room helplessly as Shadow made his way to the couch, his shoulders tight and brows drawn tightly together. He and Grudge were brothers, likely by blood as well as their bond in friendship, and my chest ached for my husband too.

"I think a hostage exchange is the only way we can do this without more bloodshed," Gunner said. "We have some of their people too—important people. Members of their elite class."

Frowning, I went to sit next to Shadow and started rubbing his back. "I thought Blakeworth only sent their 'disposable' people into battle."

"We have one of their generals," Reaper said. "And a captain, both of which have made clear they're *very* loyal to their governor. They haven't said a peep to us in their interviews."

"Blakeworth will probably want goods too," Jandro added. "Isn't that why everyone wants a piece of Four Corners in the first place? They might want lumber and sheet metal. Tools and vehicles too, probably."

"I can negotiate with 'em," Gunner said. "We can—"

"There is no price for Grudge," T-Bone growled out between his teeth. "He's *our* man, and a brother-in-arms to you. He's not just fucking livestock you can trade goods for."

"Of course he's not, I didn't mean it like—"

"T-Bone's right," Shadow cut in, his hands clenching. "Give them their general, their captain, and any goods they want. No price is too high for getting Grudge back."

Silence filled the room again, but it was a more hopeful, determined silence. T-Bone nodded his agreement with Shadow, jaw clenched hard and red eyes blinking rapidly. Dyno held onto T-Bone's arm and kissed his shoulder, their intimacy and vulnerability clear and out in the open. This was someone they loved, after all. I couldn't even imagine the pain if it was one of my men captured by the enemy.

"I'll ride over and tell Dad." Reaper was already pulling on his cut and heading for the front door. "Gun?"

"Yeah, coming." Gunner sprang up from his seat, gave T-Bone a brotherly pat on the shoulder as he passed him, and then a quick kiss to me before joining Reaper in putting his boots on.

"Ride safe," I said to both of them, my hand still moving over Shadow's stiff back.

"We'll be back soon," Reaper promised. "And let you all know what happens next." He looked at me for a long moment, like he was trying to decide if he wanted to kiss me goodbye too or not. He ended up not, instead following Gunner out to the garage with a quick slam of the door. Their motorcycles started up moments later.

"You guys are welcome to stay here," I said to the two distraught Sons.

"In fact, you should stay," Jandro added, rising from the couch. "For dinner, at least. You guys should be surrounded by family right now." He headed into the kitchen like a man on a mission.

"Thank you," Dyno said, sounding grateful but weary. T-Bone still looked too choked up to say anything. "We'd really like that, actually."

"Take the guest bedroom," I said. "Stay as long as you'd like."

T-Bone only nodded gratefully with a small glance at me, the two of them wrapped up in each other. I wrapped a hand around Shadow's bicep and planted a kiss on his shoulder. "I'm going to help Jandro cook, okay?"

"Okay." He brushed a kiss along my forehead. "I'll stay with them."

Reluctantly unwrapping from him, I stood and headed to the kitchen. "What can I do, *guapito*?"

"Enchilada sauce, please," he answered immediately, carving a raw chicken with experienced precision.

"Got it."

We worked around each other in quiet collaboration, anything to get our mind off of the situation at hand. Grudge wasn't a Demon, but the Sons of Odin had become something of a sister club to us. Him being captured was like one of our own missing. I could only hope he was just being held for the time being and not suffering.

While Jandro and I cooked, Shadow came into the kitchen briefly to grab drinks for himself and the Sons, his expression downturned and grave.

"Come here," I said to him, my fingers coated in enchilada sauce from dipping tortillas in the mixing bowl.

"Hm?" Shadow paused, clearly distracted.

"Kiss." I leaned up and across the counter toward him.

The smallest smile twitched on his lips as he leaned to meet my lips. We sipped at each other lightly, a few brief moments of comfort for both of us before he pulled away to serve drinks to our guests.

"Yo, where's my kiss?" Jandro called after him.

Shadow didn't answer, but T-Bone's throaty chuckle floated in from the living room.

"He's a whole new person," Jandro remarked in a softer voice, carefully laying out enchiladas in a baking tray.

"He is," I agreed, a note of pride in my voice. "As much as I hate to say it, I think that time in exile was good for him. He was forced to grow and make new connections. And Doc's therapy was nothing short of amazing."

"I would've liked to see it." Jandro washed his hands in the sink, then dried them on the dish towel over his shoulder. "But I'm glad you got to."

"I don't know if you would've wanted to, honestly." My throat tightened at the memory of Shadow confined to Doc's metal chair, confessions and memories pouring out from the deep recesses of his mind. "It was so hard to listen to, Jandro. I knew he'd suffered but couldn't fathom how much. I've seen suffering, but nothing could have prepared me for that."

A warm, strong hand squeezed my shoulder, followed by a kiss on the back of my neck. "He had the right people listening to him, helping him without any judgment. That's the important thing."

"You're right." I placed a kiss on his knuckles resting on my shoulder.

The food was ready a half hour later, and we called T-Bone and Dyno to our table. They didn't have hearty appetites, understandably, and Jandro thankfully bit his tongue, not making any cracks when they only picked at their food. Normally we'd be going for seconds and thirds of Jandro's enchiladas, but all of us seemed to have trouble just with our single portions.

Reaper and Gunner came home just as the table was being cleared. The Sons practically sprinted to the door, the most energetic I'd seen them today.

"What did your father say?" T-Bone demanded, well up in Reaper's personal space.

"He met with Vance and together they drafted a message for Governor Blake." Reaper shrugged off his cut and placed it over the back of an armchair. "It's being sent by a secure courier tonight."

"And?" T-Bone pressed. "What did the message say?"

Reaper hesitated in answering, allowing Gunner to jump in. "He's offering to exchange just the captain for Grudge, first. And wait to see what Governor Blake says."

"Wait to see?" T-Bone's eyes narrowed. "The longer we wait, the more opportunity they have to torture him."

"When they see we're offering a hostage exchange, they'll know he's valuable to us," Gunner explained. "They know now that we can take them in battle, so they won't hurt him too badly. And by offering a high-ranking officer in exchange, Blakeworth knows we're reasonable, if even generous."

T-Bone let out a frustrated groan, walking several paces away from the two men before spinning back aggressively. "Grudge is *not* a bargaining chip for these fucking war games. We already established that no price is too high to get him back, so why the fuck is Vance playing like this?"

"Easy, T." Reaper held his hands up in a defensive gesture. "You know I agree with you. If it was me, I'd offer up all of Four Corners on a platter to get Mari back."

My eyes locked on Reaper with shock, my heart rate doubling the moment those words registered in my brain.

"But we can't do that and still expect to win this," Gunner said cautiously, earning T-Bone's murderous glare. "If we offer the keys to the kingdom for one man, Blakeworth will gladly take it all and come at us again when we have nothing left."

"Do you *know* what we've done for Vance? What Grudge has done?" T-Bone roared in his face. "We've protected this territory for a decade. We marched right into enemy territory and rescued his precious fucking daughter! Grudge has bled and sacrificed for Four Corners, and Vance doesn't see him as valuable enough to offer a bigger prize? Fuck him, fuck you—"

"Trav, come here." Dyno wrapped his arms around T-Bone's waist and forcibly pulled him away from my men. "Sit down, take a breath."

The fight seemed to go out of T-Bone then as he sank into the couch cushions, hands cradling his head. Dyno remained wrapped around him, murmuring something private and intimate to his ear.

"For what it's worth," Gunner said after several moments of tense silence. "Reaper and I fought with them for thirty minutes, trying to make them offer the captain *and* general for Grudge, but they wouldn't budge."

He threw a glance to Reaper who nodded, chewing his lip in grim agreement. "Dad and Vance insisted on negotiating this way. Depending on what Blake says, they'll offer more. But what Gunner said is right— we can't show Blakeworth we're willing to do anything to get one man back. Even if it is the truth."

"We know," Dyno sighed, his hand making long, sweeping passes over T-Bone's back. "It's war. It's bigger than us. It's just hard when..."

"You've lost so much already," Shadow filled in quietly.

"Yes." Dyno continued to hold T-Bone with an arm around the distraught man's back, rocking him gently from side to side.

"We will get him back," Reaper insisted. "Dad and Vance *do* understand how important he is. They want to handle this a certain way, and we have to trust them."

"If we don't," T-Bone muttered, his head still bent low. "So help me Odin, if they fuck this up—"

"Travis." Dyno squeezed tighter around his partner. The affection and calling T-Bone by his given name seemed to have a calming effect on him. Dyno's voice was low and soothing. "Don't let your thoughts go that way, not yet. Let Vance and Bray carry out their plan." He looked up from comforting his partner. "When do they expect a reply from Blake?"

"Any time tomorrow," Reaper said.

"Blake will likely wait until the end of the day to send a reply. They'll want to make us sweat and panic," Gunner added.

T-Bone let out another pained groan, and everyone looked at him in sympathy.

"I think we'll lie down in your spare room if you don't mind." Dyno's dark eyes were tired, but his posture remained protective and supportive of T-Bone. "Not that we'll get any sleep."

"Of course, go ahead," I told them. "The bedding's just been cleaned. You can use the restroom in the hall."

"Thank you, Mari." Dyno stood, gently pulling T-Bone along with him.

My guys mumbled goodnight to them as they crossed the living room, and I reached out to rub T-Bone's arm when he passed me. He didn't acknowledge the contact, his mind off somewhere else as he blindly followed Dyno's lead.

Once the guest bedroom door shut quietly, Jandro turned to Reaper and Gunner. "There's plenty of enchiladas left if you guys want any."

"Thanks, man. I might have a small plate, but my appetite is shit today." Reaper rubbed his forehead. "It's early, but I might go to bed soon too."

"Yeah, same." Gunner raked his hands back through his hair. "We should head to City Hall early tomorrow, so we're there once the reply comes."

While the two of them lumbered into the kitchen, I grabbed Shadow's hand and pulled him back to talk privately. "Do you want me to spend the night with you tonight?" Lately, I usually cycled between his, Jandro's, and Gunner's beds, but tonight was different. I didn't want to leave Shadow's side for a single moment.

His large palm found purchase on my waist, the thumb of his other hand tracing my cheekbone. "If you want to."

"I'm asking you if you need me." I wrapped both arms around his waist, propping my chin on his chest as I stared up at him.

Shadow bent to kiss me, forearm sliding around me until it hooked around my lower back. "I love when you're in bed with me. I...just..."

"It's okay." I reached on tiptoes to kiss him again, smiling to make sure he knew I wasn't offended by his reluctance. "I didn't know if you'd rather be alone after today or—"

"No, I don't," he protested quickly. "I *do* want you with me, I just don't think I'm in the mood for..."

"Oh, sex?" I blinked. "Of course we don't have to. I wasn't even thinking of that."

He huffed out a sheepish laugh and smiled back at me briefly before the expression died on his face. "I'm sorry, I just can't stop thinking about Grudge."

"You have nothing to apologize for." I pushed a lock of hair out of his face and kissed him once more. "We're all worried about him. I just want to be there for you."

Shadow wrapped both arms around my lower back and lifted me off the ground to give me a deeper, longer kiss. "You're the most amazing woman, and I love you."

"You're amazing." My fingers raked through his hair as I returned every warm press of his mouth. "And I love you."

He lowered me slowly to the floor after a few more kisses, the sounds of low conversation and glasses clinking filtering through to remind us of our surroundings.

"A drink with the guys and then bed?" Shadow suggested.

"Sounds good," I agreed, then followed his lead into the kitchen.

My three other men were around the breakfast bar, talking quietly among themselves. Jandro started pouring me a small tumbler of *anejo* tequila before I even had to ask. As I took my first sip, my eyes caught Reaper's.

That smoldering green gaze was just like the first time I ever saw it the moment he walked into the service center at Old Phoenix. The difference was now, I *knew* the danger and ruthlessness behind that gaze

—I didn't have to speculate based on legends. When Reaper said he'd give up all of Four Corners for me, I knew he wasn't exaggerating. Recalling those words now lit up a fire in my belly that had nothing to do with the alcohol.

He might have taken me and tied me to his bike that day, but I was captured the moment he laid those eyes on me.

CHAPTER 10

GUNNER

Reaper was already up and pouring coffee by the time I came down from my room. "Mornin'," I greeted, earning a noncommittal grunt in reply. "Thanks," I added, reaching for the mug he poured me.

He was looking better since Mari and Shadow got back, but still not *great* by any means. He still wasn't sleeping much, that was clear from a single look at him, but he wasn't as cantankerous either, which was some improvement.

"Will your dad be up this early?" I brought a tentative sip of coffee to my lips.

"Mm-hm. Hardly anyone is sleeping well." He shot a joking accusatory look at me.

"Don't look at me like that. I was tossing and turning all night." I set the coffee down and rubbed my face once with a groan. "Everyone else still down?"

He nodded after a long pull of coffee. "Jandro will be up soon. He's still got a long day of repairs ahead of him."

"Shadow and Mari?"

Reaper shrugged, the motion tight in his shoulders at the sound of her name. "She'll be making rounds at the hospital, I assume. Shadow might stay with the Sons, I dunno. I'm not keeping tabs on them." He drained the rest of his coffee before meeting my eyes again over the rim. "What?"

"You don't have to avoid her, you know," I said. "She's taking steps. She *wants* things to work out."

"I know, I just," he rubbed his face with a groan. "I've been too overbearing in the past and I don't want to do that again. I don't want to make demands of her. She doesn't owe me anything, so I just...don't want to be in her way."

"The timing of it all fucking sucks right now," I sympathized with him. "Trying to fix what went wrong between us in the middle of a fucking war."

"Yeah," he agreed. "She's got a lot on her plate, and I don't want to put any pressure on her. The last thing I want to do is drive her away again."

"There's a middle ground between pressuring and avoiding," I reminded him. "It's not like you gotta leave the room when she pays attention to us. Unless it bothers you," I added quickly. I never knew Reaper to be jealous, but maybe that had something to do with it. He was the one all about sharing and got *me* roped into it, so jealousy wasn't something I'd considered in him. But maybe he was just better at hiding it.

"It doesn't bother me," he answered. "I'm not entitled to anything from her, and I'm glad she has all of you." He looked toward the backyard where Foghorn was stretching his wings and getting ready to crow his ass off. "It's just, I dunno. I can see she's happy as fuck with the three of you, even when things are really shitty right now. Maybe...maybe I overestimated how much she really needed me."

"Reap, dude. Come on—"

"I've always just hurt her," he cut me off, eyes hardening. "Ever since the beginning, I've been a fucking dick to her. I've lashed out at her, made her cry for no fucking reason. It's always been you guys that pick up the pieces."

A long silence stretched between us. "What are you saying?"

"The truth. You know it's true, Gun."

"I mean yeah, you're kind of an asshole but you're a..." My hands gesticulated wildly as I grasped for words. I was no good at this shit. "You have your reasons. You're a good person underneath that asshole exterior. You own up to it when you fuck up. You love her, man. And she loves you."

"I do," he sighed, eyes closing for a moment. "More than anything. But after everything that's happened...I wonder if that might not be enough to keep us together."

"So I'm gonna ask again, and I want a real fuckin' answer this time." I leaned closer to him, my forearms on the kitchen counter, and lowered my voice. "What *exactly* are you saying?"

"I'm not making any decisions about this right now." Of course he would fucking backpedal when push came to shove. "But when all this shit is over and everyone's heads can clear, I think Mari and I need to decide once and for all what's going to happen between us."

"Dude, she just needs time—"

"And I'm giving her that," he growled. "But I've also been thinking back on *everything* I've done wrong, and it's quite the fucking list. I'm not holding my breath for a mediocre-husband award, or even..." he trailed off, but I kept staring at him hard, daring him to say it out loud. "Or even if she wants to keep me around as a husband at all."

"Jesus fucking Christ, Reap." I rubbed the heels of my palms into my eyes.

"You know it's a possibility," he said. "If some woman did to me everything I've done to her, I sure as fuck wouldn't stay. Would you?"

"Fucking hell, dude. Just stop for a second." I held a palm up. "This is the same shit you always do. You get ahead of yourself, you build up this whole plan and all its justifications in your head, then you carry it out without a thought as to how it's gonna affect other people."

Reaper opened his mouth to protest then promptly slammed it shut, his gaze turning away with the realization that I was right.

"You *have* to talk to Mari if you're feeling this way," I said. "And listen to what *she* says, don't just unload everything running through your mind and steamroll over her."

"I know." He rubbed his forehead with a groan. "Fuck. Yeah I know, Gun."

"If you just drop this on her like a bomb, I guarantee you she's gonna be blindsided and get hurt even more. She's trying to have a relationship with you again. You gotta at least meet her halfway."

"You're right." He blew out a long sigh. "I know you're right." He fiddled with the coffee mug, still not looking at me. "I guess this is my way of trying to prepare for the worst."

"Making you obsess with that outcome, more like."

"I know. It's not good."

I reached across the counter and slapped his shoulder. "One thing at a time, man. Let's get Grudge back first, alright?"

"Yeah." He seemed relieved at the change of subject, sliding off of his stool. "Hades." He whistled on the way to grab his cut, and the dog came trotting to wait by the door.

I only had to look up to the perch near the ceiling before feeling Horus' talons in my shoulder. The weight of him there felt grounding, if even comforting. He guided Mari back to Shadow, and then the two of them back home. I could only hope his eyes would let us check on Grudge today.

I stroked his chest feathers. "Gonna show us some good news today, buddy?"

A soft chirp and a nip to my ear was my answer.

"You're in early, boys." General Bray regarded us curiously from across the conference room table. Ever the general, he looked refreshed and polished in his pressed uniform, his hair still a little wet from his shower. He had a steaming cup of coffee in one hand and some documents spread out in front him.

"Wanted to be here when the answer came." Reaper went to the side table to get a second cup of joe, and I followed after him.

"You might be hanging around a while." My father-in-law flipped idly through the papers in front of him. "Blakeworth is in no hurry to respond to our request."

"Are those intake forms for our prisoners?" I asked, seating myself across from him.

"Yes." The general flipped a few sheets around and slid them across the table to me.

"Got any from our battle?" Reaper asked, and I heard the shuffle of papers as his father handed him a few to read.

"Bunch of normal folks, from the looks of it," I mused while skimming through my stack. "Most of them seem to be open to renouncing their Blakeworth citizenship, which is good."

"We'll need more extensive interviews to be sure," Bray said. "The last thing we need is more Blakeworth loyalists trying to stab us from within our own ranks." His head tilted toward Reaper. "What do you make of your stack, son?"

Reaper flipped through several more pages before answering, his brow furrowing deeper with every page. "You pranking me, Dad? These are all fucking blank."

"Not a prank. Those have all the information Tash's soldiers gave us when we checked them in."

"Which is nothing."

"Correct." General Bray folded his hands on the tabletop. "Read the notes at the bottom of each page."

I scooted closer to Reaper and read over his shoulder. "P.O.W-number-19 refuses to give his name or rank. He seemed willing to at one point, but started screaming and grabbing his head. The fit passed, and he returned to silence. Medics are calling it a catatonic state."

Reaper and I looked at each other, then back at his dad.

"Medics have noted blood coming from the ears of roughly twenty percent of those captured from Tash's army," Bray reported, looking at us pointedly. "They seem to correlate with the ones that scream like they're in pain."

"And the ones that don't?" I asked.

"Catatonic state, like the notes at the bottom. They say nothing, do nothing, just stare blankly forward. They don't even respond to stimuli. The medics are pretty certain they don't even sleep."

"What the fuck are we dealing with?" Reaper stared down at the sheets as if they had all the answers.

"A zombie apocalypse," I muttered.

"Boys, I hate to even ask this but..." General Bray's hands curled into fists on the table, his neutral expression turning distressed. "The symptoms that correlate with yours from last week, the pain and the ear bleeding. Do you think it means...you've been compromised?"

"No," Reaper and I answered together.

"How can you be sure?" The general kept up his pressing stare. "If Tash's soldiers are being controlled and that thing that was in your head is how they're kept to heel—"

"I do believe you're right about that," Reaper admitted. "It felt like something was trying to crack open my brain and shove something inside. I'll bet you anything that's how they turn them from normal people to zombies. They comply just to stop the pain, then it's a gradual shift until they're puppets with no sense of individuality."

He looked at me and I nodded my agreement. "But we have our own gods," I reminded Bray. "I don't know how, but I think they're some kind of shield against what's controlling those soldiers. My head hasn't felt like that since the first time."

"Mine either. Mari and the other guys seem fine too," Reaper nodded.

"That might have been an attempt to control us. But he, it, whatever it is, didn't succeed."

"I sure as fuck hope you boys are right." General Bray still looked grim across the table. "'Cause as soon as I saw those symptoms in the reports, I *knew* it was something related to what happened to you."

"We're good, Dad," Reaper assured him. "If it turns out we're not, you'll be the first to know."

"We have to carry out certain protocols in case something like that happens," the general said uneasily. "For the good of the territory."

"Understood." Reaper glanced at me and I jerked my chin down in a sharp nod. Being family made it harder, but we would have to be removed from our duties if we became compromised, and likely imprisoned like Tash's men. That was just war, and one of the first things I learned at the academy.

"Did you find out anything about that gold pin I gave you?" Reaper asked, setting his papers aside.

"No, we haven't yet." The general frowned pensively as he took a sip of coffee. "Which is strange. We've reached out to historians, archaeologists, experts of all kinds. They've never seen anything like it."

Reaper slumped in his seat. "How is that possible? Shadow and I found Hades, Horus, and Freyja in a book."

"Maybe it's a trait of the god, entity, whatever, that we're dealing with," I suggested. "We're talking chaos, right? Maybe it's something made up just to fuck with us."

"These things tend to be archetypal, if I'm understanding correctly," Bray said. "So there must be something that already exists to draw from."

"Well, there's gods of chaos, right?" Reaper piped up.

"Several," his father nodded. "But even if we narrow it down to the right one, how does that help us beat it?"

"I don't know that it does," I mused. "I think we just have to keep winning battles. Reduce its power and its influence so it doesn't run rampant and turn all of us into zombies."

"I hope you're right." The general's gaze rested on me. "We have good momentum now. If we don't lose focus and keep winning, we can turn the tide on this. With our combined experience and brains, the battles are in our hands. But when it comes to fighting gods?" He leaned back in his chair. "I'm out of my element there."

"So are we, really." Reaper shrugged. "We're just doing the best we can."

"Let's keep doing what we're doing, then," I said.

That seemed to settle the matter. Bray gathered up the papers to stack them neatly in his folder. "So while we're waiting on this response to the hostage exchange," he ventured, peering at Reaper. "How are things at home?"

I wanted to jump in, brush things off or smooth them over, but the question wasn't directed at me.

"Things are fine." Reaper shrugged again.

"Just 'fine'?" his father repeated.

"Fine enough," Reaper answered with more hardness to his voice. "I don't need to discuss everything in my marriage with you, Dad."

"You're right," Bray relented, backing off. "It's just been a while since I've seen Mari in any unofficial capacity. I miss my daughter-in-law."

"I know, she's just busy."

"We all are. But making time for family is—"

"Can we drop the subject, please?" Reaper barked.

The general's eyes slid over to me and I gave him a sympathetic look. I wasn't about to air out what Reaper told me privately. While I didn't know Bray well, I had a feeling he'd dropkick his son for even considering splitting from Mari. My gut churned at the thought of her finding out. If she knew, there would be no coming back from that.

But Reaper and Mari both deserved the time to sort out their feelings, to get clarity and start anew, whether that was together or going their separate ways. This war hanging over our heads certainly wasn't helping with stressful decisions.

We spent the next several hours planning the next battle. Bray's lieutenants and advisers cycled in and out of the conference room until all their faces blurred together in my brain.

It was the middle of the afternoon, not as late as I expected, when Blakeworth's reply to our message finally came.

A young private stumbled in with the letter and then quickly made himself scarce, apparently taking *don't shoot the messenger* very seriously. General Bray opened it first, scanned the contents, then dropped it on the table for us to read. Reaper and I both grabbed for it, but I was quicker.

The answer was brief, only half a page of typed, double-spaced sentences. It had Governor Blake's official crest at the top, despite the unlikelihood that he wrote it himself.

"He doesn't even want the captain back?" I handed the letter to Reaper as I looked up at Bray.

"That's what he says." Bray rubbed the stubble on his jaw as he stared out the window. "I wonder if he's bluffing and trying to see if we'll call it."

"He wants his general instead." Reaper peered up at both of us. "And says we can just kill the captain? His *own* man?"

"Keep reading," I said, rubbing my temple.

Reaper's eyes returned to the letter. "Feel free to send me a souvenir. Captain Lance's finger bones will make a nice addition to the collection in my office. He'll be far more useful as a decoration than a leader of my army." Reaper's head jolted up abruptly. "What the fuck?"

"He's got to be bluffing." I shook my head, turning back to face Bray. "We beat his ass, so he's just talking a bunch of shit to make himself sound like a super villain."

"Regardless, we're not killing anyone in our custody, nor are we sending pieces of them as souvenirs," General Bray growled. "It's a fair enough trade. He can have his general back in exchange for Grudge."

"He doesn't list any other terms or when it should happen." Reaper scanned the letter again.

"Good, that means we set the terms. Is tomorrow evening soon enough?" I glanced between the two of them.

"Not soon enough for the Sons," Reaper muttered. "You think we could get him back tonight?"

"Tonight doesn't give Blakeworth enough time to prepare for whatever charade they'll want to put on for the exchange." Bray turned back to face us.

"And?" Reaper snarled. "Who gives a fuck if we rush them? They lost. Those fuckers jump when *we* say it's time."

"We still have to look like the bigger person," I reminded him. "The reasonable side. It's what the soldiers and civilians are gonna remember when all this is over."

"How we treat hostages is going to be another," Bray pointed out. "Everyone knows Blakeworth doesn't deserve an ounce of courtesy from us, but we still have to show that we're better than them."

"And what if they show up with their whole cavalry?" Reaper asked. "'Cause we all know they're not above doing that either."

"We should prepare for that," I agreed. "Giving them time to prepare for a hostage exchange doesn't mean we trust them."

"The exchange means nothing in the grand scheme of things," Bray said. "We're still enemies. All it really does is show that we care about our people enough to get one of our men back."

"I don't like it either," I said, noting Reaper's scowl. "It's politics and it's shitty that Grudge is in the middle of it. But we have to play it a certain way, because *this* is the shit people will remember generations from now—how two warring territories handled the exchange of prisoners."

"Whatever, I get it." Reaper dropped the letter dismissively to the table. "Just don't ever let T-Bone hear you say that."

CHAPTER 11

MARIPOSA

The wind howled and whipped through the canyon walls. It had been warm not long ago, but the sun hadn't touched the rocky terrain down here for hours. I kept my focus straight ahead on the slow procession lumbering toward us.

Four Corners soldiers looked over us from the ridges above, every one of them holding assault rifles. Not long after we settled at the meeting place and waited, drones approached the canyon from the north, humming and hovering over our heads. Several people looked up at the small, sleek aircraft with disgust. What an arrogant display of wealth from Blakeworth before the VIPs even bothered to show up.

The general from Blakeworth, General Arroyo, stood handcuffed between two of our lieutenants to my right. I had checked the man over for a final exam before we came to make the exchange. Arroyo hadn't been happy in our custody but was otherwise in fine health. I didn't appreciate how he leered at me while I examined him, but at this point it was nothing I hadn't experienced before.

My four men stood off to my left, primarily serving as bodyguards for me. Once the exchange happened, I was to examine Grudge as well. If he hadn't been treated well, Blakeworth would have a bigger problem on its hands.

The Sons of Odin were the only major players absent for this exchange. General Bray advised them to stay back in the city, and after much yelling and swearing, T-Bone and Dyno relented. This meeting was expected to be tense at the very best. The last thing we needed was either of them losing their cool and starting an impromptu skirmish when we were trying to put on a display of diplomacy.

I could feel Shadow vibrating at my side with barely contained anger. He would keep calm but I knew how much he wanted to explode, to take Grudge back by any means necessary. On his other side, Gunner squinted down the length of the canyon as we waited. Occasionally his eyes rolled back for a few seconds at a time, sneaking peeks through Horus while there was still a bit of sunlight left.

"They're coming," Gunner muttered. "But they're in no hurry." He looked more annoyed than anything else, and I could see why. Blakeworth was taking their sweet time and making us wait. On purpose.

It was all a game, and I hated that part most of all. Each side was trying to show they were better, more powerful. They made pokes and jabs at each other, trying to provoke a reaction while the people caught in the middle were the ones who suffered.

An extensive motorcade rolled slowly toward us—first, riders on sleek black motorcycles, then matching Hummers with shiny chrome rims on their off-road tires.

"Unbelievable," Jandro muttered.

I wanted to rub his arm in sympathy, but remained stoically facing forward. The Hummers were followed by four massive SUVs, then more Hummers and motorcycles brought up the rear.

When the entire entourage came to a stop, the passenger door of the first SUV opened. A smiling, middle-aged man stepped out casually, like he was showing up for a family barbecue. His uniform was perfectly fitted and pressed, an assortment of military stripes and medals pinned to his jacket—clear markings of a decorated general.

"Good evening!" he called cheerfully. "I'm General Rolf Larson, Chairman of the Blakeworth Military Council."

"General Finn Bray. Head of the Four Corners Army," my father-in-law replied stiffly.

"My deepest apologies for our lateness." An insincere smirk crossed

Larson's lips. "Our vehicles are not well-fitted to this terrain, so we had to drive slowly."

One of my men pulled in a sharp breath. Gunner had told me all about how they set the terms to be reasonable and accommodating, and here they rolled up with the underhanded remark that we still weren't accommodating enough.

Fuck everything about Blakeworth.

Finn stepped forward, his face a stern mask. "Where is the hostage?" He ignored the other general's first remark.

"Where is ours?" Larson countered.

My father-in-law turned his body, keeping his eyes on the enemy in front of him as he gestured to the cuffed man between his lieutenants. Larson started walking forward, prompting all the Four Corners soldiers and Steel Demons in attendance to draw their guns. My heart jammed up into my throat when the Blakeworth motorcyclists drew their weapons in response. Fuck, no. This was getting too fucking tense already.

"Hold, everyone." General Bray was the epitome of calm as he extended his arms forward and back. "You can see your hostage, general," he said to Larson. "Not another step forward until we see ours. That is what you agreed to by coming here."

"Arroyo!" Larson called to our prisoner, ignoring Bray completely. "Are you alright?" He waved as if they were neighbors across the street. Bray's jaw ticked but he otherwise didn't react to the blatant antagonism.

Arroyo grunted out an affirmative, wrists pulling slightly at his cuffs.

"Very good, glad to hear it!" his colleague called out cheerfully across the line. I'd never wanted to punch someone so badly. "Bring out the prisoner," Larson called, turning to face the motorcade behind him.

The rear passenger door in the last SUV opened, and everyone on our side seemed to hold their breath. Nobody came out for a few seconds, and then a bound man was shoved roughly out of the car, sprawling facedown in the dirt.

"Grudge!" Shadow hissed under his breath.

My hand shot out to the side to stop him and for once, I was faster. Shadow's stomach connected hard with my palm as he stepped forward, the impulse to save his friend riding him hard. He was strong enough to crash right through the flimsy barrier I'd thrown up, but thankfully he didn't. He froze mid-step, eyes fixed on the man the Blakeworth soldiers were now manhandling to his feet.

It took all my strength to swallow my cry at the first sight of Grudge's face. His hair and beard were matted with dried blood, his left eye swollen shut, lips split open and still bleeding. He was still wearing his cut, with only a thin white T-shirt underneath, also stained with blood. The difference between our two hostages could not be more obvious.

The only thing I was grateful for was T-Bone and Dyno not being there to see him like this. It would have become a bloodbath the moment Grudge got shoved out of the car.

General Bray sucked in a harsh breath as Larson stepped aside so Grudge could be brought forward.

"Hand him over." Bray extended an open palm toward the beaten man, choosing not to comment on the state he was in.

"No, pull him back. Remove him from my sight," the other general sneered.

"Larson," Bray hissed in warning. "This is not what we agreed upon."

"I didn't agree to send this scum back to your loving arms with no repercussions," argued the other man. "Give us General Arroyo first, as a sign of your goodwill."

"Our man needs medical attention," my father-in-law said. "We have a medic right here." He gestured toward me. "If he dies because of your carelessness, that'll only further increase the bad blood between us."

Larson's eyes landed on me with a leering kind of curiosity. I returned his gaze with a hard stare of my own, refusing to look meek and submissive. *I* was the one who stole Kyrie out from under his governor's nose. He hurt one of my friends, and I wasn't about to play nice. My men stiffened at my side, their protective natures and simmering anger palpable on the breeze.

Grudge sagged against the two men holding him up by his arms, his breaths coming in painful wheezes. I had to clench my hands at the sound, holding back the urge to fight my way through the soldiers to give him aid.

Completely oblivious to his suffering prisoner, General Larson grew bored of looking at me and returned his attention to Bray. "Give us General Arroyo first," he repeated. "You may have claimed one victory, but you are the ones desperate to have this prisoner back." He threw a disdainful glance at Grudge over his shoulder. "I can't imagine why. The idiot can't even talk."

Shadow's breathing labored with angry huffs at my side, like a bull. I didn't have to look at him to know he looked shit-your-pants terrifying right then. I'd never seen him, the *real* him, this eager to kill for personal reasons. A couple of the Blakeworth soldiers tightened their grips on their weapons.

"General Arroyo is clearly the more valuable of the two hostages," Larson prattled on.

"No one human life is more valuable than another," Finn shot back.

"Oh please." Larson rolled eyes. "Now is not the time to get sanctimonious. I don't want to be out here any more than you do, Bray. Just hand over the general so I can get back to cigars and cocktails."

My father-in-law held firm with a shake of his head. "I don't trust you. We exchange at the same time."

"You think I *want* to keep this waste of air?" Larson snorted. "Please, I'm eager to be rid of him. He's useless as far as extracting intel, not to mention there's blood all over my seats. The only reason I'm holding on to him is because he means so much to *you*, Bray."

"Every citizen of Four Corners is worth rescuing to us." Bray amazed me with his calm. I and everyone surrounding me seemed a hair's breadth away from tearing into these people. But my father-in-law remained ever the diplomat in tone and posture. "We'll make the exchange at the same time," he repeated. "Let the soldiers hand them off to each other."

General Larson squirmed a little. It was a reasonable request, but he didn't want to look like he was giving in to our demands. Everyone seemed to hold their breath while waiting for his response.

"Fine," he relented, stepping aside to make room for his soldiers to step forward. "Let's get this over with."

Bray copied his movements, moving aside so his lieutenants could march General Arroyo forward.

The escorting soldiers of both sides halted a few feet in front of each other, Grudge struggling to get his feet under him between his two, while General Arroyo stood proud and proper.

"Uncuff him," snapped Larson.

"You don't give orders to *my* men." Finn's jaw ticked, the only sign of tension beneath his calm facade. "Have your men untie Grudge."

"You first," sneered the other man.

"I'm gonna fucking lose it," Jandro growled under his breath.

Me too. Every word from Blakeworth was just to show-up or antagonize us to provoke a reaction. They were the playground bullies enjoying our torment and dragging it out for as long as they could get away with it.

My father-in-law sucked in a sharp breath, but otherwise nodded to his soldiers. "Remove General Arroyo's cuffs." He stared down at Larson until he ordered his men to do the same.

Each prisoner was now held only by his arms, and a few heavy seconds passed without anyone moving. It felt like a game of chicken, both of them waiting for the other to move first.

"Shall we count their steps forward together?" Finn asked finally. "And then order the release at the same time?"

General Larson rolled his eyes again. "I'm flattered, Bray, but I didn't come here to dance with you."

"You're the one unwilling to make the first step in good faith," Finn retorted, an impatient growl entering his voice. "We have accommodated your every request, even when we do not need to. Handing off at the same time seems to be the only way we get this done without more blood shed."

"How precious, I'm so touched." The general mockingly touched his hands to his chest. "Fine. We'll do this together, like a little tango."

It was a painstakingly slow process, the tension only ramping up as the soldiers approached each other with the captives in tow. Finn and Larson negotiated over every single footstep and the release of the men. But when Grudge finally collapsed into Finn's arms, we all breathed a massive sigh of relief.

"Make room, bring the gurney," I instructed the soldiers behind me. "Lay him down on his back, slowly," I said to Finn.

Our enemies standing not twenty feet away were the last thing on my mind as I prepared to examine Grudge. While Finn lowered him gingerly to his back, I snapped on a pair of gloves, then clicked on a small flashlight and handed it to a nearby soldier. "Hold that steady for me."

Grudge groaned and writhed when I started cutting away his shirt, his fists swinging up as if to defend himself.

"No, no, it's okay," I said to one of the soldiers grabbing his arms to restrain them at his sides. Grudge was so weak and disoriented, it was no issue to bat his hands away. It was hard to believe he'd only been captive for a few days. He looked like he'd been suffering for weeks.

I smoothed a hand back through his hair and leaned down to speak to him. "Grudge, sweetie? It's Mari. You're home now. We got you back, and I'm gonna make you all better, okay?"

He stopped his swinging immediately, opening his fists. "Mah?" he asked in a raspy croak.

I grabbed his nearest hand and gave it a light squeeze. "Yes, it's me. Shadow's here too. You'll probably need a hospital stay, but we'll get you back to your guys as soon as we can."

Grudge gave a weak nod and reluctantly let go of my hand.

"Hold that light up higher," I instructed the soldier and lifted my head to look around. "Shadow?"

"I'm here, love." My assassin's footsteps brought him soundlessly to Grudge's side in the next moment. "What can I do?"

"Just sit with him. Hold his hand and talk to him while I work."

If Shadow felt any hesitation about comforting another person, he didn't show it. He took Grudge's hand carefully as he sat on the ground next to the gurney. "Hey brother. You're safe now. Mari's going to fix you up."

"You might feel some stinging," I warned, clearing the blood around Grudge's head first. Then to Shadow I muttered, "What's going on now?"

"Nothing. Blakeworth's leaving." His mismatched eyes glanced up and behind me, glaring at the spot where the motorcade had pulled up. "I was so close to killing him."

"You weren't the only one," I sighed.

Grudge's head and neck looked okay. He'd obviously been punched a few times, but the swelling and lacerations weren't life-threatening. He would need plenty of stitches though, and I wouldn't rule out a concussion. I moved on to feel around his torso and he immediately thrashed in pain. "Sorry! I'm sorry, Grudge. Does it hurt to breathe?"

He nodded, his face a tight grimace of agony.

"Bruised ribs for sure, possible breaks," I noted. His chest and ribs were covered in dark tattoos, so it was hard to tell where exactly he was injured without examining him, and thus hurting him more. "He needs a hospital right away."

"I'll take him. Fold down the seats in my car and put him in there," Finn ordered. "You all can jump in and hold him steady on the way."

"We'll follow," Reaper added, his gaze rising to the tops of the canyon walls. The motorcade had already left and the drones were just now starting to fly off in the same direction. "We'll make sure you don't get any surprises along the way."

"I'll stop at home and tell the Sons we got him back," Shadow said.

"The Sons are gonna want blood," Gunner remarked with a tone of worry. "There's no excuse for treating a hostage this way."

"They have every right to want it," Finn said bitterly. "I know we all felt like ticking time bombs out there, but we have to be smart about our next move."

"Guys!" I clapped my hands once. "Talking can wait. Get this man into the general's car *now*."

The rest of my men hurried around Grudge's gurney and carefully lifted him. I stood back and out of their way, feeling a mixture of relief and wrung-out exhaustion as I watched them secure him in Finn's SUV.

No one would say that exchange went *well,* but it certainly could have gone a lot worse.

CHAPTER 12

MARIPOSA

"That hostage exchange was an absolute shitshow."

Governor Vance frowned at Finn's declaration from across the conference table. Next to him, Josh paused in his note-taking as if wondering if he should include the word *shitshow* in the meeting's minutes.

"But it *was* successful," Vance broached cautiously.

"They got their man back safe and sound, we got ours barely alive." My father-in-law was restless in his seat, clasping and releasing his hands, only to ball them into fists before clasping them again. His usually clean-cut appearance was the most disheveled I'd seen him, with his shirt collar unbuttoned and his hair sticking out in places like he'd been tearing his fingers through it. I even noticed a five-o'clock shadow on his jaw.

It was like seeing Reaper aged by twenty years. Their expressions of stress were exactly the same. Finn's military career seemed to contribute to his calm, controlled facade—something my husband never quite developed. But now, three days after the hostage exchange, even the stoic general was cracking.

"The Sons of Odin, who have supported this territory and your administration for years, don't just want blood." Finn leaned back in his seat, lifting his chin to the governor across from him. "They want the whole territory of Blakeworth razed to the ground, and frankly, after seeing the condition Grudge was in, they're justified in wanting that."

Vance shifted a nervous gaze to me and cleared his throat. "How is Grudge holding up?"

"He's stable," I reported. "But the damage is extensive and he'll have a long recovery. His two broken ribs led to some organ damage. He also received some blunt force trauma to his back, which has caused some damaged nerves and balance issues."

I had never seen anyone look so heartbroken as T-Bone when Dr. Brooks read him the full diagnostic report. At first, it was crushing sadness and disbelief, then came the anger in full force. Thankfully, the only casualties were some filing cabinets, but our biggest concern was T-Bone doing harm to himself. It took all four of my guys plus Dyno to calm him down and remove him from the hospital. Poor T-Bone fought every step of the way because he didn't want to leave Grudge's side.

It almost reminded me of Shadow's violent outbursts, except that T-Bone was conscious the whole time, and his pain was for someone else. But he still felt helpless and lashed out because there was no other way to express his pain.

"We will support the Sons in any way we can, of course," Governor Vance said.

Something about that statement rubbed me the wrong way. It sounded like lip service to me.

"Give them a home of their own, to start."

All eyes in the room swiveled toward me, most of them wide. I was probably breaching some kind of protocol but didn't care at that point. Grudge had nearly died. He probably would have if we had waited another day. "Honestly governor, they should have gotten one after their clubhouse burned down with everyone they loved in it. They're not your polished military officers, sir, but it's shameful how little they've received after all they've done for Four Corners."

"We had contracts with them, Mari. They were well-compensated for the tasks they carried out—"

"They saved *your* daughter!" I blurted out. "They're staying at our house—which you had no issue giving us—because they still live in a room above a bar!"

"The Sons never wanted a permanent home here," Josh spoke up timidly. "We offered them housing but they refused—"

"Gee, I wonder why!"

"Thank you, Mari." Finn didn't yell, but his voice filled the room with a sharp command. It was General Bray speaking, not my father-in-law. But I noticed the small smile he tossed my way down the length of the table. "I believe what our medic is trying to say is that the Sons of Odin deserve not only support, but retribution for their suffering."

Governor Vance paled. "How?"

"We need to strike harder against Blakeworth. I think it's past time we go to them directly."

"But we've won a battle. We successfully exchanged hostages. Wouldn't a negotiation be—"

"Did you read my report, Governor?" Finn's pulse throbbed in his neck. His patience wasn't only wearing thin dealing with enemy territories, but also his own.

"Yes, General. I did."

"Then you understand that Blakeworth did everything in their power to provoke a reaction out of us without a direct attack. And that says nothing of the state Grudge was in when we received him." My father-in-law leaned across the table like he wanted to get into the governor's face. "They won't attack us first, but they will needle us, harass us, kidnap our citizens, and disrespect us to our faces until we're forced to retaliate. I say, fuck giving them that chance. Fuck being diplomatic with these people. We're smarter and stronger, so let's just fucking crush them."

My guys, who had been silent throughout this whole exchange, appeared to be sharing hidden smiles amongst each other. Reaper was the first to speak.

"I'm with my old man on this one." He slapped his father on the arm.

"We can do it," Gunner agreed. "And we should. They're scared of us now."

"Grudge's captors deserve nothing less," Shadow weighed in, an icy ruthlessness in his voice.

All eyes turned to Jandro, who just shrugged. "I'll follow these boys anywhere. Fuck yeah, let's rock and roll."

"What about General Tash?" one lieutenant piped up. "If we focus a hard hit to the north, that'll leave us vulnerable to the east."

"We need to keep eyes out that way for sure," Gunner nodded. "They've got the numbers and the artillery. But if we can eliminate Blakeworth as a problem for good, it'll be a lot easier then to focus on one opponent, rather than splitting up the army."

"Andrea is still in their base," I reminded everyone in the room. "At some point, we'll also have to get her out safely."

"That's correct." Finn smiled openly at me before returning his attention to the governor across the table. "I'm suggesting we be aggressive, Vance, not stupid. Our enemies expected to crush us, and we've proven to them that we can hold our own. Now they have to rethink their attacks, which also buys us some time." He clapped Gunner's shoulder and shook him affectionately. "We have the best strategic minds on our side. It was Gunner's tactics that won us those battles. If we keep planning our moves wisely, we can't lose."

Gunner blushed redder than I'd ever seen him before, and he looked bashful for once, instead of cocky.

Governor Vance still looked apprehensive, but he gave an approving nod to his general. "I trust your judgment, Bray, and you haven't steered me wrong yet. Plus, the victories have certainly helped with morale in the city. Do what you have to."

The two men stood from the table, everyone else following suit as the general extended his hand. "We'll brief you on the next battle's plans within three days, governor."

With a shake of hands, the meeting concluded. Everyone started filing out of the room while I made my way to Gunner and planted a kiss on his cheek. "Proud of you, love."

He hugged me tightly to his side, his smile beaming as he kissed my forehead. "Thanks, baby girl."

A commotion at the conference room doorway pulled our attention that way. One of the soldiers struggled against the stream of people leaving the room as he was trying to come inside.

"General! Is General Bray still in there?" he called.

"Yes, what is it?" Finn turned from a conversation he was having with some other soldiers.

People finally stepped aside so the man could come in. He was red-faced and panting like he'd ran across the entire city, and held up a manila folder stamped CLASSIFIED. "There's been another message from our contact in New Ireland."

"Andrea," I gasped.

Finn made his way to the messenger in three long strides, taking the folder from him. "Thank you, Private."

"It hasn't been translated yet, sir," the young soldier wheezed. "Would you like me to get Lieutenant Anurak?"

"Yes, please," the general said with as much patience as he could muster.

"Yes sir, right away!" Still, the messenger hesitated. "I didn't make a copy or anything yet, that's the original note. I...I thought you should see it first, sir." With that, he took off to find the translator.

Frowning, Finn opened the folder and his forehead only wrinkled more deeply at what he saw. Just as quickly, he snapped the folder shut and lifted his head. "Everyone out. The meeting's over, go on. This is a separate matter."

My husbands and I stayed as the room emptied, all of us immediately crowding around my father-in-law once we had privacy. "Is something wrong?" My heartbeat accelerated at his reaction to the note.

Finn met my eyes and tried to give a reassuring smile, but I could still see the worry tensing up his face. "We'll have to see what Anurak says when he gets here, but something is definitely unusual. This note is coming much sooner than our agreed-upon correspondence schedule with Andrea."

"Well, that doesn't have to be a bad thing, right? Maybe she just has more to tell us."

The general sighed and flipped open the cover. "I wish it could be as simple as that but I don't think so." He turned it around and slid the paper toward me. I couldn't read the characters of course, but quickly realized what he meant. The pounding in my chest quickened and seemed to rise up into my throat.

The first line at the top looked normal enough—glyphs written with a ballpoint pen sitting on top of the first line. After that was where it all went wrong. The symbols got bigger with each row, the pen strokes deep and shaky, like Andrea had been convulsing as she wrote. The last characters on the page were around two inches high, dragging all the way down to run off the bottom edge of the paper, which also had dark smears over the ink.

"Is that blood?" I pointed, but already knew. "Holy shit, that's her blood."

"We don't know if it's hers," Reaper said, although he didn't sound convinced himself.

A hand came to my shoulder, probably meant to calm me, but it made me jump. Shadow ran his palm across the top of my back, the motion only a little soothing as he inspected the paper over my shoulder.

"Whatever she's saying, it's repeating something," he observed. "It's the same two characters over and over."

Finn spun the paper back around to face him. "You're right." He didn't look comforted with that knowledge. "Down here where she draws them really big, she didn't even finish the whole character. It's like she dragged the pen off the page and just stopped."

"Fuck." I barely realized I had uttered the curse until Jandro came up to my other side, his hand rubbing my lower back while Shadow continued with my shoulders.

"No jumping to conclusions yet." Jandro pressed a kiss to my temple. "Let's find out what the translation is first."

I held on to him and Shadow while we waited. Anurak entered the room within the next few minutes, his face taking on the same frown as his general at first sight of the message. The lieutenant brought a pen and blank sheet of paper with him but didn't seem to need them. He set them slowly on the table as he looked at us all gravely.

"I'm very sorry," he said. "But I'm afraid our contact has been compromised."

"What?" I cried. "Why?"

"What does it say?" Finn demanded.

Anurak picked up the pen, holding it poised for a moment before writing on the blank sheet. "You remember the code is based on phonetic sounds, yes? This is the sound those two characters make."

He capped the pen and stepped away from the paper which read, *HA HA HA HA HA.*

CHAPTER 13

MARIPOSA

"Comfortable?"

I was laying on my side with a pillow under my head on Shadow's tattoo table, which I was pretty sure had been a massage table at one point. I had my shirt pulled up to my waist and my underwear pulled halfway down my leg. My hip and thigh were bare, wearing only Shadow's touch as he ran a hand over my skin.

It had been a rough few days, monitoring Grudge's progress in the hospital, and then getting that haunting note from Andrea. When Shadow told me he'd finalized his surprise tattoo for me, I jumped at the chance to focus on something more pleasant than hospitals and enemies.

"Very." I curled my arm underneath the pillow, watching him set everything up. "Think I'll take a nap."

"You might," he said with a small smile. "This'll take a few hours."

"No hints?" I tried again just to prod him, knowing he wouldn't budge.

"Nope." He leaned in and kissed me quickly. "Unless you've changed your mind."

"Not a chance." Still, my eyes drifted to his sketchbook nearby, the cover closed. I knew whatever he was tattooing on me would be in there.

"You're sure?" He pulled on a pair of gloves, then spayed his alcohol solution onto a clean towel to wipe my skin with a firm, gentle hand. "Last chance to back out."

"I'm staying," I told him, the words carrying more than one meaning.

Shadow smiled as he uncapped a pen, holding my hip with one hand while he poised the tool above my skin with the other. "Then cover your eyes and take your nap, my love."

I stuck my tongue out before pulling the sleeping mask over my eyes and hugged my pillow. The next thing I felt was the light tickle of the pen moving over my skin as he started to draw on me. I had to bite my lip to not move—it was *too* ticklish in some spots.

Shadow's sketching and tattooing methods were polar opposites, I realized. He sketched quickly, making long sweeping lines and quick marks for necessary details. With the tattoo gun however, he was meticulous and slow. It was almost meditative, how much his focus narrowed during that stage of the process.

I tried to follow the strokes of the pen on my skin and match it to an image in my mind, but it was impossible to guess. Just when I thought I knew, he'd do something different in another area to make me second-guess. Whatever it was would be worth the surprise, but that didn't make me any less eager to know.

The pen lifted away after several minutes, Shadow's gloved touch lingering on me for a few moments longer.

"It looks good," he reported, excitement brightening his voice. "Just as I imagined. This is going to look amazing on you."

"Can't wait," I told him, smiling in the direction of his voice.

Another quick wipe of my skin and his machine buzzed to life to begin my outline. "Here we go," he said softly, moments before he touched the needle down and began the real work.

The sharp, scratching sensation faded to a gentle ache after several minutes, only the buzzing of his machine filling the air.

"Tell me a happy memory," I implored him at one point.

"I think this is about to become one." I couldn't see him, but heard the smile in his voice.

"Doesn't count," I teased. "What's something that happened to you before this that made you happy?"

"Well, there is the first time I tattooed you." The buzzing stopped briefly, and I heard his chair creak as he turned. "Did you know I purposely split up your sessions so I could see you more often?"

"You did?"

"Yes. You were the only woman I enjoyed talking to."

"Aww." I lifted my head from the pillow until his machine stopped again. "Kiss me?"

Shadow's mouth descended on mine in seconds. His beard felt especially, wonderfully rough against my mouth when I couldn't see it.

"Keep this up and it'll take even longer to finish," he chuckled against my mouth, kissing me once more before pulling away.

"Fine." I flopped back down to my side. "Tell me another good memory. One that doesn't have to do with me."

"That's a bit harder," he mused, gloved fingers holding my skin taut as his needles did their work. "Most of my good memories are with you."

"Challenge yourself." I probably sounded like an old professor from nursing school.

"Hm." Shadow continued my outline for several minutes before he spoke again. "I still have the first drawing I was actually proud of. I drew it in prison, after the...the cult."

"What was it of?" I asked, determined to keep his thought process in a positive direction.

"A dragon," he answered. "It was a tattoo I did for another inmate. I drew it pretty much from memory of a picture I saw in a book years earlier. I didn't even have a reference to go off of."

"Would you ever let me see it?"

"Hm." He sounded skeptical now. "I dunno. It's not very good by my standards now. But I was really impressed with myself at the time."

"I'm sure it's a fine drawing, love. What kind of dragon was it?"

"Eastern-style, like a Chinese dragon," he said. "No wings, long curving body." Shadow paused in tattooing to drag a gloved finger over *my* curves. "Lots of scale details. It was big, too. The face was on the guy's chest, then it went over his shoulder and down his back."

"That sounds amazing."

"It was okay," he mumbled, the noise and prick of his gun returning. "He was a good client too. Young, maybe sixteen. I had to stick-and-poke him over several days, but he never complained and sat like a rock."

"Do you know where he ended up?" I asked, suddenly enthralled by this story.

"No. Jandro's the only person I stuck around with from then."

"You know what I'd love to do together?" I said after another several moments of quietness.

"I can think of a few things." There was that smile in his voice again.

"In addition to *that,*" I grinned, "I'd love to just flip through all of your drawings and have you tell me about each one."

Shadow paused in his work, and for once the silence felt uncertain. "You'd *want* to do that?"

"Yes," I said earnestly. "Only if you're comfortable with it. I love how creative you are."

"Maybe." He still sounded unsure. "It's just that some of my drawings are really dark. Even some of the more recent ones. Doc told me I could use drawing as a type of therapy, as a way to process everything."

I stuck my hand out blindly, letting it hover in the air until he grabbed it. "You don't have to show me anything you don't want to," I said. "Just because you've shared your past with me, doesn't mean you can't keep some things to yourself."

The next thing I felt was the warmth of his breath, and then his lips descending on mine, full of warmth and passion.

"I love you so much," he murmured. "Thank you for just...letting me be me."

"I love you too much to let you be anything else," I whispered back.

He groaned through the next kiss, and I felt the slight weight of his chest pressing down as he leaned over me. "I'll never finish this tattoo if you keep making me want you."

"I'm sorry." I grinned, not sorry at all.

Shadow laughed knowingly, lifting my shirt higher past my waist to plant kisses on my side. His beard and the light, teasing drag of his lips tickled me until I was squirming and laughing. He carried on with a few more kisses on my ribs before stopping abruptly with a light swat to my bare butt cheek. "That's your last chance to squirm. I need you to be still for me now."

It took me a few moments to gather myself, and he probably had no idea why. Shadow's dominance was sweeter, more playful than Reaper's, but no less demanding. His tickling kisses followed by the serious command lit me up like a match. A small part of me wanted to push his buttons a little more, to see how much he would really punish me, but he wasn't familiar with that kind of play yet. It would probably aggravate him more than anything.

And anyway, what I really wanted to do most was please him.

"*Fine*, I'll be good," I sighed dramatically.

Shadow let out a delighted hum, and I utterly melted at the sound. I should have known this tattoo would be the longest session of foreplay in my life.

My artist resumed his work and I stuck to my promise of being good for him. "I'll look through my drawings to see what I feel like sharing or not," he said after a few minutes.

"Completely fine with me," I assured him.

We carried on for a while in comfortable quietness, only the buzzing of his machine filling up the empty air. His hands on me were warm, comforting without being gratuitous. Even when working on me, Shadow was a complete professional. The only liberties he took were occasional kisses on my waist as he checked in on my pain and comfort levels.

After a while, maybe two hours by my guess, the buzzing stopped and Shadow's hands fell away. I heard a soft groan as he must have stretched, then the snaps and pops of his back cracking.

"Let's take a break, lover. I need to move around," he said with another light kiss on my waist.

I smiled, tapping my lips with a finger. "Kiss me here first and call me that again."

I heard his stool wheel closer over the floor, strands of hair tickling my face first as he leaned down and captured my lips. He'd taken the gloves off and his hands were bare now, knuckles stroking my cheek.

"My lover," he murmured sensually, lips grazing mine before descending on me again.

I rolled to my back, feeling blindly for a spot to grip on his shirt and pull him down. My thighs fell apart to make a space for him between them.

"Stop," he said with laughter in his voice. "After I'm done with you."

My core pulsed with the way he said that last sentence, but I let him go with a resigned sigh. "Can I get up and stretch too?"

"Of course. Just let me figure out how to keep this hidden."

We settled for tying a towel around my waist. Shadow helped me down from the table and secured the towel for me, then told me I could take off the sleeping mask. I whipped it off eagerly, blinking at the brightness of the room after being in the dark for over an hour.

My smile was indulgent the moment my eyes landed on Shadow. He was standing, tall and imposing as ever with his arms stretched above his head. His fingers rested gently on one of the beams in the ceiling, broad chest pressing forward as he stretched.

"I missed looking at this gorgeous man for the past few hours," I purred, coming closer to scratch down his chest and abdomen.

He broke his gaze from mine shyly, a smile still playing at his lips as he brought his hands down, touching them to my waist. "Want to eat something before the next session?"

"Sure." I tilted my face up for a kiss and he bowed over to indulge me.

As we poked around the kitchen, my lower left side throbbed and ached a little. It would be so easy to run to a different part of the house and take a peek under my towel, but I resisted. Shadow did narrow his eyes at me suspiciously when I excused myself to use the restroom, but I placated him with kisses and promises that I wouldn't look.

"Unless you want to come with me and watch?" I teased.

He huffed out a laugh and swatted my opposite hip. "No, do your business. I trust you."

It *was* tricky business hiking up the towel without completely unraveling it, or exposing the lower part of the tattoo, but I stuck to my word and didn't peek.

After some time to nibble and chat, we got back to it. Shadow re-sanitized the tattoo table, then I hopped on and pulled my sleeping mask over my eyes without any complaint. He untied the towel, exposing my lower half, and I shivered at the rush of air on my freshly inked skin.

"I think I've got about two hours of work left," Shadow mused. "I can get it all done at once if you don't distract me," he added with a playful tone.

"I won't," I laughed. "I'm dying to finally look at it."

"Just tell me if you need anything, lover." His kiss landed on my neck, hot and lingering with that deep, rumbling voice of his sending shivers down my spine.

"Now who's distracting who?" I huffed.

Shadow let out a throaty chuckle as he pulled on a pair of fresh gloves, and then the buzzing started up again.

The next two hours went by slowly, which was both enjoyable and frustrating. I loved every moment Shadow's hands were on me—no matter the reason—but I was also dying to see my tattoo, his gift to me. His symbol of devotion and commitment as my husband.

At long last, the buzzing stopped and Shadow gently wiped my skin.

"It's done." His voice was neutral, a type of mask to hide however he was feeling. I knew he must have been nervous about my reaction.

"Can I look?" I was already reaching for the edge of the sleeping mask.

"Sit up slowly first," he said. "We don't want you having a spill like the first time."

"I thought we agreed there was no spill," I joked, but followed his guiding hands to sit upright.

"Stay like that for a second before you stand up."

"*Shadowww,*" I whined. "I want to see!"

"You will, I just want you to be careful. It's a big piece, and you've been lying down for a long time."

"You're just stalling," I teased, reaching a hand blindly for him. "Building up the anticipation, are you?"

His large hand wrapped around mine as he pressed a kiss to my palm. "I'm anxious for you to see it, but also a little worried you won't like it," he admitted.

"I'll love it no matter what it is. Because I love *you.*"

I felt his breath fan lightly across my hand as he sighed. "I love you so much."

I squeezed around his fingers and brought them to my lips. "Now can I please take this mask off?"

"Okay," he said after a beat of silence. "Go ahead."

I couldn't whip the thing off fast enough, then touched my feet down to the floor. My whole left side throbbed as I walked gingerly to the full-length mirror inside Shadow's closet door.

I was nothing short of stunned at what I saw, tears immediately springing to my eyes.

CHAPTER 14

SHADOW

She hates it.

I tried to stamp down the negative thought as Mari stared at herself in the mirror. But seconds ticked by and she wasn't saying anything. My heart hammered in my chest as I waited for a reaction from her. All the confidence and excitement I'd built up about this tattoo went out the window in an instant. I cursed myself for not letting her see it beforehand, that was a stupid fucking idea.

"I can cover it up." The words rushed out of me when the silence became too unbearable. "It needs to heal first, but I can—"

"Shadow." Mari turned to me slowly and my panic spiked at the sight of tears glittering in her eyes. "It's perfect. I can't...I'm sorry, I just don't know how to..." She laughed sheepishly, wiping her eyes as they started to overflow. "Thank you so much for this. I can't imagine a more perfect gift from you."

"You...like it?" She was smiling, so those were happy tears. I still couldn't always tell the difference.

"I'm completely in love." She looked at me, not the tattoo in the mirror, when she said that.

My heart was still going a mile a minute but for a different reason now. The panic had subsided and now it was bright, pure elation that filled my chest. I went to join her at the mirror, running a hand along the back of her shoulders as we looked at the tattoo together.

"I'm happy you like it."

It was the night-blooming Cereus flower, the center at her hip with the long white petals spreading out across her thigh, stretching toward her backside, and reaching up toward her waist. I added the green, thorny vines they grew on to fill in some background. The dark vines also provided contrast for the white petals, making them glow brightly against the dark, like that night we saw them together.

But my favorite part of the tattoo was the monarch butterfly sitting on a petal near the bottom center of the flower, casting a small gray shadow underneath it.

"Is this you and me?" Mari pointed at the butterfly.

"I thought it could represent us, yes," I said. "Not that I'm your shadow in the sense that I'm following you constantly, but more like we're always connected. A part of each other."

"I love that." Mari turned back to face the mirror, pivoting on the ball of her foot to look at the tattoo from different angles. "I love it so much. I love *you*. Fuck, I'm just in awe, Shadow. It's more perfect than I could have imagined."

"I'm glad you think so." My hand slapped to my chest, releasing a breath as I leaned against the tattooing table. "I'm fucking relieved, honestly. I thought you hated it for a second."

"I could never!" Mari's fingers began creeping down her hip to touch the design.

"Don't touch it yet," I warned her. "Give it a few hours. Let me bandage it for you." She headed back toward the table with a slight limp in her walk, and seeing her even in slight pain made my chest ache. She'd never complain but I knew her hip and thigh had to be sore from all the hours under the needle. Grabbing her waist, I lifted her off the floor and carried her the rest of the way, sitting her on the table's edge. "Let me be a medic to you, for once," I added with a grin.

"Excellent bedside manner, I told you," Mari beamed at me.

I taped a sheet of clean gauze over the tattoo, so her skin would be able to breathe while still remaining protected. The first few hours were the most susceptible to infection, as I was sure Mari already knew.

No sooner had I finished covering the artwork and began putting my supplies away than a small fist closed in my shirt and dragged me back to a hungry stare, lips parted and begging for a kiss.

I leaned down to indulge in a fast one, but Mari wasn't satisfied with that. Her teeth sank into my lip and held me in place, the light sting of pain rushing down to my cock.

"Mari," I groaned. Her good leg was already winding around my hip, her calf and foot gripping the back of my leg and pulling me forward. "You're hurt. Do you really want this right now?"

"I'm *not* hurt," she huffed with a pout. "And this tattoo has been an hours-long foreplay session, I want nothing else but you right now."

"A tattoo is an injury," I reminded her gently. "And yours is not a small one. You need to take it easy and heal from it."

"Okay, my leg is a little sore, but I don't care. I'm not *that* fragile." Mari's arms wound around my neck, pulling me down until my hands braced on either side of her. "You gave me this amazing gift. I've been blindfolded for hours while you touch me, kiss me, and tell me about your art. I just love you more every moment I spend with you, and I want you in *all* of my senses."

Lost for words, I lowered my forehead to rest on hers. My eyes closed and I just felt her there with me, breathed her in. How could this be real? After such a long, miserable existence, how was I able to find someone who loved me so genuinely and deeply? Who actively and enthusiastically *wanted* to have sex with me? Time and time again she reassured me, proved to me that every word she said was true.

She loved me, even lusted after me while I looked like this.

Keeping my hand high on her waist on her tattooed side, I grabbed her hip on her other side and pulled her flush to me, crashing my mouth down to hers at the same time.

"Hold on to me, lover." That was the only warning she got before I anchored her to my body and lifted her off the table.

"Always," she purred, squeezing both legs around my waist before tangling her tongue with mine again.

I smiled through the kiss as I turned toward the bed. Supporting her back and hip, I rested my knees on the edge of the mattress and began to slowly lower her down until her back met the bed. Mari scooted up toward the headboard and I followed, crawling on my hands and knees over her. Our lips never disconnected for more than a quick breath, the two of us determined to stay locked together.

When Mari settled into the pillows and brought her arms around me again, I allowed more of my weight to rest on top of her. She let out a pleased moan through my mouth, securing her legs around my waist again. Every time we came together, I worried less about accidentally hurting her. Like she said herself, she wasn't some delicate, fragile thing. My woman had endured so much. There was a steely strength in her lithe, beautiful body underneath me.

Our kiss ended with panting breaths from both of us, the need for air keeping us separated for a few longer moments. I took the opportunity to rise up to kneel and peel my shirt off. In the split second I couldn't see, Mari's hands were already on me.

Her constant affection brought out a giddiness that made me want to grin. I'd seen how women fawned over other men—usually the likes of Gunner or Reaper, always trying to catch their eye and sneak a touch inside their cut. The other guys had enjoyed the attention with a kind of smug indifference, and I'd wondered if that was a result of always catching the eye of women. To them, maybe it got boring.

With Mari, I wanted to soak up and collect every touch she placed on me, and not just because she was the only one who did so. She didn't want anything from me, except to be with me as much as I wanted her.

When my shirt was gone, Mari had one hand on the waistband of my pants, the other still running up to my chest and back down my stomach. She was kissing my scars, as she liked to do. Each one a small touch of healing on a place where I'd been cut.

"Ahh," I groaned as her teeth closed around a small bit of flesh near my hip bone. She sucked a hard kiss there, tongue flicking as her mouth pulled until she released me with a pop of her lips. "That's a good one," I mused at the dark red mark forming at the spot. My skin was hot there, the pulsing of the bruise echoing down into my dick.

"Some of my best work," Mari agreed, smiling as her lips dragged below my navel. She unsnapped the button on my jeans and pulled me out, already half hard, as her kisses continued lower.

"Fuck..." My head dipped back toward the ceiling, eyes falling shut at the feel of her stroking me. Her mouth was near my base, then I felt her tongue chasing her fist as she stroked up my length. I looked down again just in time to watch her lips seal over my crown before the blissful, wet pressure of her mouth sent my head falling back again.

"So fucking good..." I felt blindly for some part of her to touch, my hand finding purchase on her shoulder. She let out a small hum at my words and sucked me even deeper.

She likes it when you praise her, I realized.

"Your mouth...fuck, you're so beautiful..." As it turned out, talking and even forming thoughts was difficult when everything she did was this good. Mari seemed to understand the sentiment though. I looked down to see a smile reaching her eyes despite her mouth being fully stuffed.

My cock expanded with every drag of her lips over me, every hot slide of her tongue. Her free hand still wandered my body—dragging down my thighs as she shoved my pants down, running up my torso, or holding on to my waist as she sucked me harder down her throat.

Just when I was about to stop her, right before my pleasure really started building, she released me with a great gasping breath. I bent down to kiss her, sending her back to her elbows on the mattress. She was already naked from the waist down, dewy and flushed between her legs. My cock, now heavy and hard, dragged along her inner thigh as I resumed hovering over her.

We quickly made off with her top, and I had barely kicked my pants off when her thighs glued to my waist again, drawing me forward.

"Not yet," I murmured between her breasts before turning my head to draw a nipple into my mouth. Mari's frustrated groan made me chuckle, and I lifted my eyes to hers as I moved on to her other breast. "What, are you mad?"

"No, I just want *you*." She squeezed her legs around my waist for emphasis. "I told you, I already had my foreplay."

"Yes." I kissed below her breasts. "But it didn't make you come, so it doesn't really count, does it?"

"Shadowww..." she whined, her head falling back.

"Maaariiii," I taunted back at her, earning a bright laugh and her fingers scratching my scalp as I kissed lower.

Her frustrated grunts and groans soon turned to relaxed sighs and hums. I made sure not to jostle the gauze on her side, already eager for the day I could kiss her new tattoo. I kissed the small scar next to her right hip, one of my favorite places on her body. My mouth trailed lower and Mari's breaths quickened in anticipation. Just before reaching her clit, I pulled away, unwrapping my hand from her thigh to rest on my forearm.

Mari's head popped up from the pillows, shooting me a murderous glare. "Shadow I love you, but I'm seriously not in the mood for a bunch of teasing and denial right now."

"That's not what I'm doing," I assured her, running a hand up the inside of her thigh. "I just want to watch you."

I cupped my palm against her sex and got just the reaction I was hoping for. Mari's eyelids fluttered, her mouth falling open in a soft moan. I added pressure and small, circular movements with my whole hand, giving her the friction she wanted so badly. Her head fell back to the pillows as she started to lift and buck her hips against my palm.

"Yes, that," I whispered. Doc's pendulum had nothing on the hypnotic movements of her body as she chased pleasure. "I love watching you like that."

Mari's hooded eyes focused on me, the sexy, intimate eye contact making my cock jolt with need for her. "Keep talking like that. It's hot when you talk to me."

"Really?" I lifted my palm away from her, returning with two fingers to stroke and glide through her wetness.

"Yes," she gasped, thighs clamping around my wrist. "Tell me why you like watching me."

"Hm." I spread her legs apart and returned to playing with her, teasing her opening with a fingertip. "At first it was to make sure I was doing things right, but now I just love seeing you move, seeing how badly you want it."

"Want *you*," she added.

"Yes, me." I grinned, lowering another kiss to my favorite scar as I pressed a finger inside her. "But also in general. I love the sounds and movements you make when you're pleased."

She was making some beautiful ones now as I stroked her pussy, her hips tilting up for more sensation as her head tossed and she grabbed for the sheets next to her. I curled the digit inside her and dragged the pad of my finger along her slick walls, my eyes glued to everything happening above her waist.

"I love how flushed your skin gets," I continued, watching the pink of her cheeks deepen. "When your brows furrow and you bite your lips to keep from screaming."

She released her lip right then with a laugh, returning my gaze. "I should have known, with how observant you are—ah!"

Her cry released with no lip-bite to hold it in as I added a second finger, spreading them apart inside to give her that feeling of fullness she craved.

"I love it when your legs clamp around me like you never want me to leave." The first knuckles of my hand rubbed her sex as I stroked deeper within her. "How you get so sensitive that you shiver no matter where I touch you. How your nipples get so tight and dark too."

My thumb swiped her clit and a beautiful shudder wracked her body then. Fuck me, she was a vision. I knew then, definitively, that I wouldn't mind one of the others joining us in the slightest. As long as I got to watch her being pleased, whether it was by me or someone else who had the privilege of loving her.

It was near impossible to tear my eyes away from her, but as I took small, biting kisses of her thighs, I knew what awaited me was just as sweet.

Her taste.

My mouth replaced my thumb as the weight on her clit, my fingers still driving deeply inside her with long, curling strokes. I flattened my tongue against the hard little bud to the sounds of her cries reaching a new height, her blunt nails raking across my scalp as her thighs held me in place. Despite my being in control of her pleasure, her sweet body had me trapped—not that I wanted to be anywhere else.

Mari's orgasm closed around my fingers as she whimpered and moaned, thrashing against me with ragged pants. As tempted as I was to watch, I didn't pull away from her until her thighs fell apart and her pleasure ebbed away to soft pulses.

"Come here." It was a soft, whispered demand as she reached for me, her eyes still hungry under her relaxed lids.

I couldn't bring myself to obey her fast enough, planting my hands next to her sides as I crawled up, bringing my face down for a kiss, and nudging my hips into the embrace of her thighs as I lowered the rest of the way to her.

Our bodies slid against each other in a few teasing, short thrusts before the head of my cock found her entrance. I pressed into her mid-kiss, pausing at her moan and just to *feel* her slick heat wrapped around me.

"I'm good, don't stop," she urged me, hands running up my back.

I brought my mouth to her neck as I pressed deeper, sucking lightly at her pulse but not enough to leave marks. She whimpered in protest as I pulled back, drawing nearly all the way out, then drove forward deeper than before. The motion had her arching off the bed with a ragged gasp, breasts smashed to my chest.

"This." I lifted away from her neck to watch her face, taking another long drag out of her before a deeper thrust inside. "I love watching you when I do *this.*"

"Fuck!" Her face was in a beautiful grimace of pleasure as she clung to me with as much of her body as was possible.

Stripes of heat lanced up and down my back, her nails digging and grasping to hold on to me. It was a delicious kind of sharpness that radiated to every inch of my skin, and I wanted more.

"Fuck yes, *that,*" I rasped, finding her lips with mine again. "Scratch me harder."

Mari smiled before I swallowed her mouth in another kiss, my tongue and cock mirroring each other as they surged deeper, always seeking more of her to taste and feel.

"Ohh fuck!" Her nails felt like they were scoring me, testing the limit of my skin as she dug in and dragged them from my ass to my shoulders. She didn't break the skin—I knew that feeling well enough. For some reason I could only feel pain with her, and it danced on the knife edge of my pleasure, heightening all the sensations as I moved through her silky heat.

"Too much?" Mari's hands flattened to rub and soothe where she just scratched me.

"No." I kissed her jaw, sliding my arms underneath to cradle her head and upper back. "Pain from you is so, so good."

She wouldn't ever truly hurt me, not like how I'd been before. That very knowledge was what made me crave these little samples of pain from her. I'd gone without the sensation for so long, her teeth and nails in my skin gave me just enough to feel and experience it like a normal person would. Exploring the line where it blurred with my pleasure was just an added bonus.

I rocked into her at a steady, even pace while Mari changed directions with her scratching. She ran her nails across my shoulder blades now, digging unabashedly into my decades of scar tissue while I moaned into another kiss. It felt like a fire was licking at my back—too close for cozy warmth but not quite burning me yet. It matched the heat of her pussy wrapped around me, searing, but so soft and pliant that I *needed* to sink in for more.

"You're mine." The possessiveness spurred me deeper into her body, a growl escaping me as my fist closed around a handful of her hair.

"Yours," she agreed, nails scraping along the back of my neck. "And you're mine."

"My wife," I groaned, drunk and delirious on every feeling and sensation racing through my body. Everything she showed me I was able to feel. "My lover."

"My husband," Mari answered in a panted whisper, her palms holding my face to look at me. "My love."

I tilted her hips higher, increasing the friction between us with every stroke of my cock. She clutched the backs of my biceps at that, soft moans turning into sharp cries and gasps. Pleasing her in bed had become my new addiction. Reading her body, listening to the sounds she made, and feeling the changes in the way her pussy gripped me—I wanted to drink it all down like there was an endless supply.

"Fuck! Shadow, yes!" She was getting louder, curling around me tighter with each snap of my hips. Her arms, legs, and even her lips trembled with wrought-up tension desperate for release. Seeing my woman on the precipice sent my own pleasure soaring, swelling and aching with every squeeze of her silky walls.

My face buried in her neck again, groaning against her flushed skin as I drove into her, determined to see her to her finish.

Mari's orgasm triggered my own, the clenching of her sex around me stuttering my rhythm to the point of no return. I came in a rush of heat and sensitivity, every sensation heightened as she ran her nails up my back again. It felt like being struck by lightning, if that could ever be pleasurable. I shuddered and wrapped around her just as she did with me, the descent from my high slow and making me feel boneless.

I remained on top of Mari through the peak and the fall, my body still except for the great huffs of air I took. My pulse raced with dizzying speed. And still she felt so good, I didn't want to move. Her arms and legs remained hugged around me, like she didn't want me to leave either.

"I got you good back here," she mused after a few moments of quiet, palms caressing with a featherlight touch up and down my back.

"Am I bleeding?" I mumbled into the side of her neck. I didn't care if I was, except for giving her extra work in patching me up.

"No, it's just gonna be red for a while." Her fingers moved through my hair, running long, luxurious strokes over my scalp that made me want to purr like a cat.

"Good." I lifted my head to kiss her before rolling to my side. "I'll spend lots of time with my shirt off."

"Mm-hm." She grinned like she was pleased with the idea. "Never thought I'd hear you say that."

"Never thought I'd have long scratches on my back to show off." Mari rolled toward me and we fell into kissing some more—light, sweeping passes of our lips with how sated and sensitive we both still were. When we parted again, I touched the edge of her bandaged tattoo. "Did this ever bother you?"

"No." She scratched the rough bristles on my chin and smirked. "You're so good in bed, I forgot it was there."

A scoff escaped me as I rolled to my back. "Even I'm not *that* good." I smiled despite myself, running an arm around her waist to bring her down into the pillows with me. "You're just trying to give me an ego."

She wrinkled her nose and made more of her cute, frustrated

growling noises until I scooped her onto my chest for more kisses. We settled into quietness after a few moments, her head resting over my heart while I traced her first tattoo, running my fingers over the inked lines on her back.

"You know what I realized?"

"Hm?" she mumbled sleepily against my skin.

"I think I might...really like seeing you with one of the others."

Her head lifted at that, eyes bright and curious. "You think so?"

"Yes." I traced her cheekbone, torn between staring at her endlessly or getting up to draw the beautiful planes of her face. "I love seeing you being pleased so much, I don't think it would matter who's doing it."

Mari returned her head to my chest, a giddy smile on her face as she settled on me. "Then we'll try it, whenever we get another fucking break in this war." Her head quickly lifted again, the smile wiped away. "And you know you don't have to—"

"Share you in bed if I don't like it, I know." I dropped an amused peck on her lips.

"And you know I never want to—"

"Ignore me or make me feel unwanted." I pulled her up higher to kiss her more deeply, banding my arms around her back while I reassured *her* for once. "Yes, I know that, my love." I tucked her head under my chin and held her to me tightly. "I know that better than I know anything else."

CHAPTER 15

JANDRO

"I'm not fucking joking."

I bit back my smile as Mari paced in front of Reaper, Gunner, and Shadow, looking like the sexiest damn drill sergeant while the three of them stood stiffly at attention.

"You will not, under any circumstances, do anything stupid," she continued, pinning each of them with a hard stare. "Such as getting yourself captured by the enemy." Mari leaned aggressively into Gunner's face. "Getting stabbed, shot, or anything else that would put you at risk of a life-threatening injury. That goes for all of you!" She whipped around to face me and I schooled my features too late. I'd been staring at her ass and she caught me. "I mean it, Jandro."

"Yep, got it." I resumed my attentive stance but there was no hiding my smirk at her sexy-angry face. "That's why I'm hanging back on maintenance duty and not in the field killing some Blakeworth fucknuts."

Mari's features softened as she stepped closer toward me. "You understand why I can't have all of you out on the battlefield, right? I just couldn't handle the possibility of losing all of you."

"'Course I do." I reached for her, my fingertips finding placement on the waist of her medic jumpsuit. "I'm happy to not be fighting, actually."

"Really?" Her eyebrows jumped at that.

"Believe it or not, I actually don't enjoy being shot multiple times or burned alive by explosives."

"You're not a great shot anyway," Gunner jabbed, resting his hands on the multiple guns holstered at his belt.

"Yeah, come tell me that when your Mini jams up 'cause you haven't cleaned it."

"Hey, I clean my shit!"

"You really should clean them more often," Shadow muttered under his breath.

"I'm sorry, what?" Gunner whirled on him, incredulous.

"I'm just saying, you have a lot of guns and it's been humid. They're definitely accumulating moisture."

"Alright, enough." Reaper raised a hand to stop the bickering. "We need to go. Sugar?" His voice softened. "We'll watch ourselves and we *will* come back. Promise."

She nodded at him, her body language fidgeting as if she was unsure about reaching out to touch him or not. "You better."

There was a tense moment of neither of them knowing what to do. Finally she rushed forward, squeezing him in a tight hug. Reaper wrapped an arm around her shoulders, the other around her back. His face lowered nearly to her shoulder, mouth angling toward her neck like he was going to kiss her there, but he stopped himself. Mari only squeezed him harder, the full length of her body pressing against his. For a simple hug, it was intense and sexually charged. Neither of them looked like they wanted to let go.

The other two and I looked on without comment, only patient curiosity. Mari and Reaper's relationship was a component of *us,* a greater whole, while still being independently *them* at the same time. The issues they had affected us all, but it still felt wrong to step in. Fixing what had gone wrong took time, and there was nothing wrong with that. None of us were going to tell her to hurry up and forgive him so we could all be a hunky-dory family again. Reaper had hurt her deeply—I knew that well enough from the nights of holding her crying after Shadow had been exiled.

By the same token, Reap was doing his best. He treated Shadow like a friend now, not a subordinate. He was thinking before he spoke more often, listening to others' input before jumping ahead to what he wanted to do. Of course he still wasn't perfect at it, but he was trying. The man knew how to admit he was wrong, and he didn't deserve to continue being punished for a wrong he acknowledged and regretted.

It might have been at a snail's pace, but Mari and Reaper seemed to be moving in a positive direction. And the best thing for the rest of us to do, was support them both.

The two of them finally released each other, and Reaper came up to me as Mari said her goodbyes to Gun and Shadow.

"I want you, Larkan, and Slick out there after we're done," he murmured.

"Way ahead of you, Reap," I chuckled, slapping his shoulder. "You're crazy if you don't think we're scavenging some fancy Blakeworth machinery."

He grinned and thumped my chest. "Save the best shit for us and the Sons."

"Fuck yeah. Spoils of war, baby."

The three of them headed out to their waiting units. Mari came over to nestle into my side, and together we watched them go. She peered up at me once they were out of sight. "What were you two talking about?"

"Taking what's left of Blakeworth's goods after we beat their ass into submission." My arm rested on her shoulders as I dropped a kiss to her head. "I bet I can build you a whole new bike just from their parts."

"I like my dirt bike!"

"You're a president's wife, you gotta have at least two sets of wheels. More acceptably, three, but ideally, four."

"One for each husband?" she laughed.

"Something like that."

She hugged around me and lifted up on her tiptoes to kiss my cheek. "I should make sure the hospitals are all prepped and ready."

"Go on." I swatted her ass. "I'll swing by later to check on your generators."

With that, she headed off toward the two large white tents at the edge of the field. I chewed the inside of my cheek, watching her leave. We had nearly the whole hospital staff out here, and two field hospitals set up. A gnawing in my stomach cemented the reality that we'd likely be filling up hospital beds much faster than the first two battles.

We were on Blakeworth's doorstep, taking the battle to them now that we cleared the neutral zone of their spies. Gunner and T-Bone were able to piece together an aerial map of their capital city through Horus and Munin, T-Bone's raven. They marked the army's supply warehouses and government buildings, and the plan today was to take those out, essentially cutting Blakeworth off at the knees.

It was an aggressive move, and one in which we needed the element of surprise to pull off successfully. But there would likely be civilians caught in the crossfire.

After much back-and-forth and hesitation from Governor Vance, we finally decided this action was necessary. General Bray and Mari put together a unit of combat medics just to address civilians who'd get caught in the crossfire. Back in Four Corners, we posted a heavy artillery team facing east to watch for any activity from Tash but aside from that, it was all hands on deck.

I watched all the units move out until they were dark specks on the horizon. The shining towers of Blakeworth occasionally flashed as their glass panes caught the rising sun. I couldn't wait until we scaled those towers and put a Steel Demons flag at the top.

Some small part of me was wistful at missing out on the action. Battles used to be such a rush, on a different level than sex or riding or anything else. A year ago, I'd be out there right along Reaper's side, screaming like a madman while my gun lit up anyone who got in my path.

But battles took their toll on me. Even with the accelerated healing from Freyja, my back muscles still seized up. I'd been shot in both shoulders now, and the damn things couldn't move like they used to. I still got random pains in my lower leg, which Mari said was from nerve damage. Having gods around for healing didn't make me brand new, as I was beginning to figure out. They just sped up the process that was already going to happen, all the side effects and lingering pains included.

It wasn't just me who was battle-fatigued either. I could see it in the other guys. Even Gunner, who was fully in his element with that tactical mind of his.

We were tired. We wanted it to end.

And today was hopefully a big step toward that finish line.

I headed for the fleet of Jeeps and trucks we had standing by for a second wave if necessary. General Bray's mechanics were all good dudes who had taken well to me overseeing them, much like the foot soldiers who had taken to Gunner.

The vehicles were turned on and idling gently, ready to go at a moment's notice with a single radio call. Soldiers were relaxed but alert, hanging out with the doors and windows open, talking softly so everyone could hear if a call for back-up came in.

I wandered through the lines slowly, saying hello, but more importantly, listening for anything unusual with the vehicles. Everything should have been maintained and in top shape, but there was always a car or two that stubbornly didn't perform like it should.

"Jandro," one of the younger mechanics called, waving a wrench at me. "Can you come look at this?"

"Whatcha got, Holmes?" I came over, ears already pricked to the rattling under the truck's hood.

"Look underneath," the kid grumbled. "We just topped off the oil, but it's got a fucking leak."

I dropped to the ground, peering underneath the truck. "Yup, you're right. Go ahead and turn it off for me." He did so as I rose to standing. "We should take this one out of commission for now. Grab a flashlight and check out the engine for any leaks there. Did you just notice it?"

"Yeah, I think it's a pretty slow leak."

"So probably nothing that's a big break, a gasket or something is just not sealed somewhere." I patted the kid's shoulder, trying to wipe the frown off of his face. "It's not your fault man, cars are stubborn children sometimes."

"Just thought I did everything right," he muttered. He was young, probably not even twenty.

"I'm sure you did," I told him. "Sometimes you can do everything right and the damn thing still doesn't want to cooperate." I tilted my head, picking up a new grinding sound in the air from one of the other vehicles. "Like that, you hear it?"

The kid squinted as he concentrated on listening. "Uh, I think so."

"Something is messed up in there." I rubbed my chin as I turned around, trying to decipher which one of the vehicles it was coming from. "Someone didn't replace a belt, or a..."

I had turned toward the northeast and spotted a dark line on the horizon that wasn't there before, and was quickly growing bigger. I crossed my arms, watching the approaching unit with some confusion. Was there a second wave of back-ups that I had forgotten about? They weren't heading for us, but toward the field hospitals.

"Hey, who are they?" I asked the mechanic, jerking my chin toward the approaching vehicles.

He shrugged and shook his head. "I dunno."

I chewed my lip as I kept watching. Maybe Mari had called for more medics? She would have mentioned it though, and these Jeeps had guns mounted to the top, like makeshift battle tanks. A heavy sense of unease gripped me, and I shoved the mechanic toward the non-exposed side of the truck.

"Stay there. I'm gonna talk to your lieutenant," I told him, hurrying away to find his superior officer.

I hadn't jogged more than fifty feet before Lieutenant Davis met me in the center of the fleet of vehicles. "Who the fuck is that?" he demanded, pointing at the quickly approaching vehicles.

Fuck. Dread filled me up like a well of black ink.

"I was hoping you would know," I said.

"Shit." Davis grabbed for his radio. "General Bray, come in—"

He never got to finish the call. A projectile launched from a gun mounted on one of the Jeeps tore through the fabric of a hospital tent and engulfed it in flames.

Chapter 16

MARIPOSA

"I mean, don't knock it 'til you try it." A hint of smugness bled into my voice as the young medics hung onto my every word.

"Doesn't it hurt?" a woman with curly black hair asked.

"Not if the guys prepare you well enough with lots of orgasms beforehand." I grinned, despite my face heating up. "And even then, they should go slowly, use plenty of lube, and most of all, listen and check in with you for any discomfort. It should never hurt if they're being attentive to your needs."

"Do your husbands ever…?" Another medic crossed her two index fingers and rubbed them against each other.

"No, they're all pretty focused on me." Somehow I was able to stay composed and resisted flipping my hair over my shoulder. "But if you're interested in that, I might know a sword-crossing trio." I grinned, thinking of the Sons and their occasional trysts with women.

"Oh, me, me me!" Several hands shot up and a tittering of laughter and good-natured teasing rose up from my staff. Warmth bloomed in my chest. It was so much like nursing school. When you had to work long, rotating shifts with the same people, you couldn't help but become a family. A family of people who were far too comfortable discussing various body parts.

"Alright, you perverts." I clapped my hands once. "Stay sharp. I'm going to check in on the other tent."

"Don't accidentally trip and fall on two dicks," someone called as I headed for the tent flap.

I walked out to the sounds of cackling, my smile wide as I headed for the neighboring tent. We needed this, all the laughter and crude conversation. We were about to get overrun by carnage, chaos, and death. Might as well enjoy these moments of peace while we had them.

Most of the injured from battle would be directed toward the first hospital tent. The second tent was reserved for major operations, such as amputations or removing large pieces of shrapnel from victims. Dr. Books and Rhonda were chatting quietly over tea in the second tent when I stepped inside.

"They're ready over there," I said, angling my head toward the direction I came from.

"You sure?" Rhonda teased. "They sound like a pack of hyenas."

"Just conducting the usual interviews about my sex life." I shrugged, my grin returning.

Dr. Brooks hid his blush and soft laugh behind a sip of tea, while Rhonda remained stone-faced, peering at me shrewdly. "Is everything okay at home, Mari?"

I pulled in a breath, knowing the longer I took to answer, the more obvious the answer would be no. "As okay as it can be." I forced a smile. "Given the fact that, you know, we're in the middle of a war and my whole family is fighting in it."

"Forget the war for a second." Rhonda set down her tea cup and Dr. Brooks took the opportunity to check on some machinery at the opposite end of the tent. "War is hard, you and I both know that." Rhonda's steely eyes bore into me. "I'd venture a guess that neither of us ever took out the pain of our jobs on our loved ones."

"Please, Rhonda." I held up a palm to stop her. "We're both experienced enough to know that trauma expresses itself differently in everyone. My men aren't perfect but they love me. Have they hurt me? Yes. Have I hurt them? Also yes. Maybe not in the same ways, but no one has made it through the last decade unscathed."

Rhonda didn't speak, only kept looking at me with that dissecting gaze.

"There's no one I'd rather see at the end of the day than those four men out there." I pointed outside the tent. *Yes, even Reaper,* I realized. "So when you ask if everything's okay, yes. We're doing the best we can, but we're not in a vacuum, Rhonda. We can't just subtract the war from the equation, because it has taken its toll on all of us."

The head nurse opened her mouth like she was about to speak, but a thundering crash rocked the tent like an earthquake. I was nearly knocked to my feet, and Rhonda slid off the table she was sitting on and hit the floor.

"What's happening?" she demanded.

Searing heat coated my skin like a sudden fever. Bright, flickering light lit up the canvas walls of our tent. The most obvious sign came a moment later—the smell of smoke.

"The other tent's on fire!" Dr. Brooks sprang into action, grabbing gallons of the distilled water we used to wash equipment, and ran for the tent flaps.

"Oh my God, everyone's over there!" I hurried to pull Rhonda to her feet, but she moved slower with her bad leg and pushed me away.

"Go help the doctor!" she ordered me.

"I'm not leaving you alone!" I screamed back.

"I'll be alright, kiddo, those young medics need you. Save them!" She grabbed her cane and actually whacked me in the leg with it. "Go!"

I kept my eyes on her as I headed for the exit, staring at the tough-as-nails nurse until the last moment when I stepped outside. And holy fuck.

The battle was right fucking here.

Soldiers ran and shouted orders. Gunfire erupted, already making me duck and my ears ring. And right next door, our hospital was engulfed in flames.

I ran to help Dr. Brooks douse the flames with water, but it was hopeless. We might as well have been using squirt guns on a forest fire.

"Did anyone get out?" he yelled, swinging his arms back and forth to get more water out of the container. We didn't have hoses, so I copied his movements.

"I..." The horror hit me like a shot to the chest, cracking me wide open.

Fuck.

No.

I had *just* been in there, not even five minutes earlier. The medics' faces floated through my mind—their wide eyes, their smirks and giggles at the sordid details of my sex life. We were all just having a moment of lighthearted fun before a long day of work began. They were ready. They trained under me to save lives.

And, oh God no, they were *so* young.

"...I was the only one that left the tent."

The empty water container fell from my hand and my feet pressed forward, the flames already feeling close enough to singe my hair. A strong hand immediately clasped around my arm and pulled me back.

"No, Mari!" Dr. Brooks' voice sounded so far away. "You are *not* going in there!"

"I left them!" A sob rattled through my chest. "I walked away, I left them in there!"

"It's not your fault, sweetheart. I don't know how this happened."

The doctor's arms banded around me, pulling me back once he realized I fully intended to run into that tent, which had now collapsed into a wide circle of flames. The blaze didn't reach very high, but the fire was spread out. I could see some of the metal frames of the hospital beds and shelving we used. Flames just engulfed everything, covering shapes of every size. I couldn't even tell what was equipment or a person, and that made me scream a heart full of rage and pain at the carnage right in front of me.

"Mari? Mari!"

Someone was shouting my name, growing louder by the second. Dr. Brooks loosened his hold on me just a fraction and I tried to seize the chance to run into the fire, but he held on tighter when he sensed me pulling away.

"Mari! Oh my God, thank fucking everything."

Someone else was holding me now. Jandro crushed me to his broad chest, touching my cheek with a shaking hand. His eyes were tear-filled and full of relief, lips trembling as he said my name over and over.

"You weren't in that tent," he whispered. "Thank all the fucking gods, you weren't in that tent."

"Jandro, they were all inside!" I cried, trying to push on his chest to make him let me go. "I left them there! I have to go see if anyone—"

"Mari, babe." His voice hardened, holding my cheek firmly to make me look at him. "There's nothing we can do. We have to run."

"Run?" I blinked at him. "No, we have soldiers here. We have to fight. Someone attacked the *hospital*."

"It's Tash's army," he said quickly. "They overwhelmed the backup unit, a quarter of them are already gone. We have to run now."

"What?" I didn't understand, his words weren't computing. Before I could process what he said, he was pulling me away from the fire and breaking into a run. Dr. Brooks ran alongside us and I grabbed his arm. "You have to get Rhonda!"

"Going there now. The two of you keep moving!" He disappeared into the second tent that was still standing and a new spike of panic hit me. Would I see him or Rhonda again?

Jandro wouldn't let me stop or slow down to look around. Chaos surrounded us and I was still just trying to make sense of everything.

"Jandro, please wait!"

"Mari!" He barked my name out more harshly than I ever heard him say before. "If we stop, we're dead!"

"What about the other guys?" I hurried to keep up with his pace. "Has anyone called them?"

"I tried, didn't get an answer," he said. "They're busy with their own battle, or Tash might be interfering with our radio signals."

A barrage of rapid gunfire kicked up dirt right in front of our feet, making Jandro and I skid to a stop and throw our arms up to shield our faces. Before he pulled me to run in a different direction, I saw the armored Jeep with a massive assault rifle mounted to the roof coming straight for us.

"Fucking surrounded," Jandro hissed between his teeth, his hand an iron grip around my own.

"Are you hurt?" I asked him.

"No."

He pulled me around one of our own equipment vans and there, we stopped. Our backs pressed against the vehicle for cover, the two of us breathing with hard and labored gasps.

"Jandro—"

"Shh."

He turned to peer through the passenger window of the van, then carefully opened the door, making as little sound as possible. After rummaging around the seat for a few moments, he popped open the glove box to reveal a small handgun and a magazine of ammo.

Jandro looked at me and whispered, "You got your gun?"

I nodded shakily, my hand finding purchase on the weapon on my hip.

He took the gun from the glove box and cursed under his breath. There was no mag inside. The cartridge lying next to the gun contained the only bullets.

"You fully loaded?" Jandro asked me.

I nodded again. "How many shots do you have?"

"Fifteen." He dared to huff out a laugh. "And Gunner was right. I am probably the worst shot out of all of us."

"Jandro..." His name came out as a weak whimper on my lips. I didn't even know what I was trying to say.

He cupped my cheek and placed a tender kiss on my forehead. "I love you so much."

"Is this..." My eyes blurred with tears. I stared at the patches on his cut, inches from my face. The thread, the stitching. His club symbol was a skull with two wrenches crossed behind it. I'd never looked at it so closely before.

Jandro tilted my face up to his, wiping my tears with his thumbs before kissing me too softly, too sweetly on my lips, his mouth so soft and lingering, which only made me cry harder.

"If they get me first," he whispered. "Run south, back to Four Corners."

"No," I said weakly, clutching at him. "I...I can't lead them back to the city. All those people."

"If the others come back, they *have* to find you alive, Mari."

Glass exploded, raining shards down on us as we ducked low. The windows and windshield of the van were gone.

"They'll let me live if I tell them I'm a medic." I was just babbling now, my mind desperate to find another way out of this situation, one that didn't lead to the slaughter of thousands. One that didn't mean I was about to lose Jandro. Lose *everything.* "I'll...I'll help them at first. Buy us some time."

Jandro only shook his head, the warmth and love in his eyes hardening. "Do *not* let them capture you under any circumstances."

"But—"

More rapid-fire cut off my argument, bullet holes appearing in the side of the van just above our heads. Jandro shoved me next to the front tire just in time, and he rolled next to the rear tire just as a series of shots tore through the lower half of the van where we'd just been crouching.

Jandro leaned with his back against the tire, holding his gun to his chest as he peered around the back of the van. "They're right there." The sound of defeat in his voice was heartbreaking. He looked back at me. "Promise me, *mi amor,* you won't let yourself get captured."

"I..."

This couldn't be the last conversation I was having with my husband. Not this. We still had so much to talk about. So much to do together.

"Mari!" Jandro hissed through his teeth to keep his voice down. "Promise me *now.*"

"I promise." My voice had no strength, it was barely a whisper. "I love you so much, *guapito.*"

He forced a grin, though it looked more like a grimace. "You're the best wife a man could ask for." With a deep breath that seemed to calm him, he looked up briefly, then back at me. "Ready?"

I gave a shaky nod, still numbed by the disbelief that this was actually happening. He gave me no instructions because we were about to die.

Jandro returned my nod and let the back of his head fall against the van for a moment. "On three," he said, voice at normal volume. "One... two...*three!*"

I rose to my feet, pointing my gun through the shot-out windows of the van. Five Jeeps were lined up on the other side, each with a driver, two passengers, and a gunner manning the assault rifle on top. Only they weren't driving, so everyone in the Jeeps had weapons drawn and pointed at us.

There was no way we could win.

I started firing, hoping to take at least one of them out before I went down. They returned fire, and I ducked on instinct. Looking over at Jandro, he had done the same, waiting for a pause so he could resume shooting.

When we moved to shoot again, the gunner was taking aim from the Jeep's roof. When he fired, I thought my eardrums would burst. Pain split through the sides of my head, and then I was falling backwards. The van…it looked like it was about to fall on top of me.

I brought my arms up instinctively, despite knowing I'd never survive being crushed under a massive vehicle. Something grabbed around my waist and flung me roughly in a different direction. *Oh fuck, no! I can't get captured!*

I thrashed, kicked, and screamed. I couldn't hear anything besides the painful ringing in my head, couldn't make sense of up, down, or any direction. *Jandro! Where's Jandro?* I tried screaming at the top of my lungs but still couldn't hear myself.

Someone was touching me, dragging me somewhere, and I fought with all of my remaining strength, which was quickly draining away. Then something appeared in front of my face, a hand. Fingers were snapping in front of my eyes, the sound muffled and far away.

And then, a man's face. He looked familiar and I squinted in my effort to recognize him. Silver hair and kind blue eyes.

"Hey there, angel." His lips moved slowly enough for me to understand. "Sorry we're late, but Jerriton's here. Told ya we'd stand with Four Corners."

CHAPTER 17

JANDRO

Once that projectile fired off from the top of the Jeep, I knew we were done for. This was it, fucked over by an ambush we never saw coming. An attack on the hospital, of all things.

The van rocked onto its two passenger-side tires from the close impact of the missile. Mari had been shooting through the windows and the force knocked her back. Before I could dive for her, someone grabbed my cut and yanked me back as the van fell onto its side.

"MARI!" Someone had grabbed her, a guy was hauling her away from the overturned van with an arm around her waist. He was dressed in the all-black of the troops who just ambushed us. "Put her down!" I yelled, raising my gun toward them.

The guy ignored me, but something else was off. He seemed to be handling her...carefully. He sat her gently on the ground, and his partner crouched in front of Mari's dazed face, snapping his fingers in front of her eyes.

I tore out of the grip holding me and whipped around, my gun at the throat of a kid in his twenties. "Who the fuck are you?"

"Jerriton," he said quickly, raising his arms to his sides. "The People's Army of Jerriton, we're on your side."

"People's Army?" I pulled my gun away a fraction of an inch. "You the rebels that broke out of the prison?"

"Yes, sir." His eyes were wide as his head bobbed up and down in a nod. "We escorted Mariposa and Shadow back to Four Corners."

"Well shit." I lowered my gun and somehow in my shock, remembered to take in my surroundings.

There was no need for cover, as I soon realized. Jerriton was everywhere, shooting at the black-clad troops wearing similar, but slightly different uniforms. Everyone that had been shooting at Mari and me was either dead or had been detained.

"Okay, what the fuck is happening?" I demanded, turning around in a circle. At quick glances, it looked like our attackers had turned against themselves. "Did you shoot down our hospital?"

"No, I swear!" The kid shook his head, his wide eyes still on my gun. "We were on our way to help and saw *them* marching toward you. None of them even glanced at us. They were like robots, it was fuckin' weird. It was dark and we just kind of followed them in. Uniforms must've looked similar enough that it didn't raise alarms for them."

None of that shit was making sense, but I had more pressing matters to deal with. "Hey!" I hollered, walking up to the two guys surrounding Mari. "Get the fuck out of my wife's face!" I grabbed the shoulder of the guy crouched in front of her, shoving him to the side.

"Easy, man." He was an older guy, roughly Reaper's dad's age, with hair and a beard that were mostly gray. His blue eyes narrowed at me. "I've had some medical training, I'm just checking her for a concussion."

"Jandro, this is Samson." Mari was lucid enough to sound amused. "He led the Jerriton resistance that got me and Shadow home. Sam, Jandro is one of my husbands."

"Like that wasn't clear." Samson chuckled as he rubbed his shoulder, and a twinge of guilt sat in my chest.

"Sorry, man," I muttered. "Here, let me." I held my arm out to help him up.

"It's all good. Thanks." Samson grabbed my forearm and allowed me to pull him to standing. "She's fine, by the way," he added a bit smugly.

"Fuck, both of us are." I ran my hand over my head, still stunned at this drastic turn of events when we were down to our last bullets. "I don't...I don't know how many of us are left."

"Dr. Brooks and Rhonda! We have to find them." Mari held her hands out and I grabbed them to pull her to her feet and into my chest, wrapping her up tightly.

"Lady with a cane and tall, black guy with glasses?" piped up the kid I'd been talking to earlier. "Red crosses on their jumpsuits?"

"Yes!" Mari tore out of my embrace to look at him. "You've seen them?"

"Yes, ma'am. They're fine," he said with a dip of his head. "They found cover behind a pile of debris, and we took out the ones shooting at them."

"Oh, thank fuck." She slumped against me, only to lift her head again. "The guys! Did you try radioing them again?"

"I will in a sec." My hand came to rest on the back of her head, bringing it to nestle in the center of my chest again. "Just let me hold you like this for a minute."

I'd made peace with dying today. I had expected it, even welcomed it. But something—the universe or the gods—decided that today was not my day. I still had more time with my wife, my family, and I wouldn't take a single moment of that for granted.

Mari's arms came around my waist and she held on to me just as tightly.

"OUR DEEPEST APOLOGIES FOR NOT COMING TO YOUR AID sooner." Samson stood at the end of the conference table two hours later, cleaned up in a polo shirt and slacks for this meeting with the entire Four Corners leadership. Even some of Governor Vance's cabinet members who weren't directly involved in the war effort wanted to meet the People's Army of Jerriton. "We wanted to ensure things were stable enough back home before involving ourselves in other territories' disputes."

"Stable enough, meaning...?" General Bray implored him.

When Samson hesitated in answering, Governor Vance piped up. "Speak freely, sir. You've just saved my territory and will not be tried for any crimes here."

"You can trust the governor and the general," Shadow added. "They've been good to us."

T-Bone muttered something under his breath, earning some side-eyes, but Shadow's encouragement seemed to be what Samson needed to hear.

"We overthrew the governor that Tash left in charge," he said with an air of pride, lifting his chin. "And took back our territory, our home."

"Fuck yeah," Gunner muttered, his face splitting into a grin as his hand curled into a victorious fist. Louder he said, "Congratulations. It's the least of what you deserve."

"You're renaming the place, I take it?" Reaper asked, a smile also growing on his face.

"Thank you, and yes." Samson gave a lighthearted shrug and grinned sheepishly. "Probably Colorado, like how it was before."

"Once we're able, Four Corners will support you in any way you need," Vance said.

"Again, thank you." Samson lowered his gaze to the table. "After this war is over, we plan to hold elections."

"Just like the good old days." Even Reaper's dad was beaming at him from across the table. "You're running, I hope."

Samson shrugged humbly again. "I'm not sure yet. We'll see."

Vance's assistant Josh cleared his throat to grab the room's attention. "This is very exciting but if you don't mind gentlemen, we do need official reports of today's events."

"Right, of course." Finn turned to his son next to him at the table. "Why don't you start, and then we'll get into what happened with the hospital."

It turned out Reaper, Gunner, and Shadow's units had mopped the floor with Blakeworth. They demolished important government buildings and supply warehouses, just as planned. Sadly, as we also predicted, death and injury among civilians was also high. Their medic team was able to take over a well-stocked hospital reserved for the elite class, and stayed there to treat the injured without having to transport them back to our field hospitals.

After their battle was over, everyone stayed to look for more injured in the rubble. They filled the Blakeworth hospital, and still carried truckloads of civilians back to us, unknowing of the situation we were in. They never received a single one of our distress calls until after Jerriton saved our asses, which strongly suggested that our attackers interfered with our signals. Once Reaper concluded his report, all eyes swiveled to those who rode in and saved us, the real stars of the show.

"Samson, the floor is yours." Governor Vance folded his hands patiently, but I could see how he too was eager to hear this story.

"Thank you, sir. As I said, we wanted to stabilize our territory before offering aid. But recruiting a sizable army was a high priority as well." He looked to the side, toward Mari with a small smile. "We never forgot how Mari and Shadow freed us, allowing us to take our home back. I promised them that Jerriton had their back and wanted to make good on that promise. We headed out as soon as we had the numbers and the artillery."

"She told us to expect you." Finn smiled at his daughter-in-law. "To say we're grateful is the understatement of the century."

Josh cut in with another clearing of his throat. "And you said you encountered another army on your way toward us?"

"That's correct." Samson nodded. "We didn't have uniforms, the closest we could get was wearing all black. Well, this other army had all-black uniforms."

"So you figured they thought you were part of them but a separate unit?" Josh asked.

"We thought so at first, but actually no, they...they didn't seem to register as us being there at all." Samson looked visibly nervous for the first time, combing one hand back through his hair. "It was like all the soldiers had a one-track mind. There was no variance to their marching, not a single arm or foot out of place for miles. No one talked, smoked, broke formation, any of the normal shit soldiers do when they're going somewhere and there isn't a commander watching them. It was very bizarre to see."

"Would you say they acted robotic?" Reaper asked. "Like someone could control them with a flip of a switch?"

"Yes," Samson agreed. "It was exactly like that. Like a string could be cut and they'd all collapse."

"Did you interact with them at all?" Josh peered over his glasses, writing hand poised over his memo pad.

"No, we didn't want to risk a confrontation. We let them march ahead of us for several hundred yards, then followed. They were heading in the same direction, so we at first thought they might have been your own people." Samson's expression soured, mouth turning down as he stared at the tabletop. "We should have stayed closer. Otherwise we might have been able to stop them."

"You couldn't have known," I said, speaking up for the first time. "I saw them coming and thought they were another back-up unit too, at first."

"It was poor planning on my part," Gunner said, swallowing thickly. "I was so focused on keeping defenses up in the city, I didn't think to have extra guns around the hospital."

"You're not to blame either," Mari said to him. "The whole time I've been a traveling medic, no army has directly attacked a field hospital, until now. It's just not done. It's…" She took a shaking breath and I reached under the table to squeeze her hand. "It's an atrocity," she finally said, a dark heaviness in her voice.

"Mari, I know you've had an extremely hard day but if you don't mind," Josh broached gently. I wanted to smack him. He couldn't handle half the shit she'd dealt with, so fuck him talking to her like she was some delicate thing. "Can you tell us who was lost in the hospital? And your current patient count with the new intakes?"

Mari looked like she wanted to smack him too, but she took a steadying breath and placed her hands on the table. "We lost eight medics today," she began, her tone steady while still charged with emotion. Everyone bowed their heads and listened intently as she said their names. Josh quickly wrote them down, his pen the only sound in the room aside from Mari's voice. The first moments of silence and respect for those we lost today.

"We've lost twenty-nine soldiers from the backup units," Mari continued. "I'm sorry, I'm afraid I didn't know all of their names."

General Bray looked up. "May I?" At Mari's nod, he picked up a roster sheet and recited the names of the fallen soldiers, some of which I'd just been talking to before the attack on the hospital. He said the name of the young mechanic I was talking to about the oil leak in the truck, and my head bowed lower. This time, Mari reached out and squeezed my hand.

"Thank you, General," she said when he finished. "On a happier note, we have twenty-four survivors from that unit. Nine of them have critical injuries. The injured civilians from Blakeworth add another seventeen. Of those who attacked us and have been detained—"

"Should be executed," someone muttered under their breath.

Every one of Mari's husbands shot murderous looks at the random sergeant who spoke out of turn, but it was General Bray who slapped the table with his palm and jumped to his feet.

"Get out, Sergeant Burns," he barked, pointing at the door.

Burns shrank down in his chair, eyes wide at his boss. "Sir?"

"You heard me. Out. We're compiling reports, not sharing opinions. I'm not in the mood for anyone's smart remarks, so you can fucking leave."

The soldier scrambled out of his seat toward the door, muttering apologies as he made himself scarce.

"You interrupt anyone at the next meeting, I'll have you demoted," Bray growled. "I'm sorry, Mari. Please, continue."

She bit back a smile, keeping composed to deliver the rest of the report. "Of the attacking unit, we're treating twenty-two with serious injuries as well. But the most compelling thing about those soldiers is that they all show signs of major physical and psychological trauma, taking place long before the battle began."

General Bray paled as he exchanged a long, worried glance with Reaper. "How do you know this?"

"A few of them have spoken to us with no memory of the battle or how they got there," Mari said. "Nearly all of them have old injuries, burns mainly, that appear to be inflicted by torture." She took a deep breath, eyes casting over me and her other men before speaking again. "Some of them have had to be sedated because all they do is scream."

"Fuck," Reaper muttered, looking toward the ceiling.

"They all have damage to the ear canals as well," Mari said.

Finn scrubbed a hand tiredly down his face. "Do you have any theories as to what this could mean?"

"I can pretty confidently say these soldiers are being tortured or possibly even brainwashed into compliance," Mari answered. "Although it's to varying degrees. Some of them are lucid and talking to us, while others are nearly catatonic."

"Do you believe they're unaware, or possibly not in control of their actions, when they attack us?"

"That is a possibility," she said sadly. "We need to find out more to be sure, but it's clear they're not fighting of their own free will."

Fuck, I thought. *And we sent Andrea right to the center of it.*

"Is there anything else?" Bray asked, sounding more weary than I'd ever heard him before.

"There is one thing." Mari glanced at the table for a moment, looking hesitant as she chewed her lip. "The loss of eight medics coupled with a much bigger patient load is...stretching us very thin."

Now she was the one who looked weary, and I wanted nothing more than to remove her from this room and take her home to rest.

"We'll be training new medics as quickly as we can, but that still doesn't help us with our patient load right now," Mari continued. "So Dr. Brooks gave me permission to seek hospital volunteers. They won't do anything complicated, just help us with basic tasks for the patients. If anyone—"

"Me." I leaned toward her, dropping a fast kiss on her shoulder. "I'll help. Anything you need."

"I'll help too," Reaper piped up from across the table. "Just tell me what to do and where to go."

"I volunteer as well, ma'am," one of the soldiers piped up.

"What a great idea to give back to our people." Governor Vance slapped Josh's shoulder. "Count both of us in."

All around the conference table, people echoed their willingness to volunteer. Even Samson and his people from Jerriton said they would be willing. Mari smiled humbly down at the table, her shoulders just a little more relaxed than they had been.

"Thank you, all of you. I guess we can make a sign-up sheet and a volunteer schedule."

"I can definitely help you with that." Josh turned to a fresh page in his memo pad. "Everyone who's volunteering, come see me."

The meeting concluded shortly after that. A line formed in front of Josh, and Mari had to return to the hospital.

"When are you coming home?" I asked, grabbing her hip like I never wanted to let her go. I thought we would die together today, and now I didn't want her to leave my sight.

"I don't know, honestly." She looked up at me apologetically. "Maybe I'll have a break for a couple hours in the morning."

"You want me to bring you food? Coffee?" I laced my hands at the small of her back. "I can go with you, just start volunteering right now."

"We're still trying to get all the patients situated. No one's got the spare batteries to train volunteers right now." She stuck her hands inside my cut, hugging around my waist. "Food and coffee would be amazing, though."

"You got it." I kissed her forehead, running my hands up her back. "I'll sign up with Josh, then see what we got at home."

"Thank you." She tilted those beautiful lips up, kissing me a few times before we reluctantly untangled our limbs so she could say goodbye to the other guys.

No sooner had she left the room than one of Samson's officers approached me, a woman maybe a decade older than me that looked tough as nails, like she'd been in the military her whole life. "Excuse me, I didn't want to interrupt you with your wife but, you're Jandro?" Her eyes fell to the patch on my cut.

"Yeah, and you are?" I held my hand out to her in greeting.

"Nora." She stared at my hand, not taking it. "Are you Angelica's brother?"

My hand fell limply to my side, my once-calm heart rate now hammering in my chest as I stared at this woman. "You know Angie?"

Nora nodded. "I have a letter to you from her." She was still wearing a bulletproof vest and quickly worked to remove it as she talked. "I met your sister in Oregon—well, Cascadia now. She showed me pictures of you two when you were kids, and I used to babysit her daughter."

"Her daughter?" I repeated numbly. "My...niece?"

"Yes, Sofia. My lord, she's gotta be almost four now." Nora finished removing her vest and pulled an envelope from a pocket inside her sweater. "She sent this to your old address in Arizona over a year ago, but it got returned." She held the letter out to me and it was all I could do to not snatch it from her hand.

"How did you end up with this?" My hands shook as I struggled to unfold the paper. "How is she? She's okay?"

"She was fine last I saw her," Nora assured me, then added with a small grin, "Pregnant with her second baby."

"Another baby..."

I finally managed to unfold the letter, the words on the paper blurring, but the photo enclosed was crystal-clear. There was my sister, looking exactly as I remembered her the night she left. Angie sat on the ground behind a dark-haired toddler, hugging the little girl and smiling. Fuck me, I couldn't remember the last time I saw her smile like that.

And behind Angie, a man hugged around both her and the toddler, his eyes closed as he kissed the back of my sister's head. I wondered if that was Drew, who she ran off to be with, or some other guy she met there.

"Colorado was where I grew up," Nora explained to me. "When I heard about the oppression going on, I decided to move back to check on my extended family. Angie gave me the letter on a whim, saying you were probably riding all over on your motorcycle and to give it to you if I ever saw you."

"Fuck," I laughed in disbelief, still staring at the photo. "What are the odds, huh?"

"I was staring at you like a creep during the whole meeting, wondering why you looked so familiar," Nora chuckled. "It finally hit me, and thank God I've carried the letter on me everywhere since I left, just in case."

"I'm grateful," I said, looking up at her. "Thank you so much for this."

"I'm just glad I could pull through for a friend." Nora smirked. "And meet the little brother she told me so many stories about."

"Aw hell," I groaned. "I'm afraid to find out what you've heard."

"You should be," she goaded me with a laugh.

I carefully folded up the letter to read later, when I had a moment alone. "When did you last see her?"

"Oh, it's been about eight months or so." Nora tilted her head with a smile. "She's definitely had the baby by now."

"This is her same address?" I tapped the faded ink on the envelope.

"Yes, she's lived there for the past four years."

"I'll write to her myself," I decided out loud. "I know it's a fifty-fifty chance she'll even get it, but I want her to hear from me directly."

"If we get lucky and win this war," Nora shrugged hopefully, "we might even get working phone lines again and you can give her a call."

"That would be nice." I returned her smile. "Something to look forward to. Hey!" I held an arm out to indicate the rest of the Jerriton army in the room. "Do you all have somewhere to stay?"

"The governor's staff has set us up with accommodations, thank you."

"Good." I made sure to catch Reaper's eye as I tucked the letter away safely. "Well, you're welcome at our home any time. You've been there for my sister, so you're family as far as I'm concerned."

"Thank you. My wife wasn't present for the meeting, but we both love Angie, and she'd love to meet you too."

"My wife had to leave, but she'd love to have you both over." I smiled a bit sheepishly. "When she's not overworked and exhausted, I'm sure."

Nora laughed, amusement deepening the lines around her eyes. "You've certainly grown up from the troublemaker your sister told me about."

"Had to," I said with a small shake of my head. It was the simplest answer for everything that transpired in the last few years. "Thank you again. It was great to meet you, but if you'll excuse me," I touched a hand to Nora's shoulder. "I have to run home and make some food and coffee."

CHAPTER 18

—————

MARIPOSA

"You're sure you don't mind?"

I smiled at Finn, trying to ease the concerned frown etched into my father-in-law's face. "Not at all. The more information we have on official record, the better."

"You're working harder than any of us," he said. "And training the volunteers, on top of your regular job."

"It's not much to train them," I said, scanning the wall of clipboards for the patient we were about to see.

"Still, it's more than what you should be doing."

"That's being a battle medic in a nutshell." I found the one I was looking for and snatched it off the hook, quickly flipping through the paperwork to get a refresher on the patient's intake report.

He was from General Tash's army, and one of the more lucid soldiers, talking to us readily despite not remembering much. Every day he grew stronger and seemed to remember a bit more. When Finn asked to speak to some of those from the opposing army, this patient seemed like the best candidate. He was still skittish and prone to headaches, but his CT scans showed improvement and all his vitals were strong.

I looked up at Finn, sharp and handsome in his military uniform as he waited for me to finish reading the patient's chart. "Ready?"

He held an arm out to the side and smiled at me warmly. "After you."

I led the way through the hospital corridor, walking fast enough that the general had to quicken his march to stay at my side. My medic-march, as we in the hospital called it, was on autopilot at this point. I was so exhausted, I could barely perceive my walking speed anymore. I'd hardly spent any time at home in the last few days, only crashing there for a shower, quick meals, and a few hours of sleep. The volunteers were beginning their shifts soon, which would ease the burden on us slightly. I figured I might be able to manage one full day off soon.

My feet stopped robotically just outside of the patient's room and I took a moment to re-center myself. I had to be a person now, not a machine, and that took a different kind of energy.

Rapping my knuckles softly at the door, I turned the knob and cracked it open a few seconds later, sticking my head in with a smile. "Hi, John. How are you feeling?"

We called all of the male patients from Tash's army John, as in John Doe. None of them remembered their own names.

This John was fair-skinned and freckled, with strawberry blond hair and blue eyes. He'd suffered second-degree burns and severe lacerations from shrapnel during the battle. Both of his arms and his torso were wrapped in thick white bandages.

"Oh, hi. Um, good..." He squinted for a few moments as if concentrating. "Mari, right?"

"Yes, you got it!" I opened the door wider, allowing him to get a view of Finn right behind me. "Is it okay if the general sits in with us today?"

John's eyes widened as he shrank back in his bed, bringing the hospital blanket under his chin as he rapidly whispered something under his breath.

"You don't have to be afraid, son." Finn leaned in closer. "You're not in trouble, no one's gonna arrest you. I just want to listen and help figure out what happened."

"I don't know..." John broke eye contact as he shook his head. "Four Corners army, they want me to kill..."

I turned toward my father-in-law so only he could hear me. "It might help if you took your jacket off?"

"Oh, certainly." He started unbuttoning his uniform immediately. "I probably should have thought of that."

"It's okay. We're still learning everyone's triggers."

In the time it took for him to take off his jacket, a small black form had jumped onto John's bed and began kneading the blanket, purring up a storm.

"Freyja," I said in surprise. "I was wondering where you've been."

The black cat's presence immediately seemed to calm John, who held a hand out to her. "She visits me every day," he said softly.

We watched from the doorway as the cat nuzzled into his hand, walking higher up the bed until she settled into his lap.

"John?" I decided to try again. "General Bray has taken his jacket off. He just wants to listen. Is it okay if he stays for a few minutes?"

John's hands scratched through Freyja's fur. The cat seemed to soak up all his fear through his pets and give him back some bravery, at least temporarily.

"Yes, I think that would be okay," he voiced softly.

"Thank you. We'll be fast and then we'll let you rest."

Finn and I made our way into the room, he was now in his white T-shirt with the top of his uniform draped over his arm. My father-in-law took a chair at the back of the room while I pulled up to John's bedside.

"So you didn't call for morphine this morning," I noted, my pen hovering over his chart in my lap. "How was your pain level when you woke up today?"

"My headache was completely gone." There was a brightness in his voice, excitement making him light up. "I think...I think I remember more too."

"Really? That's great!" I made a quick note of it and set my pen down. "Would you like to share what you remember now or..." I let the question trail off, giving him ample permission to refuse if he didn't want the general to know.

John's eyes flicked toward Finn for a moment, then back to me. "I think, I'm pretty sure my name is Robert." He nodded to himself, as if speaking aloud made him more confident in that answer. "Yes, Robert. Some people call me Rob, I think. Yeah, I'm pretty sure."

"Excellent, this is all good news." I crossed out *John Doe #17* at the top of his chart and wrote in *Robert*. "Do you happen to remember your last name?"

He thought for a moment. "Anderson? I think it's Anderson."

"Robert Anderson," I repeated back to him. "Does that feel like it's you?"

"Yes, it does!" He beamed, looking the happiest I'd seen him since we took him in. "My name is Robert Anderson."

"Well, it's wonderful to meet you, Robert. You're making great progress." I made a few more notes on his chart. "Is there anything else you remember?"

The excitement drained from him slowly, his smile fading as his eyes took on a distant, vacant look. "I remember feeling...trapped in my head."

I glanced at Finn, who started leaning forward in his chair. "What do you mean?" I asked Robert.

"Like I wasn't in control of my body. Like..." He brought a hand up to rub at his temple. "Like someone had broken into my brain and they controlled me from the inside. I could still think and stuff but...something else was there." Robert swallowed thickly, his hand returning to petting Freyja to ease some discomfort. "I remember it just...hurting *so* bad."

"Did you hear laughing?" Finn inquired.

Robert nodded. "We all did."

"Who's we?" I asked him. "The other soldiers you were with?"

Robert shook his head. "We were never soldiers. Not willingly, anyway. But yeah, we were all crowded together, and..." He grabbed his head with his palms. "There were so many faces, so many of us in pain. I can't even remember them all."

Finn and I exchanged a look. My father-in-law was now on the edge of his seat. "Do you remember the battle three days ago?"

"Three days?" Robert muttered to himself, his brow furrowing. "The time sounds weird. It feels like longer than that but I remember flashes, like it was a dream. It doesn't feel real." Robert rubbed his forehead. "I'm sorry, I'm starting to get a headache again."

"I'll get you some Tylenol." I rose from my chair to reach over and touch his shoulder. "Thank you so much, Robert. You've been incredibly helpful."

"You're very brave, young man." Finn made his way to the door. "And you're safe now. Thank you for letting me listen."

We left Robert's room, closing the door quietly as he sank into his bed, Freyja making herself comfortable on a new spot on his blanket. Finn and I just stared at each other for a moment of stunned silence in the hallway.

"Well, what the fuck do you make of that?" he breathed out in disbelief, sliding his arms through his jacket to put it back on.

"Wanna talk it out?" I jerked my head toward an empty break room.

"Yes, please."

We headed that way to find none other than Freyja sitting on the counter next to the outdated microwave.

"What the?" Finn looked down the hallway, then turned back to the cat blinking slowly in front of him. "How did she...?"

"Gods," I said with a shrug. "You get used to them popping up everywhere."

"Huh." He chuckled softly as he resumed buttoning up his jacket. "Well, alright then." Once he was dressed as the general again, he looked at me with a serious expression. "So what do you make of our friend Robert?"

"He's in probably the best shape out of everyone from that unit," I said, leaning against the counter next to Freyja. "Most of them are non-verbal, non-responsive to stimuli at all. It's like they're not even there." I scratched the cat's cheek. "The ones who do talk, it's just babbling. They're confused and don't know who or where they are."

"So there's varying degrees of this...this trauma they've endured?"

"I think we're seeing different stages of the same process," I answered. "With Robert, maybe he was a newer addition. If he wasn't conditioned for very long, it makes sense as to why he's recovered so quickly."

Finn nodded, following my train of thought. "And the ones who haven't recovered?"

"They've probably been conditioned for much longer." I let my hand drop from Freyja's head. "They may be even too far gone to save."

"And so the ones who are speaking but confused, are somewhere in the middle," my father-in-law concluded.

"Yes, exactly. Some of them have improved slightly, but it's slow-going."

We both found ourselves looking at Freyja, blinking slowly and sitting calmly on the counter next to me. The cat seemed to grow bored of the staring contest and proceeded to lick her paw.

"Do you think she has anything to do with Robert's recovery?" Finn asked in a low voice, barely above a whisper.

"I'm almost certain of it." I smiled, petting down the cat's back. "She's basically lived here at the hospital, wandering in and out of patients' rooms."

"Amazing," the general breathed, reaching out to stroke Freyja gently.

I cannot do more for the empty vessels. Frejya's warm voice was heavy with sadness, filling the room and my head with a gentle pulse of energy. *There is no humanity left for me to nurture.*

"Did you hear that?" I asked Finn.

"No, but I felt...something." He rubbed his own arms. "Like static in the air, but not as harsh."

I repeated what Freyja said and he nodded slowly. "So they are too far gone then."

"Sadly, yes."

"What I want to know is," he rubbed his jaw, "why send a mix of them to attack us? Why not a whole unit devoid of their humanity? Rory and Shadow seemed to deal with a mix at the first battle too. Some screaming and struggling, others just...empty."

"Maybe the victims respond to it differently," I suggested after a few moments of thinking. "Some might be more susceptible to the torture, while others are more resistant."

"What would determine that, in your opinion?"

"I really don't know," I said with an apologetic sigh. Doc and Dr. Ellis would probably have some compelling theories, but digging this deeply into psychology was beyond my realm of expertise. "Torture of any kind seeks to exploit weaknesses. They can't do extensive physical torture because they need the soldiers in good enough shape to fight and march long distances."

A thought hit me suddenly. "What if they're still experimenting?"

Finn narrowed his eyes. "What do you mean?"

"Whoever's torturing them is...they're refining their technique," I said. "We have more catatonic patients from this ambush than in the first battle. That means whoever's doing this is becoming more efficient at torturing them. After we won the first battle, they realized they needed better soldiers, which for them means less humanity. Less free will."

"So they're testing their levels of control. That could explain why they attacked the hospital this time instead of meeting us in an actual battle," Finn mused. "Or this was a unit of rejects that they just wanted to dispose of quickly."

"We were still completely outmatched though." I petted Freyja again, trying to shove away the events of that day. The burning hospital tent was not a memory that would leave me easily. "If Jerriton hadn't showed up when they did, that would have been the end for us."

"But it wasn't." My father-in-law reached out to give a gentle squeeze to my shoulder. "We're all still here to fight another day."

"Yeah," I agreed with a sigh, the exhaustion settling into my limbs again. "Still kickin'."

Finn released me, his face taking on a conflicted expression before speaking again. "You know I love you no matter what, right sweetheart?"

I blinked for a moment, taken aback. "Finn, I—"

"No matter what happens between you and my son, I mean," he clarified. "You'll always be a daughter to me."

I looked down at my shoes, a mixture of embarrassment and relief surging through me. My pride was a little wounded, to be sure. I didn't want anyone outside of me and my husbands knowing how Reaper and I were struggling to reconnect. But Finn had become a father figure to me too, and with the absence of my own parents, his presence was a comfort I hadn't realized I needed.

"You know all about that, huh?" I said a bit sheepishly.

"No, very little actually. He's been just as tight-lipped as you." Finn smiled reassuringly. "And I won't pry. Lis and I just miss you, that's all. If you ever have a free moment to come by, by yourself or with one of the others even, we'd love to have you."

"Thank you, I appreciate it." I wasn't sure how much I believed him. Parents always favored their own children over their children's partners, didn't they? In all honesty, I was too exhausted to give it much thought. More patients needed to be seen. "Was there anyone else you wanted to see while we're here?"

"No, thank you for allowing me to listen." Finn clasped his hands behind his back, readily accepting my change of subject. "I should report back to the governor and my lieutenants."

"I'll walk you out."

Freyja jumped down from the counter as we left the room, tail high in the air as she trotted down another hallway.

"A god's work never ends," Finn chuckled, watching her leave.

I held on to his elbow as we walked together toward the front entrance. "Does any of this change how you're going to prepare for upcoming battles? What you heard from Robert today?"

"I don't know," he said with a weary sigh. "Ideally, we would. I hate the thought of killing people who aren't aware and have no control of what they're doing." He gently removed my hand from his elbow and turned to face me when we reached the door. "But I don't know of any alternatives," he added sadly. "If only we could target the source of what's doing this to them."

"I understand," I said. "Above all, we have to protect our own people from outside threats."

"Correct." The general smiled warmly at me. "It's good to see you at the war meetings. I hope you keep coming to them."

"If I have time," I laughed humorlessly. "Which I never have enough of. But it's been good to see you too."

Finn leaned forward and kissed my forehead. "I'll see you later. Take it easy, sweetheart."

"You too, General Bray."

I watched him walk down to his waiting SUV, then went back inside for another long hospital shift.

CHAPTER 19

MARIPOSA

"You know if I close my eyes and just forget everything that's been happening, I can almost pretend like we're not in the middle of a war right now."

I was stretched out length-wise on the couch with my feet in Shadow's lap and my head in Jandro's. At one end, my skull and neck were being rubbed, my headache being soothed away into the blissful pressure of Jandro's firm fingers. He tried braiding my hair at one point, but quickly gave up on that endeavor to massage me instead.

At the other end, Shadow thoroughly experimented with all manner of touch on my feet, just as he did with the rest of my body. My initial instructions were all he needed. He picked up the rest from the sounds I made and how I utterly melted at his touch.

"Is this helping you pretend?" Shadow asked with a small smile, running his thumbs up the length of my arch.

"Mm-hmm..." My eyelids were falling shut from relaxation. "Both of you are helping my imagination along very much."

The guilt still wasn't going away—that remained my biggest tether to reality. Guilt over the medics we lost. None of us were able to mourn them, we had too much work to do, patients that needed us, but most of whom we didn't know how to treat. And then there was Andrea.

Andrea. Tessa still didn't know about the latest message we received. What could I tell her?

I still wanted to hope that Andrea hadn't been compromised—that she wasn't under control like all those robotic soldiers from Tash's army. But what else could the note mean?

Either way, I was still determined to get her out. We suffered some losses, but we were still winning this war. Whenever Tash surrendered to us fully, we'd take over their base and find her. After she risked everything for our cause, bringing her home was the least we could do for her.

Jandro's warm fingertips came to my forehead, smoothing out the tension that built up there while I thought of Andrea.

"Keep on pretending, *Mariposita*, just for a little while. We'll be back to reality tomorrow."

I nodded, releasing a deep sigh from my chest. The hospital was full of our own people, Jerriton citizens, Blakeworth and Tash troops. We had to keep the one field hospital up just to contain the overflow of injured. The rush of volunteers eager to help did give us a tiny bit of breathing room. It was the only way I was able to take this evening off.

Even with the extra help, I expected to be on my feet for no less than sixteen hours tomorrow. So I'd do my best to enjoy this evening and release the guilt over pretending that all this fighting and suffering didn't exist.

My two men seemed to have similar ideas. Shadow's touch crept higher up my legs, fingertips pressing a delightful circular massage inside my knees. Jandro's hands moved lower, running below my collarbones to the top of my chest.

"Are you boys getting fresh with me?" My eyes were still closed, teeth sinking into my lip as I tried not to smile too hard.

"What, us?" Jandro's fingers glided down over my arms. "Wouldn't dream of such a thing."

"Mm-hm..." I spaced my legs apart in Shadow's lap to make more room for his hands. He saw where my mind was going, bringing his massage higher up my thigh. I started to squirm, sensitivity prickling along my skin from both of their touches.

The thought of having both of them had been heavy on my mind since Shadow told me he'd be interested in sharing. Now, excited flutters filled my stomach at making that a reality. I wanted to jump up, start kissing them both, and touch them at the same time. But we'd barely started and Shadow could still change his mind.

So I stretched out long between them, pointing my toes and arching my back, letting them set the pace. Jandro would be mindful of Shadow's feelings too. As I reached my arms over my head, Jandro clasped my wrists together with one hand, leaning down over me with a playful smile.

"What does our girl want?" he asked in a low voice, lips hovering over mine.

"Both of you," I whispered back, keeping my eyes locked on his while I rubbed my foot against the front of Shadow's pants, who grunted out a soft moan at the contact, his hand between my thighs squeezing slightly.

"You down for that, big man?" Jandro looked toward his friend, whose eyes kept running up and down the length of my legs.

"Yes." Shadow breathed the word out softly, but there wasn't a hint of hesitation. More like he was trying to contain his excitement.

I rolled up from Jandro's lap, looking behind me to kiss him. This would be a gentle enough start—Shadow had seen me kiss him and the others plenty of times.

Jandro turned on the couch to support my back with his chest, arms coming around my waist to kiss me over my shoulder. I let his body hold me up, leaning my weight against him as I sank into his kiss. The warm flutters extended down to my toes, where I could feel Shadow growing hard beneath his jeans as he watched us.

Shadow's hand continued his firm, kneading massage of my inner thighs, while Jandro's touch spanned my stomach and waist. Already I was languid, just wanting to fall limp and let their four hands explore me.

Jandro broke away from my mouth, dragging his lips to the nape of my neck and my upper back as he started lifting my shirt from behind.

"Come here." Facing forward again, I reached for Shadow and he scooted closer to me while Jandro got me topless. "Hi, love." I smiled, pleased to have him within kissing distance.

"Hi." Shadow returned my smile, his hands now resting on my hips as our kiss connected. My hands went around his neck, then smoothing down his solid chest to dip under the hem of his shirt. He pulled away to remove it, and I audibly sighed at the beautiful sight of him. All the while, Jandro placed kisses down my spine, amplifying the flutters running through me.

It was a nervous-excitedness with the two of them, probably because it was the first time. Despite having had plenty of threesomes by now, this one was different.

"What would you like right now?" I asked Shadow, leaning forward into him. I kissed the scar on his cheek before moving down to his neck, relishing in the soft sighs and moans he made. *You will never be neglected again.* I repeated the promise mentally with each taste of his warm skin.

"Mm, I want..." he murmured, hands running from my hips up my sides.

"Yes?" I urged him, taking a nibble between his neck and shoulder.

"I want to watch Jandro please you," he confessed.

"That can be arranged," Jandro said behind me, stroking lightly down my lower back. "Come here, *Mariposita.*"

I pulled my legs out of Shadow's lap and swung them around toward Jandro, coming to my hands and knees between my two men. Jandro's kisses continued working their magic on my spine as he pulled my shorts and underwear over my ass and down to my knees.

"Damn, I love this tattoo." Jandro caressed over my hip, admiring the Night-Blooming Cereus, which was almost completely healed. "Some of your best work, man."

"I agree." I grinned, dragging a biting kiss over Shadow's shoulder.

"I have the best canvas to work on," Shadow answered humbly.

When Jandro swiped his first touch between my legs, I gasped and Shadow let out a rumbling moan that sounded like a purr. I leaned my forehead on his shoulder, nipping at his collarbone and the top of his chest.

Jandro's touches were light and teasing, only his fingertips dragging in circles around my sensitive flesh. My hips rolled, chasing his hand for more friction, and I got swats to my ass for my impatience. I whimpered against Shadow's shoulder, looking up to see him focused on what Jandro was doing behind me.

"Kiss me," I pleaded, running my mouth up his neck.

"You kiss *me*," Shadow retorted with a smirk. "I'm watching."

I wanted to pout and whine. He *loved* to kiss and make out, and now he was refusing me? But I was also a puddled, proud mess inside. He was taking pleasure for himself, now confident enough to tell me what he wanted. It was insanely hot and made me so eager to give him all he asked for, and more.

I kissed his throat, tongue licking the hollow between his collarbones, and moved lower, sending my hips higher.

"You're making her wet, man." Jandro grabbed one side of my ass, holding me with a strong grip as he finally rubbed more firmly between my legs. He still ignored my clit, but stroked through my sensitive flesh, coaxing even more wetness out of me.

"Am I now?" Shadow's chest vibrated against my lips when he asked the question, hands caressing my face as he pulled my hair out of the way. He cupped my cheek and tilted my face up to look at him. "You like kissing me that much?"

I licked my lips, tongue darting out to lick his thumb. "I like it when you tell me what to do to you."

His lips parted, eyebrows raising like he didn't expect that answer. "You...do?"

I grinned at him, enjoying his reaction immensely. "Very much." *Take some power back, love. You deserve it.*

Shadow drew my face up to his, kissing me with a warm tenderness, like he was silently thanking me for this trust, for this freedom to explore more of a power dynamic between us. To exercise a type of control he never had before in his life.

Our kiss parted with a dizzying breath, my face lifting up with a gasp at the feel of Jandro's tongue gliding along my slit, his lips sucking and kissing between my legs. Shadow cupped my face again, bringing my gaze back to him. "Make me hard for you, lover."

I couldn't obey fast enough, my hands scrambling over his jeans as I kissed down his chest, leaving nips and bites on his body because I knew he liked them. He ended up helping me with his pants—Jandro was just too good at playing with me back there and made it impossible to concentrate.

Shadow was already at half-mast, his cock slapping his stomach softly as he shoved his jeans down. I grabbed his thick base and slid my lips over his crown, already eager for something to fill me somewhere, whether that be my mouth or my pussy.

"Ugh, fuck..." Shadow drew my hair out of my face, running an affectionate touch down my back. "That's so good."

Jandro's mouth pulled away from me, his fingers driving through where his tongue had just been and filling me from the other end. "She's the best at sucking dick, man. Literally nothing else compares."

I only had a moment to bask in the praise, drawing more of Shadow into my mouth and moaning at Jandro's fingers fucking me, when I heard a loud slap above my head.

Releasing Shadow's cock, I looked back and forth between two of them incredulously before they could save face. "Did you guys just high-five?!"

Jandro burst out laughing, lowering his forehead to my back and planting a series of kisses there. "I'm sorry, I just...I've always wanted to do that."

"He kept raising his hand when you weren't looking." Shadow was chuckling softly. "I did it so he'd finally stop."

"You guys are the worst," I groaned, bringing my forehead to Shadow's thigh. Despite me, a few snickers escaped, and then moans as Jandro's hand returned to its duty of pleasing me. His thumb rolled over my clit, fingers curling as they dragged against my walls.

"I dunno, *Mariposita,*" my cocky man mused. "Seems like we're doing pretty good."

Shadow gripped my chin in his fingers, the touch light, but firm. "I didn't tell you to stop sucking me." Oh fuck me. He was enjoying this just as much as I was, if not more.

With my next breath, my mouth was on him again, tongue and lips gliding over rigid muscle and velvety skin. He muttered curses and praised me, hands running over me with so much tenderness and care that I wanted to melt in his lap.

Ever the jokester, Jandro seemed intent on distracting me and fucking up my blowjob to the best of his ability. He kept varying the speed and depth with his fingers—fucking me intensely with his hand until I had to release Shadow's cock to cry out, only to slow the pace way down just as my release started building. That was his style, dangling an orgasm in front of my face only to yank it away when I got close.

He did that several times, even switching up between his hands and his mouth to bring me to the edge, only to leave me hanging. My knees gave out, and I laid on my stomach stretched out between the two of them.

"Jandro, please," I whined, my head resting on Shadow's thigh to give my jaw a break. I kept stroking my gorgeous, scarred man who was now fully hard and pulsing in my hand, looking up at him with pleading eyes since Jandro wouldn't listen.

Shadow stroked my cheek, the sweet touch wrapping around to caress the back of my neck. "Let her come, Jandro. She's been good."

I heard a sigh of mock disappointment from behind me, along with the rustling of clothes as Jandro got undressed. "Guess I'm outvoted."

With renewed energy I rose up to my hands and knees, Shadow and I leaning toward each other for a kiss. A loud smack on my ass was the only warning I got before Jandro's wide cock pressed through my flesh, striking deep into my core with everything I'd been needing. He barely pulled back to drive forward again when the release hit me like a crashing wave. Shadow held me up by my shoulders while I convulsed, shuddered, and barely breathed.

Even as it ebbed away and the aftershocks zipped through me, my arms gave out and I found my head cradled in Shadow's lap once again. I realized it was quickly becoming one of my favorite places to rest.

"You always get mad at me for that." Jandro grinned from behind me, gliding in and out of my body with long, slow strokes while I recovered. "But isn't the release worth all the build-up, *Mariposita*?"

"Fuck you, a little bit," I mumbled, pushing up to my hands again. Leaning back, I left Shadow alone for a moment while I wrapped my arms around the back of Jandro's neck, arching to kiss him over my shoulder. "It is *so* fucking worth it," I whispered, dragging kisses from his cheek to his ear. "I just can't help being a brat."

"Don't I know it." Jandro hugged around me, bringing my back flush with his chest as he sucked along my neck and shoulder. "I just want to make you see other realities when you come, that's all."

I laughed lightly as I covered his hands with mine, enjoying this private moment between us, however brief it was. "You like bringing the brat out of me too."

"Also true." He nipped along the back of my neck, squeezing me in a hug that was both endearingly sweet and a testament to his strength. Jandro could snap an enemy's neck with these arms, but he'd rather take bullets and jump in front of bombs to protect me.

"I love you," I whispered against the side of his face, wishing I could become smaller only so he could hold me tighter.

"*Te amo,*" he answered, loosening his arms around me with a final kiss.

I returned to hands and knees, my eyes meeting Shadow's as Jandro's hands shifted to my hips. "You okay, love?" I searched Shadow's face, his mismatched eyes, for any sign of discomfort. Jandro and I were wrapped up in each other for less than a minute, but I made the same promise to him and every one of my other men—I'd never neglect them for someone else.

Shadow returned his hand to my cheek, leaning in to kiss me in answer. My worry relaxed away as our lips pressed and our tongues tangled. Jandro started fucking me in earnest then, making me moan through kissing Shadow as his cock filled and emptied me.

"Is Jandro pleasing you?" Shadow smirked, his lips hovering over mine as his best friend drove into me harder.

It took me a moment to form a simple answer. Jandro's thickness pressing through me stole my breath away, and each drag of him pulling back felt like it hit every nerve ending in my body.

"Yes, ah! Fuck...yes," I panted in reply.

Shadow's eyes flickered from my face to watch the action behind me, his touch dragging down my chest until he kneaded a breast in his hand. Sparks of sensitivity made me cry out louder when he rolled a nipple between his fingers.

"Then I'm so much better than okay," he growled, eyes roving my entire body as I shook and swayed from the impact of Jandro's thrusts.

"You are?" I reached for Shadow's cock again, and he inhaled sharply at the contact. My pleasure swelled at his reaction. The poor thing hadn't gotten any attention for a whole minute and I needed to rectify that. "You're really enjoying this?"

He touched his forehead to mine, hands caressing me and heightening my pleasure over every inch of my skin. "Not just enjoying it. I see how right Reaper was about sharing a woman we love."

"How do you mean?" I breathed. Jandro slowed his thrusts behind me as if he too were waiting to hear an answer.

"This is...not just sex," Shadow muttered. "This is all about giving you more of what you deserve. All the pleasure you can handle." He pressed a warm, dizzying kiss to my mouth, then broke away to stare at me reverently. "I love you more than I can ever express. I want you pleased and cared for more than I could ever physically do by myself." His eyes flicked up to Jandro. "So I'm glad you have the others. You've always deserved more than one man."

"Oh, Shadow..." My throat tightened, a sob threatening to choke out as I planted kisses everywhere on his face that I could reach. "I love you so much."

"Shadow-man gets it." Jandro's palms smoothed down my back. "On our own we all fall short but together, we can be exactly what you need."

"Yes, that's it," Shadow agreed.

One of Jandro's hands came away from my skin. "Come on bro, up top."

"No!" I tried to glare as I looked back at him but couldn't hold in the laughter. "No more high-fives."

"Just one more, then I'm finished being a dumbass, I swear," Jandro pleaded.

I groaned but didn't keep arguing. Shadow rolled his eyes and relented, slapping Jandro's palm with far less gusto than the first time.

"Pretty weak, but I'll take it. All your strength's in your dick right now."

"So's yours," Shadow moaned as I gripped his length again, wetting him with my tongue before sucking him into my mouth.

All the talking finally ceased. Only slapping skin, moans, breaths, and whispered curses filled the air as the three of us found our rhythm.

Jandro tried to pace himself as he fucked me from behind, but I could feel how closely he edged toward release. His breaths grew louder and ragged, his already-thick cock swelling against my walls.

I lapped at Shadow's cock like he was made of ice cream, moaning at how he pulsed under my tongue and how Jandro filled me with each drive of his hips. With a heavy moan, Shadow pulled me up for a breathless kiss, his hand stopping mine when I continued to stroke up and down his length.

"You don't want me to touch you anymore?" I teased, smiling against his lips.

"I want to last long enough to fuck your sweet cunt."

The words were filthy, but his tone was the same warm, tender voice he always used with me. The combination of the two was like an orgasm for my brain, sparking as it processed the mental pleasure this man gave me, before filtering it through the rest of my body. His dirty talk tingled down my spine, accelerated my heart, and made my core squeeze around my other husband.

"Fuck, babe," Jandro grunted, still rocking me forward with each thrust of his cock. "Thanks for the warning."

"Sorry I, ah...fuck!"

Words left me as he reached around for my clit. He tipped me over the edge, pausing his thrusts while fully seated inside me. Both men petted and praised me as I shook and whimpered through another release, my skin now coated in a sheen of sweat. Jandro withdrew from me and kissed my back as I floated down from bliss.

"Never say sorry for feeling good," he rasped before sitting back on the opposite end of the couch, chest heaving with loud breaths, his cock erect and stiff. "Even when I do gotta take a breather," he added with a sheepish smile.

He looked so damn delicious, I wanted to run my tongue all over him. And I would, once he had a moment to cool down.

I sat up to kneeling, bracing my hands on Shadow's shoulders for balance as I threw a leg over his lap.

"Ready for me already?" He gazed up at me, hands already trailing up the backs of my thighs.

"Told you I recover quickly." I was still a little breathless but started lowering down eagerly. As wonderful as tasting him was, I was more than ready to feel him inside me.

Taking him was easier after having Jandro and a couple of orgasms already. Shadow's cock spread me open with ease, the pressure of him so filling and delicious as I sank down.

"Fuck..." His eyelids fell shut as his head tipped back, palms smoothing over my ass and running over my waist.

"No. Look at me, handsome." I placed a finger on his lips and his eyes fluttered open again. "You like to watch? Then watch me ride you."

"You fucking undo me," he groaned as I began a slow rise and lower, savoring every inch of him gliding through me.

"You're...fuck, God..." My legs were already shaking at the effort of riding him, most of my strength already zapped from earlier. Shadow was right there for me, guiding me with a hand on my waist and rolling his hips underneath me.

"You're so beautiful when you're spent and well-fucked," he whispered, the tenderness in his voice taking on a rough growl. "So good and perfect for us."

"You're so perfect for me," I panted. Our skin glided hot and wet against each other at a quickening pace, both of us swept up in this urgent need for each other. "You're mine. Mine."

"Yours." Shadow's fist closed in my hair, bringing my mouth to his for a hard kiss. "Only yours."

I leaned my forehead on his, resting my upper body against him while we crashed and rode each other down below. Turning my gaze to the side, I saw Jandro stroking himself as he watched us, his cock flexing against his hand.

"Keep going," he urged with a grin. "Don't stop on my account."

"Shut up and come here," I demanded.

Jandro scooted closer, moving up to sit on the back of the couch so I could reach him easily while riding Shadow. Bracing one arm on Shadow's shoulder, I could touch and taste Jandro with the other as I pleased.

"Oh, Jesus..." Jandro hissed, gripping the couch on either side of him as I pulled his thick head between my lips, letting the rise and fall of my body on Shadow's cock determine when my mouth slid up and down on his. "So much for that fucking breather. I'm not gonna last through your mouth doing *that*."

"I'm getting close too," Shadow moaned through gritted teeth. His grip tightened on my waist, lifting me high off his cock so I could reach more of Jandro. When he slammed me back down, he struck a new place deep inside me that had me seeing stars, and moaning for more.

"Gonna come for us one more time, *Mariposita?*" Jandro ran a touch down the front of my body, grabbing my breasts and making me whimper louder with his pulls on my aching nipples.

"She's right there," Shadow growled out. "Fuck, she's squeezing me so tight." He wrapped around me, holding me in place as his powerful hips snapped up and crashed his body against my clit.

My whole body shook from the impact and I was screaming as loud as I could with my mouth stuffed full. The orgasm hit me harder than Shadow's thrusts, convulsions sweeping through me as though I'd been electrocuted. And then warmth filling my mouth, pulsing into my core. The release of my men dragged out my own pleasure, their bodies rigid and their expressions furrowed in sexy grimaces as their moans and gasps for air filled the room.

Shadow's hands fell limply to his sides. The two of us rose and fell with his breaths, our pulses thrumming together. With me slumped across his chest and shoulder, I laid my head on Jandro's thigh, who looked to be in danger of sliding off the back of the couch.

"Don't fall," I whispered drowsily.

"Hm?" Jandro bowed forward, leaning over me to place more kisses on my back, then rested his forehead between my shoulder blades. "Damn," he panted.

"Yeah," Shadow agreed on a deep exhale, returning one hand to caress up my leg. He kissed my shoulder that was nudged against the side of his chest.

I reached for his face, stroking his bearded cheek while rubbing Jandro's neck with the other hand. "I don't wanna move," I confessed, utterly blissed out in this place with my two men.

"Me neither," said both of them in unison.

"Shadow-man, want to carry her to the shower?" Jandro suggested. "She might be sore."

Shadow grunted out an affirmative and brought his hands to my ass to secure me. He started scooting off the couch, but I held on to Jandro before we stood up.

"You're coming too, right?"

Jandro slid down onto the couch and jumped up, cock still wet from my mouth and bouncing on his thighs. "Shadow, you gonna scrub my back?"

"No."

I giggled as Shadow rose from the couch with one swift press of his strong legs. He held me easily, but I still wrapped my arms and legs around him, pressing a kiss to his mouth. "Will you scrub mine?"

He grinned. "Yes, of course."

Jandro sighed in pretend disappointment, gathering up our discarded clothing. "Don't sulk," I chided him. "I'll wash your back, *guapito*."

"Fine. I'll deal with washing your front, I guess." Then he smacked my ass with his free hand and ran ahead of us to turn on the shower.

CHAPTER 20

REAPER

I didn't love my volunteer shifts at the field hospital at first, but my time spent there grew on me after a few days. Since I had barely any medical knowledge, my duties mainly consisted of bringing the patients food, water, blankets, or whatever else they needed.

Sometimes they just wanted someone to read to or sit with them. For some reason, I found this the most difficult to do, despite it being the easiest task. But it wasn't about me, as I was quickly learning. None of my volunteer hours were about me, or how it would make me look to Mari. Admittedly, being in closer proximity to her and having her see me do this kind of work played a part in signing myself up. I had the small, lingering hope that it would help bring us back together.

Rhonda ended up putting us on opposite shifts, so Mari and I were never at the hospital at the same time anyway. I had a feeling that the crabby old nurse did that on purpose. She wasn't a big fan of mine. Not that it mattered, anyway. I got a firsthand look at what Mari dealt with every day, and after my first few shifts, I was beginning to see why she was so dedicated to it.

Day after day, after changing endless sheets on the makeshift beds, running back and forth to fetch all manner of things, or just sitting and holding someone's hand as they told me their life story, I started to think there was hope for a selfish prick like me after all.

Jandro and I worked together sometimes, although he was usually put on maintenance duty to fix machinery or the hospital vehicles. I saw Freyja every so often too. The black cat seemed to have become a fixture at both hospitals, wandering around beds and accepting scratches wherever she went. No doubt she was spreading some of that healing magic too. She put the patients at ease, which made the medics' jobs easier.

Hades on the other hand, stayed far away from the hospitals. If he followed me, he usually hung back near my bike until my shift was over. Maybe there was something unsettling about a god of death hovering around a place trying to prolong people's lives.

A slew of new patients had just arrived when I showed up today, a mixture of our own injured, Blakeworth citizens, and Tash's soldiers. Governor Vance was still optimistic about giving Blakeworth citizens refuge in Four Corners, *if* they had been conscripted to fight and didn't have loyalties to the cause. They would be treated for injuries first, and then questioned by my dad's lieutenants when they were well enough.

The soldiers from Tash's army were wild cards, though. We were beginning to question if they were soldiers at all, or people just unlucky and vulnerable enough to fall under the mind control they were subjected to. At least more of them were talking now, although a great majority of them still didn't remember their names or how they ended up here.

I stepped into the hospital tent and nodded at Jandro on the other side. Today they had him replacing filters in the air purifiers. Grabbing a pitcher of water, some towels, and snacks, I started making my usual rounds.

Most of the Tash patients were dead silent, but the ones that weren't catatonic had eyes watching me like hawks. I wondered if any of them recognized me from previous battles. The medics warned me the patients were skittish, especially around loud noises, so I did my best to speak to them in a low voice and not make any sudden movements.

One guy however, stood out as being particularly chatty and couldn't seem to sit still. Even Freyja, sitting at the end of his bed, had her ears pointed back in irritation.

The guy's head was wrapped up in bandages, covering one of his eyes. I could hear him talking rapidly to himself from across the tent. As I got closer to his bedside, I realized he was speaking Spanish.

"Hey man. Do you want some water?" I rolled my small cart up next to him and held up the pitcher. "*Agua?*"

He'd been lying on his back, but sat up abruptly the moment he heard me. The movement sent Freyja jumping down and walking off to tend to someone else. The guy tried turning to me, but his weakened state, and probably the drugs, nearly had him careening forward.

"Whoa, whoa, easy!" I grabbed his shoulders to hold him up, then placed a hand on his neck to keep his head still. "You shouldn't move so fast with a head injury. I'll get you whatever you need."

"*Señor, por favor,*" he whimpered before talking in a rapid string of Spanish too fast for me to understand.

"It's okay, buddy. Let me lie you back down. You gotta watch your head." I pointed to my temple. "*Tu cabeza.*"

He clutched my shirt and started pushing back against me, which was alarming. No patient had ever fought me before. I didn't want to use force on this guy and potentially injure him further.

"Hey man, you gotta lie down," I told him more firmly. "You're hurt. You need to rest."

"*Por favor, mi esposa!*" he pleaded. That was all I caught before he started speaking rapidly again.

"Okay, okay." I heard the word *esposa* a few more times before his strength gave out and he allowed me to lay his head back on his pillow. "Take a drink, man. It's gonna be alright."

The man accepted the water I held to his lips, swallowing several gulps and gasping before speaking, no, begging, rapidly again. He held on to my forearm and I saw a tear trail out of his one visible eye.

"Okay, listen. I'm gonna get someone who can talk to you." I patted his shoulder, then looked behind me to make sure Jandro was still in the tent. "We'll figure out what's going on with your wife, okay? *Un momento.*"

Seemingly placated, he finally released me. I moved the supply cart out of the way and headed for the back of the tent, feeling his stare on me the whole way. Jandro was elbow-deep in an air purifier when I came up next to him.

"Hey 'Dro, I need a favor real quick."

"'Course you do," he chuckled. "Why else would you come up to me in the middle of your Mother Teresa shift?"

I ignored his jab. "There's a guy here who keeps asking about his wife but it's all in Spanish. Can you talk to him?"

"Ooh, I'm an interpreter now," Jandro said with fake excitement as he pulled a small motor out of the air purifier. "Nice to know I'm moving up in the world."

"I'm just asking, 'Dro," I sighed tiredly. "Dude seems really distraught, and I know that'd be any one of us if we got separated from Mari. But I'll ask someone else if you're insulted or whatever."

"Nah, Reap. It's fine." Jandro pulled his hands out of the machine and quickly rubbed them in hand sanitizer. "I just wasn't sure if this was a friend's request or a president's order."

"A request," I answered. "I feel bad for the guy, that's all."

"Huh, you might have an empathetic bone in your body after all." Jandro rubbed his palms together. "Which one is he?"

"Bandaged head and eye." I pointed to the bed he was in. "Thanks, Jandro."

"Sure thing." My VP grabbed a pen and a notepad and headed toward the patient, whistling as he did so.

Meanwhile, I took over replacing the motor in the air purifier. It was far less complicated than replacing the same part on a bike, and I was able to watch Jandro with the guy for my own curiosity.

Jandro sat on his bed like a friend would, the two of them too far away to hear, not that I would understand anyway. At one point, Jandro turned his head and looked back at me, his expression something between concerned and confused. He started writing on his notepad then, I assumed taking the man's information.

They spoke for about ten minutes before a medic came by to check the man's injuries. Jandro shook his hand gently before rising and returning back to me. He appeared even more confused than when he first looked at me.

"Well?" I asked.

Jandro shook his head and blew out a long breath. "Poor bastard's got noodle soup for brains. Must've been near too many explosions, on top of all the other shit cracking his egg. He wants us to find his wife and daughter, but can't remember their names."

"Fuck," I bit out. "Well, we can't help without knowing that. What's his name?"

"He doesn't know, but it gets even weirder." Jandro set the notepad down. "He's *pretty sure* his wife is a white lady originally from Texas, but as you heard," he jerked his head toward the guy, "homeboy doesn't speak a lick of English."

"So how could he be married to an American?" I rubbed my jaw.

"Exactly."

"Maybe she speaks Spanish?" I offered.

"Mm." Jandro made a skeptical noise. "I dunno, it seems like all kinds of things are jumbled in his head. When I asked him what was the last thing he remembered, he said his most vivid memory is his daughter being born. However, he's again *pretty sure* she's an adult now, so his sense of time is all fucked too."

"Damn." To my uneducated brain, it sounded a lot like dementia, which the man had to be too young for. He looked to be in his late forties, early fifties at the most. But then again, he seemed in better shape than the majority of those from that unit. "Poor guy went through the ringer."

"Yeah," Jandro agreed sadly. "Who knows if he'll be able to remember those details."

"Maybe as he recovers, he'll remember more. He's strong enough to sit up and talk, at least." I folded my arms, watching as a medic gave the man a dose of something and tucked him into bed. "Mari might know how to help him."

"I dunno, man," Jandro sighed. "He might even be above her pay grade. Like if he forgot all this stuff, maybe he forgot how to speak English too. Does that even happen with head injuries?"

"No idea, but I don't think any of what those guys are dealing with is normal."

"True. It sucks either way." Jandro leaned against the table next to me. "We don't even know if his family are prisoners, dead, or just figments of his imagination."

"If he can tell us more, we should find them," I said, determined.

"Huh, look at you." Jandro shot me a look of surprise. "If Mari had said that three months ago, you'd chew her ass out for wanting to save everybody."

"Yeah, well," I shrugged. "I know what it's like having my family torn apart and not knowing if they're alive or dead. Nobody should go through that."

Jandro sniffed and pretended to wipe a tear. "My little Reaper's all grown up and matured."

"Shut up." I knocked my shoulder into his. "I gotta finish my rounds. You're welcome for the new motor in that thing, by the way."

"Aw, sweet!" Jandro rounded the table to look inside the air purifier. "And you're welcome for me being an interpreter, by the way."

"Yeah whatever, thanks man." I hesitated before grabbing my cart. "Would you be cool with checking in on him? See if he remembers any more?"

"You don't even need to ask," Jandro said while screwing the panels back on the machine. "I already told him I'd be by to chat again later."

"Thanks, 'Dro."

"Yeah, go on." He made a shooing motion at me. "Get back to grumbling and barking at people before they start thinking you're actually nice."

"So what do you suppose we do with you?" My dad peered shrewdly at Captain Lance, the hostage that Blakeworth had refused to take back. That couldn't have been good news for him, to not be wanted by the territory you served and lived in.

We were in the main conference room at City Hall—a small, informal meeting with a few people present. Dad, Gunner, Mari, and I all sat on one side of the table, with Hades at my side. Lance and the soldiers who escorted him sat across from us, Lance's wrists still cuffed as he scowled at us.

He'd been given royal treatment for a prisoner, despite complaining constantly about his accommodations. Every other day, he seemed to come down with a migraine or an asthma attack, and the medics quickly figured out it was just an excuse to get out of his cell. They were laughably bad escape attempts and he was apprehended quickly every time.

Still, we asked Mari to be present at this meeting as a courtesy. We didn't know what the captain was capable of, and wanted to ensure we had a professional in the room if he tried anything crafty.

"You could let me go," Lance suggested, his tone bitter, like he already knew how we'd respond to that idea.

"Explain to me how that would be advantageous to either of us," my dad offered patiently, as if talking to a child. "You spied on us, attacked us, captured our citizens, and now your territory is disinterested in having you back. So where would you go?"

The captain shrugged, his cuffs clinking as his shoulders raised. "I'll find my own way, like everyone does."

"You're lying," Gunner cut in sharply. "You have some contingency plan you're not telling us. If you really had nowhere to go, you wouldn't be so eager to leave."

"You ambushed *us* and took my people captive too!" Lance shouted. "Four Corners isn't the peachy little village you pretend it is. You're just as bad as us, so why would I stay?"

"We don't kidnap women for forced marriages." I started counting off my fingers. "Using said kidnapped woman to blackmail another territory for labor and supplies, using our own citizens for slave labor while we get rich. Shall I go on?"

Lance scoffed and shifted in his seat. "Someone like you wouldn't understand."

"Someone like me?" I repeated. "What's that supposed to mean?"

He sneered at my patches, eyes tracing over the word PRESIDENT. "A filthy road pirate who doesn't know the first thing about building a prosperous city."

"I suggest you think very carefully about what you say next." My father folded his hands calmly on the table but I could feel his temper, so much like mine, simmering below the surface. "That's my son you're insulting."

The color drained from the captain's face as he realized his mistake. Generals were powerful and highly respected in his world, only a few steps down from the governor, who he seemed to regard like a king. He couldn't fathom General Bray in his pressed uniform, decorated with stripes and medals, ever existing in the same world as an outlaw biker, much less sharing blood with one.

Lance's eyes snapped back to me and for a moment, I thought he might actually apologize. His mouth opened but only a soft rasp came out. His cuffed hands flew up to his neck, eyes growing wider until they bulged.

On Gunner's other side, Mari leaned forward. "Is he choking?"

"Wait." Gunner placed a hand on her forearm. "He's doing his dumb faking shit again."

"No, I don't think so." Mari stood. "The blood vessels in his eyes are popping. He's not getting air."

She'd just started rounding the table, heading for the captain when I felt Hades' dark, oppressive presence weigh down on me like a boulder. The whole world seemed to darken and slow down when his voice came in the next moment.

Reap.

His life is yours to take.

Reap him now.

I didn't hesitate this time. I had learned my lesson before.

My hand swept over my gun, finding the grip with ease as I pulled it out of my holster. I already had a finger on the trigger when I extended my arm across the table, aiming the barrel at Lance's forehead.

I squeezed, firing off my shot before anyone could react.

Lance's head threw back from the force of the shot, his hands falling limply into his lap. He was dead instantly, but that didn't concern me. I was given an order and I carried it out.

What turned my stomach was my wife's horrified expression, her face speckled with the captain's blood.

CHAPTER 21

MARIPOSA

It took a few seconds for me to catch up and figure out what had happened. In one moment, I was approaching a choking man to assist him. In the next, a gun had fired and there was a bloody hole in the man's forehead. His head had thrown back, dead, empty eyes staring up at me.

I looked across the table to see Reaper with his arm stretched out in front of him, weapon in hand and pointed at the now-dead Blakeworth captain.

Everyone seemed frozen for a long time, even Reaper was looking like he couldn't believe what just happened.

General Bray moved first, rising from his seat at the table. "Thank you, lieutenants. You are dismissed. We'll handle this from here."

The two soldiers who had escorted the captain turned and stiffly marched out of the room. Their faces didn't betray any shock or horror, so who knew what they were thinking.

As soon as the door closed after them, Reaper lowered the gun to the table, staring at it like it would bite him. "He told me to. I had to obey."

"Hades?" Gunner asked.

Reaper nodded, his expression numb.

"Then you didn't do anything wrong." Gunner reached over and grabbed his shoulder, giving it an assuring shake. "You had a reason. He must have been faking it and planned to do something nefarious with Mari."

"I know...I know." Reaper rubbed his forehead, the shock of the event seeming to quickly fade. "It just...feels like I murdered someone in cold blood."

Because you did, a small voice inside me whispered.

"Mari, honey." Finn's voice drew my petrified gaze away from the dark hole in the captain's forehead. "You've, um, got some blood on you. Do you want to wash up?"

"Okay," I answered flatly, turning like a robot toward the bathroom. "Yes, I will."

"Do you need help?" Gunner and Reaper both moved to get up from the table.

"No!" I raised my hands, moving faster toward the bathroom. "I'm fine. I just...need a minute."

Their stares weighed heavily on me as I closed the bathroom door behind me. The electricity in here was old, and the bulb flickered and hummed when I hit the light switch. The dim light struggling to stay on didn't help with the glimpses I caught of myself in the mirror, the dead man's blood speckling my face like morbid freckles. It didn't feel real, more like I was in an old horror movie as I struggled to keep the contents of my stomach in place.

I tried to breathe deeply and opened the faucet. The water trickled out pathetically slowly, and I was forced to look at myself again as I wetted a paper towel and wiped at my face.

"Why are you freaking out?" I murmured, watching my own blood-speckled lips move.

Hades ordered Reaper to kill. It was what they did together, and always for some justifiable reason. Captain Lance was our enemy. Maybe he was going to try something when I got close enough, and Hades gave Reaper the command to protect me.

I had seen men get shot. I saw them die mere feet in front of me. So why was I having this reaction?

My trust in Reaper was shaky at best, but had been slowly getting to a better place. Even when we were in a good place, I knew what he was capable of. I knew he wouldn't hesitate to kill someone if they threatened anyone he loved.

Was it the fact that it came without warning? That he was just sitting in a meeting in one moment, then a killer in the next?

Did I really believe Hades had ordered him to do it?

That question made me pause, my damp paper towel hovering next to my face. It was a cold, eerie realization that I wasn't sure if I could believe it. No matter how badly I wanted to, I knew Reaper was brash and impulsive.

And that side of him almost cost us our marriage.

Maybe it still would.

When I couldn't see any more blood on my face, I dropped the paper towel in the small trash can and washed my hands vigorously. I didn't want to go back out there, didn't want to face them and the dead man who had been alive mere moments ago.

But there was no other way out of this bathroom, so I opened the door reluctantly and stepped out. Gunner and Reaper immediately looked at me, while Finn zipped up a long bag on the floor.

A body bag.

Again, I'd seen them before. So I couldn't place why it was so jarring to watch as two soldiers lifted the bag at either end and carried it out of the room.

"Are you okay, sugar?" Reaper sounded apprehensive, like he was worried he upset me.

"I should go to the hospital," I said, bypassing his question. "Some blood might have gotten into my eyes or mouth and I should get tested just in case..."

"I can take you." Reaper started coming toward me and I found myself backing away before I realized it.

"No, thank you. I'll drive myself." I could barely bring myself to look at his face but from one darting glance, I saw the rejection and hurt he wore plainly.

"Mari, are you afraid of..." He let the question trail off as if he couldn't believe it, much less say it out loud. *Afraid of me hurting you?*

I wanted to shout *no* and wrap him in a hug. Reassure him that he did the right thing, and that I was glad he reacted so swiftly to protect me. But that small, nagging part of my heart that still couldn't trust him fully, kept me nailed to my spot.

"I'll see you guys at home," I murmured, heading stiffly for the conference room door.

IT WAS A FAST BLOOD DRAW AT THE HOSPITAL LAB, BUT I wasn't ready to go home right away.

"We'll let you know by the end of the week, Mari," Jarrod, the lab tech, informed me as he carefully sealed and labeled my blood vials.

"Thanks." I pulled my sleeve down over the band-aid inside my elbow and stood from the chair. As I stepped out into the main corridor, I spotted a familiar, bearded man walking with a medic, his hand trailing gently along the wall for balance while the medic chatted away at him.

"Grudge!" I hurried toward him, relief and elation flooding my system at the sight of him up and about. It had been a few days since I had time to check on him "You're looking so much better."

"Mah!" His face lit up with a smile, the bruises and swelling mostly gone as he held an arm out to me.

I hugged around him carefully, taking note of the thick bandages still wrapped tightly around his torso. "You taking it easy, big guy?"

"Mm-hm." He looked to the medic, a woman named Becky, who elaborated.

"Always gotta get his exercise in." She rolled her eyes, but it was affectionate and playful. "He likes to walk fast to increase his lung capacity, but these ribs aren't gonna heal overnight, mister." She poked the dimple in his cheek and it was cute seeing the friendly banter between them. Despite the communication barrier, Grudge was just likable and always seemed to make friends easily.

"Mah?" Grudge looked back at me and pantomimed writing with his hand.

Becky reached into the pocket of her scrubs to hand him a notepad and pen, then smiled at me. "Seems he wants a private conversation with you. I'll be back in a few."

"Thanks, Beck. What can I do for you?" I stood back while Grudge turned to the wall to write his message.

S said you can tell if we're related from blood? he quickly scrawled out.

"Yes," I answered. "It's a simple test. We'd only need a little blood to find out. I just got mine taken." I pushed up my sleeve to show him the bandage on my elbow.

He nodded, stroked his beard for a moment as if pondering, then returned to writing.

T & D are my family. You & Demons are too. But I'd like to know if me & S share blood.

"Of course. We can do it now if you'd like. And I'll let Shadow know and test him too."

Grudge nodded but his mouth pressed into a frown. His hand hovered over the notepad, hesitating before he wrote his next message.

I don't like being injected with stuff. Or the opposite, w/e that's called.

"Okay. So no syringes." I nodded, trying to conceal my disgust. Not at him, but the people who gave him those phobias. Knowing what gave Shadow his fear of being cut with knives, I could only imagine what had been done to sweet Grudge.

"Do the medics give you IVs?" I asked him. "The needle in the back of your hand? It's attached to a long tube with a bag at the end."

He nodded and returned to writing. *Yes, that's not so bad. It's different...in my brain. But when the doc said I needed a shot, I couldn't do it.*

"I completely understand," I assured him, placing a hand on his arm. "We could do a blood draw with an IV needle and a long tube. Would that be okay?"

Will you do it?

"Yes, if you'd like me to."

"Mm-hm." He nodded eagerly before writing again. *Becky is nice but she's not you. You're my sister.* He underlined the final word with a firm stroke of the pen.

"Aww, Grudge!" I was grinning from ear-to-ear, the shock and numbness of what happened in the conference room far away from my mind. "Don't tell the other two, but," I leaned closer to him and whispered, "you're my favorite Son of Odin."

He huffed and smirked, rolling his eyes slightly as if to say, *obviously.*

I laughed and took his elbow. "I'll walk you back to your room and we can do your blood draw there."

"Hm!" he agreed and followed my lead down the hallway.

REAPER WAS PUTTERING AROUND THE KITCHEN WHEN I GOT home. Not drinking, but he seemed to be rearranging the contents of our cabinets—something to keep him busy until I got there, perhaps.

"Hey," he called softly, setting a series of whiskey tumblers down on the counter. "Did you find out anything?"

"I won't get results until the end of the week." I hung my jacket on the back of a dining chair, going around him as I went to the refrigerator.

"They can't do it any faster for you?" he pressed. "Since you're medical staff?"

"I'm sure it's the fastest Jarrod can do it," I answered. "He's by himself and backed up. Everyone else going in for tests is waiting weeks to get results back."

"Oh. Okay."

The silence was heavy between us. Me trying to ignore him, him trying to act like everything was normal. What was normal between us anymore?

It dawned on me right then how silent the whole house was, not just the lower floor. No one else was home, and I wondered if that was intentional.

"Can we talk about earlier today?" Reaper broached quietly.

Of course. The others had cleared the house so we could have *this* conversation.

"Sure," I answered dryly, my tone betraying just how much I *didn't* want to talk about this.

"You just seem shaken up by what happened." Green eyes watched me warily. "I want to make sure you're alright."

"I'm...not." I swallowed heavily, trying to work out the knot that tightened my throat.

"Okay." I was staring at my own fingernails on the kitchen counter but could hear the heavy breath cycle through his chest. "Can you tell me why?"

"Because I never really enjoy being splattered in a patient's blood and brain matter while on my way to treat them."

I was being snippy, defensive, and we both knew it. Reaper drew in a sharp breath and I saw his hand close into a fist before flattening his palm again.

"I don't want to get into another fight with you," he said softly. "Hades gave me a command and I obeyed. Hesitation has only cost me in the past, so I chose to act swiftly this time. That's all it was. I'm sorry for upsetting you."

"You didn't *upset* me. I just..." I brought a hand to my forehead, my frustration mounting. At myself for purposely being difficult. At him for being the calm, reasonable one for once. Where was my impulsive, hot-headed Reaper? And why was I getting pissed that he seemed to be missing from this conversation?

"He hadn't even done anything." I felt like I was grabbing at straws, and maybe I was. Why did I even care? The captain had been the enemy. "You condemned him to death for doing nothing that justified it."

"That's not my decision to make, sugar," Reaper said. "The God of Death gave an order, and I'm the instrument." He straightened up. "Eduardo had also done nothing when I was ordered to kill him. My hesitance then put four people in danger, including the *governor*. I promised I would never make that mistake again." His face hardened with determination. "Especially not if you were the one at risk."

"Did you really do it to protect me?" I fired back, lifting my eyes to his. "Or did you just *love* the chance to shoot and kill someone without a second thought?"

Reaper reared back like I'd struck him, his brows knitting together and making his eyes narrow. "I've *never* enjoyed killing anyone," he snapped. "Not once in my life, even when they've deserved it. If that's who you think I am, you are badly mistaken."

"Am I?" I challenged. "You wouldn't have enjoyed killing Shadow if you had the chance?"

Reaper's eyes closed softly, his chin dipping down until he stared straight down at the ground.

"No," he finally answered, barely above a whisper. "Because I'd be murdering a brother and hurting the woman I love."

"Killing, not hurting," I corrected. "You might as well have killed me too."

"Yes, I know." He looked up to meet my gaze, eyes pained and mouth set in a hard line. "You're still angry at me for what I did. And I'm sorr—"

"I know you're sorry." I turned away from him, hand on my forehead to rub the ache that seemed to settle there permanently. Anger throbbed through me—at myself? Him? I didn't know anymore. I was being unfair to him, I knew that. But I got a twisted sense of satisfaction from lashing out at him like he'd done to me several times before. And I hated that I enjoyed cutting him down like that.

What's wrong with me? I'm no better than him.

"I thought we were getting to a better place," Reaper said quietly.

"And what place would that be?" God, why could I not *stop?*

He flinched at the question. "One where you can trust me again. Where we're happy and in love like we used to be." His fingers dragged across the counter. "I know I still have a long way to go before we reach that point."

It felt like I was kicking him while he was down, and he just kept silently taking my hits and asking for more. I hated that he was being so passive like this, but wasn't it also what I wanted? For him to stop being so bullheaded, to show more kindness, empathy and patience?

I fell in love with a hot-tempered, passionate man who took without asking. Was it possible for me to love him any other way?

"Are you so sure we'll get there again?" I whispered, focusing on a small crack in the tile. I'd fall apart if I kept looking him in the eye.

It took a long time for him to answer. "I'm willing to try, as long as you are."

Those words should have reassured me, satisfied me to some degree. But the knots in my stomach only increased as I walked off, leaving him alone in the kitchen.

CHAPTER 22

JANDRO

I was usually a solid sleeper, so I couldn't place what woke me up in the middle of the night. Being in a different bed, maybe. Or maybe sleeping in a different part of the house just fucked with my senses.

My eyes adjusted to the darkness as I lay awake, the two figures in bed next to me becoming clearer. Shadow was reclined on his back, one massive arm wrapped around Mari, who was draped over his chest. The sheet had been pushed down to waist level, just covering her ass and his lower half. Unsurprising, since the big dude gave off heat like a furnace. Even so, he and Mari seemed content wrapped up in each other, their bodies rising and falling gently with steady breaths of sleep.

For a moment, I wished I had Shadow's artistic skills. The two of them made for a pretty sexy picture.

But more pressingly, I was wide awake at an ungodly hour and probably too hot. With the sheet kicked down around my legs and my throat dry as a bone, I might have to talk to the big dude about cracking a window. Especially if I was going to be spending more nights in his room.

I swung my feet down to the floor and found my shorts, pulled them on, and felt my way blindly to the bedroom door. The kitchen light was on, an unwelcome surprise as I quickly shut the door behind me so it wouldn't flood the bedroom.

"Who fuckin' left the light on?" I grumbled, rubbing my eyes and squinting as I padded barefoot to the kitchen.

"I'll get it before I pass out," answered a gruff voice.

I blinked, surprised to see Reaper hunched over the counter on a barstool, a recently purchased bottle of whiskey now half-empty in front of him. Like me, he was shirtless and barefoot, only in a pair of sweatpants.

"The fuck are you doin' up?" I went through the cabinets in search of a glass, then filled it from the sink.

"What's it look like I'm doin'?"

I drained my water and refilled it. "Being a sorry sack of shit."

"Bingo." There was no humor in Reaper's voice as he lifted the whiskey and drank straight from the bottle.

With a sigh, I grabbed a stool and settled across from him. "Alright, so tell me why. Before you need a liver transplant."

Reaper shook his head and let out a rattling breath, which quickly turned into a cough. *And a lung transplant, Jesus,* I thought. *He needs to cool it with those cloves.*

"You heard about the thing that happened today?"

"You shooting the Blakeworth captain in the middle of a meeting? Yeah, I heard."

"Right." Reaper passed the bottle between his two hands on the counter. "Well, it shook Mari up. She got kind of...distant. I tried talking to her afterward and I think I just made things worse between us."

I grabbed the whiskey from him and took a quick swallow. It wasn't like he needed it anymore. "I thought you two were getting along. Working through reconciling."

"I thought so too, but..." With nothing to occupy his hands now, he flattened them on the countertop. "I always seem to fuck it up."

"What did you say?" My tone came out more accusing than I intended but at this point, Reaper had come to expect that from me.

"Nothing bad, I don't think. I was listening. I didn't raise my voice or lash out. I thought...I thought I did okay, but she just seemed to get angrier."

"Dude, it might not actually be your fault for once. She's stressed out. You're stressed out. We're all fighting for our lives here and none of us are in the best state of mind."

"She and Gunner got past it," he grunted out. "She's happy with literally everyone but me. And it's not about *me*, I know that. It's just..." He took a long pause, leaning back in his stool as he scrubbed his hands down his face. "I don't know if we can make it work, Jandro."

"Don't say that," I snapped. "Don't you dare give up on the best thing that's ever happened to you. To all of us!"

"I don't want to. But if she gives up on *me*, what else can I do?" His hands flopped down by his sides. "I want her to be happy even if...even if it's without me."

"She'll be heartbroken without you, man. She needs you just as much as she needs any of us."

"Does she really?" he countered. "It seems like all I do is make her miserable. I'm a constant reminder of what I did to Shadow." His eyes looked off in the distance, focused on nothing. "I told Gunner this too. All I've ever done is hurt her."

"You really want to test that theory?" I leaned across the counter toward him. "You really think that if you're gone tomorrow, she'll be skipping along without a care that you're no longer here?"

He didn't answer. Of course he wouldn't.

"You *really* want to kill what's left, you go right ahead and do that." I pointed to the front door. "That'll be exactly what she needs, one of her husbands walking out on her in the middle of a war, during the most stressful, painful time of her life. 'Cause we all know how well that went last time."

"And I was the cause of that," he argued. "The blame for Shadow leaving lies solely on me."

"And now he's back, and you're atoning for it," I said. "Yeah, it sucks you're still being frozen out by her, I know. But she's your wife. You gave her your mother's ring."

"I know," Reaper sighed heavily. "I know."

"This whole war going on right now, on top of what happened between you two," I tapped my finger on the counter, "is probably the hardest thing that will ever test your relationship. Hopefully this is the last big war of our lifetimes. If you show her you're willing to stick through this, then you can start mending things properly. But if you bolt now? Dude." I shook my head at him, hoping I was conveying how serious this was. "There is *no* coming back for you."

"I want to stay, Jandro. There is no question in my mind about that. I'm just becoming less confident that it's what *she* wants. And I..." he groaned and rubbed his eyes. "I don't want to pressure her about us right now and add to her stress. I'm also scared to death of what her answer might be."

I leaned back and took a long swig of whiskey. "I know you never believe me when I tell you this, but *man* you're sensitive."

"Am not." He reached across the counter and swiped the bottle from me.

"You are. She's under a lot of pressure and you're taking what she says super personally. Don't." Reaper lifted the bottle to take a drink and I snatched it back from him. "Because Medic Mari is exhausted and overworked just like all of us are. She's not at her best. You're not at your best." Reaper lunged across the counter and belly-flopped on the surface as I held the booze out of reach. "Are you even listening?"

"Yes," he grunted, settling back into his seat. "Basically the same shit Gunner told me—don't make any big life decisions right now."

"Exactly." I returned the bottle to the counter, placing it right in front of him while he eyed me warily. "You gotta hold on, man, for all of us. It's not just her that needs you."

"Yeah, yeah. Enough of your sweet-talkin'." Reaper upturned the bottle and took a long swallow. "I'm not going anywhere."

"Better not."

He nodded, nudging the whiskey back toward me. "I just wish I knew how much longer this is going to go on for."

"Don't we all." I wasn't much of a whiskey guy and was already feeling it, so I idly spun the bottle on the counter. "Want me to say anything to her?"

Reaper pondered it for a moment, rocking back on the rear legs of his stool. "Nah," he decided. "She knows what I want...and how I feel. I just need to be patient, consistent. Show her that I'll stick around during the hardest time of all our lives, like you said."

"Good man." I pointed to the bottle and decided to take one last swallow. "And that's the core of it, really. You're irritable, short-tempered, overbearing, and yeah, kind of a dick, but at the center of it all," I set the bottle down and spread my hands, "you're a good dude who loves his woman and just needs to get laid."

"Huh," Reaper scoffed, reaching for the bottle. "Rub it in, why don't you?"

"Nah, I'm good. That's on you to rub 'em out."

He shook his head, smiling ironically. "It's been months and honestly, I never even feel up to doing that." He paused before taking a sip. "It's just not the same."

"I hear you," I said sympathetically.

Reaper choked on his next swallow. "I sure as fuck hear *you*."

"That's mostly Shadow's fault. He's addicted to pleasing her and she gets...enthusiastic."

Reaper laughed lightly before setting the bottle down, pushing it away with a touch of finality. "Thanks, Jandro."

"You feel better, buddy?" I got up to put my water glass in the sink, slapping his shoulder along the way.

"As better as I'm gonna feel," he sighed.

"Drink some water," I said, grabbing a clean glass and filling it up from the sink for him. "Or you'll feel like hell tomorrow."

"Thanks, Dad," he snorted.

I turned to hand him the water just in time to see Shadow's cracked bedroom door close with a soft click.

CHAPTER 23

MARIPOSA

I parked my dirt bike in the small, roped-off clearing a few hundred feet from the field hospital. We created a makeshift parking lot further away from the main tent because the noise of vehicles upset the patients. I was checking on the overflow today, mainly Blakeworth citizens and a few from Tash's army. Maybe this lot would have some whose recovery was on par with Robert's, but I wasn't terribly optimistic.

The bulk of my workload had been at the main hospital in town, and this was actually my first time visiting the overflow hospital since we got all the patients and volunteers streamlined. My stomach flipped nervously as I headed for the large white tent. I knew Reaper had been assigned to volunteer here, though I didn't know what shifts he worked.

For being unable to sleep after hearing his conversation with Jandro last night, I was surprisingly alert. Maybe I was finally getting used to the sleep deprivation of the last several weeks. That, or it was my wounded husband's words running through my mind, leaving me unable to focus on anything else.

He's thought about leaving. That was the bell that rang endlessly in my head, no matter how much I recalled Jandro chastising Reaper, convincing him to stick around, especially with the war still going on.

But what if he doesn't actually want to stay?

The thought sent my stomach clenching as I approached the tent. Every beat of my heart was painful. I needed to talk to him, but it seemed like an insurmountable task after that last conversation we had.

I was a major bitch to him. It's no wonder he's thinking about taking off.

Reaper wasn't likely to approach me again, so it was on me to apologize and to have a constructive conversation without lashing out.

How the tables had turned.

I hurried into the tent and went straight for the medic station, a small area sectioned off from the rest of the patients. "Rhonda!" I couldn't help but beam at the head nurse, flipping through charts like she hadn't nearly lost her life in a battle a few days ago. "Good to see you."

"Gonna take more than a little ambush to get rid of me," she smirked back. "How you doin', honey?"

"Fine." I wasn't about to complain about being overworked and sleep-deprived. We all were.

She nodded, accepting that answer. "How are the patients faring at the main hospital?"

"Blakeworth citizens and our people are pulling through their injuries just fine. As for the John Does, recovery is still slow except for the one, Robert. He's remembering more every day. A third of them still haven't shown any signs of improvement."

Rhonda made a few notes as I spoke, nodding as she did so. "Pretty much the same story here. One is improving much faster than the rest, though he's still muddled on some details. He's only been speaking Spanish, so your hubby's been translating for him."

"Oh no," I snickered. "Do we have a second interpreter? You never know what Jandro's gonna make up."

Rhonda laughed. "He's actually been very helpful. No nonsense about chickens or anything X-rated."

"Well, that's good." My laughter died quickly as I thought of those who weren't so lucky to be speaking or moving. "Have you thought about what we should do for the ones who are still catatonic?"

"Only every single minute," Rhonda muttered. "Dr. Brooks and I need to discuss this at length and exhaust all options of treatment that we can."

"And if you run out of options?" I chewed my lip, remembering how Freyja told me she couldn't save them. If a goddess couldn't, then I didn't have much hope for modern medicine.

"Then we'll keep them as comfortable as possible," Rhonda said softly. "They are victims of this war just as much as anyone else."

"You're right about that," I said, setting down my backpack. "Alright, so what do you need from me, routine check-ups?"

"Yes, dear. The John Doe your husband's been interpreting for has had trauma to his eye, if you could take note of the swelling and any infection. John Doe number-6 needs his leg injury looked at."

Rhonda handed me a small stack of charts and I flipped through them quickly to become acquainted with each patient's needs. The moment I stepped out from behind the divider and looked out at the main patient area, my heart did that painful beating again.

Reaper was here.

He was standing at the foot of a patient's bed, talking and smiling like he was cracking jokes. I hadn't seen him smile like that in months, and that made the ache in my chest cut even deeper. He certainly hadn't smiled at *me* like that in a long time.

Reaper said something that made the patient laugh uproariously, clutching his stomach and causing other people to look his way. When Reaper grinned and leaned over the bed to fist-bump the man, his eyes caught mine and all his laughter died.

His eyes dropped just as quickly as they lifted, his lips forcing a smile out at the patient, but the bright glow was gone from his face.

I did that.

And I *hated* that I did that.

I looked down at the patient charts in my arms, trying to focus on the job I came to do, not on my husband across the room who felt hundreds of miles away. *Tonight,* I decided. *We'll talk tonight and figure this out.*

With that in mind, I set to checking on everyone that Rhonda had assigned to me. I caught glimpses of Freyja walking around as I worked, her tail in the air between the beds or jumping up on someone's bed for some healing and head scratches. She settled at the foot of the Spanish-speaking man's bed, where he and Jandro talked softly.

The man was at the end of my rotation, but his voice reached my ears several times while I tended to other patients. I couldn't catch everything he said, but there was something warm and comforting about how he spoke. The cadence and inflections of his words reminded me of my dad, which compounded the ache in my chest already put there by Reaper.

Jandro was speaking rapidly by the time I approached, his wild gesticulations making it clear that he was telling some dramatic story. His accent and tone were slightly different from the other man's and I found myself grinning as I walked up. It was so sexy when he spoke Spanish. I needed to remind him to speak it more at home.

"Mariposita!" Jandro returned my grin as I approached the bed from the other side.

"Guapito," I returned.

The patient, at first engrossed in Jandro's story, swiveled his head to look at me. He had gauze pressed to one eye and medical tape to hold it in place. Part of his head was shaved, revealing a long incision held together with surgical staples. But there was no mistaking him.

All of my patient files fell to the floor as our eyes met. My hands, my legs, and my mouth refused to work.

No, it couldn't be.

But it couldn't be anyone else. No wonder his voice had sounded so soothing to me from afar.

"Dad..." I managed to squeak out before my knees buckled, hitting the edge of his mattress. I managed to grab the bedframe before collapsing completely to the floor. "Dad!" I cried louder, his face blurring from my tears. "Oh my god, Dad?"

He looked at Jandro and then back at me. *"Tu eres mi hija?"* he asked with a puzzled expression.

"Dad!" I grabbed his hand and he startled at the touch, pulling away like I was some stranger. "Dad, it's me, Mari! You..." I felt like I was crumbling. It was nothing like any other heartbreak I had experienced before. "...You don't recognize me?"

"Hold on, hold on." Jandro came around the bed to help me up, but I barely felt him past my father's confused expression cutting straight through me. "Mari, are you sure this is—"

"Yes, I know it is!" I cried. I knew this man's face almost as well as my own. We had the same nose. He had a scar on his chin from one of the first battles he got drafted for. I *knew* that mouth frowning at me, it looked exactly the same as when I'd get in trouble as a teenager. "Dad, come on. You know me."

He just kept staring at me with a confused expression while Jandro rubbed my arms. "It's okay, babe. We'll figure this thing out. We always do."

"Dad!" My husband's words were little more than background noise in my head. "Dad, you can speak English. Why are you only speaking Spanish?"

"We don't think he's remembered it yet," Jandro said into my ear. "He's remembering a few things since I started talking to him, but it's slow-going. Please don't take it personally, Mari—"

"Dad," I sobbed, shaking with the urgent need to hug this man, to hear him call me *mijita* again and tell me where he'd been all these years. "How can you not know who I am?"

"What's going on?" Reaper walked up to us, his brow pinched in concern.

I was making a scene in the middle of the hospital but couldn't hold back my relief, my grief, and my heart breaking, all rolled into one. My father was alive but was he, really? His chart had indicated he was one of Tash's army. I sank to the floor, sobbing as I stared at the man in his bed while Jandro held and rocked me.

"Found homeboy's daughter," Jandro muttered dryly, wrapping around me tighter as if he could protect me from this pain in my body that swallowed me whole.

"What, *Mari?*" Reaper gasped, looking between me and the patient. "*She's* his, his..."

"He doesn't recognize her," Jandro elaborated. "At least, not yet."

"Oh fuck, sugar." Reaper covered his mouth, like he was holding back a sob himself. "Fuck, my love. I'm so sorry."

My dad was looking at all three of us now, the confusion deepening in his face. He spoke rapidly in a soft voice, mostly under his breath, and the sound only made me want to cry harder. That was my father's voice, and the fact that he didn't know who I was made it feel like knives in my ears.

"He's...very apologetic." Jandro interpreted awkwardly. "It's not that he doesn't believe you. He knows he has a daughter and a wife, he just can't recall their names or faces."

I swallowed hard, taking a deep breath as I locked my gaze onto the man in the bed.

"Your name is Javier Luis de los Angeles. Your birthday is February twenty-seventh. You were born in Guadalajara, Mexico and moved to Texas when you were fifteen," I said. "You married Emma Wilder on September sixth, and had me, your daughter, Mariposa Wilder, on March twenty-first." The important details of his life came rushing out of me in a single breath, but his eye shifted to Jandro as I spoke.

My husband repeated everything I said, but neither of our accounts brought a spark of recognition to the man's face.

"Lo siento, lo siento mucho." He muttered the apology with a sad shake of his head.

I didn't know it was possible to crumble anymore, but it was only Jandro holding me up as I collapsed into tears.

"We should get her home," Jandro said softly.

"I can take her," Reaper offered. "I rode the fat boy today."

They talked for a little bit longer but it was just noise to me. At some point, someone pulled me to my feet and gently dragged me away.

MARIPOSA

I was barely aware of the ride home. Reaper kept one hand over both of my palms resting on his stomach the whole way. Whether that was to comfort me or make sure I didn't fall off the bike, I wasn't sure.

His hand stayed connected to mine when we arrived and headed inside. I followed his lead numbly, not resisting nor hurrying. Reaper directed me to the couch and sat me down without a word, then headed down the hallway. I heard some distant noise as he did something but none of it was registering in my mind. All I could think about was my own father's clear lack of recognition when he saw me.

Never for a moment did I consider this as a possibility. Not from the man who taught me how to drive, how to be a hard worker, and how to appreciate tequila. Him, me and my mom—our little family was everything. It was all we had as the Collapse approached, and what kept us going afterward. Finding out he got drafted for the border wars, and faced prison time or death if he refused, was the first big heartbreak of my life.

What Reaper did to Shadow, and Shadow's leaving, was the second. And this...this was the third and the worst one of all.

"Sugar." Reaper's hands enveloped mine again as he kneeled in front of me. "I'm running a bath for you. Come and get in."

I was grateful that he didn't ask, and just told me. I didn't want to be making any decisions right now. If he had asked me, I would have just said that I wanted my dad back.

Reaper gently pulled me up from the couch and led me down the hallway to my favorite bathroom in the house. This one didn't have a shower, only a luxurious standing tub that I once loved soaking in. I couldn't bring myself to love anything right now. Not even my small collection of soap bars and scented oils that Reaper was thoughtful enough to place on the tub's edge for me.

"I'll be in the kitchen if you need anything," he said stiffly before turning to leave.

"Wait." The word choked out of me, my throat raw as my hand reached out to grab his wrist.

He turned back to face me, eyes concerned and a little curious. His throat bobbed with a heavy swallow.

"Is...is anyone else home?"

Reaper shook his head. "Gunner and Shadow are in a meeting with my dad. Jandro's trying to finish up his work at the hospital so he can come home early. But that still might be a while."

I hugged my arms around myself, standing awkwardly next to the tub. "I don't want to be alone right now. I'll just think about him too much and—"

"Then I'll stay with you." Reaper turned his back to me in an offer of privacy. "Get in whenever you're ready."

I took my clothes off slowly, feeling an odd mixture of gratitude and slight that Reaper chose to not see me naked. He was my husband— we'd spent countless hours naked together. Rationally I knew he was being respectful, considerate of the distance between us in recent weeks. But a smaller part of me felt rejected that he didn't want to see me.

Reaper turned slowly after I sank into the water. A thin layer of bubbles floated on the surface, covering me from the shoulders down. Still, he kept his eyes on my face.

"I'll be right back," he said, heading for the door. "Just going to grab a few things."

"Okay." I leaned my head against the edge of the tub, sinking a bit lower.

He returned mere moments later with his arms full of three bottles —one water, one whiskey, and one tequila. "Wasn't sure what you're in the mood for," he said, carefully sitting on the floor next to the tub. "So I brought the unholy trinity."

"Isn't there a song about this?" I mumbled, watching him set the bottles next to him.

"Not quite. You're thinking of One Bourbon, One Scotch, One Beer."

"Oh, right." A dry snicker escaped. "I'll just have water." As tempting as it was to drink myself into oblivion, I'd have many more long shifts ahead of me. Possibly in that same tent with my father who didn't recognize me.

By the time Reaper handed me the water, I was already crying again. At least it was quieter this time. I took sips of water between soft, hiccuping sobs while Reaper pulled from the whiskey bottle.

"He'll remember you, sugar." Reaper scooted closer to the tub, leaning his shoulder against the outer edge. "You're not easy to forget."

"You don't know that," I whispered, staring at my knees poking through the bubbles on the water's surface. "He hasn't had an MRI yet. We don't know how extensive the damage to his mind is."

"He's improved by miles since last week. And anyway, you're his daughter, his only child. There's no way his memory of you is completely gone."

"I know you're trying to make me feel better but please don't." My gaze shifted toward him, drifting over his forearm resting along the edge of the tub. "I know more about this than you do. And it...it doesn't look good. I'd rather face reality than have false hope."

"Okay. You're right." He shifted away, his arm dropping next to him as he took another swig from the bottle. "I'm sorry, sug—Mari."

We sat in silence for a few minutes, only taking small sips of our drinks.

"I heard you last night," I said, clutching the water bottle between my hands. "When you were talking to Jandro."

Reaper barely moved. Only his chin tipped up slightly in surprise. "What did you hear?"

"Everything."

I didn't know what made me bring it up. I wasn't anxious or sad about what I overheard like I'd been earlier that day. I felt numb, just a body sitting in a bathtub and trying to stay alive by drinking water. Maybe it felt less risky to bring it up when I already wasn't feeling anything.

Reaper let out a long breath but the silence stretched on.

"I was a total bitch to you the last time we talked," I began.

"No, you weren't—"

"I'm sorry for shutting you out while you've been trying to make things work. I didn't mean to make you feel like you'd be better off leaving." At least I could recognize and say that, even while feeling like an empty shell in the moment.

"You didn't make me feel that way," Reaper said. "How you feel, everything you said to me that day, is completely justified."

More silence passed between us, and a sliver of feeling cracked through my numb shell—the need for answers. An intense desire to know *why*.

"So why did you want to leave?" I hugged my knees, not looking at him as I whispered out the question.

"Because I've been a bad husband to you. Even before exiling Shadow."

That drew my gaze up. His brow was pinched with pain, with regret. "What?"

"Even in the very beginning, I mistreated you." Reaper gripped the edge of the tub, as if stopping himself from reaching out to touch me. "I did and said things that hurt you. I let others hurt you, like with Heather at Fight Night."

"Reaper." I leaned toward him unconsciously, my shoulder brushing against his fingers curled over the lip of the tub. "That was so long ago. We barely knew each other."

"But it wasn't the only thing." He inhaled sharply, fingers gripping tighter. "There's something else you don't know. Something I was going to take to my grave, but you deserve complete honesty."

"What?" My voice was small, my chest felt like it was collapsing around my heart. My biggest fear came to the forefront of my mind—another woman. That he'd been with someone else while I was gone, or when I wasn't speaking to him.

"I...*did* try to kill Shadow." Reaper said each word slowly. "I would have, if Hades hadn't stopped me."

The silence between us now was oppressive, creating a distance that stretched wide, like two canyons on opposite ends of a valley. I waited for the response in my body, the irreparable heartbreak. The final twist of a knife that this news was supposed to bring. But it never came. I only felt more of the same, a constant numbness tinged with a painful ache.

My eyes lifted to Reaper's, filled with fear and regret. He was desperate for me to say something, but would never ask me to. Like me, he was probably expecting this to be the end of everything between us.

"On some level, I think I already knew that." The realization came to me slowly, clarity emerging from the sharpness of many painful weeks.

"H-how?" Reaper blinked in surprise. "Did Hades tell you?"

"No. I just know you." My arms wrapped tighter around my knees. "You don't take half-measures. Exile wouldn't have been your first choice."

His head hung low. "You're right," he sighed out quietly. "And it wasn't."

"I've felt so angry and hurt for so long, I just..." A heavy sigh rushed out as I brought my hands to my forehead. "I'm tired of feeling this way. I'm tired of wondering whether forgiving you is the right choice or..." The sentence died on my lips before I could finish speaking it. I still couldn't bring myself to consider the alternative.

"I've asked you for forgiveness too many times already. Now after what I did to Shadow, to you..." Reaper shook his head—a slow, pained, back and forth movement. "It's too much to ask. I love you more than anything in the world, but all I do is hurt you."

I remained still in the water, soaking up everything he said while fighting the urge to reach for him. To reassure him and tell him no, none of that was true. I fell in love with him the fastest, the hardest. But he wasn't saying it in hopes of falling into my arms again. He was just being honest. And there was truth in what he was saying.

"Do you want to leave?" I asked quietly.

"I want you to be happy and to never feel a betrayal like what I did again."

"That wasn't my question."

Reaper sighed and rubbed at his face. "No, I don't want to leave."

"What *do* you want?"

"What I want doesn't matter," he said gruffly. "My selfish wants shouldn't factor into any decisions you make."

"Tell me, please."

He sighed again, tilting his gaze up toward the ceiling. "I want to see you smile at me again. I want to hear you tell me you love me. I want to wrap you up in bed at night and make you feel safe. I want to feel trusted and needed by you again." The back of his head touched the wall as he spoke, his gaze somewhere far away as his throat worked in a hard swallow. "And I know I have no right to ask for any of that. I'm not entitled to anything from you."

"You're still my husband." The declaration seemed to come out of nowhere, like a final thread I was desperately trying to hold on to.

"And you have three other very capable ones who treat you as you deserve."

"This isn't about you versus them," I argued. "This is about you and me."

"Then I leave the decision up to you." His gaze finally turned to me, a resigned calmness in his green eyes, like he already accepted his fate. "Keep me as a husband or not. Choose what'll make you happy and forget everything else." He pushed himself up to standing, looking down at me in the tub with such longing, it made my chest ache.

At least I could feel again.

"Take all the time you need to decide." Reaper picked up his liquor bottles and started for the door. "Whether that's tonight or when the war's over. I'll accept your decision either way, Mari."

"Reaper, wait." He was almost out of the room when I stood up, water sloshing onto the bathroom floor. He glanced back, then faced forward again when he realized I was standing and naked. That made me hurt even more. Every day, every moment of missing him and longing for him seemed to culminate in this moment and it felt like I was shattering again.

My dad. My fallen medics. Him. This whole fucking war. I was breaking apart at the seams and all I wanted was for my husband to make it stop hurting.

"Why won't you look at me?" I cried out at Reaper's back. "I'm your wife! I'm *yours!* Why…"

He was across the room in a flash, rough hands pulling me into his chest. I was dripping wet but he didn't seem to care, holding the back of my head so my face was against his shoulder so I could scream and sob. I gripped his cut to pull him closer, inhaling the whiskey and cloves with every rattled breath through my chest like I was an addict. My legs threatened to give out from underneath me but he held me up, like an oak tree rooted firmly in the onslaught of a storm.

He's shaped by storms, I realized. The losses Reaper had endured gave him armor that sometimes hurt those at his sides. He was strong, there were no doubts about that. But only now was he seeing that armor did more harm than good. He didn't need armor to be strong. He just had to be brave enough to lower those defenses.

And now, he had been. There was no ego, no pride left in him. He'd been more honest with me here next to this bathtub than probably any other moment in our relationship. I wanted more of that. I wanted my Reaper who was strong enough to be raw and vulnerable with me.

His hand continued running up and down my back as my sobs quieted. His other palm on the back of my head was a comforting weight, holding me to his shoulder.

"You'll be alright, sugar," he whispered gently. "I know it doesn't feel like it now, but you will be."

Not without you.

The thought made me clutch him harder, like he would be ripped away from me at any moment. He held me tighter in response, the hand on my back pressing me into his chest while staying a respectful distance above my ass.

I didn't want him respectfully distant. I wanted his claim on my body, consuming and without apology.

"Reaper..." I whispered his name along his neck before bringing my lips to his skin there. My tongue flicked against his pulse, the thrumming doubling in speed. His skin was so warm and mildly salty.

Reaper let out a surprised hiss, jerking in my arms at the contact. The swelling in his pants was immediate, an insistent need pressing against my lower stomach.

"Mari...sugar, are you *sure*?" His voice was a husky rasp, just further proof that he truly hadn't been with anyone but me. My husband's desire was only for me.

"No, I'm not sure of anything," I admitted, watching his skin prickle in reaction to the breath from my mouth. "Except that you're here and I want you. I've missed y—"

He moved away from me only enough to bring his mouth down on mine. The two of us groaned into the kiss, like a couple of addicts hitting a fresh high. And that was exactly what it felt like. Sparks shot through my brain and every nerve ending in my body. I never wanted to come down from this, never *not* feel the rough scraping of his stubble, the demanding presses of his tongue, his wild and passionate way of loving me.

Reaper's hand finally slid down the curve of my back to squeeze my ass, my bare skin still wet from my bath and burning hot, first from the water, and then from him. Our kiss broke for a dizzying, gasping breath and a cocky smirk filled my vision, a glimpse of the Reaper I first met and fell in love with.

"Do you want to step out?" he asked in a husky whisper, gliding a rough palm over my waist and hip. "Or I could come in."

"Out." It was the only coherent word I could say at the moment.

Reaper moved back, holding my hands for support as I stepped over the tub ledge. "Want to towel off?" He turned to grab a bath towel from the rack on the wall but I was faster, grabbing his cut and pulling him back until my mouth was locked on to his again.

He let out a moan that was more of a growl and lowered his arms, palming my ass with both hands and lifting up until my legs wrapped around his waist. In a few steps, he walked us to the vanity, perched me on the edge of the counter, and rolled his jean-clad erection against my spread open center.

"Sorry for getting you all wet," I blurted out the apology as he bent to kiss my neck, running that sinful mouth to my shoulder, where he nipped me.

"Shouldn't *I* be the one apologizing for that?" His grin was wicked, eyes dilated and hungry as his hands ran up the front of my body. He touched and looked at me like it was our first time again, like I was something precious he wanted to both treasure and defile.

"Stop," I groaned with a playful smack to his shoulder, but I regretted that word in the next moment. He kissed me again, deep and dizzying as a hand ventured leisurely down my belly.

"Stop?" Reaper teased the word against my lips as his fingertips found my clit, running over it with the lightest possible contact.

"No," I begged, holding him in place with my legs around his hips and an arm around his shoulders. "Don't stop."

"Hm, I could've sworn you told me to stop." His hand moved away and I whimpered in protest. He touched the edge of the tattoo on my hip and leaned down to inspect it more closely, fingers tracing the vines and lengths of the petals. "Is this his gift to you?" Reaper's tone was lighter, curious. "Shadow's?"

"Yes," I answered, watching his reaction carefully.

"It's well done. 'Course that goes without saying." His gaze lifted to mine. "Do you like it?"

"I love it," I breathed. "For me and him, it's perfect."

"I have to agree." Reaper smiled, his forehead nudging mine. "I'm glad that you have him. That we all have him."

"Me too."

Reaper brushed the back of his palm against my cheek. "He loves you."

"He does," I said. "And I love him."

For a moment Reaper looked like he was going to say something else, but opted to kiss me instead. The coolness from our brief conversation gave way, our passion reigniting like gasoline on a fire. His kiss started off gently but soon became a deep, demanding tongue-fucking. I felt fingers brush my clit again and whined into the kiss.

"Don't stop," I pleaded, nearly teetering off the edge of the vanity with how hard I bucked toward his hand. "Please don't stop."

Reaper pressed down on the bundle of nerves, his thumb circling it as his fingers stroked through my folds. "It feels so good to hear you beg for me," he rasped. "Fuck, I've missed you."

"I've missed you so—ohh!"

Two fingers filled me, spreading wide to caress my walls while his thumb kept the steady, circular motion right above. My head tipped back as I gave in to the sensations of him, so familiar, like I was coming home and yet so new that it gave me such a rush. With his hands busy, he placed more of those kisses on the column of my throat. Some were so soft, they felt like whispers. Others were rough and biting. Exactly like the man who gave them—so full of love but with hard, jagged edges.

I wanted so badly to touch him, to take him out of his wet clothes and feel his bare skin on mine. But my hands braced behind me on the counter, my only support under him conquering and devouring me. The steady driving of his fingers through me sent my pleasure soaring, and it wouldn't be long until my strength gave out.

"Reaper," I whimpered, head tossing as my control began to unravel. My hips and his hand crashed against each other, meeting in the middle with loud smacks of flesh. Anyone listening at the door could have mistaken it for sex.

"Mari," he rumbled, lips skimming mine. "I don't have it in me to deny you. I want you coming for me every time you choose me." He smothered my moan with another bruising kiss, fucking me harder with his hand. "And if I please you every day until I die, it still won't make up for how I hurt you."

I shattered around him then, clutching around his fingers with a release that sent my cries echoing off the bathroom tiles. He kept driving into me, prolonging my pleasure while murmuring praises in my ear about how good and sexy I was. My body sucked around his fingers when he finally removed them, both of us panting.

Reaper kissed me again with more gentleness than before, but I still had to break away to breathe. My pulse raced and I felt exhausted, but my mind felt much clearer than before. And to my shock, the most persistent feeling was a wave of intense remorse.

Reaper straightened up, that cocky smirk returning as he unsnapped the button on his jeans. The motion sent a jolt through me, but not of pleasure. My body was still feeling the effects of physical pleasure from moments ago, but right then my brain was screaming, *I don't want this. I'm not ready.*

"I don't expect to last very long." Reaper yanked his zipper down, oblivious to my internal conflict. "But I have also been dying to taste you again."

"Wait." I held a hand up when he reached for me.

He froze, brow pinching in confusion. Or maybe it was concern. "Something wrong, sugar?"

"I don't...I..." My throat tightened and I was hit with the overwhelming urge to cry again. Like I hadn't been doing enough of that lately. "I'm sorry, but...I think this was too soon."

Reaper backed away and refastened his pants immediately. He grabbed a towel and quickly returned to wrap it around me, rubbing my arms through the fabric for a moment before yanking his hands away like he shouldn't have been touching me.

"Thank you," I said, holding the towel securely over me. "I'm sorry, I'm just—"

"Don't apologize. You have nothing to be sorry for." He seemed unsure of what to do with his hands, either rubbing his jaw or crossing them over his chest. That worried, pinched expression never left his face. "Did I hurt you?"

"No." I shook my head and tried to smile at him, but it faltered and he only looked even guiltier. "No, I think I just had a moment of clarity and...physically, I'm just not ready to jump all the way back in yet."

"Of course. Yeah, of course. I understand." Now *he* tried to smile, but it looked equally as strained as my attempt. He stood several feet away from me now, the space between us feeling as wide as a canyon again.

"I'm gonna lie down, I think." I slid down from the vanity, holding the towel to my chest while the throb of my orgasm still pulsed softly throughout my body.

"Okay. Let me know if you need anything." Reaper then turned and left like he couldn't get away fast enough.

CHAPTER 25

MARIPOSA

"I'm sure this comes as no surprise." General Bray held a folded letter above his head, barely able to contain his grin. "Blakeworth has *graciously* sent us a formal surrender and offering of peace."

The conference room erupted in a mixture of cheers and raucous laughter. Soldiers hugged each other, made obscene gestures, and shouted various forms of, *Suck our dicks, Blakeworth! Bend over and take it up the ass!*

"How kind and diplomatic," Gunner mused to my right. "Right after we handed their asses to them." His feet were propped up in the chair on the other side of him. The whole feel of the room was relaxed, if even happy after hearing this news.

"You'll love this part." Finn opened the letter and scanned for a certain section to read. "We hope you will join us in leaving behind the pains of the past and move forward in a mutually beneficial relationship."

Gunner made a farting noise with his mouth that stretched on for several seconds, until I slapped his arm. "Okay, really though," he laughed. "What happens now?"

"Their infrastructure is crippled, so their economy will be limping along for several years." Finn leaned back and put his feet up in an empty chair as well. "We can offer them aid, with strict terms. Remember, it's their working class that will suffer the most. The elite families have probably all fled to greener pastures."

"Also no surprise," I muttered.

The general nodded. "How are the hospitals doing, Mari?"

"Okay." I forced a tense smile. I hadn't felt great since yesterday with my dad and Reaper, but I shoved it all down to get an early start before attending this meeting. The patients needed me. "We're good on supplies at the moment. All current patients are stable. The volunteers have been a tremendous help. The only thing is, both hospitals are full and we are still understaffed." I clasped my hands on the table. "If we have another big battle, it could overload our capacity. Our resources are going to be spread extremely thin."

"I'm glad you brought that up," Finn said, his mouth tensing. "Because there is still New Ireland to deal with."

"Have you tried communicating with them?" Gunner rolled his chair closer to me, grabbing one of my hands.

Finn shook his head and lowered his voice. "After what we've seen with Andrea and the soldiers from there, sending a messenger is not something I'm willing to risk. I never thought I'd be saying this but...I don't think we're dealing with a *person*."

Gunner and I nodded in agreement.

"For now, we have to stay vigilant," the general said. "We'll plan an attack for when the hospital has more space, so we don't overload our medical staff."

"Truthfully, sir," I squeezed Gunner's hand, "that could be weeks from now."

"Yeah, what if they ambush us again?" Gunner leaned forward in his seat, placing his chin on my shoulder.

"That's where staying vigilant comes in," Finn answered. "Samson has the Jerriton army posted around the perimeter of Four Corners. They've been briefed on what to look for. Nothing will get past them, no matter which direction it comes from. We won't be surprised again. But for us?" He smiled a little more easily. "I feel like we could use a bit of a break from fighting, don't you?"

Gunner cleared his throat. "Respectfully sir, I feel like waiting too long gives them too much time to prepare."

"I see where you're coming from son, but you heard your wife. Medical staff are already carrying a huge burden. Our soldiers are exhausted. We won't be the superior army if we keep going until we're dead."

Gunner leaned back, conceding to the general's point. "You're absolutely right, sir."

"Don't get me wrong, we will push back if we see Tash's army approaching," Finn added. "We just shouldn't get too far ahead of ourselves."

Gunner nodded his agreement, letting the conversation die as the general stood to talk to a small group of soldiers across the room. With the two of us now alone at one end of the long table, I reached for his hand to clasp it in mine again.

"I know how you feel." My other hand ran through his golden strands as I leaned in, talking low to keep our conversation private. "It feels like we're stopping right when we've gotten good momentum, but Finn is right."

"Yeah, I know he is." Gunner tugged me closer until I slid out of my chair and into his lap. He hugged around me from behind, resting his chin on my shoulder again. "We can only ride high on adrenaline and morale for so long. It's good to take a small break." He squeezed around my waist and planted a kiss on my neck. "We should ride out to the hot spring and camp for a few days."

I turned to look at him. "'We' being who, exactly?"

"All of us," he answered quickly, a grin pulling at his lips. "It can be like a honeymoon for you and your four husbands."

His grin was infectious as I played with his hair some more. "As nice as that sounds, I can't get away from the hospital for that long."

"One day, then. Just an overnight trip." Gunner pushed my hair aside, dragging more kisses along the back of my neck. "Think about it," he whispered, his breath sending shivers along my skin. "Sleeping under a sky full of stars. The hot water relaxing all your aches and pains away."

"*All* of them, huh?" I snorted.

"Whatever the spring misses, your devoted husbands will take care of." He dug his thumbs into my upper back right then, circling them into the knots of muscle that had settled there for weeks. "We'll attend to your every need, baby girl. We can even be like real cavemen and hunt food for you."

I laughed at that, leaning into his hands working their magic on my back. "You make a tempting offer, captain."

"Then accept it." I felt his smile on my skin before he kissed behind my ear.

I squirmed in his lap, unable to keep my own grin away. He was turning on the charm and it was fun seeing this side of him again. A full day away from everything, just me and my men, with no responsibilities, sounded like utter bliss.

"I'm not sure if I can get away from work, even for a day." I twirled a lock of his hair around my index finger. "But I'll try," I added when he pouted and turned on the puppy dog eyes.

"Even an afternoon would be enough," Gunner said. "I just want some time to spend with my favorite people and no one else."

Horus, who had been perched on the back of Gunner's chair, now leaned down with a chirp to nip at his hair.

"Yeah, that includes you too, you little shit." Gunner reached up and let the falcon walk onto his hand, then brought him down to perch over my lap.

I tensed at the sight of Horus' talons so close to my leg, but the bird seemed to take care and be gentle, releasing Gunner's wrist to walk toward my knees. "We'd never exclude you, Horus," I said, using the back of my hand to lightly stroke his chest feathers.

"You critters are my favorite people too." Gunner returned to hugging around my waist, dropping a kiss on my shoulder. "At least until we have kids."

"Is that so?" I leaned back to kiss his cheek.

"It's one of the things I'm looking forward to most, after all this is over." Gunner placed a soft kiss on my nose. "I want to be a better father than my dad ever was."

"You will be," I assured him, touching the stubble on his cheek. "I already have zero doubts about that."

He inhaled sharply, like me saying that caught him off-guard, and I wondered if anyone had told him that before. Then he smiled, the motion slow and unbelievably sweet like melted honey. "Thank you, baby girl."

"I love you, Gun."

Horus flapped his wings and fluttered onto the table as I shifted in Gunner's lap, turning to face him.

"I love you, Mari." He whispered it reverently, forehead on mine and holding me like I would slip out of his arms at any moment. "And thank you for trusting me with your heart again."

"Thank you for owning up about being a dick," I chuckled, darting my tongue out to the tip of his nose.

"It won't happen again." He remained serious even after I tried to crack a joke. "Who you love and who you keep—those are *your* decisions to make. We had no right to force an outcome you didn't want." He swallowed. "We had no right to treat a brother like that."

"Thank you for acknowledging your part in it," I said. "With you, I'm ready to move past this. Shadow is too."

Gunner gave me a long look. "And with Reaper?"

My heart immediately picked up a thunderous rhythm, beating against my sternum like a fist. I was taken back to yesterday, talking to Reaper while sitting in the bath, and then what we did afterward.

I could still taste the roughness of his kiss, the grip of his hands on me, and how expertly he played my body. And I remembered how quickly he stopped, his guilt-ridden face after he saw I was no longer enjoying myself.

Why did I suddenly not want to keep going? I could only determine that, physically, I still didn't trust him completely. Even if I was mentally and emotionally ready to have him as my husband again, my body, even after yearning for weeks, had rejected him.

Damn that post-orgasm clarity.

The hurt on Reaper's face had been crushing. He probably took the rejection personally, he always did. If I peeked into his bedroom, I'd probably see a packed duffle bag ready to go—just waiting for me to say the words.

But I couldn't be certain. I hadn't seen or spoken to him since he walked out of the bathroom. If I had a chance, I'd tell him I wanted him to stay. I wanted him as my partner and my lover, just that my body-brain connection was being weird about sex. I wanted to get back to trusting him fully again, with his help.

"I guess that's a 'no'," Gunner mused softly after I hadn't said anything for a while. "Or at least a 'not yet'."

I let out a long sigh, resting my forehead on his. "I want to, but it's not as simple with him."

"I know." Gunner leaned back, looking at me with a loving smile. "That's part of why I want all of us to get away. So we don't have to think about," he waved his arms around, "all this. We can just focus on us."

"You're right. And it's a good idea."

"'Course it is." He smirked. "All my ideas are great."

I snorted and began sliding off of his lap to stand, but got hit with a sudden sense of vertigo and found myself crumbling to the floor.

"Mari! Are you—agh, fuck!"

Gunner must have felt the same pain that I was feeling right then, like a sledgehammer pounding at my skull.

Something was trying to get inside my head.

"No, no!" I clutched my head, all sense of direction gone, but I must have been rolling around on the floor.

Whatever barriers I had against the previous attempt to fracture my mind were failing. I could *feel* them buckling under the weight of the mental attack. Fear struck me, thinking of my dad and all the mindless, controlled soldiers walking to their death under General Tash. *This* was how they were broken and kept to heel like dogs.

Who or whatever General Tash was, it would not stop. It hurt so fucking bad that I saw in a single clear moment that I had vomited on the floor. My hands were covered in blood, probably from grabbing at my ears.

And then whatever was attacking me broke through.

The pain stopped and I heard a clear, otherworldly voice in my head, dripping with smugness.

Aha, there you are. Bring me the underworld, the sky, and the thread that ties them together.

CHAPTER 26

MARIPOSA

I rolled, pushing shakily to my knees. Remnants of pain still throbbed in my head, but overall I felt okay.

Someone clutched my arm—Gunner. Blood trailed down the sides of his neck and darkened the ends of his hair. He was sweating and breathing hard—I imagined I was doing the same.

"You okay?" he asked in a pained rasp.

I nodded. "Did you hear that?" We said it at the same time.

"Yeah." Gunner's hands floated over my face, my neck, and shoulders, as if checking to make sure I really was okay. "What does it mean?"

"Hey, you two."

I looked up to see General Bray and a group of soldiers forming a circle around us, their faces drawn tight with concern. "What was that?" My father-in-law knelt at my side, staring at my bleeding ear.

"It...happened again," Gunner said with a tight breath. "The pain in our heads, the—"

"I thought you were certain it *wasn't* going to happen again," Finn clipped out. "You said you were protected."

"I thought we were, but—"

"Get them to the hospital," the general cut him off curtly. "Tell Dr.

Brooks it's an emergency. They're encountering the same symptoms as the Tash soldiers."

"Right away, General," a lieutenant responded.

"Finn, wait." I climbed shakily to my feet, reaching for my father-in-law's arm to steady myself. He allowed me to lean on him but looked as though he'd rather throw me in a prison cell than let me touch him. "We need to find the others—Shadow, Reaper, and Jandro. The last time this happened, we were all affected."

"I know." Finn's gaze was hard, his mouth a thin line. This wasn't my warm, kind father-in-law at the moment. He was one-hundred-percent general. "I'm afraid we'll have to hold you at the hospital until we get to the bottom of this. If the others are affected, we'll hold them too, when they come to see you."

"Hold us?" Gunner repeated, his gaze narrowing. "You mean, against our will?"

The general turned stiffly to him. "We talked about this. We agreed that if you were to display these symptoms again, you had likely been compromised by the enemy." His gaze softened just a fraction. "I'm sorry, to both of you. But we still don't know what we're dealing with, and I need to keep the territory safe."

"Wait, wait!" I slapped away the hands of the soldier who tried to take my elbow.

"Ma'am, please don't resist." The soldier's throat worked in a swallow. "I don't want to force you, but I must follow the general's orders."

"Don't touch her!" Gunner hissed. Then to Finn, "Sir, I understand what we said. We'll cooperate, but you need to understand something."

"I'm sorry, but I don't know if it's my son-in-law talking to me right now, or…something else." Finn gave a defeated wave of his hand toward the exit. "Take them."

More hands grabbed my arms on either side and forcibly started moving me in that direction. I pulled my arms away and kicked out my feet, but it was no use.

"Mari, Mari, it's okay." Gunner was trying to be calm, but I heard the undercurrent of panic in his voice. "Don't fight them, we're still on the same side. Once we see the other guys, we'll figure something out."

With a huff, I stopped trying to get away, but still turned my head to yell back at the general.

"Something's going to happen!" I hollered over my shoulder. "They're coming! They want something and you need to be ready."

After that, I allowed the soldiers to escort me without issue. We walked down the long corridor without a word, boots scuffling over the carpeted floor. We were almost at the exit, two soldiers holding the doors open up ahead, when a sudden screech sent us all ducking.

A light breeze on my back was the only indicator of Horus' flight. He made no sound as he sailed through the corridor and out the open doors, the two soldiers darting out of the falcon's way.

They took Gunner and I to one of the army's SUVs, which we got into willingly. We huddled together in the backseat on the way to the hospital, trying to be strong for each other while I knew that voice still haunted us both.

"It's got to be something to do with Hades and Horus, right?" Reaper ran his thumb over his lip, pondering the message that had rattled through our heads. "What else would be the underworld and the sky but those two?"

He, Jandro, and Shadow had been notified of what happened to us, and immediately rode over to the hospital, where they were greeted by more soldiers. All five of us had been escorted and crammed into an exam room at the hospital. The door wasn't especially secure like a holding cell, but all of those rooms were taken by the worst-off of Tash's soldiers—the ones still screaming and bleeding from the ears. Finn's soldiers stuck us in here and were standing guard on the other side of the door.

None of us had resisted. They were just doing as they were ordered, and Finn believed this to be the best course of action. But if we needed to get out, I was confident my four men could break their way through.

"But what's the thread that ties them together?" Jandro sat on the exam table, legs swinging back and forth like a child. "Fuck, I hate riddles."

"Remember when we were looking up the gods in books?" Shadow said to Reaper. "Back in Sheol."

"Yeah, and?"

"The underworld and the sky are like two ends of a spectrum. The darkness and mystery of death on one end, light and higher knowledge at the other." Shadow held his hands out in front of him, roughly two feet apart. "What's in the middle?"

"I dunno, dude. That's what we're trying to figure out."

Shadow's hands fell to his thighs as he shot Reaper a disappointed look. "Life, Reaper. Humanity. Not dead, and not in a higher state of consciousness. Where we are *right now*." The room fell silent as Shadow looked around for someone else to chime in. "The underworld is below us, metaphorically speaking. The sky is above us."

"I get it, man. But I'm still not sure what—"

"Freyja," I broke in, the understanding clicking into place like a puzzle piece. "Humanity. Life and love in all of its forms. This is Freyja's domain. She's the link between the underworld and the sky."

"Yes," Shadow beamed as he nodded at me. "Our companion gods form a trinity, of sorts."

"Okay, so this thing," Jandro pointed at his temple, "wants *our* gods? Why?"

"Because they're protecting us," Gunner piped up. "They're naturally opposing forces, right? Chaos versus life, death, higher learning— we have the natural order of things. Chaos wants to disrupt that. Our gods are what's standing in the way of chaos taking over."

A brief silence filled the room before Jandro slapped Gunner on the back with a loud *whack* on his cut. "Look at you, smart guy. Way to break it down for us."

"So, what? We have to round them up and protect them?" Reaper rubbed the back of his neck. "Hades is back at the house. We've seen some coyotes around, so I told him to guard the chickens."

"Aw thanks, dude." Jandro nodded at him.

"Freyja is usually wandering the hospital," I said. "But I don't know if she's here or at the field hospital."

"Horus took off," Gunner frowned. "I can look through him and see where he is, but getting him to land might be another matter."

"Once we do round them up, what do we do with them?" I asked.

"City Hall has a basement," Reaper answered, the first words he said directly to me since yesterday. "It's heavily reinforced like a bomb shelter, in case of attacks on the city."

"What about our babysitters?" Jandro jerked his head toward the doors. "Do we just tell them we forgot to feed our animals?"

"We're gonna have to force our way through them, unfortunately." Gunner rubbed his jaw. "Three of us should take them on, one of us should guard Mari."

"I can handle myself," I huffed.

"Lover, they're armed and we're not," Shadow said gently. "We'll have to subdue them and take away their weapons. Those of us who take them on need to overpower them quickly."

"You three take 'em, then," Jandro said. "You're the strongest fighters. I'll cover Mari."

"I dunno about this, guys." I chewed my lip, tapping my foot on the ground to release some nerves. "I'm gonna have to run up and down the halls to look for Freyja. If they call for backup, we could get boxed in."

"Once we get our guards out of the way, we'll have guns," Reaper pointed out. "Nobody wants to hurt our own allies, but I feel like this is a risk we have to take." He pinned me with a hard stare. "We *need* to protect those gods. The survival of Four Corners needs them. Shit, the whole fucking world might need them."

Trust him or don't trust him?

The question echoed in my mind, and not for the first time. Only this time, I did feel a clear, single answer. My heart, mind, and body were all in agreement for the first time in months.

Trust him.

"Okay," I said with a deep breath. "You're right. You're—"

A crackling sound from the ceiling drew everyone's attention upward. The hospital's PA system was so old and fickle, no one used it. It was easier to use radios to call each other across the building, but someone was in the control room and attempting to broadcast a message to the entire hospital.

"Attention, I need...I need every available military and medical staff in the secure holding area." The broadcaster was panting, groaning slightly like they were in pain. "John Does number eighteen through twenty-four have fucking lost it."

The use of language would have been funny if the situation didn't sound so dire. All five of us stood frozen as we listened.

"The patients have become violent toward staff without warning. Sedatives are no longer effective. Medical staff have sustained injuries trying to subdue them, and I fear some are dead. They...ah, oh fuck... patients are trying to break out of holding cells and we need help!"

"Shit." My hand flew to my mouth and I moved instinctively toward the door, only to be stopped by Reaper with a light touch on my wrist.

"Mari, who are the John Does number eighteen through twenty-four?"

"Seventeen through twenty are the mostly unresponsive ones," I answered. "With the ear-bleeding and screaming symptoms. The rest are the catatonic ones. Freyja said she couldn't do anything for them."

"So they're still being controlled. Fuck." Reaper turned to the door, a hand on his jaw.

"They must have heard the same call that we did," Shadow said. "A broadcast to every mind this Chaos thing has access to, maybe."

"Why would it tell us too?" Gunner's brows pinched. "It doesn't make any sense."

"The very definition of chaos is not making sense," I said dryly. "Are we going to help or what?"

The doors and walls were thick, but we could hear some commotion out in the hallways. Medics and soldiers must have been racing to assist, shouting as their footsteps pounded just outside of our door.

"Stand back." Shadow's light touch drew me and Reaper away from the door. My biggest husband raised a booted foot and crashed it against the door's locking mechanism. It opened easily. Shadow's kick looked effortless, like he was passing a soccer ball.

"Fuckin' show-off," Jandro chuckled, but patted Shadow's back as he slid off the exam table. "Did our babysitters take off?"

"Looks like it." Shadow stuck his head out to look both directions down the hallway. "It's pretty empty. They must have all responded to the call."

"You guys check and see if they need more help," I slid out from behind Shadow and started down one length of hallway. "I'm gonna find my cat."

"I'll go with you." Jandro followed after me.

"Meet back here," Reaper called after us. "We grab Hades from home, and take them to City Hall together."

"Okay!" I turned a corner, Jandro right at my side as I headed for one of the hospital wings that Freyja liked to hang out in. "Freyja? Freyja!"

"If you haven't tried seeing through her, now would be a good time," Jandro suggested.

"Tried it, doesn't work," I said, breaking into a jog. "But yes, that would be useful right about now."

"Freyja!" Jandro's voice echoed through the halls. "I'll feed you Foghorn if you come out!"

We ran up and down the halls, peeked into rooms, and even checked closets and supply cabinets. It felt kind of ridiculous, looking for a cat like it was the most important thing in the world. But damn it, it kind of *was* the most important thing in the world. And I hated the thought that kept popping up in the back of my mind—that she was trying not to be found.

"Let's head downstairs," I said to Jandro after nearly ten minutes of fruitless searching. "Maybe she's in the lobby."

We headed for the stairs, in too much of a hurry for the elevator. On the wall next to the staircase, a long bay of windows stretched from the ground floor to the top floor of the building. It caught my attention as we headed that way, because the landscape outside looked strangely dark, despite the sunny day.

"Oh...fuck." I stopped in my tracks the moment I realized what the blackness was, making Jandro crash into me from behind. He gripped my shoulders, sucking in a sharp breath once he saw what I did.

"Holy…fuck, that's not possible," he breathed. "How…"

"I don't know." I tried to swallow, my throat dry, like sandpaper. "We have to find Freyja."

"Yeah."

But neither of us could tear our eyes from the massive swarm of black-clad soldiers marching on Four Corners.

CHAPTER 27

SHADOW

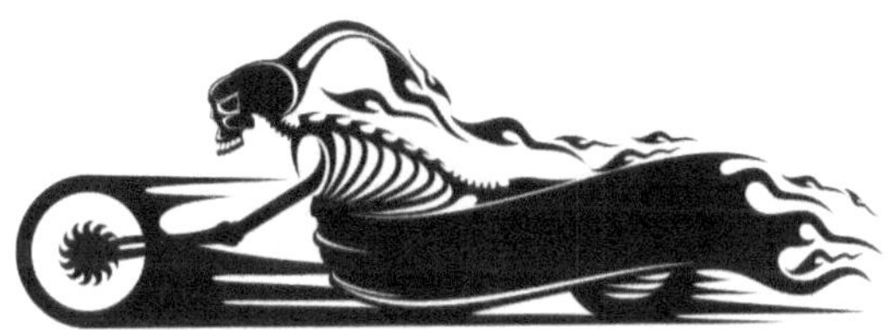

"Where the fuck even are the holding cells?" Reaper's head swiveled around, looking for a sign as we took off down the opposite hallway as Mari and Jandro.

"Probably that way." I nodded toward an unmarked door, the small window in it only showing a narrow stairwell going up. "They'll be isolated from the other patients."

"How would you know that?" Gunner asked me.

I shrugged before trying the doorknob. It was only a standard deadbolt, so I stepped back and kicked it in. "It was where they kept me before transferring me to the mainline at the prison."

"Alright, thanks, Donkey Legs." Reaper clapped me on the shoulder once. "Let's move."

I led the way up the stairwell, with Reaper after me and then Gunner in the rear—quite the shift from our usual formation.

"This is what I get for skipping fucking leg day," Gunner groaned, despite keeping a good pace behind Reaper.

"Told you," I muttered.

"Yeah I know, dude. Put me on your workout plan once all this shit is over."

The holding cells must have been on the very top floor of the hospital, because the stairs just kept going up and up.

"You sure this is the right way?" Reaper was starting to pant behind me. "I think this is an emergency stairwell."

"I wasn't sure, it was just a hunch," I said. "We can—whoa, Freyja!" I stopped right before the next landing, where the black cat waited patiently for us. "Mari's looking for you," I said, lowering to a crouch. "Tash, chaos, whatever it is, is coming for you and the other gods."

I'm afraid you're incorrect. The goddess' voice was soothing through my head, unlike the feeling of jagged knives through my brain matter like the other voice. *It isn't coming for us, but for you.*

"Me?"

All of you, collectively. The ones we've touched.

"Us?" Reaper nudged his way forward to stand next to me. "What does it want with us?"

The five of you are our ties to humanity. To cut us off from you is to weaken our connection to humankind as a whole. We exist without our animal vessels, but we cannot bond with other humans as we have with you.

"They mean to kill us?" Gunner came up on my other side.

Yes, if they cannot turn you into instruments of chaos first.

"Fuck, we have to get Mari and Jandro." I started backing up to head down the stairs the way we came.

"Uh, guys?" Gunner was pale, staring out the small, square window next to the landing. "You might wanna see this."

Reaper went next to him and I walked up the steps to see over their heads. "Holy...fuck."

The landscape just beyond the territory border was black as far as the eye could see. Thousands upon thousands of Tash's soldiers were marching on us, packed so tightly together that they looked like a single entity, and they *still* swarmed the landscape. The army looked like a slow-moving ink spill creeping closer to the city.

I moved in closer behind the other two, and looked to the south. The army spread that way too, as far as I could see. Looking the other direction told the same story.

"This window faces west," I noted. "New Ireland is east of us."

Reaper and Gunner turned around slowly, their faces stunned and harrowed. The previous attacks from Tash were a drop in the bucket compared to what was coming right now. Within an hour, they'd be tearing through Jerriton's perimeter like paper. Once they made it through, they'd sweep through Four Corners just as quickly.

We never stood a fucking chance.

"We have to get Mari and Jandro, and get the fuck out of this territory," Reaper said. "All of Four Corners is about to get slaughtered because they're looking for us."

"Reap, no," Gunner argued. "I get leading them away, but the five of us can't take on *that*." He pointed out the window. "And how would we even get out? You heard Shadow, they somehow made it *west* of us. We're fucking surrounded."

"I dunno." Reaper's jaw ticked, arms swinging stiffly at his sides like he wanted to punch something. "Fuck, I don't know what to fucking do!"

"Let's find Mari and Jandro," I said. "They might have already seen that," I nodded toward the window, "and started moving faster to get the animals."

"What about the medics and soldiers here?" Reaper wondered.

"I hate to leave them, but there should be enough of them to manage without us."

"Shit, I just thought of something." Gunner paled again. "Last time they marched on us, they burned down the field hospital. I'll bet you Mari and Jandro are heading that way to evacuate people."

"Fuck, I bet you're right. Mari's dad's in there," Reaper muttered before leaping down the stairs, taking three at a time.

I followed in the rear this time, glancing over my shoulder for a moment to see that Freyja was gone. I didn't know if she teleported or had uncanny speed, but doors and physical barriers didn't seem to slow down our god companions.

Please, please tell them what you told us, I thought—or prayed, I suppose. *Let them know and keep them safe.*

"They better not have touched our fucking bikes," Gunner announced as we made our way down.

Once we reached the first floor, we ran through an empty lobby to the parking lot outside. Jandro's bike was missing, leaving only mine and Reaper's.

"Get on," Reaper said to Gunner without hesitation as he turned on his steed, the machine rumbling to life. "Just hold on to me, don't make it weird."

My bike sounded like it was roaring out a battle cry. I backed it out of the space and turned toward the road, accelerating hard once it was clear. Traffic and signs went ignored as I weaved through the roads toward the field hospital. I only watched for pedestrians, but everyone within a mile heard us coming and no one dared to get in our way.

The field hospital was on the outer edge of town, close to the border. I kept hoping, praying that they weren't already being attacked. General Bray should have caught sight of the threat by now. He had no idea yet what they were really after, but hopefully his army would buy us some time.

I saw the top of the white hospital tent from the road and pushed my bike harder, knowing Reaper and Gunner weren't far behind. Everyone in town still acted normally, from what I could see speeding by. No one was running in a panic, there weren't any soldiers trying to evacuate large groups of people. A sick sense of dread turned my stomach and I could only grip the handlebars harder.

Something terrible is going to happen. Either thousands of people are going to die, or we are.

I crested a small hill and saw the field hospital straight ahead. What I saw beyond it nearly had me slamming on my brakes.

Blackness covered the landscape like a shadow. Seeing it closer now, without a window in front of me, was a completely different experience. I thought it looked bad enough from up there, but down here it felt utterly bleak and hopeless.

Rather than braking, I accelerated harder, pushing my bike to its limit. My teeth ground in my jaw as the wind whipped past me, eyes focused on that white tent where my wife was likely helping others before herself.

I spent the first twenty-odd years of my life in bleak darkness and hopelessness. I would not meet my end that way, or let it take my family from me.

I came to a hard stop in front of the field hospital in a cloud of dust and smoke. The smell of burned rubber followed me as I tore through the tent door, finding chaos within.

Medics were running around in a mad rush, packing up supplies in a hurry. As I suspected, many of them were moving patients as well. That was slow-going, considering many were still badly injured.

"Mari!" I barked at the rushing medical staff. "Is Mariposa here?"

"She's getting patients evacuated," someone said, pointing to the main hospital floor.

I started moving that way, brushing past people as I searched the sea of faces for hers. *There!* I didn't have the luxury of feeling relieved when I spotted her holding the arm of a man to help him out of bed.

"Mari!"

Her head snapped up at the sound of my voice. "Shadow, they're coming! Can you carry him?"

"We have to leave," I told her in response. "They're not coming for the gods, but for us."

"Us?" Her brows knitted together in confusion.

"You and your men, the ones the gods have touched. Freyja told us," I said in a rush of breath. "Where's Jandro?"

"He's driving one of the vans to get patients out." All the while, she continued helping the patient to his feet, bringing his arm around her shoulder while she held around his waist. "Shadow, we can't just leave these people here."

"Here, let me." I crouched low and wrapped my arms around the man's leg, lifting up when he was adequately slung over my shoulder. "I'm sorry if this hurts, I don't know where your injuries are."

Mari and I turned back toward the exit while the man muttered quietly in Spanish, seemingly confused, but at least he wasn't one of the violent ones.

Shit, the violent ones.

My heart nearly stopped before I turned to my wife. "Mari, how many of the catatonic patients were here?"

"I thought there were four but none of them—" She was jerked away from me in the blink of an eye. An expressionless man pulled her into his chest, covered her mouth with one hand, and wrapped the other around her throat.

"MARI!"

I set the patient on my shoulder down as gently as I could, but it wasted precious seconds as Mari's attacker started dragging her away, completely unaffected by her kicking and squirming.

He was fucking fast, even with her resistance. In seconds, he was nearly at the other end of the tent when I ran toward him, leaping off of abandoned beds and shoving wheeled carts out of my way. Others were trying to stop me, I could see them in my peripheral vision. Empty shells of people with no expression on their faces, eyes blank and hollow as they moved to cut me off from either side.

Our guns had been confiscated by General Bray's soldiers the moment we showed up to the main hospital. Thankfully, they hadn't known about my hidden knives.

I grabbed the handles hidden at my lower back, waiting for the perfect moment to send them out to my left and right. My eyes stayed on Mari when I threw them, but I never missed. My knives hit true to their targets.

Even with knives in their torsos, the controlled soldiers never stopped.

"What?" I breathed the word as I dared to look, sliding my gaze away from Mari for a fraction of a second before returning it to her.

She was getting red in the face, like she was struggling to breathe, the patient dragging her away with impossible speed. I was fast on my feet, but it felt like I couldn't catch up. And the other two bleeding from their knife wounds were creeping up faster on me.

And where the fuck were Reaper and Gunner?

With the next bed in front of me, I picked it up by the metal frame and tossed it to the side, hoping to slow down one of the fuckers coming at me. I grabbed a cart and tossed it toward the other one, then kept running. Even slowing down that tiny amount put more distance between Mari and me.

Fuck, I would've killed for a gun right then. I didn't trust myself enough to throw a knife from this distance. A stab wound wouldn't kill her, but with a gun I could be far more accurate.

Mari's attacker hit the far wall of the tent, and there he stopped. My heart leaped and I pumped my arms and legs harder to reach my woman. The man holding her seemed to be messing with one of the support poles holding up the tent's frame. He released Mari's mouth to tamper with it, but kept the other arm tightly wrapped around her neck. Mari was either trying to scream or take a breath, her hands digging and clawing at his arm.

I reached them just as the tent started to fall.

He had ducked under the canvas siding, Mari's feet scrambling and kicking as he dragged her along. The entire tent groaned as its support system began to collapse. I had a knife ready, slicing through the canvas like butter to make my way through. I had covered enough ground to reach them, and didn't hesitate.

The knife left my hand, sailing forward until it found its mark in the back of the man's neck, cutting cleanly through his spinal cord.

His feet kept moving for another few steps but his arm had gone limp, releasing Mari to collapse in a heap on the ground before he dropped dead soon after.

"Mari!" I hit the dirt next to her as she coughed and wheezed for air, quickly scooping an arm under her legs and wrapping the other around her back. "I got you," I grunted out as I rose to my feet and headed back toward the collapsed tent.

"Stop," she coughed out weakly as I made my way around the fallen structure. "We have to get the rest of them."

"I'm sorry, love. We can't help everyone, especially when we're the targets." My head whipped around in search of Reaper, Jandro, anyone. *What the fuck? They were right behind me!*

"Shadow, watch out!"

I looked just in time to see the two that I stabbed, now moving slower and uncoordinated from blood loss, stumble out of the hole I ripped in the canvas. One dragged a lame ankle behind him, but they were both still hell-bent on catching up to us.

"Fuck. Can you run?" I asked Mari.

"I think so."

I placed her feet gingerly on the ground, keeping hold of her hand. "Let's go."

We bolted together, me keeping a slow enough pace for her to stay at my side. I didn't know where to go, except away from them. With my free hand, I reached into my cut for another knife, pulling it out just as the fourth and final zombified patient stepped out from behind a van.

I pulled my arm back to throw my knife, stopping abruptly when I saw the gun in his hands.

"Get behind me!" I skidded to a stop and shoved Mari behind my back.

"The other ones are still coming!" she cried, clutching the back of my cut.

I didn't dare take my eyes off the one in front of me, who raised his gun slowly. "Throw the knife away."

The way he said it was eerily calm, almost like he was bored. He wasn't dead but there was no *life*, no adrenaline running through him. I gripped harder on the knife handle, and hated knowing that I couldn't throw it right into his chest. I didn't know how fast or accurate he was with a gun. I was Mari's only shield and couldn't take that risk.

He cocked the weapon and walked closer. "Throw it away."

"Okay...okay."

I widened my hands and tossed the knife into a bush without looking. I had more, of course, but couldn't reach for them without him seeing.

"The Sha wants you alive to begin with," he remarked, lowering the gun barrel. A small relief. "But the Sha does not mind if you are brought in pieces." He pointed at my legs and a single shot rang out.

I braced myself for the impact. Pain was not an issue but it would disable me, especially if I bled a lot. But the tearing of my flesh, the odd sensation of a foreign object cutting through muscle and tissue never came.

Instead, the man fell to his knees, teetering there for a moment before collapsing forward as dead weight. A tell-tale hole was perfectly centered in the back of his head. I looked up to see Gunner roughly fifty yards in the distance, waving a rifle over his head in victory.

"Jesus, fuck..." Mari and I ran toward him instantly. She released my hand to leap on to him in a hug. "Where the fuck did you guys go?"

"Made a pit stop at the armory for some essentials." Gunner held

Mari with one arm as he tossed a rifle to me. "Still think I'm losing my touch?" he asked with a grin.

"I'll never talk shit about you and your guns again," I said, quickly checking and loading my weapon. Jandro and Reaper were a few yards back at their bikes, arming themselves to the teeth. Two rifles crossed each of their backs, sat at their hip holsters, and each man even had one strapped to the front of their bodies amidst all the ammo in their tactical vests and slung over their shoulders. Reaper even had the automatic rifle mounted to his handlebars that he used in the first battle against Tash.

"Do we have a plan?" I asked, making my way over to get myself strapped.

"Shoot as many of them as you fucking can. Don't get captured." Reaper inserted and locked a long magazine into the assault rifle. "That's the plan."

"Everyone seems to be evacuated," Jandro remarked, noting the now misshapen tent a few yards away.

"My dad! Did he get out?" Mari squeezed in between me and Jandro and started loading a rifle.

"I got him on a truck and handed him to a medic," Jandro assured her.

"The army is mobilizing to help, but..." Gunner came up on my other side with an apprehensive shrug. "I think we're front line, guys."

"And *we're* the ones they want?" Mari blinked. "How did that happen?"

"Let's start to fan out and move backward toward the city as we start to engage them." Reaper's eyes were on the horizon, watching the enemy get closer. "Hopefully we'll make a dent, but the five of us can't take them in an open field for long. We'll need cover, so hopefully dad's troops move their asses."

"Even if they do." Gunner shook his head with a worried frown. "There's enough of them to turn the landscape *black*. I can't even estimate numbers, but they've gotta be in the hundreds of thousands. We've *never* gone up against anything like this."

"The only other option is to not fight as we go down," Reaper shot back. "Which would you rather do?"

"The one about to shoot us said we were wanted alive," I said. "So it's not a death sentence right away."

"If we get taken by them, it might as well be," Gunner said. "We'll be like *them*. Fucking zombies."

"Guys! They're really close now." Mari had followed Reaper's gaze and I looked the same direction.

Fuck, they were no longer marching but running. I could make out facial features and hair colors from this distance.

"Fan out and move back when I say," Reaper ordered. "Mari, stay between Gunner and Shadow."

We spread out, still close enough to cover each other. To keep higher ground, we all stood on top of abandoned vehicles or equipment left behind by the medics. Only Reaper was closer to the ground, and the center of our firing line.

There was no preamble, no motivating speech, or quick moments of affection with our woman. We had no time. Reaper confirmed with each of us that we were ready before he roared out, "FIRE!"

I focused on my targets, popping off clean, fast shots to the sound of bullets spraying from Reaper's automatic rifle. I could tell that Mari and Jandro were aiming for the upper bodies, while Gunner and I picked people off with head shots.

It seemed efficient for the first few minutes. Reaper mowed down the front line, giving obstacles for the people behind to step over, and the rest of us shot those moving in. But there were so many. We were only dealing with the ones right in front of us, and not the ones to the sides that crept closer into my vision.

They were still running, coming closer on three sides with no regard for fear, pain, or their fallen comrades they were literally trampling over.

"Move back!" Reaper ordered. "Back toward the city!"

I jumped down from the van I was standing on and looked for Mari, who was slower to climb down.

"Come on!" I grabbed her hand when she hit the ground and started running, with Jandro right alongside us. Only Reaper stayed put, swinging his handlebars around to spray bullets at our enemies in a wide arc.

"Reaper, come on!" Mari yelled at him.

He started easing the bike backward, still shooting, but he'd have to turn his back to catch up with us, and I was not about to let my president take that risk.

I stopped running but shoved Mari forward. "Go, I'll catch up."

"What are you doing?" she demanded, spinning and returning to my side.

"I'm gonna cover him so he can move back. Now go!"

"What about you?"

"I'll be fine. Run to Jandro and Gunner now!" I shoved her again, more forcefully. "Do not follow me." I ran back toward Reaper without another word, pulling my second rifle from my back holster as I did so.

He was swinging the machine gun more wildly, face set in a hard grimace as he sprayed back and forth in an effort to keep the enemies from getting too close. An endeavor he was quickly losing. They were close enough to shoot with handguns now, a swarm of blackness threatening to swallow us up.

"Go, I'll cover you." I came up beside him and started shooting, swinging my rifles in the opposite direction as him to cover more ground.

"You can't hold 'em off," he argued before his shots abruptly stopped, a soft *click-click-click* following in their wake.

"Just get cover and reload!" I moved in front of him, squeezing my triggers as fast as my guns could allow, which was much slower than his.

Reaper finally turned the bike around and drove toward the city. I followed after him, running backward as I fired shot after shot at blank-faced, black-clad soldiers. I was shooting men who were, in all likelihood, completely innocent. None of them deserved to be shot so callously. It wasn't their fault their bodies were being controlled by something else.

What did that one soldier call it? The Sha?

I couldn't afford to think, only act as they came closer. As I swung my rifle barrels, I almost snagged some of their uniforms. They were close enough to reach out and grab me, and some of them did. I started throwing my elbows out, trying all I could to create some distance so I could keep shooting, but there was just so fucking many.

I didn't look back. I'd be done for if I did, so I kept moving my feet back while facing forward. If they surrounded me and the others were getting away, good. I had to believe Mari and her other men got into the city and had adequate cover.

I thought I could hear someone shouting my name, but it was impossible to tell over the hundreds of footsteps all encircling me. Hands were grabbing at me, pulling my weapons and ammo away. Arms pulled at my shoulders, my biceps, weighing me down. Kicks hit me in the knees and shins, and I felt my strength faltering. I gathered up what I could with a loud bellow of effort and threw some of the Tash soldiers into the crush of people closing in on me.

But it was all for nothing.

An arm wrapped around the front of my throat, cutting off my air. My vision went to black dots as I planted my feet wide apart, refusing to fall. I'd be dead on my feet before they took me down. I'd protect my wife, my family, until there was nothing left. I'd be emptier than all of them before I stopped.

An odd sensation on my neck had me spinning, reaching to land punches on the soldiers behind me. It felt like the prick of a needle, like when Mari drew blood from me. I continued to struggle until my arms felt impossibly heavy, like boulders at my sides.

And then my legs stopped working, refusing to hold me up any longer. My eyes weren't even closed when all I saw was blackness.

CHAPTER 28

MARIPOSA

"SHADOW!" Someone's arm was around my stomach, pulling me back as I fought with all my strength to reach my husband. "Let me go, he needs help!" Tash's soldiers were swarming Shadow by the dozens—climbing and grappling as they tried to bring him down. Nothing they were doing was lethal, but there were *so* many. He was stronger and taller than all of them, but he couldn't overpower their sheer numbers.

"Shadow!" I screamed again, then drove an elbow back into whoever was holding me.

It was Gunner, who immediately pinned my forearm behind my back. "I'm sorry, baby girl. I'm so sorry."

"Why aren't you shooting?" I bellowed at Reaper. "Do fucking something!"

"I could hit him by accident," Reaper shouted back, his face pained and scowling. "We gotta keep moving into the city, get some cover!"

"FUCK YOU!" I screamed with all my might. "We are *not* leaving him!"

"Mari, there is nothing we can do right now." Reaper looked over at me and nodded at Gunner. "Don't let her go. Move further in and I'll cover your back."

Only Jandro was still shooting, but to no avail. As much as I hated to admit it, Reaper was right. Aiming at the mob that descended on Shadow ran the risk of hurting him, or worse, killing him.

"We'll get him back," Gunner whispered as he started to drag my limp, exhausted body away from the scene I couldn't tear my eyes from. "Maybe not right now, but we will. I promise you."

"Shadow..." His name became a weak sob, tearing from my throat. I couldn't see him through the crush of bodies piling on anymore. I hated that we were leaving him—us, his family. Even if it was a death sentence for us.

"Fuck, they're in the city limits now!" Gunner turned me around to face him, taking my face gingerly in his hands. "Baby girl, I need you to drive for me. Can you do that?"

"...Drive?" I only realized then we were standing next to a pickup truck. The engine was running but no one was inside.

"Mari, I really, really need you to focus right now." Gunner tapped his fingertips lightly on my cheeks, just enough to bring my attention back to him. "Drive to the City Hall building. We're gonna hide out in the basement there and figure out what to do next. Okay?"

"...Okay."

"Good girl. Drive fast." He smacked a quick kiss on my forehead, drew a new gun from one of his holsters, then hopped in the truck bed. Jandro followed him, his face a hard mask. He couldn't afford to feel anything about losing Shadow right now and neither could I.

Tash's soldiers had gotten one of their targets. Now they needed two more.

I got into the driver's seat, not bothering with the seatbelt as I hit the gas hard. As the truck jerked forward and I was forced to pay attention to the road, the scene in front of me was the complete opposite of the calmness from earlier.

People were panicking. Screaming and running in the streets. In the distance, I saw several dark smoke plumes from fires near the eastern border. Jerriton's army must have tried to stop them. It was a war zone right here in the city. We'd been trying to avoid this outcome, to keep the carnage as far away from the civilians as possible.

Now it was coming for us, and we had no option but to lead it straight into the heart of the city.

My gaze flicked to my guys in the rearview mirror every other second. Jandro and Gunner were shooting to cover Reaper, who followed behind us on his bike and turned to shoot behind him at every opportunity.

City Hall. City Hall. Make it to City Hall. That's all you have to do right now. I whispered it to myself as I white-knuckled the steering wheel through town. If my mind drifted anywhere else, I might not be able to get us there.

A hard thump on my door made me startle. Then there was another on the passenger side door, and more alongside the truck. I realized with horror that Tash's soldier's were throwing themselves at the vehicle.

"Keep going!" Jandro yelled at me from the back. "Don't slow down!"

I pressed down harder on the gas pedal, my hands already aching around the steering wheel in my fight for control of the truck. Another quick glance in the mirror showed me Reaper driving over the bodies that threw themselves in front of his motorcycle. They came up on all sides and tried to grab him, or the bike. Some of them held on and dragged behind him as he drove.

Fuck...Would we even make it to the building?

It was less than a mile away now, and most people seemed to be off the streets. I thought I caught sight of the Four Corners army shooting, but I was going too fast to see.

So close. So fucking close...

I couldn't tear my eyes from Reaper now. They must have figured out he was the most vulnerable and continued to pile on him. He was getting smaller in my mirror as more of them jumped, grabbed, and tried to drag him off the bike. One of them caught hold of his handlebars right in front, and he fired some rapid shots of the machine gun at point-blank range into the man's stomach.

We're here! We made it!

City Hall came into view, along with a long line of Four Corners soldiers and Jeeps right out from.

"Get out of the way!" I yelled, slamming on the horn as I made a beeline for the sidewalk right in front of the buildings.

Soldiers quickly dodged the truck and reassembled after I was past their line, forming a barrier between us and the mindless black swarm.

But Reaper was still out on the street.

I hopped out of the cab and climbed into the truck bed, where Gunner handed me another rifle. I took it and started shooting alongside my men, alongside the soldiers now raining fire down on the enemy, the mindless pawns of someone or some*thing* powerful enough to control thousands of minds from a distance.

We avoided shooting directly at Reaper, but I aimed as close as I dared. Jandro, Gunner, and I focused on the ones grabbing for his bike from the sides, while the army fired at the mass at large. But I couldn't ignore the heartbreaking reality that they were all centering on one target—my husband.

Reaper was fighting to shoot and keep control of the bike, which wobbled dangerously every time someone tried to grab it. When someone jumped on the seat behind him, my heart stopped.

"REAPER!" My voice was already weak from screaming for Shadow, so it didn't carry over the commotion and gunfire.

The Tash soldier wrapped an arm around Reaper's throat, taking my husband by surprise. Before Reaper could break out of the hold, the attacker stabbed him with something in the neck. The continuing struggle sent them both careening off the bike.

"NO! Reaper, no!"

I didn't realize I had jumped down from the truck bed and was running straight for him until I was being pulled back. Arms wrapped around my stomach and pinned my arms down as I lost sight of *another* husband in a pile of bodies.

My kicking and screaming was to no avail. I screamed at the sky, at Hades and Horus for not protecting my two men. I screamed at the pain splitting through my body from the knowledge that two of my husbands had just been taken from me. My voice stopped working and I still screamed. Everyone's ears had to be ringing from all the gunfire, so it wasn't like they could hear me anyway.

The binds holding me eventually loosened and I broke free at the first opportunity, picking up the first gun I saw and quickly wiping my eyes clear. Holding the rifle against my body, I spun around in confusion.

"Where...what...?"

They were all gone. Tash's soldiers had vanished like smoke, leaving only their dead behind. I turned back toward the building to see Jandro and Gunner approaching me slowly, their faces just as shocked and pained as mine must have been.

"Where'd they go?" I asked, my voice little more than a raspy whisper.

"They left," Jandro said numbly. "They took him and just fucking *left.*"

"How...why?" I looked at Gunner. "Why didn't they come for us three?"

"I dunno." Gunner stared at Reaper's motorcycle lying on its side. "I don't fucking know." Anger bled into his voice as his lower lip trembled.

The gun, now a useless, dead weight in my hands, clattered to the ground as I turned in a slow circle. None of it made sense. The more I looked at the scene all around me—bodies, guns, blood, and bullet casings—the less sense it made.

"What's going to happen to them?" The mere thought of that question made me want to scream and cry again.

Neither Jandro nor Gunner answered. They stepped in closer to me, shielding my view from our surroundings. Jandro brought my head into his chest, settling my ear over his racing heartbeat. He stroked the back of my neck with trembling fingers as Gunner came up behind me. Gunner let out a rattling sigh as he lowered his forehead to the back of my head, his shaking hands resting on my waist.

Together we could only stand, supporting and being supported by each other. None of us needed to speak to know that without each other, we wouldn't just lose.

We would crumble.

Epilogue

REAPER

"Ah, fuck!" The pain in my shoulder woke me up. It throbbed with a sharpness that felt like I was getting stabbed repeatedly. I deduced pretty quickly that the thing was dislocated, probably from falling off my bike.

"Okay, get this thing back into place, then figure out where the fuck I am." I was mainly talking to myself to make sure I was still alive, in case my shoulder wasn't a clear enough sign.

I was sitting on a concrete floor and figured out there was a brick wall behind me. When I tried to stretch my legs out, I realized that the shackles around my ankles, connected by a chain bolted to the floor, prevented me from extending my legs fully. As I became more aware of my body position, I realized my other arm was pretty sore too.

Both arms were shackled above my head. "Ugh, no wonder this fuckin' hurts."

I shimmied and scooted as much as my thrashed body would allow to press my back against the wall. Like a toddler learning to walk, I pressed slowly up to standing until my arms were in a more natural position. It hurt like a motherfucker, but I hissed and ground my teeth, pressing that shoulder into the wall until it popped back into place. The stabbing pain faded right away, lowering to a dull throb that I just knew would continue to haunt me as long as I was in here.

With that taken care of, I started looking around the room. The large, looming figure on the adjacent wall caught my eye first.

"Hey," Shadow greeted unceremoniously.

He remained sitting on the floor, heavy chains wrapped around his ankles and wrists. I wondered if the shackles didn't fit him, they were already pretty tight on me.

"Hey," I returned. "Got any idea where we are?"

"New Ireland, I assume," he mused. "Tash's compound."

The rest of the room wasn't much to look at. A concrete floor, four brick walls, a tiny square window too high up to reach, and an iron-barred door, like a jail cell.

"How long you think it's been?"

"I dunno, maybe a day?" Shadow's chains clinked as he shifted his position. "I woke up not long before you."

"Fuck." I tipped my head back until it touched the wall behind me. "We're fucked, aren't we?"

"Probably."

"You sound awfully calm about it."

Shadow shrugged, the motion moving some of his hair to reveal that a chain was also wrapped around his neck. "I'm used to dungeons, I guess. How did you get caught?"

I recounted everything that happened after he went to cover me, from the moment the others got in the truck, to getting jumped on my bike and passing out.

"Do you think the others got away?" Shadow's brows furrowed and I knew we were thinking about the same person.

"They should have, they were behind the army lines." I cleared my throat and looked around, feeling thirsty as a motherfucker but of course, there was no water in this shithole. "The inner chamber of that building is like a fortress, and they have basic necessities for a couple of weeks. They'll survive, figure something out."

"Mari will want to come after us," Shadow said.

"She better not," I barked. "She's the missing piece—the thread that ties the underworld and the sky together. If they get all three of us, I bet we're more than fucked. At least right now, we might still have a chance." I blew out a long sigh, wondering how much longer we'd be kept without water.

Hahahahaha...

Shadow and I jerked away from our walls at the same moment, staring wide-eyed at each other. Yeah, we definitely both heard that.

An odd swishing sound pulled our gazes toward the door just in time to see a forked tail dragging along the ground on the other side.

MERCILESS

STEEL DEMONS MC BOOK NINE

PROLOGUE

REAPER

TWO YEARS EARLIER

A pounding headache, a parched throat, and a queasy stomach. All three of which were becoming a lot more common these days.

Can't drink like I'm in my twenties anymore, I thought, rolling over slowly in bed so the room wouldn't start spinning.

I slid out of bed quietly so as to not wake up my flavor of the night. She wanted to get all cuddly last night and I was not having that. Most likely, she'd want to stick around once she woke up and I'd have to be an absolute asshole to make her leave. My hangover would help with that endeavor, at least.

A quick glance at the bed over my shoulder had me stifling a groan. Her makeup was smeared all over my pillowcases. I fucking just had them washed too.

I wasn't crazy about leaving her in my room with all my shit, but I sure as hell wasn't about to be here when she woke up. Somehow I managed to pull pants on without losing my balance or making a huge amount of noise. Grabbing yesterday's shirt, I held my breath as I opened the door. I didn't dare release it until I was down the stairs and out the front door.

The sun was already high on my short walk to the clubhouse, the sunlight damn near blinding. People were up and chatting, and the smell of food cooking on the grill had my hungover body salivating. I hoped Daren and Jandro pulled out all the stops for breakfast this morning.

"His Majesty graces us with his presence," my brother announced, white cigarette bobbing in his mouth as he pumped a lever on a citrus juicer.

I caught a whiff of menthol and turned my head, nearly gagging. While we had plenty in common, Daren and I couldn't be more different when it came to our taste in smokes. I liked my cloves and couldn't stomach that menthol shit. Why the fuck would I want to constantly suck on the flavor of toothpaste?

"Where you been?" Jandro turned some sausages with a pair of tongs while stirring up hashbrowns in a cast-iron pan with the other hand. "That girl wring you out?"

"Nah, I got so bored I fell into a deep slumber." I collapsed on a deck chair and threw an arm over my eyes to shield against that oppressive sun.

"You're an ass," Noelle informed me from somewhere nearby.

"So what else is new?"

I felt a kick on my shin. "Kara's nice. She hooked me up with free shots at the Shady Lady."

"That doesn't negate the fact that she's a boring lay."

Something cold touched my forearm that was thrown over my eyes. "Drink this," Daren's voice told me. "You'll feel better, Grumpasaurus."

I took the drink with my other hand, not bothering to look as I brought it to my lips. "Fuck, Daren! Did you just give me something with *fruit*?"

"Calm down, it's a screwdriver. The orange juice will help with your hangover, dick."

"You're lucky he didn't put a little umbrella in it," Jandro chimed in.

"He knows I'd disown him, that's why." I sat up to down the rest of my drink, my stomach actually settling and my eyes adjusting to the brightness of day.

The jarring sound of glass breaking made me wince, although it wasn't a terribly unusual sound for a biker club. But it was the heavy thump of a body collapsing and Noelle's, "Daren!" that shot me to my feet.

He was convulsing on the ground. Noelle rushed to grab his head so he wouldn't smack it on the concrete floor. I went to grab his arms while Jandro went for his legs.

"Shit, it's a bad one this time." Jandro frowned, his worried gaze on my brother's face.

He was right. Daren's arms tore out of my grip, every muscle tight and contracted. Even his fingers had curled into claw-like hands. "Did he eat or drink anything?" I fought to restrain him again before he hurt himself.

"Yeah, we should put him on his side." Noelle already had his face turned toward the floor, petting his hair and flushed cheeks while she stared down at him. "We got you, baby bro. It's gonna be okay," she cooed at him.

Daren never recalled us talking to him during his seizures, but she always did anyway. It seemed to work, in any case. His movements slowed, reducing to jerks and twitches for a minute before he was still.

"Hey." Noelle placed his head in her lap, smoothing her fingers over his forehead. "You okay, bud?"

Daren rolled up to a sitting position, yanking his arms and legs out of my and Jandro's grips. "Easy," I told him, holding my palms up. "Take it easy, bro. You know how these fuck with you."

"Yeah." His face was pale, eyes looking away from us as he hurried to his feet. "I'm heading back to the house. I don't feel good."

"Do you need anything?" Noelle was quick to ask, doting on him like our mother had.

"Just for all of you to give me some space," he snapped before storming off.

"The fuck is his problem?" I muttered, tapping my pockets in the hope that I had my cigarettes.

"For real?" Jandro stared at me. "Dude deals with seizures all the time that give him weird visions, and you wonder what his problem is?"

"I'm just saying, it's not like him to stomp off like a toddler." I found a smoke and stuck it in my mouth.

"I wonder if he saw something bad." Noelle worried her lip between her teeth.

"Both of you leave him alone like he asked," Jandro huffed, returning to the grill. "Swear to fuck, I don't blame him for running off when his siblings are always pecking at him."

"We watch out for him, 'Dro," I corrected. "He's the youngest of us."

"Yeah, well I'm the youngest too, so I know how he feels." He pointed at me with his metal tongs. "And sometimes, having my siblings act like my parents is fucking annoying. So just leave him be 'til he's ready to talk."

"Jesus, what crawled up everyone's ass today?" I lit up and turned my attention to the bottles of orange juice and vodka on the counter, considering making myself another drink.

"If everyone around you's an asshole," Noelle hip-checked me on her way inside the clubhouse, "might want to take a look in the mirror."

"Takes one to know one," I grumbled.

She was just upset that the guy she had a thing for didn't stick around. What she didn't know was that he used her to try to needle his way into the Steel Demons. I took one look at the bastard and knew he didn't have it in him. He bailed on her once I wouldn't even entertain the notion of making him a prospect.

Noelle would get over it. There was a guy out there worthy of her, one who wouldn't try to weasel into my club like a little bitch.

I got my belly filled with food and another megadose of vitamin C before heading back to my house. Hopefully Daren had enough time to cool down and the girl in my bed had seen herself out. Even in the stifling desert heat I walked slowly, biding my time and enjoying a post-breakfast cigarette.

Daren waited for me on the front porch—my mirror image in some ways but also my polar opposite. The outburst earlier was strange coming from him because he was usually so relaxed and easygoing, not a cantankerous hothead like me.

I tossed the butt of my black clove while he lit up a fresh, white menthol. "Hey, Reap."

"Hey." I paused before the first step on the porch. "You alright?"

"Yeah, sorry about that." He scratched his forehead with his thumb. "Told your girl to get lost."

"Thanks." I approached him and leaned against the side of the house. "Want to talk about...anything?"

He was quiet for a long time.

"I saw my own death, Reap."

That was fucking weird—both that he saw something so grave and also that he said it in such a concrete way, not in a riddle or random innocuous detail like usual.

"Oh. Shit, well." I ran a hand through my hair. "Is it cool, at least?"

He huffed out a mirthless laugh. "No. About as uncool as it gets."

Fuck, he was serious. And seeing it had obviously shaken him. His fingers trembled as he took a long drag off his cigarette.

"Well, we can prevent it, right?" I was no good at emotional support, so the president in me sought to figure out a solution. "What good is this fucking gift of yours if we can't use it to change the course of the future?"

"No, it needs to happen. It *will* happen." Daren tossed his cigarette and quickly fished for another.

"Bullshit. Says who?"

He smiled as he lit up again, like he was enjoying some secret I wasn't privy to. "It'll be okay, Reap. Just wasn't what I expected to see today." He went quiet again, now seeming peacefully resigned about everything, before his eyes bounced back to me. "I saw your death too."

"Didja now?" I pulled out a cigarette of my own. "Don't tell me— on the cafe racer in the desert with an Uzi in each hand. Wait, actually." I lit up before moving on to my better idea. "At roughly like forty-five or so. Older than now but not *too* old, you know? Please tell me I die from cardiac arrest while mid-stroke in the best pussy of my life."

Daren laughed genuinely this time, a bright sound that all the women loved. "That's a better guess than you might think."

"Yes!" I pumped a fist. "Tell me what she looks like. And seriously, do I actually die before I start having boner problems? Because that's what's *really* important."

"Sorry, bro." Daren smirked. "You're gonna be old as shit. A fucking grandpa."

"Aww man, seriously?" I huffed out a disappointed sigh. "I'm no fucking MC president worth his salt if I live to old age. We're meant to go out in blazes of glory."

"Shit's gonna change in the next few years." He got that faraway look again, tapping the ashes off the end of his smoke. "Some of it will be really fucking bad, but not all of it will be."

I snorted. "Now that's the cryptic bullshit I was expecting. But hey, listen." I walked up next to him and grabbed the back of his head for some brotherly roughhousing. "You're not fuckin' dying on my watch, okay? I mean it. If I gotta live to be an old fart, so do you."

My brother just humored me with that secretive smile again. "Fuck yeah, Reap. I'll be there for all of it."

CHAPTER 1

MARIPOSA

PRESENT DAY

I felt haunted.

I floated around like a ghost haunting my house, even haunting my own body. I didn't feel alive, but trapped inside a vessel. And I haunted those who surrounded me, namely Jandro, Gunner, and my in-laws.

Reaper's parents, Finn and Lis, were staying with us temporarily, in order to *support us*. Whatever that meant.

Ever since Reaper and Shadow were taken, and Tash's forces disappeared from Four Corners like a dark fog, my father-in-law and two remaining husbands talked late into the night. They sat around the living room or at the kitchen table, talking over whiskey in hushed voices. When I asked about these talks, Jandro or Gunner would squeeze my shoulder and assure me vaguely that they were figuring out how to get our other two back.

By the third day, I'd had enough of waiting.

I opened the garage door and started up my dirt bike, not caring who heard at seven in the morning. Foghorn answered the roar of my bike with a crow, which prompted Jandro to come running from the backyard.

"Where are you going?" he demanded, immediately suspicious as he stepped in front of my bike.

"Where do you think?" I shot back.

His face hardened, then both of his hands fell to grip my handlebars. To stop me. "You're not going anywhere."

"Let go, Jandro."

"They'll take you too, if you go," he hissed back through clenched teeth. "Underworld, sky, and the thread that ties them together. They'll have all the pieces they need, and then where will we be?"

"If you don't let go, I *will* run you over."

"Mari," Jandro pleaded, his face cracking with emotion. "Why are you doing this? You can't help them alone."

"At least I'll be doing something!" I screamed in his face, my resolve breaking with the realization that he was right. "Not sitting on my ass here. Planning, talking, and not doing shit!"

A sob escaped my throat and my vision blurred. The next thing I felt was Jandro pulling me into him, his arms cradling my face and back as he pulled me into his chest. I was sick of crying, sick of worrying, speculating, and *waiting* for something to be done. Every second that passed felt a tiny step closer to losing Reaper and Shadow. And that feeling only amplified the pain creeping into my system like a poison.

At some point, Jandro turned off the bike and led me inside. The sullen faces of Gunner and my in-laws in the living room indicated they'd caught on to what I was about to do. I didn't care. I'd happily throw myself in the path of danger if it provided even the slightest chance of getting my men back.

Jandro led me to the loveseat where Gunner sat, holding his arms open for me. I sagged limply against him, accepting his embrace with no enthusiasm, while Jandro sat down after me. The two of them wrapped around me, sandwiching me protectively between them. Under any other circumstances, I would have loved and enjoyed it. But I only felt smothered, even suffocated.

"Mari," Finn began in a choked voice, his hands clasped with his wife's from where they sat across from us. "Please believe me when I say we know how frustrating these past few days have been."

"Frustrating," I repeated in a flat voice. "That's an interesting choice of word."

"Mari." Gunner tried next. "We all want the same things. Any one of us would do anything to get Reaper and Shadow back."

These empty platitudes were sickening, literally. I felt on the verge of throwing up.

"Then why was I the only one ready to ride out of that garage just now?" I demanded, then turned to Jandro. "And why did you stop me? I thought we fought these battles *together.*"

"Because the last time we were all out there, two of us got taken away." Jandro's gaze burned into mine. "And I'll be damned if the same thing happens to you."

"He's right," Lis chimed in softly. "Rory and Shadow stepped up so you could get to safety. Your men will do anything to protect you, so please don't be reckless, Mari. You are brave and strong, but don't let their sacrifice be for nothing."

I gawked, dumbfounded at my mother-in-law's words. "How can you say that? This is your *son* we're talking about. Your last living son! And I'm not some helpless damsel, I will do anything to protect *them* too!"

"What she's saying is," Gunner voiced gently, "there are four of us and only one of you. We can't afford to lose you, Mari, because you are irreplaceable."

I wanted to scream at all of them. Why couldn't they understand? "So are all of you! I can't afford to lose any of you."

"That was an understood risk every time one of your men stepped onto a battlefield," Finn said. "You know as well as I, sweetheart, that there was some chance that not all of your men would return."

"So what's your brilliant plan, then?" I demanded. "Treat them as casualties of war and just move on with our lives?"

"No," Finn said with a firm shake of his head. "I will not consider them fallen until I see them with my own eyes." His face softened just a fraction, weariness settling into his features. "But this...force, whatever it is. We're even less prepared to deal with it than I initially thought."

"We've been hardly prepared during this whole war," I argued, looking to Gunner and Jandro for support. "We've beaten incredible odds in previous battles, haven't we?"

"Baby girl." Gunner gave a sad, heartbreaking shake of his head. "You saw the size of those mind-controlled forces. They surrounded the whole city. The five of us didn't even make a dent."

"But if you mobilize the whole army—"

"We did have casualties, not to mention damage to property and equipment when they swarmed the town," Finn cut in. "And we're still recovering from the ambush in which Jerriton helped us. It wouldn't just be dangerous to send troops to New Ireland now, it would be a suicide mission."

I sank back against the couch. "Then what do you have planned?"

I was met with deafening, defeated silence. That terrible lack of any answers had me yearning to run out to the garage and hop on my bike again.

"We don't want to give up," Jandro said finally. "We just can't see how to pull this off in a way that isn't a suicide mission."

"There has to be a way," I insisted. "There just has to be."

"If you have a plan that isn't running in blindly to save them," Finn softened the remark with a small smile, "we're all ears."

Of course I didn't. I knew it was stupid to rush out on my bike, to pick fights with my loved ones and accuse them of not caring, but I didn't know what else *to* do. I had nothing to pour my worry into, no battles to prepare for. I was running in place, spinning my wheels like a motorcycle stuck in a mudslide. It wasn't just me dealing with this, but knowing I wasn't alone was a small comfort. I didn't want comfort anyway. I just wanted my men back.

And it wasn't just the fact that they'd been captured by the enemy that weighed on me, but the timing of it.

Shadow and I had just reached such a beautiful part of our relationship after struggling for *so* long. He no longer feared hurting me or being open and vulnerable with me. It was incredible to see his confidence, to see how his journey of healing had paid off. He deserved a lifetime of happiness and love, and to imagine him being tortured again, regressing to a point of constant fear and distrust, was a pain I could not fathom.

And Reaper...

A pang of regret hit me so hard in the chest, I had to stand up and leave the room. My chest, my whole body even, felt so constricted and tight. I needed space and fresh air. I made a beeline for the sliding door in the kitchen, pulling it all the way open and shutting it behind me. Being out here, without everyone's eyes on me, was only marginally better. It didn't help that I caught sight of Reaper's whiskey in the corner of my eye on my way out.

I sat on the edge of the stoop, a soft breeze and the light clucking of chickens my only background noise as I thought back to my last moments with Reaper. Before the battle, before he was taken from me.

He had been earnest and heartfelt with me. I knew the depth of his remorse without a doubt, and he was there for me when I was inconsolable after seeing my dad in the field hospital. After everything we'd been through, Reaper still hadn't given up. I leaned on him when I was weak and told him how much I still craved him.

Then my husband gave me exactly what I craved and I *still* pushed him away.

My fists clenched as I wrapped my arms around my legs, resting my forehead on my knees as my eyes squeezed shut. Hot, angry tears threatened to spill—the anger aimed entirely at myself.

How could I? Why did I? I tried to think back to my emotional state at the time but it was out of grasp, murky like a fog. Mostly I was heartbroken that my own father didn't recognize me, and I was so, so tired. But was I still angry at Reaper? Resentful of what he did to Shadow? My tempest of emotions had been so volatile, I couldn't pinpoint how I *actually* felt toward Reaper.

My last moment alone with my husband could have been spent turning over a new leaf, rekindling the passion that burned so hot when we first met. It could have given him something to hold on to while being captured, a renewed sense of hope.

I was less worried about Shadow in a sense because he believed in our future together with his whole being. He would hold on until the very end, if it came to that. But Reaper...his own well-being was so dependent on that of his loved ones. He had already carried so much guilt over his parents, his brother, and now us.

If he believed our relationship was still irreparable, I worried—no, I was scared to *death*—that he wouldn't fight for his life. Family was everything to him, his reason for living. If he felt cut off from his family, then...

"Hades," I whispered, my lips against my fists. "Don't take him from me, please. I need him. I love him. I can't let him go yet."

As if coming to answer me, the silent black dog approached me from the side. His head lowered, eyes large and full of sympathy. Hades only nudged the side of my leg, but the sensation I felt was like a heavy blanket being draped over my shoulders. A weight, a pressure in the air that was comforting, like being wrapped in a hug.

I released one of my knees to scratch his neck, searching those impossibly dark eyes for answers.

"Can you see him? Or feel him?" Desperate hope bled into my voice. "Is he okay?"

He lives, dear daughter. Hades licked my hand, releasing a sympathetic whine. *The pulse of Reaper's life has not crossed into my realm yet.*

That was a small comfort, but better than nothing. Something bumped into me from the other side, and I looked to see Freyja rubbing against my opposite leg.

Do not doubt the depth of his love, she told me. *He is not adrift, but still yours in every sense of the word. Love will strengthen him.*

The sliding door opened behind me while I absently pet the animal gods at my sides. Their assurances sounded like little more than platitudes, probably because they too did not offer any solid plan for getting Reaper and Shadow out.

Jandro and Gunner came to sit next to Hades and Freyja respectively, sandwiching me in the middle of a cuddle pile. To top it all off, Horus flew down from his perch on the roof, flapping to slow his descent so he could land in my lap and not stab me with his talons.

"Whatcha thinking about?" Jandro leaned over and dropped a kiss on my shoulder before leaning his head on me there.

"How I was such a massive bitch to Reaper right before he was captured."

"Mari..." Both of the guys voiced my name as if to reassure me, but I held up a hand to stop them.

"It's true, don't try to convince me it's not. I keep going over our last moment together and I just..." My throat closed up, choking off my words with a sob.

"You were processing your dad and everything." Gunner reached over Freyja to stroke a tear off my cheek with his thumb. "You had no way of knowing what would have happened next. None of us did." His hand fell to pet Freyja's back. "I don't think these guys even knew."

We did not, Horus confirmed from my lap. *Our guidance led you to this moment, but we cannot see beyond here.*

Gunner startled next to me, and I remembered that he never heard Horus speak until recently.

"I just...hate that I left him feeling rejected and like I still hadn't forgiven him," I said. "Because...I do. I forgive him for Shadow, for everything." Speaking the realization out loud made me feel even worse. What kind of wife was I? To want my husband back so desperately only after he was taken away from me.

Jandro slid an arm around my back, rocking me gently toward him. "When we get him back, you can tell him that. He'll be the happiest grumpy bastard that ever lived, and this will all be a distant memory. Okay?"

I wanted so badly to believe him. We'd overcome so much before, as a group and individually. More than anything, I wanted to believe this would end happily for us. All of us alive and together.

But I couldn't ignore the cold, gnawing fear that a happy ending was impossible.

CHAPTER 2

SHADOW

Another day, another metal pipe slammed against my ribs.

I bellowed at the impact, squeezing my eyes shut as I slid against the wall to get away from my attacker. The pipe came down again on my forearm, my thigh, and then the other side of my ribs. I flinched and cried out with every hit, trying to protect my injured areas and make myself as small as possible.

It only encouraged my attacker to hit me more, which was just what I wanted.

He dropped the pipe with a metal clang, panting for breath as he reached into his pockets and slid brass knuckles onto his fingers. If my eyes weren't so swollen, I would have rolled them. What kind of pussy needed brass knuckles to hit a chained-up, defenseless man?

His punches had little power behind them, even with the extra weight on his hands. If my hands were free, I was certain I could break his jaw with a single punch. But I cried out in protest, begging and pleading for him to stop as I tried to escape the abuse.

He punched me until he was completely spent, leaning with exhaustion against the wall. Sweat coated his skin, dripping down his smug face as he slipped the brass knuckles off and returned them to his pants pockets.

"We'll play again tomorrow, big bitch," he told me, turning to the prison door.

"No." I shook my head at him, putting a grimace on my face. "No more."

Relief made me sag in my restraints as he unlocked the metal-barred door to leave, then locked it again behind him. To him, I looked sad and pathetic slumped against the dungeon wall, but the day had been a good one as far as these went.

They hadn't touched Reaper at all today.

He sat against the adjacent wall, completely silent during the beating I took. When the guard was gone, he remained staring at the door. I started cleaning my wounds with the meager amount of water I had rationed, a skill I had never fully unlearned.

"You need to stop doing that," Reaper finally said, his voice raspy from dehydration.

I paused in my washing, then continued on. "No, I don't."

"Shadow." He looked at me for the first time, one eye normal, the other a swollen, purple bruise from his beating yesterday. His speech was also off, slurred, probably from a swollen tongue. "They'll kill you."

He wasn't wrong about that. My pain reactions may have been fake, but the damage to my body was real. My muscles were seized up and stiff around my injuries. I was finding it more difficult to breathe.

But there were two of us. And if we both didn't survive, one of us had to.

I was built to withstand torture. The first twenty-odd years of my life had forged me into this. Pain had become a distant memory and abuse, my constant companion. I adapted to this because I had no other choice. Even after a much better quality of life within the last several years, my old survival habits kicked in like they'd never left.

Sure, I might die, but it wouldn't happen quickly. So far, these shit-heads with their metal pipes and weak punches didn't hold a candle to the Bathory cult that raised me, nor the sadistic bitch who brought me into the world.

"Better me than you," I said, pressing a hand to my mouth to stem the flow of blood from my lip.

"Why?" Reaper demanded. "Why are you playing into these sickos' torture fetish so that they pile on you and forget about me? You think I like watching you get beat?”

“Because I can handle it.”

“So can I!”

“I *know* torture, Reaper. And I can’t feel pain. It just makes sense.”

“So what? It doesn’t mean you should. Fuck, man.” He returned to staring straight ahead at the door of our cell. “You’ve been through enough, Shadow.”

“And you shouldn’t have to go through it at all.”

“Why the fuck not? Am I not in the same fucking dungeon as you?”

“Because you’re the president!” I had never truly spoken to a child before but it felt like I was arguing with one right then. “The club needs you more than it needs me. Mari needs you.”

Reaper huffed out a defeated laugh. “Everyone says that, but no, she absolutely fucking does not. You, on the other hand...” He glanced at me with his good eye. “You need to get back to her. And she will be pissed to find out you’re taking all the hits to save my ass.”

“She’ll understand, I think.” My bloody lip was finally clotting, so I pulled my hand away. “And we both need to get back to her.”

We were both silent for a while. There was nothing to do except talk, sleep off injuries, or stare at the walls. Meager food and water rations were brought once a day like clockwork. No one spoke about any plans for us, about the Sha, or whatever it was.

“Do you think Four Corners is still standing?” Reaper asked.

“I don’t know,” I admitted. “Mari and the others haven’t been thrown in here with us, so I hope that’s a good sign.”

“Yeah, I think we’d know if she was here.” Reaper’s throat worked in a swallow, like he wanted to say more. “I’m sorry, Shadow.”

My head had started to droop with exhaustion, but it lifted back up at that. “For what?”

“Everything.” He was looking at me with both eyes again. “You were there when we first formed the club, and I never took you seriously as a brother. I used your assassin skills, and your art for all of our tattoos. But when you needed friendship and guidance, I just let Jandro deal with you. I should have respected you more from the beginning, and I’m sorry that I didn’t.”

"Reaper, it's—"

"And with Mari." He faced forward again, closing his eyes. "I handled that so wrong. I fucked it up so bad."

"It's really okay, Reaper," I insisted. "That whole time away was actually something I needed badly. And it all worked out in the end." My eyes shifted around our cell. "Current circumstances not included."

He laughed bitterly. "No, I get it now. I deserve to be in here."

"No, you don't." I pulled at my restraints, wishing I could go to his side. "No one deserves a life of torture, Reaper. I wouldn't even wish it on the people who did it to me."

"Well, you're a better man than me."

"That's not for me to judge."

"Who, then?" he scoffed. "The gods?"

A thought occurred to me with that last question. "Have you tried your ability from Hades since we ended up here?"

"Yeah, there's nothing."

My eyes narrowed. "What do you mean?"

"There's nothing for me to see through, no death."

"We killed lots of Tash soldiers back at Four Corners. You can't see through any of them to assess the situation over there?"

"No. I've tried and they're...not empty vessels. It's not life, but there is something *in* them. Something holding on that won't let go."

I sat back against my wall, even more confused. "But you saw through the ones on the battlefield."

"Those weren't fully zombified, I don't think. Not under complete control like the black swarm that came for us."

"Why should that matter?" I wondered aloud.

"I don't know, Shadow. All I know is that it feels like I'm trying to crawl into a slab of solid concrete like it's a sleeping bag. It's just not happening."

"What about Hades?" I pressed. "Has he told you anything?"

"If he did, you'd be the first to know," Reaper said bitterly. "I'm sure you know by now these gods only intervene when it suits them."

Well, fuck.

Worse than the torture, than being separated from Mari and everyone else, was not knowing anything that was happening outside these four walls. Was Mari safe, alive? Was there still a home for us to return to? If I wasn't so exhausted from all the beatings and lack of food, it would keep me awake.

I scooted my legs to the side to lie down as comfortably as I could with a bunch of chains and restraints attaching me to the wall.

"In case it wasn't already clear, Reaper..." I started to drift off right away, my head resting on my hands.

"Hm?"

"I forgive you. For everything."

Neither of us said anything after that, but I was certain we both felt it—the finality of what the other man said. We were unburdening ourselves, making peace.

Just in case neither one of us made it out alive.

CHAPTER 3

MARIPOSA

"I've had enough of this."

Freyja had the gall to look surprised as I scooped her up from Shadow's bed. Once I had her secure against my chest, I darted out of the room in search of Hades. I couldn't bear to spend any time in Shadow's room since he was taken. It was too painful being in the room without his large presence filling up the empty space.

Hades was in the living room, belly on the floor and paws stretched forward as if waiting for me. I deposited Freyja down next to him and, after a moment of thought, decided against looking for Horus. The falcon was probably miles high in the sky, and at least I had two out of three here now.

"You all have been dead silent since Reaper and Shadow got captured, and I'm not having it anymore." I looked back and forth between the two animals, both of their ears flattening down at my confrontation. "Humans alone are no match for this thing, so tell me what you know. What is the Sha? How do we beat it?"

The Sha? Hades repeated the name in my head with a tone of surprise. *You are certain that's what this manifestation of chaos is?*

"I think so." Doubt filled my head as I thought back to when I was almost taken, and Shadow had stepped between me and a gun. "One of the controlled soldiers said the Sha wanted us alive to begin with, when he was going to take Shadow and me."

A beat of silence passed before the gods responded.

It's as we feared, Freyja said mournfully.

"What is?" I demanded. "What is it exactly?"

The Sha is the physical embodiment of Set, the brother of Horus, Hades explained. *They are direct antagonists of each other. Opposites in every way.*

"Okay, but we don't just have Horus. We have you two," I pointed out. "Doesn't that tilt things in our favor?"

The natural order has been slipping toward mindless violence and suffering for generations. The collapse of your civilization has allowed for the Sha's energy to thrive, Hades said. *The Sha exploits and weaponizes humanity's weaknesses for its own gain. It has likely been waiting for this moment to consolidate such immense power since ancient times.*

The death god's voice was so grave, so serious, but without any conviction behind it. It sounded like the fight had gone out of him, and that scared me more than anything I'd seen so far.

"Can anything be done?" I asked, fearing the answer. "Can the Sha be stopped? Or even...reasoned with? Bargained with?"

There is no reasoning with chaos, Freyja said. *No mercy to be found in pure violence, and no bargaining with a force that will never compromise. The Sha's power can only be diminished by severing its bond to humanity and the physical realm.*

"How do we do that?"

By killing its physical form, Hades answered. *Just as killing the dog, cat, or falcon we inhabit would sever our bonds with you.*

However, it's not easily done, Freyja cautioned. *As you have seen, we enhance these animal bodies just as we've enhanced human abilities for you.*

"Well, what kind of animal is the Sha? It can still be wounded, right?" My gaze drifted over Hades' flank, knowing he had a scar under that short, dense fur. He'd been in bad shape when I dug that shrapnel out of his thigh way back when I first got caught up with the Steel Demons. If I hadn't been there, the dog might have died. And then would Hades, the god, have been able to guide Reaper and the Steel Demons through all of their trials since then?

That is another concern, Hades answered after a long quiet moment. *The Sha is represented by no true animal that has ever walked the earth. In that sense, it is completely unlike Freyja or me.*

Puzzled, I stared at the stern-faced Doberman. "What do you mean?"

The Sha is a creature not known to humanity, Freyja cut in. *If it is not truly an animal that exists, there is a possibility that it cannot be killed.*

"That's impossible." I rocked backward, still floored by this information despite finding it completely unbelievable. "Everything that's alive can be killed."

Gods cannot be killed, Hades said with a slight huff. *We can, however, fade into obscurity. It is humanity that creates and sustains us, after all.*

We are known to inhabit animal vessels and forge tangible bonds with humans before that happens, Freyja added. *It is often a last resort, such as during the onset of a collapsed society.*

"So if we can't kill the Sha, we have to weaken it," I mused aloud. "And the way to do that is by reducing the belief in Set?"

It is more devotion than simple belief, but yes.

"And how would we do that? Kill his devoted followers?" I couldn't even pretend that I was disturbed to talk so casually about killing people now. Murder was the lowest crime I would commit to get Reaper and Shadow back.

That is one way, Hades remarked just as casually. *Devotion needs to be given freely, willingly, to be a true source of power. The Sha's true followers are not those he forces into battle, but who he keeps closest. Those who believe in his cause with their whole being.*

"The general's council," I blurted out, remembering the transcription from Andrea's first letter. "If the Sha is the one in power, the ones who carry out his orders are the ones closest to him."

All of which are in the fortress in New Ireland, Freyja was quick to point out. *You have seen the extent of our abilities, dear daughter. Horus' sight reaches far, but we cannot get you past the Sha's army undetected.*

"Well maybe we can lure the council out." I stood up from the floor to shake out the numbness settling into my legs. "They still need the rest of us, right? What if we set a trap?"

Hades growled irritably. *I would not advise that.*

Your husbands would never allow it. Freyja was quick to agree.

I stabbed my fingers through my hair with a groan of frustration. "Well it seems I'm the only one coming up with ideas, so if you have anything, I'm all ears."

Silence stretched on for much longer than I was comfortable.

If it is any comfort, we are still bonded to Reaper and Shadow, Hades said. *We can feel the force of the Sha's power threatening to unravel our bond so that it can penetrate their minds and control them. However, it has not yet succeeded. As long as Reaper and Shadow remain bonded to us, there is hope.*

"You can...feel them?" I fell to my knees, eyes locked onto the ancient depths of Hades' gaze. "Are they okay? Can you talk to them?"

They are holding on for now. But no, communication has not been possible. The Sha is not controlling them, but he may have cut off that aspect of our bond.

I closed my eyes, my whole body feeling heavy as my gaze lowered to the floor. "Is there anything...anything at all that we can do?" Wearily, I brought my gaze up to plead with the gods in front of me. "Please. They are bonded to you, bonded to gods! Doesn't that mean anything?"

I'm sorry, Hades said. *We have lost many bonded humans over the millenia, to other gods or even simple human violence. It's always painful on a cosmic level.*

"No." I shook my head and even let out a soft humorless laugh, I was that firmly in denial. "Not you too. You are *gods,* you can't be giving up on them!" My eyes widened as a sudden idea hit my brain with a bright spark. "Can you possess humans like you do animals?"

Hades growled, baring white teeth before he snapped, *No.*

He hesitated long enough in answering that I knew it wasn't as cut-and-dry as that. "Why not?"

We simply don't. It is not done.

"But you *can!*"

Hades barked a warning. His whole body was in warning mode—

ears back, hackles raised, and low growl rumbling from his throat. But it was too late. Now *I* was the dog with a bone.

We will not inhabit you or the others. It is out of the question.

"But why?" I demanded. "If there's no chance of it helping, then fine. But it doesn't sound like that's the answer."

Inhabiting human bodies is incredibly dangerous to those we possess, Freyja explained. *It has not been done for nearly a thousand years. Such an occupation has grave consequences.*

"Like what?"

Like losing your humanity, Hades snapped. *You will turn into an empty, used-up husk like those the Sha has discarded. Is that what you want for you and your men?*

My chest deflated, the initial rush of a new idea gone as quickly as it came. "So that's what the Sha is doing?"

In a sense, Freyja said. *He is not possessing vessels in the exact same way we would. Think of his method as reaching with hundreds of thousands of hands. Each hand grabs someone by the mind and forces submission. That is how he is able to control so many.*

I perked up slightly. "So the way you possess is different? It doesn't have to be harmful?"

It still is. Hades turned his head to direct a growl at Freyja, who arched and hissed in response. *We inhabit animals because their brains are instinctual. They are simpler, and do not object to our occupation.*

"I would not object to you if it meant saving Reaper and Shadow," I insisted. "Neither would the other two. You'd have our full permission."

That does not matter, Hades growled irritably. *Human minds are too complex to house another being for long. It doesn't matter if you knowingly permit us, your brain will unravel itself trying to process that a foreign entity is occupying the same space. We are meant to guide humans, not control them.*

Thousands of years ago, Freyja added softly, *gods would possess human prophets to communicate their commands. They could only do so for short periods of time, and the human would be wrung-out, never the same again after multiple instances of this.*

It was an abusive practice. Hades' tone softened. *Humans are not ours to be used. This is why Reaper is an instrument to me. I've had to force his hand before, yes, but I never have or will possess him to carry out a task myself.*

I slumped back, feeling more defeated now than ever. "So that's it? There's really nothing?"

We are sorry. Freyja bumped her head into my hand but I pulled away, not in any mood for affection from the cat. *We've seen many civilizations rise and fall. We hoped with all our hearts that this one would survive.*

CHAPTER 4

REAPER

The days became a blur of pain, hunger, and debilitating thirst. Not even our tally marks on the dungeon walls were accurate anymore. Shadow and I both drifted in and out of consciousness from our injuries, the exhaustion, and for me, excruciating pain on a level I never knew before.

The tips of my fingers were throbbing and extremely sensitive, bleeding stumps from where my fingernails had been ripped out. I couldn't even pick up a bowl of water to drink without intense pain throughout my whole hands. I had to drink from it on the floor, like a dog.

It hurt to breathe. Hurt to swallow, to blink my eyes. Hurt to stand up or sit down. I took it head-on at first, playing the stoic, unaffected one while Shadow kept our abusers entertained with his cries and yelps. Then they started getting more creative with me, trying new methods to get a reaction. That was when I lost my fingernails and the molars in the back of my lower jaw.

They left my teeth on the floor, just out of my reach, as if to taunt me. And they got a reaction alright, albeit still not as dramatic as Shadow. It wasn't that it didn't hurt. The pain just never stopped.

Even with Shadow taking the brunt of the torture, I was nearing my breaking point. Only that scared me more than the pain. Any more of this, and our captors would have their broken-down shell to do with as they pleased.

"Reaper," Shadow muttered hoarsely from across the cell.

At the sound of something metallic scraping on stone, I cracked one swollen eye open as far as it would go. He was pushing his water bowl toward me with his foot, the container with less than an inch of water in the bottom.

"Drink some more," he urged me.

"No...you need it." I didn't even know if he could understand me through my swollen, aching mouth.

"I'm okay. You're worse off than me, so have it. Even a little bit helps you stay alive."

I couldn't see him well enough to gauge that for myself. He sounded better than me, so he probably hadn't lost teeth yet. I knew they took some of his fingernails too because I had to listen to him screaming about it yesterday.

Or was that earlier today? I didn't know anymore.

My mouth did taste awful though, and the thought of just rinsing it out sounded more luxurious than a feather bed right then.

I inched my hand gingerly toward the bowl, my fingertips already screaming in protest at grazing over the stone floor. Before I could fully turn my body and lean down to take a drink, footsteps approached from outside our cell.

"Again?" Shadow was quick to put on his pathetic, simpering voice. "Already?"

The guards unlocked the door with no comment, and several sets of footsteps quickly crowded our cell. I counted five pairs of boots and one pair of...feet?

I tried to squint but my eyesight was terrible after all the hits I'd taken. Five people definitely wore boots with dark pants tucked into them. The figure in the middle wore some kind of dress or robe. Loose fabric grazed the floor around their legs, and as the group walked toward me, my fucked-up eyes thought I saw a glimpse of *paws*.

"Stand up, both of you," barked one of them. When neither Shadow or I rushed to move, the speaker thumped the butt of a long rifle on the ground. "You will stand before the great general, prisoners. Or you'll lose more than teeth or fingernails." He cocked a round into the chamber and I knew that was our final warning.

I couldn't use my hands to press up, so I painstakingly tried to use the wall. From the rattling of his chains, Shadow was also putting in a massive effort and getting nowhere fast. A new voice spoke, and from the eerie shiver over my spine, it could only be the robed figure in the middle.

"Here, allow me."

The voice was strange. Ancient like Hades' but with an odd cadence that sounded...wrong. Almost like a foreign person speaking English, but that wasn't it either. I didn't dwell on the voice any longer than a fleeting second because all of the pain was suddenly *gone*.

I gasped at the relief. The absence of pain felt so blissful and sweet, I thought for a moment I might have died. I looked at Shadow, I could see him now! We were still chained up in this dungeon and therefore not dead yet. I stared at my hands, turning them over in fascination. My fingernails were intact, and gone were all the lacerations on my palms and fingers. My jaw, head, ribs, everything felt normal.

"Now you may stand," the strange voice commanded.

Shadow and I rose to full height, and my eyes met several looking back at me. Before I could closely inspect the strange person in the middle, the guard to the right slammed his rifle on the floor again.

"You will not gaze upon the great general!" he hissed.

I recognized the guy, even though his head and mouth were covered in black cloth. Only his eyes were visible, brown eyes with dark, bushy eyebrows. I had met those eyes before, shook those hands that now threatened me with a rifle. He was dressed entirely in black rather than a general's uniform, but I never forgot the one man who'd betrayed me and eluded me for so long.

"General Tash," I said, my tone full of contempt. "Or his impostor, rather." Keeping my gaze averted as he instructed, I angled my head toward the strange, cloaked person in the middle. "And the *real* general, I presume."

"Ahahaha..."

The laughter was soft, nothing more than an amused chuckle, but it made every hair on my body stand on end. That was the exact same laugh we all heard, the oppressive force in our heads that tried to break our sanity, and had succeeded in so many others.

Forgetting all decorum, I stared directly at the black hood in front of me. "What are you?"

I *felt*, rather than saw, the thing smile. Like Hades, its power seemed to fill the room like it's own atmosphere.

"I am the Sha. General Tash is simply the moniker I use when necessary. When I must be perceived as...human."

"And I'm supposed to know what the fuck that is?"

Only then did it pull back its hood.

And the face underneath...didn't make sense.

I stared at a long snout, somewhat like a dog's. So that was why it sounded so weird. Black lips pulled back in a smile, revealing canine-like teeth. Its skin was a dark gray with black fur in some areas. Eerily human eyes sat below two pointed, triangular ears that were narrow where they attached to the skull and widened at the top. The creature pulled back its sleeves to reveal long, black claws at the ends of its hands, and those were indeed paws instead of feet that I saw earlier. A tail flicked forward in an almost playful manner, forked in the middle to create two shorter tails at the end.

"I don't..." My eyes drifted all over this thing, trying to make it make sense in my brain, but it just wouldn't. "I don't understand. Are you a god?"

"I am the physical manifestation of Set." The Sha grinned. "I do not make sense to you because I am no true animal that has ever existed. Chaos, by definition, does not make sense."

"Set?" Shadow repeated in a whisper, speaking up for the first time.

"Yes." The creature turned to him. "Has my brother ever told you about me?"

"Brother?" I remarked.

"Horus and Set are brothers, according to the mythology." Shadow looked just as unnerved at the sight of the Sha as I was. "They battled for nearly a century. Horus lost his eye, but he won." Shadow's features hardened as he stared down this thing in front of us. "Because the chaos, the violence you represent, it destroys everything. Even you. Do you realize that? If you win, you will annihilate humanity, the very source of your power."

The Sha turned its eerie gaze to him. It was smaller and not as broad as Shadow, but there was no mistaking the heaviness and concentration of energy that radiated from this animal-person-thing. It made Shadow suck in a breath and press flatter against the wall.

"Do you really think I'm bound by the rules of the tangible universe, human? You believe the laws of physics apply to *me?*" The Sha's lips pulled back in an unnerving smile. "If they did, then I would not be standing here. I am not meant to exist, but I do. Do *you* understand that?"

The Sha turned its snout toward me, pinning me with those creepy eyes. "Your companion gods all have real-animal counterparts and roles compatible with humans. But I," the Sha brought a clawed hand to its chest, "am not the same as your pet gods. Disorder and violence flourish in the *absence* of humanity." The Sha lowered its hands to its side, angling its gaze to Shadow. "So you are incorrect, I will not be destroyed. I will thrive."

"That's...impossible," Shadow whispered.

"Of course it is." The Sha grinned. "I *am* the impossible, in the flesh. Also," the Sha tilted its head in a curious, dog-like gesture. "I can see the attempt at repairs my brother has made on *your* fractured mind, human. It's stapled and knitted together so crudely, it's no wonder your madness escapes in your dreams. But don't worry," the Sha assured him with fake cheer. "Let me in and I'll undo all of that. Your thirst for violence will be set free, no longer caged up like you once were."

Shadow paled, and for the first time since I'd known him, he looked genuinely frightened. Not his normal nervous-because-women-were-around, but actually fucking terrified.

And then it was gone, his face morphing into a cold mask as he stepped away from the wall, pulling on his chains. The restraints stopped him six inches away from the Sha's snout, and Shadow snarled, "Release me now and I'll show you how violent I can be."

"In due time." The Sha appeared unfazed by Shadow's bulk towering over it.

"Why are you torturing us?" I blurted out in a quick demand. "You want us all gone, why not just kill us and get it over with?"

"Because you, the leaders of the resistance against me, will be more useful to me in my army." The Sha leveled its gaze at me and I felt a sensation like a rough jabbing in my brain. "The bonds with your pet gods offer some protection against my methods, but the best minds always take time to break. And it will be *so* satisfying putting you on the front lines against your own people."

I tried to hide the shudder up my spine at that. So this instance of being miraculously healed wasn't likely to last. He would start up the torture again, bring me to the brink of death, heal me, and start the horror show all over again. At least, that's what I would do if I wanted to break someone's spirit.

Even knowing that, my own self-preservation wasn't the only thing on my mind.

This thing seemed to enjoy talking, so I wondered how best to ask about Mari. Did it have her captured and imprisoned somewhere else? Seeing her suffer would be the fastest way to us losing our shit, so I wanted to believe she was still free.

"I *can* still read your thoughts even though I haven't broken you yet, human," the Sha sneered. "We do not have your woman because she is not needed to sever the protective bond of your gods."

"Not needed?" Shadow repeated. "You gave the order for the sky, the underworld, and the thread that ties them together."

The Sha grinned smugly and spread its hands out to the sides. "If I destroy the bond with the sky and the underworld, what is left to tie together?"

Fuck.

Any hope I had left was snuffed out in that moment. We were done for from the moment Shadow and I got captured. And I hated nothing more than the sinking feeling that nothing could be done to stop it. Dad and Gunner could march in with an army of millions and it *still* wouldn't be enough. The Sha would just cast its net even farther and come back with an army twice as big.

"By the way." The Sha turned to address Shadow. "Your performance of extreme pain has been most entertaining but I'm bored of it now." Shadow's face slacked in shock as that creepy stare returned its focus to me. "Guards, you will now concentrate your efforts on Reaper. High pain, low fatality." The Sha turned toward the door with a smug grin. "And make sure Shadow is watching. One more week should be enough."

The Sha's split tail brushed over my feet as it turned to leave while the guards drew knives, brass knuckles, and even a small torch.

"No, don't!" Shadow cried out in a panic from across the room. "Leave him alone and come at me!"

They ignored him and closed in tightly to surround me.

CHAPTER 5

MARIPOSA

I couldn't place what brought me here now. I'd been avoiding it over the last several days, but something pulled me to Shadow's room today. Some desperate impulse to maintain hope maybe, or the simple need to feel my husband nearby.

My walk into the room was slow, deliberate. I looked at the beam in the ceiling, the one he could touch with his fingers and stretch his upper body forward. He looked so hot when he did that, I wanted to run my nails over him every time.

I moved my gaze to the bed, running my hand over the neatly made comforter. We made so much love here, both alone and with Jandro. We talked and laughed about nothing and everything. I wanted to burrow under the sheets and curl up, to feel some illusion of Shadow holding me, always wrapped around me in a protective embrace. If I imagined hard enough, I could feel the light kisses he would leave on my skin.

The bed dipped as I sat on the edge. Maybe Jandro and Gunner and I could sleep here tonight. I didn't know, it just felt so wrong that Shadow wasn't here.

My eyes lifted to his desk, the simple flat surface only holding a lamp, a sketchbook, and a small case of pencils and pens. I followed my feet to stand at the edge of the desk, staring down at the sketchbook's cover. The edges were worn, the cover scuffed slightly, well-loved by his large, beautiful, creative hands. I stared down at the book for what felt like minutes, wrestling with myself.

Don't. He didn't want you to see everything in there. It should be his decision what you get to see.

The dissenting thoughts were weak, powerless as I reached out to touch the cover. I choked back a sob at the feel of the thick, sturdy cardboard. Shadow loved this thing. How often had he held this book, flipped it open, and turned the pages? He touched this sketchbook almost as much as he touched me. His life was documented in here, the good and the bad.

It was heavy as I picked it up, returning to sit on the edge of the bed in a daze. I just held the sketchbook between my hands, felt its weight on my lap for a few moments before flipping open the cover.

Small doodles greeted me on the first page—simple sketches, mostly of subjects in nature like plants, flowers, birds, and reptiles. In the lower right corner, he drew a highly detailed animal skull, a fox or coyote from what I could tell.

Flipping through the pages, I felt a small sense of relief that this was Shadow's 'safe' sketchbook. It was mostly rough tattoo ideas and practice sketches. He must have had a different book for the things he preferred to keep private.

I smiled at one page entirely dedicated to Freyja as a kitten. He sketched her in various poses—sleeping, hunting, and playing. The pencil lines were loose and fluid, no doubt moving fast to keep up with the boundless energy of the kitten.

As I flipped toward the back of the book, I noticed an increase of portrait sketches, rather than symbols and animals. A smiling, upper body portrait of Jandro with a chicken perched on his shoulder made me pause and run my fingers over the pencil lines. He captured everything, from the playful mischief in Jandro's eyes, to the texture of the bird's feathers. *Mi amigo,* Shadow had captioned the portrait in small, blocky letters.

I turned a few more pages, spotting the familiar faces of Reaper, Gunner, and even a few self-portraits. I spent several long minutes looking at those—it was fascinating seeing how Shadow saw himself.

One portrait even seemed to have been traced over, the same mirror image as on the opposite page, the only difference being the absence of scars.

Shadow looked like a different person without scars, still strikingly handsome but in a crisp, refined way that didn't seem to suit him.

I let out a soft gasp, my heart accelerating at the sight of the next spread of portraits.

It was me.

The sleeping faces of Mari, Shadow had titled this page.

These sketches were quick, rough studies, but his pencil lines were much softer, lighter when he drew me. One was a close-up of my face while sleeping on my side—my eyelids, eyebrows, lashes, nose, and mouth, all in exquisite detail. Like he had been lying right next to me, drawing me as I slept.

Another showed my bare back with my hair spilling out over the pillow and the sheet draped low over my hips. He copied my tattoo into the drawing as well, but his focus was on the contours of my body—the lines of my hip and waist, and even the tiny sliver of my face that was visible.

The next drawing showed me sleeping on a man's chest—Jandro's, I realized from the rib tattoos. Jandro's head wasn't in the frame, but his arm wrapped solidly around my back. My mouth was open slightly, cheek resting on his sternum and a hand over his heart.

I couldn't stop bouncing my gaze from each of the drawings, fascinated at all the little details Shadow saw and brought to life on paper. Every time I looked, I saw something new. The freckle on my shoulder, or how he made my lips curve to give me a slight smile in sleep. I felt vulnerable looking at these, realizing how Shadow's eyes truly missed nothing. They were highly intimate, these portraits. And although I was nude in every single one, they were not at all explicit.

That was not the case for the image when I flipped the page however.

My face heated at the sight of myself, laid out and bare from head to toe, with a man's head between my legs—Jandro's again.

Ecstasy was Shadow's chosen title for this piece.

My head was turned to the side, mouth open in a scream and brows pinched with tension. One hand gripped the back of Jandro's head while the other fisted the sheets next to my head. My back arched off the bed in one long, curving line. As I took in all the details, it dawned on me how realistic this portrait was. It was like going through a checklist in my head. *Those are my breasts, yep. My hips, my belly, my legs.* Shadow even drew my appendectomy scar, the one he loved to kiss so much.

There was no altering in this artwork, no ridiculously huge boobs or unrealistic waist-to-hip ratio. You would think a guy's erotic drawing would contain plenty of fantasy in there, but no.

There's nothing for him to alter, some voice whispered to me. *Having you was more than he ever dared dream of.*

Turning the page once more confirmed that, this last portrait pulling a sob from my chest. He drew me from the waist up, dressed in my medic jumpsuit complete with my red cross armbands. My face was serious, determined, with my arms crossed in front of me like I was about to tell some medics to get off their asses.

And he gave me wings.

Large, intricate butterfly wings spread out from behind me, making me look like some kind of ethereal fairy from another world. At the bottom of the page, Shadow wrote, *Mariposa, the love of my life and healer of my soul.*

A tear fell onto the page, then another.

The tears were coming faster and I had to shove the book out of my lap to not further ruin the drawing. I couldn't stop, curling up onto my side as I sobbed loudly. Just when I thought I couldn't cry over my men anymore, my well of sorrow turned out to be bottomless.

Chapter 6

MARIPOSA

I had no memory of drifting off to sleep, except for waking up with sore, puffy eyes and the heavy weight of an arm draped over me.

"Hey baby girl." Gunner curled around me tighter and nuzzled a kiss into my hair.

"Hey." My voice was scratchy and hoarse and I felt unusually warm. It took a moment to realize that was due to a blanket draped over us both.

Gunner was thankfully quiet as he squeezed me protectively, peppering kisses into my hair and on my face. None of my men would offer empty platitudes as comfort and I was grateful for that. They knew how I felt. That I wasn't okay. If anyone could understand my pain, it was them.

"You tired of being sad?" he asked after several long minutes stretched on.

"Yes," I answered automatically. I wanted this heavy, crushing despair to be gone.

"Good. Let's go." Gunner sat up behind me, pushing the blanket back as I looked at him in confusion.

"Go where?"

"The garage." He was off the bed now and grabbed my pant legs to slide me closer to him. Then he scooped under my knees and back to carry me.

"Why the garage?" I didn't resist, but just hung limply against his chest. All of my strength had been cried out.

"Because Jandro's in there."

"Okay?"

Gunner looked down at me with a wry smile as he carried me out of Shadow's bedroom. "He's been with you a little longer than me. He knows what you want when you're sick of being sad."

"And that is? Whoa, Gun!"

He did some crazy maneuver with my body that was too fast for me to follow. I thought I was going to fall for a second when he released one of my legs, but then he grabbed it again while turning me in his arms so that I was facing him. Gunner now held my legs around his waist in a straddle, barely missing a step as he walked us to the garage.

"Gunner, what is it that I supposedly want? Besides, obviously, Reaper and Shadow back."

He nudged the garage door open with his shoulder while placing a long, lingering kiss on my mouth at the same time. For the first time in days, my heart fluttered at the affection. It wasn't much, but that tiny response was the most alive and good I'd felt in all that time.

"Us," Gunner whispered sensually. "For your men to make you feel better."

Behind me, I heard the metallic clang of tools being dropped into a box. "She said it?" Jandro asked.

"Yeah." Gunner kept walking forward until he perched me on the back edge of the bike's seat that Jandro had been working on.

Jandro rolled up from the creeper he'd been lying on, white tank top smudged with black grease. "Alright, I should probably shower first though."

"Nah dude, right now." Gunner wedged his hips between my thighs, his steadying hands on my waist. "You're the only one she hasn't fucked on a bike."

"Guys, wait." I brought my palms up against Gunner's chest. "I actually don't think I'm in the mood right now."

"'Course you're not." Gunner stroked my cheek, his gaze warm and loving. "But you don't want to feel sad anymore, right? At least for a little bit?"

Oh, *now* I saw what he was getting at. Jandro told him about how we had sex right before I left to find Shadow. I had told Jandro I was tired of feeling miserable then, and it was true. A good fucking seemed like the perfect distraction, a release of all the misery I'd been absorbing for weeks before. In my exhausted, heartbroken state, I probably even thought it would make for a nice goodbye.

The sex had been wonderful, but it made leaving so difficult.

I nodded at Gunner, pulling my lip between my teeth. Like back then, I barely felt like myself, being so knotted up with fear and worry. Fuck, I barely felt human, or alive. My men knew that, and this was an attempt to give me a little bit of life back.

"Then will you give us a chance to get you in the mood?" Gunner's fingers trailed to my neck, his eyes remaining fixated on mine. "We'll stop if it's not doing anything for you." His thumb dragged over my dry, cracked lower lip. I must have looked like shit, but he was staring at me and touching me like I was the only thing he wanted. "I just want my baby girl to feel good."

I bobbed my head in a tired nod. "Okay, we can try." That was probably the most un-sexy thing I could say to get things started, but Gunner only smiled warmly as he leaned down to kiss me again.

His tongue probed gently at the seam of my lips and I opened up to him, closing my eyes and returning the sweet presses of his mouth. The light fluttering in my body returned, but it didn't grow stronger as Gunner's hands slid around my waist to stroke my back. Nor as his tongue surged deeply into my mouth and he touched me in all the right ways. He wasn't doing anything wrong, but I couldn't bring myself to feel *into* this.

Our kiss ended and I didn't find myself reaching for another.

"I'm sorry, Gun," I whispered. "I just can't."

Before he could answer, the bike shifted slightly as Jandro climbed on behind me. Warm fingers, slightly damp from just being washed, skimmed over my hips. Jandro's chest came to support my back, his form solid and smelling lightly of motor oil.

"Lean on me," he ordered gently, hands spanning across my hips and lower back. "Let us care for you."

I allowed my head to tip back, finding Jandro's shoulder there to catch me. Gunner took the opportunity to kiss down the column of my throat, and a small gasp escaped me when his teeth closed to take a sharp nibble of my flesh.

I barely had a moment to take another breath when Gunner's mouth returned to mine, his kiss biting and rough. The sting of his teeth in my lip made me squirm against the hot, solid wall of Jandro behind me.

Gunner broke away, his eyes bright and pretty lips smirking. "I think I know what our girl needs."

"Yeah?" Jandro's breath fanned over my ear and neck in a light tickling sensation that was nowhere near enough.

Gunner's hand closed around the front of my throat and my pulse immediately fired up. He felt it thrumming under his firm grip on the sides of my neck and grinned at my resulting ragged breaths.

"She needs it hard. She needs us to fuck her until she's sore and bruised and can't feel anything else that hurts." Gunner adjusted his grip on my neck so he could brush his thumb tenderly over my cheekbone. "Isn't that right, baby girl?"

His filthy words, his bites, and the weight of his hand on my throat made me feel more alive than any of the warm hugs or sweet kisses I'd received in the last few days. My pulse throbbed in my pussy, the need to be taken roughly already making me ache.

"Yes," I whimpered desperately. "Make me feel nothing else but you."

With that, Gunner returned the pressure to both sides of my neck, squeezing just a fraction tighter as he took another rough, bruising kiss from my mouth. A hard, sucking bite on the nape of my neck stole my breath away. Jandro's hands dove under my shirt as his mouth attacked the back of my neck, pawing and groping rudely on his way to my breasts.

The guys got me topless and Jandro's hard pinch of my nipples had me crying out. Already I was so sensitive and it made me crave even more sensation. Gunner got to work on removing my pants and then it was Jandro's hand on my throat, holding me in place while he sucked and gnawed on my earlobe.

"You want me to fill your little ass?" he asked in a harsh growl, his free hand still groping roughly over my breasts. "Want to ride two cocks on this bike, *Mariposita?*"

"Yes! Yes, please!" I was squirming hard against him, both to get away from the intensity of his rough touches and to lean into him for more.

Jandro released the nipple he was plucking, bracing his other forearm between my breasts to hold me still. His grip on my throat wasn't hard, but it was solid and unyielding.

"Open your mouth," he commanded.

I obeyed, sticking my tongue out while my eyes focused on Gunner, just a few feet out of reach and stripping slowly out of his clothes. I wanted his cock in my mouth, the thick bulge calling to me as Gunner rubbed a hand over the front of his jeans.

I got Jandro's fingers instead, tasting clean and lightly soapy as I closed my lips around them.

"Suck," Jandro ordered. "Get them nice and wet for me."

I did so happily, a small amount of my despair already melting away. I knew it was temporary, but it felt so good to be commanded, to be touched and taken with abandon. It was a relief for my mind to be pleasantly blank instead of racing at a mile a minute. The ache in my heart was still there, but right then it was outshined by the ache in my cunt, and the rough, buzzing friction on my skin from all the manhandling.

"Good, stop." Jandro seemed to enjoy giving me orders just as much as I enjoyed obeying. "Put your legs over mine."

He released my throat and we shifted in our rear-facing position on the bike until my thighs splayed open on top of his.

"That's right." Gunner watched us from where he stood, stroking his thickening cock that was now out of his jeans. "Spread that pussy open for me."

Jandro's fist wound in my hair, yanking my head back with a firm pull as the fingers I just sucked on trailed down the cleft of my ass. I let out a small whimper as he started to push inside. It had been a while since I'd had a man back there.

Gunner was on me in a flash, hand gripping my jaw and eyes burning into mine. "I said spread it open for me." His voice was low with warning. "Let me see you play with yourself."

A small part of me wanted to pout and refuse, to tell him to go down on me instead. But this wasn't the headspace for that. I didn't want to make this a game, I just wanted to feel. I needed a distraction from this black hole of hopelessness threatening to swallow me up. My guys were hurting too--they probably needed this control as an outlet just as much as I needed to let go.

I trailed a hand down my body, Gunner's eyes following with rapt attention as I brought my fingertips to my clit. "Like this, love?" I asked in a high, breathy voice as I began to circle and stroke.

Gunner leaned down in reply, drawing a nipple into his mouth with a heavy groan. He bit and sucked at my flesh hard, the sensitive peak feeling like it was being teased by the edge of a knife.

"Don't stop playing with that pussy," Jandro ordered. He was still working his way into my ass, adding liberal amounts of saliva as he patiently stretched me.

Gunner moved on to my other breast to continue the same treatment. My skin was already red from Jandro's manhandling and now my nipple looked bruised from Gunner's mouth.

And yet it was so good and freeing. The pain brought on a rush of adrenaline that fueled a need for *more*. More rough handling of my body, more bites and bruises until I squealed, and please, please, please, a rough fucking.

My clit came alive under my own instinctive touch, amplified by Gunner's treatment of my nipples like they were directly connected. He angled his mouth lower, sucking the sensitive underside of my breast as he forced my knees apart. He gripped the flesh of my inner thighs--hard, commanding, and perfect as his mouth trailed down. I thought he'd want to taste me and slowed my own touch, but he returned a hard pinch to my nipple that made me yelp.

"Don't stop," Gunner ordered. "Your first orgasm's on your own, baby girl. You know why?"

I shook my head, my teeth sinking into my lip.

"'Cause it's for Jandro to feel, once his cock is nice and snug in your ass." Gunner held my jaw again. "And not before then. Got it?"

I whimpered, feeling like I was in over my head. It was bad enough when they denied me, now I had to deny myself? I was already close. If I kept up my current pace, it wouldn't be much longer.

Jandro tugged on my hair wrapped in his fist, the tingling pain in my scalp a sweet reminder of his control.

"Relax," he ordered with that sinful mouth against my ear. He was fucking my ass with his hand in earnest now, the pinching discomfort easing away as he prepped me for his cock. "The sooner you relax and can take me inside, the sooner you can come."

I groaned in wordless frustration. It wasn't enough! I wanted both of them inside me *now*. My breasts were a bit sore, but I craved more pain. Spanks on my ass, more hands on my throat, or--

"Ah!" I yelped, jerking against Jandro as a hand slapped down on my clit. Gunner's hand. It was just hard enough to hurt, to overload my senses for one split second.

"You stopped touching yourself." Gunner's hand returned to my throat and now my body was absolutely buzzing. Despite the pain, or maybe because of it, that slap to my clit brought me even closer to orgasm.

"Bad baby girl." Gunner shook his head, clicking his tongue in disappointment, but his eyes flashed excitedly. "What am I gonna do with you?"

I didn't dare voice any suggestions but mentally I was begging him. *Do it again. Bite me. Choke me. Tie me up. Anything.*

"How about my cock down your throat?"

The moment my lips parted, Gunner guided me down, bending my body forward with his unforgiving grip on my neck. I took him in my mouth eagerly, my hand returning to my clit as if on instinct. Gunner waited for me to get a rhythm going first, dragging my lips and tongue over his hot, solid length, before he took control again.

His hands closed around my throat as he started to thrust his hips. He went slowly at first, then started to fuck my mouth harder. I moaned louder to encourage him and rubbed myself harder, letting his hands hold me up as I took his dick down my throat—gagging and choking and never getting enough.

When I felt a wide cock spreading me apart as it pushed into my ass, it sent my pleasure soaring. I pressed back onto Jandro, pushing away from Gunner with a great gasping breath just as my furiously rubbing hand finally released an orgasm that hit me like a mini-explosion.

"Oh fuck, she's squeezing my dick so hard. Holy fucking shit..."

A rough tug on my hair brought me upright again and sat me all the way down on Jandro's cock.

"Ohhh fuck," we said together. Jandro's forehead pressed to my upper back, squeezing a hand around my arm as he sucked in ragged breaths.

"You okay back there?" As breathless as I was from my throatfucking and my orgasm, there was still a bit of smugness in my voice.

"Almost forgot how fucking delicious your ass is." His forehead lifted away and he got back to business, swatting the right side of my ass hard as he sucked a rough kiss on the back of my shoulder. "Now bounce on this dick and let's see how bad Gunner wants that pussy."

My feet found purchase on the sides of the bike, my legs splayed open and on display for Gunner. I braced my hands on Jandro's thighs as I started to lift up and down. The foreign sensation of him sliding in and out of my ass felt better as I found balance and a rhythm. And even more so as Gunner watched me.

Jandro slapped my ass as I rode him, and I knew each side would be decorated with his handprints before we were done. With each whimper and moan as he filled and stretched me, I hoped it would entice Gunner to come take his fill.

"Please Gunner," I begged when the watching became too much and one cock became too few.

"Please what?" he rasped, his gaze focused hungrily on my pussy.

"Please fuck me. I need you too."

"You need me, baby girl?" He drew closer with an outstretched hand but instead of a throat grab, it was a gentle caress of my cheek. "You really do?"

"Yes!" I gasped, nearly in tears with how badly I needed him. "I need you so fucking bad."

And I realized this was what *he* needed, to hear those exact words from me.

Gunner leaned in, connecting our mouths in a fierce kiss. He held my cheek in a gentle hold, but the way his cock drove through me was anything but.

My head dropped back to scream as the two of them filled me, the sensation intense and overwhelming but exactly what I needed. Jandro resumed holding my throat, crashing up into my ass while Gunner pulled back.

"More...yes..." I begged with breathless pants, eyes squeezed shut as I sank into the best feelings that bordered on too painful.

Gunner splayed my legs open wide, holding the inside of my knees with a punishing grip that I knew would leave finger-sized bruises. He kissed me roughly between his thrusts, biting lips and cutting off my gasps for air with his tongue. With Jandro holding me in place, I could do nothing but take it all and plead for more.

They were merciless in how they fucked me, using me and giving me a purpose after I had felt so useless for days. I was used to some roughness, but their hard grabs, slaps, bites, and punishing thrusts took me to the edge of my limits.

And still they watched me carefully, easing back at my yelps of pain until I begged for more. Jandro's chest was slick with sweat at my back and his sexy groans of effort grew labored as he snapped his hips up against my ass. Gunner took some of my weight off of him, the long muscles in his arms flexed and tight as he held my legs. Sweat was beginning to bead on Gunner's skin too, one running down the ridges of his abs as he fucked me.

"Is that all you boys got?" I taunted when Jandro's hand began to slip from my throat.

Jandro growled in reply, squeezing tighter than before as he began to fuck my ass wildly. Gunner closed my legs, bringing them against his chest, and that dialed up the intensity to the point where my screams filled the small garage. To turn it up even more, Gunner hugged around my legs with one arm and slapped the backs of my thighs as he fucked me.

Jandro's palm crashed against my sore, stinging ass. His other hand on my throat had me seeing bright dots. The culmination of it all, the constant strikes against sensitive flesh while they both fucked and filled me was almost overwhelming. The crazy thing was, I couldn't tell anymore if it was too good or if it actually hurt too much.

I opened my mouth and my hand flailed, trying to signal for some reprieve, when one of them grabbed my hand and placed a soft kiss on my palm. That small touch of sweetness was the final piece that sent me crashing.

I came hard, seizing and clenching around both of them to the point of making their thrusts stutter, and then wringing their releases from them forcefully.

"Oh God, oh...fuck..." Jandro's arms wrapped around my middle, his forehead against my back as he shuddered and pulsed through his orgasm.

Gunner could barely stand, his hands ending up on Jandro's knees splayed on either side of the bike seat. His forehead rested on mine, strands of golden hair mixing with my dark strands.

"Baby girl," he huffed, face flushed as his eyes searched my face. "Did we hurt you?"

I took a moment to answer. I felt *everything* now that it was over. The stretch and ache in my skin and limbs rose to the surface now that the adrenaline was ebbing away.

"Yes, but," I touched a finger to his lips when his brows knitted, "it's okay. I wanted to hurt and I feel...okay now. Not good, but better."

"Hot bath," Jandro grunted against the back of my shoulder. "You're gonna be sore for a while."

"Shit, I think *we're* gonna be sore." Gunner pulled me off the bike and folded me up carefully in his arms. "You just about killed us."

"But it was good," Jandro added, sliding gingerly off the bike. "I think we all needed that."

I couldn't agree more. It didn't fix anything but the release of tension, of frustration and helplessness, made me feel lighter. After a bath to soothe my aches and pains and a few decent hours of sleep, maybe then I could think of a way to get Reaper and Shadow back.

CHAPTER 7

SHADOW

Watching Reaper get tortured was infinitely worse than receiving it myself. Like with the men who shared my cage with me growing up, I was powerless to do anything to save him.

Only this time, I had to watch it all happen to my president and friend. No amount of pulling on my chains and yelling at them did any good. Every time they left him in a limp, bloody heap, I fought like hell to escape my own bonds to help him. But not even I could loosen the chains that were bolted to the ground. With the lack of food and water, every day left me weaker.

And every day, Reaper's breathing got quieter. He moved less after every beating, and I was getting increasingly worried whenever several seconds would pass without him taking a breath.

A few times, the Sha had returned and miraculously healed him, only to have the torture start all over again. Even those days were becoming few and far between. I was afraid to fall asleep in case Reaper stopped breathing altogether.

"Reaper."

I talked to him as much as I could, just to let him know that I was still there. That we still had a life outside of this dungeon worth going back to. When I was alone in my own dungeon, I would have killed for someone to talk to other than my mother. Even when I knew they'd be going to their death, I yearned for the men who'd be thrown into my cell with me. They weren't always friendly, but they didn't hate me and they told me about an outside world that sounded wondrous and imaginary.

"Reaper." I repeated his name until I got a pained groan in reply. Metal scraped on stone as I pushed my water bowl toward him with my boot. The water was dirty and only half an inch deep, but if it would extend his life another minute, I would make sure he drank it. "There's water about a foot away from your left hand. Drink it."

A wheezing, rattling breath answered me and my skin crawled with the sound. It sounded like he had fluid in his lungs. He had a bad cough two days ago. Now it seemed he didn't even have the strength to cough.

"Drink the water, Reaper," I insisted. "I need you to hold on. Our whole family does."

His bloody fingers twitched on the floor at his side but he didn't move for the bowl. I swallowed, my own throat as dry as a bone, but Reaper needed that water more than me. His hand looked wrong too— swollen, bruised, and probably broken in several places. The guard had taken turns stomping on it this morning.

"Hey," I called when the cell got too quiet. "You with me?"

"...Yeah..."

It was little more than a huff of breath, more weak and defeated than any sound I'd heard from him before. Fuck, he would surely die without medical treatment soon. How far was the Sha willing to go to break into his mind? Had that not already been accomplished yet? I wanted to ask Reaper these questions, but more importantly, I didn't want to waste what little remained of his strength by making him talk.

The Sha had tried to pry into my head a few times since being here, but whatever protection our companion gods had over us didn't allow the Sha inside. It felt like an outsider was pounding on my door every day but never making it inside my house. I could only hope the case was the same for Reaper.

I had a sense the Sha was growing frustrated at being unable to mentally break us. But even if he didn't succeed, he could kill us even easier. Able bodies were apparently disposable and easy to replace. That was all humanity was to this thing—a means to an end.

Our cell door opened with a series of metallic clanks and a guard walked in, carefully holding a metal bowl with both hands. I was guarded, alert and tense as I watched him approach Reaper, who was painstakingly trying to move away, but there was little movement anymore that didn't hurt him.

"Look at this," the guard said with a smile I did not like at all. "A full bowl of fresh water. Just for you, puppy."

A smell hit me that I couldn't place. Something sharp and bitter that definitely was not water. Reaper's cracked, bloody lips parted with a soft pant. He knew better than to trust our captors, but he was also badly dehydrated. His brain heard *fresh water* and now he wouldn't be able to think of anything else.

The guard stood in front of him, waving the bowl from side to side in front of Reaper's face. Of course Reaper couldn't smell it when his nose was broken in several places.

"Reaper, don't drink that," I warned. "It's not water. It doesn't smell right."

The guard clicked his tongue at me. "Sounds like your buddy just wants it for himself. Can you imagine how good a drink of clean, filtered water will taste?"

"Don't listen to him," I said. "He's messing with you. Reaper, please don't drink it."

But Reaper's instinct to survive was stronger than anything else. He leaned his head forward, dried tongue out to taste. When his mouth touched the liquid inside, he jerked back with a hiss at the pain. The guard's raucous laughter echoed off the brick walls as he threw the bowl's contents onto Reaper's face.

I had to look away as Reaper shook and screamed, his throat already so raw that it was a whispery, aching sound. He reached up instinctively to wipe his face, but the stuff only transferred to the open wounds on his fingers.

The recognition of that smell hit me too late—distilled vinegar. It looked exactly like water if you couldn't smell it, and it burned every open wound that it touched.

The guard walked out, chuckling amusedly to himself at his little prank. He didn't have his mask or hood on for this visit, so I focused my gaze on memorizing his features as he locked the door. If we escaped, he was mine.

I also noticed that this particular guard didn't appear to be under the Sha's mind control. His eyes were bright with plenty of life there. He wore his expressions clearly, from the conniving smirk when he first walked in, to the peals of laughter from throwing vinegar on Reaper's face. So the Sha didn't place everyone under its control, but why?

Maybe they joined its cause willingly, I thought with disgust.

I took a mental tally of the guards the Sha always surrounded itself with. One was the vinegar-thrower, and I recalled a few more that didn't have that blank, zombie look in their eyes. It was hard to be sure with their faces almost completely covered, but it made sense for something like the Sha to have a few dedicated followers with no need to break into their minds. Not to a normal person maybe, but the leaders of my cult did it without mind control at all.

The Sha was infinitely more powerful. People would align themselves with that thing out of self-preservation, to end up on what clearly looked like the winning side. The Sha probably didn't even need to offer salvation, riches, or whatever cult leaders promised. All he had to do was not turn them into zombies.

Reaper quieted after several minutes, and I pulled as far away from the wall as I could to get closer to him. "Hey, Reap. Are you okay?"

His head was bent low, chin nearly touching his chest. Blood dripped from his lips, which meant he must have bit the inside of his cheek again.

"Reaper, please say something."

He didn't answer with words, but with a slow, barely noticeable shake of his head from side to side.

"Okay, I know. I shouldn't have asked if you were okay. I know you're not." My teeth ground in my jaw at the sheer unfairness of it. Saying sorry or wishing I could help him did nothing of use. Neither did the pep talks, but at least maybe those turned his mind to something besides the pain.

"We're going to wipe this plague off the earth," I said. "We're going to get out. Mari's going to fix you up and when you're good as new, there'll be hell to pay."

Reaper rolled his head up slowly, like it took every ounce of his strength to do so. He turned his head toward me, both eyes bruised, swollen, and unseeing.

"It's going to feel so good," I went on. "We'll kill the Sha. Kill everyone who followed him willingly and allowed him to get this powerful. Then we can just live. Go on rides every day, spend time with our wife, our family. We just have to get through this."

Reaper's lips moved in a shaky whisper and I leaned into the chain around my neck to get closer.

"What did you say?"

He repeated it and I had to hold my breath to hear his weak, whispery voice.

"...I'm...not gonna...make it..."

"Yes, you are." Desperation bled into my voice. "You have to, and you will."

"...Sorry...Shadow..." His head lolled to the side before he brought it upright again, an enormous task for a man so beaten down. "...Love...Mari..."

"Stop. You're the fucking Steel Demons MC president. You're the instrument of the God of Death. Your work is not done, Reaper. You *need* to live." He stopped talking and moving, which made my panic spike. "Reaper? *Reaper.*"

I held my breath again and listened hard for his. Finally, there it was. The weak, sick sound told me he was still clinging to life. Exhausted, and not nearly relieved enough, I leaned against my wall and allowed my eyes to shut. I needed sleep, but my desperation to make sure that Reaper was alive kept jolting me awake whenever I drifted off.

I didn't tell him the real reason I couldn't lose him in this place, but it rattled through my mind right then.

If you don't make it, then I won't either. Because I can't live as a man who sat here and allowed you to die.

I jolted awake to the sound of Reaper's pained groans, my eyes snapping open to see one of the guards kneeling in front of him.

"Get away from him!" I jumped up, pulling on my chains as far as they would allow me in hopes of scaring this person off.

The black-clad figure gave me an impassive look over their shoulder that stopped me in my tracks. *That's a woman,* I realized at the sight of blue eyes and long, dark eyelashes. The mask on her lower face covered a delicate nose bridge. Her stature and overall features were smaller than the other guards, and yet I remembered her from the Sha's personal guard detail. She'd stood in the back, shorter than everyone else. But I was too distracted by the otherworldly creature talking to Reaper and I to pay her much attention.

In any case, woman or not, she was here to enact her personal brand of torture on Reaper.

"Stop touching him!" I yelled again when she ignored me the first time. "You want to fuck with someone, fuck with me."

Her next glance at me was narrow-eyed and annoyed. "You don't have to take my help, but I'm your best shot at living if you do."

"Help?" I couldn't have heard her correctly. I was hallucinating.

The woman returned to her task, which I realized was washing Reaper's face. His sounds of pain were quiet, more discomfort than anything else. A bloodied rag was discarded on the floor next to her, while she dipped a clean rag in a bowl of actual water and wrung it out before wiping it over Reaper's face and neck.

Her passes over his skin were light, intentionally being careful of his injuries. I found myself feeling envious as I watched her tend to him. Fuck, water over my skin would feel so fucking good.

"Who are you?" I asked, settling back against my wall. "Why are you helping us?"

"He has a fever," she said by way of answer, placing the back of her palm against Reaper's forehead. "A lot of his wounds are already infected. I made him swallow Tylenol before you woke up, but it might not do much. I'll do what I can to bring water and better food, but it may not be for another day."

"You're not under the Sha's control." If she was ignoring me, two could play at that game. "You have your own mind and are on the Sha's personal guard, but you're working against him. Why?"

The woman collected her rags and now-empty water bowl, then headed for the door. She adjusted her hood as she unlocked the door, and I thought I caught a glimpse of dark brown hair. "If I tell you now, the Sha may be able to extract the information from your mind and compromise both of us." The woman let herself out and paused on the other side of the door. "But you'll know when the time is right."

She turned to leave and, with my keen sight in the darkness, I caught something with a bright and glossy pattern hidden under her hood.

A pattern that looked like snake scales.

CHAPTER 8

MARIPOSA

The hospital was where I always used to go to get my mind off things. Being busy used to help me cope.

Now, seeing Robert Anderson and some of the others who recovered from the mind control, only reminded me that my husbands were now captured by the source of that abuse. I could barely function at home, I couldn't focus at work. I was just a mess.

I had ridden out alone into the unknown for one man once. Every cell in my body wanted to go out and find my two, but Jandro and Gunner stopped me every time I attempted. They stuck to me like velcro, making sure I didn't run out and do anything stupid.

Jandro was in the day room across the hall now, spending time with patients as they recovered, but I knew he was also there to keep an eye on me. I couldn't get a single moment alone and hated how stagnant everything felt. The army was planning, strategizing supposedly, but *nothing* was being done. And every time I had enough and got off my ass, someone made sure to stop me.

I had screamed and cried and hit so many pillows over the lack of action to get my men back. I was exhausted, and nothing would release the rage at what had taken them from me.

Medics and patients alike barely talked to me anymore, so I was surprised to hear the door to the break room open. The Pop-Tart in my mouth tasted like cardboard as I turned in my seat to see my dad standing in front of the door.

He was looking better. His eye was healing and the staples in his head wound had been removed. Still, my chest cracked at the sight of him. He'd been one of Tash's victims and couldn't remember me or the second language he was fluent in.

"*Buenos dias*," I said absently to him before turning back around. Technically, he wasn't allowed in this room, but fuck if I cared about hospital protocol anymore.

He was silent for several long seconds before I heard a soft, "Morning, *mijita*."

I froze, my pulse shooting up to pound furiously as I processed those words. When I turned around again, it was with the heartbreaking fear that I had misheard him. "What did you say?" I whispered.

My dad's lips trembled and his dark eyes were filled with unspent tears. "I said good morning to my daughter."

I stood shakily from my chair, unable to believe what I heard as I gripped the armrest until my hand ached. "You...you..."

"Yes!" My dad rushed forward with his arms out. "I remember you, Mariposa."

Emotion burst so hard from my chest, I was barely aware of what my body was doing until we crushed each other into the hug I'd spent years yearning for.

I thought I couldn't cry anymore, but his thin hospital shirt was soaked through after moments of being pressed to his chest. He felt thinner and more frail than I remembered, but this hug was exactly the same as all the other ones we shared before. When he'd come home after weeks of fighting, Mom and I would cling to him like we'd never see him again. Then he'd leave again and we held onto him like we'd never let him go.

"Oh my daughter, I'm so sorry." He kissed my hair and rubbed my back. "I should have recognized you the moment I saw you."

"No, it wasn't your fault." I sniffed against his shoulder. "None of it was your fault."

"It all came back to me today," he explained, just as sniffly as I was. "It felt just out of reach for the last several days, but it all finally came back to me. I remember *everything*."

"What's better, *reposado* or *añejo*?" I asked in a shaky whisper near his ear, hardly able to believe it. If he could tell me his favorite type of tequila, I knew it was true.

A peal of laughter burst out of him. "Always *añejo*, you silly girl."

Our bone-crushing, tear-filled hug stretched on, neither of us prepared to let go. The only sounds we made were laughs and sobs. When I finally felt a bit lighter, my hold on him loosened and my dad pulled back to hold my face in his hands.

"Look at you." He beamed, eyes bouncing all over my face. "My beautiful daughter. Are you a nurse now?"

"No, that's still not allowed," I laughed, wiping my nose. "Just a medic."

"*Just* a medic," he repeated with a scoff. "I've seen you running around and working your ass off. I'm so proud of you, *mijita*."

"Oh, Dad..." I reached for his face. He was still the same but had changed so much. A weariness had settled into his eyes, I couldn't begin to fathom what being under the Sha's control had done to him.

"Mom." I remembered suddenly, my pulse shooting up. "Did she ever find you? Has she been in touch with you at all?"

Dad frowned, his brow wrinkling. "I...I don't know, *mijita*. That part of my memory still isn't all the way there. I remember seeing her face, I'm just not sure *when*. If it was the last time I left home or..."

"It's okay." I smiled at him through the tightness in my chest. "Do you want to sit down? Maybe have some breakfast? I could have Jandro bring us something."

"Ah yes, Jandro." Dad smiled teasingly at me. "He's certainly been helpful. How long have you two been a thing?"

I put a finger on my chin as I thought back to the beginning. "Seven or eight months, I think." It felt like I'd known all of my men for years already. Our time spent together might not have been long, but circumstances had forged our bonds deep.

"He seems like a good guy, but what's with that vest he wears?" Dad headed for the small break room table to sit down. "He's not part of an actual gang, is he?"

"Well, kind of." I followed him to the table, my feelings somewhere between nervous and amused. "But that's not the most shocking part about our relationship."

My dad's eyes narrowed, lips pressing together into a frown. "What do you mean?"

"I'm with him and three other men." I swallowed and stifled a laugh at my father's wide-eyed, scandalized expression. "We all consider ourselves married. I have four husbands, Dad."

"What?!"

I spent the next hour explaining the nature of my relationships and answering his many probing questions. Time slipped away and it was just like catching up with him on his weekends home on leave. Only this time, he'd never have to step foot on a battlefield again.

"And General Bray, the leader of the Four Corners Army, is Reaper's father," I explained. "I think you would like him. He and his wife are really sweet."

"So they get one amazing daughter-in-law, and I get four *very* different son-in-laws," Dad laughed. "Who's really getting the better deal here?"

A soft knock on the break room door interrupted us, Gunner sticking his head in moments after. "Hey, Dr. Brooks is looking for you, baby—oh! Hello." His blue eyes widened and he backed out toward the lobby. "I'm sorry, I didn't mean to interrupt."

"No, Gun! Come in." I waved an arm, ushering him inside. "Come meet my dad. I just finished telling him all about you guys."

Gunner's eyes bounced back and forth between my father and I as he slowly re-entered the room. "*All* about us?"

"The important parts, anyway." Dad smirked as he rose from the table, sticking his hand out toward Gunner. "I'm Javier."

"It's a pleasure, sir." My husband grinned broadly as he shook my father's hand. "Gunner." He looked at me next, warmth shining in his eyes. "I bet you're happy his memory's back."

"You have no idea." Tears welled up in my eyes as Gunner pulled me into a hug, dropping a kiss in my hair. This was the good news I needed that I never imagined I'd receive.

"You deserve this, baby girl," Gunner whispered, as if he knew what I'd been thinking. "This and so much more."

"I've heard only good things about you so far," my dad remarked, inspecting Gunner with that critical dad-eye.

"Let's try to keep it that way," Gunner joked, squeezing an arm around my shoulders.

Dad looked back at me. "So when can I meet the rest of your... husbands?" He tried out the plural form of the word like it was foreign to him.

My smile dropped. "That's the thing. Two of them have been captured by the Sha. Gunner and Jandro are the only ones here with me now."

"You met Reaper," Gunner told him. "Shadow, I don't think you've met yet."

"Oh no, you did!" The memory came to me suddenly. "Shadow was the one who carried you out of the field hospital when we evacuated everyone."

My dad's eyes widened. "You're married to *that* guy? Jesus, *mijita*, you're gonna kill me."

"He wouldn't hurt a fly. You'll see when you meet him properly." *When, not if.*

Dad squeezed my shoulder, noticing my downturned face. "If these guys are as great as you say, they'll find their way back to you."

I leaned into him, silently grateful for his support. That was my dad. It didn't matter if I had four husbands or made questionable choices in high school. He had my back no matter what.

"Thanks, potato."

The ache around my heart eased a little more when he snorted with laughter and hugged me tighter. The Spanish word for potato was *papa*, so calling him that had been a longtime inside joke. His reaction proved that he remembered it too.

"Don't think I'll be a useful soldier anymore, but let me know if there's anything I can do to help."

"There might be, actually." Gunner stroked his chin thoughtfully.

"Do you remember anything inside of the New Ireland fortress? A general layout or where certain things were located?"

Dad squinted and started rubbing his forehead. "Maybe? I dunno, I can kind of remember flashes of things. Every time I try, I get a hell of a headache."

"Get some more rest," I said. "I'll take you back to your room. The rest of your memory probably still needs time to return."

"Or I'm just old," Dad chuckled.

"That too." I took hold of his elbow. "Come on, *viejito*."

"Some things don't change," he sighed with a parting smile to Gunner.

"It was good to meet you," Gunner offered politely. "I'm glad you're on the mend, sir."

"I'll be right back to see what Dr. Brooks needed," I said, leading my dad out of the break room.

"I'll let him know what's keeping you." Gunner planted a quick kiss on my head before skipping backwards with a bright grin. "He'll be overjoyed to hear the news, I'm sure."

"Nice *gringo* you got there," Dad said when Gunner was out of earshot.

"They're all nice." I nudged him with my arm. "In their own ways."

"Four of them, huh? You really need that many?"

My laugh filled up the corridor as we walked and, damn, it felt so good to *really* laugh. "I didn't *need* that many, it just kind of happened that way."

"I trust you, *mijita*. You've always been smart. I just, fuck." He shook his head. "I never thought I'd wake up one day and see you again, all grown up and married."

"Someone's looking out for us." I squeezed his arm, steering him gently when I noticed his balance wasn't completely stable. I'd have to see about getting him a cane, if his pride would allow him to use it.

"Yeah, the snake is."

"What?"

"Huh?"

"What do you mean, Dad?" I stopped walking, peering at his face curiously. "The snake is looking out for us? What snake?"

"Oh, I don't know." His face had been relaxed, if even dreamlike, but right then, he was frowning. "I'm not sure why I said that." His expression turned sheepish. "Ignore me. I'm just a silly old potato."

Something inside me was going off like alarm bells. This was important. Gods inside animals had brought us too far for me to just ignore what he said. But my dad's already-limited strength was waning for the day, and he gripped the railing next to us.

"Let's get you to bed," I said, gently urging him forward. "I'll bring you something for your headache. Are you hungry?"

"No. No, *mijita*. Thank you."

The hospital was still overcrowded and understaffed, so his bed was wedged in a room where three other patients slept. "When you're discharged, you're coming to live with us," I announced, deciding right then.

"Mari," Dad sighed. "No, I couldn't—"

"You will," I insisted. "We have plenty of room, and you're family. Plus, when we find Mom..." I paused, focusing for a moment on that instinct inside of me that *knew* my parents were alive this whole time. Both of them.

"When all this is over, and we find Mom," I repeated, fighting to keep my voice steady. "They're building lots of houses here. You two can live with us until you have your own place."

My dad smiled tiredly as he settled into bed. "Sounds real nice, *mija*." His eyelids fell slowly, the exhaustion taking over him. "My beautiful daughter, it's so good to see you again."

"You too, Dad." I squeezed his hand. "I'll be here when you wake up."

I watched him as he slept for several minutes, battling the urge to shake him awake. What if he didn't remember me again when he woke up? Time slipped away as I just watched my dad breathe.

When a warm hand dropped to my shoulder, I looked up to see Jandro beaming down at me. "Gunner told me," he said in a hushed voice. "I couldn't be happier for you, *Mariposita*."

I stood up, allowing myself to be wrapped up in a hug by him.

"He's back," I whispered into his chest in disbelief. "I really have him back."

"You do," Jandro affirmed with a loving squeeze around me. He brought his palms to my cheeks and touched his forehead to mine. "And you'll get the rest of them back."

For the first time since Reaper and Shadow were taken, I felt the tiny spark of hope that he was right.

CHAPTER 9

REAPER

Pain was my constant companion. It woke me up, it knocked me out. It fed me and drained me. The only time it wasn't with me was when I was unconscious. Every time I got used to one kind of pain sensation, the Sha's guards would switch it up and do something new to shock my system.

The Sha never entered my mind, and from what I could tell through my pain haze, he never entered Shadow's either. Shadow was always with me too, I guess. Although I was never constantly aware of him like I was with the effects of the torture in my body.

"Drink more water," he told me. "It's safe. She brought a whole bowl for you."

I was pretty gun-shy about sticking my face in a bowl full of clear liquid after the distilled vinegar incident. Shadow insisted there was a woman among the Sha's guard who was working against him and helping us. I never saw her, I figured he had to be hallucinating. But then why would he still be in the dungeon with me if his mind was breaking down?

Maybe I was still sane, but I couldn't make sense of anything anymore. I still remembered Mari, my club, my home, everything I was fighting for. Mentally, I held onto it all for a while, but it was starting to slip from my grasp at this point. I didn't know if they'd been captured or killed by the Sha's forces or someone else.

The only thing I knew for sure was that I'd be a changed person if I ever made it out of here. Maybe I'd be a better person, or maybe a shell of the man I once was. But day after day of torture loosened my grip. Not on my sanity necessarily, but the willingness to endure. My wife's face, the happiness I once knew, was fading into a distant memory, and all I knew anymore was burning, stabbing, aching, blinding pain.

"Reaper." Shadow was starting to sound far away too. "Tell me one word. Just let me know you're there."

"...hurts..."

"I know. Can you do me a favor and drink some water? It will help you heal a little bit."

I would have laughed if I had the energy. What did he know? He couldn't feel any of it. They didn't even bother with him anymore.

"...Mah...ri..." It felt like I hadn't said her name in so long. My broken, swollen, bleeding mouth could barely form the syllables.

"She'll find a way to come for us." Shadow used to sound so optimistic, so gung-ho. Now even he didn't seem convinced by his own words. "You should go to Gunner's hot spring with her when we're back. It's a beautiful, secluded little place. It'll be perfect for you two to reconnect."

That did make me laugh, which quickly turned into a wracking, wet cough that felt like knives dragging along the inside my lungs. I probably had pneumonia. And, fuck, probably cancer from all my damn smoking. Just as well.

"Be quiet!" A guard smacked his rifle on our cell door.

"He really needs a doctor," Shadow answered.

"You think I give a fuck what *he* needs?"

"...don't..." I tried to warn Shadow, but the guard had already decided. I heard a metal clang as he began to unlock the door.

"The Sha wants him alive, right? He won't be for much longer, he's in bad fucking shape." Sweet, innocent Shadow, still thinking reason applied to these people. Still thinking he could save me, that we'd reunite happily with our family if we just kept the hope alive.

"The Sha can bring him back if he dies."

Boots scuffled across the stone floor toward me, then one snapped up to kick me in the face. The slap of cold, filthy stone hit my temple as I slumped over.

"Stop! Come hit me, you fucking coward!"

As usual, Shadow's pleas went ignored as the guard whistled for more to join him. The blows pelted down, my body already too beaten-down and exhausted to react anymore. Sliding into unconsciousness felt different this time.

I might not make it back, was my last realization before it took me under.

THE STRANGEST SENSATION WOKE ME UP. I COULDN'T PLACE it as I squinted against the bright sunlight. The feeling was so jarring, it didn't occur to me until a moment later how strange it was to see *sunlight.*

I touched my abdomen, face, and arms frantically in disbelief. I could *move.* The endless blue sky above me nearly brought me to tears as I figured out what this feeling was.

I wasn't in pain anymore.

Which meant I had to be dead.

I rolled up to sit, my surroundings even more shocking than the lack of pain in my body. I was home, in the community where I grew up. My old neighbors' RVs and cabins surrounded me on either side, with the steep canyon walls of Yavapai Point in the distance.

Taking a glance behind me, I saw *my* house exactly as I had left it. Everything looked pristine, not like an abandoned ruin like when I brought Mari here to tell her about how I grew up. It felt like I could walk around the back to find Carter lifting weights, or Nolan tilling the soil to grow vegetables. Or even Daren.

I scrambled to my feet, suddenly eager to reunite with the family I'd lost.

"They're not here, Reaper."

I whipped around at the sound of a voice I knew all too well, to see a man I didn't recognize standing where there had been no one before.

"Hades," I said.

"Correct."

The God of the Underworld looked like...a normal guy. If I passed him in a crowd, I probably wouldn't look twice. He had brown hair and eyes with a clean-shaven, unremarkable face. He walked toward me at an unhurried pace, like he expected to find me here.

"Why isn't my family here?" My eyes bounced around all of the surrounding structures. "Why is *no one* here?"

"Because you're not dead." He shoved his hands in his pants pockets, an oddly human gesture for someone who spent so much time as a dog. "Not yet, anyway."

"So why am I seeing you?"

"You're on death's doorstep, as the saying goes." Hades said it easily, even lightheartedly, like we were two strangers chit-chatting in line for food. "You're in a coma. And if you don't receive medical attention soon, you *will* die."

"Let me guess." I crossed my arms over my chest. "Mari and the guys aren't anywhere near close to breaking us out, are they?"

Hades didn't say anything, which was enough of an answer for me.

"So how long do I have here?"

"That depends." The god removed his hands from his pockets to clasp them behind his back. "You can enter your childhood home now." He nodded at the cabin behind me. "And you will no longer be on the doorstep of death, but in its realm completely. Your mortal soul will leave your body, and there is no coming back."

"And if I don't?"

Hades looked at me gravely. "Then you have until the damage to your body becomes too extensive to repair."

"So probably not long," I concluded.

Hades shrugged. "You have surprised me before. I wouldn't rule it out again."

I looked back at my front door, the flood of memories pouring in more clearly than ever. Mom got so mad when my siblings and I ran in and out of the house and left the door open when it was hot. I tried to sneak girls into my bedroom a couple times, but that damn door always had a loud creak in a certain spot.

"Will I see them again?" I asked Hades, still staring at the door.

"You may," he said as a non-answer.

I looked back at him. "Care to elaborate?"

"The underworld is not a *place*, Reaper. It is a state of being." He walked up to stand next to me, his gaze on the door. "I can assure you rest and peace in your next phase of existence. But whether you see your past loved ones again, or if you even remember them?" He turned to face the canyon behind us. "That I have no control over."

"Wait...what?" I followed after him as he began his leisurely walk toward the horizon. "What do you mean by that?"

"You may pass by your father Nolan one day," Hades said, tilting his face up toward the sky. "But you may be a seed carried by the wind, while he may be a spine on a cactus. Now, does a seed know it's a seed?" He looked at me over his shoulder, his expression amused. "And does a cactus know it's a cactus?"

"What the fuck?" I raked my fingers back through my hair. "Are you telling me that all that hippie bullshit about becoming trees and shit is real? Ugh." I scrubbed my hands down over my face. "Fuck it. I don't wanna die after all."

Hades returned his gaze to the horizon. "What you want doesn't matter."

"Right, it's all inevitable. The circle of life or whatever. Everything happens when it's supposed to. Just let me come to terms with the disappointment that there's no hell for me to throw beers back with my fathers."

"I used to think everything happened as it was meant to," Hades scoffed. "I believed that for millenia. It's different when you're a god coming to terms with your own demise."

"Oh, you're gonna die too? Perfect."

"Everything will. Even the Sha." Hades started to look wistful. "Ideas and concepts don't exist if there's no one left capable of thinking them."

"Well, that's not comforting at all." I gave him a hard look. "What'll happen to my family?"

"If the Sha is not stopped soon, all of humanity will perish in the violence it brings. You, the ones we've bonded, were our last stand against the chaos coming for us all."

My mouth went dry at his declaration. "And we're losing."

"It appears that way." Hades' tone was even, although it carried more than a hint of sadness. Maybe even regret. "We may have acted too late. A generation ago, maybe our odds would have been better. I watched over your father Finn, and almost chose him as my instrument at one point." He gave a small shake of his head. "But there's no use in wondering what could have been."

"The Sha believes it won't die when it wipes humanity off the earth. At least, that's what it told us."

"Naturally." Hades didn't sound surprised. "The Sha believes anything that favors itself."

"Hades." I gritted my teeth. This place suddenly felt wrong. If I couldn't just die to be with my fathers and brother, then what was the point? "Can you wake me up?"

"No." He angled his head toward the cabin behind me. "If you choose to cross the threshold, I'll handle it from there. But I cannot force any being toward life or death."

"They need me. I need to...fuck, I can't just *wait* here."

"I believe this is similar to what the Christians call purgatory." Hades stroked his clean-shaven jaw. "Only instead of being cleansed for heaven, you're caught between life and death."

"And you really can't do anything to move the needle in either direction?"

"No," Hades repeated. "It's not my place to interfere."

"Right," I scoffed. "That's what you use me for."

"You've been grasping for control your whole adult life," the god mused. "Now, that control is completely out of your hands. What better time to reflect? To think about how you would go through life differently if you return. Or, should you choose to move on, the impact you had with this life."

"No control, huh?" I felt claustrophobic, despite being out in the open. An itch crawled up my skin, some instinct pulling at me.

I looked back toward the cabin, at the door that would send me to the underworld. Immediately the itch stopped, replaced by a soothing, peaceful feeling. *I have to go,* I thought.

"Reaper." Hades' voice was hard, carrying a note of warning as I turned to face the house. "Do not go through that door unless you are absolutely sure it's what you want."

"I don't know. I just…" One foot stepped closer, then the other. "I don't like it here. It doesn't feel right, and that's my home."

"If you go, there is no coming back. Do you understand?" Hades stepped closer to me. "You may not see Mariposa again for a very long time."

"Fuck, Mari." The urge to walk through that door felt magnetic now, and resisting only made it worse. "What's happening, Hades? Why is it pulling me?"

His brow furrowed the tiniest amount, the only change in his otherwise calm, neutral face. "Your body must be failing. You're getting even closer to death."

"Shit." I slapped a hand to my chest, feeling like there was a fist inside my chest cavity physically pulling me toward that door. All my instincts were telling me that that place would feel much better than here. "I want to go, but…but not yet. I need to work things out with Mari. I want to become a father and watch my kids grow up—fuck!"

Calm.

That single word rumbled through my senses, lifting the hairs on my skin and echoing through my mind.

Be calm and stay. We are here with you.

"What is that?" I looked all around me. "*Who* is here?"

"Well." Now Hades had some amount of surprise in his voice. "I didn't know anyone else could be here."

I whipped around again to find another man standing in front of my parents' cabin, effectively blocking the door. Like Hades, he looked like a normal guy, but with warm brown skin and glossy black hair that hung straight past his shoulders.

"There seems to be much you don't know, old god," the stranger said to Hades, almost in a playfully chiding way.

"Leave it to a young god to still have an ego," Hades responded with a huff.

"I'm sorry, who are you?" I asked the newcomer.

"The companion god of a friend," he answered, leveling his dark gaze on me. I thought Hades' presence was heavy. This god made my knees want to buckle under some invisible weight. "Don't be afraid," he added. "I'm only here to encourage you to not choose death. At least, not until there is no other choice."

"You cannot interfere with his free will," Hades said with a snarl.

"His failing organs already are," the new god retorted. "I cannot heal as others can, but I can hold him closer to life for a short while longer." His gaze returned to me. "Until you are rescued or you die, Reaper."

CHAPTER 10

JANDRO

Mari's dad was cleared to leave the hospital the next day, and all three of us welcomed the distraction of getting him set up in our home. I felt my old caretaker instincts kicking in from when my aunt and uncle started getting old and they needed more help around the house.

Gunner and I hovered, eager to help but also not wanting to be overbearing. Mari knew her dad best and it was heartwarming to see them bantering and cracking jokes. She had more brightness in her and smiled like she hadn't in days.

"Are you hungry, Dad?" Mari was darting around his room now, checking and rechecking that he had everything he needed, while us three guys just watched her movement like the cutest tornado.

"No, *mijita*. I don't have much of an appetite lately."

"You're skin and bones, *viejito*." She poked his cheek. "You're gonna have eggs for breakfast every day. You need the calories."

"Quit your fussing, you're not my wife." Javier smacked her hand away but he was smiling. At least he was, until a deep frown settled on his face and Mari took a seat on the bed next to him.

"Do you remember her?" she asked gently. "When you last saw her?"

Javier rubbed his forehead while Mari took his other hand. "I don't...I don't know. I'm sorry."

"It's okay," Mari assured him, though it only seemed to make him more frustrated.

"It's not okay! It's, shit, it's like she's right there but I can't reach her."

"It'll come to you," I said from the doorway, trying to be helpful. "Don't force it."

They both glanced up as if noticing us for the first time. Gunner thumped me once on the back before turning away from the room. "We'll be right out here if you need us."

"Shit, good call," I muttered, following him out to the living room. I got so wrapped up in taking care of Mari, and by extension, Javier, that I didn't stop to consider what they needed most was to be alone.

"They need their time together," Gunner said, confirming that he was following the same train of thought. "And I'm sure our hovering doesn't help him remember any faster."

"You're right." I collapsed onto the couch with a sigh. "If he *does* remember the inside of the compound, you really think that'll help us?"

"Fuck, anything is better than what we got now." Gunner settled into an armchair, the one Reaper usually sat in, and stretched his long legs out toward the coffee table.

The front door swung open moments later, General Finn Bray coming through like a bull in a tea shop. He was disheveled lately, miles away from his usually clean-cut and polished appearance. His hair was mussed, his jacket wrinkled and buttoned incorrectly. Like us, he was barely sleeping and fraught with worry. The general paused at the sight of us, leaving the door wide open behind him.

"Well, I'm glad you two got some time off to relax," he growled irritably, eyes narrowing at us. The stress and lack of sleep also contributed to him having less of a filter. He and Reaper had the same scowl and temper when things were this tense. Like father, like son.

Gunner started to sit up, but I got to my feet faster. "Mari's dad is here," I said, lowering my voice. "He remembers her now, and we just got him settled in. We're giving them space, that's all."

Finn's expression softened. "He does? Oh, that's good...great, even."

A weak smile wobbled onto his lips. "I'm glad. That's something, at least."

Mari and her dad came out of the bedroom then, probably alerted to the noise Finn made when he got home. The prickly general softened even more at the sight of his daughter-in-law. "Hey, sweetheart."

"Hi, Finn. I'd like you to meet my dad, Javier." Mari stepped to the side, keeping a loose hold on her dad's arm. "Dad, this is my father-in-law, General Finn Bray."

"It's a pleasure." The two older men shook hands, with Javier throwing a teasing smile in his daughter's direction. "You runnin' an old folks home out of here, girl?"

Mari glared and slapped his arm that she was holding while Finn released a bright laugh. It seemed like everyone was put in a better mood now that Mari and her old man were reunited.

"So is one of them yours?" Javier nodded at me and Gunner.

"Thankfully not," Finn chuckled, but the brief happiness left his eyes at that moment. "My son is Rory—Reaper. One of the captured ones."

"Oh, right." Javier rubbed his forehead while glancing at Mari with a sheepish look. "You told me that. Sorry, General, my memory isn't all there yet."

"That's alright. It's a lot of new information to take in, I'm sure." Finn straightened a little, a bit of the poised general returning. "And if you don't mind me saying, Javier, you've raised an incredible young woman for a daughter."

"She made it easy." Javier nudged Mari with his elbow. "Most of the time."

"Well, don't let me keep you from getting settled in." Finn started up the stairs toward his own borrowed room, which was Reaper's personal bedroom.

With Mari, Gunner, and I never wanting to be apart for long, we spent most nights in my room, which freed up the rest of the bedrooms. Now that we had Javier staying with us, it was nice to have a somewhat full house again, even if it was under the worst circumstances.

Moving in and getting up to greet Finn seemed to zap most of

Javier's energy. He started leaning heavily on Mari as she guided him back to bed. Now alone again, Gunner and I exchanged a quick look.

"I really, *really* fucking hope he remembers," Gunner confessed quietly, reaching up to stroke Horus' chest feathers.

I nodded, choosing to keep my thoughts to myself. Javier's memory of the New Ireland compound might be the one thing that could save Reaper and Shadow.

It was all we had and barely, at that.

"AHHH! YOU MOTHERFUCKING...COCKSUCKER!"

I examined the line of blood growing thicker inside my forearm. Fucking Foghorn caught me with his spurs *again* while I was trying to collect eggs. If the rooster was so determined to not have his children become breakfast, maybe it was time to throw *him* in the pot.

"Fucking asshole." I kept grumbling on my way into the house, heading for the kitchen sink to wash the cut. I was so preoccupied with cursing out the rooster that I didn't notice Javier at the kitchen table until he spoke.

"You can trim back their spurs," he told me in flawless Spanish, raising a mug of tea to his lips.

"Oh yeah?" My native tongue flew from my mouth without thought as I turned to face him, keeping my arm under the running tap water. "You know much about roosters?"

"I come from a family of farmers in Mexico," Javier said with a nod and a small smile. "You can trim the spur with nail clippers or grind it down to the quick." His eyes shifted toward the backyard. "The challenge is not getting sliced up while you hold him to do it."

"Sounds like it would be a two-person job."

"Or three or four," he chuckled, looking back at me. "They're crafty sons of bitches. Especially when they've got a brood to protect."

"Don't I know it."

I took my eyes off of Javier to turn off the water and stem the flow of blood on my arm with a towel. When I looked up again, his elbows were braced on the table and he held his head in a white-knuckled grip.

"Javier!" I hurried to his side and placed a hand on his shoulder, but he flinched and pulled away from the contact. "Mari!" I called toward the bedrooms.

"No, don't yell," Javier wheezed painfully, hands moving over his ears. "It's too loud."

"What's going on?" Finn and Lis poked their heads out from the living room.

"Get Mari, something's not right."

I hovered protectively over Javier, not wanting to touch him or leave his side. A few drops of blood had fallen onto the table's surface. I didn't know whether to be relieved or concerned that they came from his nose rather than his ears.

"What's happening?" Mari darted in moments later, rubbing her eyes and blinking. Her face had lines in it and her hair was mussed like she'd been napping hard. Reaper's parents and Gunner were right on her heels.

"I don't know," I told her. "One minute he was fine, we were talking. And then..."

"Everybody back up. Give us space, please." Mari went into medic mode like the flip of a switch. She placed her hands on her dad's shoulders, holding firm when he flinched at the touch. "Dad, I need you to talk to me. Tell me what—"

Javier began muttering in a long stream of gibberish. I picked up some Spanish words that didn't make sense in the context, and it sounded like there were some other languages garbled in too.

Mari's face went white. "Oh no. No, no, no, no."

"Babe, what is it?" I went to her side despite her earlier request for space. She looked like she was about to fall to the floor at any moment.

"I think...he's regressing." Her gaze was locked onto her father's face, which was still propped up by his hands, mouth moving rapidly without saying anything. "He's losing the ability to speak. Or retain language, or something."

"Oh, Mari..." I was shattered on her behalf. She had just gotten him back and now...

"No." Javier's hand snapped out, grabbing one of hers. "It's not that, not that, not that..." He sounded like a malfunctioning robot.

"Baby girl, step away from him." Gunner had come up beside me, his posture defensive like mine had become. If this was the Sha trying to regain control of one of his drones, Mari was in danger. Shit, we *all* were.

"Dad, let me go." Mari's attempt to yank out of her dad's grip went nowhere, so Gunner and I stepped up to help her.

"Sorry, Javier," I muttered before forcibly breaking his hold on Mari's wrist.

Gunner and I each restrained one of his arms, pulling him back against the chair he sat in. More blood trickled from his nose, his lips still moving rapidly while his voice was at a frenzied whisper. His eyes stared blankly at nothing in front of him.

"I think we should take him back to the hospital, sweetheart," Finn broached gently.

"Not yet." Already past the shock of her father grabbing her, Mari wiped at the blood under his nose with a napkin.

"But if he's regressing as you say," Gunner began, but Mari cut him off with a sharp wave of her hand.

"It was just a guess, I could be wrong. Give him a minute."

"*Mariposita,* I'm gonna have to agree with them." The regret was heavy in my voice. Fuck, Javier and I were just having a nice chat. What the fuck happened?

"I said, give him a minute." Mari's eyes snapped up to mine. "Just trust me, please."

"Okay." I glanced at Gunner, who nodded his agreement. But both of us tightened our grip on the man's arms.

Mari continued tending to her dad's nosebleed while also checking his pulse and focus of his eyes. She asked for her penlight, which Lis scurried off to find for her. Feeling something near my pant leg, I glanced down to see Freyja winding around the chair legs and Javier's feet. The cat jumped into Javier's lap, purring up a storm as Lis returned with the light. When Mari shined it into her dad's eye, the response was immediate.

"Ah, fuck! You trying to blind me, *mija*?"

The light fell to the floor with a clatter, and I felt every bit of relief that took over Mari's face.

"You're back!" she cried, reaching forward to hug him. "Holy shit, I thought I lost you again."

"Is that why your husbands got me in a headlock?"

Mari laughed, quickly wiping tears as we released him. "Don't be dramatic. Now what the fuck was that?"

Javier rubbed his eyes. "I don't know. Feels like I blacked out." He glanced up at me and Gunner on either side of him. "You guys look like a couple of bouncers about to toss me on my ass, so it couldn't have been good."

"Dad." Mari touched his face to bring his attention back to her, carefully inspecting around his eyes, nose, and mouth. "Has this happened to you before?"

"Yeah," he remarked casually. "Couple times in the hospital."

"When was the last time?" Mari picked up her light from the floor and shined it into his mouth.

Javier smiled when she finished inspecting him and allowed him to close his lips. "Right before all my memories of you came back, *mijita*."

Mari sucked in a breath, eyes widening with a glance up at us before looking at her father again. "Do you remember anything new now?"

He thought for a moment, frowning. "I don't know."

"Mom?" Mari asked hopefully.

Javier's frown deepened. "Not...really. I'm sorry."

Mari was quick to cover up her disappointment with a tight smile. "Don't be sorry, Dad. You can't force these things."

"What about..." Gunner's eyes flicked to her in a silent request for permission. When she nodded, he continued. "New Ireland? Your time there?"

"New Ireland?" Javier rubbed his jaw. "You mean the fortress? That's what everyone called it."

Everyone froze in temporary shock, then me and Gunner were scrambling to pull up chairs and sit facing him.

"The fortress?" I repeated. "You mean the place you were deployed from?"

"Yes, I think so." Javier sounded unsure at first, then he nodded more confidently. "Yes, it used to be New Mexico."

"Do you remember the inside of the fortress?" Gunner gripped the edge of the table, as if holding himself back.

"Yes, of course. I never left before we were sent out to attack."

"Javier." I put my palms together as if in prayer. "We need to know the layout of that fortress. It could be our only chance to get Reaper and Shadow back." I looked at Mari, knowing she wouldn't disagree, but her dad's recovery was important too. Trying too hard to remember things gave him intense headaches and fatigue.

"Jandro's right, Dad," she said quietly, taking one of his hands. "They're my family, and we need you."

"I'll tell you everything I can remember." He squeezed his daughter's hand and looked once more at me and Gunner. "Because you're my family now too."

CHAPTER 11

SHADOW

"Shadow, I love you." Warm hands drifted over my face, rousing me gently.

"Mari?" I reached for her before my eyes opened, my fingers finding purchase on the slender, curving waist I'd held so many times before. "Mari!" My eyes snapped open to find that I wasn't dreaming. Her beautiful face was in front of me in the sharpest detail, from the curve of her lips to the freckles on her nose. She was here! Oh thank fucking everything, she found us.

"Mari, check on Reaper. He's in bad shape." I took her hands from my face, trying to look around the dungeon to see if she came alone or with the others, but I couldn't seem to see beyond where she sat in front of me.

"He's fine." She returned a palm to my cheek, her skin so soft and warm, I wanted to rest my whole, weary head in her hand. "I missed you so much, Shadow."

"I missed you too." I blinked, waiting for the rest of the room to come into focus. I was fully awake now, but why was it so dark? Did she sneak in late at night? Even with my night vision, I couldn't make out anything in the blackness beyond her. My stomach clenched with an instinct of warning, and I looked at Mari again. "Are you sure Reaper's okay?"

"Yes," she replied quickly. "Shadow, do you love me?"

My stomach clamped harder. "Yes," I said with a note of caution.

"You would do anything for me?"

I grabbed her wrist and removed her hand from my face again. "What are you asking me to do?"

Mari's face flickered for a split second, a quick distortion, like an image on paper being folded. I would have missed it if I wasn't watching so carefully. Despair crushed my relief like a cruel fist and I scrambled to get away from this illusion using my wife's face and voice. Maybe this wasn't a dream but it sure as fuck wasn't *real*.

"Let the Sha inside your mind, Shadow." Mari's voice had deepened, distorting into the Sha's strange cadence. "Take the leash off of the monster you're holding back. You'll feel so much better when you're free."

"No!" I scooted away as far as my chains would allow me. I kicked something metallic-sounding, probably a metal water bowl. Empty blackness still surrounded me, so I had no sense of place or proximity.

"You can't fight it forever," the Sha taunted me through Mari's mouth. "All you know is dungeons, blood, and violence. No woman or brotherhood can change what you really are."

"That's not who I am!" I hated how desperate and in denial I sounded.

"My brother tried to fix you but you are *perfect*, Shadow. You would make the perfect instrument for me."

"I am no one's instrument!" I roared back. "Especially not one who uses my wife to manipulate me."

"Oh but you will be, Shadow." The Sha sounded more than confident, like his victory was inevitable. "And if I must, I will sway you to me through Mariposa's visage. She is the one weak spot in your defenses."

"I *know* her," I bit back. "You won't fool me using her face again. She would never—"

The illusion of Mari zipped forward at an impossible speed. I flinched, trying to back away again, but I had reached the ends of my chains. She–it–sat down, straddling my waist. I bit the inside of my cheek and shut my eyes, stifling my groan. It felt just like her—the slight weight of her on my lower stomach and the squeeze of her thighs around my body. The physical memory of her was so sweet. I almost unclenched my hands with the need to touch her.

It's not her. It's not her. Don't you ever fucking forget that this is not her.

"Get off me!" I would have shoved the Sha's illusion away if I trusted myself to touch it again. But the fact of the matter was, I didn't.

And the Sha knew that. I saw it in the smug curve of Mari's lips as the illusion stood, lifting away from my body.

"You may know her, but you have not seen her for a very long time. This face," the Sha traced a hand along the illusion's jaw—Mari's jaw. The gesture was odd, even jarring, because I knew Mari would never touch her own face like that. "I could feel your relief, your utter joy when you saw this face. When you heard this voice say, *I love you, Shadow.*" The Sha's voice morphed back to Mari's for those last four words and I flinched as if they physically pained me.

It's not her. It's not her.

"You're wasting your time," I said. "I won't fall for this."

"Maybe not today, but soon." Mari's image flicked her hair back over her shoulder, and that was hard to see because she *did* often do that. "You'll start missing your wife so much, you'll do anything to see her again." The illusion traced a finger around Mari's mouth." You'll do anything these lips will tell you to."

"I won't," I insisted, but even I was becoming less convinced of that with each passing minute.

That became evident with the Sha's knowing, parting smile as the illusion of Mari disappeared. What I felt next wasn't the cramping hunger in my stomach, the weakness in my limbs, or the dryness in my throat.

It was the constant, gnawing ache of not seeing her face anymore.

I woke with a start, gasping like my lungs could never get enough air. A cough wracked through my chest. Unlike Reaper's wet, hacking cough, my lungs and throat felt dryer than the desert. I knew I was dehydrated—I'd been giving him most of my water. It had been nearly a decade since I had to, but I knew how to ration water so that I could survive on very little.

I looked around for my bowl, eager for just a little water to soothe my cough, then spotted it turned over across the dungeon near the door.

Oh fuck, the Sha.

My legs drew up toward my stomach at the memory, the dream, hallucination, or whatever it was. The Sha might not have been able to break in and control me yet, but he *knew* how much I loved Mari. He knew she was my one exploitable weakness, and pulled no punches in letting my guard down. And fuck me, I almost did.

I couldn't even process how violating that encounter felt. That it kept making me touch the illusion of my wife, that it knew exactly what she felt and looked like, all from information in my own head. Information that it had no right to see.

What I hated most of all was how right the Sha had been. I had been so happy to see her, to hear her voice, and feel her skin exactly how I remembered her. It scared me how much I wanted that, what I was willing to give just to see Mari's face again.

"No," I said aloud to myself. "It's not her. She would never want me to do this. I'm not an instrument. I won't be used."

This is how they will break us, I realized. For Reaper, they intended to break him down physically. They knew I wouldn't respond to pain, so for me, the torture would be all mental.

"Oh fuck. Reaper!"

He was still lying in the same position as the guards left him in. Shit, how long had that been, hours? A full day? Coagulated blood surrounded his body and I couldn't tell if he was breathing.

"Reaper!" I called to him, my panic rising to an all-time high. "Reaper, wake up. Do something to show me you're still there."

He remained silent and eerily still.

"Reaper!" I shouted again, pulling at my chains to get closer. "Wake up, president. I need you." When there was still no change, I tried his given name. "Rory! Rory Daley, wake up now! Get up and punch me in the face for calling you that. You know you want to."

I yelled and shouted his name until I was hoarse, his name a desperate whisper of disbelief as I slumped back against my wall. No, it couldn't be. He was my president, for fuck's sake. I was supposed to die before him.

I couldn't tear my eyes away from his body, dumbfounded by the utter lack of movement. He couldn't be dead. It wasn't *right*. My own breathing, an erratic sawing of air in and out of my chest, grew painful while I just stared at him. Like even my lungs knew how unfair it was for me to be alive if he was dead.

Only the metal clanking of a key through our cell door drew my eyes away. The door creaked noisily open and a familiar, black-clad figure slipped inside.

"You," I rasped at the Sha's female guard, the one who gave Reaper water and washed his face before.

"Shhh," she hissed at me, making her way to where Reaper lay. Her eyes looked like they were narrowed in annoyance above her mask. "I would have come sooner if you'd have stopped screaming his name," she whispered.

I didn't give a shit about blowing her cover right then. He needed help hours ago. "Is he…"

She carefully rolled Reaper to his back. The limp flopping of his hands at his sides made me feel sick. I held my breath as she brought her ear down next to his mouth.

"He's alive," she reported, and the air left me in a big whoosh. "But barely," she added with a finger on the pulse at his neck. "He won't survive another beating."

"Is there anything you can do?" My voice was heavy with desperation. I didn't know who this woman was. She could have been just another player in a game set up by the Sha, giving us false hope to break us even more. But I didn't care. Maybe I was already losing mentally because I was ready to cling on to anything.

"The others won't touch him," she said. "Not until he becomes conscious again or dies first."

"Can you get him out of here?" I asked. "Get him to a medic, anyone who will stabilize him? *Please.*"

"No. I'm sorry." The woman shook her head. "I'll be discovered if I try anything. I shouldn't even be in here."

I stared at her, helpless and confused. "Who *are* you? How are you getting by undetected at all?"

Because of me.

A voice brushed against my mind, sparking up the musty air in the dungeon. That was a familiar sensation now, but the last thing I expected to hear in this hellhole was a new god speaking.

Fear and awe mingled together in my chest. "Who's here?"

The woman's robe moved at the shoulder. She extended one arm toward the ground while the movement slowly made its way down toward her wrist, the loose fabric rippling from what hid underneath.

"What the...fuck!"

I stumbled back toward the wall when a fucking rattlesnake slithered out from under her robe to the floor. Its forked tongue darted out, tasting the air, while its unblinking eyes regarded me curiously.

Don't be afraid, my son. I will not harm you or your friend.

"This is Quetzalcoatl," the woman said. At my blank expression, she added, "I call him Q."

"You have a companion god," I said, watching the snake glide across the floor to Reaper. "Like...us."

The woman nodded, both of us watching now as Q's long body moved over Reaper's chest and abdomen. "He's a god of wisdom and knowledge. I think it's because of my bond with him that the Sha doesn't detect my disloyalty."

Q's head inched toward Reaper's face, tongue flicking out mere inches away from his mouth and nose. *I can hold him back from the underworld temporarily, but he needs more healing than I can provide.* The snake swung his head toward me. *You have not harnessed the bonds between your companion gods and your fellow humans. Why?*

"I don't understand," I admitted. "Harnessed them how?"

Ah. You don't know. Then I suppose neither do they. The snake slithered off of Reaper's chest and paused next to the robed woman. *I will return, daughter.*

"Return?" the woman repeated in a panic. "Where are you going?"

These bonded humans lack the knowledge of the potential they wield. With harnessed bonds, they may be able to rescue these two, and put an end to the Sha.

"Will the Sha detect me if you go?" the woman asked.

No. The bond between us protects you. Be patient and trust in us. Trust in the humans that will come. Q slithered toward the barred door. *When I return, you will know.*

The serpent god then left the cell and disappeared.

CHAPTER 12

GUNNER

I didn't tell anybody I went scouting alone, and as my bike's shocks groaned and protested over the rocky terrain, I realized that was probably a mistake.

Mari or Jandro would have wanted to come with me, but we couldn't risk losing any more of us to the Sha's black swarm. General Bray was trying his best to keep it together, but he was clearly distraught at potentially losing another son. And truthfully, army escorts with me would have drawn attention or slowed me down, neither of which I wanted.

We kept bashing our heads against the wall, circling back to square one, then getting pissed off at the lack of options again. The longer we sat around coming up with bad ideas, the longer Reaper and Shadow suffered. Everyone knew we were running out of time and getting no closer, which only angered and worried us more.

Every time I brought up checking out the New Ireland compound with Horus, Mari or Jandro shut it down immediately. It was too dangerous. I could end up taken too.

But I had Horus' eyes, a rough sketch of the compound's interior pieced together by what Mari's dad could remember, and we had no other options.

Still, it probably would have been smart to have left a note.

I left hours ago, so they had to know something was up by now. I just hoped they weren't following me out this way, for their own safety.

Horus was silent, a dark speck in the sky as I rode across the desert terrain below. He almost never spoke to me in the way he did with Mari or Shadow. It didn't bother me as much as I thought it would. The falcon god and I were always in sync somehow, without spoken language between us. Even when he wasn't on my shoulder or in my line of sight, I always seemed to know instinctively where he was. When I needed him, he was there, ready to take flight. Like early this morning when I snuck my bike out of the garage, he was waiting for me on a fence post like he already knew where we were going.

As I approached the compound, I started looking for a spot to camp out, several miles away from New Ireland. It wasn't like I needed to see anything with my own eyes. Getting too close risked being caught anyway—seeing them meant they had a chance of seeing me.

Roughly five miles out from the border, I spotted a large cluster of boulders that would do nicely for cover. Horus was already flying ahead of me by the time I stopped and got to work camouflaging myself and my bike.

"Thanks for the tip, Blakeworth," I muttered, rubbing some dirt on my forehead and cheekbones before covering my mouth, nose, and hair with a hood and mask. I'd brought a few different options and picked the ones that blended best with the landscape surrounding me.

Hiding my bike proved to be a bit more difficult, as there wasn't a lot of vegetation out here for me to cover it. Finally I was able to wedge it mostly out of sight between two boulders, which would have to do.

Once it was in place, I turned around to sit on the front tire and lean back against the headlight. When I found a position that ensured I wouldn't fall and crack my head open on a rock, I let my consciousness slip into Horus.

Seeing through him always felt like a massive breath of fresh air. I was lighter, freer, not held down by anything like gravity or the limits of a human body. The sense of freedom was short-lived, however, when I saw the massive compound looming up ahead.

Easy, I warned Horus with a thought. *They might be looking for you.*

The Sha is absolutely looking for me, he said back. The response startled me so much that I nearly came back to my own body. *But for the Sha, his wish to end me is personal,* Horus went on.

Why's that?

Set and I are brothers who have warred with each other since our stories were first told. We cannot coexist in harmony, it's simply impossible. One must always defeat the other.

It would have been nice to know that before we set out on this trip, you know.

Would you have done anything differently? The question sounded like a challenge.

Probably not, I admitted.

Horus was silent for a long few seconds before speaking again. *You may use my sight to learn all that you can. But know you may return alone and with only your own sight and mind to guide you.*

I'm not leaving you behind! I retorted.

You may not have a choice, my son.

Well, just don't do any stupid bird shit.

Horus didn't laugh but a feeling of amusement passed over me. The compound loomed closer and it was clear that talking time was over. I needed to observe and not miss any detail. Any bit of information could be crucial to getting Reaper and Shadow back.

The falcon banked left, taking us around the fortress in a wide loop. I noted the tall, stone walls wrapped around the perimeter—similar to what we had at Sheol, but at least twice as high. Spaced out along the top were small platforms, each with an armed soldier keeping watch. Thankfully they paid no special attention to Horus or any of the other fauna in the general area.

I counted twenty guard platforms as we circled the fortress. Fucking hell, the Sha really wasn't messing around. It turned my stomach knowing that Reaper, Shadow, and Andrea were in there. Mari's dad had been in there and had only gotten out by sheer, crazy luck.

Let's go higher and straight over the top, I suggested to Horus.

That's not wise, I have been sensed, the sky god said in reply.

Shit! By the Sha?

No. By...another.

Another? I repeated. *A god? Who?*

I'm unsure. The presence is unfamiliar to me.

Should we leave?

Horus completed one more wide loop around the fortress without saying a word, and while waiting for his answer, I tried to memorize the structures I could see within the walls.

This presence does not appear to be a threat, Horus finally reported. *It wants to meet us.*

I'm not sure that's wise, I said, parroting back what he just told me. *What if it's a trap?*

It may be, the falcon admitted.

Let's just fly overhead and see what we see, I suggested.

He said nothing in response but angled his body like a fighter jet toward the fortress. Swells of hot air carried us closer, though we were still high enough not to be identified by any human eyes.

Thousands of feet in the air, I could clearly see faces, though many were covered by hoods and masks so that only their eyes were visible. Some soldiers milled about, their faces clear and out in the open, but they were few and far between. I wondered at what point they became part of the black-masked swarm, if there were some kind of trials or tests to go through.

A coldness ran through me at the thought of everyone in the hospital back at home—people like Mari's dad whose memory came back in bits and pieces. Or the worst ones who remained catatonic. I didn't have to be a medic to know there was no one home behind those dead, blank eyes.

Run, I wanted to say to the soldiers who were still in control of their own minds. *Get away while you still can.*

Horus seemed to sense my thoughts. *They chose this.* His mental voice bristled. *The ones who do not have control are the ones who resisted. The ones who remain free needed no coercion to join the Sha's cause. They are free as long as they're loyal.*

Who would choose this? I didn't bother to hide my disgust. *To contribute to the destruction of all people?*

Who would choose to follow Hitler? Or Mussolini? Horus answered. *Perhaps they have been bribed with lofty rewards in exchange for their service, but these people made their choices.*

It was a morbid thought, but I felt a weird sense of gratitude that there were so few of them. If the majority of the black swarm was controlled, that meant they fought back. They were given a choice and said no, they would not follow the Sha in wiping out humanity, and accepted the terrible consequences.

Mari's dad had been one of those, and it made me respect him even more.

We are drawing attention, Horus warned. *We should leave.*

He was right. The scouts along the wall had started following our movement with their binoculars and more people on the ground had begun to peer up at the dark speck flying overhead. It was creepy how people turned and looked at the exact same time, their heads tilted at the same angle. Fuck, they had to be some sort of hive-mind. Like the Sha was a queen bee with the ability to control thousands of drones with a single thought.

Yeah, let's go, I agreed. *Don't make it look obvious, though.*

Horus flew in one more leisurely circle over the fortress. I prayed we'd be written off as just a normal, desert raptor scoping the place out for food. He started heading away from the compound and I almost let myself feel relieved.

Until the shots rang out.

Shit!

Horus dove hard, the ground racing up to meet us at terrifying speed. Right when I thought we would splat on the ground, he shot straight up into the air again. It was then that I realized he was zigzagging to avoid the onslaught of bullets aimed at us. He shot up and dove down, banking hard from left to right. If I'd been in a human body, it would have felt like the most sickness-inducing rollercoaster in existence.

We were almost out of range of the fortress' snipers when Horus changed direction hard *again,* this time doubling back toward the compound, and kept going that way.

Horus, what are you doing? I cried in a mental panic. *We were almost in the clear! Why are you going back?*

He is that way. I have no other chance to retrieve him.
Who?!
The other presence I felt.
The one that might be a fucking trap?

The sky god was silent as he made another pass over the top of the fortress, flying lower this time, which gave the snipers much clearer shots.

Horus, we can't! You're going to get killed.

I warned you I might, he said lightly. *If I do, then it's your responsibility to communicate with this presence.*

How am I supposed to—

A close shot cut me off, grazing just the edge of Horus' wing tip, but it was enough to knock us off-course. Horus went spinning through the air, dropping altitude fast, but was able to right himself after a few terrifying seconds.

Fuck this other presence Horus, we have to go!

We cannot.

Somehow we cleared flying over the compound again, but the snipers on this wall were ready. They coordinated their fire so that not even zigzagging could protect us. Horus dove toward the brush just beyond the wall when the shot hit.

Pain exploded up my right limb like I got shot in the arm. Horus screeched in agony as we tumbled down toward earth. I could feel the urge to withdraw from the pain, to get back into my own body to escape it, but I wasn't leaving Horus alone. To my complete shock, he was still flapping it and keeping us hovering in the air, though I couldn't begin to understand why. We were an even easier target now.

Take cover in the brush, friends. I will meet you halfway. Another voice spoke to us—low, ancient and calming.

What?! Who are you? I demanded.

I got no answer, but Horus stretched his talons out toward the cluster of bushes. The pain was blinding as he braced his wings out, preparing to catch...

A rattlesnake?

It was indeed a snake's head looming out of the top of a bush, but that was all I saw before Horus' talons snagged the reptile's midsection and continued flying on.

I didn't bother asking what was going on anymore because they weren't talking, and I thought I'd pass out from pain any minute. Footsteps now hurried after us on the ground and the panic from that overshadowed everything. Horus was slowing down, hovering so low over the ground that the snake's rattle nearly brushed the earth. In seconds, they'd be able to catch us easily.

Now, friend, the snake, who I assumed was the presence, instructed.

Horus dropped the snake, and we went tumbling. The falcon hit the ground rolling and I heard a snap that made my whole right side feel like it was on fire.

Fuck, Horus! I'm getting my bike and coming to get you.

No, stay. The command from the sky god felt unshakable. Only the slightest strain in his voice indicated he felt pain in the falcon's form. *Do not alert them to your human body. Have faith in our new friend.*

The snake was roughly twenty yards behind where we crash-landed. Its lower half coiled on the ground, head and upper body erect as it shook the rattle on its tail. The approaching soldiers could see us clearly, their faces hard and determined. This unit wasn't mind-controlled and that worried me even more. They only slowed when they noticed the rattlesnake in their way.

While most of the soldiers came to a stop in a straight line, a couple dared to take a few steps closer. The snake arched higher, shaking its rattle more insistently. The sound became a constant low hum, like static or white noise. It grew louder, making my head feel like it was stuffed with cotton.

One by one, the soldier's faces slackened into blank expressions. Their hands loosened on their weapons, arms flopping loosely to their sides. The rattling continued until all of them appeared to have been lulled into some kind of hypnotic state.

Now go, the snake said. *I cannot keep them in such a state permanently.*

Horus rolled painstakingly to his feet. He was forced to hop and flap awkwardly with his good wing, which was slow and cumbersome.

Let me go back, I said. *Then I'll carry you.*

Yes. The sky god sounded exhausted.

The last thing I saw through Horus' eyes before slingshotting back to my human body was the rattlesnake striking as he bit one of the soldiers in the leg.

THE MOMENT I WAS BACK, THE WEIGHT OF MY OWN BODY had me sliding off my tire to the ground. It took a moment for the vertigo to pass, then I shot to my feet and pulled my bike out from its hiding place. With the noise it'd make, riding probably wasn't the best idea, but Horus' wing had been bleeding badly. And it fucking scared me how worn out and exhausted he'd sounded in my mind. As a god, I figured he wouldn't be dead-dead, but I still wasn't ready to lose my falcon buddy.

I kicked the bike to life and headed off toward the fortress to find my companion god.

Well *gods* now, I guess.

Horus and the snake had covered a good amount of distance before I reached them. I only rode about three and half miles before I spotted the falcon hobbling along the ground with the rattlesnake at its side.

If he hadn't been injured so badly, I would have scooped them both up without stopping and headed straight home. But I didn't want Horus bleeding out or being injured worse on the ride, so I stopped and lifted him gingerly off the ground.

"Hey buddy. You're lucky a coyote didn't find you first."

Horus clicked his beak like he wasn't amused.

"Shit man, you're still bleeding." His wing looked like a giant mess of bloody feathers that I couldn't make heads or tails of. What I would give for a fraction of Mari's medical knowledge right now. The best I could tell was that he was shot near his shoulder joint. "I'm gonna wrap your bullet wound," I told him. "I don't know what I'm doing though, so I'm sorry in advance."

While I tore off a strip of my T-shirt, the rattlesnake slithered up next to my rear tire. His head stretched up toward the seat, tongue flicking out.

You've chosen an interesting human, sky god, the snake observed.

They are all interesting. Horus vocalized through small chirps and screeches while I tried my best to wrap his wing.

"So who might you be, snake god?" It was unnerving having a damn rattlesnake so close to me, but remembering he was more than a simple animal helped.

I am Quetzalcoatl.

I paused in my wing-wrapping. "No disrespect, but would you mind repeating that?"

Something like an exasperated sigh passed through my mind. *You may call me Q, if you wish.*

"Thanks, I probably will." I began to tie off the wrapping on Horus' wing. "So...you're a snake god, huh?"

I am known as the feathered serpent to the Mexica, yes.

"Mexica?"

You may know them as the Aztecs.

"Oh, right. So wait, who are you bonded to?"

I will explain everything, but you must take me to your other companion gods. The snake's rattle shook a little, it seemed not with warning but with eagerness. *The Sha will soon be aware of your fly-by and will act accordingly.*

"No offense, Q, but why should I trust you?" I cradled Horus carefully against my chest. I'd hold onto him for the whole ride if I needed to.

Aside from the fact that I just gave venomous bites to five loyalists of the Sha and saved you from them? Q's rattle shook a little more insistently. *I am the primary force keeping your president alive.*

"My president?" I repeated, dumbfounded. "Reaper? He's alive?"

Barely, the snake clipped.

Let's go, Horus insisted.

"Alright then." I still wasn't sure about this snake god, but he had a point about saving our asses. And Horus seemed to trust him enough. "Make yourself comfortable in one of the saddlebags, Q."

With a final, quick rattle of its tail, the reptile slithered up and coiled itself into one of my compartments. I closed it, made sure it was secure, then settled back in the seat with Horus still against my chest.

"Hang on for me, buddy." My free hand went to the handlebars and we were tearing across the landscape in seconds. I just hoped Mari wouldn't be too pissed at me for going off alone and that she could work her magic to nurse Horus back to health.

CHAPTER 13

MARIPOSA

"Where the everloving fuck have you been?"

Gunner, who had been gone all day, at least had the decency to *look* guilty as he hopped off his bike and left it running as he jogged up the driveway toward me. He was dressed in desert camouflage and had dirt smeared on his face. But what alarmed me most of all was the bundle of feathers clutched to his chest and his shirt stained with blood.

"Baby girl—"

"What happened?! Is that Horus?"

"He got shot and I think broke a wing," Gunner explained in a rush of breath as he came to a stop in front of me. "Can you help him?"

"Ohh, Horus..." The poor bird was barely conscious, eyelids closing. The shock must have worn off hours ago. "I'm not a vet, but I can do my best."

"Please! You have to." Gunner held the limp bird out to me. "I'm sorry to put this on you, baby girl, but please help him. I'll explain everything."

"You better," I muttered, accepting the bird carefully into my arms. "Jandro!"

"Mariposita!" He answered me through the open sliding door to the backyard, where he and my dad tended to the chickens.

"You remember Erica, the medic who rotates shifts with me?"

"Um, yeah. I think so."

"Can you bring her over from the hospital? Tell her we've got a bird with a gunshot and a broken wing."

"Okay." Jandro looked puzzled but still set aside his rake and came inside.

"She used to be a vet tech," I explained. "She's the best person to help."

"You got it!"

Jandro hurried to the garage, then stopped in his tracks when Gunner yelled, "Take my bike! It's faster."

Jandro was out the front door and settled into Gunner's seat within moments, then promptly screamed and jumped off. "Gun, there's a fucking rattlesnake coming out of your saddlebag!"

"What the fuck?!" I cried.

"Yeah, that's the other thing." Gunner rubbed his forehead, not sounding alarmed or surprised, just weary. "Ran into another god who hitched a ride."

I couldn't have heard him correctly. "*Another* god?"

I'm Quetzalcoatl, and I will not harm you, a warm, ancient voice soothed me.

Sure enough, a six-foot long rattlesnake moved with fluid grace up my driveway, porch, and into my house. Despite its assurance of no harm, I found myself backing away from the reptile.

Heal the sky god first, Quetzalcoatl said. *Then we will have much to discuss.*

He was right. I had a barrage of questions, but taking care of Horus was the first priority. Jandro had gotten over his freak-out and had already taken off for the hospital. I went into the kitchen so that I could lay Horus down on a flat, clean surface.

"Freyja?"

I am here, daughter. The black cat jumped gracefully onto the table, making her way toward Horus.

"How bad is it?" I watched her sniff him delicately.

Very, but he lives, she reported.

"What do you need?" Gunner was already scrubbing his hands in the kitchen sink.

"A bright light, forceps, alcohol, gauze," I rattled off. "Something to use for a splint, like a wooden dowel or something."

"I'm on it." He raced off to grab my supplies while I examined the injured bird as carefully as I could.

"I'm so sorry if this hurts you, Horus," I muttered, saddened by every one of his soft chirps of pain.

I wasn't sure how to go about setting the broken bone in his wing, so I decided I'd wait for Erica to handle that. In the meantime, I was an expert at treating gunshot wounds at this point.

I had just extracted the slug and was wrapping up the wound with gauze when I heard Jandro's motorcycle rumble up the driveway. Perfect timing!

"Erica, thank you so much for coming," I said when the two of them walked in. "I'll explain later, but can you set a broken wing?"

She blinked once, taking in the sight of animals all around us. Hades and the rattlesnake were also nearby, looking at her hopefully. With a short laugh, she then pushed her sleeves up and headed for the sink to wash up. "Believe it or not, this isn't the craziest house call I've ever gotten."

"You're an angel," I breathed with relief.

Erica quickly figured out how best to set the bone, and it was my job to hold Horus still. After the most tense count to three of my life and a firm *snap,* I fought against every instinct in my body to let the bird go. His screech rattled my eardrums, his good wing beating against the table in an effort to get away.

"I'm sorry, I'm so sorry," I whispered to him.

"We need more hands to hold this splint in place while I wrap the wing," Erica said.

The guys sprang into action, all four of us lending a hand to keep Horus still. Moments later, it was over. His wing was wrapped in two places, the thick bandages making one side comically bigger than the other.

"No flying for eight weeks," Erica instructed as she went to wash her hands again. "You can give him pain relief, just microdose in comparison to humans."

"Thank you," I breathed, pulling her into a weary hug. "Really, we can't thank you enough."

"You don't know how much this means to us," Gunner added, lifting the bird carefully to hold him against his chest.

"My pleasure." Erica grinned. "Animals are just special in a different way than humans."

"Can we repay you in any way?" Jandro asked. Her eyes only had to slide toward the backyard for him to say, "Eggs? All yours. A lifetime supply."

"Don't mind if I do," Erica laughed.

She and Jandro immediately went to collect some while I hunted for pain relief for Horus. I had almost forgotten about Quetzalcoatl until I returned with a syringe of analgesic to find the rattlesnake curled up on the living room floor, mere inches away from Gunner's feet.

"So what happened today?" I settled on the couch next to Gunner, who was still holding Horus in his arms like a baby.

"Jandro just took Erica back to the hospital, let's wait til he's back." Gunner watched while I gave Horus the painkiller through a shot in the leg. "This is big. It affects...everything."

The rattlesnake lifted up, its head and upper third of its body leaning toward me as it tasted the air with its tongue.

A shame I did not find you before Freyja did, Quetzalcoatl remarked. *It probably wouldn't have worked, but things may have turned out very differently.*

"What do you mean?"

I am of your heritage, daughter. Your blood. The unblinking, reptilian eyes focused on me. *But you already had your companion gods, so I chose to bond with your next of kin.*

"Next of kin?" I repeated. "You mean my dad?"

Sadly, no. The Sha had already taken advantage of your father's fragile mind. I was too late to protect him, but I could guard the one closest to him.

"Closest to him?" I hardly dared to believe it, but who else could it be? "My mom?"

Yes, daughter. Your mother lives, truly *lives. Her mind is safe under my protection. She is not controlled.*

I probably should have asked more questions, namely how and what proof did he have, but the only information I could process was that *my mother was alive and safe.*

"She's okay?" I squeaked out, barely aware of the tears already rolling down my cheeks. "Really okay?" Dad's memory of her still wasn't quite there, but he would be overjoyed to hear this news.

Yes, dear daughter.

Gunner pressed a kiss to my cheek. I didn't know whether he heard the entire conversation or just one side, but his smile against my skin indicated that he got the gist of it. "We'll get her back too, baby girl."

"Hey—whoa!" Jandro came through the front door right then, immediately backing up a step at the snake reared up and hovering right in front of my face. "I don't like snakes as it is, but snakes that make you cry are the fucking worst of them."

"My mom's alive!" I blurted out. "Quetzal...um, is her companion god."

You can call me Q, if you wish, the snake's mental voice sighed.

"For real?" Jandro stared in disbelief.

"Now that we're all here," Gunner motioned him toward a seat on the couch, "I'll come straight out with it—I went to the fortress with Horus."

"Fuckin' knew it," Jandro grumbled.

"Alone?" My mood shifted from elated to anger on a hairpin turn. "How could you? Without even telling us?"

"Because I knew I'd get a reaction like this," Gunner sighed. "Look, it turned out okay—"

"*Okay?* You almost lost Horus!"

"It was weird." Gunner looked down at the bundle of feathers in his arms. "I decided I had to go, and it was like he was just waiting for me to make that decision. He even seemed to expect that he wouldn't make it back."

"*What?!*"

"I can't explain it, baby girl, other than it was a feeling."

The other piece of information clicked for me and I turned back to the snake. "Wait, my mom is at the fortress? The Sha's fortress?"

She is, Q chimed in. *And she's watching over your captured men.*

I nearly slid off the couch onto the floor. "My mom is with Reaper and Shadow? How are they?"

Q took a moment to answer. *Not well. They may perish if we don't act quickly, which is why I've come to you.*

All my caution went out the window with that information. This snake could tell me to walk into a volcano to save them and I'd do it without hesitation.

"Please." The word came from Jandro now, who also seemed to throw away his dislike of snakes over what this one just said. "What can we do? We're listening."

You have not harnessed your bonds. Why?

The three of us looked at each other with blank expressions. "What do you mean?"

Your bonds! Q repeated with an air of exasperation. His tail began to rattle slightly. *Between each other, fortified by your companion gods.*

Again, we exchanged glances like kids in a classroom being reprimanded by a teacher. "I'm sorry, I don't understand," I told the snake, watching his tail.

You are lovers, yes? His tongue flicked the air in front of me. *You love both of these men?*

"Yes, of course I do."

The feeling is mutual?

"Yes," Jandro and Gunner answered solemnly together.

And you are aware that that creates a bond? The god's tone dripped with condescension, like talking down to a child. *One that is intangible but you can feel it. You know it's there as sure as you can see me with your own eyes.*

"Okay, and?" I prompted.

The bonds with your companion gods are similar. Harnessing all of these bonds is like threading strings together to make a length of rope. With this, your strengths become even stronger, more durable. You are capable of more, and can use these bonds to sense each other without touching or speaking.

"How do we do this?" Gunner leaned forward eagerly in his seat.

Q's rattling calmed as he swung his head toward Gunner. *You simply reach out for your partners as you would your companion god.*

"Question." Jandro lifted a hand.

Yes? The snake's agitated rattling picked up again.

Jandro rested his forearms on his knees. "Unless Foghorn counts, I don't have a companion god."

Human, of course you do. The snake sounded like he'd had it up to here with our stupidity. *You have two.*

"I do?"

You have been touched by both Gods of Death who watch over your whole family. I see their marks on you.

"I...have?" Jandro paled.

"The drone attack back in Sheol," I blurted out as the awful memory hit me. "When you were almost gone and I had to resuscitate you."

Clarity dawned on Jandro's face. "That's right," he said softly. "I skirted the edge of death and met Hades and Freyja. They spoke to me."

And you, daughter of my blood. The snake god swung his head back toward me. *You are bonded to all three companion gods, which is remarkable. I have never seen such a thing before.*

"All three?" I repeated.

You have the touch of love and healing. You have flown on wings and seen the world from the sky. The snake paused before continuing. *And it seems you have had your own brush with death.*

His observations—particularly the last one—were chilling, leaving me completely open and exposed. What Shadow had done was a terrible accident, one I was happy to move on from and leave in the past. I never realized Hades might have been involved in my near death experience, but it seemed obvious now.

"How do you know?"

I can see the hands of the gods on you, daughter, Q said. *I am also a god of wisdom and knowledge. The connections between the tangible and intangible are where I specialize.*

My men slid in closer to me on either side as the god spoke, subtly forming a protective shield.

What else is remarkable, Q went on, *is how perfectly balanced your three gods are. Covering the spectrum of human experience while powered by devotion from three very different civilizations. The underworld, the sky, and everything in between. Simply fascinating.*

"What does this mean for Mari?" Gunner asked. "That she has three?"

The snake god seemed pleased that we finally stopped asking the stupid questions. *A balance of harnessed bonds between three people is a rarity in itself.* His ancient voice brimmed with excitement. *But three bonds, perfectly balanced, across multiple pantheons, within one human? It has never been done, and the strength from you is powerful and focused. It may be the only way to defeat the Sha and his army.*

"How?" I demanded.

You must draw on the bonds with your gods and your fellow bonded humans. Like pulling on a rope, you can send and receive feedback through the senses. The gods are the source, and you are the conduit, Mariposa.

"I'm still not following," Jandro admitted.

"When I reach for Horus to see through him, it is like mentally pulling on a string to see if he's there," Gunner explained, then looked at me.

"Similar with Freyja," I agreed. "Although, I've never tried reaching for the other two."

Try it now, Q suggested. *Reach for your men, Mariposa. They will feel the bonds of the gods through you.*

Jandro and Gunner each grabbed one of my hands, anchoring and supporting me between them. I took a deep, steadying breath and reached for Jandro with my mind, much like I did with Freyja when I needed her.

The result was subtle, a small shift in perception, like when you blink one eye and then the other. First I was in the middle, then I shifted slightly to the left where Jandro sat next to me. He jerked in surprise, bringing me back right away.

"Was that—" He slapped a hand to his chest, breath quickening.

I squeezed his hand. "How was that? Are you okay?"

"I felt you." Jandro stared at me in awe and disbelief. "I felt you pulling me that way, like we switched places for a second."

"Yes, that's exactly it!"

"Now imagine using this in a battle," Gunner said, his brow already furrowed in concentration. "We can watch each other's backs, basically seeing in all directions."

"But what about Horus?" I looked down at the bird, which now seemed to be sleeping against Gunner's chest.

You do not need the gods' animal forms with you. In fact, it's better if they're not present. If their animal bodies are killed, the bond will be severed, Q said. *We are outside of time and physical space. Your bonded gods are always with you. You only need to reach for them.*

"And how do we prevent the Sha from breaking into our heads?" Jandro asked. "I doubt this mission will be very successful if we're writhing in pain and bleeding from the ears."

Your companion gods will continue to shield your minds from afar, Q said. *The harnessed bonds between the three of you is an additional shield. I can also provide defense, as I do with Mariposa's mother.*

"What I want to know is," my gaze shifted across the room to where Freyja and Hades looked on, "how did we never hear about harnessed bonds before?" If they had told me about this when I came pleading to them for help, we would have been ten steps ahead by now.

I am just as surprised as you, daughter. Freyja took a few tentative steps toward the snake, her dark pupils wide. *I'm well-versed in the power of love, certainly. But no bonded human of mine throughout history has ever loved another person with a companion god. You are the first I've seen.*

My experience is the same, Hades said. *Had we known of these harnessed bonds, we certainly would have shared that with you.*

Old gods can learn new tricks after all, the snake mused, tail rattling gently.

Hades only responded with a soft growl before silence fell over the room. My men and I just sat for a few moments with the weight of this information. We had our answer now. Finally, something to act on.

Gunner broke the silence first. "We need to tell Finn." He looked at Jandro and I solemnly. "If the three of us going in is the only way, he has to know."

"My dad too," I said, my gaze shifting toward the bedroom where Dad rested. "If we don't come back, they both need to know why."

"If we don't come back," Jandro pulled my hand into his lap, "the Sha will come for all of them soon enough."

"Not happening," Gunner said with a low growl. "They've taken enough from us. We're getting everyone out—Reaper, Shadow, and Mari's mom."

"Don't forget Andrea," I said.

"Andrea too," Gunner agreed. With that, he stood up, then turned around to place Horus carefully in a small nest of blankets on the couch. "Time to start making a plan. A real one," he said before heading upstairs to gather his maps.

CHAPTER 14

GUNNER

Mari's dad reacted better than we could have imagined. Maybe he didn't remember it all entirely, but somewhere in his head he knew about gods, including the one who had controlled him.

"Yes, the snake!" Javier's eyes brightened once we finished telling him everything. "The snake kept your mom safe, *mija*. I remember now."

Mari, Jandro, and I were all gathered in her father's room, suited up for riding to meet with Finn at City Hall once we told Javier the news.

And once we told Finn, we'd be riding out to New Ireland. Depending on what the general decided, we'd either go alone or with the support of the Four Corners army. No matter what, we were getting everyone back. Tonight.

Mari reached across the bed and squeezed her dad's forearm. Her lip wobbled for a moment before she steeled her features. "We're getting Mom back. I promise."

Javier, too, had to compose himself before smiling at his daughter. "If anyone can, I know it's you, *mijita*."

Mari scooted closer, bringing her arms around her father in a hug. "I love you, Dad."

"Silly girl," he chuckled, but hugged her back fiercely. "You got this, it's a walk in the park. You'll be back before you know it." He held onto her tightly for an extra long second. "And I love you too."

When they separated, Javier's eyes were hard on Jandro and me. "You guys watch over my girl."

"We will," I said, my voice just as hard.

Jandro said something in Spanish, his tone hard-edged and determined. Javier nodded just as Mari came to stand between us.

"We'll see you soon, *viejito*," she said before the three of us turned and left the room.

Normally Mari would ride with one of us, but three separate bikes awaited us in the garage. Jandro and I had our most trusted steeds ready, while Mari borrowed a lightweight Harley from Noelle. We all had to anticipate carrying at least one extra person if we made it back alive.

Hades and Freyja also waited for us in the garage. The black cat, unsurprisingly, jumped onto Mari's bike and snuggled her way inside the front of Mari's jacket.

Hades sat like a regal statue next to my bike, which *was* surprising.

We will join you for the meeting with the general and see you off to the fortress. The death god's voice rumbled with authority in my head.

"What about Horus?" I asked, throwing a leg over my seat.

Quetzalcoatl will guard the falcon here. But I must tell you all... the dog cocked his head while Mari and Jandro paused to listen. *We may not be occupying these forms when you return.*

"What do you mean?" Jandro leaned forward over his handlebars. "You'll be just a dog?"

If you succeed, then I, Hades, will exist as I always have since my inception. But yes, the creature you're looking at now will only be a dog.

"Why?" Mari unzipped the top of her jacket to allow Freyja's ears and head to poke out.

Because you will have fulfilled your purpose and no longer need our guidance in these forms, the cat goddess said.

"Shit," I blurted out, thinking back to when Horus and I last spoke. He told me he might not make it through that mission but when he did, I had no idea it might be the last time we spoke. The last time we would fly together.

We will not be gone, son, Freyja said, as if sensing my regret. *We watched over as you were born and will stand guard when your children are born. As long as humanity persists, we will always be here.*

I nodded, more to myself than anyone else. Horus had been in my life as a falcon for under two years. We'd grown so close in that time, to the point where I never imagined *not* having him. It was jarring to think about, but less so if I considered the fact that he had always watched over me.

I would have to sit with that idea later though. We needed to get moving now.

"You ready, VP?" I called to Jandro over my shoulder. Without Reaper here, it fell on Jandro to lead us out.

"Aye-aye, captain," he cracked, just like old times.

He eased out of the garage, then took off with a roar once he hit the driveway. I nodded at Mari to follow him, then drove out behind her with Hades loping at my side.

If Jandro took Reaper's place, I had to take Shadow's. It was strangely fitting with him leading our pack and me bringing up the rear to protect the rider between us.

Bonded to three gods and four men, I was convinced Mari was the key to everything. But even without the god stuff, she was everything to us. To me.

And I would be my woman's shield until my dying breath.

"You kids can't be serious about this," General Bray groaned, looking to Mari with hope in his eyes that she would be a voice of reason. "Sweetheart, tell me you're not actually doing this."

"We are," she told him firmly. "It has to be the three of us, Finn. That's the only way this has even the slimmest chance of working."

The general looked more put-together today, his uniform crisp and buttoned correctly. But he still looked weary, and his hair had begun sticking out in all directions from constantly running his hands through it. A habit that Reaper also picked up when he was stressed.

"Listen, I don't doubt these bonds with the gods you all have. I've seen the remarkable things you can do. But..." His eyes scanned over us. "Is it enough to end *all* of this?"

"We don't know," I admitted. "But it's the only shot we have, General. And we *have* to do it now. Any longer and we can pretty much expect to never see Reaper or Shadow again."

"Or Andrea, or my mom," Mari added.

"Worst case, we do see them, but it's as one of those fucking zombies coming after us," Jandro chimed in.

Finn sighed heavily, dropping his head into his hands. "There's nothing I can do to keep you from going, is there?"

"Nope. Sorry, General," I said. "And since we're protected by a fourth god now, you don't have the excuse of saying our minds are compromised."

Mari shot me a scathing look that was completely justified. I was a little salty that we got detained by the army before the last attack, even though Finn had made the best possible decision with the knowledge he had.

"I don't like this one fucking bit." Finn shook his head. "You're not my blood but you guys are my kids, and you're just heading off to be slaughtered."

"Will you support us or not?" Mari asked, cutting to the chase. "We'd rather not do this completely alone, but if you disapprove of us rescuing *your* sons, my husbands, so much, we will do it ourselves."

Her words hung in the air, a challenge demanding an answer. The silence was brief as Finn dipped his chin slightly.

"What do you need from me?"

"Armored Jeeps, rifle units," I said. "Hanging back, maybe a mile or so. We mainly need cover for when we're leaving the fortress with injured people in tow."

"Also medical staff," Mari added. "But I can't lead them since I'll be busting inside with these guys."

"I'll have Dr. Brooks send me a handful of his best," the general promised. "Anything else?"

Our side of the table was silent once again. "That's really it." I shrugged. "We need cover and support for getting everyone back home.

Other than that," my fingers tangled with Mari's at my side, "it's up to us and the gods."

CHAPTER 15

SHADOW

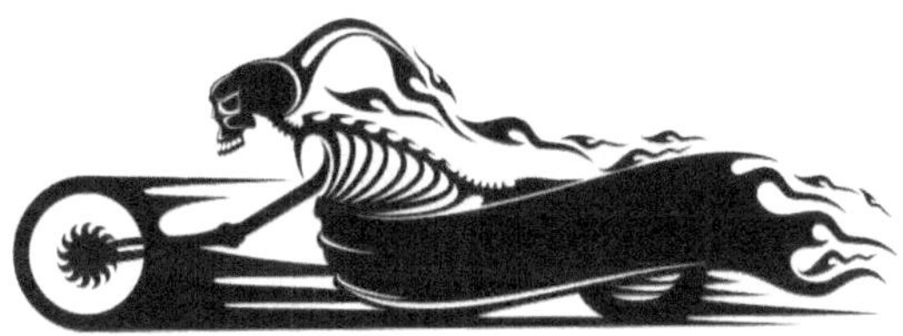

The female guard stopped by daily to check on Reaper and sneak me small, extra rations of food and water. She did what she could to keep Reaper hydrated but short of him waking up or her hooking him up to an IV, we had no way of making him drink.

It was the same routine. She showed up, checked his pulse, washed his face, and dribbled some water into his mouth. She'd let me know he was still alive, and then she left.

"He doesn't have much longer," she informed me on the third visit since Quetzalcoatl left. Her finger pressed to Reaper's neck while her ear rested on his chest. "Maybe a day, if that."

"How long has it been?" I asked after taking a careful, small, measured mouthful of water.

"Just over two days." Her brows pinched in sympathy above her mask. "I'm sorry."

"We still have a day." The words felt hollow as they left my body. I didn't really have any optimism left. I had a terrible feeling instead that if Reaper were to die, that would be it for me too.

The Sha wouldn't even need to use Mari's image to weaken me enough for control. The grief over losing my friend and president, my guilt over being unable to save him, would be enough.

Usually the woman was quick to leave but today, she hesitated. She even sat cross-legged on the floor as though she planned to stay.

"How long have you known him?" she asked.

"Around ten years, but we haven't really been close until recently." I was surprised at how easily the words came out. Who knew someone like me would be so eager to talk to another person? And a woman at that.

The guard's head cocked to the side, her eyes wide and inquisitive. "Close like...?"

"Not like that," I said. "He was, *is*, my president. The leader of our club. We never interacted much besides him giving me orders. But more recently, I guess you can say we've become friends."

"What prompted the change?" The woman glanced over at Reaper and reached over to touch the back of her fingers to his cheek. "No fever at least," she muttered to herself.

"It's a lot to explain." I shifted to a more comfortable sitting position myself, the clinking of my chains echoing softly throughout the dungeon. "But the core of it is, we share a wife."

The woman's head snapped back toward me, eyes narrowing with suspicion or confusion, I couldn't tell. "What do you mean, 'share a wife'?"

"Our wife has four husbands. He was her first," I nodded at Reaper, "I was her last."

The woman's hand drifted over her loose clothing as if searching for a weapon. "Did you buy her from one of those human auctions? Split the cost up between the four of you?" Her words carried venom now, and I bet she wished that the snake had attacked us rather than helped us.

"No, no. It's not like that," I rushed to tell her. "We don't own her, it's quite the opposite really." I huffed out a bitter laugh, recalling the longing and the heartbreak from the Sha's trick. I was fucking doomed if I stayed here another day. "She's with us willingly, and she has so much power over us. She's our whole world. We love and cherish her. She *chose* me, when I never thought in a million years she would."

The guard's tense position relaxed a little, her hand returning to her lap. "What's your wife's name?"

"Mariposa." The taste of her name in my mouth was as sweet as the water I drank.

The guard stiffened again, her eyes wide and burning into mine. "What did you say?"

"Mariposa," I repeated. "It means butterfly."

"I know what it means!" the guard snapped, her apparent vitriol coming out of nowhere. "What's her last name?"

"Why?" My own defenses rose up, confused by this woman's reaction to the mere mention of my wife's name. "Do you know her?"

"Is it Wilder?" she demanded. "Is your wife Mariposa Wilder?"

"What's it to you?" I probably already said too much since Mari's given name was unique enough, but if this woman meant her harm, I wouldn't give her another inch.

"She's my fucking daughter, that's what she is to me!"

I froze, at first in disbelief, then all the clarity dawned on me. The snake god, being hidden in plain sight. *Of course.*

"Will you take off your mask and hood?" I asked.

I didn't think she would, but the woman shoved away the loose fabrics covering head and face as though they were suffocating her.

The resemblance was uncanny. Her hair was a lighter shade of brown than Mari's and her eyes were blue instead of that shifting green-to-brown. But her nose, lips, and cheekbones were identical to my wife's. If it weren't for the deep lines around her eyes and mouth, they could have been sisters.

"I'm Emma," the guard said softly. "Emma Wilder."

"I wish we could have met under better circumstances, Emma." A sudden realization jolted me. "Your husband! Mari's father."

All of the suspicion and distrust drained out of Emma right then. She let out a soft gasp and scooted toward me across the floor until she crouched directly in front of me. If my hands were free, I could have touched her.

"Javier? Have you seen him?" she asked rapidly. "Is he...is he himself?"

My eyes dropped toward the floor, wishing I had better news to tell her. "Last I saw, he was being treated for injuries at our field hospital. When Mari saw him, he didn't recognize her."

I wasn't there for it, but Jandro had let me know what happened. By the time I'd been able to see her, we were all rounded up and held at the hospital because of the Sha trying to break into our minds.

Emma clapped a hand to her mouth, her fingers shaking.

"I'm sorry," I offered her. "His condition was improving, from what I understand. But then the Sha's forces swarmed over Four Corners. We evacuated the field hospital, but that's when we got captured."

Emma rocked backward until she sat on the floor again, her mind somewhere far outside of this prison cell. She was silent for a long time and I was too exhausted, thirsty, and hungry to get a sense of her mood.

"You love my daughter?" she asked to break the silence.

"Yes." My eyes were half-closed and Mari was all I could see. Imagining her was my only escape from this hellhole. "She taught me what love means. She's the most incredible person I've ever met. If we die in here," I let my head rest against the wall, "it'll be worth it, knowing she loved me back."

"The Sha won't let you die." Emma's voice was clipped as she replaced the hood over her hair and covered her mouth and nose again with the mask. "Him, maybe." She jerked her head toward Reaper. "But I think the Sha has a special interest in breaking and controlling you."

"Story of my life," I muttered.

Emma reached into her robes and pulled out something that made my breath shorten and my heart accelerate--a dagger with a slender but wickedly sharp blade. Just as quickly as she showed it to me, she hid it underneath her clothing again.

"It will be your choice," she whispered. "Just say the word, and I'll give you one final mercy. But you have one day, maybe less, to decide."

The gravity of what she was saying settled heavily over me. I didn't *want* to die but I wanted to be controlled like a zombie even less. However, her method of choice just might tip me in the opposite direction.

"Is there another way?" My chest felt tight as old, bygone fears began rising to the surface. "Other than a blade?"

Emma blinked, her stare curious now in a different way. Blue eyes shifted over me as if taking in my scarred exterior for the first time.

"Taking a gun could blow my cover." She stood from the floor, heading toward the cell door. "I've already been here too long as it is." Her keys jangled as she unlocked it, metal hinges creaking as she let herself out. "The next time you see me, I need to know your decision."

"Oh, my son. Have you missed me?"

The voice jolted me awake. Fuck. No. I couldn't be awake. Not if *she* was here.

My mother's gaunt face hovered in front of me, only empty blackness surrounded her. Blood dripped from her mouth and her hairline. Whether that blood belonged to me or her, as a result of the village getting massacred, I didn't know.

"You're not real." I tried to close my eyes and turn my face away, but there was no escaping her. There never was. "You're dead. You don't haunt me anymore."

"I'll always haunt you, you worthless stain. Where do you think you'll go when that woman, my earthly sister, finally ends your pathetic life?" She grinned, her teeth stained dark with blood. "And with a blade, no less. Isn't that poetic?"

"She's not like you!" I roared back. "She didn't lock her child in a cage!"

I should have done my deep breathing, should have thought of Mari to calm myself. But I was so tired, so weak and desperate. My mother's ghost showed up at the perfect time to get under my skin and dredge up everything I fought so hard to keep at bay.

"Because she had a daughter!" my mother cackled. "A beautiful, perfect daughter. Too bad the girl wasn't raised right. She was stupid enough to love you, even to almost get killed by you. You see? Men are *horrible*."

"*You* made me that way! Because you're an abusive, psychotic bitch!"

I should have saved the last of my strength rather than spend it yelling my lungs out at this ghost, hallucination, whatever she was. But I was too deep in my rage, completely lost to the storming sea of anger and hatred that used to rule me. Hatred at myself for what I was, anger at her, at everything, for never allowing me to have a normal life.

"No, you're just proof that the Elder was right. Our goddess was right! Men do nothing but destroy everything they touch. You almost killed a woman you supposedly love! She could have died just like *so* many others."

The echo of a thought whispered through my mind, *She's right...*

"You're wrong," I said in an attempt to squash the voice, but my doubt began to bleed through. I was good at killing, and little else. What if I wasn't a good man? I did hurt Mari, the one who mattered to me the most...

No, no. You've been here before. Don't go down this path again. Come back, Shadow.

I managed to find my breathing somehow, focusing my attention on a memory of Mari's face and the shallow expanding of my lungs.

My mother's image was still there, but it flickered like it was fading.

"I accept responsibility for what I did to her," I said, calmer than moments ago. "And I know you died never feeling an ounce of responsibility for what you did to me." I lifted my head, looking my mother square in the eye. "That alone makes me a better person than you ever were."

She flickered even more rapidly, like the flame of a candle under a gust of wind. "I have been a victim of *men* my whole life, including you!" She stuck a bony, trembling finger in my face. "You almost killed me too when you were born, you know."

"I wish I did."

There was no reasoning with her, no way to make her see that it had been me who was a victim of hers. The only difference between now and back then was the knowledge that she no longer had power over me. "Fuck, I wish I could've watched you bleed to death when that militia rolled in and killed everyone."

"You're a sick, evil *man*!" she spat.

"I hope you're in some kind of Hell right now," I went on. "And all the men you killed for bullshit sacrifices for your fake fucking goddess are treating you exactly like how you treated me."

"I should have killed you when you first drew breath outside of my womb!"

"I hope you feel every bit of pain I stopped feeling years ago." My life likely would be ending soon, so now seemed like the best time to unload everything I wished for the monster who birthed me into the world. "The pain isn't even the worst part. I hope you feel so utterly lonely that abuse becomes attention you're grateful for. I hope that every time you feel a shred of happiness, it's ripped away from you in the most cruel and unbearable way."

I shut my eyes against her visage, which held on stubbornly despite its flickering and fading. "If I live beyond one more day, I'll never speak of you or waste another thought on you again. Your power over me is gone, and you don't deserve to live another miserable second in my head."

A sensation washed over me, like I had been paralyzed before but now I could move. She was gone when I opened my eyes, but I didn't know if that was a victory or defeat.

Reaper continued to lie motionless on the other side of the dingey cell. I was still chained to a wall and growing weaker by the hour, mentally and physically. I had said what I'd wanted to say to my mother for years, but the closure was overshadowed by the fact that I was still in a dungeon. I would probably watch my friend die and follow him soon after. I might never see Mari again.

I needed to give Emma an answer when she returned in a day. What scared me the most was, I didn't know if I had the courage to tell her yes.

CHAPTER 16

JANDRO

I paced in front of the bikes, unable to sit still. I was both eager and filled with dread at this ride out to the fortress. It could be my last ride on this earth.

Only Hades and Freyja were with me, watching me wear a hole into the pavement like it was a spectator sport. Gunner was off with the general, finalizing the number of troops we'd need. And Mari said she wanted a moment alone while they did that. Unusual for her, but I tried not to worry. Everything depended on the success of this mission. The weight of it on all of our shoulders was no small thing.

I reached out to Mari with the god-infused, harnessed leash-bond or whatever it was. Here I thought I was the most basic dude of our group, but it turned out I had some special abilities too.

My perception overlapped with Mari's as I focused on our bond. She was out on one of the balconies, watching the tail end of the sunset fade into dusk. I felt the smooth glass of her butterfly pendant as she stroked a finger over it, heard the soft click of metal as her ring touched the necklace too. A gust of wind blew, and I could *feel* her dagger earrings swing like tiny windchimes along the sides of her face. And when she placed a hand on her left hip, I knew she was thinking of the man who tattooed her there.

She tugged back on our bond, the sensation like a string in my chest. It startled me, and I stopped reaching with a gasp and an elevated heart rate.

A few seconds passed and Mari reached for me again, amusement bleeding through our connection. I realized I could sense her proximity too. She no longer stood at the balcony now and was on her way toward me.

"Spying on me?" Mari asked with a smirk when she entered the garage, her voice echoing through the space.

"Just checking on you," I said, reaching for her with my arms now. "And trying this bond thing out since I only learned about it like an hour ago."

Mari accepted my embrace with ease, leaning into my chest. "How does it feel?"

"Honestly? I love it." I leaned against my bike, pulling her with me. "Even if we don't have the gods after all this, I hope *this* stays."

"Really?" Mari's hands wound around the back of my neck, her expression curious.

"Yeah." I folded my hands on her lower back. "I mean, I knew we always had something between us. It's just nice to feel *it*, the connection we have, physically."

"It is. And it feels so natural, like it was always there and we knew it. We just didn't see it." She smiled, tipping her head back. "Gunner's on his way back. He'll be here soon."

I swallowed, finding the question on my mind too unbearable to keep to myself. "Can you feel them? Reap and Shadow?"

Mari's smile fell with a small shake of her head. "No. I tried reaching on our way over here and there's no response, no feedback. I'm...scared of what that might mean."

"Hey." I lowered my forehead to hers. "Don't let your mind go there." But she already was. I could feel her frazzled emotions through our bond.

"What if we're already too late, Jandro?" Her fingers on my neck started to shake and I reached up to hold them.

"We don't know that," I said, trying to push steadiness and calm through my connection with her. "I don't want to have false hope either, babe. But we can't start thinking of the worst yet."

"I never got to tell Reaper I'm sorry." She brought her forehead to my chest and I immediately tucked her head under my chin, bringing a hand to the back of her head to hold her there.

"You have nothing to be sorry for, *Mariposita*. He understands."

"I don't know how that's possible because *I* didn't even understand! I pushed him away for no fucking reason."

"You had a reason, even if you didn't understand it. If it didn't feel right, it didn't feel right." I pulled away to cup her face and look in her eyes. "And you had no way of knowing this would've happened."

Mari closed her eyes and took a few shuddering breaths. When her face started to relax and I felt less tension through our bond, I pulled her back into my chest again. Whether from bullets, fire, or her own fears, I would protect her from it all.

"Do you really think we can do this, Jandro?" she whispered against my shirt.

My chest lifted with the deep breath I took before releasing it with a sigh. "You want to know my honest answer?"

She hesitated before answering quietly, "Yes."

"I do. I really fuckin' do. You want to know why?" I nuzzled the side of her face until my mouth touched her ear. "'Cause they may be gods, but we're fucking Demons."

Mari's lips twitched into a smile as she squirmed in my arms. "*That's* your reason?"

"Yeah, I mean it." I held tight and grabbed her chin to make her look at me. "They fucked with our family and tried to run away. So we're bringing Hell to them. I don't know what we'll find when we arrive, but we'll make the Sha regret ever taking form here."

She nodded, lips still wobbling slightly but the fire in her gaze had returned. "You're right."

"That's it. Get mad, girl. They took *your* men from you." I swore I felt the heat of her anger simmering in our connection too. Sex with these bonds had to be on a whole other level. Hopefully we still had them and would still be alive after tonight.

"You guys ready?" Gunner's voice echoed as he hollered across the concrete garage.

Mari pulled away from me to embrace him, but she didn't melt into his chest like she did with me. She grabbed the back of Gunner's neck and pulled him down for a rough, biting kiss. It was so fast that he even stumbled from the momentum but found purchase on her waist and kissed her back with same ferocity.

I was grinning when they both came up for air—Gunner a little breathless with a dopey smile on his face, but Mari...

Mari strode over to her bike, looking ready to not only go to war, but to burn cities down that stood in her way. She cast one last look at Hades and Freyja, who stood off to the side of our exit in silent observation.

We are with you even when you cannot see us, Hades said. *Remember that you three are not battling alone.*

Horus and Quetzalcoatl are with you as well, Freyja added. *We carry you on our wings and in our hearts, bonded humans.*

With that, Gunner and I mounted up, flanking Mari on either side. No words were needed as we rode out of the garage, we all knew none of us would come back the same.

If at all.

CHAPTER 17

MARIPOSA

Outside of our bike engines, the ride to New Ireland was silent. Externally, anyway. Gunner, Jandro, and I didn't speak, but our bonds to each other, tethered and strengthened by the gods, were full of activity.

The best I could describe it would be like having a conversation without words. Like when two partners or best friends know exactly what the other is thinking just with a look, a subtle hand gesture, or a facial expression.

It was like that between the three of us, only amplified and solidified into an invisible thread that connected all of us. Without words, touch, or even looking at each other, we expressed worries and fears at what we would find. We also reassured each other and validated each other's strength and determination. We were completely in sync, my two men and I. And when that first glimpse of the fortress broke the line on the horizon, I felt the cold, steel-like focus straighten all of our spines.

Jandro and I picked up speed, maneuvering to let Gunner hang back slightly in the middle. I didn't need to look to know Gunner was pulling his first rifle from the holster on his back. We were still thousands of yards away, and his rifle didn't have a sniper scope, but he didn't need one.

Gunner's shots broke the low, constant hum of our bikes. He took out the guards atop the front perimeter wall cleanly, despite them looking like specks in the distance.

In my head, I could see the layout of the interior, thanks to the map Gunner drew with help from my dad's memory. I wanted to veer left, to start sneaking around the back of the compound and send the Sha's zombie army on a wild goose chase. But Jandro and Gunner urged me back into the middle of our formation with our mental bond. They wanted me between them, shielded at all costs.

I gave in to their tugging, veering back to the center while Gunner drove out to take my place. He was reloading his rifle one-handed when the enemy returned fire.

The bonds made me aware of the returned fire from all angles, like I was in multiple places at once. More soldiers spread out on top of the perimeter wall. I sent Jandro a tug of warning about a cluster of soldiers aiming straight for him, and he zigzagged to avoid their shots.

I pulled out my rifle and aimed straight ahead when my shots were clear enough. My shots were true from the first trigger pull. I returned fire with no fear of the bullets whizzing past me and plinking off my bike. I hit soldiers in the chest, even the head, while keeping the balance of my bike rock-steady with my left hand. If I had a moment to think, I'd wonder if I borrowed Gunner's marksmanship and Jandro's natural ease on the bike, thanks to our bonds.

But my mind was calm and blissfully blank. Like the glassy surface of a lake, so still and tranquil. My whole body was the weapon, and my mind, the clean, efficient mechanism.

Jandro took out the ground soldiers guarding the gate to the inside of the fortress. Like me, he also had better accuracy than normal. When the men fell, he shot at the heavy chain and lock system holding the doors together. But those on the inside did our work for us.

The tall doors burst open, and an endless stream of black poured out to greet us, like ink spilling on a page.

We were ready.

The three of us pulled the pins on our grenades and tossed them. Mine bounced toward the front of the swarm, Jandro's landed in the middle, and Gunner's sailed the farthest. Three simultaneous explosions rocked our eardrums and the earth beneath our tires, but we stayed upright and drove straight through the carnage.

Did you hear that, Reaper? Shadow? Mom? We're coming for you. Another thought followed on the heels of that one. *Can your earthly body hear us, Set? We're coming for you too.*

The explosion cleared enough space for us to drive into the first courtyard and form a circle with our bikes. With the swarm quickly recuperating to close in on us again, it was time to bring out the big guns.

Our motions were fluid, well-practiced and confident as we readied our assault rifles. The spray of fire we rained down was merciless. All the panicked shouts and rapid spraying of bullets was just background noise to the cold, rigid focus in my mind. I didn't even care in that moment that these were people being puppeted and forced to attack us. They stood between me and my loved ones and would kill me first if I let them.

The swarm's assault was never-ending, but thankfully so was our gunfire. These weapons had come from Gunner's prized stash and had been altered to fit long, winding bandoliers of ammo rather than magazines. Too destructive for typical warfare, Gunner had originally procured these as collector's items. Now the three of us were draped in yards and yards of ammunition, firing endlessly into the crush of bodies closing in on us and barely making a dent.

I ground my teeth against my gun becoming so hot that it burned the palms of my hands. My whole body was numb from the constant rattle and vibration of my firing. But I couldn't stop to rest, not even for a moment. They just kept coming.

My bonds to Gunner and Jandro were wide open, keeping me aware of everything from their perspectives as well as mine. Gunner was in a precarious spot, having to swing his weapon in a wide arc to keep the enemy at bay. Every time he swung in one direction, they creeped in closer from the opposite side. Back and forth he had to do this, never missing a single shot, just to keep us covered. I felt his worry, his realization that he couldn't continue like this forever.

Really, none of us could. We had just entered the compound and how long had we been sitting here already? Minutes? Hours? We still had the Sha to deal with, and then getting our people out. Spending all our energy and firepower here would kill this mission before it ever began.

I pushed all my determination and support to my men and just kept firing. What else could I do? The bodies piled up all around us, but it did no good. Soldiers walked or jumped over them. Some started dragging or shoving the bodies away to clear more paths to us. They never, *ever* stopped, so how could we?

My arms ached all the way up to my shoulders. The gun was heavy, and while I was pumped full of adrenaline, my physical strength could only carry me so far, and I was reaching the end of my limit. My hands were surely burned and blistered from gripping the hot metal by now. As my strength faded, my shots went lower and lower, hitting at waist and leg height. I pulled up on my barrel as soon as I realized it, but my arms screamed in protest.

My guys weren't faring much better. I could feel the fatigue in Gunner's arms, taste the blood in Jandro's mouth from biting his cheek so hard. The longer we carried on, the more we began to slow down. And our enemies took every single opening they saw.

"Gunner, your left!" I cried out, still without taking my eyes off of the onslaught in front of me.

Gunner swung wide with his weapon, his weariness making him overshoot the arc and allow a pocket of mind-controlled drones to creep in closer on the other side. Jandro took them out moments before they could touch Gunner, but then that left Jandro vulnerable and I swung to protect his open side.

"Mari, watch out!"

I ducked just in time to avoid Jandro's spray of bullets over my head. Blood rained down on me, the remains of my would-be attackers.

What began as such a strong attack quickly turned into us backing into a corner. We were all defensive now, our ammunition and stamina dangerously low. Our bonds were stronger and more connected than ever—really they were the only reason we covered each other so effectively, but now they were overridden with panic.

And the enemy never stopped coming.

They crept closer with every beat, every half-second we lowered our guns and paused our shooting because our hands burned and we were so damn weary.

We're not going to make it. The thought bubbled to the surface, breaking through my confidence, calm, and razor-sharp focus. I tried to shove it back down, to override it before the guys sensed it through our connection, but the damage had already been done.

Their minds latched onto that thought and fed into it, giving it more power that threatened to shatter our resolve, to make us lose sight of the whole reason we risked everything to come here.

Get Mari out of here. I didn't so much hear my guys' thoughts as much as felt them.

"No!"

I screamed the word at the top of my lungs, a final battle cry as I used my last well of strength to lift my weapon and fire at the swarm of black.

They were so close now, mere inches away. I could see their blank, empty eyes under their hoods and many had been able to touch my bike before I shot them dead. It wouldn't be long now, just moments until one of them grabbed my leg or snatched my gun out of my hand.

Calmness returned to my mind, the panic and fear subsiding. Only instead of focus and determination, I was filled with resigned acceptance. We tried our best. I would kill as many of them as I could and see this through to the end. The end which was moments away.

I'm so sorry, Reaper. Shadow. Mom. Andrea. But especially you, Reaper. Our last moments together are my only regret.

As soon as I finished the thought, I fired my last round and my gun clicked empty.

Chapter 18

JANDRO

My thousands upon thousands of bullets ran out. And when my gun clicked empty, I still couldn't hesitate. Still couldn't give them a fucking inch.

On that last click, I swung my gun around and crashed the butt against the nearest zombie's face. His jaw broke, but he kept coming at me with dead, empty eyes. It was like the blow never registered. Even Shadow flinched when he took a hit, but this swarm felt *nothing*.

I hit him again and again and again, until I could see brain matter peeking through the bloody mess of his skull and his body finally gave out.

Killing that one took way too long. It allowed ample time for the rest of them to close the short distance and attack me from all directions. The swarm climbed over my bike, grabbing at my legs, arms, and torso.

I twisted and swung, throwing my elbows out and using my assault rifle like a police baton, trying to beat away everything that touched me. The feeling of the swarm closing in on me was amplified by knowing that Mari and Gunner were going through the same thing. If I focused on the bond, I could feel their desperation, the sensation of overwhelm and being crushed under the weight of *so* many. The mind-controlled soldiers never fucking stopped, never let up.

I was somehow still straddling my bike, squeezing the machine with my legs so hard just to maintain some higher ground. If one of these fuckers got an arm around my neck, I knew I'd be done for. It was how they got Reaper.

"Mari!"

I felt Mari's fear and panic hit a new spike through our bond just as Gunner frantically shouted her name. She had been dragged off of her bike and was now desperately kicking and swinging her gun from the ground.

Sensing her cost me a precious second of focus, and my air was abruptly cut off by an arm around my throat.

I couldn't yell, couldn't even feel the ground as I got dragged off my bike. Desperately, I pulled at the arm choking me. It didn't even feel like it belonged to an especially strong person, I should have been able to pull out of the hold with no problem, but it wouldn't even budge.

I started seeing black dots, felt my extremities going numb as I struggled for the tiniest sip of air. *It wasn't supposed to be like this. How could we fail so badly to protect Mari?*

If suffocating wouldn't end me here, the punches and kicks would surely do it. I barely felt the blows raining down on me, trying to disassociate so that Mari and Gunner wouldn't feel them and suffer even more than they already were.

Giving up so soon, my son?

I would have choked out a, "What?" if I could fucking breathe.

We told Mari this was out of the question, Hades mused inside my head. *But you are quickly declining, and we can't allow that to happen. As a last resort, I can make your body my vessel. I only need your permission.*

Do it! Do it! I screamed inside my head as I could feel the life draining from me. Who knew what the consequences of this would be, but they certainly couldn't be any worse than the fast-track toward death I was on now.

Hades went silent and for a moment, nothing was different. My vision was mostly black and my lungs had all but lost their desperate battle for air. Then a single pulse of energy thumped from my chest, like a heartbeat but different. It spread throughout my body and then every-thing was still.

And I mean, *everything*.

No more hits came down to assault me, and the arm around my neck was gone. Instead of the chaos of a swarm piling on to attack me, there was only eerie, death-like stillness.

I rolled to my side, then onto my knees to look around.

Death surrounded me, the swarm of soldiers was lifeless and scat-tered around everywhere. Mari was just rolling upright from where she had been dragged to the ground.

"Shit! Jandro, your eyes!" Mari cried out, stumbling to her feet and hurrying toward me.

"What? What's up with *your* eyes?" I retorted, scrambling backward on my butt at the sight of them. The pupils, irises, and whites of her eyes were gone, replaced by a single shade of bright, glowing green.

"Your eyes are all black." Mari fell to her knees in front of me, reaching for my face.

"Yours are green." It was so fucking creepy and weird, but honestly the least of my concerns the moment she touched me. "You're not hurt?" Creepy eyes aside, she looked fine, only dirty and disheveled from the ground.

"I was getting the shit kicked out of me but, no. I'm fine." Her fingers trailed from my face over my neck. "How about you? You don't look hurt."

"I was fucking seconds away from dying, I couldn't breathe," I confessed. "But...I feel okay too."

"Gunner!" Mari pulled away from me to look at carnage all around us. "Where's Gunner?"

"Here, baby girl."

We both looked in the direction of his voice to see Gunner standing, turning in a slow circle as he observed our surroundings. When he faced us, his eyes were replaced by a single shade of bright, sky blue.

"The gods are within us," Gunner said in a low, reverent tone. "Can you feel them?"

"Yes," Mari and I answered in unison, then looked at each other. "Hades?" she asked.

"Yes," my mouth replied, but it wasn't *me* that spoke. "Freyja." Hades inclined my head in Mari's direction first and then in Gunner's. "Horus."

"Wait, stop." I slapped my hand over my own mouth, then dropped the hand to my side. "You can control our bodies?"

I trusted these gods, I really did. And in a moment of desperation, I allowed Hades to take me as a vessel. But the fact that he used my mouth and voice to speak hit too close to home, considering we were dealing with a massive army of mind-controlled soldiers.

"Your control has not been removed." The tone of Mari's voice made it clear that Freyja was the one speaking. "Just as you can reach for your bonds between each other, you can remove us from your earthly vessels."

"No," Gunner said. "We're still alive because you've possessed us."

"You're alive because Hades is within Jandro and gave him power over death," Freyja said. She held up a hand, Mari's hand, and rotated her palm from front to back. "Your injuries are gone because I am within Mari and have given her my power to heal."

"And Gunner?" My gaze shifted toward him.

"I'm the sky," Gunner said in an awed whisper. "I can see everything. I know exactly where the Sha is. Our loved ones are in different areas of the fortress, but I can see them all."

"Well shit. What are we waiting for?"

"Wait." Freyja held up Mari's hand again. "There is a reason we do not take human vessels unless absolutely necessary. Your mind will start to deteriorate within hours. We don't want that for any of you, so our possession of you is temporary. Once we leave, you'll no longer have our abilities."

"Fine by me," I huffed. "Let's go."

Wait. Now Hades was speaking to me privately. *With your permission, I must do something before we move on.*

"What now?" I demanded of myself like a crazy person.

Look closely at the departed. Do you see them?

It took me a moment, but after some squinting, I did. Hovering over the dead bodies was some light, ethereal substance like smoke. It hovered a few feet in the air above the deceased, moving and shifting in space, like a person who couldn't get comfortable.

Their humanity was stripped away, their bodies driven like vehicles, and now they have been ejected from life altogether. I must put them to rest.

I understood right away. These people, people that *I* killed, needed peace.

Okay, I agreed.

Do not feel guilty, son, Hades told me as we approached the shimmery, smoke-like substance. *They will understand that we have set them free. I'm only shepherding them to their final state of rest.*

It was over quickly. The death god waved my hand through the smoke, which felt cool to the touch but charged, like static electricity, and used my mouth to utter one word.

"Rest."

The twisting, writhing movements of the cloud gradually stilled and then faded away into nothing. The tension in the air that I hadn't noticed before was gone. The eerie silence of the courtyard now felt peaceful, if even tranquil. No ghosts would haunt this place. With any luck, we would leave no remnants of the Sha at all.

"What now?" I turned back to Mari and Gunner.

"Now we go to the Sha and end this." Gunner's lip curled, and I wasn't certain if it was really him or Horus speaking. That could have been the sky god himself, seeking retribution against his brother, or his bonded human wanting it for him. "He already knows what happened in this courtyard and is sending double the amount of troops in hopes of overwhelming us. We'll cut through them easily and head directly for him."

"And if we can't kill him?" Mari's weird, glowing eyes shifted between me and Gunner. Now that I was getting used to it, they looked cool on her, like she was some kind of comic book superhero.

"Then we'll find and kill his council members, as we discussed," Hades said.

"The last time Set took form as the Sha," Horus used Gunner's pretty-boy lips to smirk, "he was torn apart by a pack of jackals. Some say he was trying to raise an army from the dead, and the jackals were sent by Anubis to protect their graves."

"So hopefully guns will be enough?" Mari asked, already loading up on the rest of her weapons from her toppled bike.

"They should," Horus answered. "He can certainly be killed by earthly means, but the jackal incident has made him cautious. I imagine that's why he's never revealed himself publicly. We should expect him to be heavily guarded."

Mari's gaze focused on me, but I knew it was Hades she spoke to. "Can you do the same thing to him that you did to this swarm? Kill him with a single pulse of power?"

"Sadly, no, daughter," Hades replied.

I wish you wouldn't call her that. It feels really weird coming out of my mouth, I informed him.

Hades ignored me. "With a few exceptions, gods' abilities are for humanity, not for each other." He directed my eyes toward Gunner. "I suppose that's why Anubis chose to use jackals the first time around."

"You're correct," the sky god confirmed.

Mari accepted that answer, nodding curtly as she holstered a handgun and filled her remaining pockets with loaded magazines. "Then I'll be happy to fill him up with holes and watch him fade away."

CHAPTER 19

MARIPOSA

We hurried across the fortress, making our way easily through any swarm that tried to surround us. A single pulse of power radiated out from Jandro and everyone was dead in the blink of an eye. Hades put the souls to rest, and Horus directed us closer to the Sha's inner chamber.

It all started to make sense to me as we got closer. The Sha was never seen out in public. Even his own soldiers within the compound knew him as General Tash, and only the General Council members that Andrea told us about, had a direct line to the mysterious general.

The Sha was afraid. I'd even go as far as to say that he was a fucking coward.

He knew a gun could kill him, knew his earthly body was just as vulnerable as any other body. The mysterious general persona, all the mind-controlled soldiers he threw into battle like they were nothing, it was all just to protect his slimy, cowardly hide.

The deeper we marched into the fortress, the hotter my anger burned. The Sha threw my father out into battle and stole my husbands, probably to use them as more armor to hide behind.

To my surprise, Freyja seemed pleased at my budding anger. I felt her within me and sort of outside of me, like a friend walking so closely behind me that I could sense her just over my shoulder.

Don't forget that I am also a goddess of death, she reminded me. *Death is the greatest sacrifice for love. This anger you feel now is a result of your love, dear daughter. Your passion and devotion to the men who were taken from you. Let it fuel you and guide your hand.*

Am I right, though? I asked in response. *Or am I way off base about the Sha being so afraid?*

I have never had the pleasure of meeting Set in any of his forms. Freyja's mental voice bristled. *In any case, it does not matter. You have found a source of strength. Now use it.*

Before long, we approached a set of massive wooden doors carved intricately with hieroglyphics. At any other time I would have liked to study the symbols, run my fingers through the deep grooves of the wood. It'd be even better if Shadow was with me, book in hand as we tried to decipher the ancient language together. But the thing that took him from me likely resided on the other side of those doors. I'd blast those intricate carvings to splinters without a second thought if it got me any closer to my men.

Gunner, or Horus rather, looked back to face me, those blue eyes like slivers of sky. "The Sha is in there," Horus confirmed with a jerk of Gunner's head toward the doors.

Jandro turned to me next, focusing those endlessly black eyes on me while extending a palm in my direction. "Stay back. Let us go through first."

I wasn't sure if it was Jandro or Hades speaking but I nodded regardless, tightening my grip on my handgun. We'd used all of our big guns on the initial swarm, and I prayed to the gods inhabiting us that 9mm and .40 caliber rounds would be enough to kill the Sha.

Gunner and Jandro approached the doors, flattening their palms against the wood as they began to shove. The doors gave only a centimeter with a heavy groan of wood before it halted them from pushing any further.

"It's braced from the other side," Gunner remarked. He only gave a nod to Jandro, who returned the gesture, before they began pushing again.

"Guys, what—"

I ate my words the moment I heard a massive crack, like a tree branch breaking off from the trunk. The doors moved inward, the seam between them widening as Gunner and Jandro pushed harder, arms straight out in front of them and muscles taut with effort.

No, not Gunner and Jandro. Horus and Hades.

Because no human man had the brute strength to push open twenty-foot tall, solid wood doors that were barricaded from the other side. That cracking sound must have been the bracer, snapping like a toothpick once the gods decided to give my men a huge boost of strength.

"Shit, man, can I keep this?" That was definitely Jandro.

I didn't know if Hades answered. Once the doors were all the way open, ten figures awaited us on the other side. These people wore loose-fitting pants and tunics, their heads and mouths covered, and gold pins of the Sha affixed to their shoulders.

Each person also held an assault rifle pointed directly at us.

"The General's Council, I presume," Horus said with a sneer on Gunner's beautiful face.

These were the Sha's most loyal followers, his mouthpieces and representatives for dealing with humans. The pulse of death could not come soon enough for these traitors to humanity.

"Smoke 'em, Hades." Jandro's expression morphed just as the words left his mouth, and I knew something was wrong the moment Hades took over.

"I can't." Hades sounded dumbfounded through Jandro's mouth. "The Sha has—"

They opened fire before he could answer.

Pain burned through my body before I realized what was happening. I looked down to see holes through my stomach and chest, blood spreading quickly from the open wounds. I opened my mouth to scream but couldn't breathe. Blood erupted from my mouth in a wet, hacking cough as I fell to the ground.

Freyja, heal me! Heal them! I cried out in my terrified, pain-stricken mind.

Shoot them, daughter. Use your weapons. Use that strength that was just fueling you moments ago.

But I'm shot! I'm dying!

I will not let you die, daughter. But my abilities are limited, and they will only shoot you again if I heal you completely. Shoot them while they think you're not a threat.

The goddess went silent in my mind, but I knew she was still present and protecting me. It was that knowledge that drove me to reach my shaking, blood-soaked hand to my holster. The pain was excruciating as I wrapped my fingers around the pistol's grip and used all of my strength to pull it out.

Fuck, everything hurt. Everything was burning, even my lungs. I was still coughing up blood as I tried to take in gulps of air. How I wasn't suffocating to death, I had no idea, but could only attribute it to Freyja keeping me alive.

I rolled to my stomach, every bullet wound feeling like a knife sinking deeper into my body as the ground pressed into those areas. I needed to brace my forearm on the ground to push up, but I didn't even feel strong enough to lift my head. The ground beneath me was soaked with my blood, the sight of it spreading out around me cementing how close to death I really was.

Can't do this. I can't...

You can. Freyja's voice returned with a ferocity in my head. *You will. I did not choose a weak human. You can do this, Mariposa.*

You need to do it for me. I can't even raise my arm to shoot.

The more I manipulate your body, the less healing I will be able to do. Remember why you came here. Remember the reason you're filled with bullet holes right now.

I didn't know. I couldn't remember. All I wanted was for the pain to stop, to close my eyes to the pool of blood surrounding me and be happy at home with my men.

My men. Mine.

My eyes snapped open to look ahead of me. Gunner and Jandro were also on the ground, blood soaking their clothes and darkening the earth surrounding them. It seemed they'd been able to shoot a few of the

General's Council before taking hits themselves—only seven of the black-clad figures were standing, the remaining three fallen and lifeless.

So they weren't completely invincible, just somehow immune to Hades' instant death ability.

My men, they need my help. I raised my shooting arm but could only get the gun a few inches off the ground. My hand shook, slippery with blood.

Movement drew my eye to Gunner. He released one weapon with a clatter and drew a new one holstered at his lower back. Despite being prone and bleeding, and likely in an enormous amount of pain, his shots were swift and his arm steady. Years of practice made him incredibly effective with firearms, and he took out two more of the armed council members. Their bodies dropped like stones but that left five remaining, all of whom pointed their barrels at Gunner.

"No!" I cried out, mouth pouring blood as they rained fire down on him. Not him. I couldn't lose anyone else.

Two of the council swung to fire at Jandro, who had started crawling in my and Gunner's direction. He covered his head and curled up to protect his chest and stomach, but the onslaught of bullets still struck across his broad back.

Not my men.

A swell of fury lifted my chest from the ground. My left forearm pressed into the ground to lift myself higher, my shooting arm raised and extended. I fired, unleashing hell on those who dared to hurt my family. Not just my husbands, but my parents. All the medics and soldiers we lost. The countless families torn apart because this chaos god needed slaves to spread his destruction far and wide.

I didn't aim, and truly didn't know if my hits were landing. All I saw was Gunner and Jandro, clinging to life when these beautiful, loving men should have been vibrant and full of life. All five of us still had lives to live—parties, laughter, and quiet moments. Adventures across the country on motorcycles and milestones with our future children. My men had so much taken from them already. None of them would be taken from *me* again.

My shooting was only halted by a pulse of energy radiating from my chest. It knocked the wind out of me like I'd been kicked, sending me sprawling flat on the ground again as I took huge gulps of air.

Air! I could breathe!

I pressed up to my knees, still shaky, but not as weak as I was moments ago. My clothes were tattered with holes and I was still drenched in my own blood, but the bullet wounds were gone.

"Mari, get down!"

I flattened myself to the ground just as rapid fire sailed over my head. More shooting filled the air for the next few seconds, then silence. Peeking up carefully, I saw Jandro and Gunner sitting up, looking exhausted but very much alive. The same couldn't be said for the General's Council, whose dead bodies littered the massive foyer we opened the doors to.

"We got 'em all," Jandro said with a weary breath. "Fuck, I thought that was it."

"Felt a bullet actually touch my brain. That was wild." Gunner tried for his signature easy smile, but I could see how the shootout had rattled him too. His expression changed, looking oddly serious as Horus took over. "Thank you, Freyja. You were wise to wait on the healing."

"The three of them were very near death." The goddess used my mouth to inform everyone. "I can't do much more in Mari's vessel before I must leave her. If the humans are badly injured again, I may not be able to heal them sufficiently."

Horus narrowed those endlessly blue eyes. "I don't believe there is anyone else between us and the Sha. He is expecting us."

The three of us—six of us?—got up from the floor and looked down the long corridor where another set of doors awaited. These were also carved with hieroglyphics and stretched to the tall, vaulted ceiling of the building we'd just entered.

Gunner and Jandro moved in closer to me, their presence calming and supportive. I reached out until our hands touched, just a light sweep of my fingers across their palms so I knew they were still with me.

"Let's not keep the Sha waiting," I said.

CHAPTER 20

REAPER

"What's happening?"

I'd been having a fine, dandy visit with Hades and the other god in this dreamlike state for some time, with only the occasional pull toward the door of my childhood home. But the longer I stayed here, the worse I felt.

I was sweating, shivering, nauseous, and weak. Every glance toward the cabin's door, and every inch I moved in that direction, provided a small amount of relief that was never quite enough.

"Your body is failing." Hades stared at me, narrow-eyed, his mouth in a hard line. "You're inching closer to death."

"Fuck." I closed my fists at my side and turned my back toward the cabin. Each step I took away from that structure was pure agony, like fire stripping away the flesh from my legs. But I was no stranger to pain. *It's not real,* I reminded myself through gritted teeth. *This isn't my real body. I'm lying unconscious in a dungeon with Shadow, and I have to stay alive.*

It sure as fuck felt real though. I doubled over, my stomach roiling in protest. *Just one look. It'll take the edge off.*

The glance over my shoulder only made me feel worse, like my body was punishing me for putting more distance between me and that cabin.

"Quetzalcoatl," Hades snapped at the other god.

Pretzel-what?

"Can't you stabilize him any more? He's fading."

"I'm sorry. I've reached the limit of my healing abilities." The other god's hands stretched out in front of him, palms facing each other and fingers extended like he was playing one of those kid games with a piece of string. He was still standing on the front porch of the cabin, blocking the door, his face a mask of concentration, focused on his hands. Whatever he was doing may have been fascinating to watch, but all I could think about was him being in my fucking way.

"Move." I had doubled over so far, I was now on my hands and knees, crawling toward the only place that would give me relief. "Get out of my way."

"Don't, Reaper," Hades pleaded. "You must hold on."

"Then fucking stop me!"

The death god looked truly conflicted. "I can't interfere with your free will."

"You want to hold on, Reaper," the other god added, his fingers moving like he was weaving an invisible piece of string between them. "Your wife is on her way to you."

I halted my crawling, fingers curling into the dirt beneath my palms. "Mari? She's coming?"

"Yes."

He didn't elaborate. The unspoken words felt like an additional form of torture, bringing my agony to a new level. But it gave me something to fight the pull of death that so seductively promised me sweet relief.

I rocked back on my heels, bringing my chest up despite the motion feeling like barbed wire being wrapped around my heart. "Is she going to make it? How much longer?"

"I'm sorry. I know many things, but I don't know the answers to your questions."

My palms slapped back to the ground, frustration and defeat riding me hard. "Is she okay? Does she have a chance or should I just give in now?"

"Don't give in," Hades growled, sounding more like my dog than the man currently at my side. "I will take you to the underworld if I must but now is not your time to die, Reaper."

"How about...ugh...two minutes from now?" I wasn't even certain I could last that long.

"Mariposa and her men are currently alive." The god on my porch now had a small frown on his face, his brows knitting together.

"That's all you can fucking tell me?" Sweat poured off my face, hitting the dirt in front of me, the dark spots like rain. I inched closer to the cabin and it felt *so* good, but not enough. My pain level went down from ten to 9.8. *Maybe if I just stayed close enough without actually going inside...*

"I must go." Hades clapped a solid hand down on my shoulder, and I swore the motion drew me a few inches back. "Don't go into that cabin under any circumstances, Reaper."

"Wait, what?" I took a long, agonized look up at him, too consumed with pain to figure out what he was saying. "Where are you going?"

"We'll see each other again," he said ominously. "But I must focus my energy somewhere else at the moment. Hopefully, it will also help ease your suffering."

"What the fuck are you talking about?"

But he was gone in the next moment, and I was talking to an empty space. Looking ahead of me, the strange god was still frowning, his fingers moving more rapidly than before.

"Who are you again?" I asked, desperate to focus on anything but the agony riding me.

"Quetzalcoatl," he answered. "God of wisdom for the Mexica."

"And you're here, why?"

"To keep you alive," he answered with a mild scoff.

"Yes, I know, but—"

His head jerked up suddenly, dark eyes focused on some distant point while his moving hands abruptly froze.

"I must go too."

"What?" For a brief moment, my shock and panic overrode the pain. "No, you can't leave."

"I'm sorry, I can only focus my energy in so many places at once." His eyes met mine, looking genuinely apologetic. "I cannot keep you stable and provide mental shields against the Sha at the same time. You must do as Hades says."

"You are the only thing keeping me from going through that door," I protested. "If I'm here alone, then..."

"If I stay, Mariposa has no chance of saving you," he shot back. "And all your suffering will be in vain."

"Fuck...I don't think I can do it."

"You must. Everything that matters to you rides on your survival. Your wife, your family. They need you to live."

"Fuck!" I lowered my head to clasp it in my hands, tugging at the roots of my hair to alleviate the burning ache through my skull, but it was just more pain. And I didn't dare look up, knowing that if I saw no one there, I wouldn't be strong enough to stay.

I realized in that moment what my biggest fear was—dying alone.

Even if I wasn't really by myself, if Shadow was still next to my lifeless body yelling at me to wake up and drink water, I felt so fucking alone here.

My eyes squeezed shut, fighting the need to just look at the door, now that it had no obstacles in the way. It would be so easy to just walk through, to make all of this go away...

"Damn, Reap. Lookin' strung out."

The voice was like cool water on a burn. My heart jumped but I still wasn't prepared to uncurl from my fetal position and risk seeing that door.

"I haven't seen you look this shitty since that bad mushroom trip in Mexico. Remember that?"

My head lifted an inch, but my eyes remained pressed shut.

"Daren?"

"Yeah, it's me, bro. I got you."

I unfurled myself slowly, eyes peeking open to take in the young man sitting cross-legged in front me, blocking my view of the cabin. Daren had one elbow propped on his knee, cheek resting on his fist with a lazy smile.

It took a few minutes, but I slowly drew myself up to his level. His familiar face, those green eyes we share from our mother, hardened with determination once I sat up.

"I'm not letting you go, Reap," Daren said. "I went when it was my time. It's not yours yet." He leaned forward and thumped my tired, aching chest. "I told you you were gonna die an old fucking man, right? Remember that?"

"Yeah..." I forced a smile. Seeing him genuinely made me happy, even if everything hurt like a bitch. "Crazy thing is, I actually want to live to old age now."

"I know." Daren nodded solemnly. "So your ass is sitting right here 'til you wake up. I don't care what the gods say, I'll fuck with your free will if it means keeping you alive. Shit, I'll tie you up and find a tree to hang you in, if I have to."

I swallowed, the sensation like lava pouring down my throat. I still wanted to give in more than anything, to ease this pain and be free from it all. But Daren made it just a tiny bit easier, and I was no longer alone.

"Thanks for being here." I kept my gaze focused on my brother's face, not the cabin behind him. "I miss you, kid. I think about you all the fucking time."

He flashed me that boyish grin, the one that made all the girls swoon. "I'm always around, Reap. Can't reach the world of the living anymore, but dream states are a nice little loophole."

"Can you see anything?" I knew Daren's premonitions had continued after his death. It was his warning after all that had stopped Shadow from killing Mari. "Do you know what's gonna happen?"

Daren shook his head, his expression apologetic. "It's all blank from here on. Not even the gods know. This is the turning point."

My gaze flicked up to the cabin door, rooted to that focal point until Daren grabbed the sides of my face and forcibly turned my head away.

"Don't even think about it," he growled. "You're staying put."

Dragging my eyes away from the sight felt like they were being pepper-sprayed. A fresh sweat broke out on my skin and I felt absolutely terrible. But I had my little brother with me, and I'd never pass up the opportunity to talk to him again.

"So this is all I can do, huh?" I said, refocusing on him. "Just wait?"

"Yeah," he sighed. "We wait."

MARIPOSA

The second set of doors opened easily, revealing a mostly-empty room, save for the high-backed, throne-like chair at the far end. And the creature sitting in it.

Most of the Sha's body was covered by a shroud. Long swaths of black fabric draped over its head and most of its legs and torso. But the parts I did see made my breath choke.

Large hands with gray skin and curving black claws gripped the chair's armrests. Instead of feet on the floor, there appeared to be paws underneath the Sha's body. While his body was still, movement drew my eye to the lower left side of the chair. A tail covered in short, dark fur flicked forward. It was forked down the middle, the two ends twitching playfully, if even excitedly.

The Sha stood from his throne once we came to a stop in the center of the room. Tension crackled between me and the guys, lighting up our bonds with the desire to strike at this thing. But the Sha appeared carefree, even relaxed, as he walked on those two, pawed feet toward us. He didn't seem to notice or mind how we tracked every single one of his movements. A long snout, like the muzzle of a dog, peeked out from under his hood. His lips pulled back as if smiling, revealing long rows of sharp, predatory teeth.

"You eliminated my council, despite my infusing them with my god-resistant abilities." The Sha's voice was ancient and heavy like our gods, but carried a strange cadence. Not exactly an accent, but more like his mouth wasn't built for speaking human languages.

Regardless, he didn't sound upset that his council members were dead. If anything, he seemed amused by it.

"They were just flesh and blood in the end," I said, raising my handgun to point it directly at the shroud covering his chest. "As are you."

The Sha lowered his head, pointing his snout to the floor as a low chuckle rumbled from his throat. The sound gradually grew louder, transforming into a wild, maniacal laugh as it echoed off the walls and ceiling.

My temples immediately throbbed with pain, and I forced myself to keep my gun pointed and steady. That was the same laugh we all heard in our heads, the sound that tried to break us open from the inside.

"Oh, little Mariposa," the Sha sighed once his laughter ceased. "After all this time, and everything you've seen me accomplish, you still believe that?"

"If I'm wrong, this gun will clear it up real quick."

"Are you *sure* you want to use that on me?" Bright, round eyes scanned across all three of us from under the Sha's hood. "I don't think any of you want to shoot me."

I started to lower my gun. He was right, I didn't want to shoot him. But wait, why? I was going to shoot him a moment ago, but I just changed my mind.

"Fuck!" The exclamation came from Jandro, who clasped his hands against his head. "He's in our heads right now."

Cold dread filled me. My temples continued to pulse with pain, although it was manageable. I was aware and in control of myself, but I kept looking at my gun and thinking shooting the Sha was a bad idea.

"Your bonds between each other and your pet gods are impressive," the Sha mused, his toothy grin growing wider. "But I can still slip through the cracks."

"How?" Gunner's voice was so infused with bitterness and rage, I knew it was Horus speaking.

"Easily, brother," the Sha answered jovially. "The fall of the United States was the catalyst, as you know. This ripple through the human consciousness awakened me unlike any other time before. But where your lot sought to fix it, this Collapse gave me brand new life."

The Sha curled one clawed hand into a fist and re-opened it. "So much power from so many humans falling into violence, chaos, and unrest. I'd never seen anything so beautiful." His eyes scanned over the three of us. "All of you have fed into my power in ways you can't even imagine, simply by being alive at this point in time." The Sha's eyes settled on me. "But none more so than you, Mariposa."

"Me?" My voice went high with surprise. "What are you talking about? Ever since the Collapse, I've only ever wanted to heal the damage that's been done."

The Sha tilted his head as if considering my words. "Not you specifically, but your blood. Even with all my power building and becoming concentrated, I still needed to bond to a human to take physical form." He stepped closer, to the point of looming over me. "I needed someone with a mind that was broken and weak to be the first of my many drone soldiers. Do you know who that was, Mariposa?"

There was a long beat of silence as I gazed up at the Sha's roughly-canine face under the hood, that smug toothy grin that I hated so fucking much.

"Fuck you," I spat. "My father was never weak. *You* broke him and discarded him like a toy."

"He served his usefulness," the Sha said dismissively. "But oh, that post-traumatic stress disorder," he clicked his tongue, "provided so many delightful nooks and crannies for me to settle into." The Sha perked up as if excitedly remembering something. "Your man Shadow has many of the same."

"No." I wanted to scream the word but it came out as a defeated whisper. "You did not get inside Shadow, or Reaper. They're too strong, too *good*."

"Conquering them was a most thrilling challenge," the Sha continued to goad me. "But I must award the title of my favorite conquest to either your little spy, Andrea, or," he grinned wider than ever, "your mother."

"You piece of *shit!* I'll kill you!" I finally found my voice, but my shooting hand remained stubbornly at my side. The fucker was still influencing that part of my mind that wanted to fill him up with bullet holes. I was aware, pissed beyond all reason, and could easily raise my gun to shoot a hole in the ceiling. But he had pinched down on that desire to kill or injure *him.*

And judging by how the guys at my sides struggled and grimaced, they were dealing with the same issue.

A bitter laugh erupted from my throat. "You're such a fucking coward."

"Mari." Horus barked out my name in a gruff warning, but I was already seeing red.

"*You're* weak, Set," I went on. "I'm not addressing your earthly form, I'm talking to you, the god. What kind of god needs to control thousands of people to be considered powerful?"

The Sha tilted his head, another throaty chuckle emerging.

"Mari, don't." The warning came from Hades this time.

"What kind of god," I stepped forward until I was directly under the Sha's hood, "hides behind an army of thousands? Behind barricaded doors and armed guards infused with godlike power themselves?" I tilted my face up until my nose was just inches away from that long snout. "One who's afraid of a little gunshot wound?"

The Sha growled and a burning pain sliced through my forehead, forcing me to clutch my head with a hiss and stumble backward.

"I've held back this long because your human antics have been most amusing," the Sha rumbled. "But it seems the obvious has escaped you, Mariposa. I cannot die. Look at me."

The Sha threw back his hood to reveal a roughly dog-shaped head with triangular ears. His neck was longer than a human's, but his arms, shoulders, and torso were humanoid, covered in dark gray skin and a layer of fur-like hair.

"What am I?" the Sha taunted, spreading his arms to the sides. He took another step forward, knees bending backward like the legs of a bird. "I am neither human nor animal, unlike your pets. Something like me was never meant to live." He brought a clawed hand to his chest, that toothy grin maniacal. "Therefore, I cannot be killed."

"Let's test that theory," I shot back. "Let us go. No matter how nonsensical you are, you're still made of flesh and blood."

"I think not," the Sha purred. "As amusing as you have been, I'm tired of your thorns in my hide. Chaos must spread like the beautiful sickness it is, until all humans have fallen to it."

"Coward!" I yelled in his face. "You think you're so fucking powerful, but you're afraid of us!"

"Mari!"

Whoever yelled my name was too late, the pain felt like my head was being split apart by a crowbar. My knees hit the floor, but that was nothing compared to the agony driving through my skull.

He's overpowered the bonds! I could barely hear Freyja's frantic voice in my head over the scorching hot poker driving into my ears. *I can't shield you from him, daughter!*

Buried underneath the pain splitting my head apart, my desire to kill the Sha returned with a vengeance. He had finally released his hold, but now my brain was being literally scrambled and beaten within my skull. I couldn't even tell if I was holding a gun anymore.

I'm gonna die. Oh fuck, it hurts so bad...

"You're not dying that quickly, human." The Sha's voice cut through everything—my head, my skin. It stabbed through every organ in my body, twisting and plunging deeper. "You still doubt my power? I am not flesh and blood, but a *god*."

"Stop...please..."

I hated that I was begging, but I also didn't care anymore. The pain went so deep, was so constant, that I would have given up everything to make it stop. My breaking point was miles behind me. I had been dragged across it, over jagged glass shards and with burning hot hooks embedded in my flesh. The only reason I was still alive was because the Sha wanted me to experience this agony.

"I'm just getting started with you," the Sha purred pleasantly. "I hope you enjoy these scenes as I have."

The open throne room melted away, replaced by a room much smaller, darker, and dingier, like a basement. The shift in room size was so sudden, I was taken aback by how the brick walls seemed to close in on me.

"Reaper!" I whimpered when the figure slumped against the wall came into focus.

He was filthy and bleeding, arms and legs shackled to the wall while his head hung low and defeated.

My pain never let up for a moment but at least I had something to focus on now, the whole reason I came here.

"Reaper, I'm here. Can you hear me?" I tried to approach him but couldn't sense my hands or legs. I might as well have been floating in space.

A wide, swinging movement came down too quickly for me to follow. It collided with Reaper's head, forcing him to slump lower to the floor and curl up to protect himself.

"No, stop!" I screamed, full of my own agony and sympathy on his behalf.

Robed, hooded figures crowded around him, blocking my view while they connected kicks and punches to my husband's body. I screamed loud enough for the whole territory to hear, full of pain and rage at not being able to do anything.

"Stop! Stop! You'll kill him!"

I tried to rush forward, to tear and pull at Reaper's attackers, but my hands went straight through them. I tried to get in front of them, to act as a shield, but remained in place no matter how hard I pumped my arms and legs. It was like I'd become a ghost.

"I have enjoyed taking him to the brink of death, only to heal him and start the fun all over again." The Sha spoke with a pleased purr, but his voice was like thousands of knives dragging over my skin. "Would you like to see all the ways I tortured him?"

"No...no, please! Please stop." I shook all over—pain, grief, and horror shocking my system. I could *feel* myself breaking down beyond repair.

"The big one thought he could fool me by pretending to be affected by pain. But the best torture was making him watch my guards have fun with poor little Reaper."

Something about the Sha's taunts broke off pieces of me, but not the parts I expected. He wanted me to cower, to feel terrified, weak, helpless, and I did. But seeing what he did to my men awoke something else. Instead of pleading for my own life, for mercy from the pain at any cost, the part of me that cared for my own survival broke away.

We had our gods, harnessed our bonds, and had gotten so close. Here I was, close enough to Reaper to touch and help him, and I could do nothing but watch. Pieces of me were crumbling away to dust, but that feeling of utter helplessness did something else.

Like the core of a planet, it compacted and solidified all that was left of me, which wasn't much anymore. But what remained was hardened and dense, a final shield that no more pieces could be broken off of.

If I had to die—if my men had to die—then I wanted the Sha to remember me as the bitch who gave him hell long after I was gone.

CHAPTER 22

MARIPOSA

"You're weaker than I thought." I couldn't determine the volume of my own voice, so I made sure to say and think it as loud as I could. "For a god, you're fucking pathetic, Set."

His energetic presence shifted around me without a response. The pain sensations switched up too--now it felt like hot oil rained down on me in a relentless downpour. But I was too far gone to react to the pain anymore. All that mattered was getting under this cruel god's skin, to remain that thorn in his side and live inside his head, rent-free.

"You can't even beat up one weakened, shackled mortal man yourself?" I continued. "You have to make your minions do it? Your followers should be embarrassed."

"Do you wish for eternal suffering so badly, human? Because I will happily grant that to you."

Ah, so Set had just as fragile of an ego as I suspected.

"Sure you can. You have two men chained up in your dungeon and you can't break into either of their minds to control them. You know what?" I plastered a grin on my face, despite feeling dead and lifeless to my core. "You couldn't keep my father under your control either."

"You're speaking nonsense, girl. Seems I've scrambled you well."

"Oh no, I'm still all here." I was shocked to still feel in control of my faculties, but I wasn't about to question it. "And my dad remembers me. I saw the damage you did, but it seems you underestimated his so-called 'weak and damaged' mind."

"What do you hope to accomplish with lies, fool?" The Sha was clearly agitated now, barking at me for running my mouth.

"You know I'm not lying, you idiot god." I kept pushing. "You're right in here with me. All my thoughts, fears, and desires are laid bare to you. You *could* be powerful if you really tried. But you can't do shit."

The Sha yelled something else at me, but he sounded far away and muffled like he was underwater. Pressure closed in around my head, softening and blurring the world around me until it all went out of focus. Then there was a popping sensation and...I was back.

I stared at the ceiling of the throne room. Reaper, his attackers, my pain—everything was gone.

Daughter, I can reach you again! Freyja cried victoriously before I felt her healing pulse of energy spread out from my chest to the room.

Harness the bonds now, another voice commanded. Quetzalcoatl! *I'm shielding your minds, but you must end this now.*

"What..." I rolled over and grabbed for my gun that was a few feet away. On either side of me, Jandro and Gunner came to and reached for their weapons as well.

You three are an unbreakable chain, the snake god said. *The underworld, the sky, and the thread that binds them together. You are the natural order of existence, a trinity of which the pieces must always be interconnected to work.*

"It's us," I realized, coming slowly to my feet. "It's always been us."

"No death without life," Hades said softly, black eyes trained on the Sha.

"No sky without earth." Horus raised Gunner's weapon.

"No love without loss." Freyja said the words, but pointing the gun and squeezing the trigger was all me.

The three of us hit the Sha in the abdomen.

Time seemed to stand still for a single beat, a single moment of nothingness as we waited to find out if this truly was the end of chaos' reign.

Or if the Sha had been right all along.

The creature that was never supposed to exist touched a clawed hand to his chest. His palm came away stained dark with blood. The Sha's eyes widened in genuine disbelief as he slumped back into his throne.

"This can't be...I can't be..." Those dark claws closed into fists as he snarled at us like a cornered animal. "I *broke* the trinity! How can you three harness your bonds against me?"

"You shouldn't have stopped at Reaper and Shadow," I said, aiming right between those creepy eyes. "It never occurred to you that the gods would bond with my other men? And that *I* was the link you were missing?"

The Sha growled again, only it came out sounding more like a pained wheeze. The front of his robes were drenched in blood now, and instead of a dark gray, his complexion had paled to ash.

"I am *not* dying...I cannot find your mind now, but when I do, I will rip each of your brain cells apart and ensure you feel every single one."

"You are dying," I informed him. "Because this form is flesh and blood, Set. Just like I told you. And you can't find any of our minds because, aside from the natural order, there's something else your senseless violence can't detect."

"And what would that be?" the Sha wheezed.

"Wisdom," I answered. "Knowledge and learning. That was the final piece we needed to beat you."

"You haven't beaten me yet, human." The Sha curled his blood-stained hands over the armrests of his throne and leaned forward. "And you'll never be rid of me for good. I am as eternal as violence itself."

"I know, but you'll be nothing more than an idea. A concept floating in the ether. For as long as I can help it, you'll never take a physical form again." I curled my finger around the trigger. "And you sure as fuck will never touch my family again."

I squeezed that trigger and didn't stop until my gun was empty. Jandro and Gunner joined me in the beautiful chorus of gunfire, making the Sha's corpse jerk with each shot long after its life was gone. The silence that followed after the clicks of our empty weapons was something I didn't know how to comprehend.

"We did it."

Whispering out loud didn't make it feel any more real.

The Sha's body shifted, and the three of us immediately scrambled for fresh magazines to reload.

But there was no need. The lifeless, physical embodiment of Set slumped out of the throne to the floor. Before our eyes, the Sha broke down into a dark, dust-like substance which seemed to sink or fade into the floor until it was gone.

"Never meant to exist means no body left behind when it dies," Jandro observed quietly.

Reality hit me all at once then. I dropped my gun and threw my arms around his neck in an exhausted, sagging hug.

"It's over," I whispered into his throat, a sob choking off my voice. "We did it."

"*You* did it, *Mariposita*." Jandro squeezed around me quickly, smiling wearily as he pulled away. His eyes were back to normal, the beautiful hazel color shining brightly.

Just as he spun me around and pushed me into Gunner's arms, I heard Freyja's voice in my head.

I must leave your vessel, child, before my occupation does irreparable damage to you. I've healed you all that I can.

"Wait!" I barked out loud, quickly releasing Gunner to bring my hand to my aching temple. "I need you a little longer, Freyja. We have to heal Reaper and Shadow."

I will leave you with some in reserve, but I'm afraid it's not much. I must go, daughter.

Something about that final statement felt awfully permanent, and an odd pang wracked through my chest.

Will we ever speak again? I asked the goddess in my head.

Oh yes, daughter. Freyja sounded like she was smiling. *Perhaps not with language, but I am always with you. You can always speak to me and I will answer. You only need to listen. I am so very proud of you, dearest Mariposa.*

With that, I felt Freyja's presence simply leave my body. I turned to my guys, the question on the tip of my tongue, but they already knew.

"Horus has left." Gunner cupped my cheek and lowered his forehead to mine. "But I know where Reap and Shadow are."

"Hades is gone too," Jandro confirmed. "But we'll do a proper farewell party later. Let's get our boys back."

Gunner pointed to another set of doors at the right side of the room, and together we took off running toward them.

I prayed to all the gods that brought us this far that we weren't too late.

SHADOW

Dread consumed me like a sickness while I watched Emma hover over Reaper's still body. She pressed her ear to his chest for a long time, and checked his pulse in several places. When she finally looked up, her gaze hit me like a kick to the chest.

"I'm sorry," she said. "I can't detect anything."

"Can't you breathe into his mouth?" I pleaded weakly. "Do chest compressions to restart his heart. Do anything. Please."

Emma shook her head, pulling her mask down to reveal her downturned mouth. "I don't know CPR, I could cause further damage. I'm… I'm so sorry."

"The snake god," I tried next. "Have you heard anything from him?"

Another slow, apologetic shake of her head.

I was grasping at straws and she knew it. Reaper's chest hadn't moved for hours. I couldn't hear any breathing besides my own since yesterday.

My president was gone.

I slumped back against my wall with a clatter of chains.

These fucking chains.

A ball of anger and grief expanded in my chest, and I slammed the back of my head against the brick wall with the little remaining strength I had.

Pain, now. Please.

Anything to take the edge off these emotions consuming me from the inside. I didn't know what to do with any of this, couldn't hurt myself or the people who did this to Reaper.

Emma just stared at me quietly, listening to my weak, wheezing breaths now punctuated by wracking sobs of grief.

"Have you made a decision?" she asked during a quiet moment, referring to the last conversation we had.

"No," I admitted, fists tightening at the thought of her shining blade. She wanted it to wear my blood, but it would prevent me from being a mind-controlled puppet.

She gave me a hard, impatient look. "I can't help you after I leave. I have to report to the Sha that your friend is dead."

Dead. Such a normal, mundane word for the absence of such an extraordinary man from this world.

"I have a problem with blades." Who knew why I was telling her this. Whatever I chose, my own death was near either way. "I was... abused from childhood to adulthood with knives, as you can probably tell." I gestured down at myself. "If there was another way, I would tell you yes in a heartbeat."

Emma's expression softened in sympathy. "I'll do it as quickly as possible. You won't feel any pain."

"It's not about that, I can't feel pain anyway. It's...just a mental thing."

"Oh, right."

Several beats of silence passed while I tried to gather up the courage to tell her yes. *Step into your fear,* Freyja once told me. Once upon a time, that had to do with talking to Mari, but couldn't the same advice be applied here? I would be doing this for her, for my friends and everyone in Four Corners. If I died now, my body wouldn't be used as a weapon against them. If I did this, they would have a chance.

All I had to do was say yes to a blade through my heart. From a woman. My wife's mother, no less.

"If you see Mari again," I began, taking a heavy swallow. "Will you tell her that I love her?"

Emma softened even more, the black robe of her uniform pooling around her. "Yes, of course."

"And can you tell her that..." I swallowed again, my final words made even more difficult by severe dehydration. "Tell her I'm sorry I couldn't save Reaper."

"There is nothing you could have done—"

"Please," I begged. "She'll know it's really me if I say that. That I never fell under the Sha's control."

With a heavy sigh, Emma nodded reluctantly. Large blue eyes rested on me, patiently waiting for me to say anything else.

"Tell Jandro and Gunner that I'm grateful to them," I went on. "They helped me become someone who deserved her."

Emma nodded again slowly, her expression becoming more conflicted as I talked.

"That's all," I decided with the deepest breath I could manage. "Go ahead."

The woman shrouded in black stood from her kneeling position at Reaper's side. I cast one more look at him as she approached me. At least the others would never know how much he suffered. I would take that burden with me.

"You may want to close your eyes if the sight of a blade bothers you," she offered gently.

"Just get on with it," I huffed. My fists clenched, gaze fixed on Reaper. Maybe I'd see him again soon. Maybe closing my eyes was a good idea, I didn't know. I didn't want to die like a coward, but most of all, I wished she'd hurry up so I wouldn't have to think about this anymore.

"You're being very brave." I heard the metallic hiss of Emma's dagger being unsheathed. "My daughter is lucky to have had you. I wish we could have met under different circumstances."

"That's kind of you to say." I shifted my gaze to her and immediately regretted it. Her blade was out, sharp and glinting, and it was going to cut my fucking skin. "Please don't stall anymore. If you're going to do this, do it."

Emma's breath was shaky as I went back to looking at Reaper's body. Her fingers trembled as they prodded the left side of my chest, finding the best place to stab me in the heart. It turned out to be right in the forehead of the skull in my Steel Demons tattoo.

Some loud commotion in the corridor outside the cell startled us both. It sounded like doors slamming against walls and running footsteps coming for us quickly.

"The other guards!" Emma whispered in a panic, turning toward the door. "I've been found out."

I grabbed her forearm before she could get away and pulled her back to me, bringing her dagger tip to indent the skin on my chest.

"Do what you came here to do," I growled at her. "Do it now!"

Emma's focus and resolve were gone, her attention torn between me and the cell door. Fuck. I started wrestling the knife out of her hand, determined to finish the job myself if she couldn't.

The stampede of footsteps halted right outside. "Get the fuck away from him!" A single shot fired through the bars, causing sparks to fly as the bullet ricocheted off the walls.

Emma and I both instinctively ducked, covering our heads while I tried to process the familiar female voice that had just yelled at us.

"Oh fuck, oh no. Is that Reaper? Reaper!"

I glanced up, certain that I was hallucinating, to see Mari, Gunner, and Jandro at the door. The guys struggled with the lock while Mari pointed her gun into the cell.

"I said, get the fuck away from him!" Mari's expression was feral, if even downright bloodthirsty as she angled her weapon toward her mother's back. My wife's face was streaked with dirt, sweat, and dried blood. More blood stained the front of her clothing in a reddish-brown tint, like she'd been lying in a pool of it.

This was no illusion from the Sha, no carbon copy of my wife with her gorgeous face and sweet voice trying to undo me. Nothing was polished or perfected about this image of her, covered in filth, pointing a gun, and yelling obscenities through the door.

This was...real?

"Mari?" I croaked in disbelief.

Her eyes jerked to me, the fury in them dimming slightly. "It's us," she said, her voice softer. "We're here. It's all over, love. It's going to be okay."

I couldn't afford to feel relief, joy, or anything yet. There was still the matter of getting them inside. My leg kicked out, nudging Emma who had moved away from me as ordered, still covering her head.

"Unlock the door," I told her. Then to Mari, "Don't shoot her."

"*Her*?" Mari's puzzled frown turned wide-eyed as her mother carefully glanced up, still with her hands above her head as she moved to the door. "Mom?" she squeaked out.

"Hey, sweet pea." Emma was already fumbling for the keys on her keyring. "Haven't heard you yell like that since you were a teenager."

The door opened and Mari sidestepped her mother's arms, spread in open invitation for a hug. My wife went straight to Reaper's body, falling to her knees as she placed her hands on his chest.

I felt a pulse of...something the moment she did that, like a refreshing gust of air. Right away, I noticed a slight change in my body. I could breathe a little easier and didn't feel as weak, although I was still nowhere near full strength. Mari started performing CPR on Reaper and that was when it hit me. She was here. We were getting out.

"Hey dude." Jandro and Gunner approached me, their faces trying to mask whatever they saw at the condition I was in. "Let's get you out of these, alright? Unless you're really committed to this new fashion trend."

I coughed out a weak laugh. Leave it to Jandro to make a joke right now, but it also felt so fucking good to hear him say dumb shit again. "Yeah. Get me out of these."

Gunner had to shoot the shackles binding my ankles and wrists. Good thing I trusted his accuracy. Then together they had to shoot the end of the thick chain attached to the wall that was wrapped around my neck. When it finally fell away, I could breathe even easier.

"Don't touch that," Gunner warned as I started to bring a hand up to my throat. "Your skin's all rubbed raw, man. It could get infected."

I moved that hand to the wall instead, using it for support as I painstakingly rose to my full height.

"Here, dude. I got you." Jandro nudged his shoulder under my armpit to give me further support, wrapping an arm around my waist to help hoist me up. "Can you walk?"

"I think so." My upper body wavered unsteadily on my feet, dizziness hitting me hard, and I threw my arm over his shoulders for added support. The lack of chains on my body made me feel strangely weightless. Stiff muscles in my back cramped and protested from being unused in a week.

Mari looked at me from where she knelt over Reaper. "How long has he been unconscious?"

"About three days," I told her, allowing my weight to lean on Jandro. "Is he...?"

"He's got a weak pulse. He needs medical attention *now*."

My legs buckled and I almost sank back to the floor. We didn't lose him! Not yet, at least. That pulse of energy from her must have done something. I wasn't about to question it and knew she'd tell me about it at some point. Right now, we still had to make our way out.

Gunner pulled a small radio from his cut and spoke into it, the words too mumbled and coded for me to catch. I wanted to sleep for another week, I was so fucking tired.

"I told Four Corners' army that the fortress is clear," Gunner reported to the room. "They're on their way in with medics at the front line."

"Good. Gun, can you shoot off these restraints and help me carry him?"

He fired off four quick shots, then Mari slid an arm under Reaper's shoulders and pushed his torso up. Together, she and Gunner managed to get him slung over Gunner's shoulders. "Get him and Shadow to the medics," Mari ordered, huffing for breath as she stood. "I'll be right behind you."

"Hold up," Jandro said. "What are you gonna do?"

Mari's gaze slid over to her mother, really acknowledging the other woman for the first time. "We still have to find Andrea."

CHAPTER 24

MARIPOSA

I couldn't fully process the fact that *my mother* was in the cell with Reaper and Shadow, nor that she was dressed like one of the Sha's guards and had a knife pointed at Shadow's chest when we showed up. No, she was not the priority. Nor was Shadow, honestly, once we got her away from him. He was still breathing.

My only priority had been Reaper, lying still and pale against the far wall. I used the last pulse of Freyja's healing power on him, which was far weaker than the previous ones. I didn't know if it would be enough, he looked like a corpse already. So I started up CPR immediately.

That soft pulse under his skin was the most beautiful sign of life I'd ever felt. I wanted to throw myself over his body and kiss him. *You're still here, my love. We haven't lost you yet.*

But we had no time to waste. CPR could only do so much when he needed oxygen, fluids, X-rays, and most likely several surgeries. My relief was short-lived as I watched Gunner carry him out of the cell. Reaper still had many obstacles ahead of him, but for now, I could focus on the different matter at hand.

Once the guys left the cell and started down the corridor, I brandished my gun again and held it to the side of my body so my mother could see it clearly. "You have ten seconds to tell me why you were about to murder my husband."

She blinked at the sight of my weapon and a heavy breath left her chest. With the Sha gone, she wasn't under any kind of mind control and therefore owed me a fucking explanation before we could reunite as a happy family.

"It was going to be a mercy killing," she said quickly. "We heard nothing from Quetzalcoatl, so we didn't think you were coming. I gave him the choice. His only other option was to become the Sha's tool."

I relaxed my grip on my gun just a fraction. "The Sha is dead. We killed him."

A smile twitched onto my mother's lips. "I figured as much, since you made it here."

"Why are you dressed like a guard?" Q told me she'd been watching over them, but her black garb and the fact that she was about to *kill my husband* had me rattled. "Were you under his control?"

"No, sweet pea. I made the Sha believe that I was loyal to him," she answered. "Q shielded my mind from him, so he never saw my true thoughts. I found out your dad was here, Mari, and had to get close to him. I pretended to be a loyalist for two years so I could try to save your dad, *mija*." My mom's lip wobbled, tears filling her eyes. "I know he's still technically alive, Shadow told me. But he's been so badly damaged. I *failed* him."

Only then did I holster my gun, elation and sweet relief sweeping through me.

"He's okay," I told her, smiling through my own tears. "He remembers everything now. He's living at our house. Everything is..." I had to pause, barely believing the words I was about to say were true. "Everything is going to be okay, Mom."

"He is?" She stared at me, wide-eyed. "He remembers?"

"Yes!" Giddy laughter escaped me now. "He's still recovering, but he's going to be fine."

Unable to hold back any longer, the two of us collided in a tight, clasping hug. My mom was a little shorter than me, so I kissed her forehead like I used to when I teased her about her height. She laughed and swatted my backside, squeezing me tighter.

"I missed you so much, Mom," I whimpered into her shoulder.

"Oh my sweet girl, I missed you too. Not a day's passed that I haven't thought of you." She pulled away slightly, eyebrows raised. "And *four* husbands? You have a lot to tell me, young lady."

I wiped my cheeks with a laugh. "It's not that weird. Dad already loves both Jandro and Gunner."

"Can't imagine why." She smirked. "So." She let go of me reluctantly and stepped back. "There's someone else you need to break out of here?"

"Yes," I said, returning to seriousness. "A woman named Andrea, though she probably didn't give that name here. She came here almost two months ago as an informant for us. Dark hair, blue eyes, mid-thirties, really pretty."

My mother's face went solemn, recognition lighting up her eyes. "I know exactly where she is. Come with me."

MOM LED ME DOWN ANOTHER SERIES OF CORRIDORS, heading the opposite way me and the guys came from. It became clear she was leading me to an area purposely kept separate from the rest of the fortress.

"What's this area all about?" I tried to keep the worry out of my voice, but nothing stopped the bricks forming in my stomach.

"It's a...conditioning area," Mom told me hesitantly. "For the ones newly controlled by the Sha and that were still being conditioned into full obedience. Or those who were particularly difficult to control."

As disturbing as that was to hear, it gave me fresh hope. "Then they'll probably make a full recovery, if they aren't completely gone. How many are there?"

Rather than answer, Mom stuck a key in a door at the end of the corridor we reached. Once unlocked, she pulled a handle to slide it open. The room inside was massive, like a gymnasium, and it was packed with people. Men and women of every age, size, and ethnicity filled the room. It was a small comfort that there were no children, at least.

Hundreds of curious eyes turned and stared at us. Most were wide-eyed in fear, no doubt fearing some kind of torture or illusion like the Sha had bestowed upon me. I didn't see Andrea right away, but she had to be somewhere in this sea of faces.

"Hello, everyone." I raised my hand in greeting and put on my friendliest smile. "My name is Mariposa Wilder and I'm a medic from Four Corners. The Sha has been defeated. You're all free now. You have nothing to fear." I tried to make eye contact with everyone looking at me, hoping they realized that I was sincere. "This is not a trick, you have my word. Medical help is on the way for anyone who needs it. If you have family or loved ones, we'll do our best to put you back in touch with them."

Hushed murmurs and movement rippled through the crowd as people talked amongst each other. If they didn't believe me right away, that was fine. Their minds had been manipulated and abused to the point where suspicion was natural.

"Mari? Is that really you?"

My heart stopped at the voice calling out from the crowd. "Andrea?" I answered hopefully.

A section of people moved out of the way for someone pushing through to the front. I still couldn't see her and my heart drummed louder the closer she got. When she finally came into view, I wanted to burst into tears.

Andrea had lost so much weight. Her skin was covered in scratches and scabs, and her beautiful mane of black hair, which she once took so much pride in styling, had been shaved off. But it was her. She was alive and she recognized me.

"Drea," I choked out, finally losing it. "I'm so sorry. Oh my God, I'm so fucking sorry."

"Come here," she huffed, pulling me into a hug against her bony body. "It's not your fault, I signed up for this. And...it's over, right?"

"Yeah," I squeaked out, returning her hug as tightly as I could without crushing her. "It's over. We're gonna be okay." No matter how much I said the words, I still couldn't believe them yet.

"Tessa and the kids?"

"They're good." I nodded against her shoulder. "Good, just waiting for you to come home."

"And your men? The Demons?" She pulled away to look at my face.

"Um, they're okay." I pulled in a shaky breath. "A lot has happened. We'll fill you in."

She nodded, releasing me slowly as she turned back to face the crowd of people. "It's true, everyone! We can go home."

The hesitant murmurings rose excitedly, a buzz of hopeful energy filling the air. Mom and I stepped aside, pulling the door all the way open to let people through. My mother had discarded her black guard's tunic, revealing a simple outfit of linen pants and a shirt underneath.

"I'm proud of you, sweet pea." She knocked her shoulder into mine as we started walking alongside the crowd to guide them out.

"Thanks, Mom." My hand squeezed around hers, still hardly daring to believe she was really here. That she and my dad, my whole family, would be back together soon. "Let's go home."

CHAPTER 25

JANDRO

Word must have traveled fast in Four Corners once the army deployed. Once we got back, the whole town was rallying to help. And thank fuck, 'cause we needed it.

Mari and her mom had met us in front of the compound with two hundred people in tow, in addition to the Sha's former soldiers who were still alive and in various stages of mental breakdowns due to no longer being mind-controlled.

People with vehicles volunteered to drive out and pick up those we couldn't carry with the army's first wave. Even with the extra help, Finn's units had to take several trips back and forth to get everyone alive transported out.

Those with the most life-threatening conditions were rushed to the hospital first, and no one was in worse shape than Reaper. Shadow wasn't looking good either, but his condition at least wasn't critical. If I hadn't seen him as an emaciated shell of himself in prison all those years ago, I wouldn't have recognized him in that fucking dungeon.

The next few days passed by in a blur. We were still short on medics, so Mari worked herself to the bone to distract herself while Reaper was in surgery. And I swore he spent all those days in the operating room. Every update from Dr. Brooks was a horror show. Reaper had severe, probably permanent, nerve damage in his hands. Shattered bones in multiple places, including his face. Teams of medics had to spend hours reconstructing his bones like a jigsaw puzzle. He also had internal bleeding and organ damage. And on top of all of that was the coma, which meant likely brain damage and no estimate of when or if he would ever wake up.

But his heart kept beating. He *was* alive, which counted for something. We would cross all other bridges when we got to them.

There were some beautiful moments in those first few chaotic days, though. Seeing Mari's parents reunite with tearful embraces was a sight I'd never forget. It would be one of those stories we'd tell our kids one day, the happily ever after to all the shit their parents and grandparents went through.

Calmness finally seemed to settle over Four Corners the day Reaper was moved out of surgery and into one of the recovery rooms. Dr. Brooks said there was nothing left to do now except let him heal, rest, and wait for him to wake up. And no one was more eager for all of that than Mari.

She was already at his side when I entered the room, chair pulled up next to his bed and hands clasped around his. Her gaze was locked onto his face, watching him like he could wake up any moment if it weren't for the sedative still wearing off.

"Hey," I greeted her softly as I walked in, my voice no louder than the beeps of the machines monitoring Reaper's vitals. "Finally quit working?" I squeezed her shoulder, standing behind her.

Mari grabbed my hand and looked up at me with a weary smile. "Rhonda kicked me out. Literally whacked me with her cane and said I'd done enough."

"She's right." My grip moved to the back of her neck, massaging her there. Mari's head immediately rolled back, eyelids fluttering, and her lips parted in a soft sigh, which I promptly leaned down to kiss. "You need to rest too."

"I asked Dr. B to bring a cot in here for me." She returned to looking straight ahead, at the man we were all desperate to have back. "I want to be here when he wakes up."

I bit back my argument that she should come home—soak in one of her baths, eat a home cooked meal, and sleep in an actual bed. Let us fucking pamper her for telling chaos itself to fuck off, essentially saving the entire fucking world.

I knew it would be fruitless, that she wouldn't leave Reaper's side if the whole hospital came crashing down.

"Okay," I said. "But let me know if you need anything from home, huh?"

Mari looked up at me again, guilt crossing her face. "How's Shadow?"

"Oh, big dude's fine," I told her, stroking over her hair. "I'm going to see him before I head home for stuff. They're gonna discharge him in the next day or two."

"Tell him I'm sorry I haven't—"

"Stop right there." I cut her off with another kiss. "You're not apologizing for shit."

Mari kept up her frown, so I kept kissing it away until she was finally laughing.

"We know," I whispered. "We're your husbands. We understand."

My eyes lifted to Reaper, stretched out and motionless except for the shallow breaths he took. Most of his body was casted or bandaged. It went without saying that the road ahead of him would be long and difficult. He'd be recovering from what happened to him for the rest of his life, and not only physically.

But Mari would be there. We all would be.

I bent to kiss her one more time. "Gonna check on the big dude, then I'll be back with some clothes and food, okay?"

"Thank you." She kept squeezing my hand as we separated, letting me go only at the last possible moment. It was a simple gesture, but one that warmed me up like a crushing, full-body hug. Even with all her attention focused on Reaper, she still needed me.

I left the room with my heart lifted at that sweet reminder.

"HOW'S REAPER?" IT WAS THE FIRST THING SHADOW ASKED me when I stepped into his room. He looked comically huge in his hospital bed, feet dangling off the far end and tucking his arms close to his sides if he didn't want them falling off the edges.

"Looking like a mummy, but fine. He got put in a recovery room and the anesthesia is wearing off. Now it's up to him to wake up."

Shadow shifted like he was trying to get comfortable in the too-small bed. "And Mari?"

"What you'd expect," I said with a small smile. "Had to be forced to stop working, now she's glued to his side."

Shadow returned my smile. "So she's fine."

"Given...everything, yeah."

He turned his head on the pillow to look at me more directly. "And how are you, Jandro?"

"I'm..." It took me a moment to answer. I didn't get asked that question a lot, as the guy who usually looked after everyone else. My needs were simple and few—laughs with the guys, some love from my girl, and getting my hands dirty in some machinery.

But *this,* everything that happened...it was over, but it was going to stick with us for a long time, if not forever. What Mari, Gunner, and I did in that fortress felt like a faraway dream. But also so real, like a gross film I couldn't scrape off my skin. Everything had changed, but I didn't *feel* all that different.

"I dunno," I admitted after a long silence. "I'm still processing, I guess. My muscle memory is telling me to prepare for meetings in the conference room, more fights, but I guess we don't have to do that anymore."

"Not for war, anyway," Shadow mused.

"How are you though, dude?" I directed the topic back to him.

"Fine, I'm getting discharged tomorrow morning. I got off way easier than Reaper." His jaw tightened at that. "Except for when it comes to these fucking hospital beds."

I gave a half-hearted chuckle at his attempt at a joke and decided to pry a little deeper. We had no secrets between us anymore.

"And mental health-wise?" I broached, trying not to sound like I was preparing for the worst.

But if there was ever going to be a setback to all his progress, a week of being tortured in a dungeon would probably do it.

"Oh, uh." Shadow looked surprised but not offended by the question. "I...think I'm okay." He frowned, thinking about it some more. "Not that anyone would be *okay* after that but it's like..." He paused, looking at me. "This might sound weird."

"Spill it, my man. You know I've heard it all from you."

He swallowed and continued, "It's almost like my early life prepared me for this."

I leaned back, sucking my breath through my teeth. "Okay, yeah, that is a weird thing to say."

"Physical torture," he lifted a shoulder in a nonchalant shrug, "it's nothing to me now. I knew how to ration my food and water, to conserve my energy in a cramped space. And I was able to..." He swallowed again. "Keep the brunt of the torture off of Reaper in the beginning."

"I get it. You're saying you knew how to survive because of what you'd been through. That you'd already been through worse. Fuck, you probably saved Reaper's life."

"No, that was the snake." Shadow shook his head. "Mentally...it wasn't like before, but I'm not sure how long I would have lasted. If Reaper had died, if you guys hadn't come when you did..."

"Mari told us about the choice her mom gave you," I said gently.

Shadow's fingers clenched in surprise. "She did?"

"For what it's worth, man," I crossed my arms in front of my chest, "I'm sure I would have done the same in your position. Shit, I bet any of us would."

Shadow's hand relaxed. "Thanks, Jandro. It really felt like there were no other options." He scrubbed a hand down his face with a dry laugh. "Fuck, maybe I'm not okay."

"And that is also okay." I stepped up to clap him on the shoulder. "We'll get through it, man. We're family."

"Yeah." The tension eased out of him slowly.

"You been sleeping?"

"Yeah, like the dead."

"Well that's a good sign, yeah?"

"Yeah," he repeated, nodding. "And I know what to do if that changes."

"Fuck yeah you do." I grinned at him. "And you've got people here to support you."

"I do," he whispered dreamily, like he still couldn't believe that *this* was his reality.

I thumped him on the shoulder again. "You want anything from the house?"

"Food," he said immediately. "The shit they feed us here is bullshit."

"Alright, you big baby. How many tacos you want?"

"Ten. Actually, no, better make it fifteen."

"Jesus, you trying to hibernate for the winter or what?"

"Those tortillas you use are really small."

"In your big mitts they are," I laughed, heading for the door.

"Scrambled eggs too, please," he called after me, grinning, but I knew he was serious. Eggs from my girls were gifts fit for gods.

"Sure," I mock-grumbled from the doorway. "Man, I can't wait 'til you're home so you can grab them your damn self."

"Me too," he sighed, waving at me from his bed. "Thanks, Jandro."

CHAPTER 26

MARIPOSA

"Good morning, love." I took my seat at Reaper's bedside, throwing my wet hair up a careless bun before reaching for his hand. "You'll be happy to know that I did *not* doze off standing up in the shower today. I'll call that a win."

The soft, steady beeping of his heart monitor was my only reply. His fingers remained stiff and unresponsive to my touch. I took his thumb and rubbed over the stone of the ring he gave me, like he always did when our hands connected.

"I miss you," I said to my husband who looked peacefully asleep, despite all the wounds covering his body. "We all miss you. I thought for sure you'd wake up at the smell of Jandro's cooking, but you're being stubborn now too, huh?"

Dr. Brooks said talking to him might encourage him to come out of his coma. Attempting a joke seemed like it might lift my own spirits, but the silence that followed canceled that out completely. Even when my own jokes were lame, Reaper always validated them somehow. He'd laugh, groan, tease me, or just grab me and kiss me.

The past day of sitting next to him, finally being able to *see* him, brought all those little moments pouring back. I thought of the night he gave me the ring, how nervous he was when he asked me to be his wife. When I first told him I was going to spend the night with Jandro, how terrified I had been, wondering if I'd misunderstood everything.

All the regrets came pouring back too, like the night I took this same ring off and threw it at him. But nothing replayed on an endless loop like the day before he was captured.

How I had completely melted down after seeing my dad in that state, and Reaper was there through it all. How beautifully, painfully honest he was with me, and how I threw it all in his face.

I reached up to touch his face, taking in what would become new scars long after he healed. Even with all the injuries, he was still so beautiful. My touch ran over his eyebrows and forehead, wishing I could absorb all the suffering he went through for our family. For me.

"I need you to wake up, love," I whispered. "I need to tell you how sorry I am."

There was no movement beneath those eyelids, no sign that they would crack open and show me those green irises that always made my pulse race.

With a sigh, I moved back to sit down when I heard a soft knock at the doorway. The man filling the frame made my heart skip, and a sob choked my throat.

"Shadow," I whimpered.

"Lover," he answered, stoic face crumbling with emotion.

My body hit his before I realized I was moving. The solidness of his chest was the exact place I needed to land on, and the massive arms folding around my back was the shield I needed to stay strong.

He was thinner, his ribs more prominent as I hugged around him.

"I'm sorry, I should have been around to--"

"Stop," he grunted, cupping the back of my head. "No apologizing. Others needed you more than me."

"None of you damn men will let me apologize," I laughed, wiping my cheeks.

"Because no apology is needed," he told me matter-of-factly. "You can't be in more than one place at a time."

I pulled together after a few more moments of letting myself cry on him. "So you're okay? Discharged already?"

Shadow's thumbs swept the remaining moisture off my cheek. "Yes, lover. Want to sit down?"

I led him to my chair at Reaper's side, sat him down, and promptly curled into his lap. Shadow's content sigh against my body was the only thing that eased my stress level since we got back from the fortress.

"Pneumonia and dehydration were my biggest issues," he said. "Once they treated my infection, it was just a matter of me getting rest and fluids."

I rested my forehead in the crook of his neck, soaking up all the warmth and the familiar, cozy nearness of him that I could. "Good. I'm glad that's all it was."

Shadow's gaze lifted to Reaper's bed. "Any change since yesterday?"

"Not yet."

He rubbed my lower back, fingers moving in an idle, circular pattern, staring intently at Reaper.

I gave a light scratch to the beard on his jaw to get his attention. "Anything you want to talk about?"

Shadow's jaw clenched, a harsh huff of breath leaving his nostrils. "I wasn't able to protect him."

"Now you better not apologize," I warned. "He'd never want you to become a martyr for him, pain or no pain."

"I know. He told me as much." Shadow's rubbing at my back stopped. "It wasn't even so much the torture I wanted to protect him from but the aftermath." His hold tightened around me. "Dealing with what comes *after* torture, it can be so much worse."

"Oh, Shadow..." My arms draped around his neck, I was somehow still amazed at the massive heart and empathy of this man.

"He's going to deal with things like I did," Shadow continued. "Maybe not sleepwalking, but he'll have nightmares. There will be random sounds or words that will take his mind back there. I just wish I could have prevented that for him."

"He will heal." He had to wake up first, I refused to consider the possibility that that wouldn't happen. But once he did, we would rally around him. "We can take him to see Dr. Ellis if he needs it."

"You know how stubborn he is," Shadow muttered. "He'll have to swallow his pride and accept help."

"He will," I repeated. "He's already seen the results of it in you."

"I hope you're right. It was so—" Shadow stopped abruptly, squeezing around me tighter with a sharp breath. "It was awful, lover. What I went through in a year in my old life, they did to him in a week."

"I'm sorry you had to see that." I kissed his cheek just above his beard and felt the tension melt out of him.

"It was how the Sha tried to break me," he admitted. "To control my mind. He could tell I was mentally damaged—"

"You're not," I interrupted.

Shadow returned to looking at me. "He tried to use you," he admitted, like it was a shameful secret.

"What do you mean?" I rested a palm on his chest to calm him further, knowing that was where he felt most of his anxiety.

"He...conjured up an image of you and tried to make me believe you were there with me. Your face, your voice. I could even touch it and it *felt* like you."

"But you knew it wasn't."

"Yeah, I figured it out pretty quickly." His hand rested over mine on his chest, and our smiles connected in a long overdue kiss.

The familiar elation and joy he sparked so readily in me burst to life like a bonfire. My guys were home and alive, and this kiss was the thing that cemented it all into reality.

"I love you so much," I breathed. "I'm so glad you're okay. So glad you're back."

"I told you I'd never leave," he said before kissing me again.

I was still exhausted and sleep-deprived but that mouth locking over mine, those hands smoothing up my back reinvigorated me in a way sleep and food never could. I couldn't wait to feel all my men together, their unique touches and kisses piling on me until I was breathing nothing but them.

"Something else happened," Shadow murmured when we paused for a breath.

"I'm listening," I said, moving a kiss to his forehead.

He turned his head in a way that made my lips brush against the scar cutting through his eye. "I think...I confronted the ghost of my mother."

"Really?" I leaned back to look at his face.

"It felt like I was under Doc's hypnosis," he explained. "I was aware of myself but not fully lucid. But she..." Shadow met my eyes and shook his head slowly. "She wasn't a memory. And while it's possible, I don't think it was the Sha fucking with me."

"What did you say to her?"

"Told her to fuck all the way off, pretty much." A smile pulled at his lips. "I told her she didn't control me anymore. That despite all the odds, I found someone who loves me." His eyes flicked downward to our connected hands. "Who forgives me."

I pressed another kiss to his forehead. "I bet that pissed her off."

"It did." His fingers stroked the band of my ring. "When she finally left, I felt...lighter. Like I'd been carrying her on my shoulders all this time and didn't even realize it."

I curled my fingers around his, nuzzling him for another kiss. "I'm proud of you."

His mouth ghosted over mine in a soft huff of breath. "I love you."

Our kiss connected to the sound of a fast knock at the door and then Gunner's voice. "What's shakin', lovebirds?"

"Gun!" I had barely seen him since the fortress too. As the unofficial diplomat of the family, he'd been running around letting my parents, Reaper's parents, the club, and all our other friends and acquaintances know what happened and where we were.

I started to get up but my golden man motioned for me to stay where I was. "You look comfy, baby girl." He leaned over and kissed me, lingering and sweet, with a hand on my cheek.

"How is everyone? And why do you have your sleeping bag?" I noticed the rolled up bundle slung over his shoulder when he resumed standing.

"Everyone's good. Sending their well-wishes."

"Except Slick, that guy's a turd," Jandro cut in as he entered the room, also with his sleeping bag slung over his shoulder.

"What—"

"Ah, fuck you, VP." Slick walked in next, thankfully *without* a sleeping bag, but with a folded table under his arm. "Hey Mari," he greeted cheerily as he began setting the table up against the far wall.

"Did you grab mine?" Shadow's breath ruffled my hair as he asked Jandro the question.

"It's on my bike, I'll get it in a sec."

I stared at Shadow accusingly. "You're in on something behind my back?"

"It's no big thing, baby girl." Gunner set his and Jandro's sleeping bags on my cot. "We just decided that if you were gonna stay with Reaper twenty-four-seven, we might as well too."

"Guys, no."

"*Sí*," Jandro argued. "None of us are sleeping in separate rooms again, unless under dire circumstances."

"Don't worry, I'm not staying the night," Slick called over, although he still had a little conspiratorial smile that he tried to hide.

I narrowed my eyes at Jandro. "Okay, so what are you *not* telling me?"

"Hey, we're not late, are we?" Noelle strode into the room next, Larkan following closely behind her.

This time, I did get off Shadow's lap to hug the woman I loved as a sister. "Oh, Noelle..."

"Slick! I thought you were gonna bring booze." She didn't seem to notice my somber mood, patting me on the back distractedly.

"Oh shit." Jandro's apprentice blushed.

"We brought a thirty-pack, will that be enough?"

I looked to the doorway again to see Tessa, Andrea, and all of their children spill into the room, which was now becoming *very* crowded.

Shadow stood and handed his chair to the women who just walked in. "I don't know about the beer, but we definitely need more chairs." He went out into the hallway in an apparent search for more seating.

"Will someone tell me what the fuck is going on?" Laughter was pouring out of me joyously now as I hugged Tessa and the kids. Andrea must have been recently discharged, but she already looked like her old self. She was bright-eyed, alert, rocking her new buzz cut, and glued to Tessa's side.

"Nothing's going on, really." Larkan was already fishing a beer out of the cooler. "Gun told us what happened, so we figured we'd give old

Pres something worth waking up to." He passed me a beer. "A good old Steel Demons party."

"That's...actually not an awful idea." I laughed, accepting the beer after a moment of hesitation. It was nine in the morning, but what else was I going to do besides wait by Reaper's bedside?

And it really was a perfect idea. Reaper loved his community, this camaraderie and sense of brotherhood, more than anything else.

I scanned the small room as people chatted and caught up with each other like it was any other day. Slick shuffled playing cards on the table and more people started pulling drinks out of the cooler. The only ones this party was missing were...

"Room for three more?" T-Bone's gruff voice cut through the noise as the three Sons of Odin maneuvered their way into the room.

"Sons!" I shrieked, tearing up again at the sight of them. Now it was a party.

The three of them came straight for me, T-Bone reaching me first as he swept me up into a bone-crushing hug.

"Knew you could do it, little lady," he whispered before planting a kiss on my cheek.

"Hey, hands off my wife!" Gunner called from the corner.

"As long as I get to put 'em on you next, pretty boy." T-Bone laughed as he set me down and cut through the crowd, heading straight for Gunner.

After hugs from Dyno and Grudge, I went back to Reaper's bedside and took his hand.

"Come on, love," I whispered, bringing his fingers to my lips. "You're going to be so mad if you miss this."

Everyone else in the room became background noise as I rubbed his palm and kissed each of his fingertips. My eyes never left his face, searching for any sign of awakeness.

He remained still in his bed, and when one of my men came up to rub my back, I reluctantly let go of Reaper's hand to let it rest next to his side.

CHAPTER 27

MARIPOSA

Another day passed. Then two more. And then a week. Reaper did not wake up.

His body continued to heal quickly, I wondered if it was due to lingering effects from the pulse of power Freyja left with me. I hadn't seen or felt the goddess since the fortress.

After nearly two weeks, Reaper looked mostly normal. Most of his stitches and casts had been removed, the injuries fading to scars. His beard started growing out in that time and I had shaved his face twice. But not once did I see those eyes crack open.

My other three continued to spend the nights in his room with me, going about their different duties throughout the day, but always having meals and spending the evening with Reaper and I.

Others checked in daily too, usually Reaper's parents and mine. Finn and Lis moved back to their house to give us some space. My mom and dad were falling back into their old banter again—teasing each other and being all cute and affectionate. I wish I could say I was happy for them, happy to have my family back together. But a key piece of my happiness was missing.

My emotional state was all over the place. I'd put on a cheery mood when someone came to visit, then collapse into tears at Reaper's bedside when they left. I went from hopeful to deeply depressed and back again so many times. I questioned if it was cruel to hold onto him like this.

Dr. Brooks, and every other doctor he consulted, simply did not have answers for me. Reaper wasn't on life support. He wasn't brain dead. The possibility of talking to my husband again was greater than zero, so I kept waiting.

And waiting.

It was only my mom with me today—Dad was off doing something with the guys. I wasn't in the mood to talk, which Mom thankfully understood. Dad knew how to listen to me, Mom knew how to keep the silence away.

"We had dinner with Finn and Lis last night," she was telling me. "They're lovely, I think Javi and I will be good friends with them. They told us stories about when Rory and his sister were young, and their youngest boy too."

"Daren," I said without looking at her.

"Yes, all three of them; bright, feisty kids from the sounds of it." Distantly, I felt Mom squeeze my hand. "I'm glad you had them around, sweet pea. Everyone we met here is so kind and supportive. Oh! We met the governor and his daughter too, did I tell you that?"

"No," I said flatly.

Mom continued to talk, making pleasant background noise while I studied Reaper's face. The strong column of his throat, his jaw, and his lips were just as beautiful as ever. His left cheekbone had been shattered and had to be carefully reconstructed over several hours. No one would be able to tell now, except for the new scar under his eye.

His hair was growing back from being shaved to address his head wounds. More new scars lined his scalp and forehead. Scans showed no lingering brain damage, but Dr. Brooks wanted to keep checking for several months, even after he woke up. We never really knew how the head trauma would affect him until we saw symptoms. It could be memory loss, balance issues, or even personality changes.

"Mari?"

I looked at my mom, realizing she was trying to get my attention. "Yeah?"

She gave me a pained, sympathetic smile. "I'm going to head home for the night. Do you need anything?"

"No." I gave her a brief, distracted hug. "No, Mom. Thanks for sitting with me."

She squeezed me tighter and kissed my hair. "Always. I'll bring you some lunch tomorrow."

"Thanks," I said again, turning my full attention back to Reaper.

Now that we were alone, I leaned my chest against the side of the bed with a sigh, taking his thumb and rubbing it over the stone on my ring for the thousandth time.

"I really need you to come back," I whispered, bringing his limp hand up to my lips. "Please, please, my love. We all need you. And I—" My throat closed up but I forced the words out anyway. "I don't know how to go on without you."

At some point, many tears and pleading sobs later, I must have dozed off leaning over his bed. Someone was shaking my shoulder gently.

"Baby girl." Gunner placed soft kisses in my hair. "Come to bed." We had ditched the cot and sleeping bags for a big inflatable mattress that took up nearly half the room. Somehow, Shadow still dangled off of it.

"No." I removed Gunner's hand from my shoulder, I felt particularly masochistic tonight. "I want to stay by him."

Gunner breathed out a sigh but didn't argue as he placed a final kiss on the crown of my head, then backed away.

I felt Jandro and Shadow looming over me, but they thankfully didn't try to pull me away either.

"Love you," they both said with an affectionate touch and a goodnight kiss.

Someone put a blanket over my shoulders, the weight of it settling me down over the side of Reaper's bed again where I fell asleep.

The back pain woke me up first. I sat up with a groan, still mostly asleep as I rubbed my face. Why did I insist on sleeping over the side of the bed again?

My eyes remained shut as I stretched and twisted, trying to alleviate this aching stiffness from my sleeping position. When I opened them, two hooded, but also opened eyes stared back at me.

I froze, convinced I was dreaming. But the pounding in my chest was too loud, too real. So were those lips moving slowly to whisper, "Hey, sugar."

"...R-R-Reaper?" I went from frozen to trembling. Did I get so used to watching him in stillness that it was such a shock to see him moving?

"Mari." His whisper was barely audible but his lips did move, and his hand scooted toward mine on the sheet. "...s'it really you?"

"Yes!" I wanted to scream it but could barely speak. One hand came to my mouth while the other clasped his fingers. I went to lean over him, shaking in a ball of nerves and unspent tears. "You're really back?"

"Think so." Reaper's eyes followed my movement, lids still hooded, but he *tracked* movement! He was awake, aware. The EKG started beeping faster as his heart beat accelerated.

The machine's noise grounded me in reality for a moment. "Stay calm, you're not totally out of the woods yet. We...we still need to run tests."

A corner of his mouth lifted in a ghost of a smirk. "I'm...calm, sugar. Are you?"

That question made the dam burst. Tears spilled and a sob tore out of my throat. Calm was another universe as I released everything I'd been holding back. Every fear and speculation, every unknown, every stressful moment of wondering when and if I'd ever hear his voice again, it all leaked out of my eyes and rolled down my face.

Every regret too. Never again would I ever spend a single moment with this man treating him like he didn't matter.

"I'm so sorry," I forced out between chest-heaving sobs. "Never again, I...I love you so much. I'll never...fuck, if I lost you, I don't know how..."

Reaper listened quietly while I blubbered and poured everything out. He was able to bend his elbow and stroke my hair, green eyes watching me thoughtfully. I leaned down further so he could touch my face, holding his hand against my cheek.

I started breathing normally, then he rubbed the stone on my ring and I almost started bawling again.

"My wife," he whispered, index finger stroking my cheekbone. "My sugar."

"Yes," I breathed, feeling a smile pull at my face for the first time in weeks. "My husband." I touched his face in return, still marveling at those gorgeous eyes blinking and watching me.

Reaper made a sound like he was trying to clear his throat and I sprung into action, finding a glass of water with a straw.

"Take it easy," I told him, my nose still sniffling. "You haven't swallowed or used your voice in a while."

He accepted a small, tentative drink and then tried again. "How...long?"

"You've been in a coma for about two weeks," I said. "We got you out when you'd been out for about three days already."

"Shadow?" His eyes widened with the question.

"He's fine." I squeezed his hand in assurance. "Everyone is."

I looked behind me to find the room empty, our air mattress bed made and blankets folded neatly over it. It must have been late morning for the guys to all be gone already.

"The Sha?" Reaper asked next, brow furrowed with concern. His voice was sounding stronger already.

"Gone," I said with a broad grin. "We have a lot to tell you, but...it's over, love. We beat him, got everybody out, then we were just waiting for you to wake up—"

I clapped a hand over my mouth because I wanted to scream and yell with victory. With absolute joy. There was nothing, *nothing,* left to kill myself with worry about. Reaper was awake! I had my whole family with me, and the enemy haunting us was gone forever.

"Come here." Reaper nudged a hand against my side to beckon me closer.

"Fuck," I breathed, holding the side of his face as I leaned down. "It is so good to hear your voice, my love."

"Closer," he said.

I leaned down until I was hovering just a few inches above him. He made a frustrated sound, then impatiently said, "Lips, woman."

I laughed at the realization of what he was asking for, then continued down until my mouth slanted over his.

Reaper in top shape would have held me down, kissed me like he needed my air to breathe, and would fight for every sip with teeth and tongue.

But this kiss was full of longing and relief, a sigh that released the last of our worries. He still wore compression wraps for his broken ribs, so I kept the kisses light--soft sips that didn't impact his breathing, despite the yearning I felt from him to deepen them.

He panted softly after a few moments. It was the most exertion he'd had in weeks, after all. I rested my forehead on his, held his hand and his face, not wanting to lose a single moment of contact with his skin.

"Can I...go home?" he asked after catching his breath.

"Not yet, love. Sorry." I placed a fast peck on his lips. "We still have a lot of work to do. But now that you're awake," I kissed his forehead, "we can get started, then get you home as soon as we can."

Reaper was quiet for another long few minutes, and I almost thought he fell back asleep.

"You're not...not mad...anymore?" he asked softly.

The regret rose up in me again and threatened to choke me like a rope.

"No, love. I haven't been." My fingers ran over his scalp. "I wanted to talk to you the next day, to apologize and finally move forward. But then..." My lips shook. "I'm such a fucking idiot. Fuck, I was so awful to you. I'm so, so sorry."

"Me too, sugar."

"No, stop." I brought my forehead back to his. "You've apologized enough. I shouldn't have let it keep festering."

Reaper brought a finger under my chin, tilting my face up for another kiss, which I happily gave to him.

"Love you," he whispered on my lips. "My wife, forever."

"I love you too." My hand curled around his. "My husband, forever."

He smiled through his next kiss. "Forgiven?"

"Forgiven."

CHAPTER 28

REAPER

It was another week before I was cleared to go home.

Mari and the doctor got me up and out of bed the same day I woke up. I had to use a walker to get around the first two days, like I didn't feel fucking old and feeble enough. Then I moved on to a cane, which wasn't as bad. As long as I had a wall or something for support, I could swat Mari on the ass with it.

By the time I was discharged, I could walk, eat, and do most basic tasks on my own. But there were some things, both tangible and not, that I knew were permanently changed.

The nerve damage in my left hand caused me to lose feeling in my pinky and ring fingers. I could still hold objects and grip the handlebars of a bike, but I would never be able to fully extend those fingers.

I had areas without feeling on my head too, which I didn't realize until Mari was scratching my scalp one day. We had a whole back-and-forth, much to the other guys' amusement, where I thought she'd stopped but she insisted she didn't.

Mari and the others remained sleeping in my room, staying with me through downtime and my rigorous physical therapy. The guys only went home to grab food, clothes, and to feed the animals, who I missed more than I thought I would. Even that fucking rooster.

I grumbled about never having time to myself, but I was glad for their company, for the normalcy of it. To see the guys acting like dipshits with each other and being affectionate with Mari, it was everything. They filled me in on what happened, and I formally met Mari's parents for the first time. Her dad strolled into my room, spent the first five minutes speaking exclusively Spanish, and everyone thought it was hilarious.

I was weeks behind everyone else, but the reality started sinking in for me as more time passed. It was really fucking over.

The life we wanted, the world we'd been fighting for, it was here. And it was real.

Still, it was a crushing disappointment when I was told I couldn't ride my bike out of the hospital when discharged.

"Mari, tell 'em." I flung my hand in exasperation at the medics who kept telling me no. "I can fucking walk, dress, and feed myself. I can definitely fucking ride."

"Nope, sorry, love." She looked a little too delighted to be saying no to me as well. "I'm with them. You're much better, but you still have strength and balance to rebuild."

"Shadow can give you a piggyback ride," Jandro chimed in helpfully.

The big guy stared at him. "Don't volunteer me for shit."

"Your dad's on his way with the car," Gunner said through barely-controlled laughter.

"Great," I grumbled. "Dad's picking me up. How old am I again?"

"You'll be riding again before you know it." Mari rubbed my back, the only one trying to genuinely be helpful.

My dad pulled up not long after in his black SUV, while Mari and the others would ride home and meet us there. When Dad stepped out to hug me, I was surprised to see him in his pressed general's uniform.

"Aren't you out of a job now, General?" I cracked, slapping his back. "Thought you'd be decked out for golf or whatever retired people do."

"Sadly, not yet." He opened the passenger door for me with a chuckle, then elaborated when he got into the driver's seat. "We have a lot of diplomatic threads to iron out with Blakeworth and other neighboring territories. And now that New Ireland is free for the taking, we want to make sure its new occupants can remain civil."

"Someone looking to move in already?"

"A few," he confirmed, driving out onto the road. "We have a unit at the fortress just to maintain the place and make a smooth transition once we've established some agreements."

The drive was mostly quiet after that. I wasn't thinking of anything besides getting to the house. Would it *feel* like coming home or would everything be different? I figured as long as Mari and the guys were there, I could deal with any changes the place had gone through.

It wasn't until we crossed the small bridge into our still-developing neighborhood that my dad asked, "How are you, son? I mean really."

The question pulled me out of my simple fantasy of sitting on the back patio with a cigar and some whiskey. "I'm alright, I guess. I'll be better once I have somewhere soft to land."

"This is me you're talking to," he reminded me, pulling into our long, gravel driveway. "I've seen torture, son. I've seen what it does to people."

So have I. I thought of Shadow, how timid he used to be despite being the most skilled assassin I'd ever seen. I thought of how he made strides and then regressions. And how he offered up himself to protect me in that dungeon. Since waking up, there was kind of unspoken solidarity between us. I understood him better now, and he knew better than anyone else how that experience had changed me.

I'd had a few nightmares since waking up from the coma, mostly flashes of the Sha grinning and laughing. Some other patient or random medic in the hallway would look vaguely like one of the guards who beat me and I'd feel phantom pains or a rush of adrenaline.

Mari knew. I was certain Shadow knew. The other guys probably figured out I'd have some lingering effects. And obviously my dad caught on.

I didn't like anyone in my business. I hated being perceived as weak. My first impulse was to snap at my dad that I was fine, to quit digging into me.

But I paused with the words on the tip of my tongue, still reconciling the Shadow I first met with the man I knew now.

He was no weaker now that he had gotten real help. If anything, he was much stronger now. I never saw him regress once in that dungeon. He'd only been concerned for me. A year ago, I wouldn't have trusted him in the same room as Mari. Now, he was among the only three I trusted with her.

Mari only ever wanted to help him, to ease the suffering caused by a life of trauma. In that dungeon, Shadow tried to spare me as much suffering as he could. And I knew without a doubt, the rest of my family only wanted to help me too.

"I'm okay right now, Dad," I said as he pulled to a stop in front of the house. "Some days are better than others. Some nights are hard but, shit."

The others had pulled up next to us on their bikes. Jandro was the first to hop off and open the garage door, releasing a very excited, stubby-tail-wagging Hades.

"As long as I got this," I nodded to the scene outside the window, "I'll be okay."

Dad smiled at me, relief etched into his features as he clapped me on the shoulder. "Good, son. Lean on them. They'll hold you above water when it feels like you can't breathe."

"I will." I made a decision in that moment to really act on those words, not just say them. If Shadow could, then I could.

"Let me get your door." Dad took off his seatbelt and started to get out of his seat.

"Pfft. I got it, old man. I'm not your wife, you can put away your chivalry."

He laughed but got out of the car anyway so he could greet everybody.

I stepped out of the passenger side, keeping one hand on the car for balance as I made my way around the hood. I had just made it past the first headlight when Hades caught my scent and zoomed toward me with an excited bark.

"Whoa, whoa. Hey." I leaned against the car as the massive dog jumped up so that he wouldn't tackle me to the ground and put me right back in the hospital.

He was all puppylike excitement—jumping up to lick my face, stubby tail going crazy, and rubbing into my ear scratches like nothing else in the world mattered. It never occurred to me until right then how weird it was for him to act completely like a dog.

"Hey, Hades." I held both sides of his head, trying to get a closer look into those endlessly black eyes. "You in there?"

The dog blinked and tried to lick my chin, then wiggled out of my hold and tried to sniff my pockets for treats. I knew from just a glance there was no longer a god inside this animal. He was just a dog.

When I looked up at the others, Mari answered the question in my expression.

"Since we killed the Sha," she said softly. "After they possessed us, they just...left."

"All of them?" I asked.

Mari nodded and Gunner spoke up next. "They still act mostly the same, probably because they've been with us since they were born, but...they're just animals now."

"He's still Freyja's favorite," Mari said, nudging Shadow.

"It's just because I'm the tallest and she likes to climb," he huffed.

The others gave him skeptical looks while I was still trying to process the information. "Why would they leave?"

"They haven't left," Mari corrected. "They're just not guiding us through animals anymore. And from what they said," she shrugged, "because they accomplished what they came here to do."

She was probably right. The gods came to us with a very specific purpose, but I didn't expect them to just retreat back into the void. It would take me a while to adjust to no longer being an instrument of death.

But still, the thought was freeing.

My dad helped us bring some belongings into the house and then took his leave, likely sensing that the five of us wanted to be alone together. The first thing I did was crash in the nearest bedroom. I didn't care or know whose room it was, I just wanted to lay down on a real bed in my house.

Mari's soft laugh floated in from the doorway the moment my back hit the mattress. "Do you, uh—"

"Get in here." I beckoned her in with my eyes still closed in bliss. "All you fuckers get in here."

The mattress dipped as she climbed on, then movement was all around me as the guys joined her. Mari nestled against my chest while Jandro spooned me from the other side with an exaggerated, contented sigh. I couldn't be bothered telling him to fuck off, even as a joke. He reached across my waist to rest his fingertips on Mari's side and I was damn glad he was there. That she had him while she didn't have Shadow and me.

Gunner snuggled up against Mari's back, sandwiching her between us while Shadow took Jandro's usual spot, scooting lower down the bed to rest his head on Mari's legs.

Once settled into our cuddle pile, the five of us let out a breath collectively. I couldn't explain why but it felt like a final release. The last nail in the coffin of the nightmare that had been our lives. We were all here, alive and at home. If I had any doubts, I could just reach out and touch any one of them.

Mari started laughing at our collective sigh. "So now what do we do?"

"Take naps," Gunner murmured, already sounding half-asleep.

"I'm all for that." Jandro snuggled harder against my back, purposely trying to get a reaction out of me.

Joke's on you, buddy. You're actually pretty comfy back there.

"Whatever the fuck we want." I reached back to pat his face.

Shadow looked up at Mari, idly caressing her legs. "Is there something you want to do now, lover?"

Mari seemed thoughtful, chewing her lip.

"Tell us, sugar," I urged, running a light touch over her face. "Now that nothing is in your way, what would you like to do?"

Her gaze met mine. "I think...I might want to become a doctor."

"Overachiever," Gunner grunted. Shadow growled and swung to hit him somewhere, the blow landing with a soft thud. "Ow, dude! I was fucking joking."

"Uh-huh." Mari laughed and tugged at Gunner's hair before looking again at me. "Dr. B's been talking about starting a training program. We really need a bigger team of doctors, and while I already do a lot of those duties, it would add to my credibility if I went back to school and actually got an MD."

"That all makes perfect sense," I said, trailing a finger along her jaw. "But is it what *you* want to do?"

Jandro's hand on her waist closed to hold her there. "We support whatever you want to do, Mariposita."

"I like the *idea* of it," Mari mused. "But I'm still not sure yet. Anyway, it'll be a while before the training program actually gets put together, so I have time to decide."

"Perfect." Gunner nuzzled the back of her head. "More time for naps."

She looked over her shoulder to kiss him, which exposed a long, beautiful sliver of neck to me. I leaned in to kiss her there, pausing to savor the heat of her skin on my mouth. Being able to touch her intimately was not possible at the hospital, but now...now we were *home.*

Mari's body shifted as Gunner and I subtly pressed in toward her. Just the shape of her against me, the friction of her movements, made my hands curl into fists in her clothes. It had been so, so long. I *needed* my wife. If I didn't have her, I would...

Mari faced me again, catching my mouth in a kiss that matched my own hunger. I pulled her flush to me, bringing her leg over my hip and not caring who else was around as long as I had *her.*

I rolled to my back with Mari straddling me, clumsily pulling at her clothes with my gimpy hands until a stabbing pain shot through my arm.

"Ah, fuck!" I clutched at my arm, more in annoyance than anything else. I hadn't felt any random pains in a while and it was damned inconvenient for it to be happening right now.

Mari took my arm in both hands and rubbed over the area with her thumbs. "You're okay, love. Better?"

"Yeah." It had already faded to a dull throbbing under her touch.

"It's your connective tissue back here. Maybe even your nerves too." She smirked down at me. "Maybe you're not ready for sex yet."

I huffed dismissively. "I will be the judge of that—ah!" I tried to reach for her again, only to feel my arm and shoulder vehemently protesting.

"Relax, love." Mari placed my arm back down at my side. "Don't force it, you'll make it worse."

I let out a frustrated groan, staring up at the ceiling. "We have all the time in the world after I'm better, I guess."

Mari laughed and when I looked at her again, she was pulling her shirt off and tossing it to a far corner of the room. Four pairs of eyes were now locked on her, bared to us. And from the way her hips wriggled out of her pants, she loved every piece of the attention.

"I never said *everything* was off the table." She crawled over me, one hand pushing my shirt up my abdomen.

A moment of hesitation hit me like I'd never felt before. I didn't look the same. I was thinner, although I'd get back to my normal weight in time. More scars covered me now, from my injuries in the dungeon and multiple surgeries. I'd never been a guy who was self-conscious of my looks before, so that sudden moment of doubt was jarring to me now.

I realized it was all for nothing as Mari's touch ran over me, just as indulgent and exploratory as she'd always been. If anything, she was even more eager now, making off with the rest of my clothes in a hurry. A heady thrill chased away the last of my self-consciousness, seeing that my wife wanted me just as fucking badly as I wanted her.

"Come here."

Her kiss pressed me down into the mattress, dark hair falling all around us like a curtain. She met me with every lash of tongue, scrape of lips, and sinking of teeth. It was every kiss I fantasized about when I missed her, all the pent up passion and longing and aching for months. I poured it all into her mouth and she gave hers to me.

"I won't repeat the past," she told me in a hushed whisper against my lips. "I promise."

"Neither will I," I panted, dizzy with love and lack of breath.

She stole the air out of my mouth again and again and I kept giving it to her, knowing she deserved more. I lost track of the other guys until Mari started down my body, the curtain of her hair pulled back as she lingered kisses over my abdomen. Beyond her, I saw three vaguely amused expressions looking back at me.

"Should we go?" Jandro asked, his grin widening.

"Fuck no," I barked. "The doctor says I'm not ready for the main event." I touched Mari's arm, the furthest I could reach without pain, as she headed lower. "So you fuckers better do what I can't."

"Y'all heard him." Jandro stood up, shucked off his shirt, and pulled apart his belt buckle. "Sounds like a direct order from the pres to me."

Gunner and Shadow quickly got up and started stripping as well, while Mari took an indulgent peek over her shoulder to watch.

Me? I grabbed a pillow for my head for a better angle to watch and relax.

Per the medic's orders.

CHAPTER 29

MARIPOSA

Reaper's cock pulsed with an insistent need against my belly, but I didn't want to direct my attention there just yet. I wanted to learn my husband's body again, taste his skin and reacquaint myself with the man I had pushed away for so long.

I started at his collarbones, following the path to his throat with my fingertips and then my lips. He was missing his signature smell of cloves and whiskey, but I knew that would return as our life went back to normal. Regardless, he smelled delicious and masculine as I dragged my mouth indulgently down his chest.

He had some injuries here, healing scars creating blank spots in the large tattoo covering his torso. Shadow would fill them in, no doubt, so I kissed them lightly while they were visible. Reaper had endured so much. From me, from his time in captivity, and still now, from his painful recovery. He deserved every moment of R&R that he was ordered to take.

But that didn't mean I had to deprive him.

"Come here, *Mariposita*." With a hand on my back, Jandro directed me to the side of Reaper's body while I continued to kiss him and explore lower. I wasn't sure what he and the others had planned. My focus was on a single person for the time being.

Or was it?

I paused, taking note of four other distinct sparks of excitement in my chest. They were separate from my own and easy to miss if I didn't pay attention, but still there all the same. I smiled against Reaper's skin, realizing it was the bonds between my men and I. It was *their* excitement I was feeling, an echo of the bonds harnessed by the gods. I couldn't see from their perspectives anymore, nor borrow their abilities, but I loved knowing that we still had this--a tangible connection we could feel.

A warm hand pressed between my legs as palms swept over my ass and my back. My face hovered just over Reaper's cock now, and I dragged my tongue down the length of it, unable to contain myself any longer.

"Oh fuck," he cursed, his cock practically jumping at the contact with my mouth.

The familiar heat of him pulsed beneath my lips in time with the heat blooming between my legs. Jandro rubbed and caressed me there, stoking my fire while the others threw kindling on by touching me everywhere else.

A palm slid up my back to hold the nape of my neck, then a mouth breathed harshly against my ear. "Can I have your ass, baby girl?"

"Yes." I couldn't answer Gunner fast enough, the anticipation sending a thrill up my spine to where he gripped tightly on my neck.

He used that grip to haul me up for a kiss, surging his tongue deep with a promise of what was to come. As Gunner released me, running that possessive touch down my spine, Jandro's touch skimmed my inner thighs and I felt a kiss on the back of my leg.

"Sit on my face," Jandro rasped, his kisses inching closer to my core.

We shifted around on the bed to make room for him underneath me, to allow me to continue pleasing Reaper, and for Gunner to keep stroking and kissing my back as he made his way leisurely to my ass. There was only one person missing.

I looked up to find Shadow sitting on the edge of the bed a few feet away, pupils blown wide under his hooded eyelids. He was just as naked as the others, the muscles in his arm and chest flexing as he stroked himself with a loose, relaxed grip.

"Come here, love." My voice hitched on a higher note as Jandro's mouth pressed to my pussy in a long, shiver-inducing kiss.

"I will," Shadow promised, his adoring gaze meeting mine. "I want to watch you with them first."

I smiled at my voyeur husband, keeping his gaze as I lowered my mouth to Reaper's hip. I kissed my way to his cock again, dragging my tongue over the thick organ as Jandro's tongue lapped at me. Jandro's strong fingers kneaded my thighs, spreading me apart for him to consume. A few inches away, Gunner massaged my hips and lower back, slowly treading closer to his destination.

My eyes dropped from Shadow's as I took Reaper into my mouth, gliding my lips over his silky head to the sound of a deep moan leaving his chest. I answered him with one of my own, savoring his taste while my lower body found a rhythm riding on Jandro's tongue, who hummed with delight underneath me.

"Holy fuck." The muttered curse of awe came from Gunner, his hands now sweeping forward to knead my breasts and pinch my nipples into hard points. "That's our girl. So beautiful."

"God, how could I go so long without this perfect mouth sucking me?" Reaper's hand clasped with mine alongside his ribs. "Don't stop, sugar."

My body sparked everywhere from their touches, from the praise. I went down further on Reaper's cock, mapping his shape and thickness with my tongue so I could never forget how he filled my mouth. He hissed out his pleasure, fingers tightening around mine. Jandro lashed at my clit, forcing me to rock against the delicious friction of his lips and tongue devouring me.

"Yes, baby girl. That's it." Gunner's fingers, now leaving a trail of slippery wetness and heat, finally started their way down the cleft of my ass. "Ride his fucking face. Suffocate him if that's what it takes to make you come."

"Mmm!" Jandro made a loud noise of protest but remained steadfast as he devoured me. His hand dug even harder into my thighs, sucking at my flesh and lashing at my clit like he had zero qualms with Gunner's suggestion. I could *feel* their love of pleasing me through our bond, and it only heightened my own pleasure.

Gunner's slick fingers teased my ass while Jandro ate me even more vigorously. My orgasm was imminent, a steady climb as I sucked Reaper harder and moaned out every delicious strike of pleasure consuming me.

"I want to feel you come on my cock," Reaper rasped. "Your scream, sugar. I want to feel it in your voice when you get there."

My chest was tight, heart already hammering from the build-up of pleasure and breathing through my nose to suck him. But the peak was so close, I didn't dare pull my mouth away for a breath. Gunner's fingers eased into my ass and that got me closer but not quite there. I teetered on the peak, right *there*, but not over the threshold. I could barely breathe but my body chased that release above all else.

Jandro made one small change with his mouth, sealing his lips around my clit as he stroked two fingers inside my pussy. He and Gunner stroked and filled me, Reaper thrust toward my throat, and it was that, being filled by my men, that sent me hurtling over the edge.

I released my scream over Reaper's cock just as he wanted, and he swelled and pulsed in response. Sensitivity hit me like lightning, edging me away from all the sensations. I let go of Reaper's cock and took a huge, gasping, moaning breath. I pulled away from Jandro's mouth and started scooting my hips down his body. He held me to his chest once my legs straddled his waist, his cock gently nudging against my thigh.

"So fucking incredible," Jandro whispered, stroking my back and kissing my face. "Breathe, babe. Take a breather."

The aftershocks rolled through me, making me shiver and prompting more kisses and praise from my men. When my heartbeat finally slowed, I looked up at Reaper who was still panting, cock erect and pulsing stiffly.

"Shadow, get in here," he said to our quiet observer. "Take my place for a bit. I need to calm this thing down."

With a soft chuckle, Shadow moved closer until he kneeled on the other side of Jandro.

"Did you enjoy watching?" I smiled up at him, still catching my breath as I took in all his gorgeous masculinity.

"Yes, lover." Shadow reached to stroke my face tenderly. "Seeing your pleasure is my absolute favorite thing."

I took his hand and drew him closer until he was within easy reach while I straddled Jandro. Wrapping a fist around the base of Shadow's cock, I pressed a kiss next to his hip bone. He sucked in a breath, waiting for that slight sting of pain he liked so much. I smiled up at him, teasing him with soft, gentle kisses while I stroked up and down his heavy length.

"Mari..." My name in his throat was such a sexy, desperate plea. This massive, incredibly strong man was completely, utterly mine and wanted to be nothing else.

I closed my teeth on his lower belly and sealed my lips, sucking hard on his flesh.

"Oh fuck yes," Shadow groaned, his hands digging into my hair and curling into fists.

"Damn man," Gunner observed. "Didn't know you were into that."

"I can only feel pain from her." Shadow's breath was short as I unlatched from him, leaving behind a dark red bruise. "And I only like it from her."

"Right on." Gunner's tone was lighthearted and curious, not an ounce of judgment to be heard.

I left Shadow matching hickeys on each side of his hips before running my mouth down the length of his cock, seeking his wide, blunt head with my tongue.

"Does she bite you there?" Gunner asked with a soft laugh.

"No," Shadow and I said together. "But I wouldn't be opposed to trying it," he added.

I shook my head at him. "I don't want to hurt you here."

"Fair enough, lover." Shadow stroked my neck and shoulder. "You can bite and scratch me anywhere else you'd like." He spoke to me so tenderly that I wanted to melt into a puddle at his feet.

But I sucked his wide cock into my mouth instead, sitting up tall to take more of him down my throat.

"Fuck, just look at her," Jandro breathed. He had a perfect view from down below, watching me suck and lick the man he took under his wing years ago. "Our wife. So fucking perfect." His hands slid up my ribcage, palms rolling over my breasts before he captured my nipples between his fingers.

"We're the four luckiest bastards in the world," Reaper agreed, his hand kneading my thigh.

I wanted to preen and bask in their adoration, soak in their loving touches and words until I needed it like air to live. These were *my* men, mine. All of them devoted to me before anyone or anything else. We'd had missteps, miscommunications, and sometimes had made flat-out wrong decisions that were hurtful with devastating consequences.

But *this,* all of us together, was so pure and meaningful. It was everything. This was what the war had been for. All the struggles and heartbreaking moments brought us to this, this unfathomable, unbreakable love we shared.

I lowered to kiss Jandro, still stroking Shadow with my hand as I licked inside the mouth that had just made me come so intensely.

"*Te amo,*" I whispered to him. "I love you so much. I never would have made it through this world without you."

"*Te amo, mi esposa,*" he answered, cupping my face. "I was ready to die with you every step of the way. Now I'm ready to *live* with you."

Our kiss connected again, passionate and ravenous while my legs clamped around his hips. I ground against his body, searching for the heat and solidness of his cock to fill the empty ache inside me. Jandro released me with one hand to wrap it around his base, never breaking a kiss as he rubbed the fat head against my pussy. He teased me with it for a few swipes before pausing it at my entrance so I could sink down.

The width of him spread me open and my mouth broke away to moan at the delicious pressure. My head rested on his chest for a moment while I just lowered and lifted up, relishing in the feel of him spearing through me. I sat up after getting my bearings, returning my mouth to Shadow's cock, which waited for me so patiently.

A familiar hand stroked down my back, pausing once again at the entrance to my ass.

"Yes, please," I begged Gunner before sucking Shadow between my lips again.

Jandro took control below me, holding my waist while his hips rolled up to fuck me. With my spare hand, I reached over to Reaper, figuring he'd had a long enough breather already. He had softened, but not by much.

"Yes, fuck. Touch me, sugar. Just like that." He grunted out praise as I stroked him back to full hardness.

I drew Shadow down my throat as far as he would go, then released him with a gasping breath. Leaning to the other side, I took Reaper into my mouth, still working both men with my hands.

"Holy...shit," I heard from behind me.

"You gonna take her ass or what, Gun?" Jandro slowed his thrusts below me, hands sliding around my hips.

"Yeah, yeah. She's just fucking stunning, that's all."

"Don't blame you," Reaper purred with a caress down my arm.

I sucked him as Gunner eased his way into my ass, pausing often to lube himself more as he stretched me open. Jandro was fully seated inside me, not thrusting, but flexing his cock as Gunner worked his way inside. I lifted up from Reaper, sitting back on the two other men as I leaned my head against Shadow's thigh.

Gunner and Jandro started moving and I cried out at the sheer fullness in my body.

Shadow flinched at the sound. "Don't hurt her," he warned.

"I'm okay, I'm good," I panted, rolling my gaze up to his. "It doesn't hurt, it's just a lot."

He cupped the base of my skull and I knew he was watching me for any discomfort, even though my eyes rolled back and my lids slammed shut.

Just below Shadow's hand, Gunner kissed my upper back. "Good, baby girl?"

"Yes," I answered, my face tipped skyward and back arched in a deep curve. "Oh fuck, yes."

Gunner dragged out of my ass as Jandro thrust in, their alternating movements leaving no reprieve in my body. They slid against each other through a thin wall inside me and the mere thought of that, nevermind the sensation, was so utterly erotic that I felt another orgasm building immediately.

"Oh fuck, she's getting there..."

"She's so close, I can feel her..."

I didn't know who was talking but my need for that release had me taking over the movement, riding them both as I sucked Shadow back into my mouth. This time I wanted to scream over him as I came.

My hand was still wrapped around Reaper's cock, solid and slick as I stroked him with the rising and falling of my whole body. Jandro and Gunner held me steady for balance, but the control of this ride was all mine.

Again, I was right there, teetering on the edge. My lungs burned as Shadow filled my mouth, but his moans and touches kept me going. I wanted him to feel me even if he wasn't inside me.

My thighs ached as I rode them, bouncing and grinding and taking all the cock I could. Even my arm stroking Reaper was beginning to shake from fatigue. How could I not just come instantly with four gorgeous men touching, praising, and pleasing me?

A hand to my clit did it. I didn't know whose it was, but it was like pressing on a button that detonated a bomb. The release was explosive, my scream not only reverberating around Shadow's cock but filling the whole room.

And then I felt free and weightless, like smoke drifting back to earth.

CHAPTER 30

GUNNER

I'd never seen such a beautiful display of multitasking in my life. Mari had Jandro and me inside her, then Shadow and Reaper in each hand. Her mouth went back and forth between the two of them until her orgasm rocked her to another dimension.

As Mari screamed through a mouthful of Shadow's cock, her ass clamped down around me so hard I thought for sure my dick would snap off. That *would* be the best and most epic way to lose it, but her convulsions thankfully ebbed after that first one.

Jandro stilled inside her, but I kept rolling my hips until she collapsed panting onto his chest. A light sheen of sweat coated her back, her skin tasting lightly of salt when I leaned over to kiss her shoulder blade.

"Did you guys break her?" Reaper ran a hand down her arm that still held his cock with a slack grip.

"She's fine, just gotta come back to earth." Jandro stroked a hair away from her face and kissed her forehead.

"Are you sure?" Shadow knelt next to the bed to get a closer look at her face.

"I'm fine, love." Mari laughed breathlessly, reaching out to scratch his beard. "I just need a second to recover."

"Kiss me and I'll be the judge of that." He was smiling now, quickly assured that our girl was nothing less than thoroughly pleased.

Mari's hips lifted as she reached to kiss Shadow, the movement causing Jandro and I to moan in unison.

"God, I wish I could fuck her," Reaper huffed. "I'm so fucking jealous."

"You should be." My voice strained with effort to concentrate. "It's so fucking good."

Every drag of her along my cock was on another level of pleasure. Just the slightest shifts and movements gripped and squeezed me like she was meant to fit me, even with another man inside her.

Especially with another man inside her, I realized. Mari was *ours*, and I had the privilege of sharing her with the three best men I knew. There were no words for how good it felt, all of us being together this way. Our gods were gone but I swore I felt the shockwaves of Mari's orgasm in me, like we still had a bond tethering us.

Shadow resumed standing and Mari sat up, her hands pressed to Jandro's chest. She looked over her shoulder at me, her side profile so beautifully breathtaking.

"Gunner?"

"Yes, baby girl?" I leaned into her, my chest brushing her back as I reached for a kiss. "What do you need? Tell me. Anything."

Mari's lips skimmed mine in a sweet smile. "Kiss me and tell me what *you* need."

"I need nothing." My arms wrapped around her middle, pulling her back more firmly against my chest for this small moment of just me and her. "I have everything right here."

"You're sure?" Her smile grew, the kisses she peppered on me so sweet and reassuring.

"Positive." I dragged a kiss from her shoulder to her ear, trailing along the sensitive skin of her neck for the journey. "But I might like to try something."

Mari perked up immediately. "Such as?"

I tapped Jandro's leg to get his attention. "Switch spots with me."

"Um." His eyes flicked from me to Mari. "On the bed or in her?"

"The bed, dude!" I laughed and took a possessive grab of Mari's ass cheeks. "I ain't leaving this sweet ass for nothing."

"Alright, let's see if I can do this without slippin' out."

"Bet you a shot you can't," Reaper piped up.

"I'll take that bet," Shadow chimed in.

"Thanks for the faith, bro." Jandro fist-bumped the big dude before he started moving, sitting up in the bed. He and I looked around each other to figure out the best way to move while the other two looked on.

"You're not allowed to help him." Reaper smirked at Mari, stroking himself lazily.

"What do you mean?"

As soon as she asked the question, I felt it—a contraction of muscles squeezing around my dick that made me want to stop everything and thrust into her sweet, sexy ass until I filled her up.

"That!" Reaper pointed accusingly. "You just did it, I can see it in their faces."

Shadow chuckled under his breath. "She has to help them a little."

"Nah, Jandro's a gifted mechanic. I want to see if he's got the same dexterity in his dick. His dick-sterity."

"If you want to see me do tricks with it, you just have to ask," Jandro informed him.

"Guys, I think I figured it out," Mari declared. She leaned the back of her head on my shoulder and looked up at me. "You want to lie back on the bed, right?"

"Yeah." Completely unable to help myself, I slid a hand up her ribs to grab a breast.

"So just sit down and lean all the way back. Jandro can just come forward."

"You're making it too easy for them," Reaper complained.

"You're just mad you're not one of them." Shadow was truly laughing now, enjoying our antics.

"Fuck yeah I am," Reaper huffed. But there was no bite to the words. He was just giving us shit.

"You have a lot of faith in *my* dexterity, baby girl." I checked to make sure there was enough room behind me. "I don't know if I bend that way."

"Hurry up, I'm getting soft!" Jandro yelled.

I started leaning back, holding Mari to my chest and Jandro followed us, leaning forward to stay inside her. She clenched around us again and it took work to stifle back my moan. We had to do some maneuvering with our legs, while Shadow and Reaper provided helpful commentary, but in the end, we were successful.

"Take a shot when we leave the bedroom, buddy." Jandro grinned victoriously at Reaper, who turned around and scooted toward the opposite end of the bed to lie next to Mari again.

"Whatever, I don't plan on leaving the bedroom." He slid closer to me and Mari, already seeking out her touch.

"I'll pour it down your throat, then," Shadow said as he moved closer to the other side of us.

"Damn," Reaper mused. "Didn't take you for that kind of guy."

"A deal's a deal."

"Anyway," I said loudly, running my hands over the gorgeous woman lying on top of me. "You comfortable, baby girl?"

"Very." Mari turned her head to kiss me. "Are you?"

"Couldn't be better." I grabbed her waist and rolled my hips up to press deeper into her ass, pulling a soft gasp from her mouth. "More?" My mouth scraped against her ear.

"Yes," she breathed, her voice going higher. "Please, both of you."

Her legs wrapped around Jandro's waist and the room filled with moans, creaks, and sighs as we started up again. Jandro and I alternated thrusts again, his hands planted on either side of Mari and me as his chest hovered over hers.

This was a great idea, I thought. Even while she kissed him, I could touch her and tease her. She loved it when we all touched her, it must have been some kind pleasure-sensory overload. And with some of the bond still there, I could feel some of what she felt. Her hands reached out to the sides for Reaper and Shadow as Jandro and I found a steady pace.

"Such a good girl," I whispered into her ear, punctuating each word with a thrust into her ass. "You take our cocks so well."

She answered with a moaning mouthful of Reaper, who kneeled next to us to give her better access. Her opposite hand was vigorously jerking Shadow, who stood stiffly with his hands clenched like he was trying to hold back from popping off too soon.

Yeah. Me too, dude.

Mari pulled her mouth off of Reaper, prompting Jandro to lean down and kiss her again.

"Fuck," he growled against her lips. "Too fucking good."

I could see the effort in his chest and arms as he held himself up. I could feel his thrusts fucking her harder, losing his resolve to how well she took him. Took both of us.

I was getting close too. My movement was more limited from our position but, God, her ass. Her beautiful, perfect ass that she let *me* have first. I loved fucking her here and cherished the fact that she trusted me with her body this much.

Not to mention that she was so tight and hot and felt fucking amazing back here. The harder Jandro fucked her, the tighter and more intense she felt on me.

"Fuck," I growled out through my teeth, fingers digging into her waist as I felt her tensing up, all her muscles coiling for another explosive release. If this was anywhere near as strong as her last one, I wouldn't last through it.

"Gonna come for us, *Mariposita?*" Jandro felt it too and brought a hand to her throat. It was a firm hold without squeezing, but she locked eyes with him and let out a whimpering, wordless plea. Barely a second passed before Mari wrapped her hand around his to tighten the hold.

"Oh, fuck." Jandro leaned his forehead on hers, gaze reverent as he squeezed her throat and crashed into her harder. "Oh, you want it hard. You're gonna come so hard."

Mari barely made a sound, just a tiny squeak as the orgasm rippled through her body. Her ass closed around my dick and I was done for. My release spilled out of me in a heady rush and I kept driving into her ass, trying to extend her orgasm, as well as mine, for as long as possible. A throbbing sensation that didn't match up with her convulsions made me realize that I felt Jandro's release too. He must have felt that overload of pleasure through the bond too, there was no way he couldn't.

The three of us all came down slowly in a sweaty, panting pile. Jandro sat back and sprawled on the opposite end of the bed, his chest heaving as he took great gulps of air. Mari slid off my body to the side, and I scooted away to give her more room.

"Well fuck," Reaper said, looking at a very spent Mari, now sandwiched between us. "That was hot."

"Thanks. Be here all week," Jandro panted from the far end of the bed.

"You two look wrung out," Shadow observed.

"Power of the pussy," Jandro moaned, throwing an arm over his eyes.

"And the ass," I agreed, scooting up to recline next to him. "You gotta take her ass, man," I said to Shadow. "It's incredible."

Shadow frowned in Mari's direction. "No, I'm too big."

"Well, shit. You don't gotta brag." I scooted up high to sit against the headboard. As relaxed and languid as I was now, I wanted to see what our girl had left in her.

Shadow took the spot I was just in, lying on his side as he skimmed a hand down Mari's back. "Had enough, lover?" he asked her gently.

She rolled toward him in answer, wrapped a leg around his hip, and brought his mouth to hers for a scorching kiss. Jandro and I watched them while catching our breath. I had never seen this side of Shadow before—a guy who kissed a woman with confidence and pulled her closer without hesitation. Who smiled at the private things she said to him and whispered things back that made her laugh and nuzzle into him.

"Proud of that guy," Jandro muttered, peeking under his arm.

"Me too, man." Mari rolled away from Shadow to make out with Reaper, sliding her body along his as she kissed him. "Proud of you too," I added with a nod in Jandro's direction.

"Me? What'd I do?"

"Gave him a place to go, for one." Shadow moved closer to Mari's back as she kissed Reaper, running a hand down her spine until his fingers dipped between her legs. "You also stood up to Reap and I when we were dumbasses."

Jandro sighed and propped his arm behind his head. "Someone had to question Reap to make sure he was making the right decisions. You, I knew you were just defaulting to him as president. I couldn't blame you in the same way because it wasn't your decision to make."

Mari slid lower down Reaper's body, taking his cock in her mouth while she wiggled her ass against Shadow's hand in invitation. The big guy groaned and nudged his cock where his hand had just been. His hips rolled against her ass, length sliding along her slick core to tease her for entry.

"I could have questioned him too," I said to Jandro. "But I guess I realized that too late."

"Nah." Jandro shook his head, his gaze never pulling away from the erotic scene in front of us. "If you backed me up, he would've just tossed your ass out too. I've just known him for so long, he was only okay with me telling him he was wrong." He nodded at the threesome a few feet away. "Me and her, really."

"For different reasons."

"Yeah." Jandro barked out a laugh. "You don't see *me* sucking his dick."

"Mmm, fuck...you know I can hear you."

Reaper finished the sentence just as Shadow pressed inside of Mari. Her muffled moans and the crash of his hips against her ass filled the room.

"Sorry, Reap. What was that?" Jandro placed his fingertips behind his ear. "Can't hear you."

Reaper just raised a middle finger in our direction. His face, eyes closed and blissed out, tipped up to the ceiling as Mari sucked more of him into her mouth. She rolled up to lean on hands and knees between his legs, and Shadow followed right after, kneeling behind her and never missing a thrust with the shift in position.

"It all worked out though," Jandro said, picking up our conversation from earlier.

"Yeah," I agreed. Reaper's cursing and moaning was getting louder, his fists clutching the sheets at his side. "But things are different now, aren't they?"

"They are." Jandro nodded. "None of us are the same people we used to be."

Shadow's breaths had turned to ragged groans, hips snapping with more force against Mari's perky ass. He reached around and underneath to play with her clit while he fucked her, turning her sexy moans into desperate whines as her release neared.

"But that's a good thing," I said to Jandro. "We're really a family now, not just club brothers."

A smile pulled at his face. "You got that right."

"Oh fuck, don't stop, sugar." Reaper was flushed and panting, hips driving up into the beautiful mouth wrapped around his cock. "That's perfect. Fuck, keep doing that."

Shadow bowed over Mari with his forehead on her shoulder blade, still rubbing her clit and fucking her with long, deep strokes. Our girl was getting red in the face too, moaning loudly with her mouth full and her brow furrowed with tension. All three of them were close, dancing along that knife-edge of release.

"Who's gonna be first?" Jandro smirked.

"Mari, duh," I scoffed. "Why, you wanna bet?"

"Nah." He folded his hands on his chest, awaiting the finale. "I know those two will make sure she gets hers first."

The air in the room grew thick over the next minute, while all the heat and energy and passion in the center of the bed reached a crescendo. Mari's thighs shook when the orgasm hit, her knees giving out until she lay prone between Reaper's legs. And still she sucked him with gusto, working his stiff length with her hands until he roared out his release. Shadow finished soon after, sheathing himself inside Mari with a final deep thrust and shuddering with a breathless groan against her back.

Jandro clapped slowly while the three of them stayed like that, barely moving in the aftermath.

"Stop that shit and open a window," Reaper panted, his hand tangled in Mari's hair, who rested her head on his lower stomach.

Shadow pulled out of her slowly, lifting her hair away to dress her neck in kisses. She shivered at the contact but otherwise didn't move.

"Falling asleep on us, baby girl?" I scooted closer to touch her ankle, and she shivered at that too. Our poor girl, so sensitive and orgasmed out.

"Mm no," she mumbled, but her fluttering eyelids and slack limbs said otherwise.

"Are you sore?" Shadow curled his body around hers, stroking a hand down her thigh. "We can start a bath for you."

Mari perked up at that, stretching her legs out long with a point in her toes and arch in her back. I could only sigh at the sight of her, so beautiful in everything she did.

"Bath sounds nice."

"Jandro." Reaper looked up at the VP who was opening the windows in the room. "What's for dinner?"

Jandro glared at him. "You're lucky your ass is gimpy, otherwise I wouldn't even entertain that question."

"Gotta milk it while I can." Reaper placed his hands behind his head.

"I'll help with food." Shadow placed a final kiss on Mari and rolled up from the bed.

"Thank you. At least one of y'all is useful," Jandro declared dramatically.

I slid into the spot Shadow just left, hugging around Mari's waist as I spooned her. "Guess that leaves me to help you with your bath."

"And me," Reaper said, grimacing as he sat up. "With what I can, anyway."

"With the two of you, what could go wrong?" Mari laughed as she kissed me over her shoulder.

"That's right." I grinned against her lips. "You were the key to preventing a zombie apocalypse by an evil god, so you definitely need a couple of dudes to help you with a bath."

"I'll take it as a perk." She grinned back, rubbing the stubble on my jaw. "Especially if it's from the men in this room."

"Good." I scooped an arm under her legs and hauled her against my chest. "'Cause we're the ones you're stuck with."

Mari wrapped an arm around my shoulders, drawing me in for a deeper kiss. "Perfect."

CHAPTER 31

SHADOW

Jandro and I were both pretty brain-dead after the sex, so we kept dinner simple—chicken tacos topped with random shit we found in the fridge. We all just stood around the counter, building the tacos as we wanted and then shoving them in our mouths. In other words, perfection.

"You think the governor's gonna throw another dinner party for us?" Jandro wondered after shoving his fourth taco down his gullet.

"Fuck, I hope not." I lost count of how many I ate, but I was in the middle of piling another one high with avocados and salsa.

"No?" Jandro looked incredulous. "We're even bigger heroes now, we saved the fuckin' world! You don't want to eat fancy, rich-people shit on the governor's dime again?"

"I don't want to wear too many layers of clothes and be forced to talk to boring people."

He laughed. "You got a point there." We were quiet for a moment while I chewed my food, but I felt the weight of his gaze for his next question. "Still sleeping good?"

"Yeah. Great, actually."

"Good, man. I'm glad to hear that." He turned at the sound of footsteps to see Reaper emerge from the hall—freshly showered and in a pair of sweatpants and a T-shirt.

"Yo." Reaper slapped Jandro's shoulder. "Leave me any food?"

"Yes, Your Highness," Jandro scoffed. "How's our queen?"

Reaper wandered toward the taco items. "Wrinkly from her bath and half-asleep."

"She gonna eat?"

"Maybe. You should lotion her up and ask her."

"You left her un-lotioned?" Jandro gasped in fake shock as he rinsed off his hands. "How dare you?"

"Gun's getting her started, but she'll love another pair of hands."

As soon as Jandro headed down the hall to the bedroom, I grabbed Reaper's favorite whiskey and set it on the counter. "You owe me a shot, President."

Reaper rolled his eyes but smiled easily. "How could I forget?" He finished preparing his plate of tacos and brought down two shot glasses from a cabinet. At my questioning glance, he said, "Hey, I ain't taking one alone."

"Fair enough." I finished the rest of my taco while he poured.

He slid one toward me and raised his, then paused. "I don't have the brain cells for a toast right now," he said before meeting my eyes. "But I'm glad it was you in there with me. And ah—don't." He raised a finger in warning when I opened my mouth. "Don't give me some shit about how you couldn't protect me or should have done more. You did your best, Shadow. You kept me just alive enough so that I could come home. I don't know if anyone else could have done that." He clinked his glass against mine quickly. "So thank you."

A mirthless smile came to my face. He knew exactly what I was going to say. So I said nothing, mirrored him as he raised his glass and poured the liquor down my throat.

"I'm glad you're alive and home," I said when we put our glasses down. "And I'm especially glad that...everything is in the rearview mirror now."

"Yeah," he breathed, leaning against the counter. "It's a hell of a fresh start."

"It is," I agreed.

Reaper ate his food quietly for a few minutes while I started cleaning up. Jandro didn't come back to get food for Mari, so I figured she was probably asleep now.

"Can I ask you something?" Reaper's voice took on a grave, serious tone.

"Of course." I turned to give him my full attention.

He swallowed before speaking and then nearly whispered, "The nightmares."

I moved closer to him, keeping my voice as low as his. "Yes? You're having them?"

"What do you do about them?" His expression was raw, vulnerable like I'd never seen him before our time together in that dungeon. "Besides drink yourself to death. The old me would've had no problem doing that, but I don't want to deal with shit that way anymore." He smiled wryly. "Gotta make it to old age now, I guess."

"Yeah. We all do." I stroked my beard while I thought on his question. It wasn't at all surprising that he was experiencing nightmares from what he'd been through. I just didn't expect him to ask me for help this soon, or this openly. "It might be different for you, but hypnosis worked best for me."

"How does it work?" His hand inched toward the whiskey bottle. "How is it not just reliving the nightmare over and over?"

"It can be, if you're not careful." I sat across from him and nodded yes when he motioned for more to drink. "The first couple times for me were exactly like that. I almost stopped doing it because it didn't seem to work."

"Why'd you keep doing it?" Reaper poured for us into bigger glasses to sip from and slid one over to me.

"Doc convinced me to give it one last shot, and I'm glad I did." My fingers circled around the rim of my drink. "That time, I was able to separate myself from the memories. I was there, but I was also outside of them, like an observer to what was happening. He guided me through, and I was able to stay grounded, stay in control. And it got easier from there."

"Gotta be honest." Reaper sipped deeply from his drink. "That doesn't make a whole lot of sense to me."

"It didn't to me either, not until I did it." I took a small, pensive sip. "It helps to have someone there guiding you through it. They become an anchor to you, a safety net if something really ugly comes up."

"Could you do something like that for me?"

I hesitated in answering with another swallow of whiskey. "I can try if you want me to. But Doc had years and years of doing this. I don't want to lead you somewhere that makes you feel worse."

"Ah, how bad can it be?" Reaper polished off his drink. "You think Mari could do it?"

"Reaper, I..." I rubbed my palms together, searching for a way to answer in a way that he understood. "I know you're used to bearing down and muscling through things. I am too, but that's what led to me hurting Mari and you exiling me. I'm not saying that's what you'll do, but the stuff in your head isn't something you can just soldier through."

"I get that, Shadow. But you know I'm not one for the touchy-feely shit."

"It's not that simple. You never know how long this is going to affect you or in what ways. We'll probably be dealing with this shit for the rest of our lives, so you need the right tools. That might be hypnotherapy or...regular therapy, I dunno. I'm not qualified to help you but someone smarter than me is." I downed the rest of my drink, bringing the glass down harder on the counter than I intended. "I am here for you, though. We all are."

Reaper leaned his elbows on the counter and rubbed his eyes. "Yeah I know, dude. And you're right. I need to not be a pussy about this and get some real help."

"Doc's colleague isn't far from here," I reminded him. "Dr. Ellis. She'll know what to do."

"Alright." Reaper placed his palms together, the curled fingers of his maimed hand nestled between them. "I'm glad I could come to you, Shadow."

"Me too."

"I think it helps a lot already, you know." He glanced up at me. "Knowing you've been through something similar and made it out the other side. I know Mari and the guys would never think differently of me, but..."

"They weren't there." I nodded in understanding. "Having Mari, Jandro, everyone really, is more support and care than I ever dreamed of. But what we went through...it's not an experience many people share."

"No." Reaper proceeded to pour another round of drinks for us. "And while I wish your upbringing was never inflicted on you," he paused to put the bottle away, "I don't think I'd be ready for help if it wasn't for you." He made a face as he lifted the glass to his lips. "That makes me sound like an asshole, doesn't it?"

"No," I chuckled, raising my own glass. A passing thought of my mother's ghost entered my mind and left just as quickly as it came. "I've made peace with my early life, I think."

"Really?" Reaper's eyebrows lifted in surprise.

"Yeah, we have a fresh start, like you said. I'll still have nightmares, I'm sure. The setbacks will still come. But I'm ready to move on."

"Well cheers to that, man. I'm proud of you." Reaper touched his glass to mine. "And hey." He looked at me intently. "When that stuff happens, you're not alone, alright?"

I smiled before taking my drink. "Neither are you."

CHAPTER 32

MARIPOSA

Reaper's strength and mobility recovered beautifully over the next few weeks at home. Governor Vance wanted to immediately have an award ceremony and dinner party at City Hall, but thankfully everyone else insisted on rest first.

And that time relaxing at home with my men was absolutely glorious. We slept in and took naps. We took the bikes out and rode with no destination in mind, just for the thrill of it. In the evenings, we all went to bed together, my favorite part of the day.

My parents, eager for their own private time together, moved into one of the new duplexes a short ride away from us. Jandro regularly took over eggs for them and our other neighbors.

I still worked at the hospital because there was plenty to do and I couldn't *not*. But our patient load was slowly decreasing, and at my guys' insistence, I kept my hours reasonable.

By the time the governor's assistant, Josh, stopped by to talk about the celebrations again, we had run out of excuses to say no. Everyone begrudgingly agreed, with Reaper stipulating that it had to be early in the evening so we could throw a raging after-party at our house. Just as I thought, he was not pleased to learn we threw a party in his hospital room after he got out of surgery.

"That's cruel," he insisted, pulling on a suit jacket that he had no business looking so dapper in. "Throwing a party in my room while I'm dead to the world and can't participate."

"We were hoping it would wake you up." I lifted my hair so Jandro could fasten my butterfly necklace. "But your ass had to keep sleeping for another two weeks."

"Did you at least funnel beer into my mouth?" Reaper turned down his collar and pulled apart the top three buttons on his dress shirt. Fuck, why was that so hot?

"We should have." Jandro decided to forgo a jacket for the event, rolling his shirt sleeves up past his elbows instead. The tailors altered his shirt a bit too small and it pulled snugly at the width of his chest and biceps.

Down girl, you can have him any time. None of them are going to war tomorrow. Or ever again.

"Slick wanted to flick playing cards at your face, but I didn't let him." Shadow too decided to go jacketless, since it was still daytime and warm outside.

He undid the shirt button at his throat and was in the process of rolling up his sleeves, exposing the forearm tattoo of me as a pinup girl. Okay, how the *hell* was I supposed to get through this event without dragging a pair of them to a dark corner for a quickie?

Gunner grinned at us from the mirror as he combed his hair. "I'll admit, I was really tempted to draw dicks on your face."

As usual, he was suited up nicely, everything tailored to perfection, from his jacket to his tie and waistcoat. That would only make it more fun to remove every piece later on in the evening.

I have been in the middle of at least *a threesome, if not a moresome, nearly every single night for two weeks, how can I still be this insatiable?*

"If I'm at a party, I need to be the drunkest one there by the end of the night," Reaper went on. "It's a cardinal rule."

"You were heavily drugged, if that counts?" I offered, winding my arms around his waist.

"Hmm." He lifted an arm to wrap it around my shoulders and pull me into his side. "You got a point there, sugar."

"Can we go already?" Shadow grumbled, fiddling with his sleeves some more in the mirror.

"So eager to chat and mingle with politicians again, are you?" Gunner teased him with a slap on the back.

"The sooner we go, the sooner we can get this over with."

"And then we can start the *real* party." Jandro rubbed his hands together gleefully. "I got the smoker going with a few racks of ribs already, they'll be perfect tonight."

Reaper squeezed my shoulder. "Who all is coming over?"

"I invited everyone we know," I said, swiping a final coat of mascara over my lashes. "I imagine most of them will be at the ceremony too."

Once the five of us were ready, we left the house in the waiting SUV that the Governor sent to pick us up. He sent along five armed soldiers on motorcycles to escort us, which was, honestly, excessive, but it was more for show than anything. People lined up on the streets to wave and watch us drive by.

"I don't know whether to be flattered or uncomfortable," Reaper said through his teeth as he waved back.

"Just smile and go with it." I patted his leg.

Someone hit a button that lowered the windows and people screamed louder as they got a clearer look at me sandwiched in the backseat.

"Oh no." I hid my face in Gunner's shoulder, suddenly bashful at all the attention.

He just laughed at my reaction, smiling and waving like he was born for the spotlight. "Just go with it, baby girl."

I peeked up and saw that it was mostly girls and young women walking alongside the vehicle, craning their necks to get a glimpse inside the window. When I waved at them, the brightest smiles broke across their faces as they returned the gesture. They didn't know exactly what role I played in ending the war, but that was okay. If I gave them something to aspire to, I would take that honor proudly.

The crowd continued all the way up to the City Hall building. The perimeter was roped off to keep people at a distance, but our escorts still surrounded us as we walked up to the front doors.

"No offense, guys." Jandro grinned good-naturedly at one of them. "But I think we've proven we can handle ourselves."

The guard next to him smiled back. "The governor insisted. And we're honored."

Once inside, we were immediately crowded by members of the governor's cabinet. Everyone wanted to shake hands and congratulate us —mostly my men—personally.

"You must be so proud of your brave, er, husbands, is it?" One older gentleman clasped my hand tightly and leaned in *very* close.

His hand was firmly detached from mine as I was pulled back protectively against a tall, solid chest. "We're proud of *her,*" Shadow corrected. "She saved our lives."

"Give them space, you damn vultures!" A commanding voice cut through the buzz of curious questions and everyone crowding us slowly parted to reveal Finn and Lis at the end of the foyer.

They made such a beautiful couple—Finn in his formal general's uniform and Lis in a modest, floor-length dress and a few of her statement jewelry pieces. She held on to her husband's arm, the two of them beaming at us as we made our way to them.

"Mari, you look beautiful!" Lis held her arms out to me and pulled me into a tight hug. "Thank you for not giving up on him," she said when my cheek pressed to hers. "Thank you for loving my son."

There were no words that felt adequate enough to answer, so I just squeezed her back.

She pulled away, smiling and taking my hands. "Your parents are already inside. We saved seats for everyone."

We moved slowly toward the ceremony room, which looked like an old-fashioned theater with a stage and red curtain. Lis and Finn guided us to the front row where my parents waited in an otherwise mostly-empty section.

"There she is." My dad beamed, patting the seat next to him. He looked more like the man I remembered every day with that warm brightness in his eyes and his hair growing back.

I hugged both of my parents before sitting down. "Are you guys coming tonight?" I lowered my voice to a whisper as people began to fill seats.

"We'll stop by but might leave early." Dad smiled apologetically. "This old man gets tired once the sun starts going down."

"So do these," I said, gesturing to my four men. "But they still try to party like kids."

My husbands came over to say hello and hug my parents before the lights started dimming in the auditorium. The governor and his daughter walked onstage to the sound of applause. I looked past my mom when I stood to clap, noticing the three reserved seats on the other side of her were still empty.

"Mom," I whispered, leaning over quickly. "Who was supposed to sit there?"

She looked at the empty seats and frowned. "Those biker friends of yours, I think. The three men who are always together."

So the Sons of Odin were snubbing the governor by not attending. Interesting.

Kyrie kept a pleasant expression on as she stood next to her father onstage, but I didn't miss how her eyes kept shifting to the three empty seats.

Governor Vance's speech was extremely flattering and long. I felt self-conscious from all his praise at first, then I quickly grew bored to the point where I was zoning out. I didn't know what the official story was that he was told about New Ireland, but from his speech, I got the sense he believed we saved the territory from a dictator using slave labor. That was close enough to the truth.

The governor stepped aside after his long monologue and invited Finn to the stage. Reaper's father walked up to shouts and applause and smiled charmingly from behind the podium. He looked the part of a diplomat, handsome and charismatic.

In Finn's speech, he praised the Jerriton troops who came to our aid and took a moment to speak the names of the fallen medics, soldiers, and Steel Demons who lost their lives over the course of the conflict. He even mentioned Dallas and the Sons of Odin club members who were lost before Four Corners ever became a target. That floored me, and I reached across the seats to squeeze Reaper's hand.

"I also want to extend my utmost gratitude to Andrea Marks, the widow of Dallas Marks, who went into New Ireland undercover to gather information for us." Finn's eyes scanned the room for her. "She acted selflessly to honor her husband, who gave his life selflessly so that his family could have a peaceful future. Four Corners is forever in your debt, Andrea."

Those of us in the front row stood and applauded loudly for her, with Finn's soldiers quickly following after. I spotted her a couple rows back, wiping her eyes and smiling as Tessa hugged her.

"To Javier and Emma Wilder," Finn continued, looking straight at my parents. "Not only are these two brave survivors of the New Ireland compound, they gave us the keys to save over two hundred more lives and secure a victory over this enemy. My wife and I have gotten to know you both personally over the last few weeks, and we are honored to call this kind, inspiring, beautiful couple, our family. Thank you for what you've done, and that includes," he leaned over the podium, grinning, "giving me the most incredible daughter-in-law I could ask for."

A ripple of soft laughter and applause rose from the crowd and my face burned hot.

After they each spoke, Finn and Vance took turns calling people up for awards and medals. Some were called individually, others grouped together, like the specific units who went into battle. Andrea walked onstage with her two children to accept her award. My parents went up together while holding hands. Because the Sons of Odin weren't present to accept their award, Shadow, as Grudge's assumed next of kin, accepted it in their stead.

We'd been sitting for a while and the guys were fidgeting, getting antsy. Once all the awards but ours had been given, a beaming Governor Vance strode up to the podium with his chest puffed out.

"And for the heroes who need no introduction, who not only saved our modest territory from annihilation, but also who is most precious to me." He paused to look at his daughter who, for a moment, flicked her eyes to the ground as if she was uncomfortable. In actuality, Kyrie may have never been rescued if the Sons of Odin hadn't devised the plan. T-Bone and the others insisted they didn't want credit for that mission, but it was owed to them.

A couple seats down from me, Reaper also shifted uncomfortably. I knew he didn't feel the same way now, but he had been against the mission back then and didn't feel right with being awarded for her rescue. The Sons' absence was jarring, and I hoped they would still attend our after party.

"Our gratitude is beyond measure," Vance continued. "Words and recognitions fall short of describing what the Steel Demons MC has done for Four Corners. I speak for everyone in this room, in this territory, when I say I'm honored to have met you all. May the legacy of your strength, bravery, and compassion live on for generations." He paused once more to wipe his eyes. "Reaper, Jandro, Gunner, Shadow, and Mariposa. Please come forward and accept our highest decoration, the Four Corners Cross."

The room exploded into applause as everyone stood up for us. Even I had gotten a little teary-eyed at his speech and needed a moment to compose myself before I stood. The applause never stopped, not even as each of my men accepted the medal around their necks one by one, including handshakes with the governor, Kyrie, and hugs from Finn. Once my guys were fully awarded and it was my turn, Governor Vance stepped aside and Kyrie walked up to the podium. Only then did the applause die down to silence, but everyone remained standing.

"Mariposa Wilder," Kyrie said into the microphone. "For your dedication as a medic and for saving countless lives, it is my greatest honor to present you with the Caduceus Excellence in Medicine Award."

"What?"

The squeaked-out word was lost in another round of thunderous applause. None was louder than my men clapping across the stage. I started to actually cry, taken aback with a hand on my chest. Kyrie placed the ribbon over my head with the medical award, and then her father followed with the same medal my men wore.

Kyrie pulled me into a hug, quickly whispered, "Thank you," into my ear, and then the remainder of my time onstage was a blur. Only the familiar scents and touches of my men grounded me again as they guided me back to our seats. The next thing I knew, it was time for the dinner party.

"Ah, thank fuck," Jandro muttered as we and the other guests were ushered into the dining room.

Unlike last time, today's meal was more of an informal cocktail hour than a multi-course, sit-down dinner. There were several tables with various foods to snack on, several wet bars, and pub tables to sit at. It would allow us to chat and mingle enough to be polite, then exit whenever we wanted. Maybe the governor and his staff had picked up on the fact that we weren't terribly formal people.

"Shit, I forgot Vance had good fuckin' whiskey." Reaper turned to me, playfulness lighting up his eyes. "How many am I allowed before we blow this pop stand, sugar?"

"Hm." I tapped on my chin. "Two."

"That's it?"

"We have plenty to drink at home and a whole evening to celebrate."

"I can have two whiskeys in five minutes, that's barely pre-gaming."

"Fine, three."

Reaper kissed my cheek. "I'll make 'em last." He smirked at me before heading to the nearest wet bar.

"Do you want a plate of food?" Jandro eyed one of the nearby buffet tables while Gunner checked out a selection of wines at another bar.

"Sure, not a big one though." I squeezed his forearm. "Saving room for your barbecue."

Jandro kissed my opposite cheek. "That's my girl. We'll share a plate."

He went off to get in line, leaving only me and Shadow together.

"Holding up alright, my social butterfly?" I hugged an arm around his waist.

Shadow huffed out a laugh, draping an arm around my shoulders. "I'm fine, lover. How are you?"

"Oh, good. Still reeling a little from having a bonus award sprung on me at the last minute, but otherwise fine."

He squeezed my shoulder affectionately, turning me into him to kiss my forehead. "You deserve it."

"I was just doing my job."

"One that few other people can do as compassionately and effectively as you can."

Kyrie walked up to us just then, a glowing smile on her pretty face and two champagne flutes held out in offering. "Congratulations you two! How about a toast?"

"You've done too much for me already," I laughed, but accepted the drink along with Shadow.

"Oh, it was nothing." Kyrie snagged another flute from a passing waiter on a tray. "It just felt wrong to not recognize what you did in the medical field as well as in battle."

"Thank you," I said, at a loss for any other words.

"It was my pleasure." She smiled and lifted her glass. "To peace and prosperity."

The three of us touched glasses and drank. Shadow and I exchanged a look when Kyrie threw back her entire champagne flute instead of just sipping it.

"I hope I'm not intruding but, um…" She passed her empty flute to a nearby waiter, her face flushing red. "Do you happen to know why the Sons of Odin didn't attend the ceremony? Is everything alright?"

I resisted the urge to glance at Shadow again. "I don't know, I'm sorry. We last saw them on a ride two days ago. They seemed fine, but maybe something came up."

"There's a chance we'll see them tonight at our house," Shadow offered. "You're welcome to come over too."

"Oh, no." Kyrie waved her hand, blushing harder. "I couldn't, I don't want to intrude."

"We're having a party, you won't be intruding," I told her. "It might be a rougher crowd than what you're used to, but we'll all be there. Come alone or bring a friend, everyone is welcome."

"That's so sweet of you, Mari." She laughed nervously. "But I dunno."

"No pressure." I reached out to touch her arm. "If you'd like to come, we're happy to have you."

Kyrie quickly but politely made her exit after that, leaving Shadow and I to sip our champagne and ponder.

"Does she…like the Sons?" Shadow looked at me curiously.

I grinned impishly over my glass. "I dunno, have I been dying to rip your clothes off all day?"

His eyes widened briefly in surprise before the grin took over his handsome face. "Is that so?"

"I've never spoken truer words in my life." I played with the buttons on his shirt, sliding my fingers into the gaps between them until he grabbed my hand.

"Why are we having a bunch of people over at our house again?" His voice grew low and husky, meant only for me.

"I can't seem to remember the reason for that."

"Me either." He placed a slow, smoldering kiss on my palm before releasing my hand with a sigh. "These last two weeks have spoiled us."

"I know, love." I stroked his beard. "But tonight will be fun."

"It will be," he agreed. "I've been itching to do some tattoos."

"Oy, come here and eat!" Jandro motioned to us from a table piled with several plates of different finger food.

Gunner had one arm on Jandro's shoulder while he drank directly from a bottle of wine and talked to one of Finn's lieutenants. Reaper also sat at the table on, most likely, his second glass of whiskey. He also had a cigar and was talking to one of Governor Vance's cabinet members. A few other important-looking men hovered around the table, waiting for a chance to talk to one of the saviors of the territory.

"Shall we?" I took a step in their direction, my hand in Shadow's as I looked back at him.

"With you, always," he said warmly, following after me.

CHAPTER 33

MARIPOSA

We mingled for another hour before saying our goodbyes. Once in the car, the guys became a flurry of removing ties, unbuttoning shirts, and rolling up sleeves. I knew they loved me, but in that moment, I was absolutely certain they were trying to kill me.

At home, everyone changed into casual clothes and we rushed around the house like bees in a hive to prepare for our guests. Did any of them take me up for a quickie? No. Wholly unfair, honestly.

After changing into a casual sundress, I helped Jandro prepare food while the others cleaned the house and ran out to stock up on alcohol. Shadow also set up a small tattoo station in a corner of the dining room.

The usual suspects arrived first—Andrea, Tessa, and their children, quickly followed by Noelle and Larkan, and then Slick, who held hands with a pretty young woman I'd never seen before. She smiled nervously, leaning into him for support as they walked in through the living room.

"Mari, this is Katelyn." Slick puffed his chest out, turning to beam at the girl he was clearly smitten with. "We started talking a few weeks back, she finally let me bring her around to meet everyone."

"It's so nice to meet you." I reached for her hand, utter elation in my chest that Slick had found someone. "Please make yourself at home."

"Call me Kat, and thank you. I've heard a lot about you," she blurted out, her face reddening. "One of my friends, Erica, is a medic under you."

"Small world." I smiled at her. "Erica might come over soon too. Slick, you know the drill. Help yourselves to anything. And Kat, don't pay attention to my husbands' hazing of him. It's really out of love."

"It's not that bad anymore." Slick chuckled, leading her by the hand toward the kitchen.

"Slick, ya dumb fuck! I told you not to kidnap pretty girls!" Jandro shouted, not a moment later.

"Worked out for you, didn't it?" Slick retorted.

"Ohh, he's a big man now!" Gunner taunted.

I barely had time to laugh at the situation before Noelle pulled me into the hallway. "I'm so fucked, Mari," she hissed under her breath.

"Why, what's wrong? Wait, hang on." I pulled her into the nearest bedroom and closed the door behind us. "What is it?" My heart pounded, worry spiking.

"I'm fucking pregnant!" she whisper-yelled.

"Wha—oh my God!" My palms flew to my mouth and then wrapped around her in a hug. "Congratulations!"

"Don't tell me that yet." She pulled loose from me and smacked a palm to her forehead. "I found out this morning and I'm...still in shock, I guess."

"That's okay, that's normal." I placed my hands on her shoulders in an attempt to calm her down. "This wasn't planned, I take it?"

"No, it wasn't planned! He usually comes *on* me but lately it's been all, you know, end of the world and shit, and it feels nicer when...aw fuck, you get what I'm saying?"

"Sure I do." I rubbed her arm in sympathy. "But this is the consequence of doing that."

"I know! Ugh, I'm such an idiot. I should have gotten one of those birth control things from you."

"Yeah, a little too late for that. How's Lark feeling?"

Noelle worried her lip and scratched one of the bright tattoos on her forearm. "I haven't told him yet."

I bit back my smile. "You should probably do that."

"I know, I know. I've just been trying to process this all day. I probably will tonight, since I guess I can't drink anything and he's gonna be suspicious."

"Noelle." I hesitated on my next question but squeezed her arm in support. "Do you want this baby?"

She squeezed my hand as a blissful smile took over her face. It was the calmest she'd looked since dragging me into the hallway.

"I do, Mari. I want it because I made this baby with *him*. I never really thought about it before because I assumed it would never happen. But it's...scary how much I want this baby." Her worried expression returned. "What if I fuck it up? I drank and smoked before today, what if something's already wrong? Oh fuck, what if Lark doesn't want it?"

"Calm down, honey. Take a breath." I placed my hands on her shoulders again, breathing deeply so she could copy me. "Come to the hospital tomorrow and I'll do an ultrasound. You're probably fine. Lots of people don't abstain from vices early in the pregnancy because they don't know. But we'll monitor you and make sure, okay?"

Noelle nodded, her throat still working in nervous swallows.

"As for Lark, honey, you have absolutely nothing to worry about. That man *loves* you. He will be overjoyed, you know that."

"You're right, you're right." Noelle laughed sheepishly. "I'm just freaking out."

"That's okay. It's a big change."

"Mari?" She clasped both of my hands in hers. "Will you deliver the baby for me? Like you did with Tessa?"

"Noelle," I gasped, tears springing to my eyes. "Of course I will, I'd be honored."

"I don't want anyone to do it but you." She squeezed around my fingers. "You were so amazing with her, and I don't trust anyone else as much."

"I wouldn't miss it for the world," I promised, squeezing back.

She released my hands and hugged me, her laughter and smiles now more joyful than nervous. "Guess I should tell my baby daddy what we made, huh?"

Larkan was hovering at the end of the hallway when we left the bedroom, concern darkening his face. "You okay, baby?" He held an arm out to Noelle.

"Yeah, babe." She slid under his arm, hugging around his waist with a beaming smile. "We were just having some girl talk."

They kissed and turned toward the kitchen, still wrapped up in each other. "What do you want to drink?" I heard Larkan ask, but they were too far away for me to hear Noelle's answer.

A heavy knock came at the front door and I rushed to open it, finding three tall men with wiley smiles on their faces.

"Sons!" I shrieked, jumping up to hug T-Bone who caught me against his chest.

"Little lady." He greeted me with a warm kiss on the cheek before setting me back down on the ground.

I hugged Grudge and Dyno, then halted the trio before they could get too far inside the house. "Where were you guys today?" I lowered my voice to a conspiratorial whisper.

T-Bone's charming smile disappeared, replaced by a frown and a shifting glance at his two partners. "I'm sorry we missed the ceremony. We made other commitments earlier today."

It was clear he wasn't going to say anything else, nor did the other two care to add details.

"Fine." I smacked a palm on T-Bone's chest, earning a smile from him again. "But I'm glad you guys are here."

"We wouldn't miss the *real* party," Dyno scoffed. "Where your boys at? Making fools of themselves?"

"Oh, I hope not yet," I groaned. "It's still way too early for that."

Grudge broke off from his men and embraced Shadow in the dining room. The two men clung to each other tightly and slapped each others' arms. We'd seen the Sons regularly since bringing Reaper home, but those two always greeted each other like they hadn't seen each other in months. It was sweet to see a deeper appreciation of the friendship and bond they shared.

Seeing Grudge and Shadow reminded me of the slip of paper in my bedroom. I had just gotten it from the hospital and planned to show them together. I excused myself quickly and headed back down the hall-way. My heart pounded as I retrieved the folded piece of paper from the desk drawer, the beat doubling in speed as Shadow looked at me with such love and adoration as I approached.

"Hey, lover," he said, reaching for me.

I let his protective, unbreakable embrace fall around me and planted a kiss on his mouth before producing the paper. "Do you guys still want to know?"

Grudge's eyes widened at the paper and then at me. Shadow squeezed my waist, the pulse in his neck accelerating. "Is that...?"

"The results from your blood tests, yes," I confirmed. "I picked them up from the lab yesterday. I haven't looked at them yet. I figured you guys should be the first to know."

Shadow took the results from my hand, loosening his embrace as he held it out to Grudge. "Should we do this together, brother?"

"Mm." Grudge jerked his chin down in a nod and grasped the other end of the paper in his fingers. They unfolded it together and I waited with my breath in my chest.

The two of them peered at me after a few seconds. "I don't know what any of these mean, lover. What is X-DNA?"

"Oh sorry!" I laughed, taking the paper from them. "Allow me to translate." After a quick scan of the results, a smile overtook my face as I looked up at them. "I knew it!"

"Mari." Shadow's warning growl of my name was low and playful, lighting up heat between my legs.

"You two are half-brothers," I said. "You share the same Y-chromosome, which means you have the same father. Your X-chromosomes don't match at all, which means you have different mothers."

Grudge made a noise like a scoff, glancing away for a moment until Shadow thumped him on the back. "I know, brother. He was most likely an evil son of a bitch, but he's hopefully dead now. And if he's not," Shadow clapped his shoulder, "take comfort in knowing we are huge disappointments to the old man."

"Heh." Grudge looked back at him with a lopsided smile, gesturing between the two of them and then pantomimed counting on his fingers.

"That's right. We could have a whole bunch of siblings out in the world." Shadow's jaw tightened, returning his gaze to me.

"Maybe, maybe not." I perched myself on his thigh. "But family isn't determined by blood."

"Mm-hm." Grudge nodded in agreement.

"I'm glad we know for sure, but you're right." Shadow nuzzled my face, planting a kiss on my cheekbone. "Nothing has changed. And life is so fucking good."

THE PARTY WENT ON LATE INTO THE NIGHT. I HAD ONLY SAT with Shadow and Grudge for a few more minutes when we heard Larkan's shout of, "Whoooo! I'm gonna be a daddy!" reverberate through the house.

That victory cry kicked off the real party atmosphere. People cheered, shouted congratulations, and the alcohol flowed through everyone's good mood. Someone brought out a guitar and couples started dancing in the backyard. Reaper and Shadow weren't dancers, but I had a blast being passed back and forth between Jandro and Gunner. Slick and his new girlfriend stayed huddled to themselves for the most part, but she did manage to drag him out to dance for a couple of songs.

When I headed inside for a quick restroom break, I spied a tipsy, pink-cheeked Finn with his shirt off, getting tattooed by Shadow.

"What is this?" My voice was high and probably a little too loud from my own tipsy state. "What are you getting?"

"My old lady's name, of course." My father-in-law smirked.

"Oh my God!" Shadow had indeed sketched "Alisa Forever" with a pen on Finn's chest and was currently in the process of outlining it. "How sweet. Does she know?"

"She will soon." Finn laughed.

"You crazy kids," I teased him.

"I don't recommend it until you've been together a minimum of thirty years," he added with a grin.

Time passed in a blur. I drank and danced some more, kissed my men, and laughed with my friends. It felt so, so incredibly good to have fun for essentially no reason. Yes, we were celebrating being alive but now we knew tomorrow would come. And the day after, and the next week, next month. Next year, and many more years. We were celebrating a future we never thought we would see.

At some point I kicked off my shoes and danced barefoot, the grass cool and soft on my aching soles. Spinning away from Gunner, I left our makeshift dance floor in search of a drink and place to sit to catch my breath. Reaper pushed a glass of water into my hands, then was quickly pulled away by some guy calling his name.

I was plopped down on the back porch, chugging my water, when a large man took a seat next to me.

T-Bone cleared his throat awkwardly. "We're taking off, Mari. Thanks for having us."

"What, already?" I set my water down to wrap my arms around his bicep. "You're not leaving yet. I won't let you."

He let out a rumbling chuckle but firmly removed his arm from my hold. "We've got an early ride tomorrow."

"Oh yeah, where are you guys going?"

T-Bone swallowed, taking a long time to answer and looking unusually serious. "Mari, we're leaving Four Corners. For good."

"What?" I rocked away from him, taken aback in the moment, but in reality, it wasn't all that surprising.

"Yeah. I'm glad the Demons have found a home here, but it feels like we've outgrown the place. We'd been thinkin' on it for a while, but after Grudge's whole hostage situation...it's just time for us to move on."

"I hate to hear it, but I understand." I placed a hand on his forearm. "After everything you've done, I'm sorry you weren't treated better here."

"Shit happens." He shrugged. "We'll find a place where our funky little threesome can live like kings."

The question, *What about Kyrie?* hovered on the tip of my tongue, but I decided against voicing it. Their decision was made, and while I didn't hold out hope that she would attend our party, it was clear that she had wanted to see them. I had thought the feeling was mutual, but it wasn't my place to get involved.

"You guys better visit," I said instead.

"I promise we will, little lady." T-Bone lifted an arm to wrap it around me in a side hug. "This isn't goodbye forever."

"Our house is always open to you," I told him, returning his squeeze. "Our food, our liquor, everything."

"Your prettiest husband?" He chuckled into my hair.

I slapped his chest. "No! Gunner's mine."

We laughed together, saying another friendly goodbye, until he reluctantly stood to break the news to the others.

I watched, a mixture of wistful and happy as T-Bone hugged my guys and tried to sneak a grab of Gunner's ass. The Sons of Odin were amazing allies and friends. We wouldn't be partying tonight if it hadn't been for their help. But not all paths continued in the same direction.

While T-Bone mingled with my guys, I stood from the porch and headed inside to find the other two. Grudge and Dyno were sprawled on a couch, drinks in hand and talking softly to each other.

"T-Bone told me," I said at their glance up at me.

They sat up straighter, faces apologetic. "Mari..." Dyno began.

"No, it's okay." I took a seat on the coffee table in front of them. "I understand, just..." My fingers clasped together as I tried stringing my thoughts into words. "Just be careful out there. Take care of each other. Especially him." I angled my head to indicate T-Bone, who was still off talking to my guys.

Gunner told me what happened when he and T-Bone were out in battle together against Blakeworth. He started that huge fire and went apeshit when they got captured, trying to goad Blakeworth officers into cutting out his tongue.

From how he reacted when Grudge was taken hostage too, it was clear T-Bone could be a loose cannon when those he loved were threatened. The jovial, flirtatious man still harbored a great deal of pain. Dyno and Grudge were likely the only ones keeping him grounded.

"We will." Dyno nodded solemnly, understanding my meaning.

"I'll miss you guys," I sighed, and leaned in to accept their embrace when their arms opened up.

They left our house soon after and my chest tightened at the roars of their bikes starting up. I listened until the sounds of motorcycles faded, and the Sons of Odin rode off to start the new chapter of their lives.

CHAPTER 34

REAPER

The party began to wind down not long after the Sons left. Their departure shifted the atmosphere to a more sobering one, that tomorrow we'd be living in a Four Corners without T-Bone's boisterousness, Dyno's sly remarks, and Grudge's observant silence. I owed those guys everything, which made our goodbyes especially bittersweet.

Until they broke the news, my spirits were higher than they'd been in months. The party was just like the ones we threw back in Sheol. I nursed a good buzz for hours, got a belly full of food, and shot the shit with my favorite people. It was the perfect way to end one chapter and start anew.

Then once the Sons left, everything felt a little more wistful. The music in the backyard stopped, children started blinking heavily, and people started settling on our chairs and couches after dancing the night away.

I spotted Mari on the back porch, leaning against the exterior wall as she watched Jandro and Andrea's kids playing fetch with Hades.

Mari smiled when I approached her, leaning into me when I slid an arm around her waist and pulled her back toward my chest.

"All alone, Mrs. President?" I nudged a kiss by her ear, our fingers intertwining on her waist as I hugged around her.

"Never." She kissed me quickly over her shoulder. "Just enjoying a moment of quiet."

I squeezed tighter around her hands, rubbing my finger over the stone on her ring. "You alright?"

"Yeah, I'm okay." She rested the back of her head on my shoulder. "Just didn't expect the Sons to take off so suddenly, I guess."

"Ah, they'll be back." I kissed the top of her head, then rested my chin in the same spot. "They might not see this place as home but they know we're family. Besides, T-Bone will miss hitting on Gunner too much to stay away *that* long."

Mari's laugh was bright and playful as she spun to face me, winding her arms around my neck as she stood on tiptoe to kiss me. I held her flush to me with a heavy grip on her waist, kissing her back deeper than all the short, flirtatious pecks we shared during the party.

"I want you," I groaned out when we parted for a breath.

A coy smile tugged at her lips. "I've wanted you all day."

My palms slid to her ass, squeezing and pulling her forward with not a fuck given about who saw.

"I want you to myself," I clarified.

Sharing her was great, but the five of us had been damn near inseparable for the last two weeks. I still only had partial use of my left hand, but overall my strength and mobility were coming back quickly. Certain positions and movements didn't hurt anymore, but the moment Mari and I would get started, the others couldn't resist touching or kissing her.

Not that I could blame them, especially in the aftermath of everything. It felt like we were on vacation, a honeymoon even. I'd never push the guys away, but it had been months and months since I had my wife to myself. I didn't need it all the time, but fuck me, I needed her now.

Mari's smile only grew wider at my request. "Then what are you waiting for, Mr. President?"

A spark lit up my chest. My doubts of her feelings for me were long gone...mostly. I knew she wouldn't have stayed at my side every day during my coma, wouldn't have been so hands-on with my physical therapy, and endlessly patient once I came home if she didn't love me. She apologized too many times, needlessly and tearfully, for how she treated me before I got captured. I believed she was sincere, I truly did.

But it was hearing that confirmation from her lips that she wanted me, and me alone, that smothered that last, lingering seed of doubt.

I tugged her inside the house without another moment of hesitation. The beautiful sound of her laugh followed me through the hallway to the bedrooms. I went for the nearest door, not caring whose room it was. The five of us had fallen into the habit of spending every night together anyway.

Mari closed the door behind us and headed for the untouched bed, but I tugged her back to my side.

"Not there. Come here."

I smothered her mouth with a kiss, driving my tongue past her lips to taste every part of her I could reach. My hands gripped her ass like a lifeline, encouraging her to rock and grind against my dick that was already fighting to get out of my jeans.

Mari stretched up on her tiptoes, one leg nudging around the outside of my thigh, and I picked her up so that she could straddle my waist. Her legs now secure, I turned to perch her ass on top of the chest of drawers against the wall.

The casual dress she wore, which had spun around her so hypnotically as she danced, now rode up high as her legs spread to accommodate me between them. My touch dove under the fabric, finding the warmth of her bare skin as I followed the curves of her hips and waist.

"I like this dress," I murmured, mouthing my way down the side of her neck.

"The dress or the easy access?" She reached for my jeans, pulling apart the snap and the zipper with quick efficiency.

"Both." I pulled a strap down her shoulder, lingering a kiss on the new stripe of exposed skin. "You looked beautiful tonight. Happy."

"I am happy." Mari's fingers returned to my neck, scratching through my hair as she kissed me with a smile. "Are you?"

For once in my life, I didn't need to think about the answer. Just getting by, living to another day, used to be enough. It satiated me until the next big fight, until I counted every Steel Demon patch and reeled from however many we lost. Not losing anyone was once a blessing, a rare gift that was fleeting and unreliable.

Now I knew, with as much certainty as possible, that everyone at this party would still be here tomorrow. Mari would still love tomorrow. Jandro's stupid rooster would crow at the crack of dawn, and then...the day was ours. The future, our lives, belonged to *us*.

"Yes," I said through a tightening in my throat, my forehead on hers. "I am."

We kissed while I pulled down the other strap on her dress and bunched the fabric down around her waist. She gasped into my mouth as I rolled her breasts in my hands, drawing me in closer with her legs. Together, we gathered up the fabric of the dress to keep it out of the way. From the top down and the bottom up, my wife was so beautifully, obscenely exposed.

"Oh, look at you," I groaned out at the sight of her damp panties, pressing my hand between her legs. "So wet for me already?"

"I've missed having you to myself too." A moan escaped her as I rubbed, giving her that friction she wanted so badly. "I love the other guys and never want to turn them down, but—" Her breath stuttered in her chest while I kept rubbing, sweeping the edge of my hand over her lips and clit through the damp fabric.

"But what, sugar?" It was a command, not a question. One that made her hooded eyes pop open at the bark of my voice.

"I've missed how *you* fuck me. You and no one else."

A growl tore from my throat, my fingers hooking into the edge of her panties to pull them aside. I stroked once, twice through her slick folds, just to make sure she was ready before freeing my cock and notching it against her.

"Ah, good," Mari sighed, grinning at me. "I thought you'd make me wait."

"I'll still make you come until you can't remember your name." I pressed forward, her slippery heat embracing my blunt head. "I just want to feel all of it on my cock."

Her thighs squeezed around my hips as I pressed inside, and my head fell to her shoulder with a groan. She was the best feeling—familiar, soft, warm, and just so good. When the memories of the Sha's dungeon made me unsettled and on-edge, she brought me back.

My hips drew back and when I pressed forward again, my thumb circled over her clit. And there my hand would remain until she couldn't take it anymore.

My hand motions were fast, faster than my thrusts, the pressure of my thumb consistent and unrelenting. Her first orgasm built up faster than she could catch up, her moans turning to pants, then gasps and yelps when the release hit. She gripped the edges of the dresser for purchase, her pussy squeezing and stroking around me so beautifully.

"Good girl." I eased the pressure off her clit slightly, my circling motion just a touch slower. "Shall we do that again?"

"Bastard," Mari huffed with a laugh. "I want more of this." She grabbed my waist and pulled me forward, causing me to sink to the hilt inside her and pulling a deep hiss from my chest.

"I'll fuck you twice as hard for every orgasm I get from you," I told her. "Deal?"

Her head fell back with a bright, breathless laugh. "How could I forget how terrible you are?"

"You wanted me," I reminded her, leaning forward to suck a pert nipple into my mouth, dragging my teeth on the stiff peak until she cried out.

She came again quickly with a lighter touch, still sensitive from her first one. Her pussy fluttered around me again, and it was such sweet relief to fuck harder like she wanted.

"Good girl," I praised again, biting a rough kiss on her shoulder. "How about another?"

Mari came for me three more times before she slumped back in exhaustion, her elbows propped on the dresser and her skin dewy with sweat.

"Come here, sugar." I pulled her to me and kissed her once before allowing her head to rest on my shoulder. Bracing one arm against her back, I brought the other to her hip.

She was limp and utterly spent, leaning on me as I finally released the white-knuckled control and fucked her wildly. My cock felt like solid iron after being teased and stroked by her orgasms, so ready to take my woman and burst into her perfect pussy.

Mari looped her arms around my neck, soft moans crooning directly into my ear. Her hips rocked forward, meeting the rough crashes of my thrusts and letting me plunge to new depths that had me seeing stars. But before I finished...

"One more," I rasped into her neck, returning my hand to where our bodies joined. "Come for me one more time, sugar."

"Reaper, I can't," she whined, but she still responded to my touch. A shiver raced over her skin, and still she chased the weight of my hand on that sensitive bundle of nerves.

"Oh fuck yeah, that's it," I urged her with my mouth against her rapid pulse. "Take it sugar, it's all yours."

Her hips stuttered with the build-up of pleasure, movements growing frantic and needy as she raced toward release. The shift in our hard-crashing rhythm staved off my own orgasm *just* long enough. She found the edge and hurtled herself off, the hot spasms of her pussy taking me with her.

My hands slapped the dresser as my body became boneless, the heady rush of my orgasm too good and all-consuming. Our hips kept moving, creating a feedback loop to extend each other's pleasure. And oh fuck, how I wanted to stay here, flush inside her and bliss everywhere in my body.

"Would you marry me?" I mumbled on our slow, lazy descent back to earth.

Mari's legs relaxed around me, but her pulse was still racing as she panted out a soft laugh.

"I thought we were already married." She leaned into me, resting her temple on my shoulder as she placed soft kisses on my neck. The sensation made me shiver and she hugged around me tighter.

"If we weren't already, would you?" I brushed a kiss along her forehead, then nudged my face lower to look at her eyes. "If I asked you for the first time now, after everything that's happened, would you still?"

She cupped my cheek, staring at me for a moment before answering confidently, "Yes. I would." She caught my mouth in a kiss and I poured all of the elation and relief building in my chest into that kiss. "I'll marry you again, if that's what you want."

"Hm." I ran my fingertips up her naked back, in no rush to see her clothed again. "A ceremony might be nice. With all the guys."

Mari leaned away, her blissed-out expression sobering. "Would you want to marry *me* again, after all this?"

I let out a scoff. "First of all," I tapped my index finger to her nose, "I ask these questions, young lady. Not you."

She huffed, a smirk pulling at her lips before I leaned in again, just short of a kiss.

"Second of all," I whispered. "Yes. My answer to you will always be yes."

"I want that in writing." She grinned. "In your vows."

"Don't get any crazy ideas, missy."

We laughed, kissed, and held each other lazily, lingering in our precious alone time until she mentioned that we should probably check on the party. I grumbled out a reluctant agreement and we quickly got decent before leaving the bedroom, holding hands on our way out.

The air was cooler out here, soothing to my heated skin as we came out of the hallway together. About half of the people who'd settled into the living room had taken off. Slick had his new girlfriend in his lap in *my* armchair, making out like fucking kids.

"Get a room and use condoms," I yelled as Mari tugged me away toward the kitchen.

"Whoo, I'm gonna be a daddy!" Larkan yelled from somewhere in the backyard for the seventeenth time that night.

"Or you'll end up like that guy," I added.

Mari slapped my arm. "Leave them alone. You're going to be an uncle!"

"Yeah." Truth be told, I was excited for Noelle and Lark. *It'll be our turn soon*, I thought.

Mari wanted to become a doctor and I didn't want to impede those plans, but I also really, really wanted to raise a family with her.

We'll talk about it soon. There's no rush, I assured myself.

"Where have you two been?" Jandro and Gunner were putting leftovers away, eyeing us across the kitchen counter. Behind us, Shadow's tattoo machine buzzed as he worked on someone.

"We went off to fuck, what do you think?" I snatched a rib from a plate, sucking the meat off the bone while Mari snorted and slapped a palm to her forehead.

The guys didn't bat an eye, although Gunner laughed at her embarrassed reaction.

"We have too much food. Here, send people off with these." Jandro shoved foil-covered plates at us.

"Are we kicking people out?" Mari loaded several of the plates into her arms.

Gunner yawned. "Yeah, I'm beat. Don't think I've ever danced, drank, and socialized more in my life."

"You got plans tomorrow?" I started loading up on to-go plates as well.

"No, and don't give me any." Gunner leaned his elbows on the counter and rubbed his eyes. "Let me sleep in 'til noon tomorrow, please."

"Jandro?"

"Nah, auto shop's closed for the next week while they repair the building." Jandro wiped his hands clean, casting me a curious glance. "Why?"

I nudged Gunner with my elbow. "Let's go to your fabled hot spring for a couple days. Camp out, just the five of us. And the animals, I guess."

"I'm down, but let's go late."

"Sure, sleeping beauty. We'll let you get your rest." I turned to face the other end of the room. "Shadow, you down for a hot springs trip?"

"Yes," he grunted out, not looking up from his tattoo.

"What are we doing?" Mari had just returned from handing out food and seeing our guests off.

"Hot springs tomorrow, for a few days." I reached for her waist, bunching up the fabric of her dress as I pulled her forward. "Just you and us."

"Yes! Later is good. I'll do Noelle's ultrasound in the morning." She lifted to her tiptoes to hug and kiss me again. Her skin was still deliciously warm, lips swollen and flushed from the love we just made.

"Sex, food, and booze mandatory." Jandro pantomimed checking off a list. "Clothing optional."

"Dare you to ride there naked," Gunner challenged.

"Oh boy, just watch me. You see this tan?" Jandro smoothed a palm down one arm. "The sun loves me. Now for you, that's something I don't recommend."

"What are you trying to say?" Gunner demanded in mock offense.

Mari unwrapped from me with a soft laugh and a shake of her head at their antics. That dress swished from her legs to her hips as she went over to Shadow. He paused his tattoo immediately, looking up at her with a smile. She leaned over and kissed him, nestling into his side and the big arm that came around her waist.

A clicking of nails on the floor drew my attention to the large black dog in front of me.

Hades licked his lips and sat like a good boy, dark eyes wide and innocent, no doubt begging for some leftover barbecue. It felt weird to think of him as Hades now that I knew the god no longer inhabited this animal. But calling him by another name didn't sit right either.

I knelt down to the dog's eye level, scratching the sides of his face as he licked his lips hopefully.

"I know you're not in there anymore," I said. "But I know you're always present, so I hope you can hear me."

On instinct, I paused to wait for a reaction, but there was none. Not a flicker of that ancient intelligence in those wide puppy eyes.

"I'm grateful," I went on. "Thank you for the valuable lessons you taught me. For choosing me, even though I fought against you many times. Thank you for protecting Mari and just...helping us to have this second chance."

The dog only stared back at me, ears lowered and those puppy eyes losing hope that he would earn a treat after all. With a slightly sheepish laugh, I returned to standing and went to grab a piece of rib meat.

Then I felt it.

The weight of a hand on my shoulder and a whisper in my mind.

You did well, my reaper.

Epilogue

MARIPOSA

THREE YEARS LATER

I stared at the objects on the bathroom vanity, eyes moving over each one in disbelief.

Three different pregnancy tests. All positive.

"*Mariposita?*" Jandro called out from the other side of the bathroom door. "You alright? You've been in there a while."

I was too shocked to answer in words, but a nervous giggle left my mouth. The first test I took on a whim and did not expect those results. The other two I took this morning, a day after hiding the first one yesterday. One could be a faulty test, but *three* positives?

"Mari?" Jandro began to sound genuinely worried. "If you don't answer me, I'm coming in. And you're not allowed to get mad."

"I'm okay!" I called back, finding my words finally. "You can come in."

He hesitated before opening the door slowly, poking his head in with a curious expression. "Not interrupting anything, am I?"

I laughed and felt the first rush of emotion as the reality hit me. "Come here, look at this."

Jandro looked concerned again, as I was on the verge of crying.

"What's going on, babe?" He came up next to me at the counter, looking down at the three tests laid out on the surface. "Are those..."

"Yeah," I laughed, sniffing and wiping away tears.

He looked at me wide-eyed, which was all the confirmation I needed. "They're all..."

"Yeah," I confirmed, full-on laughing joyously now. "It's really happening."

"Holy...shit!" Without another word, Jandro snatched up the tests and ran out of the bathroom with them. "Hey guys! Yo, dickwads, stop what you're doing! Important announcement! Family meeting right now!"

I followed him out to the sound of Reaper's grumbling—it was already ten AM and he still hadn't broken out of his morning grumpy mode. "What the fuck requires so much excitement in the morning?" He was in his favorite armchair with coffee and a newspaper, bare feet scratching Hades stretched out on the floor in front of him.

"Hang on, Groucho, everybody needs to be here for this." Jandro stuck his head out of the sliding door to yell at Shadow in the back-yard. "Get in here, big dude! We got something important to tell everyone."

"Where's Gun?" I spun around in the living room, noting my golden man's absence.

"He rode out to grab shit from the farmer's market, he'll be back any minute." Reaper set aside his paper and coffee and stretched with a groan in his chair, grinning at me. "Come here, sugar."

I happily obeyed, climbing into his lap to nestle against his chest. My lips rested near his throat and I kissed his warm skin there.

Reaper let out a small groan of satisfaction as his arms came around me. "What's the big news?"

"Not telling." I nipped the edge of his jaw. "Not 'til everyone's here."

"You won't make an exception for me?" he purred, lips grazing my cheekbone. "Your favorite husband?"

"Is that what you are?" I grinned and brought a hand up to his jaw, running the stone of my ring against his coarse stubble.

"I'm pretty sure I earned the title last night." His mouth trailed to the shell of my ear, nipping playfully.

I laughed, squirming in his hold. "Aren't you a confident one, Mr. President."

"I sure as fuck am when you call me that, Mrs. President."

The slider to the backyard opened then, Shadow's imposing figure filling up the space as he stepped inside. Freyja followed after him, head-butting his ankles at every opportunity.

Shadow wiped his face on a towel hanging over one shoulder, his bare upper body glossy with sweat and muscles taut from the exertion of his workout.

"What's the big news?" He bent over and picked up Freyja, flipped her upside down like a baby—*A baby!*—and cradled her against his chest.

"We're just waiting for Gunner to get home," I said, my heart pitter-pattering at the sight of his firm, supportive hold on the cat. "And then we'll stop keeping everyone in suspense."

We heard Gunner's bike roaring up the driveway a few minutes later and opened the garage door to see a bunch of grocery bags and produce boxes bungeed precariously to the back of his bike. On his handlebars, Horus chirped happily and preened his feathers.

"Jesus, Gun. Did you buy up the whole market?" Reaper asked.

"Nah, they just had a ton of good deals. I figured we could store any excess in the chest freezer. Baby girl, I got that goat cheese you like." He nodded at Jandro. "And before you ask, yes, I got a whole box of cabbages for your girls, *papi pollo.*"

"Gun, don't worry about that stuff right now." Jandro waved a hand at him. "Come inside and sit down. We've got something important to tell everyone."

Gunner's smile dissipated, his expression concerned as his eyes floated over all of us. "Is everything okay?"

"Yes!" I told him with a beaming smile, reaching for his hands. "Come on, everybody's here now."

Everyone sat in the living room, their attention rapt on Jandro and I. "You want to do the honors, then I'll present the evidence?" he asked me.

"Sure." I couldn't stop grinning, my joy and excitement impossible to contain. "I'm pregnant!"

"What?!" Gunner gasped, his jaw dropping.

Reaper clapped his hands and punched the air victoriously. "Yes! I fuckin' knew it!"

Jandro took my three pregnancy tests from his back jean pocket and laid them proudly on the coffee table.

"Wait, how did you find out first, asshole?" Gunner threw one of Hades' dog toys at him.

"He barged in on me in the bathroom," I said.

"Bullshit, I gave you plenty of warning!"

Shadow was the only one who remained quiet, if even sullen at the news. He stared at the tests on the table, a slight furrow in his brow.

"Hey." I scooted toward him on the couch, taking one of his hands. "How are you feeling about this? It's okay if it's not all good. This is about to be a huge change for us."

His odd-colored eyes flicked up to me as he squeezed my hand. "I'm happy that you're happy, I'm just...concerned. I don't know anything about being a parent. Especially a *good* parent."

"None of us do, man." Reaper leaned over and slapped his shoulder. "But we'll be fine. We're all gonna struggle through it together."

"The child-raising part worries me, but it's not just that." Shadow swallowed, his gaze fixed on me. "I've read that pregnancy is very uncomfortable, even dangerous sometimes, for a woman. I don't want your health in jeopardy, lover."

"True, you're not entirely wrong about that." I leaned into his side, letting his heavy arm wrap around me. "But a few things to consider—one, pregnancy is temporary. I'll only be carrying for nine months. Two, it's different for everyone. It could be very easy for me, difficult, or anywhere in between. And if it is difficult, I have my medical training and I know my body. I'll also have Dr. Brooks and Rhonda to monitor me throughout the whole thing."

"And you'll have us," Jandro reiterated. "We'll do everything we can to make it easier on you."

"When you're not being a massive pain in my ass, you mean?"

"Well yeah, naturally."

Laughing, I turned back to Shadow and kissed the scar on his cheek. "Does that help alleviate your worries?"

"A little," he said, still looking concerned. "Even once the pregnancy is over, there is still the whole caring-for-infants thing."

"Yeah, that's the terrifying part," Gunner laughed. "But hey, there's four of us, and we already know the kid has an amazing mom. That puts us ahead of the game already."

"We're all gonna screw our kid up, just to varying degrees," Jandro said.

Shadow glared at him. "Is that supposed to make me feel better?"

"Well, no one is gonna screw the kid up worse than Reaper, so—"

"Fuck you, 'Dro." Reaper tossed a throw pillow at him.

"Most importantly." Gunner reached across Shadow's lap to squeeze my leg. "How are *you* feeling about this, baby girl?"

"I feel…" It took a moment to find words for all the sensations in my body, all the thoughts running through my head. "I'm *so* excited! I can't wait to meet this baby and to see all of you become fathers."

"You haven't stopped smiling." Jandro leaned over and planted a big kiss on my cheek. "You're glowing already. This happiness is such a beautiful look on you."

"I'm a little nervous too," I admitted. "I didn't expect it to happen so soon."

My birth control implant was removed about three months ago. I thought it would take much longer for my hormones and monthly cycle to return to normal. The guys and I talked right before I removed it and, while we weren't exactly *trying* to get pregnant, the five of us decided not to actively prevent it either.

"The timing is perfect." Reaper beamed from his armchair. "Your parents just finished moving into their house, my dad's retiring next month, Noelle and Lark's new place will finish being built soon. Everyone will be on deck to help out, sugar."

"I might have to take a break during med school." I frowned, trying to mentally calculate timelines over the next few years. The first semester started in two months. I'd finish it before the end of my pregnancy, but would be too far along to start the second semester. I'd have to take it off and go back in the summer, and even then, I'd probably only want to be in school part-time.

With four husbands, two sets of grandparents, and plenty of friends close by, finding childcare wasn't likely to be an issue. But as much as I wanted to further my education and become a doctor, I also wanted to experience motherhood and watch my child grow up.

"I still think they should just give you the MD," Gunner scoffed. "After all the lives you saved in this territory, I don't get why you still have to go school."

"Because I don't know everything, Gunner." I leaned in front of Shadow to stick my tongue out at him.

"I don't believe that for one goddamn second." Gunner leaned toward me, grinning as he cupped my face and kissed me. "I love you so much, baby girl," he whispered, lips grazing mine. "And I can't wait to meet this baby too. Everything will work out. It always does."

"I love you too." I smiled against his mouth before kissing him and leaning up, nudging my head against Shadow's shoulder. "And I know it will. Especially when we have each other."

Shadow rubbed the nape of my neck, brushing a kiss across my forehead. "I'm fucking terrified," he admitted. "But I'm yours forever, and I'll do my best."

"You'll be amazing." I nuzzled the side of his face, a mental image of him holding a tiny infant making my heart soar. "Because you already are. I love you."

"I love you endlessly," he said before kissing me.

I turned to Jandro, who was practically bouncing in his seat. "Fuck, I'm so excited!" He yanked me out of Shadow's arms to squeeze me against his chest. "We're gonna have a fucking baby! How many more do you want after this one?"

"Jesus, slow your roll!" I laughed, smacking his shoulder. "Let me get through this pregnancy first."

"I gotta write to Angie and tell her. Our nieces are going to have cousins. Oh, I bet they'll want to come visit!"

"Slow down, *guapito*." I licked his neck, still laughing. His excitement was adorable and infectious.

"Can I speak Spanish to the baby?" His hand rubbed over my stomach. I didn't look any different yet but his gaze was already fixated there, where our bundle of love was growing.

"Please do." I scratched the back of his head, then kissed his ear. "*Te amo, mi amor.*"

"*Te amo mas, mi Mariposita.*" He kissed me, then lowered a kiss to my belly. "*Y te quiero mucho, mi bebe.*"

I let him talk softly to my belly for another minute before heading to Reaper's chair, where my first husband patted his lap in invitation.

"My little sugar cube," he cooed, running a hand over my belly as I climbed on. "Jandro's right, though. I probably will screw you up more than the others."

"Don't say that." I ran my fingers through his hair, finding it peppered with a few more grays in recent years, as I brought his gaze up to mine. "This baby is going to learn about all the amazing things you did for your family, to save and protect us. They'll learn how to be a leader, to be confident in the decisions they make, all because of you."

Reaper's green gaze locked onto mine, such bright and expressive eyes that I fell in love with. I hoped at least one of our children inherited those eyes from him.

"You're never wrong, so who am I to argue?" He smirked, arms wrapping me up and holding me close. "I love you, and I'm so grateful to the gods that you're my wife."

I knew he meant every word, especially about being grateful. Ever since waking up from the coma, he looked at the world with a renewed sense of gratitude. And I knew he would teach that to our children as well.

"I love you so incredibly much." I snuggled close to kiss him, the outside world melting away as I curled up with my first husband, the first love of my life.

My men, my loves. We beat the insurmountable odds stacked against us just for this, so we could raise a family with hope, joy, and the normal fears and worries that came with it. Our children would never experience the horrors that all of us had to endure.

And that made every single battle, against enemies and ourselves, worth fighting for.

ENDLESS

A STEEL DEMONS MC EPILOGUE

MARIPOSA

"Congratulations, *Doctor* Mariposa Wilder!"

The smile on my face stretched into a joyful grin as I walked across the stage. I was excited for the diploma I was about to receive, certainly. But my joy was primarily due to the shouts and cheers from my family in the audience.

Jandro and Gunner were the loudest, naturally. They hooted and hollered with their best attempts to embarrass me, which made everyone in attendance laugh uproariously.

All four of my husbands stood in the front row. My parents, Reaper's parents, Noelle, Larkan, their two children, plus our closest friends in and out of the SDMC, took up the seats next to and behind my men. All of them stood, clapping and cheering. For a moment, I felt bad for the people sitting farther back, here to support the other graduates.

But nothing sent my heart soaring higher than my twin five-year-olds shouting, "Doctor Mommy!" from atop their fathers' shoulders.

Our daughter, Aurora May, sat on Gunner's shoulders. She was his spitting image, from the mass of golden curls to her permanent smile and daredevil personality. Her eyes were green instead of blue, however, which made me wonder if Reaper's DNA played any part in creating her. It wasn't possible, in the strictly scientific sense. But her fathers and I had saved this territory from the impossible years ago, so I wasn't about to completely rule it out.

Our son, Daren Javier, watched me from Shadow's shoulders. He couldn't be more different from Aurora, to the point where some couldn't believe they shared a womb. Daren was all quietness and observation to Aurora's sunshiny boisterousness. His hair and eyes were dark, lips always pressed together like he was deep in thought.

Except for now. He and his sister smiled and screamed in excitement as I accepted my diploma from Dr. Brooks.

"Congratulations, Mari." Dr. Brooks beamed as he shook my hand and pulled me close for a kiss on the cheek. "So proud of you, Doctor."

"Thank you," I whispered back through elated tears, wrapping my friend and mentor in a hug. "Couldn't have done it without you."

"Nah." He pulled away to grin at me. "You were a doctor from the very beginning."

I returned to my seat to let the ceremony continue. We were the first medical school graduates of Four Corners, a small class of twelve. Five of us were women. It had been a rigorous training program, and next year's graduating class was already double the size. Most of my class already had jobs lined up in nearby territories or here in Four Corners.

Our little home was growing faster than construction crews could keep up with. People felt safe enough to start having children, and more families migrated here every day.

Already I was excited for more patients to care for, friends for my children to play with. I still woke up some mornings, sandwiched between all of my husbands, and pinched myself. Or I started looking for my battle medic jumpsuit before remembering we no longer had a war to fight. Only much to celebrate.

My family waited for me at the side of the stage once the ceremony was over. The twins hugged my legs while their fathers smothered me in kisses. I lifted Aurora, who we nicknamed Rori, much to Reaper's dismay, into my arms, while someone else shoved a bouquet of flowers into the crook of my free arm.

"Mommy, I made you this!" Rori shoved a construction paper

drawing in my face. It looked like me in my white doctor's coat, with DOCTOR MOMMY in her crayon scrawl right above it.

"Thank you, sweetie! I love it so much." I kissed her while tucking the drawing into my bouquet. "Where did everyone go?" I looked over her mass of curls to see only my husbands standing around, the auditorium cleared of everyone else.

"They went to the house to finish setting up," Jandro answered, now holding Daren against his side.

"Setting up what?"

Reaper laughed in answer. "You didn't think we'd pass up throwing a graduation party, did you?" Rori held her arms out to him, so I passed her over and he hoisted her against his side with a groan. "I got you, sugar cube."

"We just had a party," I reminded him.

"That was for completing your finals," Gunner said. "And it was like a month ago, so we were due for another one anyway."

I laughed. "It was three weeks ago!"

"You deserve another party, regardless." Shadow's hand rested on my waist, turning me toward him for a kiss. "We're so proud of you, lover."

I leaned into him, melting against his solid body. Aside from the war, medical school had been one of the toughest, most grueling experiences of my life. He and the others supporting me had made all the difference in the world.

"I have the best family that helped me get here." I held my arms out to Jandro so I could take Daren from him.

"Is there cake at home?" Daren asked me with adorable seriousness.

"Yes, son." Gunner leaned down and kissed the top of his head. "Auntie Tess and Andrea made a cake."

When Andrea and Tess got married, they insisted on making their own wedding cake, which opened up a love of baking and cake decorating for the two of them. They opened their bakery three years ago. It was down the street from Shadow's tattoo shop and a block away from Jandro's mechanic shop.

"Cake?" Rori screeched from Reaper's arms.

"Indoor voice," Reaper reminded her gently. Our running joke was that she was born without volume control. "Yes, there's cake. But lunch food first."

She tried again. "A *little* cake first?"

Reaper let out a dramatic sigh, already caving to her demands. "What does Doctor Mommy think?"

"One bite of cake before lunch." I booped Rori's nose. "Because it's my graduation."

"Me too?" Daren asked hopefully.

"Yes, you too, my boy."

Once my son got his assurance of cake, he started squirming in my arms. "Down," he grunted. He was getting to the age where he didn't want to be held by Mom, especially around others, and preferred walking on his own.

"Alright, big guy, but I'm holding your hand."

We walked out of the auditorium together with Reaper leading the way and Jandro at his side, Gunner next to me and Daren, and Shadow bringing up the rear. Small habits like these were the hardest to change.

Several of my fellow graduates were milling about outside in the early afternoon sun, taking photos with family members or chatting excitedly amongst each other. I posed with a few of them while Jandro brought the car around, a military-grade SUV he had inspected with a fine-toothed comb and custom-fitted with extra safety features for the kids.

Naturally, all of my husbands had balked at my suggestion of a minivan.

We piled in and took the short drive home, with a few of my classmates following us. Our home had become known as the party house, and we always invited everyone. Dogs, people, and cars were already crowding our driveway, which meant the inside and backyard were already packed.

"Hades!" Rori pressed her face to the window at the sight of the big Doberman on the porch and started fumbling with the door handle.

"Hey." Shadow reached over the seat and pulled her back from the door. "Don't open that until the car's stopped."

"I wasn't," Rori whined, sitting back with a pout.

While the five of us each had our own idea of leniency and strictness with the kids, Shadow definitely veered into overprotective territory. His life experiences made him never want our children to suffer so much as a scratch. The rest of us had to occasionally reassure him it was normal for a kid to fall or scrape themselves sometimes. It was how they grew and learned their own body's limits.

The moment the car stopped, Rori was out and running up the driveway like she hadn't seen Hades in weeks. He got up and loped over to her in return, tongue lolling out in a lazy smile and stubby tail going crazy over his favorite tiny human.

The rest of us stepped out, and the smell of barbecue had my stomach growling. I hadn't eaten before the ceremony this morning because of nerves. Now that weight had lifted and I could kick back with beer, food, and my favorite people for the rest of the day.

"Oh my God, who did this?" I gasped in surprise at the "Congratulations Mari & med school grads" banner hung between the living room and kitchen. The letters looked hand-painted and included small handprints around the borders that could have only been from the kids.

"We did!" My and Reaper's moms emerged from the kitchen, each with a half-drunk mimosa in hand and a full one held out to me. The two of them had become best friends over the years and were always doing arts and crafts projects together.

"I should have known," I laughed, hugging them both and accepting the drink, taking a quick sip before pushing it back into my mom's hand. "Hold that for me. Let me get out of this gown and get some food."

"Oh, I think the boys already made a plate for you." Lis turned around and yelled toward the backyard, "Finn, Javi! Mari's home, is her food ready?"

"I've been eating off her plate," my dad teased back. "Finn's marinade is just too good."

"There's plenty of it." Finn's eyes were narrowed in concentration as he manned *two* other grills with all the seriousness of a drill sergeant.

"Jandro, go help them out back!" I yelled, heading upstairs to hang my graduation cap and gown in the bedroom closet.

A few years back, we'd done some renovation to turn the whole upper level into a bedroom for us. After the war, it was rare that any of us wanted to sleep alone. Lis knew a woodworker who'd made a bed large enough to fit all five of us comfortably. The downstairs rooms had turned into bedrooms for the kids and some private areas, like Shadow's drawing studio.

I quickly smoothed out the dress I had on under my gown, stuck my feet into comfortable sandals, and came back to join the party.

"There she is." Reaper waited for me at the bottom of the stairs, my drink and plate of food in his hands, a cocky smirk on his lips.

"Thank you, Mr. President." I reached on tiptoes to kiss him before taking my stuff. He caught my lips with his teeth, prolonging the kiss and holding me in place with a sting of sensitivity that made a trail through my clit and down to my toes.

"Thank me again later, Mrs. President," he rumbled when he released me, eyes lighting up with a dark promise.

"Hm." I took a sip of mimosa. "I will if you don't pass out on me first, Daddy."

He laughed, following me into the kitchen with a hand on my waist. "Yeah, we'll see about that."

Even with parenting duties split up five ways, uninterrupted sleep had become a thing of the past. The kids were better at sleeping through the night now, but during parties, it was inevitable that at least one of us passed out before all the guests left. Usually it was Gunner or Reaper. About a third of the time, it was me.

Maybe it was less to do with parenting and more with getting older.

Sure enough, after hours of eating, drinking, laughing, and playing with the kids, my eyelids were drooping, and it wasn't even completely dark outside. Reaper ended up passing out on the couch as people started to leave. Someone drunkenly suggested drawing dicks on his face, and Jandro could *not* pass up that opportunity. Thankfully, he used one of the kids' washable markers instead of anything more permanent.

Jandro's face was a grimace of concentration, trying not to laugh or breathe too loudly, lest Reaper wake up. He dragged the blue marker tip over Reaper's cheek in slow, careful precision, even holding an arm out to keep Daren from getting too close when our son became curious.

"Papi, what are you drawing on Daddy's face?"

"It's a mushroom, *mijo.*"

"Why are you drawing a mushroom on his face?"

"You'll understand when you're older."

When the last guest left, Rori was curled up in the large armchair and nodding off. "Come on, Ror-meister." Shadow swept her up, carrying her off to get ready for bed. "Let's get your teeth brushed and pajamas on. What book do you want to read before bed?"

I suppressed several yawns as I tidied up the house while the guys got the kids ready for bed. When Reaper rolled groggily off the couch, I tried to hide my laughter but knew it wouldn't last long. He came up behind me while I washed dishes and I held my breath.

"Stop. Leave that for the morning and we'll get it." Reaper wrapped me up in a sensual hug, oblivious to the mark on his face. He had cut way back on smoking and didn't smell of cloves so strongly anymore. But his hug enveloped me in that familiar leather and whiskey scent that I wouldn't trade for the world.

"...Kay." My shoulders shook from how hard I was trying to keep it in.

"Sugar? What is it?" His eyes narrowed.

"You should," I suppressed a snort, covering my mouth, "look in the mirror."

He released me to stomp down the hallway, and I couldn't hold back any longer. Peals of laughter broke from my mouth, and then tears sprung to my eyes when I heard, "JANDRO, WHAT THE FUCK!" reverberate through the house.

"Relax, it's washable," Jandro called from Daren's room.

"It fuckin' better be!"

I went to bed exhausted but still giggling. Just another day of being married to four Steel Demons.

CHAPTER 2

MARIPOSA

T he bedroom was bright when I woke up. My eyes cracked open to find a glass of water and ibuprofen tablets on the night-stand. I scooted toward the edge to take them, mindful of the heavy, scarred arm draped over my waist.

Once I swallowed the tablets and drained the water, I retreated to the cocoon of warmth at my back, and the surrounding arm tightened protectively.

"Good morning," Shadow mumbled, his breath soft on the back of my neck.

"Morning, love." I peeked over and behind him to see that we were alone in bed. A rare moment.

"How are you feeling, Doctor?" I heard the smile in his sleepy voice and felt it in the kiss he brushed over my shoulder.

"Pretty good, just a little headache." I rubbed my temple where the ache was already starting to fade. "Not bad for losing track of my mimosas yesterday." I looked back to kiss the scar on his brow. "How do you feel?"

"Oh, fine. I only had a couple."

Shadow had cut his drinking back to almost nothing since I'd been pregnant with the twins. He didn't drink at all most days now and only indulged a little when we threw parties. He said it was because he wanted to be present at all times for the kids. Not that he was *ever* unaware of his surroundings, but since becoming a dad, he took hyper-vigilance to a whole new level.

I wiggled my ass on his morning wood to tease him, earning a throaty groan for my effort. "You're allowed to let loose, you know."

"I did," he protested, clamping a hand down on my hip to still me. "I had fun. And it was good to see *you* let loose before you start official doctor duties."

I reached back, threading my fingers through his long black hair to find purchase on his neck. "I'm glad you had fun."

"I always do when you and the kids are happy."

The smile I wore threatened to split my face. My chest sparked and fluttered as I spun in his arms to face him. Even after nearly a decade together, these men spurred these reactions in me. If anything, my love for them ran deeper now than when we were in the thick of war together.

Shadow kissed me deeply, pressing me down into the mattress as we lazily rolled together. We knew each other's bodies so well now. I had kissed every scar on him hundreds of times over, had him permanently mapped out and imprinted in my mind. He had only grown more attentive and loving as years passed. The violence had bled out of him long before he held our twins for the first time, leaving behind one of the most devoted fathers and husbands I'd ever seen.

Shadow's mouth fell to my neck, his strong thighs nudging my legs apart so he could settle between them, when a thumping at the bedroom door startled us both.

"Mommy!" Rori yelled from the other side, palm insistently slapping the door. "Mommy, wake up!"

Shadow inhaled sharply as he lifted away, but before either of us could say anything, we heard Gunner coming up the stairs. "Hey, what are you doing? Mommy's sleeping. Come have breakfast."

"But I want to show her my…"

Rori's voice faded as Gunner took her back downstairs. Shadow and I held our breaths, glanced at each once, then burst into soft laughter.

"Isn't parenting everything you've ever dreamed of?" I teased, curling into his side.

"Everything and so much more," he sighed, caressing a hand down my back.

I propped my chin on his chest to look at him, my curiosity now piqued. "Really? You were so worried in the beginning."

"I'm still worried. Every day there's something new to worry about." He flashed a sheepish smile. "At first, my worries were mostly to do with you."

"You mean, the pregnancy."

"Mmhm. Just pregnancy in general, at first. Then when we found out they were twins, well, that scared me to death."

"Me too, actually," I confessed. "I never imagined having twins. There's none in my family or anything."

"And you still wanted a natural birth," Shadow teased, playing with the ends of my hair.

"Absolutely! I mean, they were healthy, and the decision just felt right. Call it maternal instinct or whatever, but I knew it was the right way to deliver them."

"Maybe it was the divine feminine in you." Shadow brushed a kiss across my forehead. "The aspect of Freyja that's part of you."

Something clicked into place when he said that. I hadn't consciously felt the goddess since she stopped possessing my body all those years ago, but it made total sense.

"I bet you're right," I said in an awed whisper. As exhausting and uncomfortable that carrying two babies had been, it had been a surprisingly easy pregnancy. My water broke at just past thirty-seven weeks, which was considered full-term for twins. Daren came into the world first, and Rori followed four minutes later. They were small, as twins tended to be, but absolutely perfect. The guys and I rushed to the hospital in the early morning and came home with our children that same evening.

"Once they were born, and I knew you were okay," Shadow went on. "That made room for a whole slew of new worries to pop up."

"Because they were our fragile, precious, screaming, pooping infants we were all now responsible for keeping alive?"

"That was part of it." Shadow's wry smile faded, and he went quiet.

I snuggled into him, peppering kisses on his neck and running light caresses over him to reassure him. "What else?"

He hesitated a moment longer before answering. "That if either of them were biologically mine, the possibility that they might've...inherited something from me." At my narrow-eyed stare, he elaborated. "Or from my mother, or father, even. I don't know what that would be exactly, but something bad."

"Shadow." I returned my head to his chest, wrapping both arms around him. "Love, we ran those genetic tests, remember? Everything came back normal."

"I know, but I don't mean something physically wrong. Like, I was born physically normal. So was my mother, I'm sure. But neither of us ended up that way."

"Hey, listen." I lifted my cheek to look at him again. "You're not defective in any way. You never were." I found one of his hands and laced my fingers through his. "Everything you've struggled with was because of the environment you were in, not because there was anything inherently wrong with you."

"But we don't know that for sure." Shadow placed an arm behind his head, his expression thoughtful. "I never had a normal environment to compare it to. For all we know, I could have turned out the same."

"What about now?" I challenged. "And the last several years? You've been an amazing husband and father. You're the most sought-after tattoo artist in the Southwest, with a year-long wait list. Our children love you." I leaned in to hover my lips over his. "*I* love you."

His smile finally returned before the distance between our lips closed. "I love you so much. And you're right. These past few years have been just...perfect. Having you as my wife every day." He stroked tenderly over my cheek. "Watching the kids grow. Seeing the tattoo shop become what it is. I never could have imagined this before."

I let my forehead touch his, soaking up this moment of reflection with him. Every once in a while, the guys and I would have moments like these. Usually after the kids went to bed and when other things didn't need our immediate attention.

This beautiful little family, this amazing life we had—we could never forget how hard we fought for this. We nearly destroyed ourselves and each other before we made it here, and we'd never take it for granted.

"The kids will only inherit the best things from you," I said after a few moments of quiet. "They've already gotten started. Daren is drawing nonstop and Rori," I grinned at him, "she's your little shadow."

"She is." Shadow's smile grew even broader at the mention of our daughter. "I don't know how that happened. She's so much like Gunner, and with Reaper's bossiness."

I couldn't help but laugh at how true that was, sliding off of Shadow to land next to him on the mattress. "Speaking of, ready to get up and see what she wanted to show us?"

"Yes." Shadow pushed the sheet away and swung his feet to the floor. "I'm ready for breakfast even more."

I remained in bed, just watching as he went to the dresser to pull on sweatpants and a shirt. His broad back and perky ass were every bit as delicious now as they were eight years ago. Only his scars looked softer this morning, probably because of the morning light in the bedroom.

Shadow turned around once he got dressed and smirked when he caught me staring. Finally, the man had started to understand how attractive he was.

"Are you having some trouble getting up?" He approached the edge of the bed, his body tense and a wicked gleam in his eye.

My heart sped up with the thrill of his body language. "Um, no."

A beat of frozen silence passed before I scrambled for the opposite edge of the bed. Shadow reached over and grabbed my ankle easily, dragging me back toward him with an amused chuckle. He ignored my shrieks and playful protests, knowing full-well now that I wasn't actually trying to escape him.

Shadow trapped me easily underneath him, pinning me down with kisses and tickles until I was breathless. Then he swatted my ass and lifted away, leaving me wanting and weak-kneed, to get dressed.

CHAPTER 3

JANDRO

I woke up to a package on the porch from my sister, Angie, and her husband, Drew. They mailed a bunch of Christmas gifts for the kids months ago, which we figured had gotten lost. Postal systems were still inconsistent between the different territories and unreliable at best. So it was a nice surprise to find, even if it was three months late.

The kids digging through the box and playing with their new toys allowed us three dads to wake up slowly with some coffee while Mari and Shadow slept in. They had just gotten up as I was starting breakfast for everyone.

"Smells great, Jandro." Shadow came down the stairs first, a smile still pulling on his lips from his lay-in with Mari. They hadn't gotten a lot of private time lately, with her preparing for graduation and him booked with back-to-back tattoo appointments. I was glad Reaper and Gunner followed my lead in getting up early.

Shadow was headed off at the bottom of the stairs by Rori, holding up some tiny dollhouse thing. "Dad, look what I got!"

"What did you get? Can I see?" The shift in his tone was never something I thought I'd hear. Not until he started talking to Mari over eight years ago. And now our daughter threatened to unseat her as the woman who had the most power over him.

Mari came downstairs moments later, heading straight for me. "Do you need help?"

"Not from you, Doctor." I pushed a mug of coffee into her hands with a grin and a fast kiss. "Although I might need your expertise *later*."

"Mmhm, body exam sex jokes, very funny." She smirked over the rim of her coffee cup. "You said something similar when we first met. Do you remember that?"

"Me?" I slapped a hand to my chest dramatically. "Saying innuendos to a beautiful girl I was hoping to sleep with? That doesn't sound like me at all."

"You said it to all the girls then," Mari teased with a playful glare.

"But I wifed up the best one." I squeezed her shoulders and planted a kiss on her forehead. "Sit down, see what Angie sent the kids. I'll bring you breakfast." I followed her out to the living room just to snap a towel at Gunner's head. "Get in here and help."

"Jesus, fine. Be right back, little dude." He and Reaper were going through smaller boxes of Legos with our son, Daren.

"Can you handle pancakes?" I shoved the bowl of batter at Gunner. "Don't burn them."

"Fuck yeah, pancakes!" He got to stirring excitedly.

"Little ones for the kids. No bigger than a softball."

"I know dude, I got it." He poured the batter with surprising care, making explosion noises that got Daren all excited from the living room.

Dad-life had infected Gunner with a childlike excitement about all the little things. He was the fun dad, for sure. Me? I considered myself the teacher. I took every opportunity I could to show the kids how something worked, whether it was cooking or the bubbles in their bath. Shadow was the neurotic, overprotective one, although he was getting better at dialing it back. Reaper, oddly enough, turned out to be the most well-balanced of us.

While Gunner poured, flipped, and stacked pancakes, I worked on the eggs and bacon. The aroma started filling up the house and Gun's curious little miniature wandered in to investigate.

"*Listo para comer, mijita?*" I asked Rori if she was ready to eat as she wandered to my side of the counter. "Not too close, baby. It's hot."

"Papi, can I have an egg?" She stood on tiptoes, grabbing drawer handles like she was ready to climb up and swipe the whole pan of scrambled eggs for herself.

I touched her chin to bring her attention to me. "*En español, mijita.*" She knew the words, she just needed to practice saying them. There was always a teachable moment.

Rori frowned, the frustration settling into her tightly-knitted eyebrows. "I don't know how." Her voice was climbing into that whine, the one that preceded all her worst tantrums.

This was the other side to always wanting to teach them something, dealing with the impatience and struggles when they didn't succeed right away. But not everything would come easily to them, and they had to learn that too.

Thankfully, it was Reaper to the rescue.

"Yes, you do." He crouched low next to her, hugging one arm around her waist. "I'll help you. We'll say it together, okay?" Rori's attention was successfully diverted to him, a welcome distraction from her tantrum. She watched his mouth intently, mimicking him as he slowly formed the words.

"Un..."

"Un..."

"Hue..."

"H-h-hue..."

"*Hue-vito.* You got it, sugar cube."

"*Un hue-vito.*" Rori turned back to me. "*Por favor.*"

Only a completely heartless bastard would not have melted at the look my daughter gave me right then. All the times I got shot up and nearly died, when I thought I lost Mari and everyone else—it was worth it for that look alone.

"Very good, *mijita.*" I composed myself fast enough to scoop her up, tucking her against my side as I planted a big kiss on her cheek. "You're so smart, and I'm proud of you." I kissed her other cheek. "I love you."

I made a mental note to let her know how proud I was as often as possible. While Four Corners was relatively safe, it could be generations before the outside world was as safe for girls as it once was. Wherever my daughter ended up in her adult life, I wanted her to feel confident in how intelligent she was. I never wanted her to doubt for a second that she was loved.

"Huevito!" Rori repeated insistently.

"Yeah, yeah. I got your eggs right here, princess." I scooped up a spoonful of scrambled egg that had already cooled next to the stove and held it up to her lips. "Test it for me. Is it ready?"

She took the biggest bite possible off the end of the wooden spoon and proceeded to spill small crumbles of egg onto the floor. Good thing Hades was there to clean it all up.

"How is it? Good?" At her enthusiastic nod, I put her spoon aside and handed her a clean one. "Help me stir this next batch. It's almost ready. Hey!" My head whipped around at the sight of Reaper in my periphery. "Fuck off, bacon thief!"

"What?" Reaper unashamedly fed the strip of meat to Hades, who inhaled it. "He can't have eggs without bacon."

"Fuck off!" Rori parroted me, waving the stirring spoon at Reaper.

"I love you too, sugar cube." Reaper took the spoon from her and kissed her forehead.

We tried not to swear in front of the kids at first, we really did. But even Mari slipped sometimes, despite being the biggest enforcer of it. The kids' teachers didn't approve, obviously, but in the end, we decided it wasn't all that harmful. If anything, a bigger vocabulary was a good thing, right? Especially if they learned to speak two languages.

"Alright, I'm putting you down." I placed Rori carefully on the floor, then turned the burners off. "Have a seat and I'll bring you a plate, *mijita.*"

We got the kids seated with food, an endeavor that went smoothly this morning, before getting ourselves plated up.

"Thank you, *guapito.*" Mari kissed me as she breezed past me in the kitchen.

I smacked her ass before she could dodge out of the way. "My pleasure." And it really was. Taking care of my family was all I'd ever wanted to do.

The kids were hungry, but they were eager to get back to their box of toys, so they inhaled their food and squirmed in their seats.

"Slow down, child. You'll get a tummy ache." Mari wiped pancake syrup and crumbled egg from Rori's mouth. "Drink some juice."

"Papi, papi. Can you help me..."

"Finish chewing your food, son," I reminded Daren. "Yes, what can I help you with?"

"Can you help me build a... a motorcycle with the Legos I got from Uncle Drew?"

My chest swelled up so much when he asked that question, I thought it would burst. I had secretly hoped that at least one of my kids would want to build and tinker with stuff. Of course, I wanted them to pursue their own interests and not force them into anything, but I fantasized about working on projects with my son or daughter. Being able to teach them hands-on about mechanics and how things worked was a dream. One that my son just brought to reality with his innocent question.

"You want me to help you build a motorcycle?" My five-year-old had no idea what this meant to me, but all the adults in attendance did. Mari beamed at me from across the table and the guys let out soft, approving chuckles.

"Yeah! There's wheels and a bunch of other little parts, but I don't know where they go."

"Don't worry." I ruffled his dark hair, which was in thick, soft waves like Mari's, and kissed the top of his head. "We'll build you a bitchin' ride. But finish your breakfast first."

Daren wolfed down the rest of his eggs and bacon before politely asking to be excused.

He bolted to the living room coffee table just as his sister was finishing up.

"Rori, do you want to build motorcycles with Daren?" Mari teased our daughter, clearing plates from the table.

"No. Daddy, can I have tattoos?" Rori peered up at Shadow, grabbing his forearm that depicted Mari as a sexy pin-up girl.

"Again?" He smiled at her, pinching her cheek playfully. "You washed off your tattoos in the bath the other day."

"I want flowers this time. Like Mommy's. Oh, and I want a cat! Like Freyja."

"What do you say?"

"Pleeease!"

Shadow slid a glance over to Mari before giving in. "Alright. But they're getting washed off again before you go back to school."

"Her teacher just has a massive stick up her ass," Gunner declared, shoving the last big bite of pancake into her mouth.

"Gun." Mari smacked his arm but had giggled despite the chastisement.

"You know I'm right, baby girl. She said 'shit' *one* time—"

"It was 'bullshit' actually," Reaper chuckled. "I picked her up that day, and yes, her teacher was very concerned about how she expressed that the coloring project was bullshit."

"That's our girl," I laughed, collecting the rest of the dishes.

"And then the teacher came at me when *I* picked her up," Shadow continued. "Because Rori was showing off her 'tattoos' to the rest of the class. I had to explain to this lady that it was washable marker."

"She thinks we're raising degenerates." Reaper crunched his bacon with a satisfied smirk.

"All this is telling me is Rori's the coolest kid in her class," Gunner concluded.

"And thank everything that Daren is polite and sweet and *quiet*," Mari punctuated the last word with a soft laugh. "Because I could not handle two Roris."

"Speaking of." I rinsed off my hands in the sink and dried them on a towel. "If anyone needs me, I'll be building a motorcycle with my son."

Fuck, it felt so damn good to say that.

CHAPTER 4

SHADOW

"How've you been, big man?" Declan removed his shirt and folded it neatly on a chair before lying down on my tattoo bench. "You look good."

"Thanks. I've been great, actually." I pulled on my gloves and wheeled up next to him on my stool, bringing my cart of supplies along behind me. "Business is good. I got a family now."

"Good for you, man." He turned his head toward the shelf on the wall of my tattoo shop. "Is that them right there?"

I followed his gaze to the framed picture of Mari and the twins, taken just last week at her graduation party. Mari was holding Rori, the two of them smiling brightly while Daren stood next to his mom and clung to her hip, his expression more shy and withdrawn.

"Yeah." I cleaned Declan's skin with antiseptic while my chest did that elated flipping sensation. It never ceased to amaze me that my entire world was in that picture. And that it was real. "That's my wife and our twins."

"Beautiful." Declan looked away from the wall and relaxed while I began to sketch over his chest in pen.

"This has held up well," I remarked on the dragon's head on the right side of his chest, which I had done for him in prison around eighteen years ago. It was the first expansive tattoo I'd ever done, starting at his chest, then winding over his shoulder and down his back. I'd poked it entirely by hand over a period of several weeks. It looked rougher than my current style, but not as bad as I expected. I could sharpen up the lines easily, then add the color he wanted.

"Told you it still looked good." Declan grinned. "I'm not surprised at all that you're running a shop now. You always did good work."

"Thanks. I couldn't believe that was you walking outside. You bulked up, kid."

"So did you, man!" He laughed. "I didn't know whether to hug you when I saw you or run away shitting my pants."

"You never gave me a hard time," I said. "If you had been one of the guards, it might be a different story."

I finished the sketch and got his approval on it, then proceeded to start the real inking.

"Are you staying in Four Corners?" I asked between the buzzes of my machine.

"Ah, I'm kind of all over the place." A dismissive answer, but I didn't pry. We had been acquaintances but not especially friendly. I never learned why he ended up in prison, especially so young. He'd been a wide-eyed teenager back then, thrown into a cage with some of the worst criminals in the world.

I was lucky that Jandro took me in with the Demons once the inmates started rioting and breaking out. In all likelihood, Declan was not as lucky.

"I'm spending a lot of time in Blakeworth these days," he continued after a brief pause.

"Blakeworth?" I couldn't hide my surprise. He was definitely not part of their elite class, which was still struggling after we kicked their asses, despite their best efforts to save face. We continue to see propaganda coming out of there saying that their wealth and prosperity were at an all-time high because they beat *us* in that last battle. A bald-faced lie to their own citizens, and a shitty one at that.

"My line of work is...not entirely legal." I felt Declan's eyes on me as I touched up spots on his dragon and knew he was gauging my reaction.

"As long as you're not trafficking people, I won't judge what you do," I informed him.

He relaxed, taking a big breath. "Nah, nothing like that. I'm a cage fighter."

"Really?" That surprised me too, but not in a bad way. "So getting scrappy in the yard turned out to be useful for you, huh?"

"You could say that," he laughed. "It's all underground up there. The fancy doodads made laws against it, but some of them come to every fight and they love to gamble. It's very few rules, bare fists and shit. And *huge* fuckin' payouts."

"Yeah? What's your record?"

Declan grinned broadly. "I'm undefeated."

"No shit." I was oddly fascinated. As an assassin, I wouldn't make for a very entertaining fighter. But if I hadn't ended up with the Demons, I may have found myself doing very similar work. Although my socially stunted ass would've most likely ended up in a gladiator type of situation.

"Yeah, you should come see me fight sometime. Might want to leave the wife and kids at home, though. It gets pretty brutal."

I paused to sit up and stretch my hand, returning his grin. "I would, but I'm pretty sure I'll be arrested on sight if I ever show my face in Blakeworth again."

"For real?" Declan's eyes widened. "Okay, I need to hear *that* story."

We spent the next few hours swapping war stories while I tattooed him. All the line work on his dragon became sharp and crisp. I had started adding shading to the surrounding smoke, plus green and gold coloring to the dragon's scales, when we decided to stop.

"I'll be in town 'til the end of the week." Declan sat up from the bench after I cleaned his skin and went to grab his shirt. Now that I knew what to look for, he clearly moved like a fighter. "Thanks for squeezing me in, Shadow. I know you're busy as hell these days."

"It's no trouble. I actually keep my schedule pretty flexible in case something comes up with the kids." Speaking of, it was my day to pick up Rori from school. I cleaned up my area quickly, not wanting to leave a mess for my shop apprentice. "Come by in the mornings," I told

Declan. "I have to pick up my daughter, but tomorrow I can work on you for an hour longer."

"Sounds good, Shadow. We'll catch up more over a drink later, yeah?"

"Sure. See you, Dec."

"AND THEN WE PLAYED TAG, AND I WAS IT, BUT *GUESS WHAT*, Dad!"

"What happened, Ror?" I held on to my daughter's hand as we walked up the driveway together, carrying her llama backpack in the other hand. Ever since we went on a family trip to an alpaca farm a few weeks ago, she'd been obsessed with llamas and alpacas.

"I tagged everyone!" Rori released my hand and started jumping and skipping in front of me. "'Cause I'm the fastest! I was like this!" She sprinted up the rest of the driveway to the front door, where Hades waited for her on the front porch.

"Wow, look at you go!" I dug out my keys, smiling at my exuberant daughter. *That's one way to burn all that energy.*

The dog matched her excitement, returning her tackling hug with face licks and excited tail-wagging as I let us into the house.

"Hades, can you catch me?" Rori darted through the living room, circling the couches with her bright laughter as Hades chased her.

"Hey Freyja." I set our stuff down and greeted the sleepy cat with an ear scratch. She head-butted my hand once, then promptly turned around to sleep in a different position. "Fair enough, we'll hang out when it's quieter."

Freyja loved Rori, but didn't care for our daughter's tendency to tornado around the house when she was at full energy.

Playing tag at school seemed to drain her earlier than usual, though. Hades only chased her for a few minutes before she sprawled out on the couch, panting.

"Do you want a snack, Ror-meister?" We had the house to ourselves until the others got home, so the kitchen was unusually quiet and empty without Jandro whipping up something.

"Yes, please. Can I have animal crackers?"

"Sure. Drink some water for me, okay? You ran a lot today."

"Okay."

I set out her snack for her, then flipped through some upcoming tattoo sketches while Rori nibbled her crackers. Declan wanted a lion on his back, interacting somehow with the dragon once I finished adding color to the scales. I got so absorbed in sketching that I didn't notice Rori had finished her snack until she crawled up on the couch and nestled into my side.

"What are you drawing, Daddy?" She leaned on my shoulder, voice quiet and calm.

"Some tattoos for work." I brought an arm around her and dropped a kiss to her forehead. "What do you think of this lion?"

"He's hungry. He's gonna bite the snake." She pointed to where the lion's open jaws hovered dangerously close to the back end of the dragon.

"That's a dragon, silly." I tugged a lock of her hair. "See? He's scaly like a snake, but he has feet."

"Where are his wings?" Rori's eyelids blinked heavily. All that running around really tuckered her out today.

"This one doesn't have wings, but he does breathe fire." I flipped to another page where I had drawn the details of the dragon's head. "See all this smoke coming out of his mouth? And he's got feet up here too, so he's got four legs."

Rori shifted into my side and curled her legs up until she was a small ball. If she was getting comfortable for a nap, I'd be stuck here and have zero complaints about it. The others warned me our kids would want to spend a lot less time with us as they got older. I already couldn't believe how fast the last five years had flown by, so I was more than happy to cherish these moments with them.

"Falling asleep on me, Ror-meister?" I set aside the sketchbook and shifted to a more comfortable position while trying not to disturb her.

"No..." Her eyelids batted open, green eyes focusing on my arm around her. One small hand reached out, skimming over my years upon years of scar tissue. "You got so many owies, Daddy."

I tensed, and my heart started to race. I knew the kids would notice and ask questions at some point, but still felt completely unprepared for this moment. How much, if anything, should I tell her? Especially at this age?

"It's okay. They don't hurt anymore, sweetheart. They're really old." I tapped a finger to her nose. "Much older than you."

"But you got *a lot*. Like seventy-million." She followed the map of crisscrossing lines up my arm with her fingers, taking in how extensive they were. "I know! I'll kiss them better."

I just sat back, stunned, as my daughter placed messy kisses all over my arm, something she must have picked up from her mother. Mari kissed the kids' band-aids whenever they got a cut or scrape, then declared them all better before wrapping them up in a hug. Her doing that seemed to soothe and comfort them more than the actual treatment of the wound. And now my daughter was doing it to me.

"All better!" Rori wrapped her arms around my neck and smacked a kiss on my cheekbone. "You're okay now, Daddy."

Okay was the understatement of the year. I was a completely different person since she'd come into my life. Sure, my arm was now covered in drool, but fuck if I was ever going to wipe it off. I hugged my sweet, beautiful daughter and forced words out through the emotion tightening my throat.

"Thank you, sweetheart. I'm so, *so* much better now."

THE CLICK OF THE FRONT DOOR UNLOCKING ROUSED ME from sleep. My attention was split between Rori, dead asleep on my chest, and Mari entering the house.

"Hi guys—oh!" She lowered her voice to a whisper as I brought a finger to my lips. "Hi. How did you get her to fall asleep?"

"Playing tag at school," I whispered back. We shared a quick kiss before Mari went to change out of her work clothes while I carefully lifted up from the couch, carrying Rori to her room to finish her nap. Mari was nibbling one of Rori's ignored animal crackers when I returned. "How was work?" I pulled her close by the waist for a proper kiss.

"Good." She raised on tiptoes and leaned the length of her body on me through our kiss. "Two more confirmed pregnancies with twins! I'm telling you, there's some fertility mojo in the air."

Freyja hopped down from her sleeping spot right then, greeting Mari with a meow and a rub around her ankles.

"Yes, is this your doing?" Mari picked up the cat and flipped her belly up. "Anything you'd like to tell me?"

Freyja stared back blankly, pupils wide. We still talked to the animals and searched for the hints of that ancient wisdom in their eyes. They never spoke again after we left New Ireland, but that didn't mean we weren't being heard.

Mari set Freyja down once the cat started squirming in protest. "How was your day, love?" Her arms went around my waist, pressing herself flush against me again.

"Good. Had a surprise walk-in from an old prison acquaintance. He's in town temporarily, and I'll be working on him while he's here. He's safe, no trouble," I added at her tense expression.

"Ah well, that's good. Was it nice to catch up with him?"

"Yes, actually. He's doing some underground, not entirely legal work in Blakeworth." Mari didn't like fighting. She hated the Fight Nights we had back in Sheol, so I left that detail out.

She laughed softly, putting away Rori's discarded snack. "Good for him, as long as he doesn't get caught."

"I don't think he will." I went to help her wipe crumbs from the kitchen table. "Where's Daren?"

"I dropped him off at the pool with Gunner." Mari tossed a smirk at me over her shoulder. "That boy will not live to adulthood fearing water like I did. Did Rori's teacher give you any grief?"

"Not today," I answered distractedly. Her comment about Daren dredged up some worries I'd been mulling over about our son but hadn't had a chance to voice yet. "Lover, do you think Daren's okay?"

Mari paused in tidying up the kitchen, her brows furrowing together. "What do you mean?"

"He's...a little different, isn't he? Just in general."

Her expression turned thoughtful as she wandered closer to me. "He's quiet, a little shy. I haven't noticed anything wrong with him. Or do you mean something else?"

"No, it's like what you're saying. He doesn't have a lot of friends. He prefers doing things by himself, instead of playing with other kids. He doesn't get...excited about things like Rori does. I just wonder why he isolates himself like that."

"Shadow." Mari's head tilted as she looked at me, a smile growing on her face. "You know what I'm hearing?"

"No, what?"

"You're worried about our son turning out like you."

"That's not..." *Fuck. Yes, it is.*

The realization must have been clear on my face because Mari returned to standing in front of me, dragging a light touch up my chest to my neck. "Not every child can be a screaming tornado of sunshine like our daughter. Daren is his own person. If he's introverted and not the most boisterous kid in the room, that's who he is, and we should support him no matter what."

"Of course I'll support him. It's just..." It seemed so obvious now that she made that connection. My fears were rooted in my own upbringing, in the childhood I never got to have. "I worry when I see him intentionally withdraw from people. I don't want him to struggle with the same things I did as he gets older. Before I met you, I could barely talk to anyone. I don't want that for him."

Mari's fingers dragged over my neck and scalp as she listened, the touch grounding and soothing. "Our son is loved," she said. "He's so smart, kind, and creative. He's not antisocial, he's just very..." She paused to think. "Cerebral. Daren's in his head a lot, always thinking."

"You're right. He's all of those things." I leaned my forehead on hers. "He has it so good. It's stupid of me to worry."

"No, love. I think worrying is normal." She scratched deliciously up the back of my head. "We want them to have everything we didn't have and to never experience the awful things that we went through."

"I know. But we need to give them room to be themselves too."

"I wanted to wait until everyone was home to tell you guys." Mari smiled. "But you should know that Daren's teacher told me something wonderful today."

"What? What happened?" My heart lifted at the pride shining through Mari.

"They got a new student in class, a deaf girl. You know how resources are short now, so they're not sure when she'll get an interpreter."

"These kids need their own classes, with specialized instructors, so they don't fall behind," I said with a soft growl. "It's not fair to her."

"I know, love. And she's nonverbal, plus she's new, so the other kids didn't really make an effort to play with her." Mari grinned. "Except for one."

"Daren."

Mari nodded, beaming up at me. "He sat next to her when no one else did. They communicated through pictures and notes." She snorted out a soft laugh. "Well, his best attempts at notes, anyway. That boy writes in chicken scratch."

"He did that? Unprompted?" This wasn't disbelief I was feeling. I had no doubts my son could make friends. But I wanted to hear Mari say it again and again. I wanted to see it with my own eyes, just to feel this elation and pride in him.

"He did," Mari confirmed, leaning her chest on mine as she wrapped around me tighter. "So I don't think you need to worry, love. He's quiet and solitary for a kid, but his heart is so big."

"You're right." My arms wrapped around her back, holding her to me so I could rest my cheek on top of her head. "Our kids are going to be fine."

CHAPTER 5

GUNNER

"You'd really rather sit there and kick the water instead of getting in?"

"Yeah," Daren said succinctly. He was sitting at the edge of our community pool, swimming trunks and water wings on, splashing the water with his feet, but absolutely refusing to get in.

This was our third attempt, and I was hoping it'd be the charm. But we'd been here about fifteen minutes already and no such luck.

The water was shallow at this end, barely coming up to my waist. I could sit on the bottom and still have my head above the surface. Not many people were around, just a group of friends lounging on deck chairs and a couple of lap swimmers in the deep end.

I lifted out of the water just enough to put my arms on either side of Daren. "Talk to me, son. What are you worried about?"

"I told you, drowning!" he retorted with a narrow-eyed stare at me. "And sea monsters."

I held back a chuckle. Maybe telling him bedtime stories about sirens and krakens sinking ships wasn't the best idea.

"No sea monsters in here, buddy." I leaned back, spreading my arms wide below the surface. "See? You can see all the way to the bottom across the whole pool."

"Daddy Shadow told me an octopus can camouflage themselves to look like anything. So they could just be hiding."

Damn it, Shadow.

I returned my hands to the ledge. "I promise you, there are no sea monsters here. I won't let anything happen to you, you're safe."

Years ago, I said something similar to Mari when I got her to float on her back. She barely knew me back then and trusted me anyway. I was trying not to show frustration toward my own son for not trusting me. Facing fears was different for kids, I knew that.

Daren leaned forward, peering into the pool with a scrutinizing gaze. I wondered then, as I often did, which one of us made him. Rori was obviously mine. But with Daren, it was less obvious.

He was quiet and thoughtful, like Shadow, and a hands-on learner who loved tinkering, like Jandro. Some of his physical features reminded me of Reaper and Daren, the uncle he never got to know and his namesake.

But mostly, he looked like Mari. He sure as shit inherited her fear of water.

"How about this?" I said when he seemed no closer to getting in. "Hold on to me and I'll dip you, just up to your legs. We won't even get your bellybutton wet." A slower approach would probably work best for him, and I poked him in the belly to illustrate my point.

But something else had caught Daren's attention, and I followed his gaze across the pool.

A girl about his age and her mom were entering the pool area together. The girl fidgeted excitedly, her hands moving rapidly as her mother led them to an empty deck chair to set their stuff down. Her mom made some gestures with her hands and it dawned on me that they were speaking sign language.

I looked back at Daren, tickling his foot under the water to get his attention. "Who's that, bud? Do you know her?"

"That's Lily, she's my friend," he said. "She can't hear us, so we have to wait until she sees us to say hi."

"Oh, okay." I turned around again to see that Lily's mom had put goggles on her daughter's head and removed what looked like hearing aids from her ears.

The little girl looked up, and I knew immediately when she saw Daren. A big smile spread across her face, and she waved excitedly at him. Her mother caught on, and I gave a polite wave to her.

Lily snapped her goggles over her eyes, made a quick sign at Daren, then started *running* to the edge of the pool.

Oh fuck, she's going to slip and fall. I pushed away from Daren's ledge and went toward her, not thinking about how I'd tell her to be careful. I just wanted to be there to help if she got hurt.

It was all for naught, however, as Lily straightened her arms above her head, stacked her palms on top of each other, and made a smooth, perfect dive into the pool. I stopped in my tracks, utterly stunned, and I knew Daren had to be too. I'd been swimming since I could crawl, and I definitely couldn't dive like that at five years old.

"Showing off for her friend," Lily's mom laughed as she approached the pool's edge. "Hi, I'm Anna."

"I don't blame her, that was amazing." I said. "I'm Gunner, Daren's dad."

"Nice to meet you both. We're new to Four Corners, and it sounds like those two really hit it off in school today."

"I'm glad to hear it."

Lily had been frog-kicking underwater on her way to Daren's side of the pool, her head popping up just a few feet away from where he was sitting.

"Wow!" His eyes were big and round as he stared at her. "You're like a fish." He pointed at Lily, then placed his hands behind his ears to wave them like gills as he sucked his cheeks in.

Lily let out a soft sound that must have been a laugh, then signed something at Daren before beckoning him to join her in the water. He looked up at me, that same apprehension in his eyes from before. But now there was something else—determination.

"Yeah, we're still working on the whole 'getting in the pool' part." I chuckled at Anna as I made my way back over to Daren's side. Lily turned around as I approached, and I greeted her with a smile and two thumbs up. "Great dive, that was awesome!" I wasn't sure if she read lips, but made an effort to speak slowly and enunciate the words anyway.

The little girl beamed and touched her hand to her mouth, bringing her forearm down in a smooth arc.

"She says 'thanks'," Daren interpreted for me proudly. "That's my dad." He pointed at me and made another sign with his hand, spreading his fingers wide and touching his thumb to his forehead.

My chest swelled with pride. He learned quickly and was already picking up Spanish words from Jandro. When Mari's parents came over, Daren and his grandfather Javier were able to have complete, albeit simple, conversations entirely in Spanish. And now here he was, picking up a third language like it was nothing. I couldn't wait to tell the others when we got home.

"She's asking Daren to get in the pool with her." Lily's mom sat on the ledge a few feet away from my son, dipping her feet and calves into the water and signing as she spoke.

He seemed more determined to try, gripping the pool's edge in his small hands and staring down at the surface like it was his arch nemesis. I didn't want to add to the pressure he was likely already putting on himself, nor did I want to embarrass him in front of his new friend. So I moved to the side as he started to scoot, inch by inch, off the ledge.

"Do you want help, buddy?" I asked in a low voice, meant only for him to hear.

"No, I got it."

I kept my arm near him just in case, but let him be as he slowly eased more of his legs into the water. At the last moment, when he let go of the edge and hit the water with a splash, he did grab my arm with a frightened gasp. The water wings kept his shoulders and head above the surface, so he was completely safe.

I brought Daren close to me anyway, drawing him into a hug while wishing Mari could see this. "Good job, dude! I got you, you're okay."

Lily and her mom both clapped in support, which made Daren go shy and hide his face against my side.

"Aw, son, I'm proud of you." He continued to hold my arm as I lowered into the water, bringing my face level with his. "You did it! How do you feel?"

"Okay. It's not so bad." He was trying to play it cool in front of the ladies, but I could see the elation on his face, the pure rush of having conquered one of his biggest fears.

"You handled that like a champ." I resisted the urge to hug him tighter and plant a huge kiss on his face. I could wait until we were home to embarrass him. "You want to grab ice cream when we're done here?"

"Yeah!" His eyes lit up. "Can Lily come?"

"If it's okay with Lily and her mom."

Anna's hands moved rapidly as she relayed the question to her daughter. "Lily, love, do you want to get ice cream with Daren after your swim?"

Lily's head bobbed up and down in an enthusiastic nod and began signing rapidly at Daren.

"That's a yes, if it wasn't obvious," her mom laughed. "She's asking Daren what his favorite ice cream flavor is."

"Peanut butter chocolate!" My son forgot all about being afraid and started an adorably clumsy swim toward his friend. "My sister's is strawberry shortcake, but she likes everything pink. Pink and llamas."

Anna hurriedly translated Daren's words before the kids started swimming off. "Ah well, they'll figure it out," she laughed. "She couldn't stop talking about making a friend on her first day of school. I was so worried about her adjusting to living here, so her finding Daren is a huge weight off my mind."

"I'm glad to see it too," I told her, propping my arms up on the ledge. "He's a quiet kid, usually keeps to himself, so it's nice to see him coming out of his shell. Especially for someone who needed a friend." We watched the kids quietly for another minute before I asked, "Where are you all from?"

"Illinois, originally. But we moved around a lot after the Collapse and came here from Jerriton."

"Ah, it's not too bad up there anymore, is it?" We were in regular contact with the folks running the Jerriton territory, many of them were the same people who pulled through for us against the Sha.

"Oh no, we loved it up there! Sadly, the schools were lacking, especially for Lily's needs. And my husband landed a great position at the hospital here, so it was a no-brainer."

"Oh, what's your husband do? He's probably met my wife."

"He's an EMT. He was actually a medic in the Jerriton army when they overthrew the last governor."

"No shit, Mari did the same! She was a nurse, then a war medic, and now she just became a gynecologist." I folded my arms and rested my head on them, smiling at the thought of her. "She wanted to deliver babies, and now she finally gets to. The whole crumbling of civilization just derailed things a bit."

"It was the same for Colby." Anna laughed lightly. "We're ready for a quiet life. He just wants to drive an ambulance and hang out with the kiddo."

"Well, you guys came to the right place."

I looked over my shoulder to watch Daren, but he was absolutely fine. Lily seemed to be coaxing him to put his face in the water, even handing him her goggles so he could see. He pressed the lenses to his eyes and took a big breath before barely skimming the water with his face. When he looked up again, Lily clapped and encouraged him.

I already knew those two would be inseparable. Hopefully, we could talk Lily's parents into coming over so they could keep hanging out, and we could have new adults to talk to as well. Even though all of us were well known and respected in Four Corners, some of the other parents were still weirded out by four of us being married to one woman.

Logically, I could understand it—I was the same way years ago. It didn't make the judgments and assumptions any less annoying. But all that mattered was that our kids were safe. We, their *five* parents, just needed to keep providing a stable environment for them and continue being blissfully happy with our dynamic—which worked out great for childcare, by the way.

Anna and her husband would figure it out eventually and make that judgment call themselves. If they didn't want to hang out with us, it was their loss. We threw the best parties in town.

I only hoped, if they did feel that way, they wouldn't keep Lily from seeing Daren. Sending my friends away was one of my dad's favorite ways to be an asshole when I was a kid. So far, I was pretty good at doing the opposite of everything my old man did, and I had no intention of breaking that streak.

"Hey, Daren!"

My son looked up. He'd gotten as far as sticking his nose and mouth in the water and blowing bubbles. I didn't expect to see that for another six months.

I tapped a finger on my wrist, not that I had a watch on. "Fifteen more minutes, then we're getting ice cream."

"Yes! You're the best, Dad!"

I smiled and looked down at my left hand where I wore a gunmetal wedding band. Reaper's mom made them years ago for all of us guys. "I'm definitely in the top four, but I'll take it."

MARIPOSA

Standing in front of the bathroom mirror, I unwound the towel from my head and used it to scrub through my damp hair. Once my hair was dry enough, I started brushing.

The house was blissfully quiet, a rarity these days. Reaper, Jandro, and Gunner were playing some elaborate game in the backyard with the kids. They made cardboard swords and armor and planned several epic battles and sieges across the yard. Last I heard, Daren was a prince saving a village of innocent chicken-people from the dangerous giants who wanted to eat them.

In any case, it was a great way to keep them busy while Doctor Mommy got some time to herself. I had just finished my bath and planned to grab a glass of wine before joining the others out back.

I finished brushing my hair and started putting on my lotion when I heard the front door open. Shadow's soft, "Hey, Freyja," floating up brought a smile to my lips. He walked through the house, likely checking out the epic battle in the backyard before coming to find me.

"I'm in here, love," I called when his footsteps ascended the stairs.

Shadow appeared in the doorway a moment later, his lips parting and eyes taking me in appreciatively. "Hey, lover. Do you...want some help?"

I smiled coyly at him in the mirror, both of us knowing exactly where his "help" would lead. "From you, always."

He walked up behind me and picked up the lotion bottle from the counter. It was only as he poured a small amount into his palm and rubbed his hands together that I noticed the tension in his shoulder. There was some stiffness, even an undercurrent of aggression in his movements and how tightly his brow furrowed.

"How was your tattoo appointment?" I ventured.

Shadow let out a non-committal grunt, placing his hands on my back to rub the lotion in.

"Bad client?" I tried again.

"The worst," he admitted. "Changed his mind about the design constantly, made scheduling a nightmare, and he's always coming up short on his deposits with tons of excuses. I'm thinking about dropping him."

"Then you should." I leaned my head back until it rested on his chest. "There are tons of people who would love to be a client of yours. Give his spot to someone who would appreciate you."

"I know, you're right. It's so fucking frustrating because in the moment, he tries to make *me* seem like the unreasonable one."

"Well, he's full of shit." Shadow was rubbing lotion into my shoulders and I reached up to grab his hands. "Even if you were unreasonable, which you're not, it's *your* fucking business. Run it however you want to."

Shadow's lips curled into a smile as he gradually relaxed. "I thought about playing dumb and fucking up his design even more so he'd finally go somewhere else."

"That's an idea." I laughed. "Draw him a pile of dogshit, because that's exactly how he's acting."

"Tempting." Shadow kissed my cheekbone before grabbing for the lotion bottle again. "Thanks for letting me vent, lover."

"Always." I angled my head, reaching on tiptoes to kiss the corner of his jaw. "I'm sorry you had a rough day."

"It's fine." He was lotioning my lower back now, large hands spanning around to my waist. "I just need to decompress from the day."

"Is this helping?" I reached up to touch more of him, my fingers grazing his neck and shoulders.

"Very much," he purred. His hands roamed over my belly and lower ribs, firm and steadfast in his task despite me being completely naked.

When he reached for more lotion, I arched against him, stretching my body long as I reached up and pressed my chest forward. My hands massaged into his neck while my bare ass pressed into the front of his jeans.

"Hold still," he commanded. "I need to get all of you."

I brought my hands to the counter with a small pout. It turned into a breathy gasp when Shadow's lotion-slicked hands came to my ass. He kneaded and massaged each side with a firm thoroughness that wasn't entirely sexually motivated. When he set his mind to a task, he wanted to see it through, whether that was tattooing, doing a project with the kids, or covering his wife from head to toe with lotion.

My fingers curled on the bathroom counter while I fought the urge to press and wiggle for more of his thorough touch. I bit back a moan as Shadow went for more lotion and then knelt behind me.

His rubdown began on my left thigh, just under my ass. My knees felt weak at the first touch, at the pressure of his thumbs running up and down the back of my leg before circling around to the front of my thigh. He was just as thorough on my calf and shin, never missing an inch. By the time he reached my foot and ankle, my heartbeat was pounding harder between my legs than in my chest.

"Lift up your foot, lover." Shadow's breath blew warm air on my hip when he spoke the gentle command.

I did as he said, then my hands curled into fists as he pressed into the arch. His large hands massaged my foot with such care, even getting lotion between my toes and rubbing deeply into my heel.

When Shadow placed my foot back on the floor, it was more than enough for me. "Get up, I want you."

"I have to do your other leg." His tone was full of mirth as he reached for the lotion again but grew rougher when I started to turn around. "Stay where you are. I'm not done."

Growling out my frustration, I slapped my hands on the counter and faced the mirror. My skin was already flushed with the branding heat of his touch, but it wasn't enough. I wanted to *see* red marks from his hands, his mouth. I already ached for his thick cock to spread me apart.

"Better not take too long," I warned him as he diligently massaged lotion into my right leg. "The kids could come back inside any minute."

"They won't," he said confidently. "They're very busy protecting the chicken coop."

I heard a loud crack that echoed throughout the tiled bathroom and then a moment later, heat and stinging pain bloomed over my ass cheek.

"That's for trying to rush me," Shadow said, amusement filling his voice. "Now give me your foot."

The combined sensations of his thorough, gentle care of lotioning my foot and the echoing pain of my ass were a heady mixture. I loved his sweetness and affection and craved his rougher handling. He needed some control right now, so I wouldn't push him too much. I would be good and patient and let him finish his task as he wanted, no matter how tempting it was to just sit on his face.

Shadow stood once he finished my legs, and I swallowed my whine when he reached for the lotion bottle again. I was completely covered at this point. What more did he need to do?

The answer came when he reached forward and grabbed my breasts, lotion-covered palms rolling slickly over the sensitive skin.

"Is this how you wanted me to touch you?" His mouth hovered near my ear, voice lowered to a tantalizing whisper. "To get you so ready and wet for me?"

"Yes," I squeaked on a ragged breath, fighting to keep still as he ordered me.

Shadow's mouth dropped, sucking a hard kiss on the crook of my neck as he squeezed my tender nipples between his fingers. "But you're already wet for me, aren't you?"

"Check and see," I challenged him. *So much for being good.*

Shadow's hands fell to my waist, where he spun me away from the counter to face the bedroom. He did it so quickly, I was barely aware it happened until he swatted me on the ass.

"Get on the bed. Hands and knees."

I hurried to obey. Shadow was never dominant in an angry or mean way, but he was a relentless tease when I became too bratty.

"Scoot back towards me, to the very edge of the bed. Legs wider. Yes, there."

I stopped in the exact position and place he wanted me, the only sound being my ragged breaths of anticipation. If I looked back at him, I knew he'd keep denying me. So I faced forward, looking at the far bedroom door while the tension mounted higher with every passing second.

Shadow touched my lower back after what felt like an eternity, smoothing a palm up my spine before running it lower to the tender flesh of my ass.

"Beautiful," he let out softly before dropping his hand.

I pulled my lip between my teeth, fighting the urge to cry out and beg. He was so close but didn't touch me directly. I *craved* him, goddamnit. Couldn't he see how ready and wet I was?

A soft thud came from behind me, almost making me turn to look. The next thing I felt was Shadow's arms looping through my legs to hold my waist from underneath. The motion pulled my hips back directly onto his waiting mouth.

"Ohh, Shadow..." I whimpered at the pressure and friction of his lips on me, his beard rough on my sensitive flesh.

He moaned out some wordless answer, vibrations thrumming through my pussy as he ate me. His tongue and lips moved constantly, sucking and licking at me like an indulgent meal. I tried to squirm, but he held me in place with a firm grip. One hand slid low down my belly until he cradled my clit between two fingers, but he wouldn't let me rock or squirm to get more friction there. Only his mouth devouring me and his powerful grip directed where I moved.

"Shadow..." I was shaking from the intensity swarming over me from the relentless pleasure running through my system faster than I could breathe.

He let out a long "Mmmm," in reply, and only then loosened his hold enough to let me rock against his face and hands. It was the smallest tilting of my hips that he allowed, but it was enough. It allowed me to grind my clit into his firm fingers, a sigh escaping me at the much-needed pressure.

My rocking motions must have done favorable things to my ass, because his face pulled away and he slapped and grabbed at my flesh with hungry growls. I felt the sharp bite of teeth on my left cheek and gasped, only to hear his soft rumble of laughter and then a light caress and kiss to soothe the pain away.

"What do you want, lover?" Shadow's mouth was so close to my needy pussy, I could still feel the vibrations of his voice and shivered.

"I want you," I whined, still grinding into his solid fingers against my clit. "I need you."

A soft hum of approval left his mouth and then the pressure of a long, tongue-filled kiss between my legs nearly had me full-on collapsing down to the bed.

"You're so close. So beautiful." He was practically whispering to himself, taking long licks, sucks, and kisses of me between each statement. "Delicious. So perfect."

"Shadow," I pleaded, near tears. My fingers curled painfully around the bed sheet, every muscle so wound up and tight and desperate for release.

"Make yourself come. I'm not stopping you."

Oh, that smug bastard. If I could move any more, I'd back up and smother him in this pussy he liked to eat so much.

"I need more," I begged. "I need you to...to..."

"Yes?" He prompted with another playful bite on my ass cheek. "What do you need?"

"I need you to fuck me."

"Before you come? Absolutely not."

A frustrated groan dragged out of my chest and I brought my face and chest down to the bed, my arms already too fatigued to stay upright from all this work.

Shadow chuckled, shifting his hold around me to smooth a hand up my spine. Kisses rained down on my lower back, but I was paying attention to his other hand delving between my legs.

"My beautiful wife," Shadow purred, the weight of his entire hand massaging my clit in earnest now. "You've given me everything."

He really took it seriously when I said a woman's mind was the key to her pleasure. Every word hit me with such emotional intensity that translated instantly to more pleasure in my body. Especially because I knew how much he meant it.

My orgasm swept over me like a tidal wave, amplified by the pleased groan from Shadow as he watched me. His sure, confident hand carried me through the crest and the fall. The kisses and whispered praise on my skin were the cherries on top.

His hand fell away while I sucked in ragged breaths of air, my pulse thick and thrumming in every sensitive point. Then his warm hand returned to my back, and his silky, blunt head spread apart my tender flesh.

"Yes." My spine bowed into a deep arch, hips pressing back to receive him. I looked over my shoulder to see that he'd gotten completely undressed. "Fuck, you're so hot."

The early afternoon light brought a soft, even quality to his skin. No harsh shadows to accentuate his scars or the carved depth of his muscles. He still looked huge and powerfully built, but seeing him in daylight like this illustrated who he was. He hadn't been an assassin, a killer in the shadows, for years. He was my husband and a devoted dad who cherished his family.

Shadow looked up from where we joined, smiling shyly at my astute observation, but there was a roguish smirk in that handsome face too. "You are," he retorted, a blush creeping up his neck.

He pressed forward slowly, making short thrusts to coat himself with my wetness and acclimate me to his size. Even just that had me breathless and babbling, he was so *thick*. So kind and loving, with just enough dominance to make me want to quiver and melt.

Another wave of emotion had me pressing up to kneeling, leaning back until my head touched his shoulder and my back grazed his chest. Immediately, I was taken back to that service center where I'd traveled across the continent to find him. We'd been in a position much like this after he'd accepted that I'd love him no matter what and agreed to return home with me.

Shadow immediately cupped my face with a gentle hand, bringing my gaze to his. "You okay, lover?"

"Yes." I stroked my fingers through his beard, all the joy and elation of having this man's love swirling madly in my chest. "I just love you, that's all."

"I love you." He kissed me so tenderly, thumb stroking over my cheekbone, that it kicked up the swarm of emotions in my chest like a hornet's nest. We stayed like that, kissing and touching each other's faces like our very first time. I didn't even realize a small happy tear had leaked out of my eye until Shadow wiped it away. "Do you want to keep going?" he asked softly. "Or stop?"

I absolutely wanted to keep going, but I heard the backyard slider open and close before I could answer. Footsteps started clamoring up the stairs, too heavy to be either of the kids, but I still grabbed for the bed sheet to cover up.

Shadow and I froze at the sight of Reaper, pausing wide-eyed in the bedroom doorway before a slow, knowing smile pulled across his face. "Am I interrupting anything?"

"No, but," I clutched the sheet to my chest, "are the kids coming inside?"

"Not yet." Reaper wiped his brow, biting back a wider smile. "I've been attacking Chicken Village for the past hour and was gonna grab a quick shower."

He didn't move from the doorway, the unspoken question hanging in the air. Shadow and I quickly glanced at each other, the two of us grinning impishly. Still, Reaper was considerate enough not to be presumptuous.

"I'll just shower downstairs if you want to—"

"Don't be ridiculous," Shadow barked. "Join us."

CHAPTER 7

MARIPOSA

O nce he got the clear invitation, Reaper wasted no time. He kicked off his boots and tore out of the rest of his clothing with a speed that was almost comical. One of these days, I'd have to make the guys do nice, slow stripteases for me.

"You smell sweet, sugar. Did you just have a bath?" Reaper walked on his knees across the bed, and I leaned away from Shadow to greet him with a kiss.

"Yes, and Shadow was nice enough to lotion me up."

Reaper clicked his tongue. "Such a shame to dirty you up again."

"A tragedy," Shadow mused, returning his hands to my hips to press deeper inside me with a small thrust. He'd stayed hard and inside me the whole time we'd been kissing, and now my body stretched deliciously to receive more of him.

Reaper held my face and kissed me in a similar way, but with his signature roughness that sent wild thrills down my spine. He conquered my mouth, tongue pressing inside and lips scraping against mine. The weight of his hand kept me still as Shadow began a slow rocking motion of his hips.

I moaned into Reaper's mouth, relishing in the feeling of being trapped between them. Reaper scooted closer, bringing a deep arch to my back as his punishing kiss never relented. I groped up his thighs, feeling my way to his cock, only to have my hand batted away.

Reaper chuckled at my whine, his grip sliding to my throat as he broke the kiss with an evil smile.

"You get me in your pussy and nowhere else today," he said. "Once Shadow gets you nice and slick for me."

I whimpered through Shadow's thrusts dragging through me with increasing intensity, the way he stretched and filled me taking my breath away to desperate gasps. Reaper's hand on my throat was light enough for me to breathe, but I still couldn't beg and whine at him like I wanted to.

"Want to touch you," I whispered, skimming my fingertips up his leg once more, only to be denied again.

"I know." Reaper dropped another harsh kiss to my mouth, catching my lip in his teeth as he pulled away. "But I want to fuck you hard and make you come on my cock until you fucking can't anymore."

Shadow let out a groan behind me, the force of his hips snapping harder against my ass. He released my waist with one hand to crack his palm against my left cheek, the fire and sting making me cry out.

"Fuck, look at what you're doing to me." Reaper released my throat to grab my hair, angling my head down to see his erection swinging stiffly between our bodies, woefully untouched.

"Can I just taste you a little?" My voice was barely audible over the crashing of Shadow's thrusts against my ass, but Reaper heard me just fine.

He yanked my head back, fist tightening in my hair as he grazed that cocksure smile against my lips. "Taste me all you want, sugar."

I groaned out my frustration but opened my mouth to accept the kiss anyway. If I couldn't suck him, my tongue on his was better than nothing.

I never knew when these games would crop up with him, always just as torturous as they were fun. He never did this when we were alone together. When it was just us, sex was an indulgent, full-body experience, and he held nothing back.

While with the others, he liked to play. Sometimes he controlled the scene, deciding what I would be allowed or denied, but always with the intent of heightening my pleasure in the end.

It was a healthy outlet for him, I realized. The club was no longer as active as it once was, and Reaper had come a long way since loosening up on his controlling tendencies. But the bedroom was where I craved his control and where he excelled at it.

"Fuck," Shadow growled out. His thrusts grew hurried, desperate. He crashed into me at full force, using me to chase his pleasure that was just out of reach. The drag of his heavy cock through me hit every nerve ending and made me squirm in Reaper's steel grip.

"Oh, look at you, loving getting fucked so much." Reaper placed both hands on me now, one in my hair and the other on my throat. He held me still for Shadow to pound into me, the rough clap of our bodies echoing off the walls. At any point, the others could come inside and know exactly what was happening. And that heightened the thrill even more.

"I'm getting so close." Shadow's gruff voice hovered close to my ear, his forehead touching near Reaper's hand on the back of my head. "Fuck, it's just too good."

"Touch her. Make her come before I take her," Reaper ordered. His grip tightened along the pulse points in my neck, lips hovering over mine in a kiss just out of my reach. "Do you love Shadow's cock splitting you apart, sugar?"

"Yes," I choked out in a strangled whisper. Shadow's hand found my clit at Reaper's command and strummed me with practiced expertise. My body wound up tight like a bowstring between them, unable to move or ease how they tormented me from either end. All I could do was feel and take.

I whined louder, desperate and needy as Shadow's fingers walked me toward another orgasm. His cock swelled inside me and amplified that need. The sting of Reaper's grip in my hair and his pressure on my throat swept me up in a perfect, raging storm of pleasure that was nearly painful.

My orgasm hit me like a bolt of lightning, spreading through my nerves like an all-consuming wildfire. Fingers curled into the flesh of my hips and heat flooded my core. Shadow moaned out his orgasm, the sound deep and animal-like over the blood pounding in my ears.

Pressure released on my neck and the room spun, the pulses of my orgasm suddenly squeezing around nothing. Then just as quickly, a thick cock pressed into me, driving deep and taking me with long, aggressive thrusts with no preamble.

Reaper, I realized in the dizzying haze of my orgasm. He was behind me now, looking down at where he was fucking me like he promised he would. His arms were tight and corded from where he gripped me roughly. His abs flexed with each rough thrust against my ass, and his breaths dragged raggedly out of his chest.

He barely gave me any chance to recover, and I felt another orgasm building. My frayed nerve endings had no choice but to respond to the rough, delicious assault of him.

A caress on my cheek brought my attention forward. Shadow. He kneeled on the bed in front of me, his softening cock glossy with my wetness. I rested my head against his hip, so weak and wobbly as Reaper fucked me into oblivion.

"That's it. Lean on me, lover," Shadow purred with a gentle stroke over my hair. "Is it too much?"

Reaper slowed his thrusts just a fraction at the question, waiting for my response. He'd make it intense, maybe even painful. But he'd never give me more than I could handle.

"No...no, it's just...ohh, fuck!"

Another orgasm rippled out of me, much to Reaper's delight. He swatted my ass, grunted out some curses, and kept up his brutal pace. He overloaded my senses in the best ways, and I found myself grabbing and clawing at Shadow through my release.

"Yes, use me, lover." Shadow stroked my neck with light, reverent touches. The one thing he would never do was grab my throat. "Scratch me, bite me. Take what you need to let it out."

Reaper drove into me even harder at that, as if taking the offer as a challenge. I looked at him over my shoulder while clinging to Shadow's waist like a lifeline. Reaper smirked back at me before lifting a hand to smack down on my ass again. He wanted to drive me into a frenzy of orgasms and practically maul Shadow in the process.

And I was helpless to do anything but take it, holding on to Shadow with nails and teeth while I came apart.

My pleasure rose and fell in intensity, but it never felt like each orgasm actually began and ended. They rolled into each other like waves crashing on a beach as Reaper crashed into me. I groaned, gasped, and screamed, clawing at the solid wall of Shadow and making his skin bright red. He hissed and grunted but loved the pain, especially when I was rough with him during an orgasm. I could never hurt him seriously, so I didn't hold back as another bolt of pleasure stabbed through my clit like lightning. My mouth latched onto his hip bone, teeth clamping down as his body muffled my scream.

"Oh fuck, I love it when you come this hard." Shadow's grip was loose in my hair, just keeping the strands out of my face.

"Can't take much more," I panted, leaning my forehead on his lower stomach.

"Oh, you've got at least one more in you," Reaper taunted, his breath tight. He was rock-solid and expanding inside me, his forceful rhythm stuttering as he neared his limit.

Shadow stroked down my side, his fingers grazing the edge of my breast, and I shivered at the contact.

"She's really sensitive everywhere." Shadow sounded pleased, continuing a featherlight touch down to my waist and across my back. "So fucking beautiful."

"Keep touching her like that." Reaper's voice was bright with a new idea, his rough thrusts slowing down to deep, languid strokes.

My body was abuzz with the change in sensations, the gentle strokes almost more intense than the spanks and hard fucking. Shadow's touch continued up my back, bringing on another body-wracking shiver when he reached the nape of my neck. He then dragged his fingers down on either side, reaching underneath me for my nipples.

I cried out when he rolled them between his fingers, the peaks so taut and sensitive it was nearly painful. "No, don't stop," I begged when he paused.

Shadow's pleased rumble vibrated over me, eliciting another shiver, like he'd touched me with another limb. "Can you come for us one more time, lover?"

"I...I think..." I was in some hazy place between feeling numb and overly sensitive. My heartbeat wouldn't slow down, and I was exhausted.

Shadow pinched down harder. At the same time, Reaper delivered a smack to the other side of my ass on unmarked skin. The sharp sensations at both points brought my focus back, gave me something new to chase amidst the constant buzz in my body.

"Oh, fuck yeah, that's it." Reaper's thrusts stopped altogether as I rocked back and forth on his length, using him to ride the high I needed. "Fuck me, sugar."

"Spank me again," I begged.

He did so, rubbing the tender flesh in between each hard smack of his palm. My orgasm was finally building, growing like a fire as I kept pressing back and riding him desperately. Shadow kept my nipples clasped between his fingers, holding firm and steady as I came apart.

I lost count of how many times Reaper spanked my ass, but when I finally shattered, he was there with me. I sank into the mattress, well and truly spent by the shockwaves rolling over me. Reaper grabbed my hips for his final surge forward, shuddering and cursing as he spilled his release. His hands slapped to the bed on either side of me, keeping himself from collapsing onto my back.

"Still want a shower?" I asked once I had enough breath in my lungs.

He huffed out a laugh, lowering to ghost kisses along my back. "Take one with me."

I looked up at Shadow. "Sorry, you might have to rub me down again."

"Oh no." He grinned and swept hair out of my face. "What a shame."

CHAPTER 8

SHADOW

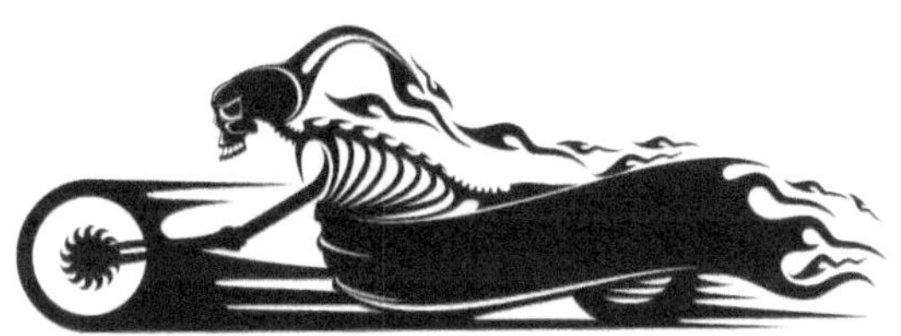

I jolted upright in bed, my heart beating mercilessly at my sternum and my skin covered in a cold sweat.

Shit, that was a bad one. The worst I've had in a while.

I sought to ground myself and catch my breath while the nightmare ebbed away. The room was dark, but I saw Mari clearly, wrapped up in one of the others as they slept. I tipped my head back and found the headboard of our bed, curled my fingers to feel the sheets underneath me.

I'm home. I'm okay.

My throat was as parched as a bone, and I itched for some light and open space. Just to calm my senses so I could go back to sleep.

I swung my feet to the floor and found a pair of sweatpants to put on, then moved silently out of our bedroom and down the stairs. Once in the kitchen, I flicked on the light and filled a big glass of water from the tap. I drank it and filled it three times before pausing to take a breath.

Bracing my hands on the edge of the sink, I stepped back and tried to assess the sudden nightmare without spiraling into anxiety.

Had I been stressed lately? No, not really. My one shitty client was gone. The tattoo shop was always busy, but I'd been able to hand more work off to my apprentice. The kids seemed happy with school and all of their activities. Rori had her tantrums, but that was normal. Everything between Mari, me, and the guys was fine.

Was it the anniversary of something? Going to prison, getting out of prison, getting captured by the Sha, or confronting my mother's ghost?

I couldn't find something concrete to pinpoint as the reason for my first nightmare in almost a year. Dr. Ellis said they would show up randomly sometimes, but there was usually some underlying cause.

"Daddy?"

I whipped around to see a sleepy, bedheaded Rori blinking at me just outside of the kitchen. She had on her favorite llama-print pajama set and was already outgrowing it, hands and feet sticking far out of the sleeves.

"Hey, sweetheart." I straightened, stepping away from the sink. "What are you doing up?"

"Um." She rubbed her eyes and avoided the question, which meant she was probably reading picture books or playing after we said lights out. "Did the monsters try to get you, Daddy?"

I smiled at her. Gunner scared the kids with stories of monsters under the bed on Halloween, but she had no idea how real monsters could be.

"They tried but they couldn't get me." I lowered to a crouch, holding my arm out to her. "Come here."

Rori shuffled over and leaned heavily on me from how tired she was. I groaned as I lifted her up, holding her against my side as I came to standing.

When did I become a dad to five-year-olds? It seemed like we had just brought the twins home from the hospital. Rori and her brother used to be shorter than my forearm, their heads fitting comfortably in my palm with room to spare. I refused to carry them upstairs for weeks, terrified that I'd drop one of our infants.

Now my daughter was a hefty weight on my hip, her legs dangling past my waist, and squirmier than Freyja when she didn't want to be held anymore.

I tickled one of Rori's feet as I turned back to the kitchen, earning a few giggles and light kicks on my ribs. "Do you want some milk, Ror-meister?"

She nodded, settling down with her head on my shoulder. *"Lechita, por favor."*

"Very good." I kissed her forehead, pleasantly surprised. "You'll have to tell Papi Jandro the new words you know."

I opened the fridge, grabbed the milk and her sippy cup, poured the milk and put the lid on, all using my left hand. I thought being ambidextrous came in handy as an assassin, but I found it much more useful in parenting.

"Careful now." I handed Rori her drink. "Don't spill."

Rori took her cup in both hands, and I refilled my water from the sink before heading to the couch to sit. We were *mostly* quiet for a few moments, the only sound being Rory's noisy drinking as she nestled into my side.

"Daddy?" she piped up.

"Yes, my dearest daughter." I curled one finger through a lock of her hair.

"Did the monster give you all your owies too?"

I froze. My mind came to a screeching halt, body tensing up so abruptly that Rori noticed it immediately. She shifted around, wearing a puzzled expression as she tried to get a better look at my face.

I knew our kids were smart, perceptive. But, fuck me, I was not ready to talk about this. When it came to the kids, I didn't know if I ever would be. I had been younger than them when the Sisterhood first started cutting me.

Becoming a dad for the first time, and seeing firsthand how fragile and innocent children were, made me want them to never experience even a mere sliver of the suffering I had endured.

Rori once fell from a play structure and cut her chin on the pavement. There was so much blood, and I panicked. I rushed her directly to Mari at the hospital, where I proceeded to spiral and freak out some more. I told Mari I couldn't do it. I couldn't be a father, I let my child *get hurt*. Rori had screamed and cried bloody murder the whole way over because I failed to protect her.

Mari then calmly explained that it wasn't my fault. Kids fell all the time and sometimes got hurt. It was normal. Their bodies were constantly growing, and it was how they learned their limits. Rori was fine after a few small stitches and a lollipop. As fragile as they were, children were also resilient.

I should have known. Somehow I survived to adulthood, after all.

While I learned to be less extreme in my reactions, it didn't make answering my daughter's question any easier. I brushed my fingers through Rori's hair, still trying to find the right words.

"No monster is ever going to hurt you." A flash of anger burned through me and I found myself growling. If that fucking cult got within a mile of my children, no force on earth or among the gods would stop me from annihilating them.

"Sometimes monsters look like nice people," I went on. "Sometimes they'll pretend to be your friend. So if anyone makes you sad or scared, or they just give you a weird feeling in your tummy," I poked Rori's belly for effect, "you don't have to be friends with them, okay? That goes for now and when you're a grown-up. Anyone at all who makes you feel bad."

"Okay, Dad," she said quietly, her eyelids drooping.

I huffed out a soft laugh and leaned down to plant a kiss in her hair. "Finish your milk, then let's go back to bed."

Once she drained her cup, I returned our dishes to the kitchen and went to tuck her in.

"Your dads will protect you from monsters," I said, bringing her blanket under her chin. "Your mom too, she's fought plenty of them. You can always come to us, Ror-meister."

Rori's eyes blinked heavily, moments away from sleep. "Daren said he would watch over me too."

"Yeah, your brother is going to be big and strong one day. Just like your dads, huh?" I kissed her forehead and started to get up from her bedside.

"No...I mean, uncle Daren..."

My heart jumped into my throat as I stared down at her, stunned. "What did you say?"

But Rori had already fallen asleep.

CHAPTER 9

REAPER

"There's the trailhead." Jandro pointed through the windshield.

"'Kay. Let me find a place to park."

"Bro, you can stop literally anywhere. There's no one around." Jandro turned in the passenger seat to grin at the kids behind us. "We've got the canyon to ourselves, guys! Are you excited?"

"Yes! Can I get out?" Rori kicked in her carseat, fumbling at her seatbelt.

"Rori, no," I told her. "Wait 'til I stop the car, you know the rules."

She stilled with a pout while Daren made signs with his hands.

"English or Spanish, son. I'm happy you're learning ASL, but we don't know what you're saying," Jandro said.

"I said, I hope we see a coyote."

Daren's hands moved swiftly as he connected the words. Every day he grew more confident with signing, and he really seemed taken with it since meeting his new friend, Lily. Shadow had even been practicing with him a bit. The big guy seemed thrilled to find something they could bond over.

"No coyotes, probably." I glanced at Daren in the rearview mirror, still signing to himself. "They'll be sleeping now and wake up to hunt when it starts getting dark."

I pulled over at the mouth of the canyon, finding a sliver of shade to park under. This place was one of the smaller canyons in the area. It didn't even have a name as far as I was aware, but it was pretty, scenic, and an easy hike. A perfect outing for a couple of squirrelly five-year-olds.

Mari, Shadow, and Gunner all had work or something else going on, so Jandro and I elected to take the kids out. It would be good for Hades too, who was currently seated between the two kids. His head was already swiveling from side-to-side, ever watchful for any threats to his tiny humans.

Hades, the god, hadn't spoken to me again since that night at the party eight years ago. But I wasn't entirely convinced he'd left this dog's body completely.

"Alright, we're here. Aurora May, don't run off," I warned, opening my door.

"I just want to seeee—"

"Come here, let me get your sunscreen and your hat on so you don't burn. Do you need to use the bathroom?"

"No. Can I pick a flower for Mommy?"

"In a second, sugar cube."

Jandro got Daren situated while I handled Rori. Hades sniffed around our perimeter as we got the kids ready, then let out a soft bark of approval and sat when he was satisfied.

I put a dog treat in Rori's hand. "Go give that to Hades and we can start exploring."

"Papi, can I sit on your shoulders?" Daren asked Jandro. "I want a better view."

"Alright, just for a little bit." Jandro picked him up and seated him behind his neck, Daren's legs draping down over his chest. "You're gonna turn your old dad into a hunchback."

"You already are," I joked, following after Rori and Hades who had already ventured into the canyon. "Rori, stay close. Don't go off the trail."

"I know, *Dad.*" Her tone was snotty, like she was already fifteen instead of five. *Ah, kids.*

"You remember what happened last time?" I couldn't resist teasing her.

"Yes, I remember!" She turned around and shot me a dirty look.

I made a similar face back at her until she laughed, then pulled her into a quick hug against my leg. "I love you, Ror. It's always an adventure with you."

On the last hike we went on, Rori went off the trail to get a closer look at a jackrabbit. She ended up walking over a young cactus plant, and Mari spent the better part of a night pulling the spines out of her feet.

The risk wasn't as high here, with the canyon being fairly narrow and mostly shaded. It felt much cooler as we started walking through, the sandstone walls curving as if shaped by water on either side of us. People liked coming here because of the paintings on the canyon walls, left by indigenous cultures thousands of years ago.

I studied the pale, faded paintings as I walked through. Naturally, I couldn't interpret them like a scholar could, but even my untrained eye could make out figures, animals, and symbols.

That circle hovering above all the figures had to be the sun or moon, clearly sacred to people who depended on the land to survive. It got me wondering if any of *our* gods had reached these people in some way, or some version of them. Did they personify the sun, death, love, and healing? Did a god of the Underworld choose someone to carry out their commands like Hades had with me?

"Look, it's Horus!" Daren pointed up at the thin stripe of sky above us where several birds with impressive wingspans soared with ease.

"Ah, not quite." Jandro peered up, squinting at the sky. "Horus is a lot smaller. Those guys are big. I'm pretty sure they're turkey vultures."

"What's that?" Daren held on to Jandro's face as he leaned back to get an even better look at the sky.

"They're scavengers, so they look for food that's already dead." Jandro turned his head and took a playful bite of Daren's leg. When our son shrieked and shook out of his grasp, Jandro exaggerated a face of disgust. "Ugh, nope. This boy's still very much alive."

Darren cackled with laughter, the bright sound echoing off the canyon walls, until Jandro lifted him off his shoulders and set him on the ground. "Go walk with your sister, my neck needs a break."

Jandro and I walked together, keeping an eye on the twins and Hades a few feet ahead of us. Rori had already discarded her hat, and her golden curls bounced with every step.

"Does it feel real yet?" Jandro knew what I meant. I asked him all the time during moments like this.

"Oh yeah." He grinned at me, rubbing the back of his neck. "Right now, it sure does. But that," he nodded ahead to the kids carefully tracing one of the wall paintings with their fingers, talking softly to each other, "seeing them explore, learn, and thrive with *us* guiding them?" His hand dropped, eyes locked with wonder on our two children. "I still can't believe it sometimes."

I patted at my pockets, searching for the phone I rarely turned on because it barely worked half the time. A few local engineers had gotten some cell towers working last year, although reliable phone calls were still a long way off. But the phone had a camera, which was the only way I really used the piece of shit.

"Aw, Mari will love that," Jandro breathed as I held the phone up.

The kids stood in a patch of sunlight, framed by bright orange poppy flowers on either side of them. Their backs were to us—Rori's hair aglow like a halo and Daren's dark and glossy like raven feathers. Their hands were stretched out in front them, still running over the ancient wall paintings with a quiet, almost reverent curiosity.

I snapped pictures of them until Hades blocked my view. Since he didn't tell me who to kill anymore, his new favorite pastime was getting into every photo of the kids he possibly could.

The kids moved on, walking through the canyon while Hades sniffed ahead and Jandro and I trailed after.

"How you sleeping lately?" Jandro lowered his voice so only I could hear him.

"Fine." My knee jerk, default answer.

"Just fine?"

I swallowed. After everything he and I had been through, and now that we were raising a family together, he deserved more than a dismissive answer. Old habits die hard. Even all these years later, I was still working on the whole opening-up-emotionally thing.

"Yeah, I mean pretty good for the most part. The nightmares don't come around that much anymore, once every few months or so."

"Your doctor says that's normal?"

"There is no normal, really. Everyone processes shit differently. But it's better than a couple times a week like it was however long ago."

"Yeah, that's true. I just wanted to check on you." He knocked his shoulder into mine. "In case you needed anything."

Always such a caretaker. It was why Jandro took to being a dad so naturally.

"I'm good, dude," I assured him. "Really. I can actually say that without any bullshit now."

"That's a first," he snorted, then shot me a good-natured smile. "I'm glad to hear it." The kids moved on, wandering deeper into the canyon with Hades while we followed a few paces behind them. "It's crazy how uneasy we feel about life being so much simpler, isn't it?" Jandro mused.

"Yeah. Like this is temporary and we're waiting for the other shoe to drop."

My fingers twitched at my side, the cigarette craving hitting me hard. It always did when I thought of our past life, all the stress and fear we were under. I never smoked around the kids, only indulging when they stayed with grandparents for a few days so we could have our adult time.

"Eight years is hardly temporary," Jandro retorted.

I rolled my eyes toward him. "Everything is temporary. I just hope this peaceful period lasts through their lifetimes." I nodded my head at the twins. "Or if it doesn't, I hope that whatever comes next doesn't touch them."

Jandro's eyes narrowed, his hand coming up next to his ear. "You hear that, Reap?"

"Yeah, yeah, it's the sound of me being a sap. You're hilarious, man, but that one's getting old."

"No, I'm serious. You don't hear that hissing?"

I paused, cocking my head to listen. There was a breeze through the canyon, plus the sounds of insects echoing and distorting through the canyon walls.

"It's just the wind, dude. I don't—"

Hades growled, low and full of warning. I hadn't heard him make that sound in years. Fast and silent as a shadow, he darted in front of the children who were none the wiser.

"Hades, move your big butt." Rori pushed on his flank to get him out of her way, but he remained stiff, blocking her path with the broad side of his body.

"Rori, stop."

She turned to look at me, dismay on her face. "But why? I want to keep walking."

"Hades senses danger, sweetie. Come back to us, both of you."

Daren grabbed her hand and started to pull her back when I heard it. Not a hissing sound like Jandro initially thought, but a rattling.

"Fuck. Guys, freeze! Don't move." Jandro and I both put our palms out. The kids stopped in place, their eyes widening in fear.

"Move up and get them behind us," I said under my breath.

"You got it, Pres." Jandro put on a smile, brightening his voice. "Hey, guys, it's okay. Just stay still and let your dads come to you. You're doing great."

The rattling grew louder as we approached. I spotted movement just beyond Hades' head and fuck, that snake looked big and close. If the dog hadn't jumped in front of the kids, they might have stepped right on it.

Hades was stiff as a board, hackles raised and low growl constant in his throat. The rattlesnake was giving a warning, and so was he—touch my tiny humans and you're a dead snake.

"Easy, Hades. That's a good boy." Jandro and I made our way closer slowly, careful not to make any sudden movements and provoke the snake to become any more aggressive.

"Dad, I'm scared." Rori's lip wobbled, her eyes darting around fearfully until Daren pulled her into a hug, placing her head on his shoulder so she wouldn't look at the snake.

"You're okay, *mijita*." Jandro forced calm into his voice, but I could hear how tense he was. "Just hold on to your brother, he's got you."

We reached the kids in one more step, then with an exchanged look and a nod, directed them behind us. Air whooshed out of my lungs with relief. I didn't even realize how tense I'd been.

Jandro and I kept our eyes forward, and one hand reached behind us to make sure our children stayed near.

"Start walking backwards," I instructed. "Slow."

Once we were a good twenty feet or so away from the snake, all four of us were able to relax.

Jandro swept Rori up into his arms, her expression still shaken as he hugged her tightly and planted kisses on her face. "Hey, you did great." He smiled exuberantly at her. "You did exactly as we said, even though you were scared. You're so brave."

With relief filling my chest, I picked up Daren, who only made a small grunt of protest, but otherwise leaned into me and hugged around my neck.

"You're a hero, kid," I told him. "That was a great thing you did, making your sister look away. It kept her calm, which was exactly what we needed."

Daren shrugged like it was no big thing, but I saw his face brighten at being called a hero. "I just didn't want her to get more scared."

It floored me how much he was exactly like his namesake, my brother. When my siblings and I were kids, I was always the asshole who scared Noelle and did stuff to make her cry. She'd run to Daren, who hugged her until she was calm. Likewise, as we got older, and his seizures got worse, Noelle always took care of him.

"You did all that and more." I kissed my Daren's temple. "I love you, son."

"Love you, Dad," he muttered, promptly wiping at where I kissed him. "Can you put me down now?"

"Alright," I groaned, bending to set his feet on the ground.

I looked over at Jandro who was gently rocking a now very tired-looking Rori. He caught my eye and smirked in my direction. "Enough adventure for one day, you think?"

"I'd say so." I ruffled Daren's hair. "You want to go Tess and Drea's for a cupcake?"

"Cupcake!" That woke Rori right up.

"Just what we need, kids high on cupcakes," Jandro chuckled, heading toward the car. "Better call the dog back, I think he's still in a staring contest with that snake." "Go on ahead." I patted Daren's back to follow them, then re-entered the canyon with a long whistle. "Hades! Come on back, mutt." He was in a darker area of the canyon and harder to see at this distance with his black fur, but when his head turned at the sound of my voice, I swore I saw...

"Hades?" I squinted across the distance, the hairs on my arms standing straight up. It couldn't be, but I thought for a second those weren't dog eyes looking back at me. They looked almost human and eerily intelligent.

"Hades." I somehow broke out of my stupor and patted my thigh. "Come here, boy."

The dog broke eye contact as he trotted over to me, tongue lolling out and his posture finally relaxed. I lowered to a crouch, scratching his ears and neck as I searched those big, dark eyes for that intelligence again. But he was all dog now, happy and smiling.

"Thank you for protecting my children," I said, then waited, searching his face for any kind of non-doglike response.

My heart stopped when those eyes met mine again, the ancient wisdom in them unmistakable.

It is not yet their time.

Just as quickly as it happened, it passed. Hades' eyes returned to wide and puppylike as he leaned forward to lick my face.

CHAPTER 10

JANDRO

"Aurora May Wilder!" I pointed my wrench across the yard. "This is the last time I'm telling you. Leave those chickens alone."

My daughter put on a big show of stomping away from the chicken coop with a pout, arms crossed over her chest. But my dad-senses knew she'd be meandering back that way once she thought I wasn't looking.

I'd been telling her all afternoon to leave them be. Some new chicks had just hatched and she wanted to pet and hold them, but getting close to the coop aggravated our younger rooster, Trombone. He had already rushed at Rori a few times, crowing and flapping aggressively. If she kept pushing his buttons, she was going to get pecked or cut with a spur.

And after I'd already yelled at her fifty times to stay away, maybe it was a lesson she needed to learn the hard way.

"Jesus, these kids," I muttered, returning my attention to the motor-cycle parts strewn out in front of me.

At my side, Larkan laughed as he stacked a set of piston rings. "I take it she's not getting a llama for her birthday?"

"Not in a million years," I huffed. "She needs to grow up, get rich, and get *me* a llama for my birthday."

"You can't have just *one* llama," Larkan's eight-year-old, Carter, chimed in matter-of-factly. "They're herd animals, so you need at least three."

"Then it's definitely not happening." I set my wrench down and wiped my hands on a rag, pointedly ignoring Rori as I gazed across the yard.

Noelle and Reaper were talking over whiskeys near the edge of the deck. Beyond them was a play fort we'd built a couple years ago. It had a slide, a small rock-climbing wall, and two solid wooden ladders to get up to the main area. Daren and his youngest cousin, Larkan Jr., who we all called Larkie, were horsing around in the fort, playing pirates or some such.

Mari, Shadow, and Gunner had gone off to ride for the day, which likely meant they went to the hot spring for skinny dipping, threesomes, and a picnic. Lucky bastards.

Not that I didn't love spending time at home with the kids and other family. Just with Rori testing my patience today, it would have been nice to have some extra backup. Rori didn't test her mother or Shadow like she did me.

"What about goats?" Larkan and Carter were still on the subject of adding animals to our little farm.

"Mari does want a couple of goats," I admitted. "She wants a regular supply of goat cheese, and to watch them headbutt us, I'm sure." I lowered my head and bumped it softly into Carter while making a *bahhh* sound.

"Have you seen those goats that fall over when they get scared?" My nephew started giggling uncontrollably.

"That does *not* sound like an evolutionary advantage," I remarked. It was funny to think about, though.

Larkan sat back, his eyes lighting up. "You should think about getting some ducks too. Duck eggs are great, man."

"Do not put more animal ideas into my children's heads, please." I shook my wrench at him. "You're lucky Mari isn't here to endorse your suggestions."

"Ah, just you wait. Pretty soon it'll be like," Larkan started drumming a beat on the table, his grin too smug and satisfied as he sang, "*Old McJandro had a farm, E-I-E-I-O.*"

"Shut your mouth." I waved my wrench more menacingly at him. "Before I smack you."

He knew it was an empty threat and carried on making the animal noises while Carter's laughter rang across the yard. Reaper and Noelle even looked our way to see what the ruckus was about just as a high-pitched scream hit my eardrums.

I looked in the direction the sound came from and couldn't stop the single peal of laughter before slapping a hand over my own mouth. Rori was running as fast as she could go, shock and terror on her face, with Trombone the rooster right on her heels.

She ran straight toward Reaper, who scooped her up and shooed the rooster away with his foot.

"Knew this was gonna happen," I groaned, getting up from the table and heading their way to assess the damage.

Rori sobbed on Reaper's shoulder and clung to his neck, her face bright red as he rocked and shushed her. He rubbed her back and glared at me over her shoulder, a look that Trombone put on his face often. Reaper hated that rooster, and I knew he'd tear into me once the kids were in bed.

"Hey *mijita*, let's see." I went to look at the red mark on her leg, which thankfully wasn't bleeding, and was promptly swatted away by a tiny hand.

"No!" Rori had twisted in Reaper's arms, mean-mugging me as hard as a five-year-old could, still crying and sniffling.

"*Mami*," I gentled my voice. "I'm trying to make sure you're okay."

"No!" she repeated. "You *laughed* at me!"

It felt like someone had rammed a Rori-sized fist through my chest. Fuck, she'd heard that? Seen it?

"Rori, I..." There was no excuse, and I wasn't about to lie, so my words trailed off, speechless.

She turned back around to cling tighter to Reaper, crying into his shoulder while he kept looking at me with that heavy stare.

"Shhh, you're okay, sugar cube." He finally broke his glare to kiss her and soothe her. "Let's get you inside and clean your owies. That rooster's not gonna hurt you again." He shot another pointed look at me before turning to enter the house.

I just stood looking after them, feeling stunned, defeated, and guilty. A pat on my shoulder roused me from my stupor, and it was Noelle at my side, giving me a sympathetic look.

"Don't feel so bad, papa." She patted my shoulder again. "She'll forgive you."

"Will she, though?" I scratched a hand over my head. "Fuck, I didn't even mean to laugh, I just..."

"Honestly, it was funny." Noelle lowered her voice to a conspiratory whisper. "Just, better to laugh in hindsight than right when it's happening. Even *she* will think it's funny one day."

"I doubt that," I groaned, pinching my nose bridge.

"Sure she will. Larkie tells people all the time about how he missed the potty a couple years ago. He thinks it's hilarious."

"That's 'cause your *boys* are foul." I grinned down at her. "Rori is a lady."

Noelle shoved playfully at my shoulder. "Go apologize to your daughter."

Yeah, that was the least of what I needed to do. Trombone would probably need to find a new home after this too.

I went inside to find Rori sitting on the kitchen counter, sniffling quietly as Reaper cleaned the welts on her legs with rubbing alcohol.

"How bad is it?" I asked.

He gave me a short glance over his shoulder. "Not bad. She just got pecked a couple times." He gathered up the cotton pads and dumped them in the trash with more force than necessary. "But I want that rooster gone. Tonight."

"Yeah. Yeah, of course. I'll go around to the neighbors in a sec and see if they want him. If not, I'll take care of it." With a hard swallow I looked past him to Rori, who was calmer but still sniffling and red-faced. "Are you feeling better, *mijita?*"

She gave a small nod. "A little."

"Good, I'm glad. I never want to see you scared or hurt." I edged closer to her, still giving her plenty of space. "I'm sorry I laughed, that was wrong. Sometimes even dads mess up and do the wrong thing."

She sniffed again. "I'm still mad at you."

"That's okay. I'm mad at me too. I wish I didn't do that." My hands flexed at my sides, wishing to give my daughter a hug, but it was more important right then to respect her space. "And it's not gonna happen again."

Just as my luck would have it, the rumble of bikes coming up the driveway announced Mari and the others coming home. Great, now I'd have to explain all this to *Shadow*, who Rori had thoroughly wrapped around her finger.

Predictably, she started sniffling louder once the door opened and her other parents spilled into the house. Mari and Gunner had their arms and fingers linked, laughing about something together. Shadow took one look at Rori and slid past them, his face hardening.

Aw, hell.

"What happened?" he demanded.

Rori hopped off the counter and ran to him, letting him scoop her up with one powerful arm and hold her protectively against his chest. That got Mari and Gunner's attention, untangling from each other and frowning at our girl's red, tear-soaked face.

"Oh sweetheart, are you okay?" Mari cooed, stroking her hair out of her eyes.

"Trombone bit me," Rori mumbled.

Shadow's gaze hit me like a cannonball to the chest, and I brought my hands up defensively. "We were all outside! I'd been telling her not to go near him all day."

"And Papi laughed at me," Rori went on.

"You *what?!*" Shadow looked more ready to murder me in that moment than during any of his sleepwalking episodes. If he wasn't holding Rori, I'm sure he would have decked me.

"Okay, let's all calm down." Mari put a hand on Shadow's shoulder and held her other arm out to Rori. "Want to wrap up in your llama blanket and relax? We can read a story."

Our daughter nodded slowly and allowed Shadow to pass her over. Once Mari took hold of her, she carried Rori toward her bedroom and shot us a look that said, *Figure this out amongst yourselves.*

"Did you seriously—" Shadow started at me again once they were gone, but Reaper stepped between us with his hand raised.

"Look, she's not badly hurt, which is the important thing. But she was really scared for a moment and that reaction," he gave me a disapproving look, "probably didn't make her feel any safer."

"I know, I know. I fucked up." My hand came to my forehead, rubbing where a headache started to build. "That's probably what's hurting her most and, believe me, I'm gutted to have done that. I'll make it up to her."

"You better," Shadow snarled.

"Probably gonna have to get her that llama after all," Gunner chimed in oh-so-helpfully.

"Great," I grumbled. "Fucking great."

"Seriously, though. She's been provoking the chickens despite you telling her not to, right?" Gunner came forward and clapped a supportive hand on my shoulder. "Now she knows the consequences, and she'll listen better next time."

"I guess, if she doesn't fucking hate me forever."

"She won't, man. And let's be honest." He brought his thumb and forefinger close together. "It was probably a *little* bit funny, right?"

"What the fuck are you saying?" Shadow growled. "Her being scared isn't funny."

Gunner whirled around to face him. "Dude, you laughed your ass off when that same rooster chased Mari all throughout the house when he got inside!"

Shadow leveled him with an incredulous look. "Yes, *Mari*. Who can handle one dumb fucking rooster. Rori is *five*."

"If she was in any *real* danger, of course I wouldn't have laughed, bro," I told him. "I'd put myself between her and whatever the threat was, like any of us would. But yeah, like Gunner said, she kind of had this coming."

"Sure, she did," Reaper cut in. "But laughing was the wrong response at the wrong time."

"I'll own up to that, definitely," I said. "And I'm getting rid of the rooster, so she doesn't continue to be afraid of him," I added with a sigh. "He's a nuisance, anyway. Foghorn's so chilled out now that he's an old man."

"I hate both of those birds, but Foghorn is easily my favorite of the two." Reaper opened a cabinet in search of more whiskey, the matter apparently settled. "If one of the new chicks happens to be male, maybe it'll bond with Rori and not act like a shithead towards her."

"Yeah, that's true." I gestured at the drinks he began pouring, beyond ready for one myself. "*Dámelo*."

"Speaking of." Gunner nudged Shadow with a chuckle. "Did you know Trombone took a shit in Mari's hair that one time?"

Shadow, who had been in the middle of taking a drink, coughed and wheezed as he doubled over the counter. "No fucking way."

"I'm serious, I had to help her wash it out. Our battle-medic wife, who's seen buckets of blood and guts and shit, was like, *retching* because of a little rooster shit in her hair."

"Poor thing." Shadow's lip twitched in amusement.

"She was so grossed out, it was hilarious." Gunner raised his index finger in the air. "But my point is, that bird is a literal shithead, and he's better off on a dinner plate."

"Not saying I disagree, but I'm going to see if anyone wants him alive first." I set my empty whiskey glass down and slid it across the counter to Reaper. "Linda down the street mentioned wanting a rooster, so I'll head over there now."

"What's wrong with her husband's cock?" Gunner's face lit up with the question like he'd been waiting for the perfect time to say it.

"Jesus, shut up," Reaper grumbled.

"Aw fuck off, you're no fun." Gunner turned away, looking out to the yard. "What are the boys playing?"

"Pirates, last I checked."

"Ooh, I want to be the sea monster!"

"Not the pretty mermaid?" Shadow cracked.

Gunner headed outside, pointing both middle fingers back at us until he grabbed the side of the playhouse with a roar.

A sense of relief fell over me as the others went to join him. It had been a tense few moments, but the kids were safe. We were all still here. Trading a rooster for a llama was miles better than a bloody shootout.

I'd take days like this over potentially losing any of them in a heartbeat.

CHAPTER 11

GUNNER

I came home like any other day, whistling a cheerful tune as I closed
the front door behind me. The last thing I expected was a very
naked Jandro *leaping* down the stairs toward me.

"Dude, what—"

He clapped a hand over my mouth, the other hand holding a finger
to his lips. I noticed he was panting slightly, the skin on his palm felt
warm, and his junk swung stiffly at half-mast.

It's not like I was offended by his nudity. Obviously we all shared a
wife and a bedroom. Over the years, us guys had become comfortable to
the point where catching each other in various states of undress no
longer fazed us.

Still, we weren't exactly in the habit of greeting each other at the
front door in our birthday suits.

"Don't say a word," Jandro whispered, glancing over his shoulder
toward the bedroom. "I don't think she heard you. But we were just
talking about this, and she wants to play a guessing game. You in?"

At my confused expression, he carefully lifted his palm from my
mouth. "It's better if you just see her. But remember, not a word. Not
even a sound."

I nodded and made the *okay* sign with my hand. Clearly, it was some kind of bedroom game with Mari. She had to be blindfolded or something and that just got my pulse racing with anticipation.

Jandro pressed his finger to his lips once more, and I nodded eagerly while making a shooing motion toward the stairs. He headed that way and I followed right on his heels, just as excited as the kids on Christmas morning.

A scent hit me halfway up the stairs—citrusy, fresh, and warm. My eager smile grew when I realized it was one of those candles Mari loved, the one she said smelled like me.

Jandro and I reached the bedroom and the sight before me was...*holy fuck*. I couldn't have made a sound if I tried, I was that blown away.

Candles flickered on the nightstands, and through the slats of the headboard, Mari's wrists were tied with a soft length of rope. My gaze trailed lower, insistent on not missing any detail. Her arms extended above her were relaxed, a soft bend in her elbows. Mari's dark hair spilled out on the pillows propping up her head and neck for comfort. A black sleep mask covered her eyes, contrasting with the pink flush in her cheeks and lips.

Mari's head rolled from side to side at the sound of our footsteps, her arms tugging lightly at her restraints as her body shifted.

"Jandro? Who came home?" she asked in a tight, breathless voice.

Oh fuck me, did he leave her hanging when he came downstairs? I wanted to slide a glance at him but couldn't take my eyes off of her.

"You're gonna have to guess." Jandro rounded the bed, moving toys and bottles of massage oil out of the way so he could lie next to her. "Isn't that what you wanted?"

Mari's torso stretched out long on the bed, arched with every beautiful, mouthwatering curve on display. Her skin was dewy and flushed, red marks around her waist and breasts as evidence to Jandro's handling.

"Oh, we're playing this already?" A delighted smile pulled at her lips, hips shifting in a way that forced me to swallow down a groan. "Well, I'm going to need some clues."

My eyes hadn't even reached the most tantalizing part, and then I really had to force myself to be quiet. She was spread eagle, ankles tied to the foot of the bed with a little slack for movement. The center of her was so beautifully open and exposed, pussy flushed and glossy with her pleasure.

"Don't leave our poor wife in suspense now." Jandro dragged the back of his hand up her side, and she startled at the slight touch.

"Jandro, is that you?"

"Yes, it's me." His caress continued up her arm. "Your mystery man is dealing with the loss of blood from his head to his other head."

"I want to know who it is." Mari tugged on her restraints again, hips rising off the bed in a clear invitation. "Shadow, are you going shy on me? Or are you Reaper, thinking of all the ways you'll torture me?"

I'd be tasting blood soon if I kept biting my tongue this hard. But oh, where to begin? She was laid out and tied up so pretty for me, like the most precious gift. Did I just climb on and sink into her like my lizard brain was screaming at me to do? She was already warmed up and ready.

No. I knew the answer the moment my hands went to my belt buckle, pulling everything loose and then off entirely. A woman who presented herself to her men like this deserved to be cherished. Savored. Worshipped.

"Atta boy," Jandro remarked when the last of my clothes came off.

"It *is* Shadow." Mari turned her face to him with a triumphant grin. "You'd only talk to him like that."

"Hmm, are you sure?" He touched a finger to her nose, then dragged the digit to her lips where she sucked it into her mouth. "No biting. You've been such a good girl, I'd hate to ruin it for you now."

While she whined and moaned around his finger, I started my touch at her ankle closest to me. Just a light caress of the soft rope holding her in place before running slowly over her skin.

I followed the curve of her calf muscle, drinking in her shiver as I traveled up to the inside of her knee.

"Hmm, way too gentle to be Reaper," she mused. "So you're either Shadow or Gunner."

I answered by closing my hand in a tight grip of her thigh, just above her knee. Fuck, I never realized before now how much I loved talking to her in bed. This whole silence thing was fucking torture.

"Oh, am I wrong?" Mari smirked under her blindfold. "Kiss me, Reaper."

No, not yet. That might make it too easy for her. I released my grip and spanned my hand wide as I moved it up her thigh. Her breath hitched, hips rising and tilting as I neared her pussy, but I roamed higher to her waist and belly.

"Oh, you're gonna be mean about it, then," she pouted, turning her face toward Jandro again. "Did you tell him to be mean?"

"Just to not say a word." Jandro dragged a hand down her opposite leg. "If it's any consolation, he's having a very difficult time and looks constipated."

Mari laughed, relaxing her head back on the pillows. "This *is* hard."

Jandro snickered. "I can confirm that that is also true."

My patience couldn't hold out forever. After running up to her slender throat, I dragged my hand back down her body, scissoring my fingers open to glide along the sides of her pussy.

Mari gasped, gorgeous lips falling open as she lifted up to press harder against my hand. I almost said something about how sexy and wet she looked, but a tongue click from Jandro reminded me to keep quiet.

Fuck me, I felt muzzled, caged. Being unable to express myself made me feel just as bound as she was. How long would I have to keep this silence up?

My teeth ached with how hard I clenched them, but I kept my touch light as I stroked and explored between her legs. Did Jandro fuck her like this or just use toys on her? How many orgasms did she have before I came home? So many questions I was dying to know but couldn't voice yet.

I crawled onto the bed, carefully stepping over her spread-open legs so I could sit between them.

"Yes, come closer." Mari grinned from under her mask. "Touch me and tell me more about who you are."

"Mean, wicked temptress." Jandro stroked circular patterns over her collarbones and chest. "The poor guy is barely holding it together, and you're not making it any easier for him."

"Maybe you should do a better job of distracting me."

Jandro answered with a growl, his hand closing around her throat before he claimed her mouth in a kiss. Without her taunting me to speak, I could focus for a moment.

I pressed two fingers inside her, watching the resulting arch of her back and her soft gasp through kissing Jandro. My other hand made another roaming pass up her body, rising and dipping as I followed her curves and hypnotic movements. Inside her, my fingers spread and curled, coaxing her slick walls into responding to me. I watched her face while her hips bucked against my hand, keeping my thumb away from her clit for the moment.

Mari broke away from Jandro, panting. A soft moan built up in her throat as she arched and tugged at her restraints.

"Any ideas?" Jandro directed the question at her but grinned at me.

"I'm...fuck, not sure." Her hips tilted from side to side, as if trying to feel my hand from all possible angles. "Feels like...Reaper? Maybe Gunner? I don't know, but it's so good." She sent a coy smile my way, now that her mouth was free. "Whoever you are, I want your cock. Not your hand."

I huffed out a soft laugh, barely more than a breath, but she heard it.

"Oh, what's that?" She cocked her head. "Tell me more."

Fuck. I needed to keep *my* mouth occupied if I didn't want to break too soon. And what better to feast on than the beautiful dessert spread out in front of me?

I scooted back, leaning down to kiss her hip crease while my fingers continued to drive through her soaked pussy.

"Reaper!" Mari declared when I dragged more kisses toward her core. "It's Reaper."

"Are you *sure?*" Jandro asked.

Mari hesitated. "Fuck, I can't remember if Gunner shaved this morning. His face is usually smoother but, ahh!"

I ran late this morning getting the kids to their swim lessons, so I did not, in fact, have time to shave.

Mari squirmed under the friction of my stubbled jaw, which I dragged along her skin just to tease her now. I'd roast her later for mistaking me for Reaper. She was getting close to figuring it out. Once I sucked that luscious clit into my mouth, angling my fingers inside her to hit that spot that drove her wild, there would be no doubt in her mind.

"Fuck!" She pulled in a sharp gasp, hips bucking desperately into my face. Her moans were smothered after a moment by Jandro kissing her. Or his dick in her mouth, I couldn't exactly see.

I savored every tremble and desperate whine with my tongue, lapping at her and demanding more. I was right at the source, and I wanted all of her pleasure. She came apart within a minute, bursting with sweetness that I couldn't get enough of. Her pussy closed around my fingers like it would never let them go, wetness filling my palm and running to my wrist. I stroked her and drank from her until she shifted away.

My woman was limp, breath sawing in and out of her chest as I crawled over her and leaned down to whisper in her ear, "Hey, baby girl."

Mari's laugh was bright as she licked my cheek. "I knew it was you."

"Uh-huh." I kissed her mouth, her lips so warm and plush, while I slowly settled my weight on top of her. "You sounded pretty convinced I was Reaper."

"Didn't want to bruise your ego. You were trying so hard to be sneaky."

"Mm-hm." I kissed her again, drinking her lips in slowly while I nudged and shifted until my cock notched at her scorching, slick center. "You want to stay tied up?"

"Yeah, I like this." Mari's grin was as bright as sunlight. "But I want to see you."

I lifted the sleeping mask away, watching her gorgeous eyes blink and adjust to the light before settling on me. Her smile grew even bigger and it literally made my heart skip a beat.

Fuck me. Not that there were any doubts that I made the right decision to be hers all those years ago, but it was moments like these that solidified just how right this was.

As time went on, our tentative, fragile relationship only grew stronger. What started as a weak sapling became an impenetrable oak tree. And our roots grew deep, supporting our children and setting them up for a better future. Not just me, but all of us and Mari were an unbreakable network. One that the gods entrusted to bring humanity back from the brink. What we had was truly endless.

"What?" Mari licked the tip of my nose after I'd been staring at her wondrously for who knows how long.

"Fuck, I just love you."

The goofiness left her face as she gazed up at me. "I love you, Gun."

She tilted her chin up for another kiss, which I happily gave her. Her legs clamped around my waist and I surged forward, every cell in my body aching to be touching her, to be part of her.

The first thrust was the sweetest agony, the exact thing I'd been craving since walking into this room and seeing her tied and spread. Our joint moan was followed by a weight lifting off the bed—Jandro getting up.

"Hey." I lifted up from Mari to look at him. "You don't have to leave."

Beneath me, Mari cackled softly while Jandro gave a sheepish grin, wiping his junk with a towel.

"I'm good, man, I got mine already. We had just, ah..." His teeth sank into his lip, a little embarrassed but also shameless. "Switched places when you got home."

"You mean...?" I looked down at Mari, and the smugness on her face said it all.

"Mm-hm," she confirmed. "I had him tied up first."

"Really?" I lifted my gaze back up to Jandro. "You liked it?"

"More than I thought I would." He waved a hand at us as he turned away. "Tell you about it later. I'm gonna shower. You kids have fun."

I returned my full attention to the woman laughing quietly underneath me. Her chuckles stretched out into moans as I sank down to her and *into* her.

"You know, *I* wouldn't mind being tied up." I dragged through her long and slow, savoring every inch of bliss and wanting to make it last.

"Oh, really?" Mari looked thoroughly pleased at that idea. "I can see you tied to a chair. Makes for a very pretty picture in my mind." She tugged at her wrist bindings, as if already eager to transfer the rope to my hands.

I slid my arms under her arched back to hold her closer. "What would you do to me?"

"Hmm—ah!" Her head threw back at my next thrust going deeper, a little harder. The bare column of her throat was so sexy, I couldn't help but take a nibble.

"Tell me or you don't get to come." I pulled away with another long drag from her silky heat.

Her gaze snapped back to me with a soft bark of a laugh. "Ha. I'd shove a gag in that smart mouth first so your talking doesn't distract me."

"Aw, but don't you love it when I talk to you?" I rolled forward again, sinking deep into her pussy while my fist closed in her hair. My hips snapped harder as I brought my mouth to her ear. "Wouldn't you want to hear me beg for this pussy? Beg you to climb on and fuck me?"

"You'd try to get out of being tied up first," she said, her breaths coming in harsher as she absorbed the impact of my thrusts.

"You mean there's a chance I'd succeed?" I sucked along the crook of her neck and her shoulder, our skin sliding and bodies flush.

"I'd let you think there was."

"Mean," I grunted.

We laughed at the same time and our lips found each other again. I slid a hand up to clasp with one of hers as we rocked together. My thrusts grew wild as I got greedier for more of her moans and rough breaths, more of the sweet pressure wrapping around all sides of my cock.

Mari came once more with a muffled cry through a kiss and a tight squeeze around my length that had me tumbling right after her. I'd been wound up like a spring since I first walked into the room, and now it spilled out of me in a dizzying rush.

I was limp on top of her, all frayed nerves and a drumming heart-beat. My face pressed into the pillow next to Mari's head, ready to fall asleep in that position if I hadn't felt her nip on my ear.

"Untie me now, please," she whispered, all sated and relaxed.

"Nah, I like you like this."

Mari's huff tickled my cheek, and I pressed lazy kisses to her face until she laughed, then sat up to untie her.

"We'll use these on you next time," she said, playfully whipping me with one of the ends of the ropes. "Jury's still out on if I'll have to gag you."

"What if I promised to be a good boy?" I caressed down her legs before plucking the knots that held her ankles.

"I'd call you a liar."

She started to sit up, but I pounced on her and pinned her back down to the bed. My attack of kisses and tickling filled the room with laughter and echoed throughout the house.

CHAPTER 12

REAPER

I slid across the open, expansive mattress until I reached her. My arm fit perfectly around her waist, and she left enough room on the pillow for me to lay my head just behind hers. It was rare that we ended up in bed together alone, and I wanted to bask in it.

Mari stirred, stretching out long with a soft groan before she laced her fingers with mine. "You're not on breakfast duty?" she asked sleepily.

"Nah. Daren wanted Gunner's pancakes, so he pounced on him. And Rori wanted Shadow to make orange juice with her, so she got him up." I squeezed around her waist, nuzzling her cheek. "You slept through all that? It was a fucking racket in here for a minute."

"Long night at the hospital, we had an emergency C-section," she mumbled, then elbowed me lazily. "You know I sleep like the dead anyway."

"Never fails to amaze me, what you sleep through," I chuckled into her hair. "Everything turn out okay at the hospital?"

"Oh yeah, everything was fine. Triplets." She elbowed me again. "Three *big* boys."

"There's Rori's future harem."

"No, don't," Mari pleaded. "They're growing so fast. I don't want to think about her as a woman yet."

I laughed into her hair, a question on the tip of my tongue. One that we'd danced around, brought up in passing, but never had a chance to really discuss before now.

"Sugar." I wrapped tighter around her, bringing her back flush to my chest. "Do you want to have any more?"

Mari turned her head, looking at me over her shoulder. "More kids?"

"Yeah."

She rolled slowly, turning over to face me. We lied next to each other nose-to-nose, her arm settling over my shoulder with her fingers stroking lightly over my back.

"I think we could handle another one or two more." Caution tinged her voice, and she didn't exactly look overjoyed.

"But do you *want* more?" I asked.

"I don't want to carry twins again," she admitted. "I'm glad we got Rori and Daren at the same time, but even though everything turned out fine, that was fucking rough. Even with all you guys to help."

"What are the chances of that happening again?"

"I don't know. Greater than zero," she chuckled. "It already happened once."

"True."

We were quiet for a few moments while she nuzzled her head under my chin. "If we do try again, it should probably be soon," she said in my chest. "Before the twins get much older."

I stroked down the length of hair covering her back. "None of us *need* more kids. The twins are perfect. They're the center of our universe, and all of us would be happy keeping it that way. Our life is perfect, sugar. Nothing needs to change if we don't want it to."

Mari sighed against my skin. "If I was almost certain I could have one at a time, I wouldn't hesitate to say yes. But so many women are having multiple births right now. There's some kind of baby boom going on and none of the doctors can figure what's causing it."

"You think it's Freyja's doing?" I wondered aloud.

"She's involved, I'm sure." Mari lifted her head to look at the cat, curled up and sleeping at the foot of the bed.

"She looked after you during your pregnancy, right?"

"They all did," Mari said with a soft smile. "She'd rub on me when the aches were the worst. Hades never let any strangers get near me. Even Horus screeched his head off when that missionary came over, remember?"

"He did a full-on hunting dive, then pulled back at the last second." I laughed at the memory. "Poor guy almost got his neck flayed open."

"Even with all that," Mari waved her hand in the air. "Pregnancy with twins is not something I'm dying to repeat."

"I get it, sugar."

"It's like," she leaned away from me, chewing her lip, "I never got to *know* them until they were born. They kept switching places, flipping around inside me. I never knew if it was Rory kicking the shit out of me or Daren."

"Well, *now* we know who the little shit-kicker was," I grumbled. Rori got me hard in the balls one time during a tantrum, to the point where I had to sit with a bag of ice on my crotch for a few hours.

"Right." Mari laughed. "But me bonding with them during pregnancy is different, I think. If I have one baby in there, I can learn about them before they're born. What kind of food or music they like, what times they're sleepy or active. I'd like to experience that, instead of wondering who's beating up my insides this time."

"That sounds nice," I said, already picturing her with a round belly again. "Too bad dads can't experience that firsthand."

Mari laughed so hard she woke up Freyja. The cat blinked at us with a narrow-eyed glare before turning to sleep in another position.

"Yes, such a shame men can't experience the joy of pregnancy," Mari said in a dry tone. "The world would be very different if they could."

"Yeah, well. Not the way it works." I pulled her back toward me until we were intertwined again—her head on my chest, our arms in a tangled embrace, and her leg over my hip. "If you want to try again, we're ready," I murmured into her hairline.

"Course you are," Mari chuckled, bringing a hand to my jaw. "I want one that looks like you," she added softly.

That statement took my breath away, and my overfilled well of love for this woman spilled over a little more.

"If we have another boy, can we name him Nolan?" I asked.

Mari nudged her nose against mine with a smile. "I'd love that. But Finn's going to get jealous."

"Finn can get the middle name," I huffed. "But no, he'll actually love it. You remember how he cried when we said our son would be Daren? He's overjoyed that we're remembering the ones we lost this way."

"What about if we have a girl?" Mari stuck her tongue out to the tip of my nose, but little did she know I'd been thinking about that too.

"Lucia," I said softly.

Mari blinked, taken aback. "After Jandro's mom."

"Yeah. What do you think?"

Jandro didn't show it much, but we could all tell the lack of information on his missing parents weighed heavily on him. He and sisters got in touch with agencies looking to reunite family members across Mexico and the Southwest, but their searches turned up next to nothing. His aunt and uncle would be moving up here next year and his sisters visited regularly, but that big question mark regarding his parents had to be a sore spot.

We might never get answers. Such was the nature of the Collapse.

"That's beautiful." Mari smiled a bit wistfully. "Make sure it's okay with Jandro though."

"I know, it's a family decision." I moved a lock of hair from her shoulder. "He seems to have...accepted the most likely outcome, so I thought it might be nice. And it's a pretty name."

"It is." Mari rolled away and stretched long with a yawn. "Alright, what do you say, Freyja?" She poked the disgruntled, half-asleep cat with her foot. "I'll have more babies, but give 'em to me one at a time, okay?"

If you insist.

The two of us froze and then looked at each other.

"Was that...?"

"I think so."

A wave of amusement passed over me, like the vibrations of someone's laughter on my skin. It brought a grin to my face and Mari looked just as giddy.

"Is that enough confirmation for you?" I reached for her, blatantly groping and pawing to pull her closer.

"I think it's the only one I'm getting." She sounded excited and nervous, her beautiful grin infectious.

"Then what are we waiting for?" I brought my wife underneath me, settling between her thighs as I leaned down to kiss her, only to be stopped by an impressively loud rumbling from her stomach.

"Breakfast." Mari laughed. "I need fuel if I'm gonna get knocked up again."

"Fine." I sighed, but lowered to kiss her anyway. "You'll be fed." I kissed her nose bridge. "Protected." Her forehead. "Adored." Her right eye. "Cherished." Her left eye. "Loved. For the rest of my days."

I sealed every promise with a kiss. Ones she knew and that I didn't need to repeat, but liked to do so anyway.

"You really can be sweet sometimes," she said, eyes glittering.

"You make it easy sometimes."

I earned another lick on my nose for that, then hauled her upright with more kisses and laughter. There was a new excitement buzzing in our touches and smiles. It matched the bright giddiness in my chest and I couldn't wait to tell everyone downstairs.

We had breakfast to eat and then more babies to make.

Thank you so much for coming on the epic ride of the Steel Demons MC! Want to know what happened to the Sons of Odin? Their book is available now!

Start reading Their Property:
Books2read.com/TheirPropertySonsofOdin

Read on for exclusive bonus content!
In appreciation of all the amazing Steel Demons fans, Reaper allowed me to publish a few excerpts from his mother's journal. I hope you enjoy this peek into the past, and seeing how our surly president learned to share. ;)

Bonus content

Excerpts & letters from Alisa's journal

LETTER FROM FINN TO CARTER
JUNE 1, 2071

Dear Carter,

Don't be a fucking idiot. Of course I was giving you permission to sleep with my wife. You read my letter. What else did you think it meant?

I talked to Alisa on the phone just before sitting down to write this. Send me your phone number in your next letter. I'm looking forward to having a heart-to-heart with you too.

Please understand. It's because I trust you as my best friend that I'm okay with this. I'm not just okay with it, I want this. What if, God forbid, I don't come home from this deployment?

There's no one else in the world I would trust as much to look after my wife while I'm away. Alisa (and my son, I just found we're having a boy!!) are the most precious people in the world to me. I love Alisa so much, well, it just makes sense to me that she should have more than one man to love her.

Yes, I know you've always been in love with her. Not a

crush, but real love. And I think she's felt the same way about you, even if she didn't want to admit to herself out of love and respect for me. I've always noticed how well you two get along and you know what? It's never made me jealous.

Why would it bother me that my best friend makes my wife laugh so hard she starts to cry? Why would it bother me when my wife tells my best friend he is kind, talented, and handsome? All those things are true.

If she wasn't already married to me, you and Alisa would be together. I'm 100% sure of that. I'm saying that can still happen. While she and I remain married.

You are not the type of guy to fuck a woman and bolt. You and Alisa know each other well, you've been leaning on each other, you've already slept together. So just be together. Go on dates. Talk to each other. Fall deeper in love. Am I making myself clear yet?

We will still have much to talk about when I get back, but I'm not worried about it. I trust my wife. I know her heart. And I trust you.

You want to know something else? I want you in my son's life. Shit, I want him to look up to you as a father too. And hey, if everything works out and there isn't a nuclear holocaust, maybe you and Alisa can have a baby together, if that's what you both want.

You know me better than anyone. I've never been one to mince words or say a bunch of bullshit. If I could say all of this to you in person, I would be. In fact, when I get home, I will do exactly that.

Take care of our woman. In every way she needs.

Yours,
Finn

Alisa's Journal
March 10, 2077

Wow. Has it really been six years since I've started this journal? I can't believe how much my life had changed since Finn's last deployment, and I found out I was pregnant.

Rory, my oldest, is now five years old. His sister, Noelle, is now two.

It's never a dull moment with those two. They go from best friends to mortal enemies at the drop of a hat. Rory is extremely bossy, but in a protective way. Noelle pushes back, though, as best as a two-year-old girl can, which usually involves lots of screaming. Thankfully, I have two incredible husbands to help me wrangle these kids.

Yes, two. Finn and I as hopelessly in love as ever. As are Carter and I. It still doesn't feel real to say that! I am truly the luckiest woman in the world to have two incredible men that love me as fiercely as I love them.

This rings especially true for the state of the world right now. I won't get into everything that's happening with the government, but as a family, we decided we had enough. We're not going to be part of this society anymore. We're going off the grid and depending only on ourselves from now on. It may be extreme, but I'm not going to expose my children to a world that will ship my son off to war against his will when he's sixteen, and treat my daughter like a piece of meat with no consequences. No fucking way.

So Carter, Finn, and I had many long, late-night conversations, pooled together our resources, and talked to a select few friends about our plan. Now, we own some land by the Grand Canyon, and are a little community of 15!

Our plan is to build cabins, but we're making do with RVs for now while we gather building materials. There's an open air market nearby where I can sell jewelry. Carter is still taking some metalwork side jobs. I have this nervous-excited feeling that we're going to be okay. Our kids are going to be okay.

I really want this community to be a safe haven for women and families. We are not completely cut off from civilization but well hidden from the authorities. The threat of being discovered is always present but everyone seems genuine so far.

Word has traveled quietly about our community. A woman and her brother showed up last week, just the two of them. No partners or children. We had a meeting before allowing them in. I felt awful, but we almost turned the brother away. When our top priority is safety for women and children, I'm wary of single men.

He, Nolan, talked with Finn, Carter, and then with me. We're the defacto leaders of this community, I guess. He came across as very sincere to all of us, and has skills we can use too. He's a farmer and has some carpentry skills too. We all like him and he's fitting in well so far, so I think we made the right decision.

Nolan has been hanging out with us nearly every day since he arrived and, well...I think I might have a crush. Finn and Carter have been teasing me about him, those jerks. Nolan is definitely different than them, but not in a bad way. He's so smart, like intelligent on another level. I asked if he went to college and he said no, he just reads everything he can get his hands on. We actually exchanged books this morning, and I got all fluttery. Just like when Finn and I first met.

But Nolan can be so shy! I can't tell if he likes me at all. He doesn't really flirt, so he's probably just being nice. He lights up when I ask about his plans for garden beds though, and gets chatty about companion planting and irrigation, haha. It's really very cute.

He knows that I have two husbands and has been respectful about it. Rori and Noelle love him. I'm distracted from the day-to-day tasks because I'm always looking for him and hoping we run into each other. Listen to me, a 30-year-old doubly married woman going on about a crush.

This morning Finn said that I should invite him over for a drink tonight after the kids go to bed. I know he wants to test some waters but what if Nolan is uncomfortable? I love my men, but I don't want to freak out the new guy!

And yet, it kind of excites me because what if he says yes?

I'm getting WAY ahead of myself, but I'm kind of thinking I would like to have one more baby. If Nolan does want to be part of us and want to have a child, Finn and Carter won't have to compete about who's the dad of baby #3. Although it is fun when they compete that way, hehe.

That is such a long shot though. First step is inviting Nolan to hang out with us. No expectations. I am a little nervous though...like I'm getting ready for a first date.

Nolan is so sweet and has a calmer energy than Finn and Carter (especially when they're together). I think he would balance them out well.

Ack, no expectations! Just relax and have a good time, Alisa. You got this.

Thank you so incredibly much for reading the entire Steel Demons MC series! If you still want more bonus content, I got you covered!

From the Shadows is a small collection of extra scenes all about our fan favorite Demon, Shadow. You can grab this mini collection for free when you sign up for my email list.

Download From the Shadows here:
https://BookHip.com/PSNHPXK

ABOUT THE AUTHOR

Crystal Ash is a USA Today Bestselling Author from California. She loves writing steamy, heart-wrenching romance with tortured heroes, especially if they're in a reverse harem. Crystal's other loves include animals, mythology, and well-crafted alcohol, most of which can also be found in her stories.

When she's not writing, she's probably drinking craft beer with her husband or trying to coax her feral cat into accepting affection.

crystalashbooks.com

facebook.com/Crystal.Ash.Romance

instagram.com/crystalashbooks

amazon.com/author/crystalash

bookbub.com/profile/crystal-ash

Also by Crystal Ash

Harem of Freaks: The Complete Series

Say Your Prayers

Steel Demons MC

Lawless

Powerless

Fearless

Painless

Helpless

Heartless

Senseless

Ruthless

Merciless

Endless

Their Property: Sons of Odin MC

Shifted Mates Trilogy

Unholy Trinity: The Complete Series

For a complete list of books by Crystal Ash, visit her Amazon page.